"MISS DOROTHY HADDEN."
SERIES 1: THE EARLY EDWARDIAN ADVENTURES – PART 1.
BY STEPHEN J. WILLIAMS

This book is based on the original internet adventure series:"Miss Dorothy Hadden" by Stephen J. Williams writing as 'William Alexander Stephens which first appeared in 2016.'

Dorothy was her uncle William's Magician's Assistant working the Theatres and Music Hall's of Edwardian London. [But she has some magic of her own!] Dorothy also assisted her brother; Detective Inspector Harry Hadden with his caseload. Together they were a formidable team fighting crime, investigating the paranormal and supernatural. They became agents for the famous Temporal Detective Inspector Jericho Tibbs, who can be found in the book series; **'THE TEMPORAL DETECTIVES'** by the same author.

ISBN-SBN: 9781739434656

TO VISIT 'MISS DOROTHY HADDEN' WEBSITE, SCAN CODE:

IMPORTANT NOTES.

[1] CAUTION:
"SOME OF THESE EPISODES CONTAIN STRONG [& FOUL] LANGUAGE, VIOLENCE, HORROR AND STRONG SEXUAL REFERENCES. They are only RECOMMENDED suitable for persons aged **18+** years."

All episodes carry a "Trigger warning" for content. This can include the following warnings: [**for example**]

Alcohol – Smoking – Strong language – Strong sexual references [including pornography & prostitution] – Nudity - violence – Witchcraft & Devil worship – Mild Horror – Mild Adult Erotica.

And other warnings as appropriate to the episode.

[2] AGE RECOMMENDATION:
"These stories contain **mild adult erotica** which is recommended only suitable for persons aged **18 years** and over."

[3] IMPORTANT DISCLAIMER:

"All incidents and dialogue, and all characters with the exception of some well-known historical figures, are products of the author's imagination and are not to be construed as real. Where real-life historical figures appear, the situations, incidents, and dialogues concerning those persons are entirely fictional and are not intended to depict actual events or to change the entirely fictional nature of the work. In all other respects, any resemblance to actual persons, living or dead, events, or locales is entirely coincidental."

[4]  CHAPTER TITLE QUOTES:

All quotes used as Chapter Titles have the person shown next to the quote in question. Where the words are traditional phrases or sayings, this has been noted. Should you believe that you know the source of any quote that has not been assigned, please contact the author with details at: **stephen.williams24@btinternet.com.**
Thank you!"

[5] EPISODES:

"The episodes are divided into CHAPTERS, as they were first originally published on the website, which produced updates on a semi-weekly basis. Therefore the episodes and Chapters can vary in length and duration."

[6] AUTHOR NOTES:

"Five bob was slang for five shillings [25p today!] - that's about 24 pounds at today's inflated values." SJW

"This Note explains a comment or action that may need further comment by the author, for the reader to appreciate what is happening; it normally concerns something about the period. For example: the currency values currently used at the time."

[7] AVERAGE READING TIMES:

"The average reading times can vary between episodes with extended episodes taking between 70 to 90 minutes, whilst the average length episode can be between 45 to 60 minutes in duration.

"MISS DOROTHY HADDEN."
SERIES 1: THE EARLY EDWARDIAN ADVENTURES – PART 1.
By Stephen J. Williams

CONTENTS:

IMPORTANT NOTES
START PAGE: 2

PROLOGUE
START PAGE: 6

EPISODE 1: "THE WORKHOUSE CORPSE WITH GOLDEN BOOTS."
START PAGE: 9

EPISODE 2: "MISS PANDORA AND HER MAGIC BOX."
START PAGE: 135

EPISODE 3: "THE STRANGE DEATH OF MRS. HANNA DASHWOOD."
START PAGE: 217

EPISODE 4: "THE HIDDEN WINDOW."
START PAGE: 290

EPISODE 5: "A TERRIBLE GLIMPSE OF THINGS TO COME?"
START PAGE: 354

EPISODE 6: "THE COMPLICATED FUNERAL OF SIR WILLIAM McKENZIE."
START PAGE: 411

ILLUSTRATIONS
START PAGE: 464

OTHER WORKS BY THE AUTHOR
START PAGE: 466

PROLOGUE.

On the 22nd January 1901 Queen Victoria died after ruling for almost 64 years [63 years and 7 months] and she presided over enormous change, not just in Great Britain but the world. Her son, Edward VII became King and ushered in the 'Edwardian Area' which was to end with the bloody conflict of the First World War; that would change the world forever.

Dorothy Mary Hadden was born on June 6th 1882 in London, the only daughter of Edwin and Elizabeth Hadden and the youngest of four siblings with a gap of ten years between herself and her older brother Harry, some twelve years parted her and her next brother, George. The oldest brother; Henry was some fifteen years senior to Dorothy.

Once a proud and wealthy family, the Hadden's had fallen from grace with the death of her Grandfather; Sir George Hadden, an amateur archeologist and Egyptologist who spend many years in Egypt searching for the 'Ark of the Convent' and any other treasure he could get he hands upon. He was not successful and died of Malaria in Cairo, some four years before Dorothy was born. Her Father and Uncle William had quite a shock when the Will was read; Sir George had died broke, even the family house had to be sold in payment of debts.

Now Sir Edwin, Dorothy's father moved his family to a modest house in Dock Street within London's East End and worked as a Bank Manager for several years.

Dorothy's Uncle William travelled back to Egypt and used his talent as a Magician to earn a modest living around the European communities within Cairo – he also collected the only item that the creditors had failed to grab - a Mummy and sarcophagus that Sir George had found some thirty years previously.

William discovered the sealed crate in a warehouse at the local port; the owner had been a friend of Sir George for many years and allowed William to send the crate home to England; still addressed to its late owner. The crate lay in the basement of the Hadden's new family home for about six years before Sir Edwin allowed the British Museum to take possession; that was after some strange happenings which Sir Edwin refused to discuss. The British Museum didn't need too many more Mummies' and so the crate – still unopened – was assigned to the basement and remains there to this day.

Tragedy struck the Hadden family yet again in the spring of 1890, when both Dorothy's parents were killed on holiday in Paris by a runaway tram. The younger children were placed in the care of their Uncle William, whilst [now Sir] Henry disappeared in Egypt, like his father, he was another amateur archeologist and Egyptologist; he had not been heard of for some years.

Dorothy's brother George joined the Royal Navy and served on various battleships around the British Empire – sending home to Dorothy, various dolls from the countries he found himself in – she had quite a collection now.

When Harry turned twenty-one, he joined the Metropolitan Police and served at several Police Stations, as he rose rapidly through the ranks and currently [1901] is London's youngest ever Detective Inspector, stationed at Brick Lane Police Station in the East End. He is Dorothy's favourite brother and the pair is close despite the age difference. As a child, Uncle William had taught Dorothy various magic tricks and she clearly had a natural aptitude for magic and eventually became her Uncles 'Magician's Assistant'.

When Dorothy was six and playing in the nursery with her dolls, she met 'Sims' and the strange creature became her favourite playmate, even when he ate her complete china tea-set! But his finder; Sir George would have nothing to do with his discovery, ordering Sims from the house and selling the Mummy and sarcophagus to the British Museum – but that didn't stop Sims returning to play with his new friend - and Dorothy introduced him to Uncle William - who treated Sims with kindness and taught him to play cards [that proved a little tricky, since Sims had the annoying habit of eating the odd card during a game.]

But William discovered that Sims had been a young and popular Magician in his own right at the court of Pharaoh Amenhoteph V, some three and half thousand years ago; they got on like a When Harry met Sims for the first time, he pulled his Police issue pistol and protected Dorothy by dragging the child behind him.

But Dorothy soon convinced her brother that Sims was harmless and Harry [like Uncle William] treated the odd fellow with kindness and the pair could be described as 'friends' - despite Sims eating Harry's new hat and gloves.

Sims ate Dorothy's umbrella and enjoyed it so much that he ate everyone's in the house! Dorothy soon learnt that Sims could sniff out a 'brolly anywhere and resigned herself to buy new one's each time. Dorothy purchased the quality umbrellas from 'Lossman & Prophet's Haberdashery' located in Eastham High Street. But she had purchased so many over the years that old man Jacob Prophet had become suspicious and believed she was re-selling the umbrella's at Eastham street markets; though it gave him many sleepless nights because he just could not figure out how she made a profit on them; everything in the markets were sold at discounted prices and he always charged top prices for his goods.

 He became so fixated that he was somehow being cheated out of money, he started to wander the markets looking for cheap umbrella's and eventually the mystery made him ill and he developed a phobia towards them; bursting into tears when one was opened near him. It proved a fatal phobia; he never used one in the frequent English rain showers and caught several colds which progressed into influenza and died.

But some good came from the tragedy; the term 'Brolliologist' could have been invented to cover Dorothy's apparent passion for them! But with the appearance of Sims came another strange visitor to the Hadden household; Mr. Jericho Tibbs, investigating a breech in the 'Time-Line' which was found to be the resurrected Sims. Unusually, Mr. Tibbs allowed Sims to stay with the Hadden's - who pleaded on his behalf – especially Dorothy. It appears that the tough, rough and dedicated Mr. Tibbs was a sucker for little girls with tears in their eyes!

As the years passed and Dorothy grew into a woman, she, Harry and Uncle William joined Mr. Tibbs's Human team for the early 20th Century Time Period and their adventures had just begun and what adventures!

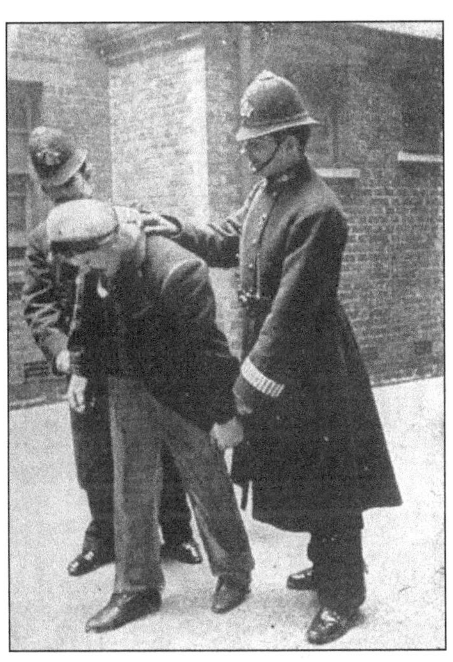

EPISODE 1: "THE WORKHOUSE CORPSE WITH GOLDEN BOOTS."

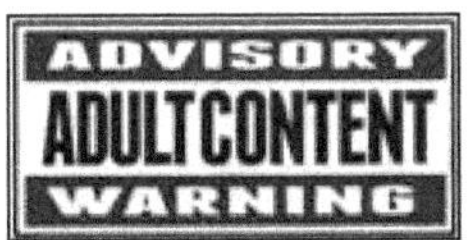

Alcohol – Smoking – Strong language – Strong sexual references [including pornography & prostitution] – Nudity - violence – Anti-religious sentiments – Mild Horror – Mild Adult Erotica.

 Approximately 70 to 90 minutes.

 Remember: **Adult Content.**

EPISODE CONTENTS.

1. 'THE THEATRE INFECTS THE AUDIENCE WITH ITS NOBLE ECSTASY'.
Start page: 11

2. 'PAY LESS ATTENTION TO WHAT MEN SAY, JUST WATCH THAT THEY DO.'
Start page: 17

3. 'DON'T JUDGE A BOOK BY ITS COVER'.
Start page: 25

4. 'PLEASE SIR, CAN I HAVE SOME MORE?'
Start page: 33

5. 'WHEN, IN COUNTRIES THAT ARE CALLED CIVILISED, WE SEE AGE GOING TO THE WORKHOUSE AND YOUTH TO THE GALLOWS, SOMETHING MUST BE WRONG IN THE SYSTEM OF GOVERNMENT.'
Start page: 40

6. 'MURDER IS BORN OF LOVE, AND LOVE ATTAINS THE GREATEST INTENSITY IN MURDER'.
Start page: 48

7. 'THE DISTINCTION BETWEEN THE PAST, PRESENT, AND THE FUTURE IS ONLY A STUBBORNLY PERSISTENT ILLUSION.'
Start page: 61

8. 'SHUN DEATH, THAT'S MY ADVICE.'
Start page: 71

9. 'ANY MAN WHO KNOCKS ON THE DOOR OF A BROTHEL IS LOOKING FOR GOD.'
Start page: 79

10. 'MAGIC IS JUST SCIENCE THAT WE DON'T UNDERSTAND YET.'
Start page: 85

11. 'I HATE THIS IMAGE OF ME AS A PRIM EDWARDIAN, I WANT TO SHOCK EVERYONE.'
Start page: 96

12. 'SO MUCH OF PREFORMING IS A MIND GAME.'
Start page: 105

13. 'HISTORY IS THE STORY OF WARFARE BETWEEN SECRET SOCITIES'.
Start page: 119

IMPORTANT AUTHOR'S NOTE:
"The names and places of some characters have been changed to protect the innocent and ficticious characters created in their stead. **The Workhouse corpse with golden boots' is a specially extended episode.** *Thank you."*

CHAPTER 1. 'THE THEATRE INFECTS THE AUDIENCE WITH ITS NOBLE ECSTASY'. Constantin Stanislavski.

Big Tom Reed sighed loudly and took a long hard swig from his hip-flask. He stared across the gas lit stage, then pulled behind the side curtain, cursing and adjusting his waist coat, thrusting the half empty flask back into his rear pocket and shouting at the young boy standing by the Performers staircase; "Arthur, for fuck sake, tell Mary to get the girls on stage, that drunken fucker has failed to appear again!"

The slow clapping audience bore truth to that statement. The 'famous Bongo Spanks' – juggler, singer and dancer was face down on his dressing room floor and quite incoherent – he had consumed several bottles of 'Bass's London Porter' and to quote the great Sir Henry Irving; "Was pissed as a rat, darling."

The girls groaned as Mary rounded them up backstage like a mother hen. "Get out there and show plenty of lace before those mad bastards pull the place apart!" she yelled.

Tom Reed hastily ushered the dozen scantily clad dancing girls onto the stage and took another swig at his fast depleting hip-flask; 'It's going to be one of those fucking nights!' He thought quickly and then grabbed his stage hand Arthur by the arm shouting: "Get down to that bloody Magician and tell him to come on early, I'll give him an extra five bob for the fifteen minutes more."

"Five bob was slang for five shillings [25p today!] - that's about 24 pounds at today's inflated values." SJW.

Young Arthur nodded and smiled, he relished carrying messages to the 'great Professor Potts' because it offered the delicious chance of catching the Magician's assistant; Miss Dorothy Hadden in a state of undress. Mind you, her stage costume didn't leave much to the imagination, to the delight of the males in the audience. He licked his lips in anticipation and ran down the rear staircase, two steps at a time, and knocked loudly upon the paneled door which bore a small chalked name board which declared: "Professor Dustin Potts – The Magic Master of the Pyramids." Arthur wondered what the hell a 'pyramid' was and why was it magical: his education hadn't been much!

A deep dignified voice answered: "Enter please Arthur." He hesitated for a moment and wondered how on earth the Professor knew who was at his door; then he shrugged his shoulders, the fucker was a bloody magician after all!

Young Arthur was quite disappointed to find Miss Hadden wasn't present; she was already on the back stage checking the props for the evening's performance. Considered by many to be gifted with real beauty; inside and out, Miss Dorothy Mary Hadden was just nineteen with a slender figure, green eyes and brown hair. She was about five feet six inches, which is tall for a woman of her time; she had a quick mind and a fine intellect. Dorothy was an excellent distraction [all Magicians assistants are used for distraction] and extremely quick performing her parts of the tricks.

But her abilities as a 'distraction' were not the real reason Professor Potts made sure Dorothy received a very good salary;

it was her skill as a Magician, in her own right, that impressed
him so. None of his friends or colleagues suspected that the old
man was a supporter of women's suffrage and that he admired
Miss Hadden's intellect far more than her physical form and
above all that, she was the only daughter of his much loved
brother Edward, now departed.

When admired and commented on by men, Dorothy would reply
with some sarcasm; "There is a person inside here, you know."
But Dorothy knew that the new century would bring great change
into women's lives and anticipated it with some passion.

Young Dorothy had only three real confidants; The Professor/her
Uncle, an old school friend: Maggie and her older brother Harry -
She wondered if Sims should be included, he had been in the
family for over sixty years!

Harry was her particular favourite, despite only being in his late
twenties, Harry Hadden was already a Detective Inspector in the
Metropolitan Police and everyone commented on his rapid rise
from young uniform Constable to Inspector of Detectives. He had
a natural gift for investigation and understanding the human
condition which resulted in some really astounding arrests,
 including the near famous murder in Lark Lane Post Office.

The dramatic conclusion resting on a stamped, but empty
envelope found on the accused. The villain was hung at Brixton
Prison some eight weeks later and Harry was promoted from
Detective Sergeant on the same day and as usual, Dorothy
insisted he say nothing about her pivotal part in the case – that
was always their secret - one of a few , the pair kept from
everyone else, apart from their dear Uncle.

The Professor nodded his agreement to the early start and his
man Mr. Skole, started to prepare his robes; the Professor's
stage costume consisted of a baggy white linen suit, desert boots
and a vivid red fez. Strangely enough, he looked like a cross
between an Archaeologist and a poor Cairo brothel-keeper! [Is
there such a thing as a 'poor' brothel keeper?]

"Tell Mr. Reed it's seven and six and inform my assistant of the
change of times." The Professor called after Arthur who raced up
the stairs.

"That piss head Bongo was given a crate of Porter by some idiot and he supped the lot, I dare say big Tom will kick his arse down the theatre steps followed by the empty bottles." Mr. Skole was chuckling to himself as he tied the Professors boot laces and positioned the fez upon his head.

Marion Edward Skole was a very tall [over six feet] part Chinese, part Scottish Valet/Stage Dresser who said that he had worked the theatres and Hall's for nearly a quarter of a century, ever since he jumped ship in London docks for a very good reason; three of the ship's crew wanted to cut his throat over unpaid gambling debts and the small problem of a certain sister who wrote to her brother [the Boson] about her delicate condition and Mr. Skoles participation in the same. She had expected a quick wedding, but was disappointed when he left her at the altar to seek his fortune in the huge Capitol city of the vast British Empire and keep his head attached to his shoulders.

His nickname among the theatre staff was 'Stick-Insect' and he always wore the same shabby dark suit and bow-tie, except on St. Andrews day, when he wore a kilt to the memory of his Scottish roots. On the Chinese New Year he celebrated those ancestors by wearing long bright ear-rings. He did look strange and received many catcalls, which he ignored until two foreign sailors followed him home one night : it was not a pleasant time, so now he just carries a Chinese lantern to honour that side of the family and walks with a slight limp.

Mr. Skole enjoyed working for Professor Potts the last couple of years; the old man paid well and treated him with polite respect. But the best perk was being close to Miss Hadden and sometimes helping her with shoes or the dark plaid stage wig that was part of her Ancient Egyptian slave costume. Such was his hidden passion for Miss Dorothy that he would groan to himself, wishing he was thirty years younger, or even twenty or even five…

Young Arthur was disappointed again, he had found Miss Hadden resplendent in her slave costume and was about to make a crude, lecherous remark [he really enjoyed that] while informing her of the change of program, but had to stick to the message because Titus was also on stage, moving a plaster prop of the Ram-headed God Amen-Ra to its stage mark.

"I know Arthur; Titus informed me of Bongo Spanks disposition and the early curtain call, thank you." Dorothy didn't even look at the boy, she found him unpleasant and smelly. He hadn't taken the hint about his body odour, even when several members of the theatre staff and performers, emptied fire buckets over him and threw a bar of soap at his feet.

He forced a grin and turned away; he would say nothing to Miss Hadden if Titus was present, then jumped in fright as he found the Professor standing behind him with a long curved sword in his hand and a severed head in the other. The Professor smiled broadly and held the gruesome object aloft; "These are for you Titus, Dotty will show you the stage marks."

As Arthur slunk from the stage, he could see Titus smiling at him and making a throat cutting gesture, among the many foul traits of young Arthur was racism and a dislike of anyone who came from Liverpool.

Titus was a magnificent African man with broad shoulders, who stood over six feet tall and was packed with muscles. He had shaved his long dark hair off, so that his appearance as a Nubian servant was authentic in every detail. The Professor had designed his costume and he really caught the eyes of the audience – especially the ladies - it should be noted.

Reginald Donald Hepple-White had travelled down from Liverpool to find fame and fortune in the theatres of London, since he was an excellent actor and Thespian [he could quote from nearly every Shakespeare play or sonnet] But found that his Liverpool accent turned Directors from casting him and coupled with a little known fact: no theatre would employ a young black man for any major roles - he struggled to find work.

After some time, his money ran out and he survived as a bare knuckle fighter until arrested for winning a bout against a local white champion – the losers [who were out of pocket] planted stolen clothing in his lodgings and he faced time in jail. But his case had fallen to DI Harry Hadden to investigate and Reggie walked away a free man, with the offer of a job from the Detectives sister. The Professor hired him immediately and found him quality lodgings with an old friend who didn't like black people, but was quite blind.

The Professor informed the landlord that Reggie was an actor from Liverpool, down in London to perform 'Othello' and he stayed 'blacked up' to remain in character – should anyone remark upon his skin colour.

The landlord didn't catch on to the deception, even when his other tenants moved out, except the old actor Randolph Bateman who resided in the small attic. Randolph was a Shakespearean actor whose glory days were long gone [if he actually had any] and he scrapped a meager living, teaching acting skills to young men. Beneath a portrait of the great Sir Henry Irving, he gave lessons for two shillings an hour and sipped sherry constantly. He liked Reggie and had him read Shakespeare aloud while he lay wrapped in a carpet under the bed. Reggie didn't think this was strange, since his uncle Rupert enjoyed something similar: he would climb into a flour sack and hide under the kitchen table for several hours. Reggie's aunt Florence believed he had acquired the strange habit when he served on various Royal Navy ships in his youth; a sort of defense mechanism that kept the older, more amorous sailors at bay.

But getting Reggie into the Paradise Theatre proved a little tougher; big Tom Reed [the Stage Manager] protested that 'no black will appear on his stage as he wouldn't have any bloody audience left and why couldn't the Professor be content with a white fella 'blacked up'. But the Professor argued, successfully, that no one in the crowd would notice Reggie really was African in descent and it would cost more to get a white man to strip down and rub himself with burnt cork every night; Reggie was the cheaper option.

A little reluctantly, big Tom agreed to the economics of the situation, but only if Reggie was paid less than white performers and Reggie finally had a job in the theatre – by the way - the Professor made up Reggie's pay out of his own pocket: that's the sort of man he was. Another great distraction, thought the Professor with some pride – he patted Titus on the shoulder - and took his start mark upon the stage for he could hear the Stage Manager, announcing their act to the shouting and clapping crowd.

Big Tom raised his arms and shouted over the noisy crowd; "Ladies and gentlemen! The Paradise Theatre management proudly presents for your entertainment the incredible professor Dustin Potts; the undisputed Master of mystery and magic straight from the Nile and the sands of Egypt. He is assisted by Titus the magnificent Nubian and Isis; a beauty with some magic of her own!" He leaned forward and gave a big wink to the audience and shouted; "And her costume is the talk of London!"

The crowd roared with anticipation and the small band struck up the introduction music for the magic act. Tom walked off stage and stood behind the side curtains with Mr. Skoles, who couldn't take his eyes off Dorothy; as usual. They were joined by Sir Thomas Astor – Smith who watched with some interest. He had a slight smile on his usually dour face and he fiddled with his well waxed moustache. He had just enjoyed his own private show: watching Miss Hadden being dressed by her maid, completely unknown to the women. His short lived smile quickly dropped as the rough man appeared and Sir Thomas softly cussed, "What the hell is he doing here!"

CHAPTER 2. 'PAY LESS ATTENTION TO WHAT MEN SAY, JUST WATCH THAT THEY DO.' Dale Carnegie.

Both Dorothy and the Professor noticed the shabbily dressed man standing in the wing, wiping his face with a grubby handkerchief and looking about: he clearly didn't belong here. Then Dorothy saw Sir Thomas Astor - Smith usher the man away, why would the owner of the theatre be in the company of such a man?

Dorothy's quick eye caught something glinting on his worn boots as he stumbled away under the firm grip of Sir Astor – Smith. But her attention was drawn back to the coming performance and she readied the first trick quickly.

As the curtain lifted, Professor Potts glanced across to Dorothy who made the finger signal indicating that the first trick was ready. He smiled and raised his arms aloft; spewing several pigeons into the air, followed by a real hawk, which circled the stage several times and dived into a large basket, held open by Dorothy who slammed the lid shut. "Stop squawking Horus and let 'Big Arthur' in." Dorothy whispered, completing the change over in just a few seconds and unseen, as the crowd ducked and dived from the crazy pigeons – they were all viewing the birds that wheeled and circled above them – another distraction.

The Professor tipped open the basket to reveal a large red & black snake, that slithered across the stage, disappearing into the small Pyramid standing on the opposite stage wing. The crowd was applauding enthusiastically, even the couple sitting in the second row, who had been splattered with pigeon shit; "Look, the fuckers are real!" They showed the shit stains to other audience members who gasped jealously; "You lucky bastards! That's good luck for a month!"

Titus dragged the richly painted sarcophagus to centre stage, he grunted and panted, his oiled muscles flexing in the bright gas lamps. He's quite a good actor smiled Dorothy; the sarcophagus was made from balsa wood and Papier-mâché: it weighted so little she could move it on her own.

Under the Professors direction, Titus turned the casket full circle and removed the apparently heavy lid, standing to one side, as the Professor explained to the audience; the box was made to hold the Mummy of the departed for the eternal sleep of death.

Dorothy stepped forward and bowed, clasping hands and the Professor announced that his 'slave' would take her place in the casket of death. She slowly entered the sarcophagus and Professor Potts bound her hands and arms, tying a black cloth over her eyes. Both he and Titus made some show of replacing the lid and the Professor called upon the Ancient Gods of Egypt to take this offering of a young, beautiful slave girl. The incantations ended when the Professor clapped loudly.

The crowd sat in silence and then gasped, as smoke poured from the casket and a strange, eerie green light emanated from the rumbling box. The Professor shouted that the Gods had been pleased with the sacrifice and when the smoke and lights had ceased, he ordered Titus to open the box.

The crowd was leaning forward in anticipation as Titus struggled to remove the seemingly heavy lid; to reveal that the slave girl had indeed been taken by the God's, who were so pleased with their offering, they left a cat behind!

The large fat cat jumped into the Professors arms and he held it aloft; "Behold the Goddess Isis has returned in her favourite form!" The crowd exploded in clapping and cheering, then watched with amazement as the cat jumped from the Professor and re-entered the sarcophagus without bidding. The Professor explained that the 'Goddess Isis' wanted to return to the Afterlife and, with her famed benevolence, she would send the slave girl back.

"The people of ancient Egypt worshiped the cat god, Bastet, as one of their highest deities. Bastet, also known as Bast, is associated with the Goddess Isis. Isis is often depicted as a female goddess accompanied by black cats." SJW

Again, the Professor and Titus made a great showing of replacing the lid, the smoke and lights returned briefly and the lid was pulled open and out stepped Dorothy: still bound and blindfolded. The crowd loved it and showed their appreciation with almost a minute or so of enthusiastic applause.

The evening's performance closed with a Mummy rising from its tomb [another incredible Papier-mâché production that stood at the rear of the stage] which, when unwrapped was Dorothy. Sims [the mummy] grinned at her from his hiding place behind the big pyramid. The swap was easily completed since Sims was a real mummy! The only person who didn't know this incredible fact was Titus: who always puzzled about this particular trick; because he knew it was bloody impossible!

The Professor's team had three encores before the next act was allowed on stage – that didn't go unnoticed by big Tom Reed - this magic act was proving very popular indeed and he now faced the awful prospect of having to pay more to keep it, he took a swig from his hip-flask and cursed; still the act was getting bums on seats and, of course, he really did fancy Miss Dorothy! but she probably wouldn't look at him twice. Big Tom glanced at himself in the mirror opposite and loudly sighed; sometimes being a dwarf was a pain in the arse, especially when it came to bloody romance!

The booing crowd drew his attention back to the stage, where "Theodore the Underwater Thespian" was reciting Shakespeare

with his head immersed in a bucket of water and had nearly
drowned. The crowd was booing because the awful actor had
survived the ordeal....

The team gathered in the 'Professor's' dressing room which was
quite spacious and drank tea. They would go over the evening's
performance and chat generally. Rosie had given Dorothy a light
summer cloak to cover her flimsy stage costume. But Titus
watched her over the rim of his tea cup and sighed; he had a
growing passion for her which he could never declare; ever.

Edwardian society simply would not accept any mixed race
relationships; as many men returning from the Indian Colonies
with Indian wives had discovered. He noticed that 'Mister Sims'
had not shown up; but then the mysterious young man rarely
did. Titus accepted a couple of biscuits from Rosie and realized
that he had never seen 'Mister Sims' out of his stage costume of
bandages! All he knew about 'Mister Sims' was that he was a
family friend of the Hadden's and had been for some years; in
fact a close childhood friend of Miss Dorothy and her brother;
Harry. Titus actually liked the strange young man with his weird
English accent. He certainly was a good magician; just the 'swap'
trick proved that. Reggie thought it was really clever that the
'real' magician appeared as an assistant; now that was a great
distraction. The little after show meeting broke up and everyone
returned to their dressing rooms.

Dorothy sat and thumbed through the cards [which accompanied
the many flowers which had been delivered to her room: as
usual!] and simply tossed them into the small bin at her feet.
Most of the flower arrangements would be given to girls in the
chorus line and other female staff of the Paradise. She stopped at
one flower which – unusually – came in a small pot. The little
green plant had clearly not bloomed yet. Curious, she read the
accompanying note: *"Miss Hadden, please accept this little fellow
into your home and heart. The instructions for his care are shown
on the rear of this note. With lots of love and tender care, he will
grow into the most magnificent and beautiful flower you could
ever imagine. Just like you have grown into a most intelligent,
talented and beautiful woman: so he will also grow into another
wondrous creation of God. With much respect and love, I remain
your greatest admirer, your Oskar."*

Totally intrigued, she carefully placed the note into her handbag and lifted the pot. It was quite heavy and she placed it on the window ledge of her dressing room: to bask in any sunlight. Rosie smiled, "So what's the bleeding thing called? I mean what will it grow into?"

Dorothy shook her head; she didn't know and that intrigued her more, as did the identity of the mysterious sender. If he wanted Dorothy to notice him amongst the many admirers she had, then he had certainly succeeded!

"The professor and Dorothy would like to draw your attention to the fact that no animals were harmed by tonight's performance: thank you!" SJW.

Dorothy sat in her dressing room stroking Isis the cat, who showed her appreciation by purring loudly and nibbling the little piece of cheese offered. The door slid open and in squeezed Rosie; "I don't know why your fussing over that little git, she's had another one of those bleeding pigeons!"

Dorothy sighed, she had hoped that only finding six was a happy miscount, but it appears Isis had lapsed again. Still, the Professor owned the birds and he did love the wayward cat; he shouldn't be too upset. It's nothing like when 'Marvelous Monty: the magic mouse man' had the dressing room next door: his grand tour of the London suburbs came to a sudden and terrible end at the Paradise Road Music Hall & Theatre.

It had cost the professor nearly two pounds to stop a potential court case against him and the theatre, by a very sad Monty, who swore he would change his act to include large dogs. That proved the downfall of the unlucky performer; he returned to his dressing room one evening – unusually, perfectly sober- and his four wolf-hounds didn't recognise their owner. The story made headlines in the local newspapers and that included the Jewish Chronicle who likened it to the fall of the Temple [eh?]. Dorothy admonished the cat over her terrible act, but Isis said nothing; she is a cat after all.

Rosie 'Legs' McMannon was Dorothy's stage Maid and looked about thirty [she never revealed her real age] a true Londoner, she loved the royal family, swore like a sailor, tippled gin and anyone not born in the East End was 'a fucking foreigner'. But she was loyal and hard working; Dorothy liked her maid and treated her well: the team would gather on a Friday night and the Professor would treat the staff to a fish supper and some brown ale. But Rosie's husband; Albert, and her two sons; Albert Junior and Edward were barred from the festivities by the theatre management, on the grounds they were: 'thieving bastards' – to quote big Tom Reed.

The one occasion they attended, the stockroom of the theatre bar was broken into and nobody could find their watches; except the Professor and Dorothy. But the worst felony was reserved for 'Theodore Timm's and his talking turkey' – the McMannon family ate well that Christmas - and the last words of the turkey were apparently; "Oh fuck!"

Rosie poured the tea and both women sat sipping the hot brew: "That's better, I really look forward to my cup of tea after the show." Dorothy confessed to Rosie who grinned; "Yep, I do love a bleeding good cup of rosy lee." Dorothy winced at the colourful language of her maid, but Rosie is Rosie, she mused and smiled as Rosie scoffed down a couple of soggy biscuits, "My old mum always said, if you drop the bleeding thing in your cup, stir it in, as it gives it balls."

Dorothy sipped her tea and then realised that Rosie was quite still, frozen in mid-sentence, as was the cat playing on the carpet. Dorothy glanced at the large wall clock; the second hand stood still and the time was 9.15pm. She knew that he had arrived and replaced her cup upon the small table and said; "Good evening Mr. Tibbs, you've just missed tea."

The young man dropped into the armchair opposite and removed his top hat, placing it on the floor, between his feet. Mr. Jericho Tibbs looked about 25 years old, but Dorothy knew he was much older than his outward appearance suggested. Mr. Tibbs pulled a magnificent time-piece from his pocket and flicked open the lid; he studied the watch face for a moment, then looked up with a small smile; "Dorothy I have a little task for you, someone has slipped into this time from the near future and it wasn't through a natural time portal."

Dorothy nodded; if it wasn't a 'natural' time portal, then someone has a time controller and that was always bad news. "What have we got to go on?" She asked, leaning back into her chair and adjusted her cushions. Mr. Tibbs ran his hand over his chin and smiled; "Not a lot I'm afraid, the disturbance of the time line occurred this morning: all we can fathom is that the two portals are linked between 1901 and 2022, to this area of the city. You remember the same link occurred back in your month of March this year, but nothing changed."

"I bet this place is very different in 2022!" Dorothy laughed and caught the sad expression that briefly covered Mr. Tibb's face; "What happens here Mr. Tibbs?" She asked, knowing that he wouldn't reveal any part of the future to a mere Temporal Agent; "What becomes of our little community?" She added, folding her arms and her smile was gone.

Mr. Tibbs held up two hands and sighed; "You know full well that I cannot comment on such matters." Jericho Tibbs had no desire to explain about the Blitz: that hurricane of death and destruction that would fall upon her small community in less than forty years and basically wipe everyone she knows and will know, from existence. He glanced at his watch and jumped up from the chair; "I have another appointment in 1344, in Paris, with a fellow who was suddenly cured of the plague by antibiotics. It should make for an interesting evening don't you think?"

Dorothy nodded and was troubled by what Mr. Tibb's was not saying; "Anything else I should know?" She had no idea what "antibiotics" were, probably some cheap French Cologne that smelt like disinfectant and could be used to murder rats.

Mr. Tibbs hesitated and then plunged his hand into his Top hat and produced an empty hand; "Do you see it Dorothy?" She looked closely and then saw several little flakes of what appeared to be gold. "It's not gold, but cheap glitter. It was found at the site of the cross-over. You must be at your best on this one Dorothy; this century is one of the most important and volatile in all of human history, with, perhaps, the exception of 2300, and we must ensure that the time line remains untainted, get that clever brother of yours involved and make sure the Professor is informed."

Mr. Tibbs bent down and stroked the still Isis gently; "I had a wonderful old ginger Tom when I was a child, he was called

'Wellington' - a real character - talking of characters, how's that mischievous creature Sims getting on?"

Dorothy grinned; "He really is trying to improve his behaviour, but he lapsed last week and found the attics - he ate all the Christmas decorations stored up there - My maid thought we had become infected with giant mice, So Uncle William ordered new ones and gave Sims a ticking off."

Mr. Tibbs laughed and placed his hat upon his head with a slap; "Goodbye Dorothy and good luck!" He was gone and Rosie slurped her tea; "My old mum always said, if you drop the bleeding thing in your cup, stir it in, as it gives it balls." Dorothy glanced again at the clock; it displayed 9.15pm.

Isis the cat rolled over her shoes, playing with a small ball. The time Mr. Tibbs had spent in the dressing room had never occurred. She shuddered and watched the rain hitting her window pane and said softly; "Should anyone really find out about the future?" Rosie finished her tea and dropped some biscuit crumbs for Isis;"What's that you say Miss?"

"Rosie, I need you to run a message to my brother at Brick Lane station, can you do that for me and please take my umbrella, the rain has started." Dorothy walked over to her writing bureau and quickly wrote a little note, folding the paper and placing it an envelope. She handed it Rosie who was pulling on her coat and large hat; "Remember, as usual, place it in his hands only."

Rosie grabbed the umbrella and grinned; "Yes of course dear, your brother is a handsome fella and I know what I would bleeding place in his hands!" She guffawed and placed both hands on her ample breasts. Dorothy shook her head in mock disapproval; "Really Rosie, what would Albert say?" handing her maid a sixpence; "He would say good bleeding luck to the lucky bugger!" Rosie chuckled, kissed the coin and pushed it into her apron pocket; "Bless you darling, I'll get the boys some chips for their supper and I'll see you tomorrow."

Dorothy watched through the small window as her maid quickly disappeared into the rainy night with the yellowing gas lamps giving poor illumination of passer-by's and carriages; that's when she noticed the carriage outside the public entrance of the old theatre.

Dottie watched as Sir Thomas Astor-Smith apparently jumped in and the cab sped away into the gathering gloom.

Dorothy wondered where the theatre owner was going at this time of night, and her mind flicked back to the sight of the shabby dressed man; how did he get in the theatre unnoticed? Why did Sir Thomas handle the situation himself; normally one of the stage hands would be told to deal with it? The man looked unwell, he clearly wasn't drunk and it appeared Sir Thomas knew him; so who was the shabby man?

"Miss Hadden, there is a visitor for you at reception." Dorothy recognized the voice of Miss Player, the theatre's Housekeeper and her quiet sharp knock upon the door. Dorothy opened the door and smiled, to be greeted with the sour expression of old Miss Ester Player, a tall skinny woman with an acid tongue and miserable disposition. "I would normally turn away visitors after nine o'clock, even yours, but this gentleman – if you can call him that – is quite insistent, he looks quite a mess. I was going to turn him away and told him I would call a constable. But he said; 'Tell Miss Hadden that the future calls upon everyone some day.' He seemed to calm down, so I asked Mr. Skole to wait with him while I fetched you." The two women descended the front staff stairs and arrived in the rear of the small reception area.

Mr. Skoles was just walking back through the theatre's staff entrance with a puzzled expression upon his face; "His gone, just suddenly dashed out the door into the street, shouting out something, you would have thought the silly bugger had seen a ghost!" Mr. Skoles explained, shaking the rain out of his short thin hair.

"Can you remember what he said Mr. Skole?" Dorothy asked, as something caught her eye, upon the reception carpet – it was tiny pieces of gold coloured glitter. Dorothy picked up some with the tips of her fingers; they were exactly like the flakes Jericho Tibbs had shown her earlier: she took a deep breath.

"Didn't quite catch what he was yelling about, something like 'Bremhaving or BremHaven', But he really did run, a bleeding cab nearly had him, at the top, near Canning Town Road." Mr. Skoles ran his fingers through his flimsy hair and patted it down; he was having drinks in the 'Royal Oak' with the widow Sissy Graves in just a few minutes and wanted to look his best, so he shrugged his shoulders and wandered off.

Big Tom Reed appeared in the foyer clutching a colourful poster advertising the latest act to grace the stage of the Paradise Road Theatre; 'The great Christian Pyle; Escapologist & Mind reader!' Big Tom pointed to the poster and with a wide grin explained; "He's top notch, is this one, last month he escaped from a Paris bank vault in less than ten minutes, a real star." Dorothy slowly examined the poster and smiled; "I seem to recall there was a little problem of bank notes stuffed in his underwear, according to the newspapers."

Big Tom waved the story away; "It was just a misunderstanding, he was cleared of all wrong doing at court and now he's going to appear at some cost." Dorothy sighed, then remembered to thank Miss Player for her help and received a grim smile in reply. The old lady returned to her desk and continued her paperwork without saying another word. Dorothy made her way back to the dressing room, where she collected her coat and hat, then, sadly realised she had given Rosie her umbrella.

Nevertheless, she strode onto the street and waved down a cab that appeared from Canning Town Road; "Thirteen Dock Lane please." She told the Cab driver and stepped in, pushing well back in the fine upholstered seat and watched the rain fall.

The shabby man filled her thoughts - why had he appeared at the theatre asking for her? Why did he dash off before speaking? Who did he see at the theatre that frightened him? The strange quote he gave Miss Player; 'Tell Miss Hadden that the future calls upon everyone some day.' Was that a clue to his identity: was he the Time jumper and why is he here?

 The cab ride was over in a few minutes and Dorothy was at home, her House Maid Ellen greeted her mistress with a big smile and helped Dorothy out of her coat and large hat. "Where on earth is your brolly Miss?" She asked, shaking water from the coat. Dottie just smiled and asked: "Is Uncle William home yet?"

Dorothy made for the drawing room and found her uncle in his favourite chair, clouds of smoke billowing from his pipe, the local evening newspaper clutched in his hands and a glass of dark rum on the side table. Dorothy leant over the old man and kissed his forehead; "I think we may have to bring Isis home with us in future Uncle William, she ate another pigeon this evening. I don't think Skole is feeding her properly."

William Hadden chuckled to himself and slapped the newspaper down, taking a sip of his rum and shook his head; "Skole over feeds the little minx in my opinion, it's in her nature to kill and hunt, never mind how much we stuff her with goodies." He re-lit his pipe and sent several large clouds towards the ceiling. "What troubles you my dear?" He added, peering over his pipe at her.

Dorothy had to smile; her Uncle could read her expressions like an open book. "Jericho Tibbs called in this evening, someone has opened a time portal between here and 2022 and it's not a natural tear, someone has dropped in uninvited and Mr. Tibbs wants to find who's clever enough to solve the problem of time travel and…….." Dorothy fell silent as Ellen bought in the tea tray and some rich fruit cake.

"You need to eat properly Miss, so I've brought some fruit cake to have with your evening tea." Ellen smiled and placed the tray down; "That's fine Ellen, thank you. I'll serve Uncle William and myself." Dorothy lifted the tea pot and strainer and filled two cups with the dark brew, then added some milk and a single sugar cube to one; "Are you taking sugar today?"

Ellen excused herself and William waved the cup aside saying: "I'll stick to my rum thank you Dotty." Dorothy also told her Uncle about the return to the theatre of the shabby man with golden glitter on his boots and that Sir Thomas had left late in a cab, just before the stranger re-appeared. Dorothy noticed the strange look on her Uncle's face and he muttered something and drew heavily on his pipe.

"I've sent a note to Harry asking him to call on me tomorrow; I'll also have a discreet word with Sir Thomas about the shabby man." [Harry wouldn't be home tonight: he and his team were working night surveillance on some suspected Irish rebels.] Dorothy sipped her tea and started to relax back in the chair. Why would a suspected time-traveller visit the theatre and wish to speak to her? And why the reference to the German port of Bremerhaven [she believed that's what he probably shouted] is Imperial Germany – somehow – involved in his visit, but then, how was she involved in all that?

She finished her tea and just for a second closed her tired eyes. The big dark man was naked standing over a sink, pushing a bright white cloth over his face. He shook his head and turned a little, "What is it Dottie? That's a real strange look on your pretty face." He grinned and dipped the cloth into the sink and wiped his face again, adding, "This bloody weather is a killer, after that bloody winter who would have thought the summer could turn out like this. The bloody city is cooking!"

He dropped the flannel into the sink and picked up a clean soft towel and ran it over his head and face. She was staring at him: he was a big man in all respects! He threw the towel on the drainer and now smiling broadly, walked towards her. "Still, I do love the way you cope with the heat by losing all your clothes! My God, I fucking love you naked my darling."

Dottie stared at Uncle William and slowly finished her tea. The man in her little day-dream wasn't Titus and she sighed with relief at that. Then regretted that thought and placed her cup down a little confused by her contradictory and erotic thoughts. She nibbled a biscuit and watched her Uncle sucking upon his pipe, deep in thought.

Finally, he grunted and adjusted his glasses; "Be careful with Sir Thomas, he's a man of ill-temper and definitely not a supporter of women's suffrage, he'll treat you like a child whilst trying to seduce you at the same time; a wretch of a man." Dorothy smiled at her Uncle's concern and sipped her tea; "I'm a big girl now Uncle William and know how to handle Sir Thomas and get some answers that we need." Reluctantly, William nodded his agreement and sipped his rum. "See if Harry can be present, I'll be happier with him there." He added, waving his billowing pipe at his niece with a smile breaking across his face.

Dorothy smiled and nodded; "Oh very well, I'll get Harry to nursemaid me. Now, changing the subject, I had a letter this morning from Lady Ann Bridgewater, she wants Pandora to perform at a large house party at Stonebridge House over Christmas and money is no object apparently. The family is returning from Germany to spend Christmas here." William groaned; "That damn alto-ego of yours is becoming quite Popular; will Sims agree to a Christmas performance I wonder?"

"I can persuade him, I think he actually enjoys the thrill of the performance and the applause of course." Dorothy looked up at the Drawing Room clock; "Heavens, it's almost eleven o'clock. Time for bed I think."

She arose and kissed her Uncle goodnight and made her way upstairs to bed, but thoughts of the shabby man drifted into her dreams, complete with golden snow and trickles of blood down dirty walls and bare floors. Dorothy awoke just after three in the morning and poured some water from the pitcher on her bedside cabinet and lit the little lamp that always stood there. The dream had definitely disturbed her and she knew that these strange visions had a nasty habit of sometimes coming true!

She sighed loudly as she caught sight of the figure sitting on her bedroom chair, legs drawn up and grinning. The strange figure with its dirty white bandages and deep dark eyes coughed loudly; "That must have been some dream Dotty or was it a vision?" His English had a strange accent, but was pleasant enough.

"Sims, how many times have I told you not to materialise when I'm at home? How on earth would I explain you to the servants?" She admonished the spirit gently; dealing with a young man who had been dead for nearly three and a half thousand years could be difficult at times! She told Sims about the offer from Lady Bridgewater and he readily agreed, slapping his hands together and laughing. "Can I do my leap from the trunk Dotty?" He asked with real enthusiasm and jumped from the chair, rolled into a ball and bounced off the wall. Dorothy sighed, but had to smile; "Sims - just calm down - you'll wake the house up!"

Sims nodded and jumped onto the chair: backwards. "We can perform the blanket trick and the genie from the bottle and....." Sims folded his legs up and gripped his knee's with both hands and laughed to himself. "We should perform together more Dotty." He added and scratched his head.

Dorothy leaned back on her pillows remembering her childhood and her strange play mate; Sims. They had such fun together, with the mad mummy making her laugh so much with his magic tricks and crazy antics. She really did appreciate how lonely her childhood could have been and she quietly thanked her late grandfather for discovering the tomb of Simhenta-Kara or 'Sims' as he liked to be called now.

It was Dorothy who gave Simhenta-Kara his new name; as a little girl, she simply could not pronounce his Egyptian name in full, so he was just 'Sims'.

"You best return to the Museum for now, we'll try and practice some tricks tomorrow, if I can find some free time." She extinguished the light and turned back to more restless sleep. "Goodnight Dotty, give my best greetings to Harry and the old boy." Sims whispered and returned to his sarcophagus in the British Museum basement, where he stood by the dusty old crate and for the thousandth time read the faded writing on the side: "PROPERTY OF SIR GEORGE HADDEN LONDON ENGLAND - HANDLE WITH CARE." He sat quietly in the dark corridor and watched the sun rise through the floor grate, then slipped back inside the casket to wait the new night.

"Sims story is told in 'THE TEMPORAL DETECTIVES' series: Book 1 – Episode 9, Amenhoteph V and the mirror of time." SJW.

Dorothy lay staring up at the dull ceiling in the darkness and her thoughts flew back in time. She was sixteen and walking – hand in hand – with Jerome [Jeb] Newgate in the fields at the back of her posh school. She had slipped away after lessons had finished and met him behind the sports pavilion. He was the nineteen year old son of the school caretaker and to her: a human Adonis. Young Dorothy was smitten with him and hung on every word he uttered and the pair walked in the late sunshine, talking and laughing. They stopped frequently to kiss, shy and clumsy at first, Dorothy enjoyed his attentions far more than she should [she admonished herself for that, but carried on] and their passions were almost overwhelming, with Dorothy allowing his eager hands into her tight blouse and his tongue into her equally eager mouth.

The summer of 1898 remained one of her best memories and a milestone in her life: the year she experienced real love. Dorothy turned and pushed the pillows against the headboard and ran a hand over her face to brush the little tears away. They always came when Jeb put in an appearance and there was nothing she could do to stop them. "Stupid, silly little girl!" She whispered and buried her face in the soft pillows, gripping them tight. The pair met many times as late summer turned into autumn and Dorothy [in her happy mind] was already making plans about her future and the handsome, charming young man figured in all of them. Then one day, Jeb didn't turn up for their rendezvous behind the white washed pavilion. Instead his younger brother Charlie appeared with a note and just smiled, handing the confused [and disappointed] Dorothy the little piece of paper, then running off without a word.

Dorothy leaned against the pavilion and read the letter that destroyed all her girlish dreams. Jeb had joined the colours [like his father and uncles had done years ago] and was on his way to Manchester for training. He told Dorothy to forget all about him and find someone new. He wished her well and that was that.

A broken hearted Dorothy returned to school and cried for a few days, comforted by her best friend Maggie Mountbatten. The years passed and Dorothy now remembered she was working [part-time, just to earn her own money] in a hat shop in Whitechapel [the spring of 1900] when her friend Maggie appeared clutching a newspaper. She said nothing and simply pulled the paper open and on page four, pointed to the new list of casualties reported from the Boar War. Apparently the Manchester Regiment had been in action near Ladysmith and suffered losses. Maggie ran her finger down the column of names and ranks: then stopped.

Dorothy followed that elegant little finger and read where it halted. Dorothy gripped the pillows and cursed. "Go away! Please God go away!" She couldn't stop herself sobbing despite many, many times telling herself that she would never cry like that again. Recovering from the shock of seeing Jeb's name amongst the fallen, she said nothing to her best friend and simply nodded, saying to herself, 'So that's that.'

Some weeks later she met James [Jimmy] O'Connor, a big Irish lad who was a student at the London University. He reminded her of Jeb in many ways and they 'walked out' together, often going to the evening music hall performances and Dorothy was totally captivated by 'stage life' and a little, by Jimmy who was funny and charming. That's when she first saw her dear uncle actually appearing on stage. Uncle William was then known as 'Willy the Wonder' performing magic tricks with a young assistant who apparently couldn't do a thing right. But the audience still liked the show and his assistant: she was a very pretty little thing with ample charms that were not hidden by her stage costume.

When Dorothy arrived home that fateful night, she had already made her mind up. She would become a magician like her dear uncle. Thus, Dorothy threw herself into the world of magic and was happily surprised that big Jimmy supported her ambitions fully. The pair quickly became lovers, with Dorothy meeting him at his 'digs' [he had rooms above the undertakers in St. Paul's Road – unsurprisingly - the rent was low and perfect for a student]. That was Dorothy's first real introduction to sex.

It was Ellen pulling the curtains back that woke Dorothy from her restless slumbers, and she eased herself up and slowly grabbed the cup of hot tea from the bedside cabinet and took a most welcome sip. Ellen stared out the window and called over to her, "I think Mr. Harry is about to get an early wake-up call Miss. Mr. Beaver is heading this way with real determination in his walk. The old bugger normally strolls everywhere. That's not fair, poor Mr. Harry only got in at two this morning."

Dottie just sighed: 'Mr. Beaver' was PC Barry Beaverfield, the local beat constable and he usually arrived to inform Harry that he was wanted [normally urgently] at Brick Lane Police Station. She asked Ellen how she knew the time of Harry's return and Ellen touched her hair and didn't look at her mistress, "Oh, I needed to go and heard him coming in. So I asked if he wanted anything, but he just wanted his bed, poor man."

Dorothy smiled, "So you spoke to him Ellen, did he say how his undercover operation went?" Ellen shook her head, "No Miss, he just wanted his bed." She didn't see or hear Dottie chuckle to herself, "And you bloody in it." Dorothy knew full well that Ellen – a young widowed woman – 'helped' Harry out with his 'night starvation' problems that all young un-married men suffered. Dottie wondered if Ellen knew about Mrs. Debra Fells or Mrs. Jane Stephens and upon occasion, another young widowed woman, Lady Samantha Crawford when she visited the capitol from her estate in Essex. Little wonder Uncle William was always telling him to get bloody married and leave other men's wives alone, even the dead ones! She then recalled that Jimmy had promised to take her to a lecture at the 'Explorer's Club' tonight. It was about the cannibal and head hunting tribes of the upper Amazon. She sighed; he certainly knew [so he thought] what a young lady liked for entertainment! But he certainly knew what Dorothy liked in the bedroom...stables, fields, and the odd 'bed & Breakfast' when he was flush with cash. At least he was no prude when it came to where they should fuck.

CHAPTER 4. 'PLEASE SIR, CAN I HAVE SOME MORE?' Charles Dickens.

A tired Detective Inspector Harry Hadden walked slowly up the steps towards the double black doors of Slaughterhouse Road Workhouse, Detective Sergeant Alistair McPearl was reading aloud from the piece of paper that the desk Sergeant had passed up to the CID office, his soft Scottish accent was quite apparent: "The body was found at 6.15am this morning by the Night Warden – Mr. Elliot - leaving for home after his shift. Couldn't miss it really, went to relieve himself before the walk home and found it on the toilet floor – throat sliced open and puddles of blood - uniform say the stiff booked in under the name 'Michael Jagger', but there's no proof that was his real name. Oh, and Doc Goldstein is on way."

Harry nodded and the uniformed Constable standing outside the doors saluted and pushed them open, the pair passed inside and were greeted by Sergeant Rollings who was eating a smelly cheese and onion sandwich; "There's nothing on the body except a brand new key, looks like it was cut yesterday; it's all bright and shiny, a door key perhaps?" He held up the key and took another bite from his huge sandwich; "The stiff's dossed down in a workhouse, but can afford to have a locksmith make a new key, strange eh?" He spat out several bits of bread and cheese as he laughed to himself.

Harry pulled the key from the sergeant's fat fingers and held it up; "Rollings you fat bastard, how many times have I told you;

no-one touches the body until CID arrive, do I have to carve it on your fat arse with a knife?" That drew a quiet chuckle from DS McPearl who couldn't stand Rollings at the best of times, he considered the overweight and unpopular sergeant an insult to the uniform. Harry handed the key to Alistair; "Get a couple of uniform boys to run it past those two locksmith shops in the High Street and Thames road, see if they can remember who ordered it and what's it likely to open."

Rollings pointed to a drab grey door marked with white chalk; 'crapper'. He laughed and pushed the half-eaten sandwich back into his coat pocket and replaced his helmet; "In there Sherlock and don't get your feet wet." The sergeant waddled down the corridor towards the front door, stopping to call back;"The Warden is still at the nick, giving a statement to Farmer; that little cock-sucker of yours." Then with a wave of his hand, the obnoxious sergeant was gone.

Detective Constable Edwin Palmer walked past Rollings without a word and stabbed a thumb towards the door behind him; "All the dossers booked in for last night are being held in the Dining room, I've got a couple of uniform boys shaking them down, but nothing obvious yet Guv." He pulled a packet of 'Woodbines' from his waistcoat and offered them around; Alistair and Edwin placed a cigarette in their mouths, but Harry declined with a 'No thanks'. Edwin lit both cigarettes with a single match and Alistair took a deep breath; "Shall we take a look at the stiff, Guv?"

"Least we don't have to wear the Lavender hankie with this one; nice and fresh." Edwin smiled and sucked on his cigarette, flicking the ash onto the dirty floor. Harry nodded and the trio pushed open the toilet door; "Fuck! I wish we bleeding had!" Exclaimed the Constable, waving his hand about his face and drawing heavily on the cigarette again for the overpowering smell of rancid urine and old feces filled the grim room. The three men stood and looked about the toilet: three urinals that had a green haze about them, one large cracked sink and three closets with no doors. "Well, it's not fucking Buckingham Palace is it?" Edwin coughed and attempted to open the large window opposite, but found it nailed shut.

The body lay sprawled upon the floor, face downwards with a large puddle of blood that had spread from the head down, creeping towards the shoulders and left arm which was held out above the head. The other arm appeared to be placed in the right pocket of the shabby brown coat. The feet were sprawled open and the left trouser leg was clearly wet. That's when Harry noticed the boots and squatted down, pointing out the little golden flakes that were scattered about the soles and heels. "That's not real gold is it Guv?" Alistair asked, pulling his sketch pad out from the inside pocket of his long coat. He licked the pencil tip and started to draw, whilst Edwin checked the closets and groaned loudly; "Some dirty fucker has left a pan of Richards!"

"Richard the Third is cockney rhyming slang for 'turd.' Should you wonder!" SJW.

He pulled the chain and stepped out, finishing his cigarette and tossing it back into the toilet. "Why the sketch book?" Harry asked his Detective Sergeant, a little puzzled, adding; "Which photographer is supposed to cover this?"

"Oh, sorry Guv, Mister Collins in on holiday in Southend- On - Sea with his wife and kids and old Jamie Lambert is in Eastham Infirmary having his piles seen to; poor old fucker!" Edwin pulled a sour face and lit up another cigarette. Harry sighed; "Welcome to twentieth century law enforcement."

Harry examined the large cut at the base of the neck and then noticed the corpse's left hand was smooth with manicured and clean nails. He sniffed the hair and could smell shampoo or maybe hair tonic: "To answer your question Alistair; no, it's not real gold. But our friend here was no vagrant, that hand hasn't done a hard day's work in its life."

Harry searched the pockets and found nothing. "I bet that fat thieving bastard has taken anything of value." Edwin quietly muttered, then noticed the odd look upon his boss's face, adding: "What is it Guv? What's caught your eye?"

Harry muttered, "Apart from being dead, he looks quite healthy and well fed." then stopped and pulled at the dead man's trouser waistband. Harry smiled and he pulled two gold sovereigns out that had been hidden there. Edwin and Alistair both chuckled and

Edwin grinned broadly; "That useless fat bastard missed the jackpot!" Harry turned the coins carefully in his hand: they looked old and worn yet were dated to 1894, just seven years ago. He grunted and placed them in a small paper bag.

"Two gold sovereigns from 1901 would be worth over a thousand pounds today [2023]." SJW.

"What the fuck is he doing in a Doss house with that sort of money?" Alistair asked, but Harry just shrugged his shoulders and walked over to the waste bin and peered in, giving it a shake.

There was just three items: a small piece of white paper which was crumpled up and looked like it had been ripped from a notebook, a bent metal spoon and the broken bottom of a small bottle, finally a piece of green cord. He had Edwin place the items into a paper bag and write the details into his notebook. Harry looked into the worn sink and smiled; "Bingo my boys, take a look."

Edwin and Alistair nodded their approval at the find; little droplets of blood around the plughole and on the edge of the sink. "The fucker must have washed his knife in the sink before wandering off." Alistair sounded almost impressed with the killer and returned to his sketching. There was a soft knock on the toilet door and Edwin pulled it open; "Hi Doc!" He exclaimed and stood aside as Doctor Rubin Goldstein wandered in and shook hands with Inspector Hadden; "Hello Harry, they told me at the station it was a throat job." Placing his 'Gladstone' bag on the floor, he took a quick look at the wound and moved the left arm about a little. "Death is certified at….." He pulled out his pocket watch and flipped open the face; "Death is certified at 8.35am and just out of interest, He's probably been dead for just a couple of hours at the most."

"Your joking Doc, he was found at 6.15am this morning." Alistair looked quite amazed, but he knew that old Doc Goldstein had quite a reputation for getting the time of death right on the button. Harry glanced down at the body; "So you think he was killed just before he was found?" Doc Goldstein adjusted his glasses and nodded; "This body is fresh as an apple picked from the tree. His cold, but not that cold considering he's been lying on a stone floor and still flexible, he's been dead just hours."

"It has to be that fucking Warden, the bugger that found him." Edwin reasoned and pulled his cigarettes out; "That or the killer was still here just before the Warden came in."

Alistair smiled and pointed to the doorway and then the window; "Remember, there's no hiding places in the corridor outside and this shit hole only has that door and the bloody window is nailed shut; so how did he get out of this fucking room without being seen?" Edwin slowly nodded his agreement; "Comes down to that bloody Warden then." And lit up yet another cigarette.

Doc Goldstein and Harry exchanged glances with a smile; "The boys from Eastham Mortuary will collect and I'll try and complete the PM by this afternoon. Good morning gentlemen; I'm going for breakfast." The Doctor raised his hat and headed for the door; "By the way Harry, the PM will confirm one fact that I already know about our deceased friend; he was a diabetic, the smell from his mouth indicates it. So he was a dead man walking, the poor soul."

"PM means Post-Mortem and Doctor Goldstein refers to the corpse as a 'dead man walking' because there was no real effective treatment of Diabetes until 1921; until then it was considered a fatal illness." SJW.

Leaving Edwin and Alistair to complete the removal of the body, Inspector Harry Hadden headed for the Paradise Road Theatre to meet with his sister Dorothy as arranged and indulge in some well earned breakfast. He hailed a cab and sat writing up his notes as the cab threaded through the busy streets of London's East End. There was something very odd about this case and Harry wondered what the man was actually doing; booking in Dosshouses, when he had lots of money? He pulled Dorothy's note from his coat pocket and re-read it. The dead man was almost certainly Dorothy's 'shabby man' – as she referred to the stage intruder – there couldn't possibly be two similar 'tramps' wandering around the East end with their boots covered in gold tinsel. Was it the same gold tinsel that Mr. Tibbs had shown her; which means that the 'time-traveller' that he [Mr. Tibbs] was after is already dead; murdered, but by who and why?

He certainly wasn't killed during a robbery; he was playing at a vagrant. Whoever killed him didn't find the valuable coins or wasn't looking for them. Harry sighed and looked again at the date that Dorothy had written; 2022. Sweet Jesus, what was London like in over a century's time? Why the 'time-traveller' here and what was was his purpose or mission? Too many bloody questions and so far: no answers. He thought and jumped from the cab when it stopped outside the stage door of the Paradise Theatre. He paid the cabby and strode up the back steps and into the theatre, giving the door keeper a wave. Old Charlie sat back down in his small office and finished his tea. Mr. Hadden was a very regular visitor to his sister Dorothy and Uncle William: he was well known to all the theatre staff.

Dorothy was dozing in the chair, getting an occasional glance from Rosie who was knitting by the door trying to hear what Dottie was muttering in her sleep!

Dorothy was back to last Sunday, in the bedroom of Jimmy's flat, naked on the small bed, giggling a little as the big man pushed hard and groaned a little. She had wrapped her long legs around his back and gripped his shoulders with both hands, their eager tongues exploring each other's mouths. Jimmy gasped, cussed and quickly pulled from her, holding his erection tightly. But it was no use, he groaned loudly and ejaculated. Dorothy waved her hands about and pulled a face as the hot liquid spattered her chin and neck, some landing in her hair. He gasped and lay back next to her as she grabbed up a small towel and carefully wiped her hair and neck. She gave him a hard slap on the arm. "You dirty bugger! You got the damn stuff in my hair now."

"They were using the 'withdrawal' method which is only effective about 78% of the time. Dorothy was playing with fire here!" SJW.

Jimmy managed a chuckle and ran a hand a hand over her taunt stomach, "Well, darling girl, if I had let that lot go inside of you, we would have to get married, no mistake." He leaned up on his elbows and took a breath, again running his hand down her stomach. "I like the idea of you waddling around the place, full of my little one. So, we should get married, but not yet. I need to graduate and get a bloody job that could pay for a young wife and some kids." He patted her tummy and chuckled, "So, sorry my darling it's only – for now – goes in your mouth or up your bum." He slumped back and Dorothy prodded him grinning, "So we're getting married are we? Is that a proposal James bloody O'Connor?"

He leaned over and kissed her cheek, "Aye, I suppose it is my darling." He wiped his face and grunted, "Least I wouldn't have to shoot me bloody stuff all around the sodding place." Dottie giggled and grabbed him, pulling his head to hers and they kissed again. He grinned, placing her hand on his cock. "Do you fancy going again? You know I last at least ten minutes more the second time around." She jerked him a couple of times and smiled, "So, you reckon you can last eleven minutes now?" Jimmy sat up and gave her pink bottom a little slap, "Cheeky cow! I'll show you!" The pair rolled on the bed laughing, kissing and whispering. Dorothy sat up and saw Rosie smiling at her, "Nice dream sweetheart? Who's this bleeding Jimmy character?"

Dottie smiled and sat back, "Put the kettle on please Rosie, I'm gasping." Rosie nodded and placed her knitting down and chuckled, "Did you manage to get it all out of your hair? It's a real bugger when that happens, ain't it?" And walked to the small paraffin stove. Dottie slapped a hand over her face, a little embarrassed, and then chuckled, what the hell; Rosie probably knows more about bloody sex than Casanova does. She had admitted to being 'quite wild' in her pre-marriage days.

Rosie still had a good figure and would easily be regarded as 'pretty' by most men that met her. But their attention would invariably be centered on her breasts. They were large, firm and still pert. Everyone commented on them with Tom [the stage manager] saying they were the 'pride of the theatre'. Few of the men would disagree with him. Her only 'rival' in that arena was Dorothy who easily matched her for long legs and whose breasts were only slightly smaller: not that many men would complain about that!

Rosie handed a tea cup to her and their hands touched. They

both smiled and Dorothy felt a real strange sensation, especially in her stomach. She sipped her tea and was about to say something when Rosie chuckled, "I like men, but unless you get one that knows what he's doing, you can end up full of a bleeding nipper you don't want and can't afford. Do you know what I mean darling?"

Dorothy slowly nodded and said quietly, "I always heard....well, that it's better with another woman if you just want some fun without any little consequences. After all, another woman can't get you in the family way, can they? And a woman would certainly know her way around a woman's body....you know, how to please them...." She stopped and finished her tea, feeling really strange to be having this conversation with Rosie. But then – strangely - it seemed quite natural to speak like this with her and Dottie felt at ease which made her feel a little odd about it: in a nice way. But this subject would appear again – quickly. They both sipped their teas and smiled at each other.

CHAPTER 5. 'WHEN, IN COUNTRIES THAT ARE CALLED CIVILISED, WE SEE AGE GOING TO THE WORKHOUSE AND YOUTH TO THE GALLOWS, SOMETHING MUST BE WRONG IN THE SYSTEM OF GOVERNMENT'. Thomas Paine.

Dorothy had to sit down and Rosie pressed a cup of tea into her hand; "My God, I only saw the poor wretch alive yesterday and now he's dead!" She sipped her tea and recounted to her brother how the shabby man had called into the theatre, but fled into the night before speaking to her. Now he wouldn't speak to anyone; ever. Dorothy told Harry about the strange quotation the man had given Miss Player and the words he shouted before running into the street.

Harry placed his cup upon the small table and accepted the bacon sandwich from Rosie; "Bremerhaven, that's probably what the man was shouting." Dorothy waved away a similar sandwich, but accepted a couple of digestive biscuits;"Bremerhaven, that's the big navel port in Germany." She picked at the biscuit, her appetite dead as the shabby man.

"Where the Kaiser intends to base a great fleet to rival our Grand Fleet, [based up at Scapa Flow, in Scotland] and never pay mind about all the teeth grinding and Sabre rattling it causes." Harry was enjoying the sandwich immensely; Rosie knew how to knock up proper bacon sandwich. He caught the look on his sister's face and lowered the sandwich, wiping his chin with a hankie; "What is it Dotty?"

"In March, there was an assassination attempt on the German Kaiser and it nearly succeeded. It was in Bremerhaven. Had it been successful, his son would be Kaiser now and maybe Europe would be breathing easily again." Dorothy stood up and paced the room, despite protests from Rosie; "Then the assassination of Mr. McKinley only last month - he was a good man - how will his death and not the Kaisers affect the future of this century?" She added, thinking there had already been many high profile deaths and the new century was not two years old yet. Was that a clear portent or omen for the future: lot's of deaths? She sighed and stood by the small window and folded her arms, remembering and wondering about Jericho Tibbs reaction to her question about the future.

"The 25th American President; William McKinley was assassinated on September 6th 1901 by a gunman who was a self-confessed 'Anarchist'. The other deaths she refers to, may be the death of Queen Victoria and the Queens eldest daughter, also called Victoria who died some months after her mother; she was the mother of Kaiser William II." SJW.

"Rosie, will you see if any letters have been delivered for me or the Professor please." She asked and her Maid departed, closing the door quietly. Dorothy checked the outside corridor and spoke quickly to her brother about the visit of Jericho Tibbs, the latest violation of the Time Line in March and the glitter found at the scene of the latest cross-over, the significance of which, wasn't lost on Harry; "If our man's the Time Jumper, then he didn't last long here, which was probably unintended, he had no idea that someone was going to murder him!" Harry sipped his tea and suggested Dorothy sit down and eat something, adding; "There is another person from the future here, the one who crossed over in

March but has apparently done nothing or failed in his attempt to assassinate the Kaiser or maybe managed to stop it; who really knows?" He said, shrugging his shoulders.

"So we have another person from the future loose in the East End, probably with lethal intentions towards some powerful person or institution that will maintain the current future or change it. For the moment we don't know which scenario is correct." Dorothy's brain was working at full speed as she paced the little room, then stopped suddenly and smiled at her brother; "Maybe the shabby man made contact with Sir Thomas because he would know how Sir Thomas influenced history by his work with the Secret Service; all that would be known in a hundred years surely?" Harry nodded at that.

"He probably told Sir Thomas about some event which will happen quite soon as proof of his truth. Sir Thomas simply could not resist such an offer; to discover the future before it happens and maybe alter it to his or Britain's advantage?" Dorothy added and picked up a biscuit and scoffed it down with a small smile.

Harry liked that reasoning and nodded again; "So the shabby man came disguised as a vagrant and cleverly frequented Dosshouses as a cover, while trying to make contact with Sir Thomas who he would know had influence in these times?"

Dorothy smiled a little: "If he hid himself in Dosshouses, the people he interacted with would have little chance of creating major changes to the Time Line that wasn't in his plan; now that would have been clever thinking indeed."

Harry could only agree with his sister's deductions and then asked about Sir Thomas Astor-Smith; "So he clearly knew the man, that's interesting and as you spotted, the man was ill; Doc Goldstein believes he was suffering from Diabetes, which means they still haven't cured the damn disease a hundred years from now."

Dorothy sighed; "The poor soul, carrying about a death sentence, so much for progress..." Then she tapped her chin with long slender fingers and looked a little puzzled, speaking her troubled thoughts out loud; "It was not a natural hole in the Time-Line, so the shabby man came back deliberately. Why on earth would he risk coming to a time that could offer him no extra medical help for his condition? Why did he take that risk when he was already seriously ill?"

Harry nodded his agreement at that thought and said; "It was a one-way trip, he would have known that before he travelled; so he must have had a very good reason to risk his life so? Then we have Sir Thomas who is a powerful man in this time period; a Mason in the new Prince of Wales Lodge I believe; that's real power right there. Is he [Sir Thomas] the reason for the visit?"

"Do you think he had a hand in the man's death, I mean he left the theatre really late and had ample opportunity to visit the Doss house, or arrange for others to carry out the awful deed?" Dorothy sat down and added; "But why did he try to contact me twice? What message was he going to impart? What on Earth do I have to do with someone from the year 2022?"

"Maybe Sir Thomas has answers to those questions." Harry spoke quietly and finished his tea. They both nodded in agreement and Harry added; "It all points to Sir Thomas, whatever way we hash it up, I will need to speak to your Patron and I'll keep you out of it for now; that'll please Uncle Willy!"

Dorothy smiled at that, then said; "Why did the shabby man want to speak to me? I believe he appeared on the stage to see me and again, he came to the theatre with a strange message to get me to see him. What did he want to tell me?"

"Maybe, he knew something about Sir Thomas, and his possible connections with the incident in Bremerhaven? I've heard the stories about his links with Military Intelligence and the Special Irish branch, he uses the patronage of the Paradise as cover - for his comings and goings – quite clever really; who would suspect a Theatre owner was a powerful secret government agent!" Harry added and pulled on his coat and hat; "I best head back to the nick, I'll see you later." He kissed her cheek and left for Brick Lane Police Station, passing Rosie on the back stairs, clutching the Hadden's mail.

"Bleeding hell Mister Harry, I had to pay a penny to old sour face [Miss Player] to get a letter some twit didn't put a stamp on; she had to pay the postman for delivery and expected the bloody money from me." Rosie waved the envelope about and Harry smiled, pulling a penny from his waistcoat; "Here we go Rosie, I hope the letter's worth it." Harry started to descend the stairs when Rosie laughed; "I have never seen such odd writing, I'll give you that."

Harry stopped and turned back; Rosie placed the letter in his open hand and commented; "Well, if you can't trust your big brother, who can a girl trust?" She smiled broadly, thinking of that big strong hand sliding up her dress; she quickly shook the thoughts from her mind and adjusted her hair; but he is such a strapping, good looking young man she sighed to herself. He only had to bloody hint and my knickers would be down or off.

Harry studied the envelope, leaning against the stair rail; the writing was definitely odd, he certainly had never seen print like it and the corner had been rubber stamped in Eastham Post office with 'A Penny to pay'. He opened it very carefully and unfolded the single sheet of paper it contained and read the contents with great interest: *Dear Miss Hadden, I have followed your careers, both on the stage and as an agent for Mr. Jericho Tibbs, with growing interest, particularly the latter. I must warn you not to interfere further in the present assignment; we will deal with the Kaiser and alter the current Time Line so that sanity and decency continue to exist in our civilized world. The sad alternative is a world of murder, immorality, madness and mass death. You have been warned. The 3rd Priest of CHRONOS.*

Harry pushed the envelope into his pocket and asked Rosie to pass a message to both Dorothy and the Professor; to meet at 'Romanov's Grill' in the High Street for lunch: which would be on him. Well, he certainly had a couple of suspects now for the murder of the shabby man. One: a powerful local business man with Masonic connections and two: A powerful Secret Society trying to the change the future by murder; definitely not the usual suspects for a Doss house killing. Worse still; he couldn't reveal either to his men or the Detective Superintendent [himself a local Mason] and so Harry returned to Brick Lane Police Station with a heavy heart and deep in thought. Jericho Tibbs had certainly mentioned the 'Priests of Chronos' on several occasions previously; a powerful group of men sworn to control the destiny of mankind by any means and that included murder, abduction and blackmail. But Mr. Tibbs was adamant they did not have possession of time travel.

The secret society had been formed in the middle of the last century and it was claimed they received 'divine' revelations by possessing the mythical 'Ark of the Covenant' which one of their group had discovered excavating in Egypt. The rumours spoke of a machine that could see both the past and the future apparently ordained by God himself and they cursed humanity for allowing fear of God to control human destiny. They believed humans should control human destiny! But one, silly little thought kept popping into his head; why on Earth didn't they put a stamp on the damn letter?

Harry was relieved to see Dorothy tucking into her mixed grill and sipping some wine; the lunch date was a good idea and the Professor nodded his silent agreement. Old Mr. Romanov himself came over to the table and welcomed his guests – he and the Professor were old friends - they had met as young men on the S.S. Sea Path: Romanov and his family fleeing yet another pogrom and the young William Hadden returning from Egypt.

The Romanov's [like many Jewish families before them] settled in the East End and thrived. Solomon Romanov was a first class cook and his little restaurant had became popular with the middle classes seeking good food and entertainment; a Balalaika band was on hand to provide music and Cossack dancers to leap about the place with great skill. It was a very popular venue after a night at the theatre or music halls. When asked, how a Jewish family came to have the same name as the Russian Imperial family, Solomon would always tell the story about his grandfather David, who decided their name was too Jewish and attracted the wrong attention, so he changed it saying;"If we're going to throw away our old family name, then the new one should be the best and grandest around!"

It didn't save him; a mob burnt down his little farm house killing him, his wife and daughter; the young Solomon just escaping the same fate by hiding in a passing bullock cart; that's when he decided it was time to move elsewhere. He had an Uncle [on his mother's side, who was a skilled tailor] in London's East End and so he moved his young family to the relative safety of England. He had explained previously why he served English dishes at lunch time and Russian in the evening; "The young professional's like to have a good lunch and the offices around here abound in them; so I cater for their tastes, but the evening clientele want something different and a little exotic." It was a winning formula.

His son, David, ran the small Pawnbrokers in the same street, which loaned money against anything of value including, it was rumoured: artificial limbs, wigs and even false teeth! The family considered themselves totally English and pictures of the King and Queen were proudly displayed in the dining room.

But it was when Harry mentioned the sad case of the shabby man that Solomon became interested in the conversation; he recalled that his son David had dealings with such a man, lending the fellow money against several small gold crucifixes over a period of months. They were quite genuine with hallmarks from Queen Victoria's time; except one.

Harry asked; "What made that one appear not to be genuine?" Solomon laughed and patted Harry on the shoulder; "The Hallmark was quite impossible my young friend. It was a square letter 'd' which means it was Hallmarked in 1903; quite bloody impossible!" The table fell silent until the Professor asked what had happened to the little crucifix; "The shabby man as you call him, returned several times and pleaded with David to buy it. The poor fellow seemed quite desperate and David had made good profits on the others, so he gave him some money for it. He may still have it or could have sold it as a meltdown." Solomon spoke quietly and was surprised when Harry quickly left the table, heading for David's Pawnshop five doors down from the restaurant. "Well, that's one way to escape the bill." Muttered the Professor with a broad grin, and would settle the bill himself, but Solomon waved that aside saying; "You are family my old friend, it's a treat for my beautiful Goddaughter Dorothy." Who always thought it was odd that her Godfather was Jewish!

Harry left the small Pawnshop and tucked the crucifix into his waistcoat pocket. It felt quite strange to be holding the future in one's hand. The cross had apparently been made in 1903 – a good two years into the future - and Harry was also intrigued that objects from the hereafter, could travel backwards with the Time traveler.

But it conjured up concrete evidence that the first Time Jumper, who had lived here since March, was also dressing and acting as a vagrant; living on the proceeds of their sale. So what part is Sir Thomas playing in all this and what the hell is he [the suspected Time Jumper] here for?

That's when a disturbing thought popped into his head and Harry realised he needed Dorothy to identify the dead man as the person she saw on stage and also get Mr. Skoles to identify the body as the man who returned to the theatre that night. He would also have to ask David Romanov to identify the body as the crucifix seller - basic police procedures – cross the 'T's and dot the 'I's. Harry sighed and waited for a passing cab; he would get the visits to the morgue arranged at Brick Lane Station. His mind was turning the facts over and over again, that's when another realisation came to Harry; the second breach of the Time-line had bought the dead shabby man here and had he overlooked the possibilities that the pair could have been working together or working against each other?

Dorothy stepped from the cab and was pleasantly surprised by the street that the McHannon's resided in. Ostensibly she was there to deliver some sewing materials to Rosie, but couldn't shake the strange feeling that she hoped for something else as well. Rosie was waiting on the step and warmly welcomed her in explaining that the boys were at school and Albert was at work. They had the house to themselves. She helped Dotty off with her coat and hat. They both walked to the kitchen and Rosie put the kettle on. There was small talk and Dorothy handed over the materials she had acquired. They both stood with hands on each other's as they exchanged cloths. They both smiled at each other and said nothing. A good few seconds passed.

"For piss sake darling, come on, we both know you want to try it!" Rosie said and keeping hold of Dottie's hand, they ran up the stairs and into the bedroom, helping each other with their clothes until both were naked. They were laughing as they jumped on the big bed and embraced, whispering and kissing gently. Then Rosie's hands went to work and soon the pair were kissing passionately and threshing about on the bed. Dorothy had to slap a hand over her mouth as Rosie's head pushed between her legs. With her tongue and mouth she caused Dotty to shake and moan, having a big orgasm which left her trembling a little. The two women 'played' until Dorothy suddenly sat up, she could smell burning. They both stared at each other and then ran down the stairs to see light grey smoke billowing through the kitchen door. "The fucking kettle! I forgot about the bleeding kettle!" Rosie shouted and using a tea towel managed to submerge the kettle in the sink. It was hot as a steel furnace.

Still quite naked, the pair laughed and embraced each other. Rosie really kissed her and said quietly, "Well my darling, I think our naughty little relationship is off to a bleeding hot start!" they laughed and kissed some more, slowly slipping onto the cold floor. Dorothy travelled home that afternoon with quite a smile on her face and feeling like she had slept for a month. She was so relaxed and happy she started to giggle like a happy school girl. She stared out the cab window but thought about Rosie's big breasts and how wonderful they felt and tasted. Then she slowly grinned; her [Rosie's] honey-pot certainly had lived up to its nickname and she licked her lips; the taste was still there and she certainly wouldn't clean her teeth until bedtime!

CHAPTER 6. 'MURDER IS BORN OF LOVE, AND LOVE ATTAINS THE GREATEST INTENSITY IN MURDER'. Octave Mirbeau.

Harry's thoughts were interrupted by the calling of his name and title; quite loudly."Inspector Hadden!" Alistair came running up, panting and wheezing, he grabbed Harry by the arm; "For Fuck sake Guv, I've just legged it from Victoria Street; there's been another fucking murder!" Victoria Street was a very 'posh' area of the East End; consisting of large, detached Victorian villa's standing in private grounds. Nearby was Albert Park [named after the Prince Consort who died in 1861] and a small boating lake; the poor of the East End were not invited to enjoy such amenities and anyone who had the audacity to try, was quickly evicted by the Park Keepers.

Hailing a passing cab, the Inspector and his Sergeant quickly climbed aboard and Alistair called to the driver; "Seven Victoria Street please mate!" Harry pushed back into his seat and realized who resided at number seven Victoria Street: Sir Thomas Astor-Smith. "What's the story?" He asked with real concern in his voice. Alistair took a couple of deep breaths and recounted what has happened so far: The body of Sir David Astor-Smith had been found by the French windows of his brother's study with his throat cut and the place turned upside down. No less than four members of the household staff had seen the killer running across the rear gardens and climbing a six feet brick wall topped with metal railings.

"Uniform has it closed down and Superintendent Taylor has taken charge; he's calling in more assistance from White Chapel nick, they're searching gardens and buildings all round the house. They are circulating a description of the suspect and that's where it goes fucking nuts Guv." Alistair coughed and pulled his cigarettes from a pocket and lit one with trembling hands, he took a couple of draws upon it and added quietly; "The suspect is a male dressed in a long shabby coat and trousers. All the witness stated they could see his old boots had pieces of gold coloured tinsels on the heels and soles. They got a clear look as he scaled the bloody wall with some ease. It was the shabby man; but that's fucking impossible! He's on a slab in the bloody morgue and this only happened minutes ago!"

Harry lifted his hat and ran his fingers through his dark hair; they had an impossible murder on their hands with the chief suspect apparently already dead before the crime was committed!

The cab dropped the pair off and they made their way inside, passing several uniform constables searching around the grounds and street. Harry examined the body very carefully; Sir David had been killed from behind with the assailant slitting his throat with almost surgical skill and precision. The knife was sharp and straight; like a surgeon's scalpel?

Harry knew that whoever killed the 'shabby man' had committed this. The similarities between the two murders were obvious; especially the clean cutting actions on the throats; the same skilful hands were involved in both killings. Robbery was not the motive. Sir David had over six pounds in his pockets, a gold watch and three gold rings upon his fingers. The small household safe – smashed open – still contained notes and had several pieces of expensive jewellery left inside. Robbery certainly wasn't the motive here; someone was desperately looking for something that Sir Thomas had possession of; did the murder succeed or did he leave empty handed? He looked about the room; it had been turned over with almost fanatical precision, not a drawer left unopened and cupboards smashed into. Even picture frames had been broken open and a couple of floorboards ripped up. This sort of frenzied search would have taken time and Harry deduced that Sir David must have disturbed the man and was murdered by the searcher. Harry noticed by the French doors and on the carpet by the desk, small strands of gold tinsel.

They were identical to the strands found on the shabby man's boots. Alistair pointed to the glittering tinsel and shook his head; "For fuck sake Guv, how did a corpse get off the morgue slab, make his way across the East End and then turn over this place; finally cutting the throat of that poor bugger?"

Harry shrugged his shoulders and kneeling down, took a long hard look at the late Sir David Astor-Smith's face and build. "Sir David strongly resembles his brother; not quite twins, but in a gas lit room you would easily mistake him for his brother." Harry spoke quietly to Alistair who was penciling notes into his little black book, stopping to suck his pencil and reply;"That's what Doc Goldstein said – the pair are like pea's in a pod - but he said there's over a year between them, with Sir Thomas the older brother." Harry nodded and rubbed his chin, thinking about the relevance of the look-alike brothers to these brutal killings.

Edwin came through the door with a strange look on his face; "You'll never guess what the fuck has happened down the morgue Guv!" Harry and Alistair exchanged looks and Harry said; "What happened Eddy?"

"Some bugger broke into the morgue offices last night and ransacked the property store, but all they nicked was the property bag belonging to the workhouse corpse. They made off with his clothes; everything, including the boots!" Edwin smiled and lit another cigarette. Alistair sighed loudly; "Thank fuck for that; otherwise we would have a Zombie killer on our hands." Even Harry chuckled at that comment and looked back at the corpse of the late Sir David Astor-Smith; why did the killer come dressed as the dead shabby man? What purpose did that serve, he would have known we [The Police] would hear about the morgue burglary?

Then Harry had another thought; was the killer sending a message to Sir Thomas? Was the killer the first Time-Jumper and why did he kill the newly arrived traveler? Then Harry reasoned one awful answer: stop him talking to Dotty could be the answer.

"Do you think that Sir Thomas could have been the real target Guv?" Edwin coughed and sucked on his cigarette; "I've got him in the Library. He doesn't seem that upset by his brother's horrible murder in his own study; a real cold fish that one."

"Get everything you can from the scene. Old Doc Goldstein will try and do the PM this evening. I'm going to have a word with Sir Thomas." Harry walked to the door and something caught his eye on the carpet, just by the fireplace. He picked it up very carefully and the three officers stared at the strange object for some time before Alistair muttered; "What the fuck is it?"

None of the Officers had seen anything like this object; it looked like smooth polished metal but didn't feel like it and was shaped like a miniature conch shell with a small wire protruding from one end. It was extremely light and glinted in the glow of the gas lamps. "I really have no bloody idea Alistair, but surely I know someone who might." Harry placed the object into his pocket and headed for the Library; this could be a very bloody interesting interview.

Dorothy walked with some modest speed down the High Street, occasionally tapping her umbrella on the pavement. She window shopped for a few moments at the Lady's Hat shop and moved on. Dottie turned down the next street into St. Paul's and headed for the small red door to right of the undertakers and pushed it open, walking quickly up the un-carpeted stairs. There were two apartments at the top of the dark stairs. She tapped on the door marked with a brass letter 'B'. Dottie had to knock again before she heard movement and the door was jerked open. Jimmy managed a smile and ruefully ran a hand over his unshaven face. He smiled a little, "Hello Dottie, I was just having a drink and reading a magazine." He stepped back and she entered, placing her umbrella in the rack and removing her hat. "What's the magazine?" She asked with a little smile. Jimmy now smiled broadly and rubbed his face again, "You'll like it, really dirty, disgusting stories: written by a retired French brothel madam. Well written I must say: certainly puts lead in your pencil!" She hung up her coat and Jimmy now started to laugh, he leaned against the wall with one arm and shook his head in disbelief. "For fuck sake Dottie! You walked here from your house with sod all under that coat except your bloody shoes!" She just smiled.

The old bed was creaking and groaning as the lovers fucked passionately, rolling, entwining, groaning and whispering, as if someone could overhear them. They finished their lovemaking in the 'Missionary position' and Dottie received his urgent seed in her mouth and didn't waste any. They lay back for a few minutes listening to each other breathing hard, then sat up with Jimmy against the headboard and Dorothy in his arms, facing the bedroom door. They shared a glass of whisky and a cigarette, talking quietly.

Jimmy had an arm around her and took a draw on the cigarette. Finally, he took a breath and asked quietly, "Have you told your Uncle William about us yet?" Dottie guessed that question would pop up – yet again – and sipped the whisky, holding the glass up to his lips. He shook his head and repeated the question. She held the glass the in both hands now and slowly shook her head. Jimmy actually groaned and stubbed the cigarette out in the old biscuit tin lid on the bedside table. After a few seconds he said quietly, "Why not? That's a fair question isn't it?" She could hear the subdued anger in his voice and sighed. "You know damn well what he thinks about your bloody political activities and views on us. He took a week to calm down after you insulted just about everything he stood for, so what do you expect me to do? I love my Uncle....and I won't break his heart, do you understand that?"

Jimmy eased from the bed and stood naked by the little window that overlooked the undertaker's rear yard which had several coffins stacked up, under a canvas sheet. He folded his arms and said nothing as Dottie pulled the covers up a little and finished the whisky. "Can we just enjoy our time together? Oh Please Jimmy." She said quietly and leaned back against the headboard.

He took a deep breath and finally said, "I think he's just an excuse you use. I think it's me your ashamed of...a useless Irishman who was expelled because of his political beliefs and now scrapes a living working for a fucking east end undertakers as a fucking 'box-boy'. With no real future and you don't want that. Do you?"

Dottie slipped from the bed and placed both arms around him, whispering that he was just a little angry and she certainly didn't think he was useless. She admired him sticking by his principles and.... She didn't finish what she was saying because he pushed her arms away and sat on the bed, grabbing his cigarettes and lighting up another. She stood in front of him and ran her fingers through his thick dark hair. Jimmy pushed her hand away and inhaled deeply. "Just go. Just go home Dorothy, I want to think,

think about us." He said quietly and stared at her and she could see the restrained anger in his eyes.

She knew that there was no reasoning with him, whilst in this mood, so she nodded and said she would get her hat and coat. He just nodded his agreement and smoked. Dottie walked to the door and said a quiet 'Goodbye' and wiped a tear away, standing naked in the drab hallway. She slipped on her boots and tied the laces, then fixed her hat and slowly pulled on her coat. She didn't have the courage to tell him that she had argued with Uncle William over his refusal to even meet Jimmy again. He wasn't welcome at the house or theatre. Uncle William had asked Dottie to end her relationship with the young man now, at once and for good.

"He's toxic for you my girl, like poison. You'll spend your life looking over your damn shoulder, watching for the authorities to lift him. Then what? Dragging your sorry self to a prison on visiting days? The police watching everything you do? Then think of dear Harry...For God sake girl, if they found out his sister had been seeing a man who supports the damn Irish rebels, his career would be over! Do you want that?" Uncle William hadn't sugar coated his objections to Jimmy and Dottie – sadly – knew his words were the truth. Harry's career would be over, ended by association – through his sister – with the Irish freedom fighters, who were considered terrorists by the British Empire. She knew that would happen, despite being unfair, harsh and brutal. Dottie knew she was between a rock and a hard place, and so, with a heavy heart and great sadness, she left the flat and walked slowly down the busy street and headed for the cab rank in Pool Street. With her head bowed a little, she stood outside the Draper's shop and waited impatiently for a cab to arrive: the rank was currently empty.

A big dark carriage pulled up right in front of her and the driver leaned over, tapping the door with his whip, but talking to Dorothy. "You'll struggle to find a cab at this time of day Miss Hadden. But the gentlemen wish to speak with you and I'm sure they'll allow me to run a lady like yourself home." She stared at the big rough man and wondered how the hell he knew her name!

The door opened and the two men gestured her in, both holding up their identity cards: they were officers from the Special Irish

Branch and Dorothy recongnised – vaguely – the older man. She had seen him with Harry at the Police station. The young one almost smiled, "Please get in Miss Hadden, we wish to have a little chat with you about your very foolish association with a certain James O'Connor." He gestured to the empty seat opposite them and added, "Please get in Miss Hadden. It's really not up for discussion."

"The first Special Branch, or Special Irish Branch, as it was then known, was a unit of London's Metropolitan Police formed in March 1883 to combat the Irish Republican Brotherhood [later IRA, Real IRA etc.] The name became Special Branch as the unit's remit widened to include more than just Irish Republican related counterespionage. From Wikipedia."

She climbed in and eased into the seat: the carriage didn't move. The younger man held up a brown paper file and again, didn't smile. "Your brother has assisted our inquiries on many occasions and has proved most useful and productive for the department. He's a very good copper and both he and your Uncle William are known patriots. Our intelligence indicated you were a loyal subject of the new king, but now there are a few clouds. You and us will dispel those clouds, won't we?"

Dorothy slowly nodded, gripping her umbrella tightly with both hands and cursed her foolishness, especially being quite naked under her coat! She thought, 'Oh my God, what if they arrest me and I'm searched....' She pushed that dreadful thought away and sat up straight. "How can I assist you?" She said very quietly and the men exchanged a glance and sat back in their seats. The older man smiled, "Your boyfriend is far more involved with the Irish terrorists than you would ever believe. We know who he associates with and they are – for the most part – hardened Irish fighters. You know the sort that wouldn't hesitate in shooting a young constable or exploding a bomb killing women and children, for their cause. But we strongly suspect, he puts up a façade for your benefit and I'm sure you'll co-operate with us....and assist us in putting him and his evil colleagues in prison or at the end of a rope."

Dottie shuddered at the mention of hanging, but remained quite composed and just nodded. "How can I assist you?" She repeated very quietly and now the younger man smiled. "It's really simple Miss Hadden, you are going to help us snare him and his cohorts before they kill some poor bugger." The older man leaned forward and gestured to her coat, "I think you'll play the part quite well, being a stage actress. But walking London streets naked apart from a coat tells us you won't mind acting the part of a tart, a high class one, but a tart. You see, we want you to play up to O'Connor's boss in their little terrorist cell. Find out where they meet and we'll do the rest. With such assistance to the Crown, any dark clouds will disappear and everyone will be happy and your dear brother will still have a job....career in the police service. From our observations of you and O'Connor you won't mind too much about offering sex to get the information we want. I'm sure you won't find that too arduous from we've discovered and recorded in our surveillance of you two."

"We'll be in touch Miss Hadden with the details of your mission." The younger one tapped the ceiling and the cab pulled away. "Now, we'll drop you off at home and I suggest you say nothing to your Uncle or Harry about this matter. Should you do so, we may have to cancel the mission and you know that would mean dragging O'Connor in, then you and of course, your immediate family members. Harry would find himself at the local Labour Exchange the following morning. Do I make myself clear?"

Dottie could only manage to nod and both men smiled, "We'll be in touch shortly Miss Hadden." They dropped her off at home and she ran up the steps, brushing a few tears away. The following day Dorothy waited in the handsome cab and adjusted her hat; "Here he comes." She said, smiling. Uncle William pushed back in his seat and gently straightened his legs. Harry appeared at the door and smiled; "Room for one more and then a jolly jaunt to the morgue."

Dorothy kissed her brother as he squeezed in and settled next to her. "Skole is making his own way; Uncle William gave him the cab fare and apparently he has another date with the merry widow." She added with a big grin. Uncle William stated that David Romanov had already left for the mortuary and was more than happy to help – mainly - because it gave the opportunity to see and speak to Dorothy. Young David had shyly loved her since he was a boy and his desires had grown over the years. No other woman came even close to igniting the same passion, which he felt for his 'Cousin' as they affectionately called each other; he looked forward to meeting her again; even if it was in a morgue!

"Are you alright with this Dotty?" Harry asked with real concern in his voice and gripped her hand. Dorothy nodded and said quietly; "I see Sims most days and his been dead for three and a half thousand years; at least this one is quite fresh!"

Uncle William laughed and tapped her hand with a big proud smile; "That's my girl!" Harry pulled the strange object from his jacket and the Professor and Dorothy studied it closely. They came to a joint conclusion: they had no bloody idea what it was made of or what it was for. Frustrated by this minor failure, Dorothy asked Harry to recount the interview with Sir Thomas and give details of the murder scene. Harry relaxed back in his seat and outlined what had taken place.

"To say it was an odd interview is an understatement; he [Sir Thomas] sat calmly sipping whisky and smoking a cigar by the fireplace, like he had just seen a dead rabbit at a shooting party and not his brutally murdered brother! He did offer me a drink and a cigar; but I declined both and asked him what happened. Apparently the Butler heard noises from the study and couldn't find his Master [Sir Thomas] so he fetched the spare study door key, from the Housekeeper's pantry and he and the Footman George unlocked the door and found the dreadful scene with Sir David dead by the French doors. They rushed over to the body and through the French doors, watched as the shabby man ran at speed across the garden and he scaled the wall with great ease. The butler and George with the two Journeymen [gardeners] watched the suspect escape and all noticed the gold flakes about his boots."

Harry hesitated for a few seconds, as they all heard the cabbie shouting at some idiot who had wandered into his path. "Bloody charming language I'm sure." Muttered Uncle William and then smiled at Dotty; "I trust you didn't hear any of that?"

Dorothy just grinned and shrugged her shoulders; "I've heard worse at the theatre on a Saturday night and that's only from the staff!" Everyone chuckled and Harry continued; "Sir Thomas has no idea who would burgle his study and take nothing of value. He believed his poor brother was murdered by the thief. He wasn't home at the time of the murder and only found out when a

Footman called at the Paradise Theatre and informed him of the tragedy. He had no idea why his brother had called upon him without an appointment and that is why he wasn't present when he did call. He remembers the shabby man appearing at the theatre, but claims that the man was drunk or suffering some kind of confusion; he says that the fellow claims he was related to Miss Dorothy and he desperately needed to tell her about the Germans!"

"So the study door was locked; Sir David must have entered through the French doors or how else did he get in; does he have a key to the place?" Uncle William rubbed his chin and added; "What the hell do German's have to do with Dotty?"

"According to Sir Thomas, he and Skoles escorted the man from the Theatre and the strange shabby man disappeared into the night. Sir Thomas says he has not laid eyes on him again and only heard of him when the murder in the Workhouse made the papers." Harry finished with a shrug of his shoulders and then sat up; "Bremerhaven. The shabby man shouted that at Skoles and it's definitely in Germany!"

"But what on earth has that to do with me; I've never been to Germany!" Dorothy chuckled; "Besides, how could the shabby man claim to be related to me and not you; that doesn't make sense even if he was a very distant relative!" and then pointed through the cab window; "We're here."

David Romanov was the first to view the body of the 'Shabby Man' and nodded to Harry that the corpse was NOT the crucifix seller. Mr. Skoles came next and stared at the dead man's face for some time; "That's the man I saw at the Theatre Sir." He said simply and was allowed to go on his date with the widow Sissy Graves.

Dorothy didn't flinch when Mr. Kelly [the Mortuary Attendant] pulled back the sheet covering the corpses face and closely examined it. She sighed and shook her head; "That's him Harry, the poor soul."

Harry sat in silence during the carriage ride back to the theatre, whilst Uncle William and Dorothy chatted about the coming evening's performance. The one negative result regarding the dead 'Shabby Man' means that the suspected 1st Time-Traveler [who apparently crossed over in March 1901] was the one who had sold the crucifix's, whilst the newly arrived 2nd Time-jumper tried to contact Dorothy and that probably means Dotty could be in danger; as the original 'shabby' man has almost certainly killed twice already. The other question that troubled Harry was why become active now after so many months hiding here?

It also means; that both travelers probably had dealings with Sir Thomas. Everything keeps coming back to that man. Harry smiled at Dotty and knew that she would have to be protected until they could capture or kill the suspect. Harry reasoned that if he [the suspect] has been selling the crucifix's to survive; what happens when he runs out of money?

But the killer was certainly seeking something other than money, when he searched Sir Thomas's study, but why did he leave all that cash and jewels behind when he's supposed to be struggling for money? What was he searching for that was obviously far more important than grabbing cash for his survival?

A strange, ominous thought came to Harry; what if he doesn't care about surviving; that would make him a very dangerous foe indeed. Then Harry smiled to himself; the answer to protecting Dorothy at all times lay with Sims. The group discussed the questions raised by the dead man and agreed that Sims would shadow Dotty at all times – which he happily agreed to do and appeared in her dressing room on cue – disappearing only when Rosie came to dress Dorothy for her performances. Soon as Sims disappeared the two women played their little games in the small dressing room as Dorothy changed into her stage costume. They were both giggling like naughty schoolgirls, totally unaware of the man watching them from behind the mirror. The old Paradise Theatre had many secrets and the hidden tunnels, peep-holes and two-way mirrors were just some of them.

Harry sat in his office at Brick Lane Police station and his dark thoughts roamed around the several murder cases that had been allocated to him. But the 'shabby man' killings were his priority.

Nothing was heard about the 1st 'Shabby Man' for nearly a week, but the PM results had arrived; Sir David's was simple: having his throat cut killed him otherwise he was quite healthy. For the second 'Shabby Man' the result was the same; having his throat slit killed him too, but the Doc had been right about the fatal untreated Diabetes and it was almost terminal. Doc Goldstein estimated that the man would have had just months, before death. He could also report that the man had never done heavy manual labour and had two toes missing on his right foot; they had been surgically removed. His last meal had been a beef curry with rice, washed down with beer. His teeth were also worthy of note; they were misshapen and many were missing completely: he clearly neglected his teeth.

The 'shabby man' murdered in the dismal workhouse toilets had been about forty years of age and had been no manual worker. Harry regretted not having been able to search the body before that fat and light fingered bastard Rollings had got to it. He had re-read all the statements from the others living in the grim workhouse at the time; no-one, it appears, had any kind of conversation with the murdered man.

The Inspector grunted his disbelieve at that; the man had been there for days and spoke to no-one; except the warden who booked him in as 'Michael Jagger'. Workhouses were notorious for chatter and gossip; after all, the men had little else for social interaction; but talking amongst themselves.

Harry read the Warden's statement - yet again - about finding the body on the floor of the toilets, just before going home at the end of his shift. For some reason, the simple fact that the warden used the workhouse toilets wouldn't leave his thoughts. It almost matched the niggling little thoughts, about why on earth the supposed powerful priests of Chronos didn't put a stamp on that damn envelope! The warden was a certain John Ellis, who had worked there for two years after leaving the merchant navy, where he had served some twenty-seven years at sea. The Governor of the workhouse had vouched for his character, when Alistair interviewed him. Harry sighed and leaned back in his chair; "The devil is in the detail." He muttered to himself and thought - again - about the unstamped letter and the warden using the workhouse toilet.

But the strangest find was the small and clearly new tattoo on the right shoulder; no one had a clue what it depicted – it seems to be a snake swallowing its tail - Harry tasked Alistair to find the tattoo artist if he could.

Alistair drew the tattoo in his notebook for future reference and explained to Harry that both locksmith shops had drawn a blank on the key – but both had agreed on one fact -the key probably opened a drawer, cupboard or large chest or trunk. The Doss house warden confirmed that the dead 'Shabby Man' had no baggage with him and that struck a chord with Harry; 'If you can bring objects from the future, why didn't the dead man have nothing with him except the key?'

Harry polled out the paper 'evidence' bag and tipped the contents onto his desk. He picked up the crumbled piece of paper; it appeared blank on both sides and clearly had been torn from a small notebook. Why throw a blank page of a notebook away? He held the paper up to a wall gas lamp and stared hard at it for about a minute. Harry carefully smoothed the paper out upon his desk and from the top drawer, pulled out his magnifying glass and peered hard at both sides.

"Fuck, there is something here." Harry whispered and realised that, whoever had written on the page above this one, had pressed quite hard and you could just make out some letters impressed upon this page. There was a C, then nothing legible, followed by the letters 'ON'. At the very bottom of the sheet, Harry could make out a single O with a tiny 'star' immediately above it. What the hell did that mean? He mused and placed everything back in the bag; after copying what had been revealed, then reopened the bag and took the spoon out. He stared at the discoloured bowl of the spoon and sighed; no real evidence there and using his hankie lifted the broken bottle's bottom to his nose: it had a strange smell and he knew it was opium mixed in water and he wondered how many vagrants could afford to buy opium? And of course, where any of these items actually connected with the dead man?

"Harry didn't associate the spoon and its discoloured bowl with drug use because 'Chasing the Dragon' didn't really appear until the 1920's – generally - in Heroin use. Currently [1901] injection or taken in liquid was the common form of imbibing the drug. With opium, smoking was the most popular form of indulgence." SJW

He leaned back in the chair and stared at the ceiling. No useful revelations came about anything he had discovered. The police investigation seemed to have stalled, but various Work Houses were raided and many tramps and vagrants questioned, but Harry and the team drew a blank; then Mr. Jericho Tibbs paid another visit; this time to all three members of his human team at once and Sims of course!

CHAPTER 7. 'THE DISTINCTION BETWEEN THE PAST, PRESENT, AND THE FUTURE IS ONLY A STUBBORNLY PERSISTENT ILLUSION.' Albert Einstein.

The group sat in the living room drinking tea and eating cake; even Dorothy enjoyed a large slice of Mrs. Harvey's [the family's cook] rich fruitcake and a couple of biscuits. Sims was shouted at because he ate his cup and saucer after finishing his tea and so enjoyed a second cup served in a small vase!

It was Uncle William that noticed Mr. Tibbs was about to arrive; he suddenly held up his hand to silence the conversation and said quietly; "The old Grandfather clock has stopped ticking and I can't hear the traffic outside." Sims was about to eat the vase when Dorothy pulled it from him and gave his hand a gentle slap; Sims giggled and then said; "Hello Mr. Tibbs!"

Jericho sat on the large sofa by the fireplace and placed his hat upon the floor, pushing his dark wavy hair back and smiling; "Good evening people, I have some information you may wish to receive." Mr. Tibbs informed his team that small changes had occurred to the current Time-Line, thankfully nothing drastic, but changes nevertheless. It appears that Sir David had died just months before his death was due; he should have drowned when his small Fishing boat sunk on Loch Lomond, whilst on holiday in Scotland the following March. His early death had made very small alterations to the all important Time-Line. But it was his next statement that had everyone sitting up; it was about the dead 'Shabby Man'.

No soul had been collected at the point of departure [humans call it death], Jericho had searched the Collection Records for Humanity and found no collection was scheduled for that time and place; he had that fact on good authority; from the Angel in charge of Collections!

Sir David had been collected and processed correctly. But the Shabby man was missing. Jericho had spoken to the late Sir David, who admitted entering his brother's study by the garden; having found the doors open whilst walking in the gardens, waiting for his brother's return. He didn't even see the man come from behind the curtains as he surveyed the wrecked room. Then pain and darkness came over him quickly. Sir David quickly found himself sitting on the desk, staring at his own corpse until a very pleasant young lady appeared and walked him away to the bright light.

Jericho accepted a cup of tea from Dorothy and continued; "He states that the visit to his brother was about money; he had a serious gambling problem and Sir Thomas had been bailing him out for the last few months. He also added that that it was him, that Dorothy saw leaving the Theatre that night, after finding his brother had vanished from his office at the Theatre, probably with the original Time-Jumper." Jericho added; "Sir David couldn't understand how his brother left the office, his Secretary Mr. Kelp was sitting outside the office door and never saw Sir Thomas leave."

Dorothy crossed her arms and said quietly; "Sir Thomas's office is located in the attics of the Theatre; the door where Kelp [the Secretary] sits is the only entrance and its three floors up!" Harry nodded and said; "I think we may have to have a very close look at his office." Everyone agreed with that.

The meaning about the shabby man's soul took a few seconds to sink in for the team and Dorothy caught on first; "He can't be collected in this time because he doesn't belong here." Mr. Tibbs nodded his agreement at that impressive reasoning and added; "If a human is killed and dies in another time span other than his own allocated one, the Soul is lost because no Collector is on hand to guide it on its way. Our friend will have no idea what has happened or where he is; they can fall prey to the Dark Prince in some cases."

That remark sent a shudder up Dorothy's spine; the Dark Prince was God's nemesis and was always on the lookout for lost souls to collect. "That's the problem; he's classified as a 'Lost Soul' – it's lost somewhere in time between 1901 and 2022 - the year he died and year he was from. I have my team from the early 21st century working on that one. Like you, sadly, they still haven't discovered the Time controlling device." Jericho finished talking and sipped his tea, then sighed: "I best bring you up to date with the German Problem."

Mr. Tibbs then outlined why the existing German Empire could be a problem for the time-Line and frankly, for the future of all humanity. He confided to the shocked group that Germany would be the focal point of vast and murderous wars sometime in the 20th Century. These wars will transform human society and change the world; totally.

"Wouldn't it be better to stop all those deaths before they can happen?" Harry asked Jericho, who smiled and shook his head; "Sorry Harry, those terrible deaths are required for humanity to move on, without them the current system would endure for at least another fifty human years and that's not acceptable to himself [God]; he does have a plan, you know."

"Humans move forward over the bodies of other humans." Uncle William muttered and accepted a refill from Dorothy who asked Jericho about the Priests of Chronos and the Kaiser. She was told that the Kaiser was the very catalysis for all this change and the so called Priests had discovered that fact; probably from the original 'Shabby Man'.

Harry placed his cup down and said quietly;"Which member of the Priests of Chronos did the 'Shabby Man' come into contact with?" Everyone glanced at each other and Mr. Tibbs smiled; "You and Dorothy make quite a team. Sir Thomas must be a member of the Priests because he had dealings with the killer, who else could he [the shabby man] have possibly told, that held such a position of power?"

"That also explains why the unstamped letter arrived after the stage incident." Uncle William grunted and pushed more fruit cake into his mouth. "Sir Thomas is known for being tight as a fish's bum; little wonder there was no damn stamp on the bloody letter." He added and grinned.

Harry showed Mr. Tibbs the strange object he had recovered from the murder scene and Jericho examined it with interest, finally pushing it into his pocket and smiled; "Its a small communications device from the early 21st century, like a telephone, it allows people to talk to each other but without wires." Harry nodded and asked; "Our friend must have being talking to someone else; does that mean, yet another person from the future is here?" The group sat in silence until Dorothy said quietly; "There have being only two breaches of the Time-Line and thus only two persons have crossed over and one of them is dead. Does that mean someone who exists here, is at the end of this device, but who?"

Uncle William rubbed his chin and glanced about the group with a grim smile and muttered; "Sir Thomas?" Everyone nodded their agreement at that deduction. Mr. Tibbs orders were simple; find the 1st Shabby Man and neutralize him and recover the Time Device; and be bloody careful doing it!

The following day came the funerals; the first was held in the morning with cold damp winter weather. The coffin was lowered into the ground without ceremony by two burly grave diggers who then stood to one side with their flat caps removed, as Dorothy insisted upon saying a small prayer. The two men exchanged a wry smile and both stared at Dorothy, who looked stunning in 'Mourning Black'. "Worth some fucker dying just to see that piece of skirt." The younger of the two whispered and grinned, leaning on his shovel. The other man just smiled again. Harry and Alistair stood bare headed as Dorothy asked for God's mercy for the man's soul and then all assembled spoke the 'Lord's Prayer' out loud – even the two grave diggers - who at the end of the prayer, slapped their hats back on and started to throw earth on the coffin. "Being an unknown with no family to pay for a proper funeral, our friend

there has received a 'Paupers Funeral' – that means no proper headstone or other marker - the grave will practically disappear in a few years and the only record of his passing will be our Police reports." Harry explained to a sad Dorothy who wondered why no Priest had officiated; "I had asked Father Andrew from St. Mary's to perform the service but his curate informed me that the Father was in Hackney; visiting his sick mother." Harry added and fumbled about in his pockets for some coin to give the grave diggers. The light drizzle tumbled down and Dorothy opened her umbrella and looked down at the nearly filled hole; "He must have family somewhere?"

Harry almost smiled and whispered; "Maybe in the year 2022, but don't hold your breath waiting for them to arrive." The pair smiled and Harry sent Alistair to fetch a cab from the main road; they had another funeral that very afternoon and they needed to quickly rendezvous with Uncle William who was also attending. Dorothy glanced at the older and bigger Gravedigger who tipped his hat: he was an ugly brutish man but had a wonderful smile. "Oskar Bellend at your service my lady." He said quietly and pulled off his hat and did a little bow. Now that made Dottie smile and she pushed her arm through Harry's and thanked the big man quietly for his attention.

Alistair, clutching an umbrella, headed for the cemetery gates to flag down a cab, leaving Harry to tip the grave diggers and walk Dorothy towards the roadway. She couldn't help herself and glanced back at the big gravedigger who lifted his hat to her, yet again. "Big ugly bastard, but he's good to the local street kids apparently." Harry said quietly and Dorothy just nodded. She admonished herself about thinking of the big rough fellow in an intimate manner, but still smiled.

The second funeral that afternoon was bathed in winter sunshine and was a lavish affair with a hearse covered in flowers and several carriages following. At least a dozen of the undertaker's staff walked beside the coffin, followed by fifty or more mourners on foot. Crowds thronged the pavements, many of the men with hats removed, and all stood in respectful quietness as the long cortege passed them by, heading for Forest Gate Cemetery and the ornate family vault of the Astor-Smiths.

Dorothy, Harry and Uncle William walked quietly among the mourners following the hearse in the warm winter sun. "You couldn't get two more different funerals in one day." Muttered Harry and smiled at Dorothy who had her arm through his. That's when both saw David Romanov gesturing from the pavement, waving his hat at them.

The three quickly walked from the procession and joined a grim looking David outside the Railway Arms Ale House. He gripped Harry by the arm and said with a mixture of excitement and fear; "The 'Shabby Man' was in my shop trying to flog another crucifix and I gave him a guinea for it, just like the others!"

"Did you see which way he made off?" Harry asked with some tension in his voice. David nodded; "I can do better than that; I followed him. He's in there." Young Romanov nervously grinned at Dorothy and pointed to the Railway Arms Ale House.

Harry and Alistair checked their pistols and sent David, with Dorothy, to fetch reinforcements from Brick Lane Police Station. Harry quickly decided on a plan – until help arrives - Alistair would watch the rear of the premises and he and Uncle William: the front of the large building. They did have one advantage: both doors to the front of the premises could be seen from their position. They awaited reinforcements in the gathering winter gloom until two gunshots rang out.

"The rear of the pub!" Harry called out, drawing his pistol which caused the crowds about him and Uncle William to scatter. The pair ran to the rear of the pub, in time to see several people scrambling from the rear entrance and one big man shouted at Harry; "Mr. Hadden, the boys still alive, the publican's daughter is a Nurse at Eastham Infirmary, she's got him!"

Harry and Uncle William exchanged concerned looks and pushed their way into the pub's rear bar.

"If it wasn't for Miss Alice Sherwood we would be arranging a service funeral and Kate would be a young widow with two small children to bring up on her own." Harry spoke quietly to Dorothy across the sleeping figure of Alistair, bandaged about the chest and head. The smell of disinfectant pervaded the air of the small hospital room and Edwin managed to get the bare window open a little. "Jesus, the Doss House smelt better!" He muttered and lit up a cigarette, trying to get some more fresh air through the slightly raised window by sniffing at the gap.

Dorothy looked with great sympathy and sadness at Alistair; but comforted herself that he should live thanks to Nurse Alice Sherwood – the Publicans daughter - who by chance, had called on her father to arrange her mother's surprise birthday party and found herself saving a young Detectives life, on the beer and sand covered floor of her dad's pub.

"Edwin and I can sit with him until he comes round and Kate

manages to get her mum to watch the children." Dorothy smiled at Harry and Edwin agreed;"Alistair's Brother George, you know the Tram Driver, has been told and he's on the way; if the bloody trams are running on time." Dorothy allowed herself a little chuckle at that and gripped Alistair's hand.

"Kate is on her way and so is your brother George; so you sleep and get stronger." She whispered against his ear. Harry stood and motioned for Edwin to take his seat and nodded to Dorothy; "Doc Goldstein has patched up our murderous friend and he's sitting in a cell at Brick Lane nick waiting for me to have words."

Harry pulled his coat on and pushed back his hat; "Let me know if there are any changes Edwin." Harry gave Dorothy a little wave and headed from the hospital; his thoughts were on how the last few hours had unfolded.

Apparently Alistair had been standing some yards from the rear entrance of the Railway Arms Ale House when the 'shabby man' appeared in the doorway: the pair stared at each other for a few seconds and the 'Shabby man' dived back inside. Alistair slowly followed, pulling his service revolver from the inside coat pocket, and crouching slightly, he entered the rear door; pistol in hand. The first shot struck him on the upper chest and he slammed against the big wooden doorway, collapsing onto the pub floor; the second bullet skimmed his head and embedded into the floorboards.

The 'shabby man' had raised his pistol to fire a third time into the helpless Alistair when four burly Dockers took matters into their own hands and tackled him. They beat him so hard that he would need treatment from Doc Goldstein in his cell at Brick Lane Police Station.

Nurse Alice Sherwood had saved Alistair's life with quick and effective treatment at the scene, mainly stopping the bleeding and letting him breath clearly. But the Four Dockers actions mystified Harry a little; the Police weren't exactly their favourite people, so he asked one after taking his Witness Statement. The reply became a legend around the nick!

The big docker wiped his face and blew his nose into a dirty hankie and said simply; "Well it's like this mate; you bluebottles are our bluebottles and we don't take kindly to fucking strangers doing 'em up; that's for us to do!" Harry had to smile and pushed a mug of hot tea to the man who would never consider that he was any kind of hero.

The Surgeon attending Alistair had praised the young Nurse for her treatment and confirmed to Dorothy that the girl had indeed saved his life; as a thank you, Dorothy arranged for several complementary tickets to the Paradise Road theatre and a free dinner at Romanov's on Alice mum's birthday. Miss Sherwood was overjoyed that she could now really surprise her mum for her special day. Harry had an inkling that the pair would become friends; they were both strong independent women with courage to match, what he didn't know was they would have a mutual 'love' interest: him!

Harry caught a cab back to Brick Lane police station and he greatly anticipated the coming interview with the mysterious 'Shabby man' – he felt quite strange - that he would be talking to a man who won't even be born soon!

"That's a bloody rum do at your nick son." The Cabby called down to Harry as he guided his horse through the market traffic of barrows and shouting people. Harry stopped scribbling in his notebook and yelled back;"What are you talking about Charlie?" The old cabby pointed his whip at Harry and shouted; "That big fucker that nearly had your mate – the Scottish lad – he killed himself in his cell with two fucking Constables standing there!"

Harry sat in total silence, a little stunned by the news he had just heard as the cab pulled up outside Brick Lane Police Station and he could see crowds around the entrance; a mix of sad and angry citizens, eager reporters and unhappy constables desperately trying to hold them back.

Harry paid Charlie and pushed his way through the unruly crowd, arriving at the front desk, where Sergeant Rollings, sweating and swearing as he directed Constables to remove the small, but rowdy, crowd from around his desk. He frantically pointed to the rear door [which led to the cells and charging area] and yelled; "Down there Hadden, Mr. Taylor wants to see you right away!" He eased his bulk down upon the rough little chair behind the desk and wiped his brow. Harry nodded and headed for the door which was opened by a thin Constable who had apparently lost his helmet in the earlier melee.

"He did it right in front of them; just flopped over the bleeding desk and was dead as a bag of nails!" The young Constable said quietly as Harry walked through the doorway. Harry said nothing and made his way past the holding cell and towards the now quiet Interview Room, which had Superintendent Taylor standing outside with Doctor Goldstein. Two nervous looking Constables were trying to explain what the hell had just happened.

Doctor Goldstein turned to Harry, wiped his glasses and sighed; "It's poison Harry, from the smell it's probably cyanide. How he got hold of it is anyone's guess, but I'll do the PM straight away." Harry stared into the small grey room and saw the still figure of the Shabby Man sprawled across the large wooden desk, face contorted and blood around his mouth; he was still handcuffed to his chair.

"How the hell could he put poison in his mouth with his wrists handcuffed?" Harry asked the two constables who had been in the interview room when he died. The older man, Constable Edmund Tanner shook his head; "No idea Mister Hadden, he was sitting there with a strange smile on his face and he quietly said something really weird and seemed to start chewing. His mouth moved about and he just slumped forward, dribbling blood. He hadn't been given anything; not even a cup of tea!" Harry patted unhappy Edmund on the shoulder and nodded; he had known old 'Sixpence' since he joined Brick Lane Station and knew he was a good, honest copper. "Alright Eddy, what was the weird stuff he said, can you remember?"

"Constable Tanner's nickname was 'sixpence' because a six penny piece was called a 'Tanner' in English slang." SJW.

Constable Tanner screwed his face up and shook his head; "No Mister Hadden, not exactly, but something like: "We are all just ghosts here my friends; nothing but ghosts and lost memories; if he gets his way." The younger Constable; Clive Collins wiped his face and added; "I thought he said: "We are all just ghosts my fellows; nothing but ghosts for memories; if he gets his way in all this." Harry nodded and Superintendent Taylor gripped his arm; "What the fuck does that mean? Who the hell are the ghosts here'? Get a grip on this Hadden and quickly!"

Taylor grunted and walked away, passing Sergeant Rollings who stood by Harry and chuckled;"You may need a séance to question that fucker!" He wiped his round face and smiled, adding; "Well, at least you caught Sir David's murderer, his brother will be pleased about that."

"What do you want Rollings?" Harry spoke quietly as he shuffled through the dead man's property – it wasn't much - a couple of shillings, some pennies, a handful of bullets, a Borchardt C-93 pistol, two small gold crucifix's and a black & white photograph of a large detached house. Harry turned the print over and rubbed his chin with some amazement, the writing scribbled on the back stated: 'STONEBRIDGE HOUSE – CIRCA 1974.'

He pushed the photograph into his pocket and repeated his question to Rollings, who moved the coins about with his finger; "That old vagrant in the holding cell wants to speak to you." Harry nodded and tapped the fat Sergeants fingers; "I know how much is there; make sure all this reaches the property store." He grinned at Rollings and walked over to the holding cell where the thin constable, he saw earlier, was giving the old man a cup of tea and a cheese sandwich.

"This is George 'Catman' Lewis; once the scourge of CID and the best cat burglar in the business until he broke his leg." The young constable laughed; "Rumour has it that he fell badly while being interviewed by Taylor when he was the Inspector at Forest Gate nick." The young constable laughed again and walked off.

Harry tapped the bars; "What can I do for you George?" He could see the old man was well down on his luck, he looked thin and grey, with clothes that a scarecrow would be ashamed of. He was quickly pushing the large sandwich into his toothless mouth after dipping the bread in his tea. He looked up and smiled; "I think you may want to give me a couple of bob Mister Hadden, for I can help you with the strange shabby men, sadly now both dead before you could have words."

Harry nodded and fumbled in his pockets and pulled a half-crown out, flipping the coin towards George who caught it with great dexterity. The old man shoved the coin into his ragged trousers and looked about through the bars of his cell. He wiped his mouth and spoke quietly, looking around the whole time. Harry threw the old man another half-crown at the end of their little chat and headed for the street and the Paradise Theatre, now with a grim expression, for if what the old cat burglar had said was true; then the entire case was turned on its head! He stood on the kerbside and raised a hand to an empty cab and climbed in; "Bollocks!" was all he said to himself.

CHAPTER 8. 'SHUN DEATH, THAT'S MY ADVICE.' Robert Browning.

Harry read the autopsy report on the second dead shabby man with interest; he had been killed by a lethal dose of Cyanide taken orally; probably concealed in the broken tooth Doc Goldstein had found. He was another walking dead man; he had found untreated tumours about the stomach and lungs – fatal tumours - which would have caused death in just a few months.

The presence of the clever suicide device, told Harry that the man could plan and execute his own passing when necessary – and had done so. He would have been hung for the murder of Sir David and the attempted murder of Alistair; not to mention the other shabby man! He had escaped all that and frustrated the investigation by killing himself before being questioned. Harry thought deeply on the co-incidence that both men were actually fatally ill and quickly came to the conclusion that it was no co-incidence; especially if old George, the former cat burglar, was right in his story. He handed the report to Dorothy, who sipped her tea and nodded; "This is no co-incidence Harry; old George is probably telling the truth and we've been pushed right up a blind alley!" Harry placed his cup down and paced the room as Dorothy passed the file to Uncle William.

Harry addressed the pair quietly; "Two dying men recruited to play a strange, but well planned game. They meet up in the London Road Workhouse and never noticed old George wrapped up in blankets against the wall; according to George, they both had answered a Personal Advertisement, placed in the Eastham Gazette that promised the terminally ill a chance to care for their families and earn some good money. They certainly knew each other and according to what George overheard, they didn't like each other. George tells us that that the man who died at the station was really well dressed and no vagrant; he told the other that he wasn't required and the plan was going well. He cussed several times about their 'employers' and the contact they sent him too; he was about to double-cross them for his own ends. He called his 'employers' a pair of stupid pricks and liars." He picked up his cup and took a sip, then continued.

"But he was determined to complete his mission for the money promised to his family; that's when they argued quite violently, pushing each other about, until the Warden appeared and threatened to throw them both out. George believes the 'shabby man' had changed his mind about whatever was planned and said he would warn "her" about the plan. They started to argue again and were both ordered to leave the Doss House or the warden would fetch a Constable. The well dressed one threatened the other; making a cutting motion across his throat and then left; still quite angry. I believe the 'Her' he mentioned was you; Dorothy. The poor fellow was going to make his threat real and that's why our second time travelling friend killed him. George said the 'shabby man' collected his meager possessions and hurriedly left the Work House. He had no cases with him; just a large brown sack – the sort sailors would carry their stuff in – apparently he looked terrified. We still haven't recovered that sack. I think Sir Thomas was the 'contact' who was about to 'double-cross' their employers and so our murderous friend broke into his house, looking for something. But in walked Sir David, the look-a-like brother and our friend seized the opportunity to get rid of the 'double-crosser' and killed him, not realizing it was Sir David until it appeared in the Newspapers. I checked with the local paper and found the advertisement was paid in cash and not on account, so we cannot trace the advertiser and it was placed in March of this year." He finished his tea.

"All the Newspaper staff can say: that it was a young couple who placed the advertisement and they were quite a handsome pair. The address given was Stonebridge House in Victoria Gardens, Forest Gate. The four men who answered the advertisement were sent there. But the paper's staff couldn't be sure that our two dead men were two of the four who answered the advertisement; I showed them pictures of our two. So are they still recruiting the almost dead and for the same purpose; time travel? Edwin and I called upon the residence to find the place locked up. A surly servant informed us that the owners of the property had been away for some two years; in Germany of all places!" Harry sat down and pushed fingers through his dark hair and sighed. "I spoke to the family solicitors and the house has been in the same family since 1790; the Bridgewater's. They made a fortune in textiles with several Mills up North and two clothing factories here in London that specializes in Military uniforms for various Governments. They also own large Country Estates in Yorkshire, Scotland and Saxony, in Germany."

"German connections again and again; the gun was German and the house in the picture is owned by a family with German connections." Dorothy pushed back in her chair and placed a hand on her head; "The Kaiser, according to Mr. Tibbs, is the catalyst for two horrendous wars in this century and he is Emperor of Germany. Does all that connect with Stonebridge House?"

Then a real look of real surprise covered her face and Dorothy started to empty the contents of her bag onto the table and slowly rummaged through the items until she pulled an envelope up. "I knew that name and address rang a bell!"

Harry took the letter and quickly read the two pages, he looked up with a grim expression on his face; "Lady Ann Bridgewater and Stonebridge House; the very place our dead shabby man was carrying a picture of, apparently taken in the year nineteen hundred and seventy four!"

Harry tapped the photograph and added; "They [The Solicitors] really didn't recognize the house from this picture at first look; apparently it has grown an entire new wing, gained a garage block and a new roof. But the grand entrance and middle block are unaltered. I have the place under very discrete surveillance."

Uncle William lit up his pipe and muttered; "Yet another co-incidence; I don't think so!" Dorothy nodded her head and sat down;"In the letter, Lady Bridgewater informs me that the family will be in residence over the Christmas holidays and she does mention some prominent guests including someone we all know: Sir Thomas Astor-Smith."

The three exchanged glances, the 'co-incidences' were mounting up and that probably means nothing is a co-incidence!

"If George was right about the two shabby men being recruited locally and in this time, then Jericho would have reported souls being collected, but remember, none were. So these two must have come from another era and old George has it wrong." Uncle William had exposed the big flaw in George's story; the lack of souls upon their death; a sure sign that the dead men didn't belong here in 1901.

Dorothy picked up the photograph and studied it carefully, then stretched out her legs and jumped up from her chair; "Old George is probably telling the truth about what he saw and overheard in the Workhouse, he just had the years wrong, and if I'm right, we need to speak to Mr. Tibbs – Sims!" Dorothy yelled and stood patiently waiting for him to arrive.

Sims rolled in from the curtains and leapt to his feet, as if waiting for applause, which he didn't get. Dorothy spoke quickly and made Sims repeat the message for Mr. Tibbs verbatim. Sims gave a big grin and waved goodbye. Dorothy sat back down and poured herself another cup of tea; "This shouldn't take long, more tea anyone?"

Harry and Uncle William chuckled, accepting their refills, and the three sat quietly watching the fire in the small grate, flicking and hissing. Dorothy gave it a couple of prods with the poker and then looked up. Sims returned, but with no answers because Mr. Tibbs accompanied him. "I was intrigued by your questions Dorothy and I think you have hit the nail on the head." Jericho dropped onto the sofa, placing his hat upon the floor; "There were two crossings from 1974 that were never traced, but the Time-Line remained unaltered; until now. Both 'shabby men' produced no souls to be collected here and could easily be the pair from 1974 and therefore, you're reasoning that we have another pair of Time Jumpers here makes sense." Jericho accepted a cup of tea from Dorothy and settled back on the sofa.

"My human team in the late 20th century reports that an advertisement was placed in the local paper – almost an exact copy of the one placed here - and with the same address: Stonebridge House!" Jericho sipped his tea and Harry nodded to Dorothy; "Well done Dotty, old George was right about what he heard from the two men, arguing in London Road Workhouse about their generous hosts; except he obviously wouldn't know; that the pair were recruited in 1974 and not now!"

Harry stood up and poked the slumbering fire, until sparks flew and flames leapt about the pieces of smoldering coal. He added quietly; "Someone is playing a very clever game with us. The tinsel left at the crossover point was a very deliberate plant for us to find; to point the finger at the two tramps, as the travelers who had just arrived. But why did the 1st shabby man to arrive, kill the new traveler? Why did he dress up as the dead man to kill Sir David? It was a wonderfully effective diversion – we believed that the dead pair had jumped from 2022 - when in fact they had arrived from 1974. Whoever is behind these cross-over's is bloody planning something big, and is using their ability to time travel effectively and masking their real intentions."

Everyone nodded their agreement at those deductions from Harry. "So we have two Time Jumpers that came from 2022 to here, almost certainly to meet up with the pair from 1974. That means Stonebridge House and the Bridgewater's are definitely connected with this." Dorothy spoke quietly and placed her cup down.

"It also means that we still have two travelers from 2022 around the place, one turning up in March and one in November [1901] and we don't have a single clue to who they are!" Uncle William sighed and lit up his pipe.

"Getting the first man to frequent Romanov's pawn shop, selling crucifix's in that month fooled us into believing he was the traveler who arrived in March, with the crucifix from 1903 a deliberate plant to ensure we believed he was a time traveler and would obviously assume he was struggling to survive here, but his clean and well fed condition should really have told us a different story; especially when the second man popped up and murdered Sir David!" Harry said and Dorothy nibbled a biscuit, thinking deeply about this shocking turn of events. They had been played and landed by a master; they all knew it; but who was that master? The silence in the small room was palatable. "The Priests of Chronos." Dorothy muttered and everyone nodded their agreement.

"Your Christmas performance at Stonebridge House is now the focus of this investigation and if Sir Thomas puts in his expected appearance, we need to be present and get to grips with what's actually happening and most importantly; find the damn time controller!" Uncle William sucked on his pipe and everyone agreed with him – including Mr. Tibbs - who slapped his top-hat on and added; "I think we need to discover the identity of the master-mind behind all this quickly and put an end to their plans for the sake of future humanity." He disappeared, leaving the team to ponder his words.

Ellen handed Dorothy the sealed note and didn't smile, "Delivered by a big rough man who had the blooming cheek to ask me out for a drink! I told him where to go and he just smiled at me."

Dottie stood by the fireplace and read her instructions, the shock at discovering who was the 'Cell Boss' of the little Irish Fighters group made her run a hand over her face and take a deep breath. Rory McLeish was certainly a 'friend' of Jimmy's and had made some very suggestive remarks to her over the time she and Jimmy had been together. Jimmy had laughed them off as banter between good friends, but Dorothy, as a woman, had suspected there was more to them than she or Rory would have admitted. Her mission was simple, get McLeish to reveal who he received orders from and report it back to her 'handlers'. She eased herself down and stared at the fire, again – because of Jimmy – she was between a rock and a hard place. She tossed the note in the flames and watched it burn. She knew where McLeish would be: the Irish pub in Sackville Street. Sighing, she called Ellen and the pair headed up the stairs: she needed to change and told Ellen to inform her uncle that she would be visiting a friend for the night. Dottie knew that Ellen would cover her story if asked.

Rory McLeish was a big affable [apparently] Irishman with thick dark hair and eyes, with the build of a championship boxer. He was a generous man and would always stand a fellow Irishman a drink, if they were down on their luck. He lived in a room above the Irish pub and the ladies who worked the kitchen, supplied his meals and even did his laundry. He was sitting at the small table by the door, supping a pint of the 'black stuff' [Guinness] when he heard the shouting: it was a woman. He rose and walked through the door, to see young Dorothy Hadden waving her umbrella and shouting after someone. She looked quite upset and so, he went to her aid. It appears some rogue had tried to snatch her bag, but she had belted him with her umbrella which was now bent like a banana! They sat at the table and Rory had the barmaid give Dottie a large whisky. He offered to buy Dottie a new brolly, he could get them from Eastham market and would drop one around the Paradise in the morning. They chatted – a little about Jimmy – and mainly what's wrong with the bloody British Empire. Rory was surprised to find that Dorothy had a real good grasp of politics and he really laughed, when she said that the Empire builders were like burglars in someone else's house. He kept the whisky coming and finally, took hold of her hand and informed her that he would warn Jimmy off – no violence used – if she wanted. A little tearful she asked if he would really do that for her? He nodded, saying he would do anything for her and for once, he actually meant it. Big tough Rory had fallen for Dottie and in a big way.

Dorothy gripped the big man's shoulders and gritted her teeth, he was thrusting hard and fast and she could feel every stroke laying in the Missionary position on his big bed, her head against the rough headboard and her legs up around those big shoulders. She would have sworn that she could feel his large cock in her stomach. What really got to her, was the orgasm she had with the big rough man. She never expected that and it came as quite a surprise. He gripped the headboard and fucked her even harder and she had another one! Finally, he finished, cussing and sweating. He certainly didn't pull out like she asked him. But she wasn't too bothered. Rosie had fitted her with a 'Dutch cap' for this assignment and Dorothy was really thankful she had. She cleaned herself up with a soft cloth whilst Rory pissed in a well worn chamber pot in front of her, and then offered it. She was very reluctant to do that in front of him, but Rosie's instructions were quite clear, "Bleeding take a piss as soon as possible afterwards, if the bugger cum's inside!" Really embarrassed, she followed Rosie's instructions and that made Rory a very happy man, if he wasn't happy enough. He loved watching women pee!

He rolled a couple of cigarettes and lit both, giving one to Dottie. He lay on the bed, with Dottie held firm and the pair smoked in relative silence. Then stubbing out the cigarettes, he took hold of Dottie's head and turned her face to him and French kissed her for some minutes, his big hands enjoying her breasts. He pulled down some pillows and pushed Dottie onto them, she was now kneeling on all fours and he mounted her again. That lasted some minutes and Dorothy was now actually a little tender and a bit sore. He finished in her again.

He slipped from the bed, watching Dottie clean herself up again. "I've a meeting with a man across the river darling, so I can't hang about. I'll meet you at the Paradise and take you for some lunch." He picked up his discarded trousers and searched the pockets, pulling out a handful of coins. "Here we go sweetheart, it's your cab fare home. I would – of course – taken you home myself, but as I say, I have a meeting to attend and I just have to be there. The man doesn't like people who are late and you get your bollocks shot off if you don't turn up!" he laughed and dropped five shillings on the bed.

Dorothy stared at the two half-crowns and felt like a cheap whore. But she kept her head and smiled, thanking him. Then as she slipped from the bed casually asked, "So who's so bloody important you have to run off and leave me alone." He pulled her close and passionately kissed her, slapping her bum hard with a big hand. "Never the mind my little darling. It's best you don't know for your own bleeding sake." He dressed quickly and left, with Dottie grabbing her coat and clothes. She pushed her boots on and stuffed her clothes in the big bag. Now only wearing her hat and coat she crept down the stairs and caught sight of Rory climbing into a cab. There was another standing behind with the driver smoking. With quite a smile, she said, "Follow that cab and be discrete about it. I think my old man is seeing another bloody woman!" The cabbie laughed and threw his cigarette down: and Dorothy made sure she sounded exactly like Rosie!

She paid the cabby from the money Rory had given her and added a good tip. "Well, roll me in sugar and call me an apple pie." She whispered to herself, standing around the corner from a big Villa near the entrance to Albert docks. She knew the place by reputation only: it was a high-class brothel ran by a certain madam Eleanor!

Dorothy stared across the road at the black carriage waiting by the closed tobacconist's and saw the driver lift his whip to her: she recongised the man, it was the same driver that the Special Irish Branch used. He had followed her and done a good job; she had been peering constantly from her cab and didn't see him behind. It had been with him that Dottie staged the so called bag snatch earlier. She opened and closed her broken umbrella a couple of times, giving the pre-arranged signal and the carriage pulled away: the driver would return to his boss for further instructions. Dottie stared up at the big house and sighed: her brother had told some real ribald tales about the Madame and her 'posh knocking shop'.

Dorothy was a little amazed at first, "Where the hell does he get the bleeding stamina from? He's had me twice and now he's having more fun in a bleeding brothel!" Then she thought better of those comments and realized that a brothel was a wonderful place for the Irish Brotherhood to meet. A group of men going into a brothel would attract little attention: even from the police. She slipped through the unlocked gate and walked around the side to a door marked 'Trade only' and peered through a window. That's when a woman's voice said, "Can I help you darling?" After jumping a little she turned and smiled. It was woman in say, her mid twenties, wearing nothing but a bodice, stockings and panties. She was smoking a big cigar!

"I'm Rosie." She said quietly, thinking fast. The woman smiled and blew smoke everywhere, "The bloody madam doesn't like me to smoke cigars around the clients. I don't bleeding know why not, the bloody men smoke 'em in there." 'Rosie' muttered how unfair that was and gripped her bag. "Bloody right darling, are you the new girl the madam is expecting?" Dottie half smiled and before she answered, the woman pushed open the door and shouted, "Henry! Henry, tell madam the new girl is here!" A hard, dark voice shouted back that he would. The woman almost shoved Dottie through the door laughing, "Bleeding glad to see you darling, the bloody Irish boy's are in the back room playing poker and madam needs all the girls she can get. You'll certainly earn some decent wages tonight I can tell you."

Dottie just nodded and turned to find an elderly woman covered in expensive lace and feathers staring at her. "Who the bloody hell are you? Where's Edith?" She asked, leaning on her thick wooden stick. "I'm afraid Edith couldn't make it madam, so she asked if I could cover her, if that's alright with you." Dottie really was getting good at thinking on her feet. The madam nodded, "Are you ready to work sweet thing? Do you know what makes men happy?" Dottie nodded, slowly unbuttoning her coat and opening it. She was of course, still stark naked! The old madam laughed so much that the other girl had to hold her up. "Fucking hell my darling, that's the best bloody reference any girl has ever shown me! Get to the kitchen and have some tea and something to eat, then Dawn here, will show you the nursery. The men in there need a firm hand and someone to change their diapers. Let's see how you cope with them buggers."

The old lady limped off, still laughing to herself and Dawn showed Dottie where the kitchen was and told the big man who was preparing sandwiches and pies, to feed the 'new girl'. Dorothy got chatting with the big man who was called Sven and yes, he came from Sweden. He had worked for the madam for some years and clearly enjoyed his job. He confided to 'Rosie' that the pay and perks were good. Dorothy said that was nice, he was so cared for. Sven laughed, "I get good wages, somewhere free to live and as a perk can fuck one of the girls each fortnight. I can tell you now my fluffy little rabbit that I'm picking you each time. You're a lovely little thing and boy, will I make you scream." She thanked him for his 'compliment' and he laughed again, "By Odin's beard, you are head and shoulders above the girls here – except maybe Dora – and I will definitely take you as my perk." He slapped a huge pie on her plate and grinned, "I bet that pretty little mouth can handle something that big." 'Rosie' just smiled and sipped her very welcome cup of tea.

Dawn appeared and handed her a long white apron and maids cap. "As the madam said, you're working the nursery, there only three in there tonight but they're all horny and misbehaving so you'll need this." She gave Dorothy an evil looking riding crop adding, "The bleeding more you use it, the more they love it. Come on follow me, I'll show you where to change." Dottie followed her up to the second floor, listening to music from the downstairs saloon. There was also much laughing and noisy conversation. Dottie casually asked about the Irish boys and Dawn sighed, "Madam doesn't like them here. They only pay for the room, don't have a girl too often and bring their own bleeding booze. Old man Collins organizes it."

Dawn pointed to a green door marked 'Nursery & Punishment'. "This is it and good luck, not that you'll need it! Hang your coat and hat in here." She opened the plain little door opposite and it revealed a cupboard with coat hooks and a small table, which strangely enough, had a pair of women's thigh length leather boots on it. "Oh shit, little Kathy must have left them. She normally does the nursery, but she has the week off, her two

cats have the shits and she really loves those little bastards."
With that, Dawn walked off down the hallway to a room marked,
'Oral Pleasures'. She gave a little wave and opened the door,
shouting, "Who's bleeding first then!" Dorothy now realized why
Dawn was carrying a 'spittoon' under her arm.

Dottie slipped into the cupboard and thought hard, she had a
lead as a detective would declare. Dawn had said 'old man
Collins' organized the poker games which probably covered the
Irish Brotherhood meetings, where they plotted a little treason.
That's when she noticed there was a peep-hole in both opposite
walls. She couldn't resist and peered in. There were three bored
looking men, quite naked apart from large diapers and pacifiers
in their mouths. She had slap a hand over her mouth to stop
laughing outright: the tall man sitting on the floor was none
other than old Charlie who looked after the stage door of the
Paradise! Still trying not to laugh, she opened the other peep-
hole and saw Dawn kneeling between two naked men and taking
turns with their erections. The spittoon carefully placed next to
her. She didn't recongnise either of the men. That's when she
heard the whistles and shouting. There were heavy boots running
up the stairs and she slowly closed the cupboard door, realizing
that the bloody place was being raided!

She could hear shouting and cussing as the nursery men were
dragged away and Dawn's voice yelling 'that the coppers were all
cock suckers!' Dorothy shrugged her shoulders; well Dawn would
certainly know what she is talking about! She grimaced as the
door was pulled open and a sweaty young copper pushed back
his helmet and smiled, "Come on darling, but what the hell are
you doing in the cupboard in your coat and hat? You are a bit
bloody overdressed for this place." Dorothy held a finger to her
lips and gestured the officer from the Royals Dock Authority
Police in.

*"At this time, there were no less than five separate Dock
police authorities covering all the major docks in London and
Tilbury [Essex]. They were amalgamated into the Port of London
Police Authority in 1909. You really wanted to know that...." SJW.*

She was actually going to explain who exactly she was working for, but the young constable seemed to have the wrong idea. The kinky boots lay on the floor and Dorothy was sitting on the table, coat open with the happy young man between her legs. She held tight to the swaying and creaking table with both hands, with her head against the wall. He was very enthusiastic in his fucking and didn't attempt to kiss her, which she was grateful for because he clearly neglected his teeth and the young man's breath could have stripped wallpaper! He gripped her arse so tightly that she had his finger marks on her bum cheeks for a couple of days.

He quickly finished and pulled up his uniform trousers and braces up with quite a smile on his face. Dorothy was now concerned about her 'Dutch Cap' and the pounding it had received tonight. She eased off the table and closed up her coat, then wondered about the Irish crowd? Had they been arrested? If they had, their identities would be known and her job was done. The young copper peered out the door and checked the stairs: the place was quiet as a morgue. He replaced his helmet and gestured down the stairs and they made their way down with Dottie walking quite awkwardly from the three sex sessions she had indulged in tonight. The copper really smiled at that and looked quite proud.

Dorothy slipped out the rear door and quickly made for the night stand for local cabbies near the Bascule Bridge. There was one cab standing there, the horse with its nose in its feed bag. The driver stood next to his faithful equine friend, sipping a mug of tea and smoking. That's when Dorothy checked her coat pocket and realized there was none of Rory's money left, she actually cursed, then putting on a brave face and smiling, walked up to the cabby. She couldn't go home but old Charlie would let her in at the Paradise. Then realized he had been nicked! She would have to go home or sleep bleeding rough, which certainly wasn't recommended for young women in this area of London. There was nothing for it; she would have to throw herself on the mercy of this sole cabby. Then she had a wonderful idea. "I say sir, could you run me to Brick Lane police station please?" The cabby must have been about forty but seemed pleasant enough. He nodded and gestured for her to get in. "What you need the coppers for miss? Are you alright?" He seemed genuinely concerned. Dottie nodded and confessed she had no money on her, but she knew some of the coppers on the night shift and they would certainly lend her the fare. He now chuckled, "Right darling, I'm to believe that if I run you to Brick Lane nick, some nice copper there will pay your fare?" Dottie nodded and he threw the cigarette down and chuckled again, "Blimey I thought I had heard them all, but that is a cracker. You best hop it my girl before I do call a copper!"

Dottie really smiled and now actually pleaded with him, saying all that she said was true and he would be paid. He sighed and looked her up and down, rubbing his rough face, "Where did you just come from, the only house down there is bleeding madam Eleanor's. Are you one of her girls who escaped the raid tonight?"

Dorothy stared at the pavement which was now getting wet with the light autumn rain. She really didn't know what to say. The cabby sighed, "That's why you have no money, she couldn't pay any of her girls from the nick." He stuck the empty mug in his coat pocket and gestured to the cab. "What, you going to give yourself up are you darling? Is that why you want the nick?" He was now laughing and removing the horse's feed bag. He turned and said, "Go on, off you go darling before the local beat man picks you up." Dorothy shrugged her shoulders "I have no-where to go, unless I go to the nick. I don't want to be around here at this time of night."

He sighed and stared at her pretty but very unhappy face. "Alright sweetheart, you are down on your luck through no fault of your own. After all, you weren't to know that coppers would raid the old madam and not get paid." Dottie asked if he knew what happened. He shrugged his shoulders, "All I know is that the coppers raided the place and took everyone away." Dottie wondered if they included the Irish boys, she bloody hoped so.

He walked to the cab door and opened it. "I haven't done this in bleeding ages, but get in darling and we'll work something out." Dorothy eased in and the cabby stood by the window and smiled, "I run up to the old St. Mary's and park in the grounds. You can pay me in kind and walk up to the nick. Is that agreed?" Dottie just smiled and the driver leapt into his seat and the cab pulled away, the hoof beats loud in the quiet of the night. It was turning colder by the minute and Dottie pulled her coat tighter. She really wished she had some warm knickers on or frankly bloody anything!

The driver explained that he didn't want the bloody pox since he loved his missus and wouldn't give her that. So she could 'play the flute' for the fare. Dorothy agreed and he sat smiling and sometimes groaning as she went to work. He wasn't big but certainly was a mouthful and Dorothy found herself thinking, 'Where's bloody Dawn when you need her!' After about ten minutes of hard sucking, he patted her head and told her to swallow and waste none. "Now that's a good girl!" he finally gasped and ejaculated with some force. Dorothy did as she was told and wiped her mouth: she would have given a fresh gold sovereign for a cup of water. She didn't watch the cabby as he disappeared back down the High Street heading for North Woolwhich probably. She trudged up the High street and saw the welcoming blue lamp. "Now this has to be some kind of bloody story, get thinking girl." She pulled her coat around and realized the weather was changing. "Probably start to bleeding snow, that's how my luck is running at the moment." She was certainly right about that. Little flakes started to appear from the dark night sky.

Dottie walked quickly up the steps and through the open door, taking a deep breath and didn't smile at old sergeant Harold 'Poker face' Gordon – the night duty station officer – and placed her bag on the counter. "Am I glad to see you Sergeant Gordon, you'll never guess what happened to me!"

He rose from his chair and walked around his desk, placing his mug of tea down. He looked quite concerned, "Are you alright Miss Hadden? What happened?" She took another deep breath and explained that some rogue must have lifted her purse while she waiting at the cab rank and that left her without any money to get a cab home. He sighed, "Not that bloody rank outside the old Paradise was it? Some sticky fingered bast....blighter had struck there twice this week already. One for your brother's CID boys I think. If old Charlie or Tom Duggan had been there, they would have run you home and collected the fare later."

Dorothy nodded and was about to ask if she could borrow some money for a cab when the sergeant yelled for 'George', and a big elderly copper appeared, smoking and drinking tea. "George mate, run Miss Hadden home would you? Give you something to do instead of sitting on your ar...backside all bleeding night." The big man smiled and said he would bring the carriage around the front. The sergeant turned to Dorothy and smiled, "Old George will run you home Miss. Give my regards to your brother, a good lad that one. Actually knows about bleeding police work!"

She thanked the old sergeant and waited outside for George, watching young constable Clive Collins walking up the steps, gripping a boy – about thirteen or fourteen – by the arm. He smiled at her and jerked a finger to his unhappy prisoner, "Little Herbert Monk, been flashing at the nun's at St. Mary's again." The boy grinned at her and she realized he had his cock in his hand! "Hello darling, like what you see?" He said. PC Collins gave him a slap about the head and sighed, "He's real dirty little bleeder miss and his brother is curate at St. James's would you believe!" Dottie couldn't help but giggle a little as her carriage rolled up and George jumped down and pulled open the door. "Soon have you home darling." The big man smiled as he helped her into the carriage, rewarded with a little glimpse of ankle and bare leg.

He slapped the reins and the carriage moved away with old George wondering why the young lady wasn't wearing stockings: his wife wouldn't be seen dead in public without hers. Still, it was a whole new century and the youth of today were different, sort of doing their own thing. But there was still one certainty: a man like him would fuck a girl like her [given half a chance] at the drop of a hat. With a smile he headed his horse towards the Canning Town Road.

CHAPTER 10. 'MAGIC IS JUST SCIENCE THAT WE DON'T UNDERSTAND YET.' Arthur C. Clarke.

The snow was falling in little gusts and the streets were covered to a depth of four or five inches. The Paradise Theatre was bedecked with Christmas decorations and Harry helped Dotty down from the carriage and they made their way inside. The theatre foyer was cold as the outside; big Tom Reed was trying to get the small pot bellied stove, standing in the corner of the Reception Office, to produce some heat, any bleeding heat!

Miss Player, wrapped in a very dull shawl, stood in the doorway; moaning about the cold and how useless big Tom was at fixing things. "Get Skoles, he can usually get the damn thing to work." She looked up at Harry and Dorothy; but didn't smile or offer any greeting. Miss Player really didn't like Christmas or anything that made other people happy. Dorothy asked her if Mr. Skoles was around; Miss Player shook her head and said simply; "With the Merry Widow." Dorothy nodded her understanding and pulled her coat tightly around herself. Harry asked big Tom if the Professor was about.

Big Tom Reed looked up from the reluctant stove and smiled; "I'll get Miss Player to send Arthur for him. How you getting on with the dead tramp? I read about it in the papers; quite a shock I can say. I only saw him here that night; alive and kicking. Then he's dead, with his bleeding throat cut."

Harry and Dorothy exchanged glances and Dorothy asked big Tom; "You saw him that night he came to the Theatre?" Big Tom nodded and Dorothy remembered that big Tom – The Stage Manager - had appeared in Reception to hang a poster about some awful new act, just after the 'shabby man' had ran from the Theatre.

"Yeah, he passed me on the street outside. I was collecting the posters for the new act from the Printer's delivery boy when he ran past me; shouting." Big Tom hit the stove a couple of times with a poker; it produced no improvement.

Dorothy half-smiled and said; "Did you hear what he was actually shouting about Tom?" She jumped slightly as Tom gave the stove another whack with the poker. "Oh yeah, he shouted the same thing a couple of times and ran up Canning Town Road; a cab nearly had him." Tom pushed the stoves little door open and racked about inside; cussing under his breath.

Harry tapped Tom on the shoulder; "What did he shout Tom?"

Tom looked up and grinned; "Brem & Havers, go to Brem & Havers."

Dorothy folded her arms in amazement and surprise; 'Brem & Havers' was a shop and warehouse on the docks that specialized in magic supplies and furnished props and curtains for theatres. It had been established in the early part of the last century by German immigrants and was the first choice of supply for many Music Halls and Theatres like the Paradise. It was also the first choice of top-class magicians from Europe and even America.

Harry gripped Dorothy's arm and lead her to the rear staircase, whispering; "I have no doubt their workshops and warehouse has glitter and tinsel scattered all over the place from the props and costumes they make."

Dorothy nodded, still a little angry with herself for making the bloody connection with the supposed 'Bremerhaven' and not 'Brem & Havers' which – as Harry stated – would certainly have lots of gold tinsel. "I wonder if they are still in business in 2022." She spoke quietly and smiled as Uncle William appeared from the stage staircase, pipe in mouth and followed by Titus; resplendent in a three piece suit with Fedora hat and walking stick.

"You look very striking Titus, who's the lucky lady?" Dorothy grinned and Titus broke into a huge smile and laughed, raising his hat to her and pointing to Uncle William; "No such luck Miss Dorothy, the Professor and I is paying a call upon the Reverend Wendell Rashwood to help with arrangements for the Children's pantomime. I'm to play a magic Genie apparently." Uncle William slapped the big man on the shoulder and blew a little smoke, then with a quizzical smile asked; "You two look like the cats who found the cream." They both nodded and Dorothy ruefully explained about the revelation of 'Brem & Havers', which made the Professor laugh out loud, shaking his head in amazement; "How the hell did we miss that one?" Both Dorothy and Harry shrugged their shoulders: they couldn't answer that! The decision was made and the little group headed back to the foyer to catch a cab to the docks.

The unhappy wretch young Arthur was made to stand outside in the cold and falling snow to flag down a cab; his teeth chattering in the wind. As Harry helped Dorothy into the relative warmth of the cab, Titus slapped Arthur on the back and pushed a penny into his shivering hand; "Thank you my boy." He said with a wonderfully posh, condescending voice. The cab pulled away and Arthur snarled and cursed loudly, throwing the coin with some anger against the wall of the Theatre. Several ragged young children scrambled after it, pushing and slapping each other. A big boy with rags wrapped around his feet won the uneven fight and ran off, clutching his prize; a big bag of hot chips beckoned, to share with his kid sister who had moaned about her empty stomach rumbling all day. There were no free school meals or fresh milk for hungry children in these days. Or even shoes for frozen little feet.

Brem & Havers" was located a few yards from the entrance to
No. 2 Gate: Albert Docks, in a small street which contained no
less than twelve pubs, four café's, a pie and eel shop and two
brothels. Their carriage pulled up outside the discrete doorway
which displayed a small sign; "Franz Bremmer & Wilhelm Havers
– Theatre & Magic supplies: Established 1749". Someone had
written in red chalk below; "Jews get out."

"Idiots." Muttered Uncle William and ran the bottom of his boot
over the chalk marks, whilst Dorothy wrapped the coat about her
and tapped Uncle William upon the shoulder; "I didn't know that
they were Jewish?" Uncle William nodded and grunted; "Very old
German Jewish family, but they have been here so long, I think
they're now an old English Jewish family!" His finger tapped the
'Established 1749' part of the sign and smiled. Dorothy chuckled
at that and everyone trooped into the shop with Harry muttering;
"Yet another German connection!"

They were greeted by Mrs. Isabella Serenity, a seemingly frail
woman in her early fifties, wearing a blue smock which had
splatters of white and red paint. She smiled at her guests and
quickly dropped the paintbrush into the small tin of red paint
upon the counter. A mannequin of a Minstrel Clown was being
refurbished by her skilled hands; "He's called 'Quinn' and will
grace the main tent's reception area of 'Jolly Joshua Robert's
Travelling Minstrel Show'. He really is from America you know."
Isabella grinned and wiping her hands upon the discoloured
smock, returned to her counter.

"Have you ever seen this man in here?" Harry didn't waste time
and showed Mrs. Serenity a photograph of the shabby man who
had died at the Police Station. She slowly placed her glasses
upon the end of her nose and stared at the picture for a few
moments; "My, my; he doesn't look well, does he?"

Briefly, Harry told Isabella about his death by self-poisoning in
the Police cell and so, she stared at the photograph again and
nodded that she had seen him before and he looked a lot better
alive. "The name he gave was Mister Mark Boland and he said he
was a Musician. But he looked a Military man to me. Anyway, he
was here to collect the cabinet for his employer – there were two
other men with him - quite rough and burly characters, they
looked like Dockers. But I had already been told that he would
appear to collect the Chinese Cabinet. He paid up the storage bill

in Sovereigns. It was quite expensive because the cabinet had been stored for some four years. They manhandled it upon a cart and were gone." Mrs. Serenity rubbed her chin and smiled; "It made my staff a great deal happier to see the back of that thing; beautiful as it is."

Harry nodded and asked why. "Over the years it was stored in the basement, all sorts of strange happenings were reported by the staff – especially the Night-Watchmen - until Mr. Elliot took the post; we must have employed a dozen men over the years it was here. None lasted more than a couple of months." Isabella handed back the photograph and admired Dorothy's hat."Why didn't they stay Mrs. Serenity?" Dorothy asked, adjusting her bonnet as Uncle William and Titus looked about the various theatrical items on display.

Mrs. Serenity rolled her eyes and smiled; "Ghosts, my dear, ghosts!"

It appears that the Night-Watchmen all reported ghosts emerging from the cabinet; Chinamen, Frenchmen, Americans and even a couple of Roman soldiers! They [the Night-watchmen] didn't hang about long enough to ask names or why they were here; they just ran from the building and never returned. Only Mr. Elliot reported no incidents with the cabinet and so had remained the Night-watchman for the last couple of years. Strangely enough, after the cabinet had finally been collected, he resigned his post and hasn't been seen since. Harry asked for Mr. Elliot's address, it would certainly be worth having a chat with the ex-night guard. Then a niggling little thought popped into Harry's head; Elliot? Where had he heard the name 'Elliot' before in this investigation? He pushed his hand through his hair and said quietly; "Who owned the cabinet Mrs. Serenity?"

"Oh, you'll know him my dear." She started to prise the lid from another tin of paint and smiled; "Sir Thomas Astor-Smith, the poor man; a terrible thing about his brother, though I never met him, the poor soul. Sir Thomas stored the cabinet here some years ago, but he visited it regularly, sometimes with friends; like the gentleman Mr. Boland who collected it."

Everyone glanced at each other and Uncle William asked if they may see where the cabinet was stored and Mrs. Serenity agreed; lighting a small lamp, she lead them down to the basement and a large empty space in a quiet corner. They all noticed that the floor was covered with gold tinsel; it was everywhere. "I have some around my boots already." Uncle William muttered and Mrs. Serenity explained it comes from the Circus equipment they store down here. When asked by Dorothy, Mrs. Serenity didn't know where Sir Thomas Astor-Smith had taken the cabinet; she assumed it had gone to his home in Victoria Street.

The party left the famous old shop and walked a little down King William Street in anticipation of hailing a cab. The snow was starting to thicken and fall in large swirling flurries. Harry gripped Dorothy's arm and said quietly;"We searched Sir Thomas's house and there was no sign of a dark Chinese cabinet, but when that miserable servant of the Bridgewater's showed us into the study; to wait for the Butler, guess what was standing in the corner of the room at Stonebridge House?" Dorothy smiled and pushed snow from her face; "A black and gold Chinese cabinet?" Harry grinned and nodded. A handsome cab pulled up at the corner of Queen Anne Square and everyone squeezed in; firstly Uncle William and Titus were dropped off at Reverend Wendell Elijah's Rashwood's home then Harry and Dorothy made their way back to the Paradise Theatre and hopefully, a little chat with Sir Thomas.

They climbed the small rear-staircase towards the attic rooms which served as Sir Thomas's theatre offices. Sitting outside the only door to the rooms was Mr. Mathew Kelp; Sir Thomas's personal Secretary. He looked up from the little desk and smiled at Dorothy; He adjusted his half glasses and imagined her naked apart from that little hat she was wearing; he smiled broadly and wiped his face with the back of his sweaty little hand.

"Is Sir Thomas in?" Harry asked directly; he didn't like the way that the skinny little man stared at Dorothy. Mr. Kelp clasped his hands together and nodded; "He came in some ten minutes ago, I'll announce your visit. Please wait here." Mr. Kelp rose from the chair and knocked loudly upon the door; "Sir, Inspector Hadden and Miss Hadden are here to see you!"

Silence was the reply, so Mr. Kelp repeated himself, knocking very loudly upon the door. "I don't understand why he's not answering; He went in just ten minutes ago and I've been here the whole time." Mr. Kelp sounded quite puzzled and a little concerned. "There are no other exits apart from this one." He added and shrugged his shoulders. Harry banged upon the door and shouted; "Its Inspector Hadden Sir Thomas, I need to speak to you!" No answer.

"Please open the door Mr. Kelp." Harry ordered and the little man struggled with the large brass door knob and admitted with some surprise in his voice, that the door was locked. He fumbled in his waistcoat pocket and produced several keys held together with steel wire. "I sure he won't mind; he could be lying ill or injured." Harry indicated to the door and Mr. Kelp tried a couple of keys before finally turning the lock. He pushed open the door and all three entered the room which was illuminated by two gas lamps; there was no sign of Sir Thomas. "This is impossible; I saw him come in and he never left!" Mr. Kelp exclaimed with some real surprise. All three looked about the room: there was a completely empty desk apart from "In & Out" baskets which were also quite bare, with a huge "Sea Captains" chair that looked well worn and Harry asked where the other door went to. Mr. Kelp pulled it and slowly Dorothy peered in; "Harry, I thought you said it was sat at Stonebridge House." Standing in the corner was the Chinese cabinet!

Both Dorothy and Harry inspected the beautiful piece of furniture very carefully; but the doors were firmly locked. Dorothy sighed; "It appears quite solid, I cannot find any hidden catches or levers and it's against a solid wall." Harry pointed to the floor; "Not a sign of gold tinsel anywhere. Could this be a copy?"

Dorothy asked Mr. Kelp if he possessed a key for the cabinet and he nodded that he didn't; "Only Sir Thomas has a key for it, I believe Miss." He replied, shifting his feet and looking thoroughly uncomfortable.

"How long has this cabinet stood here?" Harry questioned the nervous looking Secretary, who admitted that the cabinet had been here as long as he worked for Sir Thomas; some three years. Dorothy agreed that Mr. Kelp had worked that length of time for Sir Thomas, even before she became her Uncle's assistant; Mr. Kelp had been Sir Thomas secretary. Harry sighed loudly and looked about the room; it contained just the cabinet, a full length gold edged mirror, a small chest of drawers and hanging on a coat rack was something odd: a full set of yellow sailor's waterproofs, with a pair of black Wellington boots discarded upon the floor.

Dorothy noted that the window had been screwed down and was frosted; unusual for an attic room three floors up; who on earth could peer in from out there? Harry was examining the yellow coat and trousers, then the boots.

"I can smell salt water on them, quite fresh it would appear, like they were just used." Harry pointed to the floor beneath the coat stand – there were several little puddles of water - and he dipped a finger in and tasted; "Sea water." He added quietly. Both wondered how you could get fresh sea water in the middle of London; near Christmas and in heavy snowfalls. Who would go sea-fishing in this weather?

Harry and Dorothy really wanted to search the rooms thoroughly; but knew they could not – Harry quietly pointed out that a Search Warrant would be required - signed by a Judge–in–chambers and no Judge he knew would grant that, with no concrete evidence of any alleged crimes against Sir Thomas.

Reluctantly they had to leave the offices untouched and return to Dorothy's dressing room. They left Mr. Kelp to lock up and were soon enjoying a very welcome hot cup of tea, brewed by Rosie and a slice of hot buttered toast, smothered with thick strawberry jam. Dottie squeezed Rosie's hand and smiled: another little 'playtime' had been arranged at Rosie's house tomorrow. That evening, Harry joined Dorothy and Uncle William before their evening performance and accepted a steaming cup of tea from Rosie, before she left for home, to cook dinner for her family. "I'll be back at six to get you ready for tonight's show." Rosie told Dorothy, pulling on her hat and heavy coat. Then she grinned and laughed; "Ave I got some news for you Miss, bleedin' Skoles is getting' 'itched to the merry widow!"

Apparently Skoles had proposed to the widow Sissy Graves and was accepted so now the wedding would take place in the local Registrar's office at Easter.

"A brave man that Skoles." Muttered Harry with a broad smile and Uncle William had to agree, but Dorothy was quite happy for the pair which made Rosie laugh; "I heard that her old man was more than happy to jump from that ship in the Albert Dock!" The late Mr. Graves had been a docker who supped too much ale before falling from the SS 'Denver Falls' tramp steamer some three years ago. Still chuckling, Rosie headed for home.

When Rosie had departed, Harry bought Uncle William up to date with the case. Uncle William sat smoking his pipe and then smiled; "Napoleon Bonaparte," He said simply and puffed on his pipe, settling back in his chair. Harry looked quite bemused and Dorothy asked her Uncle to elaborate about the late French Emperor; which he did.

In 1814, the year Napoleon first abdicated, the French Emperor had received a delegation from the Chinese Emperor and a very special gift; a beautiful gilded cabinet which was suppose to be magical. Legend tells that the three Chinese Ambassadors entered the cabinet and simply disappeared!

"This incident was subject to a temporal Detectives investigation by Jericho and his team. It can be found in Book 3 – Episode 5 of 'THE TEMPORAL DETECTIVES' series." SJW.

But after Napoleon's defeat at Waterloo, he was again exiled and took the cabinet with him. After his death, the whereabouts of the cabinet was lost and it has not been heard of for many years. Harry rubbed his chin, deep in thought; "Quite a find for the Priests of Chronos, if Sir Thomas is a member of that little Group and I really think he could be."

"The rumour is that; Napoleon was a founding member of that unhappy bunch." Uncle William sucked on his pipe and their discussions were interrupted by a knock at the door. Dorothy opened it and smiled at Edwin, who asked for Inspector Hadden urgently. Harry rose from his chair and invited Edwin in, who stood by the fireplace and removed his hat; "Jesus Mr. Hadden, you'll never guess who's been found dead!"

"Another murder?" Dorothy exclaimed and Edwin nodded. She handed the young detective a cup of hot tea, which was most gratefully received and sat back in her chair.

"He was found in the front room by the fireplace; shot in the back twice." Edwin sipped his tea, gripping the cup with both hands to warm them. "Who?" Harry asked, pulling on his overcoat and reaching for his hat, Edwin looked up from his tea cup and said simply; "Kelp, Mr. Kelp; Sir Thomas's secretary."

The dingy ground floor apartment had several police officers inside, with Doc Goldstein and Harry standing over the body of the late Mr. Mathew Kelp. Edwin crushed out his fag upon the fireplace grate and waved to the door. "It's Jamie Guv." The photographer and his assistant had arrived; Jamie Lambert walked with a slight stoop - still suffering from the recent operation on his piles - but he grinned at Harry and Doc, telling Freddie [his young assistant] to place the camera down.

"I know they're gone, but I still feel the bastards some times." He spoke softly to them and stared down at the body; "Two in the back; that'll do it every time." Jamie started to unpack his equipment, whilst his assistant prepared the camera. That's when Edwin drew Harry's attention to the doorway again; Uniform Constable 'Lofty' Roberts had stopped Dorothy in the doorway, but Harry indicated that she could come through.

Dorothy gripped Harry's hand and the pair went to the corner of the room and held a whispered conversation; Harry was not pleased by what Dorothy told him. She had dispatched Sims to see Mr. Tibbs about questioning the Collector who had dealt with Mr. Kelp and the return message was quite surprising; there was no collection scheduled: Mr. Kelp was a man out of his time or had already sold his soul!

Harry couldn't believe it, "That would mean of the four Time-travelers that crossed over from 1974 and 2022 respectively, three are now dead [if Kelp was one] who is the remaining one and did he commit this murder and if so, why." He said quietly, but Dorothy was already ahead of him; she smiled; "But we know for a fact that Mr. Kelp had worked for Sir Thomas, for at least three years. So he couldn't been any of those time travelers, which means he was a devil worshipper and had already traded his soul; that's the only answer left to us, but I don't buy that. I think he was a jumper, but appeared some time ago, maybe even several years. So we still have the pair from 2022 to find and deal with."

Harry nodded his agreement at his sister's superb reasoning. "But why kill Kelp?" He asked and shrugged his shoulders; "Why kill Sir Thomas's secretary, for what reason?" He added and the pair walked back to the body, which lay face down - sprawled in front of the fireplace - which had no fire lit. Dorothy pointed out that the temperature outside was just below zero, with snow and ice, so why didn't Mathew Kelp have a fire burning? They both looked about the dingy room and Harry rubbed his chin. He was a little surprised that he missed that one and examined the fire place; it was stone cold, there hadn't been a fire there for some hours; now that was unusual in weather like this. Dorothy stared about the shabby room and then back at the late Mr. Kelp. She walked over to the small table by the unmade bed and picked up a photograph; "That's odd, big Tom told me that Mr. Kelp wasn't married, so what's he's doing in this wedding picture and where's Mrs. Kelp?"

Edwin took the photograph from her and stared at the couple. "Guv, come and look at this wedding picture of Kelp's and take a good look at the woman." He held the frame up and Harry left Jamie taking his gruesome pictures and walked over. "I don't recognise her; not from around the theatre anyway." Dorothy said softly, peering over Edwin's shoulder.

Harry stared at the picture and slightly smiled; "Dotty, Like Edwin, I've seen this woman before; Stonebridge House and the surly servant who showed us in. That was her."

"There are more connections with Sir Thomas and that damn House that simply cannot be co-incidences. Edwin, get young Farmer to visit the new widow and find out what Mr. Kelp was doing these last few hours." Harry instructed the keen young detective, who nodded and disappeared from the room. He and Dorothy stared back at the body; "Who was he really?" Dorothy asked; she knew he wasn't from around here [the east end] and he always kept himself to himself; no-one even knew he was married!

Doc Goldstein closed his 'Gladstone' bag and pulled on his thick overcoat, he tapped his hat and placed it upon his head; "I'm finished here Harry. I'll let you have the results of the PM as soon as I can." Harry nodded and the pair shook hands. Doc Goldstein tipped his hat to Dorothy and made his way down the stairs to the bitterly cold street.

Freddie Cable [the photographers assistant] was packing away the camera and tripod, he turned to Dorothy and smiled; "The boss and I are always looking for really pretty girls, you know for postcards and modeling hats and coats; that kind of stuff. Here's our card, we pay five shillings an hour for a girl as pretty as you

Miss." He handed Dorothy his card and the pair [Freddie and Jamie] followed Doc Goldstein down the tenement stairs. Dorothy sighed and pushed the card into her little handbag.

"Are you going to take him up on his generous offer; after all, five bob is good money." Harry smiled broadly at his sister, who tapped her bag gently; "No, but there are girls in the chorus line that really could use some extra money."

Harry chuckled and called for the uniform constable on the door to fetch the Undertakers, who were waiting in the street. Dorothy looked about the dismal room and couldn't draw her attention away from the cold fireplace. Who would stay in a room with no fire in this weather? She stepped carefully over the late Mr. Kelp and examined the surround, grate and chimney.

"Harry, there's not been a fire in this grate for some time; there are cobwebs at the base of the chimney!" Harry knelt next to his sister and ran a hand around the brickwork; cobwebs and dust; had a fire been recently lit in the grate, there would be neither. He stared at the body and sighed; "He was killed elsewhere and brought here." He concluded.

Dorothy nodded; "The family downstairs told Edwin that they heard two distinct shots around four-o'clock, but I'd wager that Doc Goldstein will tell us that he was killed much earlier. That means, someone went through all the trouble of staging the shots to cover the real time of his murder - why?"

"For an alibi." Harry said simply and they both stepped away from the body as the men from Church's the Undertakers arrived. Constable Tanner stuck his head around the door; "Mr. Hadden, you best have a word with old Henry Gates - he owns the small Tobacconist shop that's right opposite here - he says that he definitely heard the two shots. But he had full view of the front of the tenement block and its side entrance down the alley; no one came out until Mrs. Zolskisimi [who found the body] ran into view, screaming in the street, shouting fucking murder!"

Dorothy and Harry exchanged glances; this tenement block only had a front and side entrance; where did the killer go? Dorothy folded her arms and sighed; "If Kelp was a follower of the Dark Prince, then I strongly suspect that the man who employed him could also be such a devotee; after all, those types of people tend to stick together quite closely in all matters. Maybe that is the answer to why he had no soul after all."

Harry nodded and muttered; "Sir Thomas; Mr. Tibbs has always said the Priests of Chronos were Devil Worshippers; that makes sense." Harry rubbed his chin and shouted to a young uniform constable; "Find out who rents out these rooms." The baby faced constable nodded and disappeared. Harry turned to Dorothy; "I wonder who owns this slum tenement block? I have a feeling Kelp didn't live here." Dorothy smiled at that reasoning. But something about the photograph of Kelp's wedding disturbed her thoughts; if Kelp didn't actually live here, why was the bloody photograph on the side table? They left the cold grim scene as the undertakers collected the late Mathew Kelp.

Dorothy didn't have a pleasant meeting with her 'handler's' in the snug bar [where women were allowed] of the 'King George Hotel'. It appeared that the Irish boys admitted nothing, had nothing on their persons and were released without charges.

But they were pleased about the revelation of 'old man Collins' arranging the 'poker' game and paying for the room. The younger man showed Dorothy two photographs; the first, a strikingly good looking young man with a wonderful smile and told her he was 'Edward Thomas Collins' aged twenty-eight and from Cork city. He was a hardened Irish brotherhood member suspected of killing a Dublin police officer during a shoot out in a bar that was being raided. He had escaped and now was desperately sought after. The second photograph was a much older man with rough features and two scars on his chin. He was Joseph Collins aged forty-one from Dublin who had quite a criminal record going back to when he was eleven. Mostly theft and violence including gun running! They both smiled [Dorothy's handler's that is] and said that both men had three things in common: they loved Ireland, adored booze and finally, couldn't resist a beautiful woman.

Her new assignment was simple [to them anyway] find which one is the 'Collins' that ran the local Irish Brotherhood cells. They had 'disappeared' somewhere in east London and Dorothy was already 'known' amongst the Irish community here, so she could move freely amongst them. She asked about Rory McLeish and the younger man chuckled, "You won't be seeing him around for a while, he's on remand in Brixton prison for kicking shit out of your now ex-boyfriend O'Connor." Dorothy wondered why she hadn't heard from either man for a while: one was in prison and the other in hospital. She certainly had a talent for picking bad boyfriends; Rosie wouldn't be pleased about the latest news of her [Dottie's] 'love life'. Dotty was partially disappointed in McLeish: he had promised 'no-violence' towards Jimmy while explaining the 'breakup' of their relationship.

The older man sat back, sipping his brandy and almost smiled, "We do have one clue – perhaps – to their whereabouts. Madam Eleanor was interviewed by us and she seemed to recall [she couldn't be positive] that a 'friend' of hers who runs some good quality girls had spoken about a man who matched the older Collins description hiring a couple of her girls. They were paid well apparently. It's thin I know, but here's that madam's address, you see her and make sure if old Collins wants another tart, you take the job and let us know if it's him."

Dorothy took the paper and read the address, nodding slowly. She would plead with Rosie to come on this assignment to watch her back and quickly inform her handler's where the man was. This 'mission' could be quite unpleasant and she would convince Rosie to help when they were in bed together. It worked.

CHAPTER 11. 'I HATE THIS IMAGE OF ME AS A PRIM EDWARDIAN, I WANT TO SHOCK EVERYONE.' Helena Bonham Carter [but Dorothy could have said it!]

It was the third meeting with the 'madam' that proved really productive: she had received a message from the barman of the 'Pig & Whistle' in Waterloo Road that one of his 'guests' had asked for a girl from her. His name was Collins. The fee would be ten bob [50 pence today!] So Dorothy dressed accordingly and even Rosie was impressed, "Bleeding hell darling, you really do look like a high priced brass [prostitute], one of those girls that work Piccadilly Circus and the west end theatres!" Dorothy was wearing a heavy faux fur coat [down to her ankles] matching hat, boots and gloves but underneath she only had a black lacy bodice that was low cut, [with suspenders] very naughty black panties, and stockings.

They caught a cab and headed for the pub. It was packed and had a really huge man working the door. He must have been well over six foot with a face that betrayed a career as a street fighter. But he had incredible blue eyes that could have been mistaken for sapphires. Both women noticed his big hands and he had a little smile on his face. He stared hard at Dorothy and she realized – with a little horror and some panic – that he may have recongnised her. He was throwing a shouting, drunken young man into the snow and the angry drunk staggered off, shouting threats and insults. The big man now smiled at Dottie and Rosie, "Sorry about that ladies. The boy had far too much to drink, I'll have words with Maurice [the barman] about serving drunks. Now how can I help you Miss Hadden?" He had a voice that certainly matched his appearance: it was deep and betrayed a slight Scottish accent. But Dorothy and Rosie exchanged a very concerned glance, he had certainly recongised Dottie!

Dorothy swallowed hard and managed a sweet smile, "Thank you, I'm here to see Maurice myself actually…he's ….Well, he's helping me with something…..I…" Dorothy couldn't think of anything to say that would justify her appearance at such an establishment. Rosie pitched in, "God help us another bleeding one who thinks that you are that flipping actress!" She turned from an open mouthed Dottie and grinned at the big man, "Christ darling, if she had a sixpence for every time someone said that, she could bleeding retire and live in Buckingham Palace!" Her and Dorothy both laughed and gripped each other as the big man rubbed his rough face: handsome he was not. "Well, my darlings, you certainly fooled old Oscar Bellend. I would have gambled me old mum that you were her." But the way he smiled told Dorothy that he didn't believe Rosie's story one little bit. Then she quickly recalled where she had heard that very odd name before: at the funeral of the 'shabby man', Mr. Bellend had been one of the bleeding gravediggers! But Rosie was struggling not to laugh, 'bloody Bellend! What a bleeding name, but I bet no fucker takes the piss out of it, well not to his face anyway!' she thought and tried desperately to restrain the giggles.

"You must have seen me…me look-a-like on the stage then?" Dottie asked, keeping a big smile fixed to her face. He nodded and rubbed his hands together, "Oh yes my dear, many times at the old Paradise, and she's my Friday night treat on my day off. Bloody love the show, really interested in magic and all things supernatural." Rosie nodded, "Yeah, I understand she's popular, but we're freezing our bleeding knickers off out here!" and gestured to the doors, adding, "Can we get in and have some bleeding gin and warm up, me darling?" He rubbed his chin and pushed open one of the doors, "Have a nice time ladies and shout for me if you need anything, Oscar will always be at your service Miss Hadden. Always." They slipped past the big man who filled the doorway and stared at each other with Dorothy whispering, "He knows full well it's me." They squeezed through the rowdy crowd and managed to find a space by the bar which was being worked by a tall man who was wearing the most obvious and ridiculous wig. There were also two barmaids who had clearly been employed because they were pretty and well endowed: they certainly weren't the fastest barmaids in London and they repeatedly asked Maurice what the bloody prices were. Soon as he saw Dottie and Rosie, he walked over and leaned on the bar whispering, "Old Mrs. Pike send you darling?" [Mrs. Pike was the name of Dottie's madam.] Dottie nodded whilst Rosie asked for a couple of gins.

They quickly finished their drinks and Maurice gestured them behind the bar and up the dark stairs, telling Rosie to wait for her friend in the snug bar. Dottie made her way to the grim upper hallway; Maurice had said the Collins was in room 3. She softly knocked and a hard voice asked who it was. "Rosie from Mrs. Pike." She replied. That made her smile, she hadn't told Rosie – yet – about using her name. The door slowly opened and out of sight, standing behind it, the man told her to come in. For some reason, Dottie felt a little fear, but found her courage and walked in. She turned and saw that it was not either of the Collins she was after and decided to exit from the situation really fast. The man was skinny, in his fifties with a well worn face and really dark eyes. His hair was graying and unkempt, which matched his vest and trousers. He had no shoes on and his braces hung down. He really smiled, "Get your bloody coat off darling, I haven't all night."

Dorothy was about to blurt out her 'exit' story, but he stepped forward and grabbed her arms, pushing her onto the bottom of the bed. "Just keep your gob shut unless I have my cock in it. I play rough, so keep the fucking noise down. I only like to fuck arse's so get that fucking coat off and get your fucking dress up.

I'll pull your knickers down myself." He roughly pulled her onto her stomach and dragged her coat off. He chuckled, throwing it on the floor. "Now that's a good girl! All ready for old Shamus to fuck your arse."

Laughing he dragged down her panties and slapped her bum really hard, holding her down with some hidden strength. Now Dorothy was shouting and he slapped her bum again telling her shut the fuck up or he'll take his belt to her and she wouldn't get paid. Turning her frightened head, she could see he was holding a large black wooden dildo in his hand. "I'll open up your brown flower with this – it may hurt – then fuck you hard." He grinned and pushed her down on the bed with some force. She screamed again which really annoyed him and he struck her quivering arse with the dildo a couple of time, saying angrily for her to shut the fucking well up. He now tried to insert the dildo in her anus but Dorothy was struggling too much, so he grabbed up his thick belt and slapped her pale buttocks with it, really hard, which made Dorothy scream like a banshee. "I'm going to fucking enjoy teaching you to behave with paying customers you fucking little whore!" He raised the belt again, but the door had crashed open and a huge figure came quickly in.

The big man picked up Collins by his neck with one hand, and threw him against the wall. Collins grabbed under the pillows and pulled a small 'Smith & Western' revolver out. He didn't have time to use it because Oscar moved with incredible speed and grabbed the old man's hand. Dorothy actually winced as she heard Collins wrist snap. Oscar calmly took the gun and simply bent the barrel downwards which absolutely amazed her and tossed it on the floor. The look on Collins face was priceless and curled up against the wall covering his head with his arms, groaning in real pain.

Oscar turned to Dottie, now standing over the sobbing Collins, and said quietly, "He's a vicious old bastard, but he's old. But I'll hurt him some more if you want, for what he tried to do to you."

Dorothy, open mouthed at what just happened, shook her head. "No, no leave him Oscar and please get me out of here." She was staring at the bent gun and still couldn't believe what she had seen the big man do. He gently took hold of her arm, picking up her coat with his free hand. "Come on, your friend is in the snug. I'll get you a cab." Dorothy pulled on her coat and snatched up her hat. They walked quickly down the rear stairs and Dottie asked why he had interfered – though she was really bloody grateful that he did – and the big man didn't smile, "I don't like women being hit; my old mum suffered it for years with that old bas...with my father. Well, until I was big enough to put an end to it. He didn't lay a hand on her after I….Well, that's enough on that. I won't ask what a lady like you was doing here and what for, but I had a feeling you didn't wish to be here."

Dorothy reflected upon the dangers that 'working girls' faced if they weren't in the relative safety of a brothel. She had seen and faced it herself and now saw prostitution for what it was. But Dorothy was now further amazed that Oscar had sensed just how she felt and realized that there was far more to the big man than just muscles and an ugly face. They stood at the bottom the stairs and Dorothy had to stretch up to kiss Oscar on the cheek. "Thank you." She whispered softly and the big man smiled, almost shyly and gestured to the door, "Your friend is in there Miss Hadden. I know I will see you again, I have already bought the ticket for Friday night!" They both chuckled and Dorothy joined a very relieved looking Rosie who was on her third gin. Dorothy took the glass from her and drained the contents, making Rosie chuckle, "Needed that, did we? Well, is it him?"

Sadly Dorothy shook her head, "No, just some sick old pervert who liked to abuse women. Oscar sorted him out...and Rosie, you'll never believe what I saw the big man do!" Rosie now interested leaned close, "Christ, what did he do?" But Dorothy looked about, "Come on, let's get out of here, Oscar's getting us a cab." The girls made for the door, having to push through the mass of happy, drunken customers and back out into the street. A cab was waiting with Oscar talking to the driver. He turned and smiled, opening the cab door. "Here we go ladies; Alfred will run you anywhere you want. I hope the rest of your night is more pleasant Miss Hadden."

Rosie jumped in and Dorothy followed, stopping to whisper to Oscar another 'thank you'. He just smiled and closed the door, walking back to the pub entrance. There was drunken sailor staggering and swaying, his trousers half down, waving his cock about and shouting.

As the cab plodded through the snow, Dorothy suddenly sat up and said to Rosie, "For heaven's sake Rosie! Oscar! He has to be the bleeding Oscar that sent me the strange little plant. Do you remember?" Rosie looked a little puzzled for a second or two and then nodded. The little plant was thriving on the window ledge of Dorothy's dressing room and they still don't know what the hell it was!

When Dorothy explained what he did to Collin's gun, Rosie just stared at her and said quietly, "Maybe he was a strongman at a circus or something. You should hire him as a bleeding close bodyguard. You'd sleep better at night...and so would I." Dottie smiled, "I couldn't afford it: regretfully." Rosie chuckled, "I'm damn sure he would take his pay in another form other that bloody money!" Dorothy just sighed, but smiled again: he probably would! They only stopped once before returning to the theatre with Rosie going to the news-stand by the underground station and telling the big happy woman - who was smoking a cob pipe – "to tell father that the parcel never arrived." The woman nodded and said nothing. Rosie re-joined Dottie, who was rubbing her abused bum cheeks discretely in the cab and they set off again. "I don't think the Marquis de Sade has thought his perverted pleasures through: well, not from the point of the bleeding person on the receiving end." She informed Rosie who just chuckled, "I'll kiss it better and rub some bleeding cream on it darling." And she did.

Mrs. Pike [Dottie's madam!] wasn't happy about losing a regular customer [evil old Collins] but the money she received from Military Intelligence put a smile back on her face and just days later, passed Dorothy another message. A certain Mr. Collins had asked for a girl to visit him at a posh east end hotel 'The Royal Devonshire' and she assured Dottie that it wasn't old Collins the pervert; apparently he had caught a ferry back to Dublin and his shop. He was a bloody ladies hat maker! So, with Rosie in tow, [who carried a cricket bat] she headed to the hotel and spoke discretely to the Night Porter who she slipped half a crown as instructed by the madam.

The little man quickly pocketed the money and told Dorothy it was suite 4 on the second floor. The pair made their way up the staff stairs and found the door. Dorothy knocked and waited, with Rosie standing at the end of the corridor, keeping a close eye. The door opened and she was hit by music, laughter and loud conversation. There was a party going on! A young man stood smiling, glass in hand, he took a sip and quickly shouted over his

shoulder in a thick Irish accent, "Joe! The entertainment is here!"
He grinned and gestured Dorothy in, "I thought there would be
two. I think Joe wanted two." Quick thinking, Dottie signaled for
Rosie to join her. "Ah, now that's magic!" He said loudly as Rosie
appeared and finished his drink. Another man, a little older
appeared grinning, "Come on ladies, I'll show you were you can
change and we're all expecting a good turn. Mrs. Pike said that'll
you'll do a real good turn for the boys!"

As they entered the room, Dorothy realized it was a bloody stag
party and clearly the men thought her and Rosie were the
bleeding strippers! They were shown a side room which was a
small writing room or study. Yet another man appeared – not
Collins – and gave Dorothy a gold sovereign. "I'm Joe. Now
ladies, do a turn each to get the boy's blood rushing and then
touch the velvet to get the buggers hard. We'll shove the groom
to you and you can take care of him. If he can't mage the pair of
you, I'll take care of that myself. [He really smiled at that] If you
want extra money [he pointed to one of the doors near the bay
window] you can use the second bedroom. What you charge is
up to you but your guaranteed to make a fair few bob, there's
eleven of us here and if you get us all hard, you'll earn a decent
nights pay. Now, help yourself to food and drink. Have a bloody
good time, because we certainly will!" He wasn't Irish and walked
away, joining in the singing of a very foul naughty music hall
favourite. Dorothy sat on the chair by the desk and had to smile,
"A bloody stag do! Do you think Mrs. Pike is taking the piss?"

Rosie just grinned and held her big bag with both hands, "Well,
who's getting the spare one? That's five each and one going
bleeding spare!" Now that made Dottie laugh, she hadn't seen
either of the men in the photographs shown by her handlers.
"Another walk up the bleeding garden path." She muttered then
both heard the cheering and applause, apparently the groom had
appeared. Rosie pulled the door open a little and peered out, a
man was centre of attention, having his hand shook by everyone,
getting slapped on the back and drink s shoved in his hands.

Dorothy stood behind and sighed, the young man was real
handsome individual with sandy bloody hair and blue eyes. Then
she realized that she knew him! She jumped back, telling Rosie
to shut the bleeding door. "For heaven's sakes Rosie! The groom
is bloody Clive Collins, a Constable from Harry's nick and he
knows me!" Rosie groaned and asked "How the hell do they get

out of this?" Dorothy paced the small room and then went to the window and stared out, she turned slowly and asked Rosie if she had a head for heights. Rosie rubbed her face and nodded, "If the bloody situation calls for it, why?" puzzled by Dottie's apparently mad question.

Dorothy pulled up her coat and then her dress and petticoats, tying them as best she could and told Rosie to do the same. "Well, the bleeding situation calls for it. We're going for a little walk." Rosie stared at her as she pushed the window right up. "This hotel has a ledge running around the building that the sodding window cleaners use. Come on." Both women slipped through the window and crept around the ledge. Several people leaving the "Apollo" Theatre opposite all stopped and stared as Dottie and Rosie found an open window and eased through. They dashed past two naked honeymooners on a big bed and through the door into the corridor. The pair on the bed was so engrossed they hadn't noticed!

CHAPTER 12. 'SO MUCH OF PREFORMING IS A MIND GAME.' Joshua Bell.

Titus looked resplendent in his 'magic Genie' costume and stood smiling, arms folded; "The maid who brought the tea remarked that I really did look African!" He chuckled and threw up both arms shouting; "Abracadabra! And Reggie is transformed from a respectable white man into a magical black man!" Dorothy giggled and adjusted her feathered bonnet. She was now in her costume as 'Miss Pandora' – one of the few women magician's working the Edwardian stage - and she looked stunning; of course!

Rosie gave Titus a big smile and said softly to Dorothy; "Titus could work his magic on me any day." Dorothy just sighed and stared at the clock in the small room that Lady Bridgewater had given the magic troop to change in. "It's almost time. Rosie, check to see if the people are in the drawing Room please."

Rosie nodded and disappeared through the door, passing Harry slowly walking in. "No sigh of Sir Thomas – yet." He said and removed his hat and coat. "I have men discretely posted outside and young Farmer is in the audience." He slapped Titus on the shoulder; "Jesus Reggie, you really do look like a magic Genie." Reggie just smiled and folded his arms. "Amazing what burnt cork can do." He said quietly.

"Can you check the stage marks and props please Reggie?" Dorothy asked the big man and he disappeared too. Harry closed the door and sighed; "Sir Thomas owns the tenement block where Kelp was found and the other residents all confirmed that Kelp never lived there. But his wife, sorry widow, confirms that Sir Thomas used that particular set of rooms for some really odd guests that turned up. She and Kelp had married in secret because Lady Bridgewater doesn't employ married women as maids. She feared she would be sacked if her ladyship found out."

Dorothy sighed; "Now that's real bloody discrimination." She muttered and smoothed her light coloured trousers down. Harry smiled – a little bemused – "Trousers really don't suit a woman." But smiled broadly, then added; "Doc Goldstein confirms that Kelp had been dead over six hours before those bloody shots were fired. He had been murdered elsewhere as we suspected." He carefully lifted the lid of the big ornate trunk standing by the door and almost jumped out his skin; Sims leapt out and happily shouted; "Surprise!"

The strange mummy grinned and bowed. He didn't get any applause and Dorothy waved him back into the trunk. "Keep an eye on big Arthur and get keep the excitement down." Sims just nodded and leapt back in the trunk, slamming the lid behind him.

Harry stared at the decorated box and rubbed his face; "I didn't see your bloody big snake in there. It was empty apart from that lunatic Sims." Dorothy grinned and held up her hands; "Yes, that's called magic!" Harry chuckled and turned, the door opened and Rosie stuck her head in; "They're all in and Lady Bridgewater says you can start. Titus is on his first mark." Both Harry and Dorothy could hear Lady Bridgewater announcing 'Miss Pandora and her magic box.' which – for some reason – made Harry grin. He gestured to the woman [Lady Bridgewater] and didn't smile; "Her and her husband fit the description of the couple that the newspaper staff say placed those damn advertisements except they were apparently in Germany at the time and their passports prove it!" Dorothy just sighed and headed for the makeshift stage behind a huge embroidered curtain.

Harry followed and slipped into the audience and was surprised to find a very special person sitting in the front row; the Prime Minister's eldest son; James, the forty year old heir to his father's title and estates. Young Farmer pushed up to Harry and nodded to the VIP; "This family [the Bridgewater's] move in some big circles." Harry leaned back against the wall and folded his arms, searching the audience; there was no sign of Sir Thomas. But his experienced eyes caught site of a young man sitting alone by the door, who kept looking around and wiping his face. It wasn't that hot in the damn room despite being filled with many ladies and gentlemen.

"The prime Minister was Robert Arthur Talbot Gascoyne-Cecil, 3rd Marques of Salisbury, He died in 1903." SJW.

"Keep a close eye on him." Harry whispered to Detective Constable Farmer. But everyone's attention turned to the small stage as the curtains parted. Titus stepped forward – amid the applause – and lifted the trunk onto a small bare trestle table; which everyone could see under and around.

Dorothy came forward and Titus lifted the lid and tipped the trunk onto its side. It was apparently empty. Dorothy ran her 'wand' around the inside and Titus slammed the lid down. Dottie called out some magic words and Titus reopened the box. 'Big Arthur' slipped from the box and Dorothy scooped the snake up and held him aloft. The crowd applauded really enthusiastically and she replaced the wriggling snake back and Titus closed the lid.

She tapped the box with her wand and Titus pulled up the lid; Sims leapt from the trunk and rolled about the floor, bouncing like a ball. Then stood and bowed. Dorothy introduced her 'assistant' Mr. Sims to a very appreciative audience. Titus closed the lid and Dorothy waved at the trunk and when reopened; several pidgins flew from it, fluttering above the amazed crowd's heads. Even Harry was impressed.

Titus closed the lid and on Dorothy's command; opened the trunk again. The body of Sir Thomas rolled from the trunk and lay on the makeshift stage; his eyes open and his face contorted in a horrific stare. There was absolute silence for a few seconds until Dorothy screamed and everyone realized that this was not part of the bloody act!

Harry leapt forward and grabbed Dorothy, rushing her from the stage as young Farmer attended the lifeless body of Sir Thomas. The audience fled the room in shock and horror. Apart from two ladies who fainted. The show was over – quite prematurely – and Rosie gave Dorothy a big mug of hot tea in the large side room which served as her dressing room to calm her nerves. Harry was most reluctant to leave her, but Dorothy insisted he see to the late Sir Thomas; that was his duty as a policeman.

"Now that's what I call a fucking show stopper." Titus whispered to Rosie who couldn't help but giggle loudly despite the terrible circumstances.

Harry carefully went through Sir Thomas's pockets and pulled a strange object from one; a very ancient figurine of a big breasted woman who appeared to have horns protruding from her head. 'A sign of a devil worshipper?' He wondered.

It took some hours to sort the chaos out following the late Sir Thomas's dramatic appearance on stage. Everyone in the audience had to be interviewed and the nervous young man Harry suspected; turned out to be an ardent admirer of Dorothy!

Lady Bridgewater didn't appear too upset at Sir Thomas's demise at her Christmas magic party; she just moaned about all the forthcoming gossip about her and her house by malicious persons making hay from her discomfort. Strangely enough; neither Dorothy nor Harry were surprised by that.

Harry and Dorothy were checking the body – again – now covered with a clean white sheet. Constable Dave Farmer appeared and gestured for Harry to come. "Two officers from Military Intelligence want to speak to you Guv. They're both navel captains." Harry and Dorothy exchanged a knowing glance; they both knew that the late Sir Thomas had dealings with the Secret Service; he was probably part of it. Then he wondered how they appeared on scene so quickly? The answer followed quickly too: they had Dorothy under surveillance? Harry told Dave to look after Dorothy and met the two well dressed young men in the morning room. The conversation was clear and concise; Harry was to report directly to them and no-one else regarding the death. He was only to make a brief statement to the press about the matter and not to speculate on why the man was murdered. Harry nodded his agreement and then blatantly asked the secretive pair if the late Sir Thomas was a colleague of theirs! They both just smiled and said they would arrange for removal of the body. Harry nodded and watched as three men dressed in neat black suits appeared, carrying a plain wooden box. They removed the body in minutes and the strange and secretive team disappeared in two blacked out carriages.

Harry and Dorothy walked down the steps of the now almost deserted house with Constable Farmer walking quietly behind. They would pick up a cab and head back to the theatre. Young Constable Farmer coughed and spoke softly to Harry; "Guv, I recongnised one the coffin carriers. He used to be a PC over at Forest Gate nick. The last I heard he had been seconded to the Irish Branch a couple of years ago. I believe he's never returned or spoken to any of his old friends at the nick. He sort of….well, disappeared and he certainly recongised me, but didn't make any attempt to acknowledge our past friendship."

Dorothy was a little distracted; she had watched the two men from 'Military Intelligence' depart, from her window. It was the very same men who had basically 'blackmailed' her into working for them over the Irish brotherhood!

They stood by the kerb and waited on a cab; Harry nodded and told Dave to keep that information to himself. Dave rubbed his face and almost smiled; "I don't know if this is relevant, but he was subject to some strange gossip and rumours while at the nick and after he left." Dorothy asked him to elaborate on that.

Dave pulled his heavy coat about himself and thrust both hands into his pockets; "Well, lots of other coppers said that his story about joining up after a couple of years in the navy didn't quite ring true. We had a couple of ex-sailor at the nick and they often said he just didn't seem right. Never really made any friends at the station and kept himself to himself."

Harry nodded and held up his hand as a cab appeared at the

corner of the road. Dorothy also pulled her coat around; it was starting to snow again. "What wasn't right about him Dave?" she asked and Constable Farmer shrugged his shoulders; "He didn't have any family and friends and just seemed to have appeared. Never spoke about his family or friends outside of the job. One of the old sailors – PC Askwell – said that the ship he claimed he served on - HMS Hood - he [PC Askwell] had never heard of."

They climbed into the cab and headed for the theatre. After a couple of minutes, Harry pulled his companions closer and said quietly; "There's a blacked out carriage following us and not very discretely." Dorothy chuckled; "I think that must be novel, the police keeping the police under surveillance." Even the normally dour Dave had to chuckle at that.

Everyone [of the team] assembled back at the theatre and Rosie made tea for all. Dorothy and Harry were not surprised however that Mister Jericho Tibbs arrived – stopping time for everyone else – and chatting with his two human agents for this time. Harry showed him the strange figure taken from the dead body of Sir Thomas. Mr. Tibbs knew exactly what it was and what it was capable of.

He and Dorothy were to receive quite a shock; he informed the pair that it contained a time portal! This strange device would have allowed Sir Thomas to jump to any time he wished; provided he had another object for the year he wanted to visit. So – apparently – he could only jump backwards in time.

Dorothy grunted; "That means he couldn't have jumped to 1974 or 2022 and if the other travelers had similar devices, then their trips were all one way only." Harry nodded at that and Jericho expressed real interest in the whereabouts of the Chinese cabinet, which did indeed once, belong to Napoleon Bonaparte, who was a priest of Chronos. Uncle William had been spot on with his deductions.

Harry turned the figurine slowly and carefully in his hands and spoke quietly to Mr. Jericho Tibbs; "So, it's a Mesopotamian fertility symbol that's about four thousand years old?" Jericho nodded; "It's quite safe now; I've removed the damn time portal from it. Not linked to any particular time period, it's what we call a 'free range' portal. You normally need a key object to operate it. Say, if you wanted to go back to medieval times; you would need an object from that time."

Harry looked puzzled; "So why did Sir Thomas keep Napoleon's supposed magic cabinet if he possessed this little item?" With a smile Jericho told him that the magic cabinet's time portal had been closed long ago, when Napoleon himself had used it on a couple of occasions and drew the attention of himself and his team of Temporal detectives.

Dorothy took it from her astounded brother and stared at the strange carving in the shape of a very big breasted woman. "Why the hell did he appear in my bloody box?" She asked Jericho who shrugged his shoulders; "Can't help you there Dorothy. Maybe that was just an accident or the portal was attracted to the box because Sims used it. Who knows?" Dorothy handed it back to Jericho and poured the tea from a big china pot.

Harry accepted a most welcome mug of tea from Dorothy; "Sir Thomas had been stabbed at least four times. Probably by the same person who murdered Kelp. At least we know that Kelp was also a time traveler from 1974 and probably had been here for some years." Jericho nodded; "His real name was Mathew Hines and he was born in 1948 in London. He was an exception to the other's that appeared from there; he was healthy. I can't find any modern attachment with Stonebridge House or the Astor-Smiths."

Jericho sipped his tea and continued; "Sadly there was no soul collected from Sir Thomas, so we know that he was on the Dark Side. He was a historic figure that belonged to these times and so being a devotee of the Dark Prince is the only explanation of no soul. His actual scheduled date of death was in 1910. So there have been a few minor changes to the future time line which have been deemed acceptable."

Dorothy sighed; "So the trail goes cold and we still don't why all these people from the hereafter were here." Harry sipped his tea; "Not quite Dottie, young Farmer has discovered the address of Mr. Elliot that mysterious night watchman and we're going to pay him a little visit." Dorothy smiled; "I take it I'm coming too." Harry sighed; "How could I stop you."

Mr. Tibbs took his leave and re-started time, so Harry asked Rosie to fetch a cab. They would call into Brick Lane Police Station and collect detectives Farmer and Palmer. Dorothy always chuckled when Harry said their names together; "Sounds like a bloody music hall act." She said and Harry had to smile.

Detective Constable Edwin Palmer sat opposite Dorothy and smiled a lot. He had a terrible concealed passion for her and he loved just being in her company. But his attention was drawn back to the conversations in the cab. Acting Detective Constable Dave Farmer was bringing Harry [and Dorothy] up to date with the mysterious Mr. Elliot.

"He lives alone with three cats in a dingy flat above a bloody Undertakers! Apparently his wife died some years ago and he has never remarried. He's now working at Odd fellows Hall as a caretaker and Custodian. Apparently he's reliable as a Swiss watch; never turns up late or misses a shift; Seems to spend most of his spare time in the bloody library." Farmer spoke softly, flicking through his notebook.

"Poor man's universities; Libraries I mean." Harry muttered and stared out at the sparse traffic, which was unusual for Christmas Eve in the East End. The snow was still coming down and would cause problems for people and traffic after the short Christmas celebrations were over. But there was some really good news; Harry's Detective Sergeant Alistair McPearl was making a good recovery and would be at home to celebrate Christmas with his family. Dorothy really smiled at that news.

Dorothy liked young Farmer; he didn't seem to care about the rumours and gossip about him being 'a bit queer'. The young man was clearly a little effeminate and quiet spoken; but he had the makings of a first class detective. Harry had already noticed his sharp mind and attention to detail; that's why he had given the young man a chance by taking him into his team.

"We're here Guv." Farmer said and pushed his notebook into the folds of his heavy dark coat. Dorothy really grimaced as the undertaker's black horses and carriage pulled from the side gates of the funeral parlour and headed up the quiet street. "Must have a job on." muttered Edwin as he pulled open the carriage door.

"Now that's shitty for the family; bloody Christmas Eve." He added and jumped into the snow; cursing because it came up past his ankles. Harry helped Dorothy down and they went to the side entrance and knocked loudly on the shabby door.

Mr. Elliot opened the door and sighed; he gestured for them to come in. Dorothy was surprised – pleasantly – Mr. Roland Elliot was in his mid twenties and built like a rugby player. He had big hands and dark hair and eyes. Most women would certainly regard him as handsome. They walked slowly up the rough wooden stairs and he opened the top door and gestured them in. "I've just brewed some tea; if anyone wants a cup and mind the cats. They're curious little things and will be all over you." His voice was soft and firm; Dorothy was really impressed with the young man. The room was a surprise too; it was clean and well furnished in stark contrast to the front door and stairs. There was a good fire in the grate.

Two fat black cats appeared and jumped on a vacant chair, watching the visitors. "That's Clare and Kath. The little ginger one is Maggie; but she's a shy little thing and will probably stay hidden; Now anyone for tea?" Roland said and headed for the door opposite.

"We're here to ask you some questions about Sir Thomas and his cabinet. Do you have any objections to that?" Harry asked, unbuttoning his coat. Roland stopped by the door and nodded his agreement. He didn't have any objections. He actually smiled. "That's all anyone has asked me since he [Sir Thomas] fell out of that magic cabinet in the middle of the show. Now that's what I call a dramatic death."

Harry stood with hands on hips and didn't smile; "I need to know what was your relationship - if any – was with him." Roland shrugged his shoulders; "There was no relationship as you put it. I was the night watchman and his cabinet was amongst many items that I looked after. I only met him twice. The last time was when he came to the shop to tell the old lady [Mrs. Serenity] that he was removing the cabinet. He gave me five bob for looking after the damn thing." As the pair talked, Dorothy's sharp eyes fell upon the crowded mantelpiece and saw three photographs standing there; one of a grand looking old lady, holding a big cat and two wedding pictures. She gripped Harry's arm and pointed to the fireplace. "Harry, why does Mr. Elliot have a copy of the late Mr. Kelp's secret wedding photograph on his mantelpiece?"

Harry – really impressed – said quietly; "Now that's a bloody good question Dottie." He turned back to Roland and waited for a reply. The young man sighed and folded his arms. "Mathew was married to my sister Lucille." He said sadly and walked to the fireplace and lifted the picture with obvious affection. "That's how I got the job. Mathew recommended me to Sir Thomas and got me the job with the magic people. Sir Thomas believed he could trust me if Mathew recommended me I suppose."

He replaced the photograph and added; "Does anyone want tea?" Harry shook his head; "Could he trust you Mr. Elliot?" Roland smiled; "Well, I kept my mouth shut about his damn cabinet for two years, so I suppose he could." He eased himself down into the armchair by the fireplace and clasped both hands on his lap. "Strange bedfellows weren't we; a Knight of the realm and a bloody disgraced ex-naval officer; now a bleeding common night watchman."

Harry pulled off his hat and said; "Do you want to tell me about it?" Roland gestured to the sofa; "Maybe the pretty lady would like to sit?" He ran both hands through his dark hair and sighed. "Like I said I met him twice. The first time was at a boy's only party above the 'Golden Eagle' pub in North Street. I won't go into details with the young lady here, but I think you get the picture."

Harry held his hat and nodded. "Go on please; we're not here to hunt down homosexuals so please say what you need to say." Roland stared up at the ceiling and then back at Harry; "He paid me five bob [five shillings] for sex that night. I was desperate I needed the money; I had been slung out the navy – quietly – and couldn't find work. " He smiled; "He looked a little shocked when he found out that I was the man Mathew recommended, but couldn't go back on his recommendation to the magic people; probably thought I would try and blackmail him or something, if he had me dismissed."

Dorothy eased herself down on the sofa and really wanted that cup of tea offered by Roland. Harry ran a hand over his face and glanced at Edwin who was scribbling in his notebook. "What was so special about the cabinet Roland?" he asked, holding his hat with both hands. Roland held up both hands and chuckled; "Ghosts Mr. Hadden. The bloody thing was full of ghosts. Little wonder all the other night watchmen disappeared. But they didn't bother me. They came and went with Mathew; Sir Thomas never came there when I was on duty; except when he moved the damn thing." Harry joined Dorothy on the sofa and nodded for Roland to continue.

"Every time someone was to appear Mathew would turn up; always at night. I would unlock the side entrance and they would depart with Mathew in a big black carriage. I remember the two shabby fellows well; they were both ex-navy men, but in a very different navy to mine. Undersea ships; can you imagine that? Well, I knew something had gone wrong when I read about their deaths in the local paper. Mathew really panicked over that and told Lucille he would speak to Sir Thomas. Then Sir David was killed and I knew that something big was going on." He stared at the fire and looked back at Harry. "Then a really important bugger appeared from the cabinet. Mathew was totally overcome by him. Called him Sir all the time and couldn't do enough for the bugger. He [the visitor] only stayed for a few hours and then disappeared back into the cabinet."

"Who was the man?" Harry asked and Roland grinned, throwing up both hands; "Bloody Napoleon Bonaparte!" He chuckled. Edwin laughed and slammed his notebook shut. "Jesus Guv, I'm wasting my time writing this fairy tale down. No wonder the navy slung him out; he would make H.G. Wells look like he wrote historical bleeding novels! He's off his bloody rocker!"

Harry waved him into silence and told Roland to continue which he did. "Then came a couple of Druids – at least, that's what they looked like to me - now they looked like men of learning. They spoke to each other in some strange language. I thought it was Arabic. Mathew made me laugh when he told me they were bloody priests from Ancient Egypt! He said that one of them called Tha actually designed and built the bloody Great pyramid. He said that the pyramid was a bloody big cosmic time machine!"

"Priests of Chronos." Harry whispered to Dorothy who nodded

slowly. She really wished Jericho Tibbs was here to listen to this.

Edwin was now laughing outright about the latest revelations from Mr. Elliot, but Dave Farmer stood silent and was listening intently.

Roland ignored Edwin's laughter and continued; "But it was the third fella that made my blood run cold; a big man with a shaved head and well scarred face. He looked a killer; plain and simple. He never said a word. I think he's name was Herod or something like that. Mathew told me that he did really dirty work for the two Egyptians and I knew he was right. He made my blood run cold. Then surprise, surprise; Mathew gets murdered, followed by Sir Thomas. I think you'll find that evil looking sod was guilty of those killings." He ran a hand over the nearest big fat cat and didn't smile adding, "One thing I thought odd was that people only appeared with Mathew. I asked him about that and all he said was 'bloody Mesopotamia!' I didn't know what he meant by that."

Harry glanced at Dottie and thought about the figurine: Mr. Tibbs was adamant that the Cabinets time portal had been removed some years before all this took place: did Mathew use the figurine to collect the historical figures? Then why keep the cabinets?

Edwin shook his head in disbelief; "Christ, our murder suspect is some mad paid killer from Ancient bloody Egypt. I've heard it all now. This nutter should write bloody books!"

Harry and Dorothy again exchanged a knowing glance and Harry rose from the sofa and helped Dorothy up. Roland eased from his seat and folded his arms. He didn't smile. "I also know that they're probably after me now and I need to vanish. Like those buggers from the cabinet. But the cabinet is gone."

Harry stopped walking to the door and asked where the cabinet had gone. Roland wiped his face; "Lucille tells me that Lady Bridgewater had the cabinet in her house taken to the garden and broken up, then burnt. Just hours after you [the police] left her house after Sir Thomas's body fell out that damn trunk."

Harry thanked the young man and the team left, with only Edwin still laughing about the tale imparted by Roland. "He doesn't

need investigating; just a nice soft cell and a straight jacket!"
Edwin chuckled as young Farmer waved down a cab.

Dorothy waited until her and Harry was home before speaking
up. They were waiting for Uncle William to return from the
Children's pantomime. He had gone earlier with Titus to the
performance.

She sipped a most welcome cup of tea and said quietly; "The
other wedding picture on Roland's mantelpiece was also quite
interesting. It was clearly Roland in his navel uniform and the
young bride looked a little odd." Harry – a little intrigued – asked
why she looked odd. Dorothy smiled; "It's something that only a
woman would notice; her wedding dress." Harry smiled; "Why
was her dress so odd Dottie?" Dorothy smiled over the rim of her
cup; "The style was very old fashioned; probably from the late
Regency period. Maybe 1810 or thereabouts, not the most
fashionable dress to wear in the new century. Except of course,
there were no camera's – apparently - in the early 19th century."

Harry slowed lowered his cup; "It's not unusual for homosexual
men to marry; especially if it quells rumours about them.
Because Homosexuality is a serious criminal offence and such a
marriage can offer protection." Dorothy smiled; "I wonder which
navy young Mr. Roland was thrown out of; the one fighting
Napoleon perhaps?"

Harry ran a hand over his face and stood; "I think I need to
speak to Roland again." He said quietly. Dorothy nodded; "What
about lady Bridgewater; are you going to interview her?"

Harry shook his head; "That's a bloody big no no. The Deputy
Commissioner [of the Metropolitan Police] has already let my
Superintendant know that she is off limits in this investigation.
Her family has really powerful connections with the present
government and they want no scandal. None." Dorothy sighed
and finished her tea. She gestured to the brown paper bag Harry
had placed on the table. "What's in there?" She asked as Harry
pulled on his coat.

"Oh, just the stuff found on the first dead shabby man from that
God awful toilet." Curious; Dorothy lifted the bag and peered
inside. Harry noticed the look on her face. "What is it Dottie?" he
asked, a little concerned and Dorothy reached in and pulled out

the piece of paper and the new key. With her free hand she rummaged in her handbag and pulled out her notebook of magic tricks and another key.

"Harry; this page was ripped from my notebook." She placed the notebook down and flicked it open to where a page had been torn out. She then held up the two keys. They were identical. Harry ran a hand over his face; "What does your key open Dottie?"

Dorothy held the key up and said softly; "It opens Uncle William's Dressing Room at the theatre." Harry sat back down and slowly took the key. He said nothing for a few minutes, then asked; "What trick was written on the page? There's nothing on the page except some letters." Dorothy didn't smile and placed the paper on the table and asked Harry to fetch a candle. Harry lit the candle and Dorothy waved it beneath the empty sheet of paper whispering; "Uncle William's security system. The page is blank until you heat it gently and... there we go!" Harry watched a little amazed as the drawings and lettering appeared. "Which trick is it? He asked again. Dorothy stared at it and sighed; "How to vanish from a locked room, leaving no trace. It's similar to what we use to escape from locked trunks and stuff like that. It's a very old stage trick. Sims tells me that he even used it and that was three and a half thousand years ago."

Harry sat back down and pushed his tea cup away; he needed a whisky. Dorothy rose and went to the drinks cabinet; she must have read Harry's mind. "Maybe Sir Thomas knew more about magic than we ever could guess." She said quietly, pouring two large whiskies.

"Why the connection with Uncle William and why did the original 'shabby man' try and contact you? Unless he was actually after Uncle William and knew he could contact him through you. We never did solve that." Harry accepted his whisky and sighed; loudly. "I think we've actually only scratched the surface with this case." He muttered. They still had no idea what Sir Thomas's plan was, how the Bridgewater's were involved; both now and in the future and why did the conspirators fall out and start killing each other? He sipped his whisky and sat back. Dorothy patted her brother's shoulder; "Well, we've reached a dead-end except for young Roland and I think when you return, he would have flown the coup; probably to another time and place. Maybe back to his wife waiting for him in the early 19th Century."

"I think Mr. Tibbs will have to deal with that one himself. I strongly suspect that Lucille – the grieving widow – will have also vanished." Harry said and sipped his whisky. He paused by the blazing fire and tapped the whisky glass; "Do you think they – the 'shabby men' – were somehow trying to contact Mr. Tibbs through you or Uncle William? Pass on a message perhaps?"

Dorothy smiled a little; "At least Mr. Tibbs will be happy about Farmer and Palmer treating Roland's confession as total bloody nonsense; well, maybe Dave Farmer won't. His reaction to the story was quite……quite strange." Harry nodded; "His mum is a Medium, so maybe he's a bit more open minded to it all."
The door flew open and that made the pair jump. Santa Claus stood in the doorway, complete with present filled sack and a very happy mummy behind him; he shouted "Merry Christmas children!" Dorothy started to laugh; it was Uncle William!

Harry jumped up and poured 'Santa' a large glass of rum. "You're a bit early Santa, but always welcome." He handed Uncle William the glass and Santa accepted it with a huge smile. He slapped the sack on the floor and pushed back his furry red hat. "The kids loved it after the pantomime. Everyone received a little present and [jerking a thumb towards the grinning Sims] he made the little buggers laugh. It was a performance I really enjoyed."

"You may not be too impressed with what I have to say Uncle William; everything has apparently ended in utter failure." Harry refilled his Uncles' glass and gestured to the armchairs. "You may need to sit down for this one."

CHAPTER 13. 'HISTORY IS THE STORY OF WARFARE BETWEEN SECRET SOCITIES'. Ishmael Reed.

The Christmas Eve party had been arranged at the Hadden's house with everyone invited; including Rosie's light fingered husband and two boys! Mrs. Harvey seemed more than happy to prepare a large buffet and Ellen with Dorothy's and Rosie's help got the house ready. Uncle William made sure that everyone knew HE was playing Santa and filled his sack with presents for all those invited.

Titus was surprised to find that the Hadden's had invited him and young Arthur [the stage hand that Dorothy disliked] and he kept thanking the pair; Uncle William and Dorothy. They brushed that aside with big smiles; he was part of the team and was most welcome. They would all gather at the house on Christmas Eve, the theatre being closed until Boxing Day. Harry, chuckling, confided to Dorothy that he would have tie up Edwin Palmer to stop him coming, when the young detective heard that girls from the chorus line had been invited!

Dorothy and Harry visited Eastham Market to pick up some late presents. They made for the small café in Queen Street and enjoyed tea and toast in the crowded café, packed with people who had the same idea. They found themselves sharing a table with two docker's wives who insisted they have some whisky in their tea. The two 'ladies' laughed and swore, burdened down with full shopping baskets. Dorothy sipped her tea and smiled at the expression on her brother's face. To say their language was ripe was an understatement.

They finally managed to leave the café and waited on the snowy pavement for a cab. Both had to laugh as they heard the singing from the café; "They certainly know how to celebrate Christmas in the east end." Was all Harry said on the matter. That's when the blacked out cab pulled up next to them and the door flew open. A big man in an expensive suit jumped out and removed his cap; "Mister Hadden sir, my boss would like a quiet word with you." He gestured into the cab and smiled.

Harry and Dorothy carefully peered into the darkened interior and Dorothy had to grip Harry's arm in utter shock. Sir Thomas Astor-Smith sat, leaned back on the well upholstered seat, checking his fob watch. He smiled at the pair and pointed to the seat opposite him; "Do jump in Mr. Hadden and Miss Hadden. We can chat while my cab takes you home."

Harry and Dorothy stared at each other. Harry shook his head; "Dorothy can take another cab home, but I'll certainly join you for a little chat." Sir Thomas smiled; "Come on Inspector, you will be both perfectly safe. I need you to arrange a little meeting with your other boss; Mister Jericho Tibbs." Dorothy nodded to Harry and the pair climbed in. The big man joined the driver after closing the door behind them and the carriage pulled away.

Sir Thomas sat back and smiled at the pair; "I believe Mister Tibbs says that you two are his best human agents for this particular time period and place. I certainly couldn't disagree with that. I want you relay a little message to him about a meeting that I believe he wouldn't want to miss. The Chief Priest of the Brotherhood of Osiris wishes to speak with him. You probably know the brotherhood as the Priests of Chronos."

Harry nodded; "So you faked your death, may I ask why?" He gripped Dorothy's hand and stared at Sir Thomas, who chuckled; "Necessity my inquisitive friend. In the early 21st century the concealed Dictatorship that rules this good country has – by accident - discovered time travel and even as we speak; are are sending agents back to alter history in their favour. I had to deal with two of their more unfriendly agents; frankly I only just managed to prevent the damn assassination of the Kaiser back in March; that was a close run thing. Had they succeeded in their endeavor, the future would have been a very different place. For once, the Brotherhood and Mister Tibbs find themselves on, basically, the same side. I have no doubt he will tell that no soul was collected from my 'death' because I am a follower of the Dark Prince. That is quite correct. But on this occasion it was because I didn't actually die, well not terminally." He chuckled again.

"The brotherhood has the power to resurrect, to recall the soul, if they get to the body quickly enough. I am now Thomas...." He stopped and pushed his watch back into his pocket, adding; "It's enough for you to know that I now live quite a different life under a new identity."

He tapped the ceiling a couple of times. "Tell Mister Tibbs that we will meet him in the basement library of the Natural History Museum on Boxing Day this very year, at about seven o'clock in the evening. It really is to his advantage to make an appearance. The shadow government of this county has a very evil plan under way that will seriously affect humanity in the early 21st century. I'm sad to admit that it beyond the powers of the brotherhood to prevent it. We will require almost divine help."

Harry nodded slowly and asked; "Are the Bridgewater's part of that Brotherhood or agents from the so called dictatorship?" Thomas _______ didn't smile. "They are agents of the shadow government that really run the world of the next century and are quite ruthless. They really don't have the best interests of humanity on their agenda. Be careful Harry, you have fallen under their spotlight and if they think you are a threat to their plans, they will terminate you." Dorothy leaned forward; "Was your Mister Kelp one of them?" Thomas nodded and sighed; "He was quite loyal to me, but his real loyalty lay with his masters from the future. They arrived here with amazing stories how they come from various times in human history. But they are all from the future, hence they know so much about the past. Apparently future technology is incredible and they can fake anything they want, including to pose as people from the long dead past. They can be whoever they say they are. They easily control the feeble minded and gullible future generations ruthlessly with clever deceptions, fabrications, lies and technology, especially the technology. It appears our future generations fool easily!"

Dorothy whispered to Harry; "Like photographs, crucifixes and anything else they need to." Harry nodded at that and thought about Roland Elliot's statements. How much of those were lies and falsehoods. He leaned forward and said quietly; "Roland Elliot stated that you paid him for homosexual sex, is that true?" Thomas actually smiled, which surprised the pair. "Oh yes, that's quite true. He's such a handsome, fit young fellow I couldn't resist. Pity he worked for the other side. I think they hoped to blackmail me into working for them. Their latest plan is to kill some foreign genus that I've never heard of and prevent his scientific work entering into world history. Why, I have no idea."

Dorothy asked what the scientist was called and Thomas shrugged his shoulders; "Some German name I think, Burnstein or something similar, apparently the man changes the world of scientific thought completely and creates weapons that can destroy entire cities in a blink of an eye. Apparently that doesn't suit their plans." [See episode: **'The year of miracles.'**]

The carriage came to a halt and Sir Thomas pushed open the door and both Harry and Dorothy could see they were outside their house. Sir Thomas gestured to the door; "Please relay my message to mister Tibbs or millions of souls will be lost. I'm talking about deaths in their hundreds of millions across the world." Harry helped Dorothy down and Sir Thomas pulled the door shut and the carriage sped away in the fresh falling snow.

They stood silently in the falling snow for a few seconds and then headed up the steps. "I wouldn't be more surprised if I woke up tomorrow and found that I was the bloody Pope." Harry muttered and they headed for the front door. Dorothy stopped and wiped snow from her face; "There was something odd about Sir Thomas and I can't put my blooming finger on it."

Harry shrugged his shoulders; he had not noticed anything odd about the man; except that the bugger should be dead! Ellen let the pair in. They found Uncle William in his study; teaching Sims to play Bridge. The discussions between the team were lively to say the least.

The guests gathered around seven o'clock and the party was soon in full swing. The music was supplied by four members of the band from the theatre and everyone was 'persuaded' to perform.

Harry played the piano and everyone remarked just how good he was. Dorothy and some girls from the chorus line accompanied him, singing popular songs from the theatre and then everyone joined in. Big Tom was helped up onto a chair and sang a song with some very questionable lyrics; but everyone found it funny and not offensive. Miss Player sat in a quiet corner and sipped her sherry. She really didn't like being happy or happiness generally! Young Arthur sat next to her clutching a small glass of Guinness and watched the girls singing. He had some pretty disgusting thoughts about what he would like to do to them; especially Dorothy. He saw Titus smiling at him, like he knew what the boy was thinking and dropped those thoughts. But everyone agreed; the party was a huge success.

 Christmas day was a quiet affair in the Hadden household; several people having hangovers contributed to that fact. Harry was slumped in the armchair by the fire, sipping yet another glass of lemonade. He held his head gently and groaned when Sims rolled into the room and jumped to his feet. "Keep the bloody noise down Sims." was all he said.

Sims grinned and folded his arms; "Jericho says thanks about the offer from the priests of Chronos and he'll drop by tomorrow to see us all. Where's Dorothy?"

Harry jerked a thumb towards the ceiling; "Laying down – again – she had a great time last night, but she really isn't use to alcohol." Sims nodded; "Oh, I can help her and you. I know a sure fired hangover cure from my youth back in Egypt."

Now Harry was interested in that and asked what it was. Sims grinned; "It's an ancient remedy that really works. It's made from fresh Nile crocodile's testicles, ground up and mixed with cow's milk and…." Harry stopped him there and advised Sims not to explain the miracle cure to Dorothy; ever.

Sims just sighed and disappeared as Ellen opened the door and gave Harry a very welcome mug of hot tea. "Dinner may be a little late; Mrs. Harvey can't bring herself to stuff the Goose yet. Despite several cups of tea and some dry toast." She chuckled and looked around the empty room; "Do you know sir, that I thought I heard another voice in here." Harry just smiled and sipped his tea. He placed the cup down and dozed.

Uncle William walked slowly in and settled down in his favourite armchair and lit his pipe. "Dorothy's feeling better, apparently Sims gave her some ancient hangover remedy and it bloody worked. You should try it Harry." Uncle William really couldn't understand why Harry was laughing; bloody Sims was all he said. He made a point not to mention the ingredients to his sister.

Uncle William was talking about the letter from Harry's eldest brother; Sir Henry Hadden who was excavating in Egypt. He had sent a pile of photographs and a crate containing some objects from his latest dig. They had arrived with the last post on Christmas Eve. Uncle William said there were several small statues and figurines, boxes and vases. Harry was only half listening and then remembered the figurine that had been found with Sir Thomas's body that contained some kind of time controlling device. He also remembered that Jericho Tibbs was adamant that the Priests of Chronos didn't have the ability to travel in time.

He slowly rose from his chair and groaned loudly at his own stupidity. "Uncle William, I think we've been lead up the garden path and our actions could have placed Jericho Tibbs in serious danger. I've just realized what Dorothy thought was odd about bloody Sir Thomas." He headed for the door and almost bumped into a very subdued Dorothy, though she was feeling a lot better.

"I bet you were going to say that he looked a little younger than the last time we saw him when alive." Harry said to her. Dorothy stood and thought for a second or two; "You're right Harry. I struggled to think what was odd about Sir Thomas and it was that he looked years blooming younger."

Harry nodded; "That's because he IS years bloody younger than the Sir Thomas we've been dealing with in this year of nineteen hundred and one. That was a younger version of himself. We've been suckered; Sir Thomas is a bloody double agent for want of a better expression. He works for the people from the future and is a member of the Priests of Chronos and I wonder where his real loyalty lies?" Harry rubbed his chin; "I'd bet you a pound to a penny that Sir Thomas's body has vanished from the morgue, because he is now no longer dead in this time period. His much younger version has changed that."

Dorothy sighed; "The time device found by his body explains that he had the ability to travel in time, so what's to stop a younger version of himself turning up now; he's not likely to bump into a dead version of himself and so it was safe for the two to be in the same time and place. Now Harry, that's a brilliant deduction."

Harry pointed to Uncle William; "Thank the old boy for that, oh, and our dear brother Henry." Dorothy looked quite puzzled by that until Harry explained further. The team quickly came to the conclusion that Sir Thomas must have travelled to some point in the future and found that he was apparently now murdered in 1901. So his still young version had travelled back here [1901] to investigate. Jericho had let it slip once that 'time-travelers' didn't age in any time that was not their pre-ordained time period [the time between birth and death].

"Little wonder that he said he had another identity here and now. He must have been a good ten years younger than the age at which he died." Harry said as they walked to the dining room for Christmas dinner. "We'll send Sims to Jericho after diner." Uncle William muttered and rubbed his hands together; "Come on Harry, let's be new men and serve the ladies their lunch!"

Dorothy chuckled at that and sat with Ellen and Mrs. Harvey as Uncle William and Harry dished up Christmas dinner with big smiles. She felt a little sad about Sims not joining them, but he really didn't understand Christmas, even after almost sixty years in the family. Then another thought crossed her mind; everyone in this room will be dead at some point in the future and Sims will still be around. Then she thought about the fact that 'time-travelers' didn't age if they kept moving between time periods, not their own. Now that was a thought for mere mortals to consider.

"Bloody good idea Harry, try getting a cab on Boxing Day morning." Uncle William slipped from the Police Carriage and pulled his coat about him and adjusted his top hat against the fresh flying snow. Harry helped Dorothy down and told PC Davis to sit inside until they returned. He was the 'Early turn' driver of the Police carriage at Brick Lane Police Station and had been persuaded by Harry to drop them off. He had stared for some time at the strange fourth member of the Hadden group.

The young man was dressed well, with a heavy coat and bowler hat, with scarf and darkened glasses. "Poor fucking bastard, what sort of life does he have, with his face and hands disfigured by fire. I'd sooner be dead." PC Davis muttered to himself and settled down in the cab after wrapping the horses in their blankets. He pulled out a penny dreadful magazine and read about a grisly murder on Westham's patch. But he was still smiling about poor Clive Collins stag party: apparently the two tarts had fucked off before doing anything. But what puzzled Joe Simpson [the best man and organizer of the party] was the tarts left the gold sovereign behind. PC Davies shrugged his shoulders and thought, well; at least they were honest reluctant whores!

He read with some curiosity about a strange sighting at a posh hotel in the city, two young women had stood high on a ledge exposing their privates [both had their skirts pulled up] and then ran around the building, vanishing into an open window! The magazine had titled the story as 'The curious case of high honey-pots exposed for Christmas'. But the strangest part – and the most unexplainable bit – was one waving a bloody cricket bat about!

Uncle William took them down some slippery rear steps to a big dark door marked; 'TRADESMEN' and banged loudly. "It's not what you know but who you know." He told them, adding; "Old Lionel has been the day porter here for years. He knew your father well." They waited for about a minute and the door was pulled open and 'Old Lionel' welcomed his visitors with some warmth, though he did stare hard at Mister Sims. Dorothy had to smile when she heard the old man mutter; "Looks like a poor version of the bloody invisible man."

"The novel; The Invisible Man' by H.G. Wells, was first published in 1897 and became a stage play. The invisible man could be seen because he covered himself in bandages." SJW.

Lionel lit a couple of paraffin lamps and handed one to Harry; "Everything is closed down for the holidays, so the gas is off. The basement library is quite a walk. Few people would go there after dark." He turned and unlocked a big glass cabinet and pulled a bunch of keys from it. Dorothy had to ask; "Why wouldn't they go after dark, Lionel?" The old man chuckled; "Because it's filled with blooming ghosts miss. There have been more sightings of spooks down there than you can shake a stick at. All types of visitors: workmen, scholars, cleaners have all reported strange noises, voices and even figures about the place."

They followed down some steps to a basement that had several doors and he unlocked one. The corridor was long and appeared to slope downwards. They passed one very old wooden sign that declared 'ARCHIVE STORAGE' with a white arrow underneath. "It use to be the old Archive storage before it was converted into a library for the naughty stuff."

 Harry, smiling, asked him why the books stored there were considered 'naughty'.

The old man chuckled again; "Put it this way sir, the Pope wouldn't approve of monks and nuns reading some of them." Everyone laughed a little at that. They stopped before a huge wooden door, with steel bracing and a lock that looked like it belonged in the Bank of England vaults. Lionel held an equality big key and pushed into the lock. It opened easily and Harry helped him push the damn thing back and open.

Lionel gestured in and muttered; "After you good people; I'm heading back to my office and make some tea. They don't pay me enough to go in there after dark, even with frigging police protection!" He patted Harry on the shoulder and wandered off down the corridor, disappearing into the darkness. They entered slowly and Harry held his lamp up; the place was huge with numerous bookshelves extending right up to the ceiling. There were some statues scattered around and a large table with high backed chairs. There were several books and manuscripts scattered around the table, including a couple of paraffin lamps. Uncle William went to the table and lit one of the lamps; "Someone has already been here. The damn thing was still warm." He lit two more lamps for Dorothy and Sims. "We'll split up but keep in sight of each other. If the Priests of Chronos are meeting here tonight, I bet they don't come through that big door."

Harry held his lamp over a large open book on the table and laughed loudly. "I wouldn't look at this one Dorothy, not while you're an unmarried woman anyway." Sims held up his lamp and gestured towards the staircase that allowed people to visit the upper hall of book shelves. The statue standing a few feet away from it had caught his attention. "That's an Egyptian Priest, a statue of the chief Priest of Amen-Ra, probably from the big temple at Thebes." The little group wandered over and stood staring at the life size figure, everyone agreed that it was quite a superb sculpture.

Harry pointed down the hieroglyphs at the base and asked Sims to translate. Sims stood for a good minute, hand on chin, staring at the symbols. Finally, he sighed; "Well, the nearest translation in modern English is something like 'Everything is time'. It's an old Egyptian saying about life, death and time." Dorothy took hold of the 'Ankh' symbol in the left hand and pulled at it. They stood back as the statue slid quietly back, revealing a dark recess. She shone her lamp down; "Steps going even further down." She said softly.

Uncle William patted her shoulder; "I always said you'll make a top class magician." Harry had to agree with that and with Sims in tow, descended down the steps. Uncle William and Dorothy sat at the big table and tried to resist looking at the open books and manuscripts on the big desk.

"It's censorship for poor people. Only the wealthy and academics get to see these treasures. Flipping typical." Dorothy muttered and pulled off her coat and Russian style fur hat; the place was really warm. She looked about and couldn't see any form of heating about the old library. She slowly lowered her lamp and wondered why the damn place was so warm. Uncle William finally gave into temptation and pulled the beautifully illustrated book from medieval times to him. He had to smile; "We have a knight here that's fighting a dragon in a very strange way. He's naked apart from his boots and the dragon appears to be wearing a dress." He turned a page and laughed some more, then made a disapproving noise. "Tut-tut, I'm sure monks and donkeys didn't behave like that."

Dorothy gripped her Uncle's hand and nodded her head towards the other end of the table, she managed to whisper; "We have a visitor." Her and Uncle Williams, open mouthed, staring at the figure that appeared at the end of the huge table. The big man was dressed in Elizabethan clothes, complete with white ruff about his neck and sword hanging at his hip. He had a large feathered hat and was clearly African! He gave a big smile with plenty of white teeth and bowed a little; "You must be Miss Dorothy Hadden and you sir, must be William Hadden; for I understand that Harry Hadden is a much younger man."

Uncle William rose slowly; "If that was a magic trick, then it's a bloody good one!" Dorothy – still gripping his hand – also stood up. "You seem to know us sir, how is that?" She asked, her voice trembled a little. The big man bowed again; "Wilson Franklyn my lady; Mr. Tibbs assistant just back from1594 and at your service. The other's are on their way pronto." Dorothy and Uncle William exchanged a glance and both remembered Jericho talking about his team. He had mentioned that one of his assistants was an American from the 1970's. Dorothy managed a smile; "Welcome to 1901 Mister Franklyn."

The man chuckled and pulled off his glamorous hat; "Thank you my lady." He was joined by a young man, dressed similarly who was cussing and moaning about his tight breeches, "I've no chance of bloody children now, these bloody pantaloons…." He stopped and grinned at Dorothy and Uncle William."Blimey Wilson, Alex has a real rival there. Put them together and you have a real pair of beauties." Wilson just sighed; "You'll have to excuse the lad his words, he was a flipping medieval monk when last breathing!" The young man smiled; "Owen Jones."

Jericho appeared – also dressed for the period – accompanied by a tall, elegant lady in a Tudor dress that showed off her ample bosom. Uncle William and Dorothy exchanged another glance; the young woman was absolutely stunning, a real beauty. She smiled and strode right up to Dorothy and placed a kiss on her cheek; "Jericho has said so much about you and your brother. It's great to finally meet you at last." Dorothy nodded and said 'Ditto' quietly.

Jericho jerked a thumb at the woman and said; "Lady Alexandra Cappanni: one of my current assistants. Now, our Sims said something about Sir Thomas has gone time-travelling?" Uncle William nodded and explained about the younger version turning up. Jericho folded his arms and sighed; "That makes the Priests of Chronos quite a dangerous foe now. They will have contacts going back to ancient times. They could change the entire future to suit their plans."

Wilson looked around and adjusted his ruff; "Well, I somehow don't think they will actually turn up now. I think they wanted us to know they have moved up the power stakes ladder." Jericho folded his arms and asked Uncle William about the other possible time travelers; Elliot and his wife. That's when everyone turned to the priest's statue as Harry and Sims emerged from the dark staircase. They were laughing and Harry stopped and gestured to Jericho and his team. "That was a real interesting little journey down a secret tunnel."

Sims giggled; "The bloody thing comes out in the Underground Stations toilets on the Cromwell Road." Harry was dusting himself down and had to chuckle; "There's like a cleaner's cupboard with a false back and when we pushed it open, mops and buckets went everywhere. A right noisy entrance and then the bloody door opened and the old station cleaner was staring at us; well mainly at him." Harry jerked a finger at Sims. "The poor old sod ran screaming out the bog and was last seen running down the Cromwell Road!"

Everyone chuckled at that and Jericho sat on the big table and swung his legs. "Well, I now wonder what they were trying to achieve here and how that would change future history they didn't like?" That's when another figure appeared at the end of the table; a tall, very pretty young woman wearing a pale cream 'jump suit'. She pushed a little glass orb into her pocket and smiled. "Mister Jericho Tibbs I presume?" she said quietly. Everyone stared at her and then at Dorothy. They certainly could be sisters at least. "Must be a descendant of ours." Harry whispered and a shocked Dorothy could only nod.

Jericho jumped from the table and introduced himself. The young woman smiled again and looked around the grand room. "It's appropriate that we meet in a room full of censored and mostly forbidden books of human knowledge: something your boss would know all about." She folded her arms and gestured to Uncle William, Harry and Dorothy; "I bet you have kept their futures from them Jericho. Forbidden knowledge of the future is a dangerous thing and we now can travel back and change outcomes as we wish." She turned to Dorothy and didn't smile; "You will rue the day you came under the spell of Mister Jericho Tibbs my poor girl. Your life will never be your own and you will die in great misery and regret." She turned to Uncle William; "Your days are numbered old man, the die is cast and you won't escape unless you jump through time. As for you young man [talking to Harry] you will die suddenly and terribly in your bed and become a willing and obedient slave of an ungrateful master."

She finally turned back to Jericho; "Those of us that have lived through thousands of years of human endevours will achieve our freedom; he will be powerless against out technology which will match his. Tell your master that Jericho; there will be a new family ruling and a new dynasty." She pulled the orb from her pocket and smiled a final time; "You may have won this little battle Jericho using your slaves, but we will win the war; after all, we have all the time in the world." Then she was gone.

Jericho sighed and managed to smile; "The novel Frankenstein comes to mind here; the creation turning on its creator. What price the Human Hubris?"

"A bloody coup d'état planned to overthrow God! Now that's a turn up for the books alright." Dorothy whispered to Harry who just nodded; speechless for once.

After thanking old Lionel – again – the Hadden's headed home, hopefully to enjoy the rest of the Christmas holidays. And Dorothy had some good news from her 'handlers', they had apprehended Collins at last [it was the older man] and she was stood down from the case. But it wasn't the end of her dealings with Military Intelligence: they would re-appear soon.

Dorothy had heard rumours about James O'Connor: he had been released from hospital and apparently took the early ferry from Liverpool back home to Dublin: making no effort to contact her. Mister McLeish walked free from the court after O'Connor failed to appear [he had left for Ireland] and so with no evidence or victim; the case was dropped and apparently he headed north to Manchester still under close observation from the Special Irish Branch. His parting gift to Dorothy – he clearly knew about her involvement with the Irish Branch - was to send her a dead songbird through the post as a warning. He also enclosed a ten bob postal order [50 pence in today's money] as payment for her 'services'. Rosie stopped her tearing that up and cashed it in Eastham Post Office for a bottle of gin for the pair.

It appears that 'in-fighting' between the 'Priests of Chronos' had spilled onto the streets of east London in 1901 but – according to Jericho Tibbs – the current human time-line had changed little. The 1st 'Shabby man' had indeed been related to Dorothy and The other Hadden's through her 'Uncle Geoffrey' who Dorothy currently doesn't know and has never met! [See episode: **'The love letters of Mrs. Victoria Frogmore'**.] The 2nd 'Shabby man' had arrived to both assassinate Sir Thomas and the first 'Shabby man' who was believed to be about to betray their plans to the Hadden's, and thus to Jericho. With the death of the 2nd 'Shabby man' another assassin was sent: he was simply called 'Herod' and arrived through a portable time device. He quickly killed both Mr. Kelp and Sir Thomas, dumping Sir Thomas's body into Dorothy's cabinet as a warning.

But Sir Thomas had discovered on a trip to 1906 – from 1893 - that he had been murdered in 1901! Thus his younger self took appropriate action and broke with the 'Priest's of Chronos' completely and set up in business himself. It should be noted that the young woman who resembled Dorothy in the basement of the library, was indeed a descendant of Dottie's. It was her fourteen times removed grand-daughter!

The 'Bridgewater's' part in all this was never really clarified and Stonebridge House in 1974 was now in the hands of different owners, the Bridgewater family sadly having died out after World War II with the death of the only male heir during operation 'Market Garden' in 1944 at Arnhem. The house was now occupied by the De Brose family who were French in origin. At the time – 1974 – Mr. Phillip De Brose was a famous fashion photographer and his wife a local GP. Jericho investigated in 1974 and could find no connections with the 1901 incident whatsoever, except that their chauffeur – a certain Mr. Lester Graham – had simply and totally disappeared one evening, never to be seen or heard of again. Jericho knew something drastic had happened to the man because he's soul was 'missing' from the current time-line. But there is no resolution to that mystery: yet.

THE END

EPISODE 2: "MISS PANDORA AND HER MAGIC BOX."

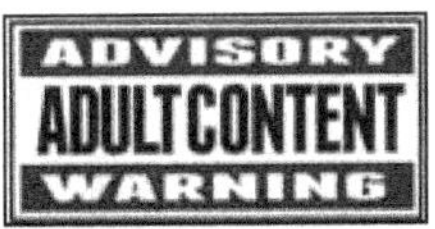

Alcohol – Smoking – Strong language – Strong sexual references [including pornography, prostitution & incest] – Nudity - violence – Witchcraft & Devil worship – Mild Horror – Mild Adult Erotica.

 Approximately 45 to 60 minutes.

 Remember: **Adult Content.**

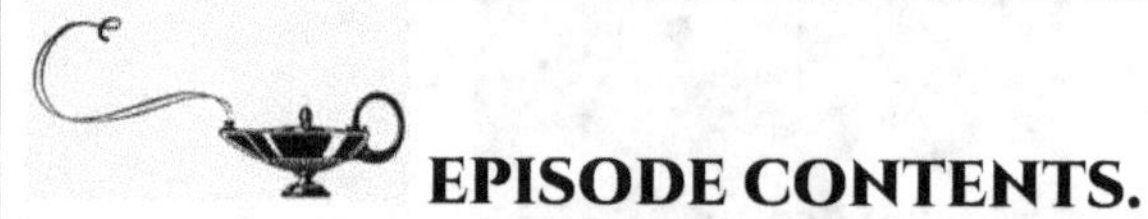 **EPISODE CONTENTS.**

1. 'ONLY TWO THINGS ARE INFINITE; THE UNIVERSE AND HUMAN STUPIDITY, AND I'M NOT SURE ABOUT THE FORMER.'
Start page: 137

2. 'THE ONLY WAY NOT TO THINK ABOUT MONEY IS TO HAVE A GREAT DEAL OF IT.'
Start page: 143

3. 'ONE PICTURE IS WORTH A THOUSAND WORDS.'
Start page: 147

4. 'DEATH IS EVERY MAN'S FINAL CRITIC, TO DIE WELL YOU MUST LIVE BRAVELY.'
Start page: 151

5. 'THE GREATEST TRICK THE DEVIL EVER PULLED WAS CONVINCING THE WORLD HE DIDN'T EXIST.'
Start page: 156

6. 'FOR THE FEMALE OF THE SPECIES IS MORE DEADLY THAN THE MALE.'
Start page: 161

7. 'CLOTHES MAKE THE MAN. NAKED PEOPLE HAVE LITTLE OR NO INFLUENCE ON SOCIETY.'
Start page: 166

8. 'CONFESSION IS GOOD FOR THE SOUL.'
Start page: 171

9. 'THE DEVIL DOESN'T COME TO YOU WITH A RED FACE AND HORNS, HE COMES DISGUISED AS EVERYTHING YOU'VE EVER WANTED.'
Start page: 177

10. 'THE SHOW MUST GO ON.'
Start page: 181

11. 'IT DOESN'T MATTER WHAT YOU DO IN THE BEDROOM AS LONG AS YOU DON'T DO IT IN THE STREET AND FRIGHTEN THE HORSES.'
Start page: 187

12. 'IT'S GOOD TO BE THE KING.'
Start page: 193

13. 'GOD CREATED SEXUAL DESIRE IN TEN PARTS THEN GAVE NINE PARTS TO WOMEN AND ONE TO MEN'.
Start page: 200

14. 'THERE IS NOTHING MORE DECEPTIVE THAN AN OBVIOUS FACT'.
Start page: 208

IMPORTANT AUTHOR'S NOTE:
"The names and places of some characters have been changed to protect the innocent and ficticious characters created in their stead. Thank you."

CHAPTER 1. 'ONLY TWO THINGS ARE INFINITE; THE UNIVERSE AND HUMAN STUPIDITY, AND I'M NOT SURE ABOUT THE FORMER.' Albert Einstein.

The naked man ran full speed towards the old stone wall, tossing aside the strange clown mask and jumping the old crumbling construction, falling awkwardly, but managed to stand. Now limping a little, he made his way down the gentle slope and stood panting at the edge of the shallow, fast flowing stream, and looked towards the small stone arched bridge that crossed the dividing line of the two big estates. The river was that line and it separated the estates of Sir William Colt and Lord Fredrick Falstaff – 14th Earl of Camlet – and now the naked man, limping badly, headed down the stream and hid under the bridge, taking controlled breaths and cursing his luck.

He gripped his ankle and cussed, it was swelling and so he

plunged his foot into the cold running water and gritted his teeth. He stared up at the woodland he had just ran through and could now see several figures appearing amongst the trees and faintly could hear shouting. A big Blackman was gesturing down towards the river and he cursed again and in some pain set off again. He now headed towards Yfel Woods and disappeared into the mass of dark forbidding trees and undergrowth, feeling the chill of the place he wrapped his arms about him and realized his teeth were actually chattering.

He walked [or rather limped] for some minutes and finally had to rest, sitting upon a moss covered stump and held his head with both hands. His head was full of strange thoughts and dark fear stalked every one of them. He took several deep breaths and the hard cold realization that he had lost everything slowly crept over him and he sobbed. After a couple of minutes he rose and now limping badly headed deeper into the woods without any real clue where he was headed or what he would do next. That's when he stopped and stared at the beautifully carved and painted 'Gypsy' style caravan, sitting beneath two big trees. A pair of dark black horses was tied nearby, enjoying the deep lush undergrowth for their dinner. He walked slowly towards the quiet wooden trailer and stopped suddenly: far in the distance he could hear shotguns being fired.

He took a deep breath and shouted, "Hello! Please, I need help!" and repeated himself, covering his genitals with both hands. The top half of the rear door came open [it was designed like a stable door; you could open separately both top and bottom] and a head and shoulders appeared. It was an old man with an incredible head of silver hair and matching beard. A cob pipe hung from his mouth and he stared at the naked forlorn figure and smiled a little.

"Please help me! I was caught by my lover's husband and now he's after me with a bloody shotgun! Can you help please? Please can you help me?" The naked man shouted, looking around, thinking fast. A big dark puff of smoke appeared from the old man's pipe and he slowly removed it. He stared at the man and slowly nodded, opening the bottom half of his door and easing himself down the small steps, and then sat on them. He was wearing a clean white blouse and bright red trousers with black braces and black boots that reached his knees. He removed the pipe and gestured with it to the man, "Caught with an angry man's wife were you?" He said with no emotion in his voice and the naked man nodded.

The old man chuckled, "That happened to me a couple of times in my younger days and once I had to hide in a pig sty. It wasn't pleasant, but it was better than having me bollocks shot off!" He now laughed and eased himself up, and indicated for the man to follow him into the caravan. The naked man, now a little relieved, didn't hesitate in following the old man up the short steps. "Hope she was worth it." The strange old man muttered and looking around closed both the top and bottom of his door. The naked man was thanking him profusely and lowered himself to the floor and stared about the place. There were two 'bunk' beds, both covered with multi-coloured blankets and cooking utensils hanging from the walls. He noticed an old fashioned, single shot musket hanging above on the beds, complete with a well carved powder horn. Next to that was a small canvas bag which he assumed carried the balls that the gun fired. There were several small, beautifully carved wooden chests piled on the other bed.

The old man rummaged around the chests and threw a heavy bright red and black blanket at the man, then lit a small paraffin stove. He held up a black kettle in one hand and asked if the man wanted tea. The man wrapped the coarse blanket about and nodded, thanking – again – the old man for his kindness. The old man drew on his pipe and smoke billowed from it. "I'm Noah Whorton, but I'm mostly called 'Chanter' or 'old Chanter' by the young people."

The naked man nodded and pulled the rough blanket close, he half smiled, "Chanter? Isn't that short for 'enchanter' or magician?" Now that made the old man smile as he placed the kettle on the flickering flames of the little stove. "Ah, a man of education, I like that. Yes, I am what my nickname indicates, a man of magic." He grunted and produced two china mugs, a small black teapot and a jug of milk from the small cupboard beneath the stove.

The man coughed, "So you do magic tricks, making people and things disappear, saw the odd woman in half and stuff like that?" He chuckled and relaxed, leaning against the strangely warm wood of the wall. The old man smiled and scooped some tea from a bright coloured tin. "I can do that sort of magic for the 'gorgers' but my people know and appreciate that I can perform much,

much more than that." Chuckling to himself, he spooned tea into the little black tea pot.

"The term 'Gorger' was a derogatory slang expression used by travelling folk to describe people who were not travelers themselves, basically, the rest of us!" SJW.

The man nodded and asked if the old man could lend him some basic clothes, he really needed to get away from this place and sort the mess he had gotten himself in, out. The smiling old man chuckled, "I can help you with that young man. You can quickly disappear to a place where no-one will know you and certainly won't be found by an irate husband." The man now smiled and nodded, "I would be most grateful Noah if you could help me, I would really appreciate it and I would reward you well, very well in fact."

The old man, clutching a thick rag, lifted the boiling kettle and poured the water into the tea-pot. "Very well young Mister Cope, I'll assist you." He shook the tea pot gently and smiled.

The man looked a little perplexed and ran a hand over his face, "How do you know my name Noah, I never told you what it was....." The old man chuckled, "See, now that's magic!" And young Mister Jordon Edmund Cope laughed and shook his head in amazement. "Now that's some fucking good trick Noah!"

Noah grinned, "Young man, you haven't seen anything yet!" That's when Jordon noticed the old man had only poured one cup of tea and now cradled it with both hands. He said quietly, "A man like you will really appreciate the irony of this. Of that I'm sure."

"I don't understand.... what do you mean Noah, how do you know what kind of man I am?" Jordan said with a little fear creeping into his voice. Noah sipped his tea and sighed. "You're a lair, cheat, thief, con artist, seducer, kiddie's fiddler, brute and womanizer with no morals or scruples whatsoever. I do have that right don't I?"

Jordon sat in silence and nodded. The old man had hit the nail on the head; he was all of those things and – in rare moments of regret – had called himself those very names. He stared at the smiling Noah and a terrible feeling of fear and dread swept over him and he slowly staggered to his feet, but his throbbing ankle wouldn't allow him to stand and he sank back down and almost tried to hide under the blanket.

He watched with growing horror as Noah pulled the old musket from the wall and slowly pulled the hammer back. "I always keep 'old Bess' cocked and ready Mister Cope, so I don't miss an opportunity to send the master a worthy soul." Jordan was now screaming and begging, trying to stand. He felt the urine running down his leg and he screamed Noah's name as the old man aimed and fired.

The heavy little ball smashed through the blanket and tore its way through Jordan's heaving chest and he fell back against the wall and gasped a couple of times and the darkness swept over him. Old Noah lowered the musket and waved the smoke away with a hand. He walked over and slowly closed the dead man's eyes and open mouth. The jaw flopped back down and Noah shrugged his shoulders. He stood waiting and rubbed his face, then finished his tea. He sat on the opposite bunk and nodded. Few things surprised the old man and the non-appearance of a Collector for young Cope's soul was one of them!

He gripped his musket and smiled – a little – the bastard had already sold his soul to the Dark Prince or he had travelled here from another time. He rubbed his chin and cussed a little, this could now be tricky as fucking Temporal Detectives would be on their way and quickly. He needed to lose the late Jordon Cope and move on. That's when the door was pulled open and young Tess stuck her head in and stared at the dead man on the floor. She was about to tell Noah that the other families were arriving. Tess gestured to the late Mister Cope and sighed, "Oh Grandpa, not a bleeding again!" The old man just smiled and told her that the tea was fresh and there was a clean mug next to the stove and she should help herself.

The young woman lifted her frilly skirt and stepped over Cope, kissing the old man on the forehead. "I best tell Ollie that we have something to get rid of – again." Noah chuckled and gave his grand-daughters bum a slap. "Good girl, I've always said you are just like you darling mum." The girl poured herself some tea and topped up the old man's, mentioning that there are several men in the woods and some are armed.

Noah grunted, "They're after that bastard. I saw it all." He tapped the side of his head. "The filthy piece of crap was caught in the nursery with the eight year old daughter of the family. Wore a mask so that the poor little thing wouldn't recongnise him. Thought no-one would notice him slipping away from the big party. But he was caught red handed. The kid's father went after him with a shotgun but I did the job for him. The bastard is now with the master."

The young woman nodded and sat next to her grandfather, "But what do we do now with him?" The old man chuckled and finished his second cup. "Dump him somewhere that nobody knows him and let the bloody coppers puzzle over it." The pair left the caravan to find Ollie and make preparations to dispose of the late Jordon Cope. Old Noah stopped by the edge of the clearing and watched the group of men approaching through the trees; he fixed a smile and walked nonchalantly towards them shouting, "Can I help you sirs."

Ollie and Moses stood by their horses and smiled at each other, Moses spoke quietly, "I have just the place to dump the stiff; the bastard doesn't respect me because I'm black and thinks I won't slit his throat because of the money he makes for old Chanter. This will be a little reminder and make me feel better to see the cunt squirm for a while." Ollie chuckled, "Come on, when those fuckers have pissed off, we'll get the stiff bagged up and head for the east end and surprise your little disrespectful friend. I think old Chanter will see the funny side."

They walked to Ollie's wagon and saw the large group of men moving off towards the river. Ollie wiped his face and neck, "Tess thinks old Chanter off'd him because he fucked up part of his big plan. He [old Chanter?] had spent a lot of time and money cultivating that kid apparently. She would have been quite an asset to the family and now that fucking idiot [Cope?] has fucked that all up. The kid will be closed off to us now. Shame really, she could have made us a lot of money when she grew a bit and the master would certainly have been pleased at her successful recruitment."

Moses could only nod his agreement, but he was more than happy to return to the east end. There was a high class prossie [prostitute] that he really wanted to use and she certainly didn't mind fucking a Blackman for money – if they could afford it – and he would use he's usual cover story that explained why a black fella was dressed so well and had so much money. He may also run into that cocky bastard Ally fucking Cadbury and settle for once and all, who was 'The Man' with a blade.

Old Chanter sat on the steps of his caravan and smoked his pipe in the fading light of this warm spring evening. He had seen the beautiful woman in his vision, "But like a viper under that beauty, she would be welcomed by the master with open arms. Two people in one body: one lovely and charming, the other dark and deceptive." He tapped his pipe out and headed inside, "Bloody Moses had better rein in his anger and passions with this job, or we'll all swing." That thought made him stop and grimace.

CHAPTER 2. 'THE ONLY WAY NOT TO THINK ABOUT MONEY IS TO HAVE A GREAT DEAL OF IT.' Edith Wharton.

"It's a real pity Mary my girl, you have such a pretty face and punters pay well for a pretty face. You're bleeding showing everything else, so you may as well expose it. As I said, there's plenty of money in it." Young Henry 'Flash' Reynolds sighed loudly and adjusted the big lens and checked the lighting again. He smiled broadly as his model settled on the bed and positioned herself – as directed – for the photograph. She stared to one side, making sure that the camera would not capture too much of her face, then pulled the thin lacy nightdress to one side and opened the back slit, exposing her peach shaped bum.

Henry smiled and said quietly; "Hold!" and removed the lens cover and checked the seconds passing on his little fob watch. "Done!" and gently pushed the lens cover back on. He now removed the plate and placed it on the small table, loading a fresh plate. "I don't know why you're so paranoid about it. These pictures sell for good money, a lot of money and the clients who buy them are not the sort to hang around the bleeding docks!"

The girl turned and sighed, "Flash, I've told you a dozen times I don't work the docks! I have some regular clients and they won't like me doing this. One's a bloody Bishop for Christ sake!" Flash grunted, "Liar, liar pants on fire! I bloody picked you up at the bleeding Albert docks, so don't spin me that old tale thank you very much. Dumb or gullible I am not!" 'Mary' chuckled, "That was just an off day and I was actually visiting a friend." Now that made young Henry laugh, "Yeah a friend whose name you were not yet acquainted with!"

Mary shrugged her shoulders, "He was a friend of my older brother's and his ship had docked. I was just there to invite him for dinner." Now Henry laughed again, "Christ, that's a new word for it: dinner I mean. How much did his dinner cost him?" Mary just smiled at him and said quietly, "Two pounds and he paid in sovereigns." Henry whistled, "Bloody hell, you must be a fucking good shag for that sort of money. But then, looking like you do with that body and innocent face, I quite believe he would pay that sort of dosh."

"£2 in 1902 would be worth about £240 in today's money! The average prostitute at the time probably charged between five and ten shillings and they would be the 'High-Class' call girls!" SJW.

Henry told her to change position, on all fours with her head down and back to the camera. Mary was now exposing her vagina and anus to the camera. He told her to bring a hand around and grab a cheek, opening it a little. She did as directed and he said "Hold!" quietly and consulted his watch again. He replaced the lens cap and said "Done!" Mary relaxed and sat on the edge of the bed and smiled at Henry, "So for this session I get thirty bob [£1 and ten shillings] and how many more are you taking today?" Henry removed the plate and thought for a second or so, "About twenty....maybe only fifteen. We'll see. Are you in a hurry then? Got another two quid punter lined up?"

Mary shook her head, "For your information Flash, I am being taken out to a real dinner. A posh place in Eastham run by a lovely Jewish family and it won't cost me a penny." Henry rubbed his face after loading another plate, "I know the place: it's Romanov's, the Russian restaurant. The food is good there, as is the music and dancers. Come on, who's taking a working girl like you there?"

Mary just shook her head, "Wouldn't you like to know!" and laughed. That's when they heard the loud thud and furniture been turned over, coming from the hallway. [Henry's studio was his large front room of his house and his developing room was the spare bedroom] They both thought the same thing: a bloody police raid! They both stared at each other and Mary jumped from the bed grabbing up her coat. But there was silence and certainly no coppers came crashing through the door. In silence they walked to the door and opened it, peering into the dimly hit hallway.

"For Christ fucking sakes!" Was all Henry managed to say and the pair edged out and stared at the naked man lying on the remains of the small occasional table, the big flower pot smashed on the bare floorboards. His legs were spread and his head was thrown back with the eyes and mouth open. They edged closer and could see the blood dried around the dark hole in his chest. Henry finally managed to gasp, "The poor bastard has been shot!" They both stared down the hallway and could see front door lying open.

"How the fuck did he get in when he was dead?" Henry whispered and Mary gripped his arm, "You mean why did someone dump him here and get out without us seeing them? For Christ sakes Flash, he didn't walk in under his own steam. That wound is old, the flipping blood has congealed. " Henry just nodded and said, really puzzled, "Why the fuck is he stark naked? And who the hell dumped him here and more importantly, fucking why?" Mary whispered that she didn't know and took a deep breath. "I can't be here when the coppers come! The bloody detective they'll send will know me and….well, I just can't be here!"

Henry stared at her and sighed, "He's nicked you before or are you out on parole?" Mary just stared at the body and nodded, repeating, "I can't be here." The young man shook his head, "They'll try and stitch me up for the killing and you are my only witness so you are talking to the damn coppers!" He gripped her arm, "I'm fucking not swinging for a murder I had nothing to do with."

Mary managed a smile and gripped his hand, "Think about it. You came home and found a dead man had been dumped in your hallway. That wound is old and he's already stiffened up. He's been dead sometime, they can't pin it on you. Say he's been dead six or eight hours and where were you all day with loads of witness? At the picture palace photographing the new acts. You were there all day and have loads of witnesses to back you up. See, you're in the clear!"

Henry released her arm and nodded, "You're fucking right, I have the perfect alibi. They can't pin this on me. Besides I don't even know the poor fucker. Never seen him in my life, so why would I kill him. Add to that, I don't even have a fucking gun!" Mary kissed him on the lips and whispered, "Let me go and keep me out of it and I'll make it worth your while." She kissed him again and gently pushed her free hand against his crotch adding, "That weekend in Brighton you are taking, I bet you would like a little company/"

Flash kissed her, lingering for a few seconds then smiled. "I've never been with a two guinea tart – until now!" Mary grinned and managed to gather her things and left quickly with Henry agreeing to wait a couple of minutes before calling the coppers. He walked to the corner and watched the people passing by, rushing home in the fading light of the spring day. He must have only waited for a couple of minutes when he saw the tall, well built constable stroll into view. Henry took a deep breath and waved his arms about and shouted, attracting quite a crowd around him and of course, the young constable.

Henry shouted;"Someone has dumped a dead man in my fucking hallway constable! I just opened the front door and there he was, he must have been dead for hours. I've been out all day!" The crowd gasped in shock and the constable blew his whistle several times to attract officers on neighbouring beats. Old man John Scott – the tobacconist – joined the crowd and shouted that he would send his boy Charlie – on his bike – to Brick Lane nick to fetch the CID. The constable seemed quite happy about that as the crowd followed Henry and him back to the house. The young constable actually knew what he was doing and kept the crowd out of the house and Henry close by. Regardless of what he had said, he was a suspect until Mister Hadden cleared him.

Mary watched from the cab rank and sighed with relief. Flash could be on the bloody stage himself with that performance. She opened her small handbag and checked the paying-in book she always carried. She had over a thousand pounds in her savings account from her 'little jobs' over the past year. She would now head home and change for dinner. At this rate she would never have to concern herself about money: ever. It was her freedom and independence. She wouldn't be forced by her family into marriage when the family fortune dwindled away. She had slowly recovered from the shock of finding that her parents had died practically broke. She was determined never, ever, to end up in the bloody poor house or marry some bastard just to survive.

A cab pulled up and she shouted her address to the driver and jumped in. She needed to leave before that bloody detective appeared on the scene: he would recongnise her immediately and the questions that followed would be hard to answer with lies. He would see through her at once. Mary had no rational explanation why she was here at this time of day, when she should have been up west at a dress fitting.

The cab pulled away and she eased right back into the seat, keeping well away from the windows. What a fucking turn up for the books: a bloody murdered stiff being dumped in Flash's hallway. She wondered why and by whom. But she knew one fact, bloody Detective Inspector Harry Hadden would find out and she hoped he would never discover her little walk-on part in the bloody mystery killing.

The black police carriage from Brick Lane nick passed her in Queen Street and she pushed well back into her seat.

CHAPTER 3. 'ONE PICTURE IS WORTH A THOUSAND WORDS.' Fred R. Barnard.

"His repeated the same story so many times I think I'll bleeding dream about it tonight." Constable Harris spoke quietly to DC Farmer who scribbled in his notebook and nodded a couple of times. He stared down at the naked corpse, and then looked about the small hallway. "It's the strangest bloody story about a murder I've heard in a while. He's saying that while he was out working, someone dumped a corpse in this hallway and then fucked off. Old Doc Goldstein reckons the stiff has been dead at least six or eight hours. Our friend says he left early this morning and only came back at six, just before the shout went up."

Harry was kneeling by the body examining the bullet hole really carefully and stood, shaking his head, "Do you know Dave, I would swear blind he was shot with a bloody musket ball! The wound is all wrong for a jacketed bullet. Could be a single ball from a shotgun, a heavy gauge shotgun, but it looks like a bloody musket ball wound: It's huge but almost round. But we'll leave that to a Firearms expert. There's no blood so he was definitely killed elsewhere and dumped here. But why here? That's going to be key to this mystery." Harry was already thinking about retired Colonel Jethro Kirkbridge who lived in Westham: his collection of antique weapons had appeared in various magazines and more importantly; he was an acknowledged expert in old firearms.

Dave sucked his pencil and smiled, "Our witness – if you can call him that – is a bit dodgy himself. You've seen his little studio and the photographs he takes: nothing extreme, almost classical but still illegal. Do you think the stiff could be a bloody warning from someone who has a beef with him?" Harry sighed, shrugging his shoulders, "Could be a frame up attempt, we'll see what he says when we interview him. He's a suspect all-right, even if he has an alibi provided by a theatre full of people. It's all down to the time of death. If it's over eight hours then he's our number one suspect. Tell Edwin to run him down the nick and get a full statement from him as a witness. Then we'll have something to go on when we dig deeper. Let's have a look at the naughty pictures." Dave showed him into the front room and Harry poked about the place, picking up the undeveloped plates. "Get these developed, let's see what's on them."

Dave held up a small bunch of keys, "Took these off him. A house key for the front door – which he said wasn't locked this morning when he left – a couple of cabinets or cupboard keys and this one. Say's it unlocks his bank Box." Harry took it and turned it in his fingers. "Uncle William, Dorothy and I have a Bank Box each at the Provincial in Eastham High Street. This looks identical to ours." He held it up and read the small number on it, "113. His bloody box is near mine!" He handed the key back to Dave and rubbed his chin, "Bank Boxes are not cheap, so naughty photographs must make a fair few bob."

"Bank Boxes would now be referred to as 'Safe Deposit Boxes'." SJW.

Dave chuckled and unlocked the big black cabinet and pulled a box file out marked 'Nudes – Young – one shilling'. They flicked through the hundred of photographs in the big box and could see all the girls were teenagers; there was no 'under-age' stuff. So Dave pushed it back and pulled down another, marked 'Naughty nudes – young – Half-crown'. The girls were all adults, but exposing their private parts fully. "Very tasteful, I don't think. I wouldn't my want my sister amongst these." Dave muttered and pushed it back. At the bottom was a big box marked, 'Private & erotic – women and girls – five shillings'.

They opened it and studied the pictures. Dave chuckled, "Tut Tut, very naughty but still not really that bad. I've seen a lot worse. You know women actually doing it with blokes and other women. These are quite tasteful; he does have some skill and artistic merit." Harry just grunted and slowly pulled out one photograph of a young woman with her back to the camera, completely nude apart from a ribbon in her hair. One arm was lifted so that her fine breasts were exposed but her face almost covered. "A shy one who doesn't want her face revealed. I find that a little odd, all the other girls – we've seen so far are not that shy - Why doesn't she want her face shown?" Then he chuckled and stared hard, tapping the photograph adding, "Except she didn't realize the window at the side there. It's practically acting like a mirror. You can see her face in it I think." He rummaged in his pocket and produced his little magnifying glass and held it over the photograph. He said nothing for good few seconds and grunted again. "I think, when we get those plates developed, we'll have this part of the picture enlarged."

Dave took the picture and studied it, "Do you know her Guv?" he asked quietly and Harry just shrugged his shoulders, "We'll see." Was all he said. They walked back into the hallway and Harry took one last look about and then pushed his hat up and smiled a little. "Dave, get the boys in here and take the place apart, I want every nook and cranny searched. If there's a bloody mouse hiding around here I want it found. I want the bank box checked, see what's in it. Get a warrant from old judge Daniel's; that will make the bank manager happy. He can tell head office he had no choice in the matter." Dave finished scribbling his tasks down and pointed his pencil at the stiff, now being photographed by old Mister Lambert and his young assistant. "Guv, do you think old Lambert would know Reynolds? After all, how many bloody successful photographers are there in the east end, they must know their rivals wouldn't they?" Harry smiled and tapped his arm, "That Dave is a fucking good suggestion." He turned to Lambert and asked if he knew young Henry 'Flash' Reynolds.

Mister Lambert folded his arms and stared down at the body and then patted his camera a couple of times. "Only by reputation and it was good for professional photographs but certainly thumbs down by what he photographed and who he worked for." Harry was now interested and asked what he meant. Mister Lambert didn't smile, "He does a lot of work for John Vicar apparently and I don't think he was paying the young fellow to take family pictures." Dave nodded, "I take it, that's John Vicar who runs the Dock gangs." Lambert said 'yes' quietly. Harry sighed, "It appears Mister Vicar is expanding his criminal empire. We've heard he's taken over a couple of brothels down the Vic Dock Road. The previous owners didn't have much say in the matter. So it makes sense that he's getting into the dirty pictures business. Where there's dirty money, there's John Vicar."

"Except the opium trade and distribution. Few would go up against madam Tong and her gang of cut-throats. Remember that mutilated torso we found last year? The silly bastard went up against her and we still haven't found the remains of his merry men, not a trace of four grown men!" Dave said and pushed his notebook and pencil into his coat pocket. Harry rubbed his face, he certainly knew about madam Tong. She ran the opium gangs around the east end with her HQ in a tea shop in Lime House. She was utterly ruthless and it's rumoured she cut the throat of her young brother for having his sticky fingers in the till. Madam Tong also ran a couple of high-class Chinese brothels and used under-aged girls to staff them. They were shipped in from China and smuggled out the docks to bypass immigration. According to his 'snouts' [informants] there was a shipment of five young girls due to arrive next week. Harry wasn't happy when told that the oldest of them was just thirteen. He had passed the intelligence up to Scotland Yard's Vice squad and heard nothing back. DC Palmer had told him that a friend in the squad had informed him that madam Tong was 'hands off' at the moment and they wouldn't be raiding her anytime soon.

Shockingly, the young girls had apparently been left to their fate. Harry wondered if there would be so little done if the girls had been white and abducted from a posh school. It left a nasty taste in his mouth and some real feeling of shame in his heart.

Harry remembered his 'chat' with the Inspector in charge of the Vice-squad over a pint in the Denmark Arms last Christmas. Apparently madam Tong must have powerful and influential patrons. On no less than four occasions his [the Vice Inspector] requests for warrants had been turned down with no real explanation. He told Harry that to get permission for a raid needed the Assistant Commissioner's express say so. He didn't paint a pretty picture. Harry and Dave walked to their carriage as the undertaker's arrived. Harry sighed, just another day in the east end. The face in the window now haunted Harry's mind and he stared out the cab window in deep thought.

CHAPTER 4. 'DEATH IS EVERY MAN'S FINAL CRITIC, TO DIE WELL YOU MUST LIVE BRAVELY.' Edward Abbey.

Reggie [Titus] carried the chest and placed it sideways on the table and lifted the lid, showing it was empty. He pulled it upright and closed the lid and stepped back, arms folded.

Dorothy stood at the side of the table and spoke loudly, waving her hands about and gestured towards the ornate chest. Slowly the lid lifted and a little smoke floated up, swirling and turning until it vanished. Two bandaged hands appeared, gripping the edge of the chest, followed by a bandaged head with two dark eyes. Then the mummy leapt from the box, spinning and tumbling in the air, landing perfectly on his feet. "How's that Dottie!" Sims shouted and took a bow. He didn't get any applause, Reggie just chuckled, "Heaven's Mister Sims that was the worse piece of over-acting I've seen you do in quite a while!"

Dorothy groaned, "Sims, this is supposed to be a dramatic bit, a little creepy and frightening. Not a bloody mummy that's thinks it's an acrobatic clown!" The stage rehearsals for Dorothy's up and coming performance as 'Miss Pandora and her magic box' show weren't quite running to specification. She still hadn't caught on to the tittering and giggling from the male staff at the theatre when she announced the show's name. Even Uncle William and Harry couldn't say anything because she was so happy about her beckoning 'solo' act. Only Titus had voiced some reservations about the name and received a blank, slightly puzzled look from Dorothy. Sims also appeared to be innocent of the conjecture [and amusement] the name caused. But the flyers, posters and cards had already been printed when Rosie [it had to be Rosie!] pointed out why the name was drawing laughter and derision. Over a cup of tea in the dressing room she explained why the title of the show was a little in-appropriate, and a bit naughty, but decidedly funny.

Dorothy sipped her tea and nodded. "Thank you Rosie, I do understand the connection with my honey-pot [vagina] but the name remains. The core principle of the show is a magic act that uses Pandora's Box and it releases all manner of magical things. The name stays regardless of what some dirty minded individuals think or snigger about." Rosie grinned, "Just don't take any jobs at a Gentleman's Club: you'll get thrown off stage in bitter disappointment!" Dorothy just peered at her over the rim of the tea-cup and simply didn't understand what Rosie meant. Rosie was still laughing when she answered the knock at the dressing room door.

Rosie pulled open the door and announced, "A very handsome young policeman to see you Miss Dorothy!" Dave farmer slowly wandered in removing his hat, "Thanks for that Rosie, any tea on the go?" Rosie sighed, "What a bugger, these days the young men only want poor Rosie for her bleeding tea." Dave chuckled, "And the bacon rolls of course. Mister Hadden swears by them." Dorothy gestured for Dave to sit down and Rosie took his hat and coat. He smiled again at Dottie and clasped his hands together. "I've been tasked by Mister Hadden to check out an alibi for a certain Henry Reynolds, sometimes called 'Flash'. Apparently he was here from about eight o'clock yesterday morning until around about five o'clock. Harry tells me you were here all day, doing your rehearsals for the new show, so I can cut the work load down to just one interview: you. It will save me a pile of time not talking to everyone else, since what you say is good enough for Mr. Hadden….and me of course."

Dorothy placed her cup down, "Do you mean the photographer that was here?" Dave nodded and Dottie folded her arms, "What on earth has he been involved in? He seemed a very nice fellow, very professional and quite charming." Dave didn't smile, "it's murder Miss Dorothy. He says someone – for whatever reason – dumped a shot man in his hallway whilst he was here taking pictures. He needs to be eliminated from the investigation or he becomes the chief suspect. So was he here all day yesterday?"

Dorothy crossed her legs and smoothed down her skirt and slowly nodded. "Yes I think he was, I remember he was very interested in the act and of course, very interested when the chorus girls rehearsed!" Dave chuckled at that and scribbled in his notebook. Dorothy continued, "He was still here when I left just before five. I had a dress fitting at Madam Elaine's booked and he and I stood outside waiting for a damn cab. He let me have the first one that arrived which I thought was quite gallant of him." Rosie refilled her cup and sat back down; she gave a knowing look at Dorothy but said nothing.

Dave stated that was good enough for him and left a couple of minutes later. Rosie coughed and waged a finger at Dottie, "That wasn't quite true was it? You left about three if I remember because you mentioned that you'll share a cab with Reggie. I don't remember seeing that bleeding photographer after that."

Dorothy sighed, "Oh Rosie, I'm not about to tell Dave Farmer about my private life. Besides, big Tom told me the photographer left about five so it doesn't alter anything, now does it? Big Tom can be trusted implicitly." Rosie just smiled, "Still a little white lie." Dottie just chuckled and asked if there were any biscuits, then she saw the look on Rosie's face. "Alright, alright, I'll tell Harry about my little indiscretion with detective Farmer and admit I sneaked off early for my dress fitting. But it doesn't alter the fact that the photographer was here until five o'clock because big Tom did see him and told me this morning when we chatted in the theatre foyer. Tom's word will be good enough for Harry as it was for me. Now, does that make you feel better, that I will confess my dreadful sin to dear Harry?" Dorothy stretched her legs out, adding she needed a nap and Rosie nodded, a little happier now.

Doc Goldstein washed his hands in the deep sink and dried his hands on a thick white towel handed to him by his assistant. He watched Harry and Edwin examining the musket ball and Edwin placed it in a paper bag and wrote in his notebook. "It's probably from a musket made around the 1840's. Probably a Crimean piece, But the ball could have been made any time before the 1870's when full jacketed bullets came in for the new rifles. You were lucky there Harry, your boys found it on the floor under the corpse. I believe it must have been dislodged when the body was moved and dropped out of the exit wound. A nice piece of luck."

He gestured to the corpse upon the slab and rolled down his sleeves. "Quite a healthy individual aged between thirty and forty I would guess. The shot killed him, no doubt of that, standing and facing his killer for certain. There are traces of rough red fibres in the wound: probably a blanket or maybe a coat. He had been dead at least six hours before the body was found." Harry nodded his thanks and spoke quietly to Edwin, "It's a close run thing. Reynolds says he was at the theatre from eight to five and the body was found at 5.35pm. He's off the hook if his alibi holds out." Edwin stared at the corpse as the morgue assistant threw the white sheet back over it. He lifted the sheet and pointed to the feet with the toe-tag hanging there. "He has grass and mud on his soles, must have been barefoot in the garden or bloody something. Who runs around the fucking garden stark naked?"

"Now all I would like is a name to tell the Coroner, over to you Harry." Doc Goldstein chuckled and wrote on the clipboard with a flourish. Harry held up his hands in mock despair, "We have absolutely nothing to go on Doc, Missing persons came up blank and we checked back two years. Old Lambert will produce a mug shot and we'll send it to neighbouring forces and that's about all we can do. Unless he's done time and we get a match with fingerprints, he'll go under as an unknown." Doc pulled the sheet back a little and lifted a pale white arm, "Perhaps this may help identify him. He could be a devil worshipper or maybe an ex-sailor of some kind to have this inked on his arm." Both Harry and Edwin stared at the strange red devil tattoo complete with fork. "Make sure old Lambert gets a shot of that." Harry said quietly and was now concerned by this strange twist to the case. He now really needed to inform Jericho Tibbs about the possibility of devil worshippers in the area. He smiled a little: Sims could relay that message and would be overjoyed to accomplish it for him and Dottie, especially Dottie!

Harry sat in his drab office and reviewed the case so far, with Dorothy confirming Reynolds was off the hook, the investigation had reached a halt. Unless the strange tattoo yielded new information, he slowly closed the thin file and sat back, hands clasped together and thought – again – about the face in that naughty photograph. His thoughts were disturbed by Dave Farmer sticking his head around the door. "Guv, the front desk just had a wee lad at the counter with this." He held up a note and Harry waved him in. He took the note and grunted, Old George [the former cat burglar] wished to see him in the snug bar of the Denmark Arms, across the street from the nick. It mentioned half a crown and so Harry knew the old ex-con had some information to sell. He eased from the seat and slapped on his hat. "Come on Dave, we can get a pint before lunch." Strangely enough Dave didn't disagree with that!

Harry sat with the old man, watching him swallowing down the pint of porter, wiping his toothless mouth and clearly looking for another. Harry sent Dave for another round and asked George what he had for him. The old man looked around the almost empty pub and didn't smile. "There's rabbit and pork [talk] on the treats [the streets] about your drum [home or house] well, about a gooseberry pudding [woman] there and I'm not saying it's your skin & blister [sister] but it ain't good. The word is she's moonlighting [the act of working a second job] and making loads of pie and mash [cash!] doing two-thirty [dirty] pictures and being a brass flute [prostitute] for wealthy toffs. I thought you had guessed when you collared [arrested] that Reynolds geezer [man] but I hear he's been kicked out without being sheeted [charged]. Just saying mister Hadden and I mean nothing by it."

Dave handed the little man another pint and sat down. Harry took his whisky and said nothing except, "Carry on George." George sipped his ale and coughed, "Me peers [ears] heard that she even goes with rich darkies for the right ackers [money] and salts it away in a bank box. It ain't right Mister Hadden, but worse than anything else, I hear madam Tong is taking a butcher's hook [look] at what she's up to. Just saying mister Hadden."

Harry pushed half a crown across the beer stained table and George grabbed it, finished his pint and slipped away. Dave said nothing but sipped his pint and stared down at the table. Harry finished his whisky in silence and gestured to the door. "Come on

Dave; let's see what the boys have turned up at Reynolds's place." They left the pub and flagged down a cab. Dave broke the silence and asked if he should speak to other members of staff at the Paradise Theatre to confirm the photographers alibi. Harry slowly nodded, "Speak with big Tom, he's straight as an arrow." Dave took a deep breath and knew that the fucking situation was really serious if Harry doubted his beloved sister's words.

CHAPTER 5. 'THE GREATEST TRICK THE DEVIL EVER PULLED WAS CONVINCING THE WORLD HE DIDN'T EXIST.' Charles Baudelaire.

Mary's trick for this afternoon was staying at a decent hotel in Westham and she had to slip the kitchen porter half a crown to show her the back stairs which only the staff used. The fat sweaty old man had asked her for 'a turn' when she finished her current job but she smiled and said 'no' – but politely – and tossed him an extra shilling for his disappointment. Now she was naked on the big bed, gripping the headboard with both hands and cussing under her breath. Her 'client' was a big man in all respects and he was thrusting hard and fast. She could feel the sweat from his hands and body on her back and thighs. Finally after some minutes he swore and groaned as he finished inside her. Leaning over, he kissed her shoulders and neck and then patted her bum – hard – saying that was worth every 'fucking penny'. He had if fact paid two gold sovereigns for his pleasure and certainly thought it was value for money.

He lay back against the headboard and lit a small cigar, giving her a gentle push. "Get me a whisky darling….and one for yourself if you wish. I have a proposition for you my little sweet thing that you will be certainly interested in. It means good money and plenty of it." Mary walked a little awkwardly to the drinks tray and poured two whiskies and returned to the bed. He accepted the glass and sat up, patting the bed, indicating for her to sit next to him, which she did. He wrapped an arm around her and smiled. "What's on your mind sir?" she asked, sipping her very welcome whisky and wondered why he was putting on this phony story about bloody America!

"I return to New York in ten days and I want to hire your services again. I'll pay your going rate, no question there. I'll give you the times and dates before you leave. There should be at least ten pounds in it for you and if you're a real good little girl, I'll slip you something extra." He cupped her right breast and gave it a squeeze. "Next time, I'll enjoy your back door so bring plenty of grease." He chuckled and placed his half smoked cigar in the ashtray and sipped his whisky. Mary just nodded and wondered how the big Negro really made his money. "It's a bit extra for 'Greek' and you're a big man so you'll have to be gentle." He smiled at that and nodded. "I won't go too deep – the first time – but once your little brown flower opens up I'll enjoy it how I like." Mary just nodded and sipped her whisky, staring at the big ornate clock on the master bedroom's fireplace. She would have to leave soon; she was expected back at the house.

He squeezed her tit again, "I have two colleagues from the city [New York?] Arriving in a couple of weeks and I'm sure they'll want to hire you. They're wealthy men so charge them the same or a little more, they won't mind, they know quality tits and arse when they see it." Mary said 'yes' quietly then asked if they were coloured like him and he nodded. He gestured to himself, "Black as the Ace of Spades, like me!" and laughed. He dropped her tit and ran his hand down her taunt stomach, "If you're not careful darling, you'll be fat with a black baby in a couple of months and I hope you have an understanding family." But the big man was thinking ahead, yes, his two 'colleagues' would definitely hire this darling little tart and fuck her somewhere discrete and he would be there to 'welcome' them too. Oh, sometimes he was so cunning it simply amazed him. So he thought.

Mary just smiled again and thought 'no fucking way!' Should she have an unexpected 'misfortune', then she knew a nice doctor who would help for the right price. Not for her, some bloody cut-throat abortionist in a back alley house with a dirty knitting needle and bucket. She finished her drink and said that she had to leave or she would be missed at home. The big man smiled and nodded, finishing his drink, "Fetch me another darling, before you go."

Mary did, then dressed and left. She really needed a hot bath. Clutching the note that the big man had handed her about their next rendezvous, she made her way down the backstairs and through the rear kitchen doors. Mary would flag down a cab at the front of the hotel. She checked her handbag and smiled a little at the two gold sovereigns lying there. Her little 'nest-egg' was growing daily and she may now have to visit the bank again and deposit what she had made this month. It was nearly thirty pounds!

"Performing an abortion or trying to self-abort was against The Offences against the Person Act of 1861 and carried a sentence of life imprisonment." SJW.

The old kitchen porter watched her go and wiped his sweaty face with a tea-towel and wondered where he had seen the high class brass [prostitute] before. As he mopped the kitchen floor, he suddenly smiled and chuckled to himself: he had seen her leaving – via the stage door or tradesmen entrance –at the bloody Paradise Theatre! A couple of cooks asked what the old man was laughing about, he didn't answer but said softly under his breath 'You'll be opening your posh legs for me when I pop in the bloody theatre and make you an offer you can't say no too.' That thought made him attack the dirty wet floor tiles with some gusto. He was now a very happy old would be blackmailer.

Harry was disappointed with the search results, nothing really bad was found, but young Constable Irving had discovered two ledgers and Harry sat reading the entries with some growing interest. The notorious gang boss John Vicar appeared several times as did a couple of local councilors. But what really caught his eye was several entries of payments to a model called 'Shy Mary' and he knew who exactly they referred too.

Edwin was reading the other ledger and coughed, then chuckled, "Reynolds's has recorded receiving thirty bob from a certain 'Alabaster Sedgwick' for a set of naughty pictures with a model called 'shy Mary' he also notes that Sedgwick was willing to pay the going rate for her services at a private party he was organizing for a Friday night at his other house. But Reynolds's had to tell him no because she only works afternoons. Now that's strange, not many prossies [prostitutes] would turn good money like that away. Why can't she work nights?"

Harry didn't smile, "Because she doesn't have any real excuses to be away from home of a night. She's living a bloody double life: a respectable woman moonlighting as a very high class tom, and making a small fortune by the look of these ledgers. Apparently her clients pay a minimum of two sovereigns for her services, but she only works afternoons. I think I know why." He slammed the ledger shut and stared at the ceiling in silence.

"Sweet Jesus, she's probably earning more than the damn Commissioner and must be some kind of bloody stunner to pull that kind of money off punters!" Edwin rubbed his chin and continued reading, and then sat up, "Boss, this entry is for this Friday afternoon and Reynolds's says that Sedgwick has paid him five pounds in advance for 'shy Mary' to be photographed at his other house whilst he [Sedgwick] watches. The dirty bleeding photographer notes that 'shy Mary' has agreed and old Sedgwick can fuck her there for two sovereigns!" Harry didn't smile but nodded, "We'll find the address of this other house and raid the bastards." Edwin smiled a little, "Won't that get up the Vice squad's nose Guv?"

Now Harry smiled, "Fuck them. This is our case now and we can charge young Reynolds with living off immoral earnings and supplying prostitutes."

"I'll find all the Sedgwick's in the borough and there can't be too many called bloody 'Alabaster'." Edwin slammed the ledger shut and grinned, "Should make for an interesting Friday afternoon." Harry just nodded: it certainly would, but it could be catastrophic for his family's reputation. He had some hard thinking to do and would he compromise his oath and duties as a police officer?

Harry re-opened the ledger and flicked – again – through the pages. The same name had appeared with several large amounts of money: Noah the Chanter. Harry had heard of that name but couldn't remember when or why.

Rosie looked up from her knitting as Dorothy came through the dressing room door, hot and bothered. She pulled off her coat and hat without ceremony and dropped into her chair. "For heaven's sake Rosie, get the kettle on, I'm gasping. Had to actually run for a cab and this spring weather is blooming too hot, I'm sweating like a horse." Rosie smiled and put the kettle on the small paraffin stove and spooned some tea leaves into the black teapot. "How did the costume fitting go? It's not too revealing is it? Harry and your uncle won't be impressed if you're bleeding nicked on stage for outraging public decency!"

Dorothy laughed and sat up, "it's no worse than what's worn by ladies on stage in Paris." Rosie grunted, "Yes, but this ain't bleeding Paris is it." Dorothy agreed with that and explained since she was a woman magician; she had to be her own distraction. Rosie was clearly puzzled by that statement and asked why Reggie couldn't be the distraction for the act. "Because he's a man. The ladies may be staring at him, but not all the men will be followers of dear Mister Oscar Wilde!" Now that did make Rosie laugh. Dorothy stood and stretched, "I really need a hot bath before the show tonight."

Rosie admired Dottie's hat and asked if it was yet another new one. Like most fashionable young women of the time, Dorothy changed her hats frequently. Dorothy nodded, "The young woman from Madam Jacqueline's delivered it this morning and made the fitting adjustments herself. She's really talented and very pretty. It was the second time she called this week at home, she had to leave my new summer bonnet with Harry."

Rosie nodded, "Is that the nice girl who does the hats for the Chorus line too?" Dorothy accepted her most welcome cup of tea and nodded, "Yes, she also delivers to some of the others acts. The 'Nightingales' new bonnets were all supplied by her." Rosie eased back in her seat, "I'm surprised those old canaries can afford to use Madam Jacqueline's." Dorothy sat up, "Well done Rosie. I need to pay Madam Jacqueline for the stage costumes, so I'll have to visit the bank Friday afternoon and get the cash out."

Rosie sipped her tea, "So you'll be out all Friday afternoon and unavailable, if anyone asks?" Dorothy held her cup with both hands and said 'yes' quietly. There was a knock and Rosie opened it, smiling. She knew Dottie was expecting this visitor with some anticipation: yet another new hat!

John Milligan stood by the corner, near the small news stand, and read his newspaper keeping a close eye on the stage door. He scratched a couple of times and cursed the warm spring weather. His target had already entered the theatre and now he waited for her to re-emerge. He smiled and folded his paper as the young lady strode down the steps, clearly looking for a cab. But John waved the first one down and eased his bulk in and told the cabby to wait. She was now standing on the pavement right near the cab, looking a little disappointed.

He opened the door and leaned out, "Hello darling, remember me?" The young woman stared at him, nodded and gripped her handbag. "Get in sweetheart, we have something to discuss and I'm sure you'll want to discuss it in private. It concerns me keeping my mouth shut about your visit to that fucking Yankee Blackman. You see I don't think three and six is quite enough and I'm sure we can work something out." She slowly smiled and climbed into the cab.

Moses stepped from the doorway of the little tobacconist shop, pushing his new box of imported cigars into his coat pocket. He watched the cab turn into Wolfe Place and then saw the empty cab approaching and held up his hand. "So, that's where else you perform my little darling and why the discrete meeting with the odorous fat man? Interesting." He told the driver to follow that cab and there was ten bob in it. Moses slipped in, smiling. The driver flicked his whip and sighed, "The bloody second 'follow that cab' today! What the fuck was London coming too?"

CHAPTER 6. 'FOR THE FEMALE OF THE SPECIES IS MORE DEADLY THAN THE MALE.' Rudyard Kipling.

Harry stood looking at the naked dead man, sprawled on the bed, his face contorted with puddles of blood everywhere that covered the blankets and sheets. Especially the pile of pillows which had soaked up his blood really well. Dave tapped his notebook with his pencil, "The stiff's name is John Milligan, he was a petty criminal in his youth, but has been clean the last ten years – apparently. Worked as a kitchen porter at the Tabernacle Hotel. The old man on the desk downstairs said he returned to the lodgings [the place was really an up market 'doss house'] about six o'clock last night looking really happy which was unusual for him. Never saw him again, well not alive anyway. Says his young friend arrived this morning because he hadn't turned up for work, knocked and when he didn't get an answer peered through the keyhole and saw this." He gestured to the dead body with his pencil. "They called the local beat constable who did a good job. Got assistance from the nick and kept the witnesses in hand until they were taken there. We can interview them at our leisure."

"It's a right bleeding week for naked dead men ain't it." Edwin was searching the big wardrobe which lay open with its contents thrown about, "Someone really was looking hard for something. They didn't take their time turning the place over, did they? Must have been in a real hurry."

Dave sucked his pencil, "Well, considering they just cut open the stiff's neck I don't think they were going to hang about, would you?" Edwin had to agree with that.

Edwin continued searching amongst the chaotic mess, looking in open cupboards and drawers. He found nothing of interest. Then he saw a thin bright coloured, tin amongst the fat man's discarded underwear and picked it up and pulled the lid off. He chuckled, "Take a look at this Guv, the dirty old bastard has quite a collection of naked young girls and a couple of them were supplied by Reynolds's apparently." Harry asked how he knew that for certain and Edwin held one up, "On the back someone's written 'one shilling' from 'flash'.

Harry stared at the bedside table and pushed the two dirty glasses with his pencil. The scotch bottle was still half full. "He had a visitor. Get them bagged up for fingerprints." Then he looked closely at one glass and smiled, "Heads up boys, his visitor appears to have been a woman, there's lipstick on the glass. Not much but it's there."

Dave shook his head, "Could a woman inflict an injury like that? I mean he's a big man and they cut his throat real deep. Would a woman have that kind of strength and guts to do something like that? Also the bloody knife is missing, so they took it with them."

Harry peered closely at the body and could smell real bad body odour, the dead man really stank of perspiration. But there was another smell, much sweeter. "Unless he liked really feminine after-shave I can smell perfume on him." Harry said quietly.

Edwin, still flicking through the 'naughty' photographs said,

"Could be a real big tart with arms like a guerilla." Dave laughed at that. Edwin threw the box back on the floor and picked up the man's clothes which were tossed on the floor in a heap. He lifted the large trousers and felt in the pockets. "Has over ten bob on him. So robbery wasn't the motive." Dave agreed and said the clothes were clearly discarded in a hurry, was he about fuck someone? Edwin now chuckled, "Don't know, but someone certainly fucked him good and proper!"

Harry didn't smile, "Well someone was certainly looking for something by the state of this mess. But did they find it? I want the room searched again, and tell the boys to make a good job." Edwin agreed and called the two uniform lad's waiting outside the door. "You heard the governor, take the place apart, floorboards, cupboards, the bleeding bed and even window surrounds. Get to work lads!" The two constables pulled off their helmets and jackets and set to their given task.

Harry and Dave left Edwin to deal with the undertakers and doctor and walked down the stairs from the third floor and stopped by the front door. The uniform constable standing there called them over and gestured to a couple of young boys standing by the gate. "Those two want to talk to you Mister Hadden, They say John Milligan spoke to them yesterday afternoon, gave them a couple of pennies to fetch a cab for him which they did. They say they hung about deciding what to do with their unexpected riches and saw him putting a real well dressed, posh lady into the cab and wave her off."

"Fuck! That means the woman being the killer is all wrong. He must have been cut up after she left because he was still breathing when she went." Dave cussed and scribbled in his notebook. Harry – looking strangely relieved – told the constable to take the boy's details and he gave him a sixpence to hand to them for their help. He rubbed his chin, "So why was the big man murdered and by who?" He muttered to himself.

"Dave, get uniform to trawl the cab ranks and find the cabby who picked up the woman. We'll start with her. Why a supposed lady of quality would be visiting old John? Unless….It's our tart 'shy Mary' but why would she?" Harry said and the pair walked to the street corner, ignoring the crowds shouted questions. But they stopped when an old vagrant, sitting on a garden wall waved them over. "It's old Silas, he is a former Marine apparently."

Dave said and pulled a shilling from his pocket and pushed it into the old man's held out hand. "Thank you Mister Farmer." He whispered in a hoarse voice and scratched his filthy beard, looking around. "I saw the woman leave, a really pretty piece but didn't look happy. Far from it I'd say, but soon as she left a big black fellow went straight in there. He must have been just behind the fat man. He came out a few minutes later and walked off towards King Street, probably to grab a cab himself."

The detectives exchanged a glance and Harry asked if the man was well dressed and the vagrant nodded, saying he hadn't seen a 'toff' black fellow before. They watched the old man wander off and Dave shook his head, "That don't make sense, why did the stiff take off his clothes after the woman left? He must have been dressed to put her in the cab for Christ sakes; otherwise every body would have noticed him!" Harry nodded his agreement with that and hailed a passing cab. "Remember what old George said about the woman liking 'darkies', maybe she had a boyfriend or pimp who took exception to the fat man. Then there's the fact that she only went with wealthy clients, so why entertain John Milligan. He was just a kitchen porter living in slum digs. He certainly couldn't afford her prices. Now that bit definitely doesn't make sense."

They climbed in the cab and headed back to the nick. They would interview the lodgings clerk and Milligan's young friend from the hotel. The nervous clerk couldn't help much because he really knew sod all! But the young man – a certain Robert Hyde – had the detective's undivided attention with the story that he related between several cigarettes and two cups of tea.

Dave wrote his statement watching Harry dragging every little detail of his conversation with John Milligan out. It transpired that the fat man had confided to his young friend that he was about to come into some money – good money – and get to fuck a posh tart in the bargain. The young man had warned him about going through with his plan [John's plan] but he wouldn't listen. He would arrange to meet the woman outside the Paradise Theatre where John believed she worked and blackmail her into paying ten pounds and force her to fuck with him. The detectives both winced at the mention of the theatre and Harry now knew he would have to act. But they would wait until the Friday raid and catch everyone in one swoop.; Harry sighed heavily at that thought.

She lay in the warm bath and sponged herself carefully, paying particular attention to her crotch and stared at the late edition of the local newspaper and shuddered a little despite the warm water. The headlines were about the terrible murder of a local hotel kitchen porter. She eased herself up and gripped the sides of the bath, thinking about what had transpired during that fateful afternoon encounter with the horrible fat and smelly blackmailer. She remembered with some horror and disgust the feel of his hands on her breasts and bum. His pitiful thrusts and the feel of his cum inside her as she lay, almost silent, under his smelly bulk. At least the ordeal ended quite quickly as he struggled and couldn't raise his cock for another attempt. She had left his shabby dirty room with his pungent body odour still clinging to her. She wouldn't go through that ordeal again now; he was dead, murdered with his throat split open.

Now she shuddered and started to sob, thinking about Moses and his unrestrained anger and the action he had taken to retrieve the ten gold sovereigns. She had wanted none of that; she would have paid and suffered the loss. But Moses was a different kettle of fish. She knew full well that he had killed the fat man and now she would have to live with her silence on the matter.

Now a little better composed she eased from the bath and examined the bruises on her breasts and thighs. The fat man had been a brutal pig in taking her and she couldn't find any sympathetic thoughts about his violent passing. The big problem outstanding was that Moses couldn't find the ten sovereigns she had paid the dead man for his silence. How was that possible? Where could he have hidden them so well in such a short time?

Moses had made him strip and found nothing on him or his clothes. Refusing to say where they were, John had angered Moses and when angry, Moses was capable of anything: including savage murder. Then she wondered if Moses had indeed found the money and kept it for himself. She actually didn't care about Moses' dishonesty in the matter; she could suffer that loss, in payment of ridding herself of the nasty blackmailer.

She knew she should quit now, but the money was rolling in and the good life beckoned. Just a few more tricks and she could lay low for some months until all this blew over. Moses would take care of her, she could rely on him, after all he had killed for her. She wrapped her bath robe around and headed for the bedroom, her family would be assembling for the evening meal and she needed to act like nothing had occurred. Pouring herself a stiff whisky she stared at her refection in the bedroom mirror and wondered who exactly she was now. She heard the maid shouting that dinner would be served in half an hour.

Harry was disappointed in that the search of Milligan's dingy room had turned up nothing new or decisive. But Edwin had located the address for a certain 'Alabaster Sedgwick' in Eastham. He grinned and slapped a piece of paper on Harry's desk. "Got him!" Harry lifted the paper and was surprised, very surprised. He shook his head in some disbelief, "Fucking Father Alabaster Sedgwick! The fucking Parochial House at the bottom of the High Street." He rubbed his chin, "Now, I don't think our good father would hold a porn shoot there, so little wonder Flash recorded that they would use 'the other house'. All we need now is to find that bloody 'other house'."

Edwin grinned again, like a cat given a giant bowl of cream. "Done. I have that address too." Harry just nodded and stared up at the ceiling.

CHAPTER 7. 'CLOTHES MAKE THE MAN. NAKED PEOPLE HAVE LITTLE OR NO INFLUENCE ON SOCIETY.' Mark Twain.

Dorothy rushed back to the dressing room, full of excitement. The young woman from Madam Jacqueline's had just delivered her new stage costume for 'Miss Pandora and her magic box' show. Rosie slowly un-wrapped the costume as Dorothy quickly stripped naked. "I shouted to Reggie and Mister Sims, I want them to see it first. Uncle William and Harry are on their way, so when everyone's together I'll pose sitting on Pandora's magic box. Then that nice young photographer will take the pictures for the show's promotion. Get the kettle on Rosie, we are having visitors."

Rosie sighed, "For God sakes Miss! Get in the bleeding dressing room. What if someone waltzed in here without knocking? And there you are, standing in just your bleeding birthday suit!"

Dorothy smiled, "Well, they certainly wouldn't rush to the owner's office and complain would they?" She carefully grabbed the costume and disappeared into the small changing room leaving Rosie a little wide-eyed and frankly concerned. But before she could voice her thoughts, Reggie and Mister Sims appeared and they moved the magic trunk into position by the window.

Reggie was in his stage costume and looked magnificent and Mister Sims…well, he was 'wearing' his bandages as usual. "It's best by the window; the photographer says he needs all the light he can get." Reggie explained as Mister Sims's lifted the lid and peered in. Rosie lit the paraffin stove and placed the kettle on and giggled to herself. "That girl has bleeding balls of steel."

Young Reynolds's the photographer set up his equipment and smiled at everyone. Harry hadn't nicked him yet for his little pornography business and he didn't know that Harry was just waiting for Friday afternoon to pounce. Flash shouted "I'll take one of you solo sitting on the box. Then Mister Sims standing in the box. I'll follow that up with Reggie standing arms folded behind the box, then the team altogether. Is that OK?" Dorothy shouted back that was fine with her.

Uncle William and Harry arrived just in time: Rosie was dishing up the tea. Harry smiled at young Flash and for some reason that made Reynolds feel uncomfortable. Everyone gathered in front of the window for the well anticipated preview of 'Miss Pandora and her magic box'. They were not really disappointed. Just a little bit amazed……..

Dorothy walked from the little dressing room and sat on the box, smiling broadly. Then she noticed there was total silence in the place except for Reynolds flash pan igniting. 'For fuck sake I can sell these for a guinea a piece!' he thought and now was working at some speed to load the plates. 'If she turns around and shows that incredible arse, I'll get fucking thirty bob a print.' His happy thoughts were now running wild and he took a couple of deep breaths. She could earn him a fucking fortune and if she did some really naughty poses, he could fucking retire to the south of France.

It was Harry that broke the silence, he ran a hand across his face and managed a smile, restraining from laughing. "Dottie my innocent little sweetheart, I can tell you now, if you appear on a

London stage dressed like that, I would have no choice but arrest you for outraging public morals, public indecency and several other charges." He now laughed softly to himself.

Uncle William wiped his face and neck with his hankie and finally managed to say, "Dorothy Mary Hadden, take that disgusting dress….well whatever it is, off – now!" then a bit flustered, he added, "But not right now you naughty girl! Get back in the changing room. For heaven's sakes Rosie, do something!" A shocked Dorothy eased off the box and did a little twirl which made Reynolds break into a sweat with his hands trembling as he loaded the plates. 'For fuck sake, that arse could make a guinea a print on its own! Oh fucking thank you God!' For an aspiring pornographer he knew he had found his Holy Grail of making money: lots of it!

Dorothy gestured down her flimsy outfit and didn't smile, "You don't like it? Do you need a better view to make your minds up?" She turned around and everyone received a fine view of her incredible peach shaped bottom: the 'costume' was really totally transparent at the back and no panties had been supplied. Madam Jacqueline obviously thought Dottie would supply her own. Strangely enough, Dottie hadn't. In the excitement she had forgotten that one very important little thing.

There was total silence until Reynolds actually gasped and with shaking hands operated his camera quickly. That one pose alone would make him a small fortune and he thought seriously of proposing right here and now. But he had another problem: his fucking erection was killing him!

Rosie stepped forward with a dressing gown and draped it around a very disappointed Dottie's shoulders. Reggie stood in silence and Mister Sims noticed that his mouth was open. "What do you think big man?" He asked and Reggie whispered, "I think I've died and gone to heaven." Sims nodded at that and chuckled, folding his arms as Rosie marched the shocked and protesting Dorothy back to the changing room.

Sims saw the sad look on Reggie's face and tapped his arm, "Reggie, Dorothy is like Uncle William and Harry: they see the person and not the colour." The big man slowly smiled and wiped his face, he had never looked at young Dottie like this before or had such thoughts and feelings. He swallowed hard and mumbled

"Thank you mister Sims." But his heart was totally lost now and he didn't mind a single bit. But his bloody erection was killing him! Reynolds, leaning on his camera tripod gestured to Reggie and Sims, "We can still get your shots done lads. Take your position first please Mister Sims." Reggie was grateful for that, he needed to excuse himself for a moment or two and find some really cold water. Well, he actually needed ice-water if he was honest. What stuck in his mind were her nipples: "Like a blind cobblers thumb!" He muttered to himself.

Whilst that was going on, poor Uncle William had to sit down and gripped his cup of tea with both hands; they were trembling a little. A smiling Harry tipped some whisky from his hipflask into his cup. "I'm sure Rosie will make alterations to make the damn thing acceptable. I can't think what madam Jacqueline was thinking of." Uncle William sipped his tea and whisky mix and grunted, "Yes, it needs a decent pair of knickers and a bloody damn corset….If she showed that sweet little bum on a London stage, we would all be bloody arrested!"

Harry actually chuckled, "If she showed that bum on the stage, we would be killed in the damn rush." Uncle William looked a little puzzled and asked, "Rush for what?" Harry now laughed outright, "Men proposing bloody marriage!" Uncle William shrugged his shoulders and smiled a little, thinking that every dark cloud had a silver lining. "Next time I invite an eligible, very wealthy young bachelor over for dinner, she can wear that damn outfit and do some parlour tricks, what you think Harry?"

Harry sighed, "The bloody dining room would be knee deep in proposing men." They now both laughed and sipped their most welcome tea.

Dorothy sat, a little sad, and sipped her tea, occasionally glancing across to Rosie who kept smiling to herself and giggling a little. "It's not that bad Rosie, I'm sure you can make some alterations to make it acceptable to Uncle William and Harry. It was very expensive and I won't waste money."

Rosie looked up with a big grin on her face, "Bloody hell my darling, Mister Harry was right. If you wore this on stage, they would close the whole bleeding place down without a second thought and your poor bleeding Uncle would probably end up in the London Hospital with a nervous break-down!"

Dorothy slowly smiled to herself and whispered, "Well, I know for certain that Reggie liked it – liked it a lot – I could bloody see that he did!" It appears that Reggie's short costume kilt had betrayed what he exactly thought of her flimsy costume! Her eyes had widened at the time and she had some really strange thoughts and feelings about that discovery. She settled back in the chair and placed her cup down. Rosie was saying something about stitching silk panties into the thing, but her voice faded as a delicious but rather naughty daytime vision swept over her. She and Reggie were dancing close in a packed ballroom, their fingers entwined and bodies pressed against each other, slowing moving across the polished floor with grace and poise. Their eyes were locked together and their lips just inches from each other as the music played. That's when Dorothy noted they were both stark naked! The other patrons of this strange ballroom were clapping and cheering the pair as they glided across the room. Dorothy glanced down and whispered to the smiling Reggie, "I say darling, do you need a bleeding license for that?" He just grinned in reply.

"Well, we need some silk thread for this bleeding thing. I'll have to get some from old Maggie's haberdashery tomorrow; it'll cost at least ten bob Miss." Dorothy sat up and smiled at Rosie, "What's that Rosie." She asked, a little shocked at her dirty daydream. Rosie sighed and repeated herself and Dorothy agreed to spend the extra money. She folded her arms and thought about Reggie and it was quite pleasant, if a little erotic!

That night Dorothy stood in the wings watching the 'The Nightingales' leave the stage to modest applause, most of it through sympathy! Reggie joined her saying 'Good evening Miss Dorothy.' They both stood in silence for a few seconds and Reggie said quietly, "I really did like your costume Miss, if my opinion means anything to you."

Dorothy smiled and touched his bare arm. "Thank you Reggie, I'm glad someone liked it and your opinion is always of value to me." She didn't remove her hand and the pair smiled at each other. He looked about and whispered, "If I had my way, the only costume you would wear is your birthday suit." Dottie giggled, "That's very naughty of you Reggie, but I do appreciate the compliment and it would save me an awful large amount of money!" They both laughed and then moved to their opening stage marks. Big Tom was announcing the act and the 'professor' appeared pushing a reluctant pigeon into his Fez.

As they parted, Dorothy whispered, "Oh, by the way I really could see that you liked the costume or was it what was inside, you liked the look of?" Reggie just smiled and nodded. Then they were on the stage with the curtain rising and the audience applauding. 'Professor Dustin Potts' smiled at his two assistants and the show started with half a dozen pigeons appearing from his Fez! Sims smiled, watching the looks passing between Reggie and Dottie, and then disappeared into the big trunk for the next part of the show.

CHAPTER 8. 'CONFESSION IS GOOD FOR THE SOUL'. Anonymous.

Mary, originally dressed as a 17th Century witch, complete with broom and pointed hat, was now naked apart from the hat and the broom had been used by the perverted father for something completely different from sweeping the bloody floor! She was bouncing up and down on the happy old pervert in front of the quiet fire. He was gripping her slim waist and watching her breasts swaying as she rode him. He groaned a lot and thanked God on several occasions. Where he obtained the necessary two gold sovereigns from was anyone's guess. His Sunday plate collection usually amounted to around ten bob and that was on a good day.

They both stopped as if frozen, the door to the big reception room flew open and several police men rushed in followed by Harry, Dave and Edwin. Harry cursed loudly: they must be running late with the raid and clearly had missed Reynolds. But they gathered around the surprised pair in a loose circle and Harry removed his hat and said softly, "Hello Mary, I'm sorry love but you're bloody nicked!" Father Sedgwick groaned and cussed like a docker pissed up on a Saturday night. Not quite the acceptable language of a man of God. The pervy priest wouldn't actually be charged with anything, since hiring and fucking a 'brass' in the privacy of the Sunday School/Church Hall reception room, wasn't actually an offence in these times!

Mary just folded her arms and said quietly, "Hell Mister Hadden, you could have waited until the old boy finished. He'll probably want his fucking money back since he didn't cum!" The priest groaned again and Mary sighed, "Oh, forget I just said that." Edwin placed his jacket around her and she lifted off the priest who now smiled a little. He eased up on his elbows and weakly smiled at Harry, "Hello Harry, I hope this doesn't mean that my invitation for Sunday lunch is withdrawn?"

Harry just smiled and told the priest to get up and cover himself. He asked where Reynolds was. Mary answered that, accepting a cigarette from Edwin, "He's gone and pissed off Mister Hadden, he didn't want to hang about and now I know why." Harry rubbed his chin, it was clear that someone had tipped the photographer off and it appears it wasn't Mary. "We started early because he said he had another appointment." She added, smiling at young Edwin who found his tie and collar was now trying to strangle him!

Dave, scribbling in his notebook, asked if she knew where that appointment was. Mary laughed and flicked ash on the floor. "Oh yeah, I can tell you mate. Fucking Australia!"

She was escorted to the police carriage as Father Sedgwick hurriedly dressed. Dave sighed, "Where do you know the brass from Guv, if I may be so bold." Harry looked around the place and picked up the broom, then quickly dropped it, wiping his hand on the father's discarded cassock. "Oh, Mary works for Madam Jacqueline and deliveries the dresses and hats. She's a regular visitor to my house because Dottie orders lot's of ladies stuff from the shop. She also delivers stuff to the Paradise where I've seen her several times."

Dave sighed, "Not anymore." Harry just nodded and they slowly followed the others into the churchyard. That's when they noticed the two boys sitting on Miss Mable Doris Canning, no, not her personally: her large ornate tomb. Dave gestured to them, "Isn't that the two boys who told us about the posh woman, sorry, bloody Mary, getting into the cab outside Milligan's?" The boys sauntered over and the bigger of the two removed his rough cap and smiled, "Hello Mister Hadden sir, Was it a good bust? Did you get all the fuckers?" Harry winced at the boy's language but nodded. Dave chuckled, "Yeah, we got most of them, you cheeky little sod."

The smaller lad wiped his runny nose on his jacket sleeve and grinned, "We know you didn't bleeding get them all. The other two went half hour ago. Took a cab to…" He never finished because the other boy pushed him hard, "Frank, you fucking dimwit, we ain't got any fucking money yet!" The younger boy bowed his head and mumbled something about being sorry. The older boy just sighed, "Bleeding sorry won't put some grub on mum's table will it you dimwit." He turned to the highly amused Harry and shrugged his shoulders, "Sorry about that Mister Hadden. I'm still training the little fucker." Now both Harry and Dave laughed outright and Harry tossed a shilling to the boy who grabbed it with a big smile. "What have you got for us?" Harry asked, still chuckling.

"That bent photographer left in a real bleeding hurry. He was helped by a big black fella who carried some of his equipment and boy, they weren't bleeding happy about something. They were having a bit of a row; it was still going on when the cab arrived." Harry was now interested and asked if the boys heard the address given to the cab driver. He nodded, pushing the coin into his pocket and scratched his head, now not smiling, "It's hard to remember exactly Mister Hadden, you know, we were bleeding watching the dirty old father and the tart and…." Harry tossed him another shilling and boy snapped his fingers, "I just bleeding recalled Mister Hadden. They told the cabby it was the Paradise Theatre!"

Harry and Dave exchanged a look and Harry thanked the boys and headed for the remaining police carriage and told Pc Whitlock to make for the theatre. They jumped in and the carriage pulled away. Dave was still chuckling, "I think Charlie [the older boy] will teach young Frank [the younger one] how to get through this life and he'll do it really well." Harry had to agree with that. He stared out the window and saw Father Sedgwick chasing the boys around the graveyard with the broom. They were too fast for him and were sticking out their tongues and holding up two fingers, as they made off.

They arrived at the theatre and had one thought: was 'the big black fella' that the boys said was with Reynolds, was he the man who killed Milligan? Harry [and Dave of course] was really concerned about Dorothy and Rosie. They could have a killer in their rooms! Harry checked his service revolver and Dave did the same. They leapt from the cab, only stopping to toss the cabby his fare and ran up the steps. They made their way to Dorothy's dressing room and pulled their guns out with Harry reaching the door first, and found it wide open. Dave followed close behind. They stopped and lowered their guns and both sighed with real heartfelt relief. Dorothy –quite naked – ran straight to Harry and grabbed him, sobbing loudly while Dave – trying not to look at Dottie and failing miserably – walked slowly over to Reggie who was standing over Moses who was spark out on the floor, the big knife still clutched in his hand. Reggie let the kettle drop and almost smiled, "He didn't think I would really have a go at him armed with a kettle, so it was a lot easier than I imagined."

A sobbing Rosie grabbed up a dressing gown and pushed it on Dorothy who was calming down now her big brother was here. There was a smashed camera and tri-pod on the floor and the room stank of burnt flash powder. Dorothy pulled her dressing gown around and sat, still shaking while Rosie took the kettle [which had quite a dent in it!] and said she would 'make some fucking tea'.

"What the fuck happened here and where's Reynolds?" A grim Harry asked, replacing his revolver and gripping Dottie's hand tightly. Rosie – now a lot calmer – lit the small stove and wiped her tear stained face. "That bleeding snake Reynolds turned up offering our Dottie serious money to pose naked. He said he would pay two sovereigns for a session of photographs. But Dorothy told him to bugger off and that's when the big fellow pulled the knife and said he would cut my throat if she didn't pose!"

Dave was handcuffing the big man and checked him, saying "Reggie did a bloody good job, he's out cold!" He carefully picked up the knife and wrapped it in a rag from the stove. Rosie continued, "The bastard stuck the knife under my nose and told Dottie to bleeding choose: get naked and posing or watch him slice my bleeding throat open!" Dorothy interrupted, "I had no bloody choice, so I stripped off and that seemed to calm him down. [Becoming calm with Dorothy taking off her clothes wouldn't happen to many men...] Reynolds was shaking and shouting, saying this wasn't in the effing plan, so I don't think he knew what the big man was up too."

Dorothy gripped her brother's hand and then wiped her tear stained face, "Reynolds took some pictures at the big man's insistence. It was horrible, I had to bend over the chair and open…..” She stopped talking as Harry stroked her hair. Rosie filled the teapot with tea leaves and took up the story, “Then there was a knock at the door and I shouted bleeding ‘ENTER!’ I really don’t know why! And it was Reggie and the big man threatened him with the knife soon as he came in. I couldn’t believe my bleeding eyes when Reggie calmly picked up the kettle and threw the hot water at him. Then – still can’t believe it – wacked the bastard right across the head with the kettle! He went down like a bleeding sack of shit!”

Reggie smiled a little, “I did some boxing before Miss Dorothy got me this job, so I pretty well knew that I could handle him, big as he is.” Clutching her dressing gown, Dorothy eased from the chair as Rosie announced the tea was made. She placed both arms around Reggie’s neck and kissed him. To say he was surprised was an understatement, but, boy, did he smile when he realized her dressing gown had come open! Dottie mumbled ‘thank you’ several times and gripping her robe sat back down. Rosie handed around the tea and grabbed Reggie too, giving him a smacker which lasted far more that it should have. Strangely enough, Reggie didn’t mind.

Big Tom appeared in the doorway and scratched his chin looking at the smashed equipment and the big man laid on the floor. He slowly smiled, “Ah, you are practicing for the new show Miss Hadden. It looks quite exciting….” Harry didn’t let the little man finish and asked him to send the stage hand Arthur to fetch assistance from Brick Lane nick. Big Tom – a little puzzled – nodded and wandered off, shouting for the boy who knew how to hide from any kind of real work.

Dave prodded the unconscious Moses with his boot and asked what happened to Reynolds’s. He was a little concerned about the big man: he should have come around by now.

Rosie now chuckled, “He must have panicked seeing the big knife being waved around by that nutter and he grabbed up his bag and ran….” She now laughed and pointed at the small dressing room door, “And hid in bleeding there!” Harry walked over to the door and rattled the handle: it was obviously locked from the inside. “Come out Flash, it’s no point staying in there. There’s no other door and no window mate. So unlock the bloody door and come out, there’s a good man. You won’t face any charges for what the lunatic with the knife did." There was no answer and Harry sighed. "Is there another key?"

Rosie rummaged around the stove and in her bag. She shook her head, "Sorry Mister Hadden, the only key I think is in the lock and the spare's bleeding in there too. Sorry." Reggie walked over and asked if Mister Hadden wanted it open and Harry nodded, "Yeah, let's get the idiot out of there."

Reggie simply put his shoulder to the door with some force and it crashed open prompting Rosie to whisper in Dorothy's ear, "Now there's a decent big man that's useful for a lot of things." And winked: Dorothy sipped her tea and smiled.

Everyone stared into the small room: it was empty!

Reggie stared about inside with Harry and said quietly, "Now that's one vanishing trick that definitely should be in a show." Everyone agreed with that. Dorothy checked the room out and whispered to Harry, "Its bloody impossible Harry! I mean, we know how Sims pulls off our vanishing tricks, but this is simply incredible. Where did Reynolds go?"

Harry rubbed his chin and muttered, "Now that Dottie is a bloody good question, but I have no answer unless....." he stopped in mid sentence and shook his head, lowering his voice, "Unless he was capable of time-travel. Remember Jericho said if someone has a time control device they can simply vanish from sight, anywhere." Dorothy nodded and pair returned to the others where both Reggie and Dave were bent over Moses. Dave looked up and shook his head, "There's blood coming from his nose and left ear. I think he's dead Guv."

Harry saw the look on Reggie's face and gripped his shoulder, "It's OK Reggie, you killed him in self-defense of the girls. That's allowed in law. So don't worry about it. No jury in the world would convict you, adding to that, you didn't mean to kill him, did you?" Reggie nodded slowly and stood, he was clearly upset at this turn up. Dorothy gripped his arm and said softly, "You did the right thing Reggie, that mad bastard could have killed Rosie...or me, or...." She took a breath, "Or raped us if you hadn't done what you did."

Harry agreed with his sister and told Dave to fetch the police ambulance, but heavy boots and the shouting of Inspector Hadden's name cancelled that order. The boys from Brick Lane nick had arrived. Dave stood and lit a cigarette, "Gov, the bleeding paperwork alone on this will take us a week."

Sadly, Harry knew he was right!

Dorothy was still gripping Reggie's arm and the pair smiled at each other which didn't go un-noticed by the astute Harry. But he muttered: "Let the cards lay where they fall." He smiled a little, but with a big sigh.

CHAPTER 9. 'THE DEVIL DOESN'T COME TO YOU WITH A RED FACE AND HORNS, HE COMES DISGUISED AS EVERYTHING YOU'VE EVER WANTED.' Oscar Auliq-Ice.

Noah Whorton sat cross-legged with his back to the rear wall of his caravan and held the ancient book open on his thin knees. The five people crammed into the small caravan where all listening with real interest and in total silence. Noah was loudly speaking in Latin, which the book had been written in some nine hundred years ago. He stopped speaking and stared at the faces of his 'congregation'. "There you have it brothers and sisters. Our master's promise in his own words. What was written in this ancient book is as good today, as it was when written. No hell for followers of the master. No judgment by the cursed angel of death who has never been human, so how dare the creature judge us humans!"

There was a murmur of agreement amongst his 'congregation' and Noah slowly closed the book and kissed it. He placed it back in its metal tin and turned the key, which always hung around his neck on a gold chain. He stood and held his arms aloft, "Brothers and sisters let us praise the master and celebrate all his dark works!" Everyone rose as one and started to chant the master's name, whilst a couple bottles of whisky appeared and were passed around. One young woman knelt down and gripped the cock of the nearest man. They were all, of course, stark naked!

The orgy was in full swing when loud knocking disturbed the party and the nearest man to the door, opened it slightly and turned to Noah, who had his grand-daughter bouncing up and down on him with some enthusiasm. "It's bloody Sigmund, he says it urgent!" The old man nodded and 'Sigmund' slipped in and squeezed past the others and knelt down by Noah who was telling the girl to speed up. Sigmund smiled at her and said "Hello Tess, I see the old bugger is in good health." The girl gasped, rocking back and forth, "He certainly is, he's already had Morag!"

"What is so bloody urgent that it can't wait until we finish the celebration of the master?" Noah muttered, caressing Tess's big breasts which were now filled with milk betraying her 'delicate' condition. Sigmund didn't smile and ran a hand over his sweaty face, "That twat Henry is back. Says Moses is probably dead and he had to leave in a hurry. Says that cunt Harry Hadden busted them all, so there's no more money from the porn and bloody prostitution rings you set up. Sorry boss."

Old Chanter gave Tess's bum a slap and told her to fuck someone else, this was business and he needed to deal with it. She – reluctantly – climbed off him and found another man quickly. Noah grabbed up his big coat and pipe and the pair headed for the door and stood at the back of his wagon. Noah lit his pipe, thinking. Had he made a mistake sending that arsehole Cope's soul to the master? His dark thoughts were disturbed by Sigmund who smoked a smelly cigarette and said softly, "The twat said it all started when a body was found in his hallway. He believes Moses dumped it there as some kind of sick joke. I have no bloody idea why the loony would do that?"

Noah sucked on his pipe, "Brother Moses always had a warped mind, but he sent many a deserving soul to the master. If he is dead, we will celebrate his return to the master. But we now have the problem of what to do with Henry Reynolds and can he be still of use to us?"

Sigmund grunted, "Chanter, he always made money for the brotherhood with his skills."

Chanter sighed, "Alright, alright, tell him to visit 'the voice' in York City. The voice will set him up with a new identity and equipment. Give him fifty pounds to recruit girls and tell him it's his last chance to succeed. Go on." Sigmund nodded and threw his cigarette butt down. "There is a small bonus to all this Chanter." He smiled and pulled the little magazine from his pocket, adding, "I know how much you love that bastard Hadden, but take a look at this. It's a sample, Reynolds's says it will sell like good opium and having read it, I agree and will really get up Hadden's fucking nose!" Noah took the magazine and chuckled, "At the least the twat has talent and an eye for making money. Tell him I love this and get his arse to York City. Now!"

Sigmund walked off laughing and Noah finished his pipe and with a small smile returned to the orgy. He would drag Tess off whoever was fucking her and finish what he was doing before the interruption. He had executed Cope because he tried to fuck the little girl without permission. Cope had been a stranger in the village and somehow conned his way into the big house and the family nursery. Chanter had seen it all with his 'third eye' – an amazing gift from the master for all his loyal service – and decided Cope was a perfect gift for the master to enjoy. Besides, he had interfered with the brotherhood's plans for that little girl. Her 'doting' nanny was a member of Chanter's Coven and had already started work on the child. They rarely failed when they grabbed them so young. Another five years and she would have been initiated into the brotherhood. Noah chuckled, 'with all these bloody Suffragettes about, we may have to call it a 'Personhood'.

He dragged Tess from a disappointed fellow, who of course, said nothing and bent her over his bunk. He smiled as he thought of the great Inspector Harry Hadden squirming and cussing as he read Reynolds new magazine. Noah thrusted slowly and whispered, "The fucking little lap dog of that big cunt Jericho Tibbs!"

The topic of conversation at the Hadden's dinner this night was the vanishing pornographer Reynolds, well, until Uncle William finished his soup and chuckled to himself. Dorothy asked what was so funny and Uncle William sighed. "My dear girl, your dressing rooms are part of the old building, built in early part of the last century and it was really a brothel – but they did put on the odd show – the knocking shop was called 'Paradise on Earth' [so that's where the theatre got its name from!] And there were little tunnels and secret rooms all over the place so that the madam's could keep an eye on the girls.... And allow some special clients to view the entertainment on offer. I would slap two gold sovereigns down now that if I check your little private dressing room, there would be a spy hole or secret door."

Strangely enough, no-one took the bet on and Uncle William would check her dressing room in the morning. The conversation then changed to how the hell Reynolds's knew it was there! Uncle William didn't know the answer to that, but two people at the theatre might know, after all they had worked there for years. Mr. Skoles and Sean, the stage door keeper. He had been there since he was a boy and must know the place like the back of his hand whilst Skoles had certainly worked there for almost a quarter of a century.

Dorothy was not happy at this revelation and voiced her fears. "What if some dirty sod has been peeping in on me? I mean, I'm naked in there sometimes." Harry smiled at her, "We'll check the place out tomorrow and if there is any kind of peep hole will seal it up for good." That didn't comfort Dottie much as she thought about the men who could have seen her naked over the year she has worked for Uncle William and used that dressing room: sometimes having sex with Rosie!

Harry explained that the case papers went to the superintendent and old man Taylor [the superintendent] had shouted "If Miss Hadden was my young daughter, I would have done more than just batter the bastard with a damn kettle, I would have shot him!" So there were certainly no charges against Reggie, who sitting next to Dorothy just smiled, then grinned when she squeezed his hand under the table and whispered "Thank you Reggie" yet again. Miss Hadden was certainly thinking of ways to thank her and Rosie's savior which her Uncle and brother may not approve of! Rosie had placed an idea in her head when the pair had a private and quiet conversation about Reggie. Dorothy just had to smile and then 'tut-tut' a lot, but she agreed with Rosie's crazy and naughty idea!

Harry spoke about 'shy Mary' who was on remand in the notorious Newgate Prison and charged with several counts of prostitution and more importantly 'accessory to willful murder'. She would appear at crown court and could be hanged if found guilty. He didn't give much for her chances since Moses was dead and couldn't tell the court the part she played in his crime, if any.

Dorothy made everyone smile [except Harry and Uncle William] when she announced that she would be happy to appear as a 'character' witness for the girl. Uncle William ended that idea by simply saying "NO."

Harry spoke quietly with Dorothy outside her bedroom door, he needed to confess something and Dottie listened carefully, Harry leaned against the door and took a little breath, "Dottie darling, I need to confess something that weighs heavy on my heart." Dottie touched his face and smiled, "What is it dear Harry?" He took a deep breath now and said, "I doubted you Dottie – just for a very short time – I doubted your word, your virtue, your….Well, now I feel rotten and please do forgive me?" Dorothy chuckled and kissed his cheek, "I' haven't a blooming clue what you are on about dear brother, but I can forgive you just about anything. Love you." and kissed him again. Harry whispered, "Love you Dottie." As she closed the door and he walked away a much happier – and relieved – man.

Dorothy leaned against the door and took a couple of breaths and smiled, whispering to herself, "Oh darling Harry you have really no idea about your little sister and it will always stay that way. If you ever turned away from me I would simply die."

CHAPTER 10. 'THE SHOW MUST GO ON.' Anonymous?

Dorothy sat in the cab and peered out the window at the busy streets; she had never been in this part of the east end before and felt like a tourist in her own city. It appeared to house everyone from the British Empire with a lot of people from China thrown in! She saw Indian gentlemen with bright turbans, women in beautiful colourful Sari's, Jewish men in big black hats and long beards and several African men and women. She assumed the poor whites were from Eastern Europe and perhaps refugees from Tsarist Russia. There were numerous Chinamen [and women] everywhere and she knew that Lime House was a melting pot of people's and cultures. The cab stopped outside a big tenement and the driver pulled open the door, hat in hand.

He looked concerned, "Are you sure this is the address miss?" he looked about keeping a firm grip on his whip. Dorothy eased from the cab and also looked about. "Yes, if this is Gladstone House." He sighed as she paid him and said quietly, "As arranged, I will return in two hours, that's exactly two hours from now." He tapped his pocket watch and added, "That'll be just after four o'clock. Now are you sure I can't just run you back home?"

Dorothy smiled, genuinely touched by his concerns for her welfare and safety, "No, I'm visiting a very dear friend and will certainly be safe whilst they're around!" The cabby nodded, replacing his cap, "So be it misses, but this is not a safe area for a pretty young woman of class like you." He looked about and lowered his voice, "Young white women disappear from around here and God knows what happens to the poor girls, so watch yourself and only use licensed cabs if need you one before I return."

He climbed back up into driver's seat and grabbed the reins, "I'll be back on time miss, perhaps a little early so that you don't have to stand in the street waiting. If you don't appear I will call the coppers!" Dorothy had to smile at that and waved the dear man off. She turned and saw two black men sitting on the steps of the tenement, they were both in their late twenties or thirties, but appeared quite well dressed for the area. One stood up and Dorothy realized he easily matched Reggie in height and size. He pushed back his bowler hat and smiled a little. He was certainly a handsome man with that smile of his. "And what is a pretty piece of cake like you doing in this dump?" He removed his hat and did a wonderful bow. Dorothy had to smile and asked if they knew Reginald Hepple-White.

Keeping his hat in both hands the big man nodded, "Are you the white lady magician that Reggie works with? You certainly match his description of her." Dorothy nodded and asked if he was in. The big man pointed to himself, "Aloysius Cadbury at your service and like the chocolate, dark, sweet and irresistible!" He bowed again. That made Dorothy laugh and she did a little curtsy which made both men chuckle. Aloysius gestured to the door, "Room 7 on the second floor Miss Hadden and if any of the cocky lads get out of order with you, just say you're a friend of 'Ally the blade' and they'll treat you like the Princess of Wales!" Dorothy winced a little at the mention of a blade and wondered how the man got such a nickname, then remembering the crime –ridden area she was currently in, really didn't want to know the answer! She thanked the pair and walked quickly up the steps, knowing full well that both men were watching her.

She was really surprised the hallway was clean with a notice board and boxes for mail. She stopped briefly to read the notices and found people advertising all kinds or good and services. Then she really smiled, someone had pinned Reggie's story [from the local paper] of the fight in her dressing room on the board. With a smile she headed up the stairs and knocked at No.7. There was no answer so she called out her name. She heard movement and the door slowly opened.

Dorothy actually wasn't surprised and she managed to smile, then giggled as Rosie pulled the door open and gestured her in. Rosie was clutching a huge red dressing gown around herself and just smiled too. "It's a bit big for me – it's Reggie's – we weren't expecting a proper lady like you to show up here." Dorothy nodded and saw Reggie standing in the doorway of the bedroom, looking quite sheepish and perhaps a little embarrassed. He was apparently naked apart from a bright red towel wrapped around his lower part. Dorothy smiled, "I popped around to say a proper thank you with a little present."

Rosie chuckled and sat on the big black sofa, "I did the bleeding same darling!" Dottie grinned, "I think I know what the present was." She said quietly and they all laughed. Rosie jumped up, "I'll put the bleeding kettle on." Dorothy agreed with that and removed her hat as Reggie mumbled about putting on some clothes. Dorothy stopped him and unbuttoned her coat slowly, "I best give you my present too." She said softly and let her coat drop to the floor. She was naked apart from her boots!

Now Rosie really did laugh and tossed her dressing gown away. "Sod the tea darling! Come on." She grabbed Dottie's hand and both strolled past the astonished [but smiling] Reggie into the bedroom. He dropped the towel and nodded, closing the door. Both girls leapt on the bed, giggling and Dorothy actually gasped as Reggie walked towards them: "Sweet Jesus! Did you borrow that from a bleeding horse?" she exclaimed, but Rosie just laughed and rummaged on the bedside cabinet, holding up a small jar; "I have the magic potion!" she declared and unscrewed the cap on the jar of Vaseline. The girls spent several minutes swapping the monster between their mouths before Rosie lubricated it, her fanny and then Dorothy's with plenty of the 'magic potion' and a very happy Reggie mounted them, taking turns with each. Dottie found herself face down, gripping a couple of pillows with her arse in the air and Reggie pounding her from behind. She was having quite an orgasm with Rosie beneath her, feasting on her 'oyster' as Rosie called it. Then the girls swapped over and Reggie fucked Rosie hard and fast on her back whilst 'French Kissing' Dorothy who was sitting on Rosie's happy face! Then to everyone's surprise, there was a loud snapping noise and the old bed parted into two pieces with the headboard now lying flat on the floor. They were all laughing, with Rosie wiping tears from her face as they managed to crawl from the wreckage of the old bed: under the weight and activity of the threesome, it had simply collapsed. They sat on the floor gripping each other with some unrestrained amusement. Finally Dottie pushed Reggie on his back and climbed on him, "Now where the hell were we!" Rosie grinned, "You know what they say about falling off a horse?" Dottie, now moving back and forth with some vigor chuckled, "I certainly do and he's certainly some kind of bloody stallion!"

Dorothy had discovered that Reggie was a big man in all respects and she was delighted about that, but had been a little afraid and nervous that she couldn't cope, and was very appreciative of all the help Rosie gave her and things certainly worked out alright. Reggie had taken turns to finished in both of the women and lay knackered on the floor, even a hot cup of tea laced with whisky couldn't get the 'monster' to raise its head. So they kissed their farewells and the girls helped each other to dress and left.

The girls stood arm in arm on the pavement and waited for the arranged cab. They were both smiling and still laughing about their visit to Reggie. "He said that was the best presents he has ever received in his entire life." Dottie adjusted her hat and knew that both of them would need a hot bath and really liked the idea of sharing one with Rosie, whose knowledge on enjoying sex was quite a revelation. The things the pair had indulged in with happy Reggie and each other was like the stories in those naughty 'Penny Dreadful's' which were so popular with readers who liked something on the 'Dark Side'.

Dorothy declared later 'that she was now a sexual Suffragette!' She didn't just want the damn vote, she wanted [no, demanded] a good shagging as a right for every woman! Rosie – laughing –

pointed out that if they ever marched, the bleeding banners would make interesting reading. And get them arrested!

"Penny Dreadful's' were risqué underground magazines of the late Victorian and Edwardian era. They contained 'shocking' crimes and gossip that the main stream papers and magazines certainly wouldn't publish!" SJW.

But the most important lesson Dorothy received was Rosie's knowledge about contraception and in particular 'the Dutch Cap' method which allowed a man to finish inside the women with [apparently] little fear of pregnancy. Dorothy definitely had a visit to an amicable chemist [Rosie recommended one] on her agenda. But for this afternoon condoms were in fashion. Well, only one actually, it was re-usable and Reggie nicknamed it 'Geronimo' because that's what he shouted [with some joy] as he mounted the girls. Dorothy was amazed at its length: it was about the same size as one of her long evening gloves, used for the Opera, balls and proper theatre!

Rosie thought it was the same size and material that vet's used for gloves to examine horses!

The cab pulled up and the driver looked quite relieved to find Dorothy standing there and upon seeing Rosie, believed she was 'the friend' the 'lady' was visiting. Rosie's appearance and clothes would be in keeping with the area and she would certainly pass un-noticed on these streets.

Dorothy and Rosie exchanged several secretive hot kisses in the cab before reaching the theatre. Dorothy grabbed her hand and they ran up the steps together. They needed to arrange the collection of props for the premiere opening of 'Miss Pandora and her magic box' which was opening at the small Victoria Theatre this very evening.

Sims had noticed the change in the relationship between Dottie, Rosie and Reggie. But he just ruefully smiled; the little girl he had doted on for years and loved dearly was now a woman. He also really liked Rosie and Reggie and so said nothing about what he knew to anyone. Not that he talked to many people! But he did wonder if the clever and astute Harry had, or would catch on. The Stage manager looked a little concerned, but did smile a lot, as he spoke with 'Miss Pandora' just before he announced the act. He wiped his face and stared hard at her costume and wondered if there were any plain clothed police officers in the crowd. Still, he admitted to himself, his own Chorus Line didn't wear much more and her 'naughty bits' did had some reinforced cover on them. Finally he made his decision and the act hit the stage, before a packed audience at seven o'clock that evening. "The fucking show must go on." He reasoned to himself.

There was thunderous applause and lots of 'wolf-whistles' as the curtain rose and Dorothy went into her act. For most of the men in the audience, Dorothy could have stood and read out loud the obituary column of the local paper: and they still would have enjoyed the show. But they [and everyone else] were soon mesmerised, fascinated and somewhat amazed by the 'tricks' on show. No-one had a damn clue how Dorothy preformed the broken vase trick and it received massive applause.

Titus carried out a large Egyptian vase and placed it down, then lowered it so Dorothy could run a sword around the apparently empty inside as the audience watched in near silence. There were gasps and shouts as Sims [the mummy] appeared from a large sarcophagus which was placed by the front of the stage. He really over-acted just lifting the lid and stepping out, but the audience loved it. With some agility and dexterity he slipped inside the vase and it was stood upright and Titus placed a thick red cloth over it and stood back. Dorothy made some loud incantations, walking around the pot, gesturing and bowing to the ancient Gods of the Nile. Then at her bidding, Titus produced a large, evil golden axe and smashed it down upon the cloth covered vase. He did this two or three times as the crowd screamed and gasped.

Titus stood back and Dorothy begged the Gods for mercy on the poor soul of the mummy and slowly the red cloth began to move and lift. Slowly it raised a couple of feet in the air whilst the audience held its breath in silence, then the cloth fell away and the mummy jumped to his feet and bowed – really over-acting this time!

The crowd went nuts and the noise was almost deafening. Mr. Donald Yates [the stage manager] wiped his spectacles and face in utter amazement, in twenty years of music hall, he had never seen anything like it. Nor – apparently – had the crowd who gave 'Miss Pandora and her magic box' an incredible five encores. The first time it had ever happened at the small theatre. That didn't go un-noticed by Mr. Yates who was already consulting his pocket diary, working out how many dates he could offer Miss Pandora. What surprised him was her lack of a manager or agent. It was the first time he had direct dealings with a female over a Music Hall act!

Harry and Uncle William quickly joined the modest celebration in Dorothy's dressing room after the show [they had been in the front row] and Harry surprised everyone by producing a cold bottle of champagne and Uncle William the glasses. The toast was the King [of course] and Miss Pandora and her team. Dottie smiled and lifted her glass to Rosie and Reggie, if they could find time to come together again, they would have a real celebration and champagne wouldn't be needed. The crowd streamed from the theatre after a good evening's entertainment.

A certain retired naval captain – Mister John Stubbs – had left his private box and waited for a cab. He finally managed to find an empty one and told the driver 'Buckingham Palace' and climbed in. The driver shrugged his shoulders and would drive to the police gate in Grosvenor Place. If he's a nut, they can sort it out.

Captain Stubbs paid the cabby and waited for the policeman on duty to open the black metal gate. The cabby blew his nose into a crisp white hankie and watched, a little surprised, as the constable saluted the man and said 'good evening sir'. Captain Stubbs made straight for the private apartments of the King, slapping a rolled up magazine against his leg. Having been 'friends' and a servant of the King for almost thirty years: he knew full well what 'Bertie' liked and he had just seen it.

CHAPTER 11. 'IT DOESN'T MATTER WHAT YOU DO IN THE BEDROOM AS LONG AS YOU DON'T DO IT IN THE STREET AND FRIGHTEN THE HORSES.' Old Edwardian saying – apparently.

Rosie and Dottie lay sprawled out on the bed, both naked, with their backs to the big dark headboard and shared a cigarette and glass of whisky. Dorothy ran a hand down Rosie's happy face. "Now that was bloody incredible darling, but I really miss a big cock!" Rosie chuckled and drew on the cigarette as Dottie sipped the whisky. "I have to agree on that my love, 'touching velvet' is wonderful but I do love a big cock and a man who knows how to use it!" They giggled together and Dottie smiled to herself. She had several lesbian encounters at her posh school, but nothing like what happened when Rosie took her.

"I suppose we are part- time bleeding lesbians." Rosie muttered and they swopped over, with Dottie cautiously trying the remains of the cigarette and quite liked it but coughed a couple of times. "I think the expression is bisexual my dear." Dottie corrected her and Rosie grunted – a little puzzled – "What, like you mean both men and women can ride the same bicycle?"

Dorothy could only smile and mutter, "That's bleeding near enough!" and they both laughed again with Rosie lifting her blouse watch from the bedside table, she smiled at Dottie and finished the whisky. "It's almost one o'clock dear, and we have a little time for a bit more fun. Are you game?" Dorothy nodded, handing her the cigarette to stub out in the shoe-polish tin lid that was the ashtray. Rosie grabbed her and whispered, "Now this is really dirty but you'll love it, rollover."

Dorothy rolled onto her stomach and felt Rosie pulling her bum cheeks apart and so she lifted up on her elbows, a little shocked but still game. "I do hope you rinse your mouth before you kiss me or anyone else." Dottie murmured as Rosie went to work with some determination and real delight. Dorothy gasped a little; she certainly never had another woman's tongue buried in her 'brown flower' before and she loved it!

"Touching velvet was a Victorian expression for having lesbian sex and a 'brown flower' was a woman's anus – should you wonder." SJW.

Dottie was groaning a little with real pleasure and wondered why Rosie had stopped, then she heard the footsteps and both turned as the bedroom door swung open and the man stood there, hat in hand. "Fuck me Rosie, I suspected you were seeing someone on the side, but I'm truly happy it's a right bit of raspberry jam. God girl, you had me fucking worried there!" With real relief showing on his face, the big rough man walked in and sat on the old chair by the window. "Ain't you going to introduce me to the pretty little raspberry jam darling?"

Rosie just sighed, "Albert, this is Dottie, a close friend of mine; we work together at the Paradise. Dottie this is my bleeding old man Albert. There, now we all know each other." Still a bit shocked, Dottie smiled and said very quietly "Hello Albert, lovely to meet you at last." That made Albert laugh and he tossed his hat on the floor and pulled down his braces. He said to Rosie, "She's a good 'un, she is. Since you're in your birthday suit and clearly up for it, you can pretend its bleeding Saturday night and let me have my treat." He pulled off his shirt and vest and smiled again at Dottie, "You'll excuse us whilst I fuck the missus and I'll really bleeding enjoy it with you watching darling."

Dorothy found herself nodding and then really stared at Albert as his trousers and underpants came off. She ran a hand over her face: little wonder Rosie could handle Reggie's big cock with ease, bloody Albert was built like a breeding stallion! She sat on the chair –still naked – and watched with real pleasure and sexual excitement as Albert mounted Rosie and basically, to use the naughty colloquial expression, he fucked her brains out. Rosie screaming, moaning, gasping and swearing [a lot of swearing] was the evidence for her conclusion in this matter. They changed positions a couple of times and Dorothy took the small whisky bottle from the bedside cabinet and poured herself a glass and enjoyed a cigarette with it.

Albert groaned and thanked God, then rolled off Rosie, who lay back breathing deeply. Albert pulled himself up on his elbows and asked for the whisky bottle which Dottie handed to him. He took a swig and handed it to Rosie. Albert took a deep breath and smiled, "Now darling [he patted the bed] do you want to take Rosie's place?"

Rosie swigged the bottle and gave Albert a slap, "You can't dump your load in her, you'll have to bleeding pull out, like you use to before we got married." Albert shrugged his shoulders, "That's OK with me, but if she wants I'll do Greek on her. She should be ready [laughing] after what I saw you doing to her bloody brown flower!" Rosie slapped him again, "No way, you'll bleeding split her, she's not ready for a big one in there, yet." Dottie stood and climbed on the bed saying softly, "Withdrawal is fine by me." Albert chuckled and patted Rosie, "Sit on the chair and watch darling….and don't finish the bloody whisky or fags."

Rosie grunted and sat on the chair, smiling a little as Albert serviced what he called 'his little bit of raspberry jam'. And the 'Jam' loved it. Like Rosie, she screamed, groaned and cussed as Albert worked his own kind of magic. Dottie experienced a couple of big orgasms and screamed the place down, scratching Albert's back [which he didn't mind] kicking her legs about which actually trembled afterwards. He kissed her forehead and whispered, "That's lovely girl, but I have to finish before me bleeding balls burst!" Dottie managed to gasp a 'yes' and Albert pulled from her and she quickly knelt before him, mouth open. Albert was more than happy as he watched 'the raspberry jam' take the lot in her mouth and then wash it down with what remained in the whisky bottle. He stroked her face with a big grin. "I abide with the old saying, my darling: It doesn't matter what you do the bedroom as long you don't do it in the street and frighten the bleeding horses!" They all laughed at that and the afternoon's sexual entertainment had come to an end.

Dottie stayed for tea with the McHannon's – they had fish and chips – and caught a cab quite late, for home. To say that she had been sexually satisfied by the big rough man was an understatement. It had been agreed to meet up again – on Sunday afternoon – because that's when Rosie's two boys's played football for the local church team. They [the boys] would be gone all afternoon. Dorothy waited in real anticipation for that Sunday afternoon.

She really needed a hot bath because she actually stank of sex. Ellen [her maid] didn't think it odd that she [Dottie] ordered a bath as soon as she arrived home. The Hadden's family dinner was disturbed that night by a visitor. This was really unexpected: it was an equerry from the King himself!

Captain Stubbs apologized for disturbing their meal and relayed his message to a very amazed and frankly shocked Hadden family. Miss Hadden – as Miss Pandora – was requested to perform her magic act at a private party which the King was hosting for some of his closest friends!

Uncle William had to sit down and have a large glass of dark rum to placate his nerves and sipped it with delight and real pride. His darling girl was going to perform for the King!

Captain Stubbs explained the royal protocols for such a private performance and added that the fee for the night was thirty pounds which would be paid in gold sovereigns. For some reason that made Harry smile.

"That would be about £3000 in today's money." SJW.

Harry was standing, hand on chin, staring at the big chalk board on the wall of his office. It contained the five major cases that CID was currently working on. The first was a simple larceny that had gone wrong and the robber had smacked the poor elderly shopkeeper with a crow-bar. The old man was still unconscious in Eastham infirmary and if the doctors were right, he wouldn't recover and it would be a murder hunt. The description of the assailant could match a couple of thousand Dockers and so Harry had little expectation of a quick arrest.

The second was straightforward murder. Two thieves had fallen out over the split of their ill-gotten gains [from robbing a post office] and one had stabbed the other to death and ran off. He was believed to be hiding out on Forest Gates ground. The suspect was a certain Jonah Hesston from Woolwhich and the dead man's brother-in-law. East end families being what they are, his sister had said nothing about the killing of her husband!

The third one troubled Harry. The body of an infant was found half buried in St. Giles churchyard and the post-mortem couldn't ascertain the cause of death. The current theory was a sad, grief stricken unmarried mother had interned her dead infant in church grounds herself. Normally the church wouldn't allow a 'bastard' to be buried in sacred grounds. He had described the case to Dottie and Rosie when they asked about it and the pair had cried for nearly an hour.

The fourth case was a little interesting, a dead body found

floating in the river Thames. The man was stark naked and had nothing to identify him except a fabulous tattoo of Christ on the cross. The cause of death was obvious and that's why it was a murder inquiry. Someone had shot him through heart at close range. The bullet type was known too, it came from a hunting rifle! Few people from the east end went hunting.

The fifth and final case was the other naked dead man. The one found in Reynolds hallway. Despite intensive enquires with other forces, nothing had turned up. It remained a total mystery.

Harry sat down thinking about the Reynolds case and had to smile. Uncle William was right about the old 'Paradise' brothel and its secret corridors and peep-holes. Dorothy was not happy when it was discovered that the mirror in her small dressing room was in fact a small door! Uncle William and Harry had walked the tight dark corridor and found it came out in the men's toilet by the rear tradesmen entrance. The exit panel was concealed behind the cleaner's cupboard. Harry placated Dottie by saying that there was no trace of a peep-hole, just the secret door, so no-one has been watching her. He omitted to say that it was a 'two-way' mirror! What fascinated Harry was how the hell Reynolds knew about it. He had no real connections with the theatre and so that part of the now closed case remained a mystery.

He sat thinking at his desk until Edwin and Dave's sniggering drew his attention to the pair, who was together around Edwin's desk. He asked what they found so amusing and Edwin held up a magazine. "You ain't going to like this Guv. It's a 'penny dreadful' and its main pictures and story are about someone we think you know. Sorry Guv, but my mate in Vice gave it to me. Says they have managed to grab and burn most of the copies." He stood and walked over, placing it in Harry's hand.

"The article is called 'Miss Pandora shows her magic box' and the pictures aren't nice either." He smiled at Dave when he said that. Both men had thoroughly enjoyed the naughty little magazine and managed to get a couple of copies to keep for themselves. Harry slowly flicked through it and just sighed. The pictures showed Dorothy in her 'uncensored' costume and they had 'close-ups' of certain areas of interest, as the article declared them. Harry knew Reynolds was behind this. But it was the 'juicy revelations' [as the magazine described it] that really caught

Harry's attention. It claimed 'a reliable source, close to Miss Pandora ' had stated that the pretty little magician was involved with numerous men – both poor and upper class – as long as they had big cocks. It said that she particularly favoured big Black men and also was particular to a little bit of touching the velvet. Not once did they actually name 'the pretty, dirty little magician'. Harry tossed it into the waste bin and said nothing, except he asked Edwin how Alistair was getting on at the police convalescent home in Hove.

*"DS Alistair McPearl is Harry's sergeant who was shot and wounded in the episode '**The workhouse corpse with golden boots.'** He's currently on sick leave."* SJW.

Harry decided he would keep the details of the shabby little magazine to himself – for now – and maybe tell Uncle William when he comes down from the clouds over Dottie's unexpected royal summons to perform for the King.

The magazine didn't stay in the bin for long! Old man Cyril [one of the station's cleaners] had it out and took it home to read with much joy and some wanking.

CHAPTER 12. 'IT'S GOOD TO BE THE KING.' King Edward VII. Apparently...

Dorothy pulled the curtain back a little and turned to Sims at her shoulder, "Notice what's odd about the King's audience?" Sims chuckled, "I certainly do, they're all men." Reggie joined them and tapped Dottie on the shoulder, "If you're uncomfortable with this, then just cancel it. I'm sure Mister Sims – like me – doesn't mind forfeiting ours fees for the night." Dorothy gently touched his arm and smiled, "No, it's far too much money to walk away from. I now know why old Captain Stubbs insisted I wear the original costume, the one that appeared in that awful little magazine. I believe this would be called a Stag evening. Come on, let's get ready."

The magic act was announced by Equerry who looked ancient and Dottie giggled when Reggie stated that the old man in the white powered wig and funny costume had probably announced entertainments for the King's ancestor: Henry the Eighth!

The applause was loud and long when Dorothy appeared and she went straight into the act. First up was Sims disappearing from his sarcophagus which really drew some gasps and clapping. Then Dottie did the old favourite; producing half a dozen pigeons from a previously empty vase. The team noticed – smiling broadly – that Dottie received huge applause by simply turning her back on the audience and walking a little. She mesmerised the men with the movements of her exquisite peach shaped bum and she deliberately shortened her stride so that her arse wobbled a little. She whispered to Reggie that since they're paying thirty bleeding quid, she had better give them their money's worth. Smiling, he whispered back, "You are an angel with a devil's mind and I love it!"

She also received huge applause by simply raising her arms when facing the crowd. Her pert magnificent breasts drew as much noisy appreciation as her bum did. The king's 'friends' were clearly enjoying the show. For the King himself, he sat on the edge of his chair with a pair of opera glasses almost permanently fixed to his eyes. He was in the front row – of course – being served drinks and cigars by the ancient announcer. The only time he lowered the glasses was to eat a complete steak and kidney pie – twice.

The show finished after two encores and Dorothy was instructed that the King will meet her now. When Reggie draped her travelling cloak around her shoulders, the ancient equerry coughed and said it wasn't necessary. She followed the old man down several corridors and was shown into what looked like a study with a blazing fire in the big ornate fireplace. She produced her best curtsy when Bertie appeared, praising her costume and act. He particularly liked the 'mad mummy'. He told her that she could call him sir and rubbed his hands together. "Now Dottie – may I call you Dottie? [She nodded and said 'yes' quietly] I want to show you my pride and joy." Dorothy couldn't help herself, she chuckled and said softly, "Quite a few men have wanted to show me theirs." Bertie laughed, "By god you're a frisky filly and there's no doubt about that. I just know that you're up for a good time."

He gestured her over to the object sitting in the centre of the room. Dorothy just stared at the strange contraption and looked around it, very bemused by its odd structure, it was more a 'Chaise Lounge' than a chair, with extra arms and space beneath. She felt Bertie squeeze her bum cheek – again – and chuckle like a naughty schoolboy. "I had it designed and built to an idea of mine. It allows me to enjoy the ladies without the poor fragile creatures having to endure my lovely, but bulky body directly upon them. I call it 'my sex throne'. I have an identical one in my Paris home, but this one was built by English craftsmen. I say Dottie darling, do you wish to try it? Sort of be crowned by sitting on the sex throne." He squeezed her arse cheek and grinned.

Dorothy sighed, "Is that a royal command sir?" Old Bertie chuckled, "If you wish, but if you're a good girl I will attend one of your proper performances on stage and afterwards you WILL be able to say 'performed by Royal Command'. I suspect few of your contemporaries can announce that!"

Now Dorothy chuckled, "I think I will have already performed by Royal command long before that!" Bertie laughed outright and gently slapped her bum, "My word! You're a wonderful saucy young filly and I like that." He started to pull off his clothes and Dorothy felt compelled to help him, thinking 'the bloody things I do for my King and Country!'

Bertie soon had Dorothy out of the costume he loved so much to gain access to something he loved even more. She lay on the strange chair, gripping the soft arms and stared at the ceiling: it had a beautiful pattern of swirls and flowers. The 'strange contraption' [as Dottie called it] was quite comfortable and she asked Bertie, who was thoroughly enjoying her charms about the space below. Sweating already, he told that it was for another woman, she could kneel under it with her bum in the air and he could go from one to another with little difficulty.

Dorothy was impressed with that and wondered how many women had shared this experience; together. At least it worked and the Kings huge belly was restrained from bouncing all over her. But he sweated profusely and the sweat splashed her frequently. She sighed and wondered if she would be allowed a bath before being dismissed from royal service. Now both his hands enjoyed her breasts and he really seemed to like them. That's when Dottie heard he groan loudly and face contorted, just for a second or two she almost panicked, thinking he was having a bleeding heart attack! But he had just finished. She hadn't insisted he 'pull out' because he was the bleeding King after all, and besides Rosie had taken care of that major problem and Dottie was wearing a discrete 'Dutch Cap'. He certainly hadn't felt or noticed it, but then he was busy fucking her, hard and fast, well, best as his age and bulk allowed.

They now sat on the big leather settee - still both naked - whilst Dottie spooned Mock-turtle' soup into his happy mouth from a silver tureen shaped like a swan. He also enjoyed a couple of huge sandwiches while watching Dottie doing moves from her teenage ballet lessons days. He wiped his mouth with a crisp napkin and eased of the settee, "Interval over my little vixen. Back on the chair please! Oh, it's good to be the King!"

Dottie found herself face down on the strange chair and 'dirty Bertie' [he loved that name] as she called him was now enjoying something that was quite illegal [at the time] and Dorothy gritted her teeth and held tight to the chairs arms. Bertie had said he would play the 'gardener' and take care of her 'brown flower'. And he did. When he finished, he groaned saying that he had well watered it and Dottie knew he had, she had really felt his finish and now needed the toilet. "Like a bloody enema." She had whispered to herself.

*"Edward commissioned famous Paris cabinetmaker Louis Soubrier to create what he called a "Siege d'Amour" or "Love Chair". Installed in Edward's private room at La Chabanais, the elaborate gilded device allowed Edward to continue having sex without crushing his partners with his enormous girth. It was also rumoured that the chair allowed Edward to have sex with two women at once, yet while the chair does feature a second cushion on the lower level it is unclear how this was supposed to function." Extract form the website: **www.todayifoundout.com** – quoted with thanks!" SJW.*

Her second royal command performance now over, Dottie left the palace by the secret entrance in Birdcage Walk: riding in a black carriage with darkened windows. The driver and his assistant never spoke to her and dropped Dottie off at home and sped away into the darkness. She avoided her family and ran her own bath; she certainly wouldn't disturb Ellen at this time of night. But her first port of call was the toilet. As she sat there, she found herself chuckling softly and remembering some of the really disgusting things 'Dirty Bertie' had said and done to her. She stared at the mirror opposite and gave herself a mock salute saying softly, "You my girl were tested by the very best and came through with colours flying. God save the King!" Then giggled and headed for a most welcoming bath.

Dorothy lay in the tub, thinking. She had earned an incredible thirty pounds tonight with her magic act. She was well pleased, until she thought about the sex afterwards. Had 'Dirty Bertie' hired her for sex and the show just came along with it? Then there was the ancient retainer who handed Dorothy the envelope with half a dozen gentleman's personal cards and told her they wished her to perform at their private parties too.

'Shy Mary' came immediately to mind; she had been a real high class prostitute and according to Harry made a small fortune in a short time. He reckoned within a couple years at that rate, she would be set up life and her plan was to marry well and raise a family in total financial security. All on her terms: a totally independent woman. Dottie sighed and eased from the tub quite reluctantly and dried herself. She certainly had some more serious thinking to do, one of the cards was from a bloody Duke of the realm and she recognized all the other names too, an Earl, two very wealthy city bankers, a retired major-general and the last was the most interesting of all: a very famous painter who was reputed to have made thousands from his skill and was in demand all over Europe and America.

That made her think of the United states. Now there was country that a strong independent woman would probably be welcome and be able to thrive. Oh yes, she had some serious thinking to do alright. Her discussion, with Rosie – at the theatre – about America would be interesting.

Harry lowered the morning paper and just had to laugh. Edwin and Dave looked up from their desk and wondered what had tickled their boss this morning. Few articles in the paper moved him to laugh. He held up page three and tapped on the small columns, "Look at this boys, 'shy Mary' must have more lives than the average cat. The jury has bloody acquitted her of being an accessory to willful murder and the judge only fined her over the prostitution charges!"

He laughed again, "Apparently she paid the fine in bloody gold sovereigns!" Edwin and Dave laughed with Dave slapping the desk, "I bet it was bloody two sovereigns, her usual price." Harry slowly nodded, "Your bloody right, it was." Now everyone laughed as Sergeant Simon 'steamy' Potts wandered in, quietly wondering what had tickled CID today. Since young Harry Hadden had taken over the Criminal Investigation Department, the atmosphere had improved in leaps and bounds. The bloody crime 'clear up rate' had also improved dramatically under his stewardship. If the Metropolitan Police had a 'Poster Boy' then it would certainly be Inspector Harry Hadden.

"What's up Steamy?" Harry asked dropping the paper on his cluttered desk. 'Steamy' placed a couple of brown paper files on Harry's desk and almost smiled, "The 'Of Interest' circular has arrived from Forest Gate and Brixton – its a few days late – contains only a couple reports of real interest. A large gypsy family is camping in woods behind that naval architects house near the cemetery. He [the architect] does all kinds of secret work for the Admiralty, so Military intelligence is twitching. The head of the gypsies is that strange old man Noel Whorton; you know, the one we had the complaints about last year." Harry snapped his fingers, "He is known as 'Chanter' because he's regarded as some kind of magician. He must be the man in Flash's ledgers!" Edwin and Dave gathered around Harry's desk now with real interest.

Sergeant Potts tapped the files, "The other one is real strange, a silk merchant lodged a complaint at Brixton nick that a guest at his party touched up his little daughter in the nursery. Apparently the dad caught him naked in bed with the kid and chased him with some of the other party guests. The suspect, a certain Jordon Cope is known; a con-artist who can play the toff really well. He's also known to like little girls, the piece of crap. Well, anyway, they chased him – stark naked – into the local woods but he had disappeared completely. They couldn't find a bloody trace of him and a couple of gypsy families living by the cross-roads couldn't help either."

Dave shouted across, "Guv, that naked stiff from Reynolds porno palace had grass and mud on his bare feet!" Harry rose from his chair and told the sergeant to contact Brixton nick – urgently – and discover the name of the head gypsy of the families that were present in the woods. He spoke to Dave and Edwin as they waited outside the nick, "Can't be a co-incidence, Noel Whorton is known as 'Chanter' and appears in Flash's ledgers and he was back in the area, days ago. Then we have the naked man at Flash's house who must be the pervert from Brixton, where, surprise, surprise, there's a gypsy family right there at the time."

Edwin smiled, "Christ Guv, if Brixton says the gypsies are from Whorton's family tribe, we've fucking nailed it!" Harry nodded and smiled a little, then saw Reggie jumping from the bus outside St. Mary's church. He strode across the busy road and removed his hat, not smiling, "Excuse me mister Hadden, but could I have a word. It's about that man I....accidently killed. I have found out who he was working for."

Now that took Harry back a bit, but he knew Reggie was an honest man, so this could be pivotal to the case. Harry told him to continue and Reggie said quietly, "There's a man who lives in my tenement – a certain Aloysius Cadbury – who knew, by reputation, another Black fella who was known to use a big knife and really enjoyed using it apparently. He worked for a strange old gypsy man. I think the man I killed, was a certain Moses Washington. Aloysius says his not been seen around for a few days and has apparently vanished. But, that's not only why I'm here….." Harry, now quite excited, slapped his arm, "Bloody excellent Reggie. I know the bloody name of that old gypsy and it certainly ties up. Thank you my friend. Come on boys, we're heading to Forest Gate!"

Reggie watched the happy detectives jump into the police carriage and disappear into the High Street traffic. He replaced his hat and waved down a cab, telling the driver 'Paradise Theatre'. Maybe it was for the best that Harry stopped him from speaking about Dorothy. But she was mixing with bad company. He sighed and stared out the window. He hadn't been quite honest with Harry how he found out about Moses and his gypsy connections. He now regretted his stupidity in allowing Aloysius to fool and deceive him over Dorothy.

It was a very unhappy drive back to the theatre for the big man.

CHAPTER 13. 'GOD CREATED SEXUAL DESIRE IN TEN PARTS THEN GAVE NINE PARTS TO WOMEN AND ONE TO MEN'. William B. Quandt.

"It's a packed crowd tonight Miss Pandora, all four privates are booked!" Mr. Yates was more than happy with this magic act, it's was certainly getting bums on seats. Dorothy smiled and watched the happy old man disappearing behind the heavy front curtain to announce 'Miss Pandora and her magic box' to a hugely excited audience. There was thunderous applause and cheering as the curtain lifted and Dorothy's team went into action.

Aloysius Cadbury leaned forward and placed his hands on the edge of the private box, which was just left and close to the stage. He had a wonderful view of Dorothy in her flimsy costume and definitely was enjoying what was on show. His friend chuckled, "I prefer the costume she wore in that dirty magazine, but her best outfit is her bloody birthday suit!" Aloysius nodded and smiled, he had seen the woman up close and had spoken with her and knew that Miss Dorothy Hadden was far deeper than anyone could guess. His rooms were next to a certain Reginald Hepple-White and what he heard through the thin walls of Reggie's bedroom had made his mouth water and his big cock erect. He stared down at Dorothy and knew that he wanted her above anything or anyone else and had already made up his mind to have her.

He had white women before – all prossie's – but this supposedly 'respectable', beautiful young woman clearly liked black meat and that meant he had a real chance to fuck her. Then a strange thought crept into his head; he didn't just want to fuck her, he wanted her for himself. Now that made him laugh a little with real surprise, but then he watched her moving around the stage and knew that's what he actually wanted. He sat back and regretted that he and Max [the young man sitting next to him] hadn't fucked little 'shy Mary' as arranged, but her bloody arrest and incarceration had ended that promising assignation!

He studied the big 'Nubian Slave' and suddenly realized that

Reggie was key to his seduction and possession of Miss Hadden. Ally knew that all he needed was a proper introduction and his charm would do the rest. He ran a hand over his face and thought hard, and then an idea dropped into his mind: Reggie had disposed of that mad bastard Moses Washington who had recommended 'shy Mary' to him. Now, Miss Hadden's brother was on the case of that and Reynolds, so if he gave Miss Hadden information which would help her beloved brother…..The idea grew and developed in his head and by the time the standing audience were applauding the finish of a really good show, Ally had a clear plan.

He and Max stood outside the small Victoria Theatre, waiting for a cab in the evening drizzle when he saw Miss Hadden and Reggie [and the woman who had also visited Reggie] climbing into an obviously pre-booked cab. He watched it trundle down the still busy street and really smiled. "Max, I think it's time to arrange a little poker game with our old friend Reggie."

Max just shrugged his shoulders and raised a hand as an empty cab appeared; it sailed straight past. "Racist bastard!" Max yelled and folded his arms in disgust as the cab stopped and picked up an elderly white couple. Ally just slapped his arm, "Come on, we'll catch one down by the docks. The cabbies there will pick up anyone." Ally walked carefully, planning his seduction of Miss Hadden. This naughty little fox was certainly worth the chase.

Reggie had a terrible poker game in Ally's rooms. He had lost nearly five pounds by the time he called a halt to his impromptu involvement. He owed Ally the Blade all that money and – without borrowing it from someone – couldn't pay his debt. And he knew that you always paid your debts to Ally the Blade! But Ally [for once] was more than amicable to Reggie paying by doing something for him in lieu of the money. Reggie listened without comment at what Ally wanted him to do, besides it sounded quite innocent [but Reggie knew he was lying to himself just to feel better about it] and so Reggie believed he had escaped from being knifed in some dark alley by simply asking Dorothy to call around to his rooms.

Dorothy could get no answer from Reggie despite knocking twice: loudly. That's when the door opposite opened [No.9] and a certain Aloysius Cadbury stepped out and smiled, "Ah, good afternoon again Miss Hadden, I'm afraid Reggie had to dash out

and commanded that I entertain you until his return." Dorothy
looked a little disappointed but smiled at the gallant young man
who bowed a little. "May I offer you a little whisky while you
wait?" Dorothy hesitated and then remembered that Reggie said
Ally the blade' was quite a gentleman around women.

She stepped in his doorway and – for a moment – thought she
had been transported up west to some luxury house standing in
Piccadilly or Westminster. It was packed with exquisite, beautiful
and very expensive furniture and paintings. Dottie was actually a
little shocked by what she saw. "Please, I'll get us some whisky."
And he walked to a drinks cabinet that wouldn't be out of place in
a Mayfair Villa.

He gestured to the huge dark leather settee, "Please take a seat,
and I'll fix us a libation." Dorothy eased herself down, realizing
Ally had a superb command of English, considering he was
supposed to be an 'East end bad Boy'. He definitely was an
enigma and that made him interesting to her. He was also very
dark, mysterious and handsome. Oh, yes, she was interested!

They sat sipping their drinks in silence for a few seconds and
Dorothy had to ask him about his exquisitely furnished rooms.

Ally smiled, "I have – apparently – good taste." He chuckled,
"Being honest a couple of very nice ladies furnished it for me and
I paid them well for their service. They advertise in the Tatler'
you know." Now Dorothy was impressed, "I noticed that this
tenement is really well looked after, the place is nice and clean
and Reggie says the rents are very fair. The landlord must be
quite a decent fellow, clearly no slum landlord."

"I sincerely hope he's not! I know him quite well actually." Ally
said as Dottie lowered her glass, "Ah, so that's how you gained
these rooms and had them furnished how you want. Reggie told
me they come furnished. You know the landlord." Ally nodded, "I
really do know him well, because it's me. I own this block and
several others around East London." He raised his glass, "Here's
to decent landlords everywhere: black or white." Dorothy raised
her glass, "I'll certainly drink to that Ally, but how, I mean..." Ally
stopped her before she embarrassed herself.

"You think I'm a bad boy don't you?" he said quietly and Dorothy
nodded slowly. Ally eased from his seat and quickly re-filled their

glasses. "My family hails from Jamaica and my ancestors were very clever people. To my great shame, my great-grandfather owned plantations in Jamaica and Trinidad which worked slaves for profit. Yes, black people owning black people. But that was the times they lived in. People who don't know me think I'm called Ally the Blade because I'm good with a knife and quite the bad boy. But the nickname comes from my very posh private school in Canterbury. I was called that because I was a fencing champion."

Now Dorothy laughed and sipped her drink, "Now I know why people say you shouldn't judge a book by its cover!" Ally sat back down and shook his head, "Miss Hadden – may I call you Dorothy? – [she nodded with a smile] I must tell that I know all about Moses, the lunatic that attacked you and your maid. You see, he also came from a good wealthy family in Jamaica. His two brothers are what we English, like to call decent chaps. But, oh dear, Moses certainly wasn't one those. He seemed full of anger and resentment about his parents and their preference for his brothers. Frankly, he was a very angry young man who was filled with darkness. I know he pretended to be my friend but hated me because of what happened at school."

Dorothy sat forward, really interested now, "He went to your posh school? Really?" Ally nodded, "If I hadn't been there, he would certainly have been fencing champion!" They both laughed at that and Ally leaned forward, his mood becoming more sombre, "I shouldn't do this Dorothy, but I think you'll be very interested in what I have to say. It's about the man who held Moses leash. The man who paid Moses after his parents cut off his money." Dorothy whispered for him to continue.

Ally sipped his drink and looked at the fireplace, then sighed, "Moses worked for a man called 'Old Chanter' who is the head of a large gypsy family. Where they travel follows death and crime. He's quite a legend among some travelling folk but many others hate him for what he does. They say he has sold his soul to the devil and received the power of the 'third eye' and use's it for profit and gain. By all accounts, he is a very unpleasant old man and someone to steer well clear off. I know for a fact that Reynolds worked for him and probably still does, if the old man hasn't had him killed yet. I ask that you never tell your brother where this information comes from. Can you promise that?"
He stood and refilled the glasses again as Dorothy absorbed his

words. Harry would be delighted with this information and accepted the whisky from Ally who now sat on the settee with her. He smiled and patted her hand, "Please do not betray me on this?" Dorothy smiled and nodded. She had been right about Mr. Cadbury, he was definitely a handsome man, especially close up and he smelt wonderful, probably French Cologne. "Why have you told me this Ally?" She asked softly and his hand remained on hers. "I was utterly outraged that a real lady like you was threatened by that animal and knew that I should act. But Moses was a 'brother' and we had schooled together and so I wrestled with my conscious and thankfully, it directed me to do what is right."

Dorothy smiled at the young man and he smiled back, now gripping her hand. He lifted that hand and kissed it slowly, whispering that he never wished to let it go. Dorothy placed her glass down and said nothing. They both said nothing and Dorothy could actually hear her heart beating. His mouth came close to hers and she hesitated for a second or two and they came together, embracing and kissing with some passion which actually really surprised the pair. Her hat came off and both their hands fumbled at the buttons on her coat, their lips never parting for a second. Her brain was telling her to put a stop to this, but her body was saying something else and on this occasion: her body won the argument.

The passionate young couple became lost in the joys of sex. Rough, dirty sex: the type Dorothy had read in the really explicit underground books and magazines. Albert had let her 'borrow' some [to give her some idea's....] to enhance their next meeting in the bedroom of his house. Dottie put her new found knowledge to good use with her 'Black Stallion' and if Mr. Cadbury was honest, she dominated the sexual activities and he certainly wasn't complaining! The things she did would have cost him many Guineas with a high class brass, so he thoroughly enjoyed what was on offer and it was basically anything the pair could come up with. They changed positions several times, using the big bed, the floor, the large set of drawers, walls and even the toilet [this apartment had an inside privy, so they didn't have to rush down the bottom of the damn garden]. Alley finished three times during the marathon two hour sex session: once in each of the willing Dorothy's orifices and she enjoyed each grand finish. Finally they lay gasping and panting on the floor in each other's arms and made plans, kissing and whispering, their hands still unable to keep off each other. To quote Dorothy at the time: "if Albert had 'fucked her brains out' previously then Ally had 'fucked her to heaven and back' and she didn't have to die to enjoy it!

She sat in the homebound cab, legs slightly apart, and her mind revisited the afternoon's sex session and found she was smiling and getting wetter between her legs with each delicious thought that re-enacted the serious fucking she had received at the young man's hands. Then she thought about Reggie and she sighed a little, but had realized that he and Albert were sex partners and Mr. Aloysius Cadbury was something completely different. And that could cause enormous problems for her…and her family. She was clever enough to realize that she had only three real options in the matter; continue seeing the young man who was a sexual God, in secret, and face all the problems that carried, tell Harry and Uncle William that she was involved with a Blackman who was a known criminal and 'bad boy', or end their relationship before it became imposable to end.

Those thoughts weren't as pleasant as her earlier ones and she sat back, head in hands, lost in all her problems until the cab stopped and the driver shouted down to her. As she walked to Rosie's front door, she now realized that she didn't regret the incredible sex but it could cost her dear; almost everyone and everything she cherished and held close. It would plague and dominate her thoughts for some time.

Dorothy smelled the beautiful basket of flowers that Rosie had brought from the theatre and ran her fingers around the card. Then saw Rosie peering at her with a little smile. "They from him?" She asked and Dorothy nodded with quite a smile on her face. Rosie handed Dottie her tea and sniffed the flowers. "Well, he knows how to thank a lady, I'll give him that." She sat down and sipped her tea. Dorothy sat back, gripping the card. "I'm going to have to end this…." Rosie quietly chuckled, "So, you have a young man totally gaga over you who is handsome, charming, bloody shit wealthy, fucks like a bleeding breeding stallion and actually knows how to treat a lady and you're going to tell him to bleeding piss off?"

Dorothy sighed, "It's not that Rosie, it's just that we have no future, none whatsoever, together. And I need to face that brutal reality like a grown woman and not some dumb love-struck Schoolgirl mooning over her first crush."

"Well, now I am bleeding confused, how exactly do you two love-birds have no future together?" Rosie slurped her tea a little puzzled. Dorothy sat back, turning the card in her hands. "I left out quite an important detail about him Rosie and it's because of that little detail, we can never really be together." Rosie was now really intrigued and she placed her cup down thinking, then blurted out, "Oh shit, he's not one of those queer men who go with women to dispel bleeding rumours and keep the coppers off his back, is he?"

Dorothy managed a little smile, "No he couldn't be an Oscar Wilde if it came with gold bars. It's something else and he certainly can't change it. Bloody impossible to do that." She saw the look on Rosie's face and said quietly, "He's black Rosie. Like he says himself: black as the ace of spades." Rosie sat back and nodded with her reaction really surprising Dottie. "Well, you've been with a Blackman before….Ah, that was sex and this is something quite different ain't it?" Dorothy smiled, her dear friend knew her better than she had ever imagined.

"I need to tell Harry about what Ally said, but how do I achieve that without compromising myself and my relationship with Ally? It's quite a conundrum, isn't it?"

Rosie shook her head, "No it ain't darling. Just get someone he trusts to tell him. Simple really….someone like Reggie would be just the ticket and he will certainly do anything for you."

Dorothy grinned and relaxed back in the chair: Rosie was right; Reggie was perfect as the messenger for this task. Rosie jumped up and held out her hand, "Come on darling, Rosie will cheer you up and bleeding do herself some good in the bargain. " Dottie rose and took her hand and the pair headed for the upstairs bedroom. Rosie's boys wouldn't be back from school for at least an hour and Albert wouldn't be home until well after five. They could have a little 'playtime' fun and soon Dorothy was lost again in the joys of passionate physical sex. It certainly made her much happier and temporarily took her mind off the 'Ally' problem. The two naked women rolled about the bed, indulging in various sex positions, laughing, groaning and moaning. Then Dorothy sat up: she could hear a voice, so they both lay quietly together until Rosie groaned loudly; "For fuck's sake, I forgot it's coal today! That's 'big Bryan' with two sacks of bleeding nutty slack!" For some reason that made Dottie laugh. Then she heard the man shout up the stairs; "Rosie darling! It's about payment this week, are you up there?" Dottie prodded her – smiling – and said quietly, "Now, what on earth does he mean by that my dear?" and giggled. Rosie shrugged her shoulders; "Well, I sometimes keeps the money that Albert gives me to pay the coalman for myself and Bryan don't object to payment in kind. It means I can treat myself to a new hat when I want."

Now Dottie laughed outright and playfully slapped her friend bare bottom. "You best call him up and we'll pay for your coal for the rest of the bloody month!" Both girls laughed as Rosie yelled down, "Come up Bryan, my friend and I have a proposition for you!" They both heard his boots running up the stairs in some urgency and the little dirty man appeared in the doorway, pulling down his braces with a big sooty grin on his face: especially when he saw the naked Dorothy sprawled on the bed, legs open in anticipation. Dottie turned to Rosie and had to mention that 'big Bryan' was a man of small statute. Rosie just smiled as Bryan quickly pulled down his grubby trousers and Dorothy learnt why the man was called 'big Bryan'.

He jumped on the bed, kicking off his boots and mounted the giggling Dorothy without as so much as saying 'Hello' and fucked her hard and fast as she wrapped her long legs around him. Rosie grunted – running her hand over his heaving backside – "This has to be worth free coal for the rest of the month Bryan?" she asked. Thrusting and groaning, he managed to mutter his agreement and Rosie chuckled, slapping his bum. "Good, then it's my turn next!"

Dorothy gripped his sweaty dirty shoulders and groaned: she was having an orgasm already and Bryan now held onto the shaking headboard with both hands and plunged into her with some force. Fucking like this he didn't last long and quickly finished, but stayed in her until Rosie slapped his arse again and he lay on his back as the two women set about raising another erection using their mouths and hands.

Rosie was soon bouncing up and down on the happy coalman as he abused Dottie's big swinging tits with his mouth and hands. He groaned and then smiled broadly, "Rosie darling, thanks for this but I shouted up for you because Albert had already paid me for the coal for the month!" Both women just stared at him and then at each other. The coalman just smiled again.

Harry stared about the dismal camp which had been erected upon wasteland near the river. Apparently the derelict factory [now, no more than some walls and the odd doorway] had made cannon-balls for the navy! But the large abandoned site proved popular with passing gypsy families and now several caravans were present. As soon as the three police carriages appeared, people appeared from every nook and cranny. Harry jumped out with Detective Inspector Albert Carney [Forest Gate CID] and the pair strolled straight into the camp whilst uniform officers and other CID officers remained by the broken gates. It wasn't a raid – yet – and Harry was 'feeling out' the situation. The last time police had gone in heavy, it ended in a near riot with several constables injured. Harry had decided that a 'quiet' approach may produce dividends. "He'll be out; he won't let anyone else talk to us." Harry said quietly to Albert, who lit a cigarette and just nodded.

A small of group of gypsy men formed around them and Harry announced who they were and that they wished to speak with the family elders. A couple of big men shouted for them to 'fuck off and leave them alone, they had done fucking nothing'. Harry gestured with his hat and said they were only here to speak with the elders. That's when Noah Whorton appeared with Sigmund just behind. "What can we do for you fine gentleman?" He asked removing his pipe and Harry asked if he was Noah Whorton, also known as Chanter or old Chanter. Noah nodded, "What's it to you?" Harry smiled and told him about 'Flash' Reynolds and his ledgers, pornographic pictures and running from the law. Then asked if he knew the late Moses Washington, who was suspected of killing a certain John Milligan, then there was Mister Jordan Cope who was killed by a antique musket and he [Harry] had the ball in his pocket, wondering if Noah owned such a musket and would balls from his ammunition bag match this one? The effect was electric with Sigmund throwing a punch and shouting "Get rid of the fucking gun!" at some young men. That was enough for DI Carney who blew his whistle, only to have it expelled from his mouth by a right hook. Harry kicked Sigmund in the balls and shouted for his lads to 'get fucking stuck in!' And they certainly did, drawing their truncheons and piling into the melee. The CID officers grabbed anything at hand and pitched in. Harry ducked a piece of wood and saw – with a small smile – Dave whacking a big man over the back of the head with a metal pipe. Harry didn't smile when the big man rubbed his head and just stared at young Dave. He chased Dave through the broken gates waving his fists. Dave wasn't seen for a couple of hours and was found hiding in the toilet's in Victoria Park, whilst the big man was nicked down Vic Dock Road [Victoria Dock Road], still apparently looking for Dave. The big man was really angry that Dave hit him from behind!

Harry sat in the small cubicle and shyly smiled at Nurse Alice Sherwood who dabbed iodine on his cut hands and forehead. She asked after Dottie and Uncle William, making Harry smile and say quietly that they were fine. The very tall and elegantly attired doctor was reading his clipboard with a smile, "So Inspector, we have two broken arms, two unconscious; apparently from having truncheons batter their brains out, two with loose and missing teeth, one man missing an ear and various cuts and bruises all round on no less than fifteen men. Oh, and my favourite, the removal of a police whistle from a certain Inspector Carney's nose. All in all, quite a result. I understand you used a 'softly-softly' approach?" Harry smiled and nodded. The doctor lowered the clipboard, "Well, I really wouldn't like to see the outcome of an aggressive approach." He walked off twirling his stethoscope; he had some really bad Hemorrhoids to look at. [Are there any good hemorrhoids?]

But he couldn't detract from Harry's happy feeling: Noah Whorton and most of his band of cutthroats were banged up; they had recovered a musket and bag of balls which could prove decisive. They were being matched by a firearms expert. Then hundreds of pounds in coin and notes, found in Noah's wagon and a big fat stash of pornographic material including some under-age stuff. But he couldn't get anything on the whereabouts of Flash Reynolds. He had vanished – like he had from Dorothy's dressing room – and the only possible sighting came from York City. Aside from the gypsy pornographers and murders, there were rumours circulating that notorious gang boss John Vicar had gone into partnership with another underworld boss: Septum Newman [who ran the African & Indian gangs] and Madam Tang [who ran the Chinese and Asian gangs] was not happy about that strange little 'partnership'.

"Bloody odd bedfellows." Was all Harry said when informed of the new criminal 'Entente Cordiale' affecting the east end. He had also noticed the chill in the relationship between Dorothy and Reggie. But they were professionals and it clearly didn't affect the stage shows. But there was one happy note: 'Miss Pandora and her magic box' had proved very popular despite the ribald comments about the name.

The family came together for Sunday service with the Reverend Rashwood and Dorothy had time to reflect upon the week that had just passed.

Dorothy walked from church on Harry's arm; head a bowed a little, and – again – managed to stop the tears coming. She glanced behind and saw Rosie walking with Albert, her two boys some yards away. Rosie gave her an understanding smile. The two were close enough now, not to need words on certain occasions. Her meeting with Aloysius had crushed her spirits and reduced her to dreadful hard sobbing. She had rushed – almost hysterical – from his apartment and ran for several streets before almost collapsing against a Draper's shop window. It had taken several minutes to compose herself and try to hail a cab.

She had arrived at his door, smiling in anticipation of another incredible sex session and simply let herself in [the door was unlocked as usual: Mr. Cadbury's reputation prevented any local thief from raiding his home!] and pulling off her coat and hat shouted for her lover. He appeared in the bedroom door, smoking a cigar and didn't smile. "You're late." Was all he said. Dottie just grinned and slowly unbuttoned her blouse, "It's better late than never darling." She said softly, pulling the last button open revealing no corset, just her heaving breasts. He drew on his cigar and blew smoke towards the ceiling. "I played poker with some of my friends last night and I lost. But it wasn't for money Dorothy. They are all business associates of mine and Max's so we rarely play for money, just for fun and dares. Do you know what I mean?" Dorothy shook her head and slowly folded her arms, her smile fading a little. He sighed, "Well, I had a full house and went for the kill, but bloody Septum Newman laid down a straight flush so I have to pay up. It's a matter of damn principle, a matter of my word and honour which I hold dear. So that's that."

She knew that the man Ally mentioned was the boss of a gang that terrorized the locals, running prostitutes and protection rackets for shopkeepers and the like. Harry had mentioned that he and John Vicar were 'associates' in several illegal businesses' and the man had an evil, harsh reputation which had been well earned. His 'trademark' was a hammer and other people's knees.

Dorothy wiped her face and asked quietly, seeing the look of concern on his face, "What did you gamble away dear?" Ally shrugged his shoulders as if uncaring. "I gambled you. There's no soft way of saying this Dorothy, so I'll just say it. This weekend you are his. From tonight to Sunday night you'll stay at the 'Devonshire' with him. Do everything he asks and keep him happy. I know you'll do it because you love me and that means you'll do anything for me. It's not like your some innocent little girl is it? Christ, I've fucked you in your mouth, honey-pot and up your arse, so you know what it's all about. You just have to be the same happy slut with him. For a woman like you that shouldn't be a problem, should it." He pulled out his fob watch, "He should be here soon to collect his prize, so button yourself up. You won't need to send for your maid to bring any clothes or that. With septum's reputation, you won't need them."

He walked to the fireplace and threw the cigar in. Dorothy stood in silence and asked if he was 'fucking joking'. He turned and shook his head, "No, I'm not. As I said, it's a matter of honour and principle for me. I lost and will pay up. You fuck Black men so it not a problem is it?" Dorothy was now in a state of shock. He stared at her, "Now what's the bloody matter? You will do this for me, for my reputation and honour. It's just a weekend and he'll fuck you as he likes and when it's over, that's that. I'll buy you a nice necklace or something, whatever you want or fancy so you'll gain from this unfortunate arrangement, won't you?"

He walked over and gripped her arms, then smiled. "Do this little thing and we can stay together, my love. It's just dirty sex with another Black man and you've done it before. Just don't enjoy it too much!" He laughed and went to kiss her. She hit him with some real hidden strength and he actually staggered back a little, shocked by the punch and the strength of it. "You bloody fuck him yourself you dirty bastard!" she shouted and was out of the door, hitching up her skirt and petticoats, running down the stairs and into the street. Aloysius stood and rubbed his chin, then walked to the drinks cabinet and poured a large whisky, sipping it slowly. Mister Septum Newman wouldn't be impressed or pleased with this and he certainly wouldn't be a man to disappoint, especially over poker. He adored the game and would let no-one renege on a bet. Well, not if they valued their knees. The last one to try that was held down on a table and had a hammer applied to both. Aloysius finished the whisky and poured another, cursing Dorothy for the situation she had dropped him in. He felt no guilt for his part in it!

"This requires careful thinking and a few lies. I can – hopefully – shift the blame for failure to pay up to someone else...." He now smiled as his quick mind leapt into action.

Dorothy sat in the local Library, drawing attention from staff and patrons because of the look upon her face and the fact she had no coat or hat, which was unusual for women in these times. Finally a friendly female Liberian came over and asked if she could help and all Dorothy could say was to get her a cab please.

That very night, as Rosie was dressing her for the early evening performance there was a knock at the door and Rosie opened it expecting Reggie or Mister Sims, instead there was a huge rough man who removed his hat and didn't smile, "I have a message from Mr. Newman Miss Hadden. He says he has dealt with your boyfriend and the matter now lies in your hands. He says that the debt is now yours and you will pay it. He will send details of which weekend you WILL spend with him at the Devonshire. He reminds you that he always gets debts paid, one way or another." Rosie told him to 'fuck off' and slammed the door.

They held each other close and a tearful Dorothy whispered,
 "Now what the fuck do I do? I can't tell Uncle William and certainly not Harry. That bastard [Newman] has powerful friends and they are certainly not frightened by the police!" Rosie held her close and the pair cried for a few minutes until they heard young Arthur shouting, "Ten minutes please, ten minutes!"

Dorothy took several deep breaths and nodded, then headed for the stage, Rosie close behind. How Dorothy performed that night made Rosie proud and she shed a few more tears about it. It appears that none of the others suspected anything. The note from Newman arrived the following morning – delivered to the theatre by hand – and specified the fate and time she was to appear at the hotel reception. It said not to bother bringing many clothes: she wouldn't need them.

That afternoon a very nervous Reggie came to see the girls and told them that Aloysius had scarpered and the word on the streets was that Septum Newman was after him. It appears all his smooth talking, lies and pleas had fallen on deaf ears. Apparently a hammer and the immediate loss of working knee-caps had made him flee. Reggie now confessed to a shocked Dorothy about his part in her 'seduction' and begged for forgiveness. Dorothy slowly nodded, saying she could forgive Reggie for his betrayal and that he could continue working in the act, but everything else between them was over. He left in silence after quietly thanking her.

Dorothy now knew she had no choice in the dreadful matter: she would have to pay the debt, with her pride, dignity, self-respect and worse of all, her body. Her greatest comfort in these dark times was Rosie who insisted – no demanded – she accompanies her to the hotel. Dorothy even managed a strained chuckle when Rosie produced her cricket bat! "We'll do this together darling. I'm sure that pig won't object to that after all, he plays fucking poker and a pair is always good to have." Rosie said stroking Dottie's hair and plying her with whisky.

Dorothy left the post office after posting a letter to George [her sea faring brother] and waited for a cab. She was about to raise a hand when a bright carriage pulled up right in front of her and the door opened. The big black man inside was dressed like a Duke with a very expensive suit and a bright top hat in his hands. He gestured to her and she looked about and saw the driver standing next to her: he was also a big man with a very unpleasant expression on his face. He also gestured her to enter the cab, saying quietly, "Mr. Septum Newman would like a word Miss Hadden."

She was shaking a little and stepped in very slowly. The rough man closed the door quietly and she felt the cab pull away. Mr. Septum Newman smiled and placed his hat upon the seat. "Would you please indulge me for a few minutes Miss Hadden, I have a story to impart. Will you please listen?" Dorothy nodded, her legs were actually shaking and her stomach had filled with ice. He eased back in the seat which his bulk easily filled and ran a hand over his completely shaved head. "Some years ago my son, my only son Washington was down by the river with several school friends and like most boys, they were pushing and insulting each other, playing as men, the men they liked to be. But it got a little out of hand and a couple of the boys knocked him down and he lost his footing, tumbling headfirst into the river. In fear, the other boys ran off, leaving Washington struggling, you see, they didn't know the boy couldn't swim."

Oddly enough, he now smiled a little more and continued, "But by the grace of God, there was boatman heading down river and he saw the boy struggling in the water and knew the fierce current would soon take the poor young soul under. Without hesitation, he pulled off his boots and jacket, plunging in the water. He dragged my boy to the bank. He had saved my young, precious son's life. I tried to reward him, but he would have none of that saying any decent man would have done the same and I knew he would have risked his life to save anyone in trouble in that water. Old man, young woman, child or adult. It didn't matter to him if they were white, pink, yellow or black. He wouldn't even take a bottle of whisky or gold sovereigns, even though I could see by his old clothes he had little. Then there was his face, disfigured, not a sight many ladies could take too. I was to discover he supplemented his meager living by street fighting: he was a bare-knuckle man and lived in slum lodgings. Yet he would take nothing for saving my boys life. He was known in the circles I move in as the 'the beast' because of his many disfigurements. Yet he was clearly more human than many who called him that. What a cruel misnomer Miss Hadden, don't you think?"

Dorothy could only nod and wonder why the man was telling her this tale. Mr. Newman clasped his hands together and nodded, "You have a Guardian Angel Miss Hadden. A real gold plated genuine Guardian Angel because he came to see me and I would have given him anything. Anything. But all he asked was that I cancel your ex-boyfriends debt and leave you alone."

The carriage rolled to a halt and Dorothy could see she was outside her house. She managed to whisper, "What's his name Mr. Newman?" The big man shook his head, "He asked me never to reveal his current identity Miss Hadden, so I will stay silent on the matter. But I believe you know him. Appearance can be so deceptive can't it? Young Aloysius all handsome, oozing charm, the great seducer and yet he's little better than a graveyard rat. And 'the beast', ugly, disfigured, shunned and ridiculed with an inside beauty that angels would envy. A strange silly world isn't it?" The driver pulled open the door and then Mr. Newman said softly, "There is no debt now Miss Hadden. The matter is at an end. Goodbye."

Dorothy stepped from the cab and ran up the steps and into the house, heading straight for the drinks cabinet and poured a large whisky, her mind reeling from what just happened. Then she thought about 'the beast' and wondered when she had met such a man? She certainly would have remembered him! And why had he helped and protected her when he could have had anything from Newman, especially when he had nothing? She swallowed down the whisky and coughed. Who the hell was the 'the beast'?

So, it was a very subdued Dorothy that sat in church that Sunday with Uncle William and Harry who had no idea what had taken place over the last week. Harry had tried to get her to explain her melancholy disposition but Dottie was a good actress and smiled his concerns away. But she couldn't get 'the beast' out of her thoughts. Aloysius was gone from them, but would remain inside her as a warning of how deceptive humans can be: especially when it was obvious to everyone including her, but who had refused to see it, blinded by passion.

THE END

EPISODE 3: "THE STRANGE DEATH OF MRS. HANNA DASHWOOD."

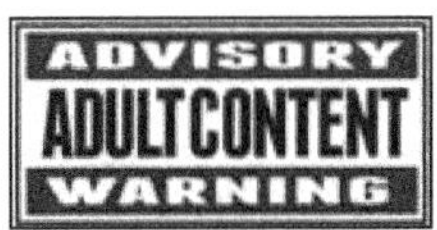

Alcohol – Smoking – Strong language – Strong sexual references [including some mild BDSM] – violence[including murder and assault] – Mild Adult Erotica.

 Approximately 45 to 55 minutes.

 Remember: **Adult Content.**

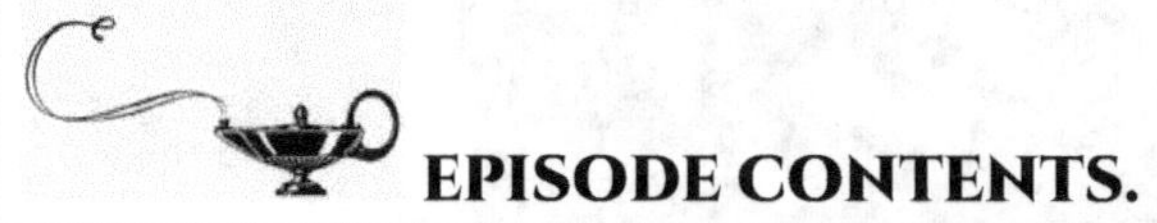

EPISODE CONTENTS.

1. 'BECAUSE [LIKE A PIECE OF RARE CHINA] I AM BREAKABLE, AND MENDABLE, BUT DIFFICULT TO MATCH.'
Start page: 219

2. 'BICYCLE FACE!'
Start page: 225

3. 'I GIVE MY MIND THE LIBERTY TO FOLLOW THE FIRST WISE OR FOOLISH IDEA THAT PRESENTS ITSELF.'
Start page: 233

4. 'EVERY HOUSE GUEST BRINGS HAPPINESS, SOME WHEN THEY ARRIVE AND SOME WHEN THEY ARE LEAVING.'
Start page: 240

5. 'AFTER A VISIT TO THE BEACH IT'S HARD TO BELIEVE WE LIVE IN A MATERIAL WORLD.'
Start page: 250

6. 'ONE MUST WORK WITH TIME AND NOT AGAINST IT'.
Start page: 260

7. 'A MAN WHO STUDIETH REVENGE KEEPS HIS OWN WOUNDS GREEN.'
Start page: 264

8. 'REGRET IS A FORM OF PUNISHMENT ITSELF.'
Start page: 276

9. 'INFORMATION MAY INFORM THE MIND, BUT REVELATION SETS A HEART ON FIRE.'
 Start page: 284

IMPORTANT AUTHOR'S NOTE:
"The names and places of some characters have been changed to protect the innocent and ficticious characters created in their stead. Thank you."

CHAPTER 1. 'BECAUSE [LIKE A PIECE OF RARE CHINA] I AM BREAKABLE, AND MENDABLE, BUT DIFFICULT TO MATCH.' Miss S.A. Roberts.

"You certainly know how to show a girl a good time. When you said breakfast, I thought it would be Romanov's or the New London grill or something. Not bloody Big Charles's 'Night Owl Lunch stand' in King Street!" Dorothy sipped her tea and just had to smile at her brother. He waved her comments away; "Finish your bacon sandwich; I'm due in Court at 10 o'clock. I can't believe that Norman Grimes has gone 'not guilty' with three separate witnesses all seeing him beat up the damn fellow."

Dorothy sighed; "You know what the sign says above the door at the Old Bailey; 'Never plead guilty'. He's following good advice. What's he charged with?" She picked up the bacon sandwich and stared at it. Harry sipped his tea; "Grievous bodily harm. He knocked out the other fellow's front teeth." He sighed and took the bacon sandwich off Dorothy; disappointed that she had only nibbled at it. "Waste not; want not." He muttered and finished it off.

"How's that love lost admirer of yours doing?" Harry smiled and sipped his tea. Dorothy rolled her eyes and sighed. "Apparently big Tom has told him to stop sending those blooming flowers and sweets. He's also warned him off hanging about the stage door. But Miss Player says he's purchased enough tickets to attend every evening performance for the next six months. If he's silly love notes was money I would be able to retire." Harry chuckled at that. That's when Dorothy gestured towards the door and smiled; "I think some of your merry men are here Robin." She said quietly.

Harry turned and gestured Edwin Palmer over. The young man smiled broadly at Dorothy and removed his hat. He placed both hands upon the table and lowered his voice. "There's been a body found in 'Summerton Manner'. You know; that old house that has been boarded up for donkey years. Some bloody kids got in and found the stiff on the floor, in what must have been the music room. A woman in her thirties apparently; old Doc

Goldstein is already on way. Constable Tanner is on scene with the new boy; Grieves." Dorothy sipped her tea; "Summerton House has been closed up for at least twenty years; ever since young Lord Harley-Coats simply disappeared Christmas Eve 1882, Now that it a real mystery right there. No one has seen or heard of him in all that time. Apparently; he told his butler he was just popping out to deliver some late Christmas presents and simply vanished."

Harry nodded, finishing his tea; "Well, he can't be a suspect for this one; if there's foul play." Dorothy smiled and placed her cup down and buttoned up her light summer coat. Edwin headed for the door to wave down a cab and Harry paid 'Big Charles' four pennies for the breakfast.

They walked to the door and stood by the large window and watched the traffic and people passing. "He's probably had to go to Queen's Square to get one." Harry said checking his watch. He sighed; "I wish bloody Alistair was back off sick leave. I could always rely on him to cover me. Typical; a big court case and a bloody body found on the same morning." Dorothy patted her brother's arm; "Goes with the job; as you always say." Harry nodded and Edwin arrived in a cab and pushed the door open; "Had to go to bloody Queen's square to....." Harry just said; "I know." and helped Dorothy in.

As the cab trundled through the busy streets, Dorothy reminded him she was away [with Rosie acting as her Lady's maid] for the weekend with Mrs. Caroline Styles at her grand estate house in Richmond. Harry smiled, "Uncle William and I are really pleased you are making such friends. Her husband is a local councilor and was the one who managed to get the bloody council to erect street lighting in some of the poorer areas." He patted her hand, "Have a lovely time Dottie and really do try and enjoy yourself, relax and forget about the show for a while."

Dorothy smiled at her brother but sighed inside. She had – now considered foolish - a little argument with Mrs. Styles in front of several other members of the Whitechapel Ladies Cycle Club about what clothes a lady should wear when cycling. It was a daft argument and Dottie regretted how it ended. She had stated that a women wearing far less cumbersome clothing would be able to cycle better and best of all, if she defied convention and cycled naked, she could beat anyone who was dressed up despite ability or age! A steely eyed Mrs. Styles had smiled and said simply, "Prove it Miss Hadden, since you appear to be the font of all knowledge about proficiency in ladies cycling." The other ladies all agreed that Dorothy should place actions where her mouth was and prove her theory. To make it interesting, Mrs. Irene Gains soon was taking little bets on the outcome, after it was decided that Dorothy would complete two circuits of the Style's extensive grounds: stark naked! She would 'race' against a woman of her own age: Miss Delphi Rossington-Jones who would wear the conventional dress that ladies wore when riding their steel steeds of liberation.

"The humble pedal cycle was an icon of the Suffragette movement and was considered a symbol of free-movement and liberation for women everywhere!" SJW.

Mrs. Rossington-Jones excitedly announced that a grand total of six pounds and nine shillings had been 'collected' and if she won, that money would be donated by the club to the poor orphans of the borough. Dottie also announced the same outcome and all the ladies agreed with it. As Dottie dourly whispered to Alice, her cycling friend "So, the only time starving children are fed or clothed is when I show my fanny to everyone." Now that did make Alice laugh and she admitted throwing two and sixpence in the hat.

Mrs. Styles had made her own announcement and invited all the ladies to her London estate for the grand occasion which would take place over the following weekend. She would 'close' the grounds for the race and only club members would be present for the actual contest. When Dottie informed Rosie of the strange Predicament she found herself in, Rosie laughed so much that Dorothy had to make the damn tea because Rosie couldn't get out of her chair for some minutes!

It was a fifteen minute ride to Summerton House and Harry paid the cabby and they made their way up the overgrown steps to the massive double front doors. They had clearly not seen any paint for nearly quarter of a century. Constable Tanner stood by the door – looking thoroughly bored – he saluted Harry and jerked a thumb inside; "On the left Mr. Hadden. Doc Goldstein and the new man are in the second room on the right."

Harry chuckled and said quietly to Dorothy; "Funny isn't it? Jim Grieves has done eight years service and made Detective sergeant last year, but because he transferred in from Popular Nick to replace Alistair; he's the bloody new boy." Dorothy smiled at that and wondered what her brother's new sergeant was like. They made their way into the dusty and somewhat smelly house. There were cobwebs everywhere and the smell of damp and neglect filled the dim place. They could hear quiet voices coming through an open door and walked in. Dorothy was well impressed – physically – with her brother's new sergeant. He was a strapping young man with thick dark hair and matching eyes. To any woman he was easily very handsome and quite attractive.

He smiled at her and Harry. "Hello guv. You're going to love this one. Either Doc Goldstein has gone off his rocker or we have a real queer one here." Harry just nodded; "Well, I don't think Doc is off his head quite yet, so what's queer about the body?" Doc Goldstein was kneeling by the body and looked up. He didn't smile but rubbed a hand over his chin. "This may sound strange Harry, but I think this poor woman drown!"

Now that did make Harry chuckle. "Are you sure doc; we're an awful long way from the sea." Doc Goldstein eased himself up and held up a single finger; "Try the puddle that surrounds her. Its sea water and I think her lung and chest cavity is full of water; like her nose and throat. She drown Harry, the only marks on her are on both shoulders; slight bruising to both and apart from that; nothing else of note until I do the PM."

Dorothy carefully and slowly approached the body of the woman sprawled upon the dirty carpet and held a hand over her face in shock. After a few seconds, she managed to say; "Harry, I know this woman; it's Hanna Dashwood!" Harry gripped his sister's arm and asked if she wanted to sit. She shook her head; "For heaven's sake; she was a regular with me and the girls cycling on Sunday morning before Church!" Harry nodded; he knew that the 'Whitechapel Ladies Cycling Club' met every Sunday morning – before Church services – and that the women all knew each other well.

"When did you last see her – alive – Dorothy?" He asked and Dorothy shook her head; "She missed our get together's for a couple of months and everyone was starting to get a little concerned; she was a founding member after all." Harry stared down at the body; "Did you ever meet her husband?" Dorothy again shook her head; "All I can say is that Hanna didn't have a good word to say about the brute." Now that did catch Harry's interest.

"Did he knock her about?" he asked and Dorothy breathed deeply and nodded with real sadness. "Over the last few months, she stopped trying to hide the bruises. We all knew when the brute was home again. Hanna would have marks about her face and arms. Apparently he use to spank her with his belt; a real nasty piece of work by all accounts." She knelt down by the body and just shook herself with real sadness. "If this turns out to be murder; you won't have to look far for the suspect; except he probably has the best alibi in the world." She whispered.

Harry rubbed his chin and spoke directly to Jim grieves; "Get someone to go round the house and see if the bastard is still there." Jim nodded and slapped his bowler hat on, but Dorothy stopped him; "No point; Captain Dashwood is probably still at sea. He left a week ago for Argentina and certainly won't be back for at least another couple of weeks."

Harry sighed; "Well there goes our best suspect for the murder – if it is murder – that's some alibi; on a ship at sea with dozens of witnesses and no way to go anywhere."

Doc Goldstein stopped scribbling in his little notebook and tapped it with his pencil; "I'll get the PM done soon as I have time. We should have some results for you tomorrow Harry." He shoved the notebook and pencil into his coat pockets and placed his hat on. Harry thanked him and turned to Jim; "We'll handle it as murder for now. People who drown usually can't make their way to abandoned old houses and lay down in the bloody music room. Someone had to dump her here and that's good enough for me to treat this as suspected murder."

Jim nodded his agreement and shouted for Tanner to fetch Church's the Undertaker. Dorothy sat on the edge of a very old fashioned – and dirty – armchair and looked about. Everything reeked of decay and neglect; except the harpsichord. It sat by the window and looked like it had been delivered from the shop only yesterday. She eased herself up and went over to it. Her long fingers strummed a few strings and found it was perfectly in tune. Who would deliver a brand new instrument to a derelict house? And perhaps, more importantly: why? She thought. "Harry, this is bloody odd. Everything in this room is old and decayed. The piano looks like it's full of dirt and woodworm. But this harpsichord is almost perfect; looks brand new." Harry left the body and stared at the instrument; Dottie was right; it looked like it was delivered yesterday!

Dorothy ran a hand down its neck and spoke quietly. Tapping the wood near the base; "The Supplies label or shop address has been removed. Why would anyone do that?" Harry admitted he didn't know. Dorothy walked back to the body and knelt down by the late Mrs. Hanna Dashwood. Something about the body bothered her and she couldn't quite put her finger on it.

"I bet you're thinking the same as me miss?" Jim smiled at her and gestured to the body; "No handbag. My mother and sisters wouldn't be seen dead without their handbags." He chuckled. But Dorothy stared back at the body and gently lifted an arm. It came to her in a flash and she called Harry over. "Take a look Harry. Hanna's wearing a winter jacket with a winter skirt. I strongly suspect that her underwear will be winter issue too. Why the hell is she dressed for winter in the middle of a very warm summer?"

Harry knelt by the body – again – and sighed; "Christ Dottie, none of us blokes would have spotted that. But what's the significance of it?" Dorothy stared back at the Harpsichord; "That's another strange thing to add to the list; first Hanna drowned when the nearest ocean is about fifty miles away, secondly she's found in an abandoned and derelict old house in a room full of old decaying instruments except a brand new harpsichord; and finally wearing her winter clothes in the middle of a hot summer?" Harry helped his sister up and they walked to the front door and stood in the warm sunshine; looking up at the old house. The downstairs windows were all boarded up. The signs of decay and neglect were everywhere. "He was just twenty three when he disappeared. No trace of him has ever been found. Apparently the solicitors Brice & Playfiar's are trustees of the property. They don't seem to be spending much on the upkeep." Harry said and checked his fob watch again and said quietly; "Time to grab a cab and get to court. I'll drop you off at the theatre on the way."

They walked down to the main road and Harry waved down a handsome cab. He explained to the driver; first, the Paradise Road theatre, then the old Bailey. The young cabbie nodded and Harry helped Dottie into the plush interior. Harry saw the look on his sisters face; "What's up Dottie?" He asked and Dorothy didn't smile; "There's something really odd about that old house, but I can't – for the moment – put my finger on it."

Harry chuckled; "Knowing you Dottie, you'll figure it out; no matter how odd the damn thing is."

Dorothy almost smiled, but then shuddered a little; "Do you know, that all the time I was in that dreadful place; I felt I was being watched." Harry patted her hand; "Steady girl, you'll be seeing the Eastend monster next!" That made Dorothy chuckle and she gripped her brother's hand.

Holding up her skirt, she quickly walked up the steps and past the empty, stage door office and made her dressing room in good time. She pushed in and wondered where Rosie was. Then she heard her voice from the change room and pulled open the door. Rosie was standing holding out a cup of tea and curtsied, "Madam's tea is bleeding poured!" Dottie giggled and pulled off her hat. Rosie was naked apart from a small apron and maids cap. The pair kissed and Dottie whispered, "Now this is what I call service."

Dorothy didn't bother undressing and sat on the chair with Rosie between her legs and enjoyed the attention of Rosie's fingers and tongue. She was holding up her skirt and petticoats and groaning softly when she could hear knocking at the door. Both women ignored it and Dorothy found her cup of tea was stone cold when Rosie finished pleasing her young lover. But she did find a note pushed under the door. It was from Reggie. He had quit.

 **CHAPTER 2. 'BICYCLE FACE!' Dr. A. Shadwell.**

Dorothy and Rosie sat in the cab and re-read Reggie's note. "It's just plan daft and just his pride talking: bleeding male ego that's all." Dottie said and sat back, pushing the note into her handbag. Rosie agreed and asked what the plan of action was. "We'll have a sensible adult conversation and since I know he has brains, he will listen and agree." Dottie said quietly, and then saw Rosie Grinning: "Yes, and if that don't bleeding work, we'll just pull up our bleeding skirts and tell what he'll miss most about Miss Pandora and her magic box!" Dottie sighed and then laughed, hugging her friend. She had certainly missed Reggie in that department.

They arrived at his tenement and Dorothy paid the cabby. They walked up the stairs and knocked loudly at his door. It was opened by a quiet, morose Reggie who just stood aside and let them in. Rosie brewed some tea in the small kitchen, listening to Dorothy explaining about his return to the show being the right and logical thing to do. She said twice that he was forgiven for falling for the seducers plans and that she [Dorothy] knew he had been fooled, like she had. Rosie could hear silence, and then laughter. Now with a smile, she lifted the tea tray and walked in saying, "Thank bleeding God, you've sorted that out, Dottie you were right about adult conversation...." She stopped in mid-sentence and almost dropped the tray with laughter. Dorothy was standing in front of a very happy Reggie with her skirt and petticoats pulled right up. She had forgotten to wear any knickers this morning, not that Reggie was complaining. Rosie shook her head with some amusement and placed the tray down as Reggie pulled of his shirt. "Come on you little tart, let me get your bleeding corset off." She said as Dorothy pulled off her hat and coat.

It was a good two hours later that Dorothy and Rosie left Reggie snoring naked on the bed and caught a cab home; both smiling and now relaxed. Rosie sighed and shifted awkwardly on the seat, gripping Dorothy's hand, "Bleeding hell, twice each in two hours. I don't think he had emptied his balls all week."

Dorothy just smiled, sitting with her legs open and smoothing down her skirt. "Well, I think he bloody well has now. Problem solved, thanks to your brilliant plan." They both started to laugh and gripped hands. "Now for that bloody bike ride." Dorothy muttered with a small smile.

Rosie was still chuckling as they boarded the tram and they

placed their overnight bags under the seat and Dottie paid the conductor. "I can hear you Mrs. McHannon's." Was all she said and that made Rosie giggle even more. "I do hope they have a bloody camera man there, I'll happily pay a guinea - if I had a bleeding guinea – to see you stark naked, pedaling a bleeding push bike around the grounds of that big house!" She slowly rummaged in her big handbag and pulled out a packet of mint humbugs and offered Dottie one, "Come on, get it in your mouth darling, you'll enjoy it."

Dorothy slowly took the sweet and whispered, "Blimey I can't count the number of men that have said that to me." and popped the sweet in her smiling mouth. Rosie nearly choked on hers and squeezed Dottie's hand with some affection. "I do hope you don't get bleeding Bicycle face rushing around those county roads!" Rosie laughed again and Dorothy just shook her head in mock despair. "More likely to get a bloody frost-bitten fanny and sore bum cheeks." Dottie muttered and smiled at the Conductor, paying the three penny fare for each of them to Hammersmith. They enjoyed the ride on the new tram system which had only opened for service a couple of years ago. Both were impressed and pleasantly surprised by the short time the journey took. It would have been quite expensive in a cab.

"A certain physician in 1897 had warned women cyclists about the dangers of 'Bicycle Face' caught from riding their bikes. He stated that it could ruin their looks! It was, of course, total bollocks, but it was the Victorian era, wasn't it.… " SJW.

Mrs. Styles welcomed them to her grand house with some apparent affection and confided to Dorothy that she was really impressed that she had turned up. "I really thought you would find some excuse to back out of the bet. But I am so pleased you didn't. It shows that you're dedicated to the spirit of freedom for women!" Dorothy now discovered that Mrs. Styles was a 'closet' Suffragette. And she showed Dorothy her suite – normally the Butler or housekeeper would do that – and said that all the arrangements had been made. As she left Dorothy and Rosie standing in their magnificent Tudor style room, she turned and informed them that Miss Delphi Rossington-Jones had arrived, boasting that her seamstress had made her a wonderful new outfit to cycle in. Then Mrs. Styles actually made Dorothy [and Rosie] laugh when she admitted that men would find Dorothy's outfit their choice of cycling attire for women, regardless of how wonderful Delphi's costume looked. She added that dinner was at seven and there would be over twenty guests. She tapped her chin and said that she would sit Dorothy next to her young friend who was home on leave from the navy. She slowly closed the door and departed.

"I think the old bird actually bleeding likes you darling." Rosie muttered and bounced up and down on the bed. "Christ! It's like a bowl of porridge, bleeding wonderful." Dottie joined her and agreed. That's when Dorothy spotted the portrait above the small fireplace and sat up, "Take a look at that Tudor gentleman Rosie, I bet he had the bleeding prim and proper ladies of the Royal court wetting themselves." They both jumped from the bed and went over and studied the picture. Rosie had to nod her total agreement. The young man had thick dark hair and brown eyes – piecing brown eyes – and a small smile on his mouth. He was clearly of mixed blood with a slight darkening of his impressive features. Dottie believed in could be of European and North African blood, maybe Egyptian or Persian. [Now Iran] but, in any generation he would certainly be considered a handsome man, a very alluring handsome young man. Dorothy read the little plate beneath: "Sir Henry Capstone circa. 1510 Anno Domino. I am a gift from England's new sun."

"Bloody hell, he's a right good looker, no bleeding mistake, but what does Annie Dominoes mean?" Rosie asked, admiring the long dead young man. Dorothy chuckled and said, "It means 'after death' and England's sun was a young Henry the Eighth who had been crowned King the previous year. He was still a young man then, considered by people at the time, as one of England's most handsome men!" Now Rosie chuckled at that, "Well, he certainly aged into a bleeding old misery guts, lopping heads off his numerous wives and kicking the Pope up the bum!" Dottie had to smile at Rosie's somewhat base, but succinct appraisal of Henry's most notorious and famous achievements.

Rosie now started to unpack their cases, but Dottie stood staring at the portrait and sighed, "To think he was a young man, full of hopes, dreams, passions and life. Now he's gone, leaving just a small portrait of his face as he's only legacy and proof that he even lived. Makes you think doesn't it?"

Rosie held up a small pair of shoes, "These riding shoes darling?" and Dottie nodded, "Since I won't have much else to worry about, I had quite a light weight pair made. I've tried them out and their comfortable and functional." Rosie smiled, "I would have thought the bleeding saddle would be the most important bit of equipment, since your darling pink bum will be bouncing up and down on it without any protection." Dorothy laughed, "Well, genius, thanks for pointing out the obvious and I have obtained a sheepskin cover for that!" She looked back at the portrait and sighed again. "Come on; let's find a suitable dress for dinner." The reception room was packed with well dressed guests and there was polite and quiet conversations abounding. Dorothy was a little besieged by fellow ladies of her cycling club who all asked – basically - the same question, "Was she really going to do it!"

Dorothy announced she was, with quite a flourish and many kissed her with real pride. Then Mrs. Styles announced dinner and Dorothy heard her say, "Henry darling, would you please escort Miss Hadden into dinner." She turned and smiled, then really smiled, no, she actually grinned. Mrs. Styles formally introduced the couple to each other as social protocols dictated. "Miss Hadden, I would like you to meet a family friend: Henry George Capstone, a Lieutenant Commander in his majesty's most royal navy."

The young man took her hand and kissed it whilst Dottie did a very fair curtsy. She had to take a little breath, the 20th Century Henry Capstone was – in Dorothy's own words – 'fucking gorgeous!' In fact, - in her mind – the bloody portrait hanging in her bedroom had magically come to life and was made flesh.

They sat at the well laid and grand table, making small talk. To Dorothy his words were liquid chocolate being poured into her very receptive ears. The young man was absolutely charming and witty and his smile could melt an iceberg. Finally, she had to mention the painting and he laughed [which Dorothy adored] and said that the young man in the painting was indeed his ancestor and namesake. The name Henry was very common in the family and had passed down the generations along with the original Henry Capstone's genes. Between the courses, the pair locked in conversation and Dottie found that the man was very, very knowledgeable about the Tudor period.

"Reading about my ancestor Henry gave me the desire for the

sea. He was – at the time – a seafarer himself. From what I have discovered, he could have been part-time pirate, buccaneer or privateer serving King Henry who was trying to construct an English navy to police England's moat [the English Channel]. But he found time to amass a fortune, get shipwrecked – twice – marry three times and father six children. The marriages were a bit naughty, since he had an English wife, a South American one and a Spanish one too. All at the same time I'm afraid! Sadly, it's always been rumoured in the family history that he also had a couple of mistresses so I wonder where he found the time for his sea going adventures!" Henry lifted his glass, "To my ancestor and to you Miss Hadden, because without the gentle beauty and comfort of the fair sex, a man's life is a passionless cenotaph of desires."

They tapped glasses and he leaned close and whispered, "Are you really going to do a lady Godiva in the name of Women's liberation and free choice?" Dorothy sipped her wine and nodded, "I am sir. I will do it for my sisters everywhere." The young man smiled broadly, "Then my little Amazon, I salute you and your sisters and may they succeed!" They both laughed, not even realizing every eye was upon them. Especially Mrs. Style's who sipped her wine and smiled. Henry confided that he would love to cheer her infamous bike ride, but men were excluded from the event. Dorothy just smiled.

When the sumptuous meal ended the sexes split [as convention dictated] and Dorothy found herself playing Bridge with three friends form the Cycling club. The two major topics were poor Hanna Dashwood and the handsome young Henry Capstone. Dorothy fended off questions about Hanna by saying it was confidential and her darling brother was tight-lipped on such cases. Regarding Henry, she just made small talk and smiled a great deal. The party broke up just before midnight and Rosie met her at the bedroom door, lamp in hand. Electricity hadn't quite reached here yet. Rosie wanted to know every little detail about the dashing young man, as she undressed Dottie. Rosie listened with great interest, finally saying, "Well if that handsome bugger leapt out of his bleeding painting, he could wreck my ship and explore my regions without any bloody arguments!"

The pair sat up in bed, sipping tea and talking quietly with the brilliant morning sun streaming through the open curtains. The 'race' was scheduled for 10am: after a good breakfast of course and Dorothy was a little nervous about it now. But happy Rosie comforted her and made Dottie laugh. They kissed gently several times and finally, Dorothy took the cups and placed them on the bedside table. She pushed Rosie on her back and starting by kissing her face, neck, shoulders and big breasts. She certainly lingered over them. They giggled and rolled gently around the bed, playing until the love making started in earnest.

Mrs. Styles stood in the grand doorway of her magnificent house, hands on hips, staring at the sky with a small smile; there were no reports of rain for the area reported in the local papers, which had just arrived. The headlines were interesting, "Suffragette's plan naked protest to humiliate Government!" she whispered to herself, with one paper declaring that all of western civilization was at risk if these damn women paraded around naked with no shame. Another demanded a trial for all those involved and imprisonment for the ringleaders. She sighed and walked to the dining room for breakfast, telling her butler to ensure that Miss Hadden received copies of the papers.

It was the arrival of a local Police Inspector and several uniform constables that signaled the authorities were taking the situation seriously. Inspector Haines and Sergeant Grimshaw were shown into Mrs. Styles study and – unsurprisingly – served tea. Mrs. Styles explained at length, that it would take place on private property; there were no cameras allowed and certainly no men. It wasn't a Suffragette protest [even if it really was!] and would outrage no-one's morals with the nudity [since they were all women]. The 'public' certainly were not invited and that included the press and the police. She also pointed out that Miss Hadden had performed before the King. The dour Inspector sipped his tea and simply shook his head. "No." was all he replied.

 With a heavy police presence around the grounds, Dorothy and Rosie watched from the bedroom windows and laughed together. They were particularly amused by the actions of the other guests, who stood chatting with police, sharing tea and sandwiches with them. "Only could happen in bloody England." Dorothy muttered.

The police remained until nightfall, and then thinking it was safe, withdrew. That evening there was some unplanned and unusual entertainment for Mrs. Style's guests in the large ballroom. Everyone gathered and cheered the indomitable Amazon on her trusty bike as she pedaled around the large room in nothing but her shoes and a very, very long blond wig, cleverly and carefully tied with ribbons in the important places. Then to everyone's surprise and delight she was joined by Miss Delphi Rossington-Jones in a matching outfit. All the ladies wanted to join in, but at such short notice, only two appropriate length wigs could be found. So they contented themselves with much applause and supporting cheers.

Dorothy cycled slowly past a very happy young man who loudly applauded and held up a thumb, "Good show old girl! Make those oppressed Tudor women proud!" Dorothy just smiled at him, watching Rosie whispering in his ear. After another incredible dinner every one retired to their rooms, well, not everyone.

Mrs. Styles spoke with young Henry as the evening broke up, talking closely together at the foot of the grand staircase and the pair exchanged quite a passionate kiss and Mrs. Styles headed for the empty bedroom next to Dorothy's and with a glass of whisky clutched in one hand, slid the secret panel back behind the large wardrobe and settled in, peering through the two-way mirror at Dorothy's big bed. She smiled and sipped her whisky as she was joined by Mrs. Richards and Lady Du Ville. They both pulled up chairs and Mrs. Richards took the bottle of whisky from the cabinet by the window and poured a glass for herself and Lady Du Ville. "The 'Tudor Room' has never failed to deliver a good show and I understand the slutty common tart Miss Hadden call's her 'ladies maid' is joining in tonight. Henry is delighted that the rumours about Miss Hadden appear to be true. She and the common tart will be excellent additions to our little parties. He believes with a little seductive work he can get the pair to perform with bloody dogs!"

Mrs. Styles chuckled and Lady Du Ville sipped her whisky and said quietly, "That's my husband's favourite: he keeps a couple of well endowed Irish Wolf-Hounds for that purpose at our Normandy estate. I will certainly invite Mademoiselle Hadden and her trollop maid for a small summer vacation." Her French accent was quite clear and Mrs. Richards just smiled, already re-filling her glass.

"It's a pity this little bicycle race couldn't have taken place there darling Chloe, we British are so damn stiff when it comes to nakedness. I'm sure your local Gendarmes wouldn't not have bothered you or Count Du Ville over such a petty matter." Mrs.

Richards spoke softly and Chloe nodded and laughed, "I think you are right Ellen, he pays them enough to keep their noses out of our business, besides, knowing our local police, they would have insisted in being spectators!"

Ellen leaned forward and asked Mrs. Styles about their own entertainment after this show was over. Mrs. Styles smiled and said quietly, "Young Gareth the footman and little Joanne the upstairs maid will be dropping by in about an hour. You will particularly enjoy her Chloe; she has no qualms about being pissed on and performs as a human toilet when required. A thoroughly disgusting, dirty little creature with the morals of an old Paris street whore, yet she looks like butter wouldn't melt in her mouth. Bless her!" Lady Du Ville now smiled broadly, "I am always amazed where you find these creatures from my darling. You really do have a knack for finding talent that would make the master smile with pleasure." Ellen agreed with that and sipped her whisky, then sat up as the bedroom door of 'The Tudor Room' opened. The portrait of Henry Capstone had worked its magic yet again. "It's Showtime." Whispered Mrs. Styles and allowed Ellen to refill her glass.

CHAPTER 3. 'I GIVE MY MIND THE LIBERTY TO FOLLOW THE FIRST WISE OR FOOLISH IDEA THAT PRESENTS ITSELF.' Robert Greene.

Titmarsh the local poacher sank deeper in to the bush and gripped his shotgun, then rubbed his face, "Well, I thought I had seen it bloody all! But that takes the bloody cake!" He whispered to himself and just had to smile, shaking his head, he slipped away in the darkness. Some yards away, at the rear of the big stables, three hurricane lamps lit part of the small gravel path and the playful antics of the three naked people. The young man had his arms around the giggling young woman, both watching the other woman cycling slowly around the lamps with some trepidation. Her language was quite ripe and centered on her bum rubbing the bleeding saddle despite the sheepskin cover and her bleeding fanny exposed to the cold night air.

Dorothy said softly, "Well, it will keep the bloody thing fresh!" The bike was soon abandoned and the three slipped back in the house to continue their games. Rosie sat at the end of the bed watching the pair having some really passionate sex in the Missionary position and admired the young man's heaving arse as he pounded Dottie hard and fast [which she always enjoyed], she rubbed herself with some vigour and really couldn't wait for her turn. The couple changed position with Dorothy now on top, riding Henry like a Grand National winner. They were panting and groaning from their exertions and Rosie couldn't wait any longer. She joined in, and Henry had her sit on his face with Rosie discovering to her delight, that he was as good with his tongue and fingers, as he was with his big cock. Rosie found herself in her beloved Missionary position, cussing and moaning under his wonderful assault. He finally had to finish in her and lay back gasping and grinning, then smiled broadly as Dorothy cleaned her other lover up with her mouth. He managed to whisper, "Ladies, if this is women's liberation then I'm a supporter. You can have the vote or anything else you bloody want!"

The two girls went to work with their mouths and fingers and soon had young Henry back in shape for more intense fucking. They found out to their further delight that he had the stamina of a breeding bull, let loose in a field of happy cows. He certainly didn't disappoint: their stifled screams and cussing paid tribute to that. They stopped a couple of times for whisky and cigarettes, with the girls rushing to the toilet to pee, laughing together. Then the fucking resumed with real dirty sex and it certainly made Dorothy's eyes water despite Rosie beneath her, helping out with her mouth and fingers. The girls swapped and Rosie now gripped the headboard and cussed having an anal orgasm that would have made the Victoria Falls look like a tap dripping. Dorothy, underneath, yelped, saying she was having a bleeding cum shower. But she certainly didn't mind: not one little bit.

The dawn was creeping through the curtains when the trio finally collapsed on the bed, cuddled together, and Rosie managed to recount the incredible score. "Sweet bleeding Jesus Christ, we've been at it for almost four solid hours! I'm bloody knackered!" Dorothy could only moan a little in reply, she had – to quote the modern term – 'tapped out'. Henry lay snoring on his back and the two women snuggled up to him and slept.

The three 'ladies' behind the mirror had been so transfixed by the dirty sweaty sexual shenanigans they hadn't bothered to indulge in any themselves! Mrs. Styles dabbed her face and yawned, declaring that Miss Hadden wasn't a two guinea whore: she could demand – and get – a large white five pound note for her sexual endevours and the other ladies all agreed. "She's an absolute must for the parties and that filthy trollop maid of hers would certainly take on dogs or horses for a little tip!" The Countess muttered, tired but happy with the show. The ladies headed to their rooms to sleep until lunch. Mrs. Styles had decided that Miss Hadden [and her maid] were now her 'best' friends and would receive invitation to the next orgy and black Sabbath for her master.

Dorothy and Rosie lay in the bathtub in relative silence, both enjoying the wonderful hot water and bath salts. Their 'Dutch caps' lay in the sink having a thorough soak too. Dorothy laid thinking about the genetic and name co-incidences that surrounded the stunning young Mr. Henry Capstone. Her animal passions had now given away to rational thought and she run a big sponge between her legs and started to wonder about the young man. It was Rosie that finally put her thoughts into perspective. "Bloody hell, our Henry certainly takes after his ancestor in many bleeding respects doesn't he? I mean he's a sailor too, can handle multiple women - thank fuck! – and is almost the dirty buggers twin!"

That didn't make Dottie happy and she sat up, "Rosie, I've just had a thought, what if he's a….." She stopped in mid-sentence, realizing who she was talking to. Rosie didn't know about Mister Jericho Tibbs, time travelers, angels and demons and of course, the real truth about Mister Sims. "What if he's what?" Rosie asked, taking the sponge with a little smile. Dorothy thought fast, finishing her sentence, "What if he's a married man? I'd feel really guilty about what happened then." Rosie sighed and shrugged her shoulders, "Well, I'm a bleeding married woman, so that could even things out!" Dorothy had to chuckle at that, but her mind was turning over the 'facts'. In her experience of bloody time travelers and from what Jericho had told her and Harry [and Uncle William too] Henry had the appearance of a bloody time-traveller!

But then, Mrs. Styles belonged in this time and place, after all, she was married to a prominent business man who definitely must be from this time. She eased from the bath and grabbed a towel. But her mind certainly wasn't placated by those basic logical thoughts. With a deep sigh, she realized she needed to look more closely at this young man and probably his friends too. Now Dorothy had her detective hat on – so as to speak – and she dried herself slowly, thinking there are over thirty bedrooms in this big house and Mrs. Styles placed her in the 'Tudor Room' which contained a picture of a supposed long dead ancestor who just happened to look exactly like her young friend. Was that by accident or design?

Dorothy shook her head, that didn't make sense, why draw attention to those supposed co-incidences if Henry was a time traveller? Then she looked back at Rosie – her supposed Ladies maid – and wondered if Henry had a valet. They would know all about his movements. She would start there. Dorothy was a little unhappy with herself and wondered if she had started to mistrust all men [except Harry and Uncle William] after the Mister bloody Cadbury incident: and then Reggie's unexpected 'betrayal'. But her faith had been restored a little by 'the beast'. Now that was some mystery she needed to apply her investigative skills to, after all, there can't be many men around the east end matching his description. "Come Rosie; get your bum out the damn bath. Let's get some breakfast." Rosie sighed and eased reluctantly from the tub. Dorothy pulled on her bath robe and asked quietly, "Does our sexual Adonis have a man servant?"

Rosie picked up a towel and thought for a second or two, then nodded, "Yeah, apparently a nice lad called John Thomas." She giggled, "Can you image going through bleeding life with a handle [name] like that?" Dorothy now smiled at her, "Thank you darling, that's most interesting."

The girls dressed and headed for their breakfasts, Dorothy to the grand dining room and Rosie to the servant's quarters. Dottie gave Rosie a little assignment and sat at the table and engaged in polite conversation with some of the other guests. Most would be leaving this afternoon – after luncheon – and she peered at Mrs. Styles, chatting away to another woman, the topic was 'is Britain really a democracy!' Dorothy ate her well buttered toast and wondered what she found odd about the woman: she appeared to look quite tired.

Mrs. Styles turned to her and smiled, "Oh Miss Hadden, Henry asked if you wish to ride before lunch? He would – of course –

asked you himself, but he's at the stables picking a horse. Shall I send a message saying you agree?" Dorothy smiled and nodded, "Yes, I would enjoy that Mrs. Styles. A ride before lunch would be most invigorating and increase the appetite." Mrs. Styles said it would be done and really smiled - again. For some reason Dottie thought of a snake peering at a rabbit! Then she thought: is Mrs. Styles pointing her towards Henry for a reason? But what was that reason? But what troubled her most, was why did the 'Tudor' Henry capstone's picture hang in a bedroom in Mrs. Styles house?

The pair was adhering to an old English custom of the summer months: they were rolling in the hay. Dorothy was on all fours, spitting hay from her mouth as Henry fucked her from behind pulling stands of the bloody stuff from his hair and torso. Dorothy was pushing backwards and couldn't help but moan, keeping an eye on the two big men bailing hay just yards away! Their horses stood idly by, but were more than happy to nibble the damn stuff. Then Dorothy was on top, leaning forward, gripping his shoulders and pushing herself up and down with real passion. Dottie started to moan quite loudly and so she slapped a hand over her own mouth as Henry enjoyed her swinging breasts. They finished in the Missionary position and lay in the hay, talking quietly with each other. Henry consulted his fob watch and pointed out that they couldn't miss luncheon: there would be too much gossip and they had Dorothy's reputation to consider, she was an unmarried woman after all. That's when Henry dropped his bombshell; he was married to Abigail and had been so for about a year. They had no children yet but he grinned; stroking Dorothy's shocked face and stated they were definitely trying on that score. He leaned across and kissed the silent Dorothy. "You two will get on like a house on fire. You're both committed and passionate about some things....and you fuck like cheap Piccadilly whores! She'll love Rosie who will get on really well with Sarah."

Dottie managed to ask who the hell Sarah was. And Henry smiled, picking straw from her hair, "Oh, that Abbey's maid, like you have wonderful Rosie, she has Sarah. The pair are quite similar in fact, Rosie and Sarah I mean, they take it up the bum really well and don't scream the damn house down!" he stood and held out his hand. "Come on sweetie, let's get some lunch. I'm returning to London with you and I'll arrange for you to meet Abby and Sarah. She'll certainly invite you over when I'm away at work, being quite a nice little foursome I suspect." Dorothy took his hand and he pulled her gently up. "I'm sure she'll introduce you two to her friends. The Carter's are our favourites, Irene is probably one of the best lesbian lovers there is and Peter doesn't mind men either. Then there's the Newcomb's from Bermondsey, they are quite outrageous and Kate has a collection of bloody toys that would shame the Spanish Inquisition." They dressed quickly and walked the horses back to the groom, who knew full they had not been riding: there wasn't a drop of sweat on their mounts!

The two big men stopped wielding their pitch-forks and passed a flagon of cider between themselves, watching the couple walking up the drive to the big house. "Nice tits and arse, but a bit skinny for me." The smaller one stated and that made the bigger man laugh, "Come on Tom, if you had that perched on your cock, like he had, you wouldn't say that!" They both laughed and with the short break over, went back to bailing hay, ignoring the other couple fucking just yards away.

Rosie gasped as the young man finished and rolled off, she was surprised – and somewhat disappointed – that John Thomas had lasted all of fifteen minutes! "With a bleeding name like that, I expected better, a lot bleeding better." Rosie muttered to herself and pulled down her skirt and buttoned up her blouse. He was lying there grinning and jerking his cock in anticipation of more.

He was unlucky, Rosie had to go and make her report. She had a piss behind the water barrels at the back door and headed up the gravel path to the house. She couldn't make head or tail out of what young John Thomas had said, but she knew that Dorothy probably would.

After lunch, Dorothy lay sprawled on the big chaise lounge in her room and flicked through a magazine, but she really wasn't reading it. Her head was full of what she and Rosie had learnt about the dashing Henry Capstone, his wife and mistress [who was good friends!] their friends who loved to take part in orgies and the very wild sex games that took place on Henry's modest estate. Then there was the strange information obtained from the laughably named 'John Thomas' the valet.

It appears that Henry was a man of mystery – apart from his sexual exploits of course – vanishing for weeks at a time. The real teaser was that he served in the navy yet was rarely at sea. Apparently he worked at Admiralty House just off Trafalgar Square in some obscure department. All the valet knew was that it was referred to as 'Section 7'. But the most important clue or discovery Rosie made – using her ample charms – was that Henry carried a very old compass everywhere and it was rarely out of his sight. Apparently it had been made in the 1480's and was a direct link back to his ancestor and namesake. The original Henry Capstone had owned it and it had been passed down the generations. Dorothy knew that she needed to see that compass. Then she chuckled to herself: how the hell would she know if it was a time portal! Soon as she had confirmed her suspicions, she would tell Sims to inform Jericho Tibbs about Henry Capstone.

The other really important piece of information Rosie had discovered was that Mrs. Styles had been Henry's lover too. But – for some undisclosed reason – the pair had parted, yet remained friends. Henry also remained her husband's 'business associate' and Mrs. Styles husband had been particularly successful dabbling on the Stock market lately. Dorothy wondered if that success was down to information supplied by Henry: if he was a time traveller he would know which shares were about to rise and fall. Was that the reason Mrs. Styles remained 'friends' with Henry? Money: and lots of it?

Did she keep the young man and his 'wife' supplied with new lovers using the picture in the bedroom to arouse interest and then push them together? All in all it wasn't a pretty picture: planned seductions to keep the cash rolling in?

The train was late by some four minutes and steamed into Fenchurch Street station not entirely oblivious of the fact. The driver was cussing and being cussed at by the Station master. Dorothy and Rosie walked with Henry from the concourse and said their goodbyes at the taxi rank. He had supplied them with his address and told them to pay a visit on his wife! Dorothy listened carefully as he jumped into the first cab, telling him 'Admiralty House, Whitehall'. The second cab pulled up and Dorothy told him 13, Dock Lane, Eastham.

"What a bleeding set up he has! His wife in bed with his mistress and all their bloody friends joining in, I bet the devil would love to cast his net at one of their parties." Rosie popped a strawberry in her mouth and enjoyed it. Dorothy had purchased a punnet from the fruit seller who had a barrow outside the Rail station. Dorothy sat quietly, a fat strawberry at her lips and thought about what Rosie had just said about the Devil. A very disturbing thought popped into her head; had Rosie and she just had sex with a devil worshipper? Or the leader of a witches coven? Both parties had the same sexual practices. "Warlock." She said and ate the strawberry with Rosie leaning forward saying, "What's that you say? Bollocks?"

Dorothy laughed and Rosie just stared at her. The cab dropped Dottie at home and then set off for Rosie's address. She had given Rosie more than enough for the cab fare and so Rosie would treat her boy's to some fish and chips and her and Albert could enjoy a couple of bottles of porter.

The anticipated note arrived just before diner, hand delivered by the wonderfully named 'John Thomas' from Henry, giving details of a special costume party his wife was organizing for the next weekend. The invite included Rosie and stated there would be fireworks, in and outside the bedrooms! She pushed it into her handbag and went into dinner. They had a guest tonight: Miss Alice Sherwood who Uncle William sat opposite Harry. Dorothy and Uncle William both sat smiling at each other and Miss Alice Sherwood. Harry squirmed in his chair but warmed up to the charming and very pretty lady as the dinner proceeded.

Dorothy smiled as the pair chatted: Alice would make a fine wife! She wondered how long before Harry also knew that.

CHAPTER 4. 'EVERY HOUSE GUEST BRINGS HAPPINESS, SOME WHEN THEY ARRIVE AND SOME WHEN THEY ARE LEAVING.' Confucius.

Dorothy was reading the East London Gazette with some interest as Rosie checked her stage costume and made more tea. "It says that her husband – Frank Dashwood – is due to dock in London on Saturday. He doesn't know yet that his wife is dead, since his ship; the SS Polar Queen cannot be contacted at sea since she's already sailed. He has been away for at least three weeks after sailing to Argentina with a consignment of bloody Ice-cream! And is now heading back from Argentina with a cargo of beef."

Dorothy lowered the paper and smiled at Rosie; "He has the perfect alibi for the murder of his wife. He was hundreds of miles away at sea with dozens of Witnesses who would – of course – notice if their bloody Captain disappeared."

Rosie poured more tea and looked a little puzzled; "I thought the poor woman drown?" She asked and Dorothy nodded; "She drown all right, with someone holding her under the damn water. The bruising on her shoulders clearly indicated she had been held down."

"So its bleeding murder then?" Rosie asked, spooning a couple of sugars into her big mug of tea and easing herself down opposite Dorothy. "Yes, Harry is treating it as murder; according to the autopsy she died some four days before her body was found. That lets her violent and nasty husband off the hook." Rosie nodded and handed over a couple of biscuits. "Why did the murderer dump the body in the old house?" She asked; a little intrigued with young Harry Hadden's latest case. Dorothy shrugged her shoulders; "Maybe he hoped that it wouldn't be found for some time. After all, no one normally goes near the place. But some street kids found the old kitchen door open and wandered in. They found poor Hanna in the old music room."

Rosie leaned back and sipped her tea; "Another bloody mystery chalked up to the old house. First the young Lord disappears, then his aunt is found dead in bed – strangled – and the young footman is stabbed to death in a bar room brawl. Not one bleeding murderer was caught. That old Inspector was as much use as a bicycle is to a fish." Dorothy smiled at that; old Detective Inspector Roy Games hadn't been the best detective the Metropolitan police had. He left a spate of unsolved serious crimes when he retired. Harry did manage to clear up a couple of the 'Cold Cases' but he really didn't have time to look at all the outstanding murders.

There was a knock at the door and Rosie jumped up and answered it, she turned to Dorothy; "It's a Mrs. Lucille Bellman for you." And she showed the elegant woman in. Dorothy rose from her chair and placed the cup down, Mrs. Bellman was the young wife of the new owner of Paradise Road Music Hall and

Theatre. She also had just recently joined the 'Whitechapel Ladies Cycling Club' and so Dorothy had been getting to know her.

There was quite an age difference between Mrs. Bellman and her husband – a rich textile merchant and mill owner – of some twenty one years. He had admitted to big Tom [the stage manager] when he visited the Paradise, that he had purchased the theatre as 'an amusing little project'. Tom hadn't smiled at that revelation; but at least it had kept the place open and the staff [and performers] employed.

The women chatted over tea and Mrs. Bellman seemed very interested in Dorothy's brother's investigation. Dorothy explained at some length that she wasn't privy to certain aspects of Harry's investigation for confidential reasons. Mrs. Bellman just peered over her tea cup and nodded. Dorothy cleverly – and discretely – swung the conversation away from the murder and asked how Lucille had met her new husband.

Dorothy was a little surprised that Mr. Bellman was her second husband; her first had died in a collapsed mine in South Africa. He had been a Mining Engineer. She had been widowed just eighteen months when she met Mr. Bellman – also a widower – whilst he was on holiday in Johannesburg. They had married and returned to England together. She admitted it had been hard to become a step-mother to three grown up children, who clearly resented their father marrying again so soon after their mother's death.

But what did surprise Dorothy was Lucille's reluctance to discuss the 'Boer war' that had only just ended in South Africa. She made no comments about English actions regarding the Internment camps and the horrific suffering they caused innocent women and children. Lucille's silence was deafening on the subject, with Dottie assuming she and her husband were ardent supporters of the Empire: regardless.

The conversation turned to the late Mrs. Hanna Dashwood and Dorothy was actually shocked – and surprised – to find that Lucille knew Hanna well! Little wonder she was so interested in Harry's investigation. Lucille told her that it had been Hanna singing the praises of the cycle club that had made her join. She was clearly upset that she hadn't been able to see and speak to poor Hanna before she died.

"The camps were a great slur on the English Government at the time: thousands of women and children [1 in 4 children] died in them, huddled together in dreadful conditions under guise of stopping them supplying aid and comfort to their men folk fighting the English. They were basically the forerunner of the Nazi Concentration camp if we're honest. The 'Boer war' is now referred to as the 'South African war' which officially lasted from 11th October 1899 to 31st May 1902." SJW.

"You must have been the last person to speak with her at the club before she died. Even if it was a few months ago." Lucille said and sipped her tea. She asked Dorothy – twice – if Hanna had mentioned her friend from South Africa. Dorothy shook her head; she couldn't remember Hanna mentioning that.

Dorothy was totally intrigued at how the pair knew each other. Lucille just smiled; "We had been friends since childhood. Hanna and her sister would come to my father's house to play with me and I would go to theirs. Her [Hanna] sister Marigold married my older brother; John. Didn't you know that Hanna was South African?" Dorothy – reluctantly – had to admit she didn't. Now this was a turn up for the books; Hanna was South African and murdered just a week before her childhood friend turned up from the 'old Country'. What were the chances of that?

Dorothy asked Lucille if she knew Hanna's husband – Frank Dashwood – well. Lucille didn't smile and she placed the cup down; "Hanna wrote me on several occasions that the brute had set about her again. If he hadn't been abroad on his damn ship; I would be pointing the finger of suspicion directly at him."

Dorothy had to agree with that sentiment. She asked about any planned changes for the theatre by its new owner. Mrs. Bellman smiled broadly; "Oh Edward [Mr. Bellman] loves the theatre and music halls. He's particularly looking forward to your magic act. He's fascinated with anything to do with magic, the supernatural, spirits and all things mythical. Your Uncle William would enjoy a conversation with him about such things. I believe he's scheduled a visit to here on Saturday night to watch you and your uncle."

Lucille then asked about her stay with Mrs. Styles and did she meet the dashing young Henry Capstone? Dorothy nodded and Lucille leaned forward, "His wife is quite a character I know her well." and really smiled. Dorothy kept her composure: were the new owners of the theatre bloody devil worshippers or witches! Then realized they may just all be 'Bohemian's'.

"Bohemians, used in this context, meant sexually liberated or morally corrupt people: with which, depending on your point of view, of course!" SJW.

The ladies were interrupted by young Arthur knocking loudly on the door and shouting that the back stage was ready for the afternoon rehearsal; the 'bloody' Irish singing family had finally buggered off and the small stage was now free!

"Sorry for the colourful language." Was all Dorothy said and Lucille laughed out loud, tapping her hand. "Don't worry about that Dorothy. My father was a sea-captain and so I'm use to ripe language!" The pair rose from their seats and Rosie showed the lady out.

Dorothy stood thinking; is that another bloody co-incidence? Father was a sea captain and Hanna's husband is one and both women came from South Africa. Rosie closed the door quietly and almost smiled; "Real strange one that." She muttered and fetched Dorothy's stage costume. "Why strange Rosie?" Dorothy asked, slipping off her long dress.

Rosie shrugged her shoulders; "The Van Gralle's are South African refugee's who now run the hat shop in Greek Street. She doesn't sound bleeding like them at all. If she hadn't said where she came from; I would have thought bloody Wales by the slight accent she has."

Dorothy unbuttoned her blouse and nodded; she had detected some kind of accent but obviously thought it was South African English. Then she realized that the late Mrs. Hanna Dashwood also had a slight accent; the same accent. She wondered what the significance of that was. She left the theatre by the stage door and waited at the bottom of the steps for Uncle William.

She pulled her light summer coat about herself and watched for a cab. The evening performance had gone really well; Reggie now had more parts in the act and was carrying them out with superb timing and skill. Dorothy nodded to herself that Uncle William had been right about his talent. But then Uncle William normally was! Rosie and she certainly appreciated his other talent!

She caught sight of an empty cab turning into Paradise Road from Canning Street and held up her hand. That's when the big figure stepped from the shadows of the Tobacconists shop and walked up to her. He was a big man in a shabby suit and hat. He struck Dorothy with the back of his hand and held her tight – screaming – down on the pavement. All Dorothy saw was the shiny blade in his other hand. She tried to wriggle from his grip and realized her nose was bleeding. He seemed to grin as he lifted up the knife whose handle was wrapped in a hankie to avoid leaving fingerprints. That's when the struggling pair was joined by another figure; equal in size to the attacker. He grabbed the knife arm and spun the desperate and surprised attacker around like a rag doll. The two men rolled on the pavement, cursing and shouting.

Rosie had appeared at the stage door and screamed; running down the steps to Dorothy's assistance. She grabbed Dorothy up and bundled her into the cab and told the shocked cab driver to 'fucking go!' He slapped his whip across the flank of his horse and the cab sped away from the dreadful scene.

Dorothy watched from the cab seat as the her savior beat the knifeman with his fists. She could actually see splatters of blood hitting the pavement and the fighting men's clothes; then nothing. She had fainted.

Rosie helped Dorothy from the cab into her front parlour and Ellen the housemaid – really shocked – rushed to help. Rosie eased Dorothy onto the big sofa and told Ellen to fetch cold water and clean towels. Dorothy was visibly shaking and all she could remember was that shiny knife above her head as she lay sprawled on the pavement.

"Thank bleeding God that big man was there! Thank bleeding God!" Rosie whispered and embraced Dorothy as she now wept, sobbing long and hard, drawing deep breaths of sheer relief and real fear about what could have befallen her. Ellen reappeared with the water and towels; her own hands shaking.

After a few minutes, Dorothy's nose had stopped dripping little specks of blood and she sat breathing deeply and wiped her face and hands with the towels. "Why me?" She whispered several times. Dorothy knew that she had escaped being brutally murdered on the busy pavement in bloody broad daylight.

Uncle William crashed through the door and Dorothy ran straight to him and he embraced her tightly; wiping tears from his face. "Thank God!" he said, his voice breaking up with emotion. He held her close for some minutes and then eased down back on the sofa. Rosie sat next to her; the two women gripped hands and Uncle William poured out glasses of brandy with visibly shaking hands. "Get this down you; both of you before you go into shock." He ordered them and they accepted the glasses and sipped slowly. Dorothy took a deep breath and murmured; "Why the hell did he attack me!" she shouted; now a little angry. Uncle William told them that Harry would be on the way and told Ellen to get a message to the police station; telling Harry that Dottie was alright. Ellen was gone in an instant, not even bothering to grab her hat or coat. She never reached the police station because Harry came bursting through the front door.

Ellen told him that Dorothy was a little bruised and upset; but otherwise fine. Harry visibly relaxed a little and ran into the parlour to embrace his sister with real affection and relief.

"Thank God I sent Jim with a message for Dorothy to the bloody theatre." He told Uncle William who handed him a glass of brandy. Dorothy eased herself back down on the sofa, she now who her savior was; Harry's new detective Sergeant Jim Grieves.

Dorothy sat sipping her brandy; how the hell do you say thank you to someone who risked their own life to save yours? But her attention swung back to the conversation that Harry was having with Uncle William.

"He came to the nick on temporary transfer with a solid reputation for honesty and reliability. It was well earned for doing the job and doing it bloody well. He knows how to look after himself; he's boxed for the force and won every match. Few buggers would get in the ring with him." Harry told Uncle William who had dropped into his favourite armchair and was filling his beloved pipe. He lit his pipe and nodded; allowing himself a little smile. "Do we know who the murdering bastard is?" he asked and Harry nodded; "A couple of the older lads at the nick quickly recongnised the bastard – despite his face being well pummeled – when Jim dragged him in. The bastard was only released from Brixton prison nine weeks ago. He had done seven years for assault and theft. He's used various names of the years; Tom Gates, William Burton, Max Styles…."

Rosie interrupted him; "Did you say Max Styles Mr. Hadden?" Harry nodded and Rosie leaned back on the sofa and sighed; "There was a nasty piece of work around the docks some years ago called Max Styles; liked to use a knife in fights. He was a real bad one; everyone said he would swing one day."

Harry told her to go on with her story. Rosie took a big swig at her brandy and wiped her mouth; "He worked for John Vicar's Gang - who worked the docks stealing cargos - as some kind of debt collector. I heard he got nine years for using his knife once too often. Gossip was he had to jump ship about ten years ago; several of his shipmates were after him for unpaid gambling debts. He's not English, but likes to make out that he is. He's a foreigner from some city with a strange name. Everyone laughed about that place because of the name."

Harry was now thoroughly intrigued – as was Dorothy and Uncle William – and he asked Rosie what the strange name was.

"The expression that Rosie used; 'he would swing one day' refers to being hung. Capital punishment – the Death penalty – was in force at the time." SJW.

Rosie smiled a little; "You won't believe it, but people said it was called hairy banana's ass." Everyone exchanged a puzzled glance until Dorothy sighed and actually chuckled [much to the relief of her Uncle and brother] she sipped her brandy and muttered; "I think they mean Buenos Aires, the capital of Argentina."

Harry folded him arms and groaned; "Yet another connection with the bloody sea and the late Mrs. Hanna Dashwood; her husband makes regular trips to Buenos Aires. Can that really just be a co-incidence, I don't bloody think so!"

Uncle William asked Rosie to return to the theatre and tell Big Tom [the Stage manger] that's the performance tonight would be cancelled; he would certainly know the reason why. But Dorothy eased herself up and shook her head. "No, my nose is not swollen and I feel alright, besides the show is sold out tonight and so we must abide by the old saying; the show must go on!" Dorothy actually chuckled a little and Uncle William gripped her arm with some real pride; "That's our girl Harry!"

Dorothy finished her most welcome brandy and headed for the door; she was going to soak in a hot bath. She stopped and asked Harry; "By the way, what was the message you asked Jim to deliver; thank God." Harry smiled; "To tell you that dinner at Romanov's was on me after tonight's performance." Uncle William muttered, "Thank God for that."

"Well, please include Jim in that. It's the least we can do; buy him a decent dinner!" Dorothy grinned and headed for the bathroom with Ellen just behind.

Harry nodded at that and Uncle William chuckled and said softly; "I understand that our young hero is a big strapping lad. It's about time our girl had a decent young man in her life." Harry just smiled and headed for the door; "Tell that loony Sims to keep an eye on Dorothy." Uncle William nodded; that was a very good idea; Sims could keep a very close idea on Dorothy and no-one could see him unless he [Sims] wanted it.

Dorothy – a little embarrassed by all the fuss – had to accept three encores from the appreciative audience that night; word of her ordeal had spread around the East end. She was cheered off the stage to find flowers all over her small dressing room. Big Tom gave her the thumbs up and sighed to himself; he utterly adored Dorothy and knew that he would jump naked into a starving lion's cage armed with just a spoon to defend her.

The little dinner party was very lively at Romanov's that night. Old Mr. Romanov wouldn't hear of taking any payment for the meals or entertainment. Dorothy was his God daughter and he fussed over her. It was rumoured later that he had stopped big Jim, as the party broke up and forced the young man to take a bag of gold sovereigns as a thank you. He really did love his special God daughter very much! Probably as much as his son David did. But the young man was of faint heart and that never would win a fair lady. So, he watched her from afar and dreamt. Sims took his guarding duties seriously – unusual for the strange young man who normally took nothing seriously – Dorothy had to keep ordering him away when she needed some privacy. The following afternoon Harry turned up and bought Uncle William and Dorothy [and Sims of course!] up to date with the prisoner 'Max Styles' or whatever his name was.

"He won't say a bloody word. Not even to the lawyer appointed to defend him. He just sits in his cell and smiles at everyone. Old Detective Inspector Albert Carney [the DI at Forest Gate nick] has been given the case by Superintendant Taylor because of my relationship with the victim [Dorothy] and so I hoping old Ray will keep me informed of any developments." Harry dropped into an armchair and accepted a cup of tea from Ellen. He sipped and added; "The SS Polar Queen should dock on the evening tide tonight and I'll be there to greet it. See what Captain Dashwood has to say about the murder of his wife."

Uncle William grunted; "We really need to know why the brute attacked poor Dorothy. If it's connected to the murder of Mrs. Dashwood, then what the hell the connection is and why?"

Harry nodded; "We'll keep Dorothy under guard until we discover why Styles picked on her to attack in bloody broad daylight on a busy street!" Dorothy placed her cup down and clasped her hands together; "What did the autopsy discover?" Harry didn't smile; "Just confirmed what old Doc Goldstein suspected. She drowned; there was salt water in her lungs, throat and stomach, even up her nose. He believes that the bruises were caused by a strong person holding her down. So it's definitely murder on that evidence alone. I think we have the suspect in custody already [Max Styles] but it's linking him to the late Mrs. Dashwood that could be the problem. We could do that with the sea captain; he's a regular visitor to Buenos Aries and that's where the suspect apparently comes from. But it's all too thin to present at court – at the moment - so we need to discover something concrete that links the captain to Mr. Styles and the murder of course."

"That's going to easier said than done. The good Captain has the best possible Alibi in the world. He was on a different continent when his wife died." Uncle William muttered and sucked on his pipe and blew smoke everywhere. Harry had to agree with that statement.

Dorothy leaned back in her chair and tapped the arms with her fingers; "Are we sure that's it sea water in her lungs? I mean; why drag the poor woman out to sea when you could easily just murder her in the damn bath. Just stick some salt in and everyone may believe she died way out at sea. Surely the bath tub is a better bet?"

Harry liked that idea and finished his tea. "I think Dottie could be on to something there. Murder in the bath tub is hell of a lot easier than taking someone out to sea, killing them and dragging the body all the way back to an old house. You've a greater chance of being caught if you move the damn body about."

Uncle William lowered his pipe; "How do we know – for certain – that the water in her lungs and other places is actually sea water?" Harry smiled; "Well, the only way to find out is get some sea water and compare it with what was found in the body."

Dorothy chuckled; "And how do we go about that?" Harry grinned and jumped from his seat; "Well my dear little sister; we'll have a day trip to the bloody seaside!"

CHAPTER 5. 'AFTER A VISIT TO THE BEACH IT'S HARD TO BELIEVE WE LIVE IN A MATERIAL WORLD.' Pam Shaw.

The train from Fenchurch Street arrived at Southend-On-Sea Victoria station right on time. Harry helped Dorothy from the carriage and Jim Grieves leapt down, carrying a canvas bag that clinked and rattled. "Sounds like I'm a travelling drunk with my bottles hidden in the bag." He said quietly, smiling. The trio passed through the gates handing over their tickets to a gray haired collector who smiled at Dorothy. She was dressed like a lady of real quality with a light blue summer coat, small straw hat and a matching blue parasol. Her carefully picked outfit did make

Harry smile and he wondered if it was for Jim's benefit. She walked next to Harry as Jim went ahead to grab a cab from the stand outside in Victoria Avenue.

Jim asked the young cabbie about hiring a small boat for the afternoon. The cabbie jumped down and held open the door. He pushed back his shiny black bowler and nodded; "Try old man Robert's; he has a boat moored near the pier. It's called the 'Sea Spray'. He's reasonable and looks after his passengers." Jim nodded and climbed in, quickly joined by Harry and Dorothy. The team chatted and laughed together as the cab trotted towards the High Street which was quite busy with locals and day trippers. They passed the big pub called the 'Royal Stores' and headed down Pier Hill towards the sea front. The famous pier came into view. They were impressed and Harry pointed out that it was the longest pleasure pier in the world.

The cabby shouted down that the little whitewashed shed some yards from the pillars of the pier was where old Robert's operated his boat hire. They could see a single mast sloop moving at anchor some yards from the shore. "That will do nicely." Muttered Harry and the team left the cab. Jim paid the young driver and gave him a good tip for his help.

The three walked down towards the shingle and found old Captain Robert's sitting on a chair reading – of all books – 'Moby Dick'. He was in his early fifties with a complete head of white hair, tall and slender with no jacket. "Now he bloody looks like a sea captain." Jim chuckled. Dorothy noticed that he had huge hands, well worn from work. He looked up and slowly closed his book and stood, hands gripping his braces.

Harry held up a hand in greeting and asked if he was Captain Roberts. The man nodded and stared hard at Dorothy, then almost smiled. Harry explained that they needed to hire his boat for a short trip to the mouth of the estuary to collect some sea water. Captain Roberts now stared at him and began to chuckle; "You want me to take you out to the mouth and back to collect sea water, have I that right young man?" Dorothy noted that he had a deep voice, laced with authority and a slight Welsh accent hidden inside.

"Yes, that's right Captain Roberts, we need to collect some sea water and return to London tonight." Harry tapped the canvas bag Jim was carrying. The captain now chuckled outright; "I've mastered this little sloop for five years here and I've never heard such a thing. What are you scientists or something?" Harry just smiled and shook his head; "No, London police officers needing to get some sea water." He gestured to Jim and himself. "The lady is not of course, she's my sister along for the trip."

Captain Roberts just nodded;"Well, to take you out to the mouth will cost ten shillings I'm afraid." He jerked a thumb to his boat, adding; "I would normally charge five bob a person for such a trip but your sister is real little stunner. She can travel as my guest." He grinned and reached down for his big dark woolen jumper and gestured for them to follow him down to the row boat. "Float! Float! Where are you boy?" he shouted, pulling on his jumper and sighing loudly; "He's more blooming elusive than the Scarlet Pimpernel if there's work to be done."

A thin young man appeared from the back of the hut, rubbing his eyes and mumbling something. He pulled on a black woolen hat and smiled at Dorothy. He looked like he hadn't eaten a decent meal since he was born. The captain just sighed; "His real name is Tom Float. Yeah, he wants to be a skipper and he's called blooming Float. You couldn't make it up, could you?"

The Londoners had to laugh at one. The captain told the young man to get row boat ready. Float grinned at Dorothy and headed down the shingle. Harry pulled four half crowns from his pocket and handed them to Captain Roberts who kissed each coin and pushed them into his big black boots. "Thank you mate, now have any of you been on a sloop before?"

Harry shrugged his shoulders; he hadn't and Dorothy certainly hadn't. Jim nodded that he had. The captain looked hard at him and smiled; "Guessed right about you, where did you do your training man?" Jim wiped his face and said quietly; "The Exmouth." Captain Roberts nodded; "Royal eh? How long in?" Jim now smiled; "Eight years man and boy. Took the Queen's shilling at fourteen and was on the old 'Colossus'." Captain Robert's slapped his shoulder; "Come on mate, let's get the bloody boat ready for these land lovers."

Jim was more than happy to take the captains place at the oars with young mister Float. The captain was more than happy to let him. He sat talking to Harry as they approached his boat; he was a little intrigued why they had come all the way to Southend to collect blooming sea water. Harry explained it was case they were working on. He wiped his face with a bright red hankie and nodded. "Must be a strange case my young friend if you need to collect ruddy sea water?"

Harry just nodded. They transferred to the sloop easily and Captain Robert's hauled up the anchor and positioned himself at the small wheel. Jim helped young mister Float get the single sail up and they were off. Dorothy sat on the stern seat, under her parasol and laughed, telling them that she felt like Cleopatra on her Nile barge.

"Well, you would be Queen on any Jack tar's boat my dear!" The captain shouted back to her and turned to Harry; "I bet that little sister of yours has them queuing outside your dad's door." He chuckled and waved at a passing fishing boat. They made the 'mouth' in good time and Harry, with Jims help filled the three big bottles with fresh sea water. The job done, Captain Roberts turned the boat around and they headed back to the pier.

Dorothy and Harry sat in the small cabin and checked the bottles, making sure the corks were tight. Harry sighed; "We should make it back before eight and I can get down to the docks and meet our captain Dashwood when he comes in on the late evening tide."

Dorothy nodded; "Will you be treating him as a suspect when you question him?" Harry shook his head; "No, I'll be ever so sympathetic and play mister nice policeman, see what he says about his late wife. Currently he has the best alibi for it I've faced in a long time." Dorothy – satisfied with the integrity of the bottles – pushed them back into the canvas sack and watched Jim and young Float adjusting the sail.

Captain Roberts, gripping the small wheel with skilled hands started to chuckle and mutter to himself. "What's amused our good captain?" Dorothy said and placed the bag on the floor. Captain Roberts turned from the wheel and smiled, quite bemused, obviously. "Did you say Captain Dashwood?"

Dorothy nodded and the old Captain chuckled again; "You wouldn't be talking about Captain blooming dirty Frank Dashwood?" Harry and Dorothy both exchanged a surprised glance and Harry said yes very quietly. The captain sighed and stared back out to sea. Harry just had to ask; "Do you know him captain Roberts?"

The captain nodded; "Yeah, I know dirty Dashwood. Worked for a few shipping lines during his time and sacked from a couple too. He's a good captain at sea, knows how to handle the big steamers, but his personal life got him in trouble a few times. I understand he works for a South American line these days; they'll take anyone with a Master's ticket for steam and sail."

Harry eased himself up and gripped the small table as the sloop pushed through some strong running water. "What sort of personal trouble would that be captain Roberts?" The old captain shrugged his shoulders; "Only rumours about the man I'm afraid. Stories like he had a wife here and one in Buenos Aires. Then, there's the story about his first wife, I can't recall her name, but she died in strange circumstances when he was out at sea. I understand the coppers looked really closely at him, but couldn't prove a thing against him. He had a cast iron alibi being out at sea, so they dropped any case against him I suppose."

Dorothy and Harry just stared at each other with the same thought; his first wife had died in strange circumstances and that simply was no co-incidence! Harry pushed a hand through his dark hair and asked the captain about how Dashwood's first wife died. The old captain turned the sloop a little to catch more wind and spoke quietly; "Don't quote me on it, but it was said that the woman was found dead in the bath. Apparently she suffered some sort of fit and slipped under the water. I heard later, that the authorities concluded she had accidently drown."

Now both Dorothy and Harry were really interested. Dorothy, swaying a little on the bench, also gripped the table and asked: "Do you know anything about the poor woman?" The captain shook his head; "No, not really, just that a couple of lads I have a pint with when they're back on dry land said she was a woman from the valleys. She was Welsh I suppose. Don't know much more than that except her brother wasn't happy about the verdict and had to be dragged from the court." Dorothy leaned back on the bench and was actually feeling a little sea sick. "Why is he called 'Dirty' Dashwood captain Roberts?"

The captain laughed and turned the wheel a little; the pier was coming into view. "Women my dear, he loved women. Bit of a ladies' man so I understand. They say he had a wife and a mistress in Argentina and another two women over here apart from his late wife!" He shouted at young Float to pull the row boat in [which was tethered behind the sloop] and help the passengers board. Young Float and Jim would row Dorothy and Harry back to shore; the captain would stay on his boat, since he actually lived aboard.

Dorothy and Harry said nothing to Jim as they rowed back to shore and disembarked. Harry gave young Tom Float a shilling for his help and efforts, which made the young man, grin broadly. Harry told Jim about the captain's revelations as they walked back to Pier Hill and caught a cab back into the seaside town. Harry and Jim insisted upon trying the local – and famous – cockles, which were landed at the little hamlet of Leigh-On-Sea. Dorothy took one look at the 'things' and wouldn't touch them. But she did enjoy the fish supper from a local 'chippie' particularly the battered cod. She did have a few chips and Harry finished off what she left.

The meal was washed down with ginger beer. Jim insisted that he pay for the meals and also brought everyone funny hats as a souvenir of their unorthodox day trip. Dorothy's was adorned with two crabs whose claws made a little love heart and she accepted it with a shy smile. Harry was more than happy with his pirate hat and Jim wore a 'captains' hat with some mock pride. Laughing and joking, arm in arm they made their way to the cab stand outside Brightwell's Drapery store.

The contented trio caught a cab back to the rail station and was back in London before nightfall. Harry left for the docks with Jim after dropping Dorothy off at the theatre. Rosie welcomed her at the stage door; complete with cricket bat in her hands! Uncle William was armed with his faithful walking stick. Dorothy just had to smile; "You two could defend the blooming Alamo." She muttered and headed for her dressing room with Rosie in tow, who wanted to know all about Dorothy's hat that Jim had given her.

Dorothy and Rosie jumped from the tram with some grace and headed for the London Hospital. Dorothy had to smile, looking at Rosie striding out next to her complete with cricket bat under her arm and the canvas bag containing the bottles under the other.

"I didn't know you were a cricket fanatic Rosie." She asked and Rosie just grinned; "It was young Gerald's favourite toy and I certainly know how to use it. I can bowl too. He made me play for bleeding hours when we were kids."

They were shown across the road by a helpful young policeman who was directing the busy traffic. He particularly wanted to help Dorothy across the road and she thanked him with a small smile and a little wave of 'thank you'.

The young police man on traffic duty stared at Rosie and her bat; he rubbed his chin and watched the ladies disappear into the hospital. Maybe the bloody nurse's were starting a bleeding cricket team or something. Women these days were doing all sorts of strange things; even demanding the bloody vote! Next they'll be hanging about pubs; drinking, wearing trousers and smoking and demanding the same pay as men. Christ, will the devil be let loose on the world if that ever happened. He grunted in disgust and turned back to the traffic.

"The London Hospital was to become the Royal London Hospital in 1990." SJW.

Dorothy just nodded and didn't ask any more questions about the bat. She knew that Gerald had been Rosie's much adored younger brother, who had died at just thirteen with pneumonia in the very hospital they were about to visit. Rosie would still talk about the boy with great affection. All he ever wanted to be was a cricket player and play for England. Apparently he had quite a talent for the game and despite his young age had played – as a junior – for the local team.

Christmas was always a sad time for Rosie; Gerald had succumbed to his illness on Christmas Eve 1881. Her husband Albert had confided to Dorothy that Rosie still kept the unopened present she had bought the boy and taken to the hospital; only to be told that he had died. She kept it in a small shoe box in her bedroom with other little memories of the boy. Dorothy pointed to the grand hospital entrance and consulted the note Harry had given her. "It's a Doctor Paul Shaw who will take a look at the water. Apparently studying the sea is a hobby of his."

The Reception porter watched the women approach and also wondered why one was carrying a cricket bat. But he did smile at Dorothy; what a fucking little cracker, he wouldn't let her out of bed for a month if she belonged to him. He tipped his hat and asked if he could assist the 'ladies'. Dorothy waved her note and mentioned Doctor Paul Shaw. The old porter sighed and shouted for 'young George. "The boy will take you the doctor's laboratory. You'll never find the damn place otherwise." He muttered as 'young George' appeared from the small office. He was built like a stick insect with a uniform that was clearly far too big. He ran skinny fingers through his vivid red hair and grinned.

'Big George' [the senior Porter] told him to take the ladies to Doctor Shaw. The boy smiled at Dorothy – really smiled – and gestured for them to follow him. "His lab and office are out the back; next to the morgue." He said with a little chuckle.

The little group passed through several drab corridors, past full wards then into two outside alley's and back inside again. They passed the canteen which stank of cabbage and back outside again. "Sweet Jesus, if I'd know we're going on a bloody expedition I would have worn me boots." Rose said to Dorothy who was reading each sign as they passed. Finally, they reached two dark doors and 'young George' pulled them open and gestured, with a smile, to a dimly lit quadrangle that was behind them. "The bright yellow door is the good doctors, just knock and his assistant will deal with you."

Dorothy thanked him and the pair headed for the yellow door. George shouted after them; "I get off at six girls. Meet you in the 'Feather's' and I'll buy you a gin." He shouted with a real big grin and smoothed down his uncontrollable red hair. He was really disappointed; Rosie stuck up two fingers and shouted back; "Stick your gin up your bum, you cheeky little git. My mistress is a lady of bloody quality. Her bleeding father was a Sir, so piss off!"

Rosie hammered at the door with her bat as Dorothy just sighed and shook her head; still, what did she expect; Rosie was Rosie!

The door was jerked open and a very dour young woman in a clean white apron stood staring at them. Dorothy held up her note and said quietly; "Inspector Hadden sent us with some…." She didn't finish; the young woman smiled broadly; "Oh, you're from Inspector Hadden. Do come in, how is the dashing Inspector?" Rosie nudged Dorothy and whispered; "I think she fancies your brother. Not really bleeding surprising that."

Dorothy just nodded and followed the young woman through a drab little office with bars over the window and into Doctor Shaw's small, but very well equipped laboratory. The woman announced the pair as 'those ladies from Inspector Hadden are here doctor!' She stood, arms folded, unsmiling.

Dorothy and Rosie both stood and stared. Doctor Paul Shaw was a strapping young man in his twenties with dark hair and eyes. He was built like a Greek or Roman wrestler from ancient times. Under his long white coat, he wore a very expensive suit and shoes. He smiled at the pair and both women realized that the good doctor was really handsome as well.

"Sweet Jesus, he could stuff his stethoscope up my blouse any day." Rosie whispered to Dorothy, who just returned the young man's smile and held out her note. The doctor took the note very slowly and then kissed Dorothy's hand; "Harry said his sister Dorothy would drop the samples around, so you must be Miss Hadden; the stage actress." Dorothy just stood and nodded. The pair was interrupted by Rosie. "She's a Magicians assistant doc; not just an ordinary actress. She has real talent. Now where do you want these bleeding samples? You must be use to handling samples I suppose." Rosie slapped the bag on a nearby chair and folded her arms. She smiled broadly; Christ, you could warm your bleeding hands on the look between these too.

The young doctor just nodded and finally released Dorothy's hand – with great reluctance it must be said – and lifted the bag up."I'll get the comparison done as quickly as possible. I'll have a porter bring…..no, I'll bring the results myself tonight. What time does your performance conclude Miss Hadden?" He stood clutching the bag like a sleeping child. Rosie sighed; their eyes hadn't left each other; not bloody once!

Dorothy managed a small shy smile and said about nine o'clock. Harry and her Uncle William should be there as well. The doctor nodded – still clutching the bag – and there was a silence between the two. Rosie, chuckling to herself, finally said; "Well, let's get going Miss. I'm sure the young doctor can't wait to get his hands on your bleeding samples."

The doctor nodded enthusiastically at that thought and held out his big hand and Dorothy placed hers in his and they stood staring at each other. "Yes goodbye until tonight Doctor and thank you." Dorothy managed to whisper. Doctor Shaw just smiled; "My pleasure Miss Hadden. I will see you tonight." He lifted her hand and kissed it again. It was another few seconds before both took their hands back. Rosie was now grinning; "Come on darling, I'm gasping for a brew."

Dorothy just nodded and the pair left the good doctor standing in his laboratory still clutching the bag. Outside in the dim lit quadrangle Dorothy waved a hand over her face and muttered something about checking her costume. Rosie just laughed out loud; she could see Dorothy was a little red.

"Come on sweetheart; let's see if we can find our bloody way out of here before we die of bleeding old age." Rosie tucked her bat under an arm and the pair attempted to find the entrance. It took then almost twenty minutes to find the elusive doorway.

And then, they had to follow a couple of morgue porters pushing their trolley to the children's ward to collect some Scarlet fever victims. The bigger porter also asked if they wanted to visit the 'Feather's' pub with him, when he's shift was finished. He was disappointed too when Rosie stuck her bat under his big nose and told him where he could stuff 'the bloody Feathers Pub!'

Miss Rachel Parkington slowly eased the bag from the doctors arms and pulled the bottles carefully out. "I wonder why that dreadfully common woman was carrying a ruddy cricket bat Doctor." She said examining the neat labels attached to each bottle. Doctor Shaw just smiled; "I have no idea Miss Parkington but an angel, flying low, has brushed me with her wings."

Miss Parkington adjusted her glasses and sighed; bloody men, they go totally stupid over a pretty face and figure. The woman is a common bloody stage actress and he's a fine, dedicated doctor doing essential research. The pair would obviously have nothing in common. Thankfully, his father simply would not approve of a stage actress in such a distinguished family. Now her brother was a different matter; a Scotland Yard Detective Inspector and like his friend, the good doctor, dedicated, respected and upstanding. Not to mention bloody handsome!

With that thought to comfort her jealous mind, she sat at her bench and turned back to Doctor Shaw; still standing in the middle of his lab with both hands clasped in front of him. His smile was enormous. She sighed loudly; "Shall we begin doctor?" with real sadness and impatience in her voice. Bloody men had no idea about which woman was best for them; no bloody idea.

The good doctor sighed too and slapped his hands together; "Right, let's see what my angel has left me." Miss Parkington just shook her head in disgust and re-read the labels. "Shall we start with the body fluids?" The doctor nodded and walked back to cluttered table and pulled a notepad from the top drawer, easing himself on a stool. He started to write a little poem and was soon interrupted by his assistant who tapped the table with a large specimen jar and simply sighed loudly; very loudly.

The good doctor just smiled and placed his pencil down.

CHAPTER 6. 'ONE MUST WORK WITH TIME AND NOT AGAINST IT'. Ursula K. Le Guin.

The cab halted around the corner as instructed and Dorothy slipped from the seat and stood on the pavement, quickly joined by Rosie. The cabby took his fare and a good tip and said 'goodnight ladies'. They walked a couple of yards and stared at the impressive London Villa. It was almost in darkness and Dorothy nodded, "Very clever, the parties must always be held at the rear, with the guests entering and leaving in Rayleigh Road. That way, none of the immediate neighbours will even realize a party is underway. Come on." The pair walked down the quiet street and turned in Rayleigh Road and saw two big men in dark suits and bowler hats standing by the rear gate. Dorothy gripped her invitation card and they walked up and both smiled, with Dorothy holding out the card.

She really smiled as the bigger of the two took the card and smiled broadly, "Good evening Miss Hadden." Was all he said. Rosie stared at him and said quietly, "Blimey it's Oscar!" He gestured them in, but not before Dorothy slipped him some coins and whispered in his ear." He nodded and resumed his watch on the gate. His companion said something and they both laughed. They quickly dived onto the grass and watched Henry's Valet welcoming other guests at the French Windows. Rosie was a little puzzled as they sneaked around the rear of the building, "If we're not going in darling, why are we bleeding wearing these naughty costumes?" she asked Dottie.

"It's our excuse if we're comprised or caught sneaking around somewhere we shouldn't be. We just say we're new and got lost." She quietly replied and smiled: there was a slightly open window right next to them. "Now that's a bleeding piece of luck." Rosie muttered and they removed their coats and placed them in Rosie's big bag. Dorothy had to chuckle when she saw the cricket bat sticking out. "What have you got that for? I mean I know why you carry it, but how do you explain it?" Rosie grinned, "If asked, I just say it's in case someone would like a spanking. After all, this is a bleeding perverted party ain't it?"

Dorothy could only nod and looked her friend up and down. Rosie was attired as a 'Paris Maid' with a frilly black [short] skirt, matching bodice that really couldn't hold back her big breasts, stockings, white apron and maids cap. For herself, Dorothy's costume was her stage outfit – an Egyptian slave - with the panties and corset removed. It was quite revealing and Rosie whistled softly, "Now, I think if we're bleeding caught that can get us out of anything." With that, they climbed through the window and found themselves in Henry's study.

The lamp on the desk was still lit and Dorothy noticed there were several books and manuscripts scattered around his busy ornate desk. She turned one around and studied the page it was open to. "A book about the etiquette and protocols of the Tudor Court of Henry VIII and the early reign of Elizabeth the first." Dorothy said quietly and now she was puzzled, if, as she suspected, Henry was a time-traveller from the Tudor Times, why the hell was he reading up on it?

Rosie tapped the book nearest to her, "Take a butcher's hook [look] at this. It's all about the rituals of bleeding witchcraft in the late Medical age." Dorothy looked at her and sighed, "That's medieval age my darling." Again, why was he looking up these subjects, if, as she also suspected, he may run a witches Coven? "It doesn't make bleeding sense unless…." She folded her arms and sighed. Rosie was grimacing at a vivid woodcut illustration of two young witches burning at the stake in a German City. She looked up, "Unless what darling?" she asked.

"Unless his leading everyone up the blooming garden path. What if he likes people to think he has the ability to travel in time….or run a witch's coven? Maybe he's using his incredible likeness to his ancestor to seduce women and indulge in a sexual free-for-all. Like, say with his 'mysterious and supposedly secret' work at the Admiralty? Maybe all we have here is a bloody Baron Von Munchausen!"

Rosie shrugged her shoulders, "Is that some kind of bleeding Italian opera about time travel or witches then?" Dorothy just smiled and nodded. Rosie was close enough with that statement; besides, it would take far too long to explain!

 "Come on Rosie; let's confirm what I'm thinking by finding that damn compass and stealing it!" they started to search the study and within a few minutes Rosie called her over to the small plant pot table by the door. "Is this what we supposed to be bleeding looking for?"

Dorothy smiled and lifted the compass from the table, "Well, that proves my point Rosie; no self-respecting time traveller leaves his time portal lying about." Rosie just smiled and shook her head, "I'll run with the story that he's just a Casanova with a bleeding good line in seduction. We bloody fell for it!" keeping a tight grip on the compass the girls headed for the window, then slipped out and walked quickly back to the rear gate. Oscar opened it and smiled again, "Goodnight Miss Hadden. You were never here." Dorothy reached up and kissed him on the cheek and he slipped her a note. She pushed it into her coat pocket and the girls headed for the busy street corner, where they knew they could pick up a cab.

They returned to the Theatre and changed back into their proper clothes. Rosie put the kettle on and Dorothy sat in her chair and held up the compass, "It's quite a beautiful little thing isn't it?" Rosie grunted, and said it wasn't much use around here. She turned back to the kettle and spooned some tea leaves into the big black tea-pot. Dorothy pressed the little button just above the north symbol [like you would get on a pocket watch of the day] and Rosie turned, saying she could murder a biscuit and found the chair empty. The tea pot shattered on the floor.

Dorothy stared at the skinny man as he raised the axe and slammed it down, splitting the log in two. He looked up and nodded. There was no smile on his well worn face. "What be you need mistress?" he said wiping his face with an equally rough hand. Dorothy managed a smile, he was dressed like a medieval peasant and she could smell him from where she stood. Finally, she managed to say, "What year is this sir?" He rubbed his face, clearly not understanding. He repeated himself, cradling the axe in his arms. She thought fast, "Now, this anno domino, the year. What year sir?"

He now nearly smiled, "It be one after Harry took crown."

Dorothy now knew it was 1510AD. She had indeed travelled in time and Henry Capstone was no bloody Baron Von Munchausen! She staggered back a bit, and then wondered how the compass would allow her to return. She stared at and saw another little button under the South symbol. "North takes you to 1510, where does South take you." She muttered and thanked the man, then realized she had sunk in the soft earth up to her ankles. Lifting her skirt a little, she slowly made her way from the little shack and the puzzled man. Then, praying hard, pressed the 'south button'. Rosie turned, saying she could murder a biscuit and found Dorothy sitting and staring hard at the compass.

Dottie stared at her and managed a smile, "I think there's some left in the tin darling." The realized that's how Henry covered his tracks, no time would pass until he returned! His mysterious disappearances must be when he does his 'secret' work for the admiralty. Her throat was dry and her heart was beating hard: she had just travelled in time!

Rosie handed her a cup and sat down. "Darling, how did you get that bleeding mud on your shoes? It ain't rained for days." Dorothy smiled, "Now that's magic!" and forced herself to smile and was a little embarrassed that she couldn't think of anything else! Rosie just grunted and asked what happens now. She didn't know, but there was a knock at the door and Rosie opened it, smiling at the visitor. "You must have smelt the bleeding kettle going on Mister Sims!" he wandered in and removed his hat, "No thanks Rosie, I just want a quick word with Dottie thanks." Then added, "In private please."

Rosie shrugged her shoulders and headed for Reggie's dressing room and soon as she left, Mister Sims sighed, "What happened Dottie, a jumper was recorded from this very time and place and Jericho wants answers: now!"

Dorothy held up the compass, "You need to report to Jericho that he has a nest of time jumpers to deal with. But they won't be going anywhere, this is their time portal." Now Sims smiled and took the compass, "A short trip I take it?" and Dorothy nodded, "A real bloody short one!" He pushed the compass into his bandages, "Jericho will probably drop by for this one himself and tell you what a great job you did." Dorothy just smiled. She now realized that time travel could be the answer to the long cherished human desire for immortality. Then she shivered a little, thinking about what Henry Capstone would do now, once he realized that his precious time portal device had been stolen. She knew that Oscar wouldn't betray her, not after what he had been offered and she had his address in her coat pocket.

Henry shouldn't suspect her because she and Rosie never turned up at the party, besides he wouldn't be here much longer once Mister Jericho Tibbs and his team turned up. She wondered about Mrs. Styles and her husband and realized that Henry was almost certainly supplying the business man with information and taking a cut of the profits: The Styles would have never been suspected because they were not the one's breeching the Timeline. Dottie also wondered just how long Henry had lived in this time period and who else was he working with. Was his wife also a time traveller? Then she stopped thinking about it: it would give her headaches! She would definitely leave it to Mister Tibbs.

CHAPTER 7. 'A MAN WHO STUDIETH REVENGE KEEPS HIS OWN WOUNDS GREEN.' Sir Francis Bacon.

Harry sat at his cluttered desk and rummaged through the paper Bags, examining each item carefully; all had clear indications that they had been soaked in water; there were tiny specks of dried salt encrusted in the fabrics. Jim held up a pair of panties and chuckled; "Never thought I would have to sort through some poor dead woman's knickers looking for bloody clues." He said and dropped them back into the bag. Harry slapped a fine white blouse down and tapped the desk; "We would never have spotted that the late Mrs. Dashwood was – for some reason – wearing her winter clothes in summer without Dorothy. Now what the hell is the significance of that?"

Jim shrugged his shoulders; he didn't have a bloody clue about woman's clothes except they were usually expensive. Harry sat back in his chair and picked up Captain Frank Dashwood's statement. He waved the paper about. "Three pages of I don't know, I wasn't there, I have no idea, I know absolutely sod all about my wife's murder. That sums up this useless piece of paper."

Jim leaned on the desk and stared at the clothes strewn across the already busy desk. "Maybe the old house is a big clue; I mean why dump the bloody body there? Surely, the murderer would have known that it would be found." Harry checked his fob watch and stared at the little window of his grim office. "Well, let's have another look at the place. Dorothy said there was something strange about the outside but couldn't put her finger on it. I think another visit is in order."

Harry stood and collected his hat from the wall hook and stared one more time at the bags of clothing. "The bloody clues are all there and at the old house. We just need to see them." Jim jumped to feet and slapped his hat on. "I'll grab a cab. Do we pick up Dorothy from your house or is she at the theatre?" Harry smiled; "At the theatre, guarded by the east end's answer to beefeaters; bloody Uncle William with his Regency dueling pistol and mad Rosie with her cricket bat!" The two men chuckled and headed for the street.

They reached the station doors when Sergeant Rollings called after them. Both Harry and Jim couldn't stand the fat obnoxious sergeant and they didn't hide it either; but then few of the sergeant's colleagues liked him and most of the station's clientele Certainly shared their views.

"Inspector Carney called in when you were making mud pies at Southend. Said that he's still saying nothing except he won't be in the nick for long and certainly won't go to prison. A real cocky bastard by all accounts."

Harry nodded and said 'thanks' quietly. That's when the thin man standing before the desk removed his hat and spoke directly to Harry; "You really should warn the local schools about the bloody monster mister Hadden. Tell the kids not to go near that awful blooming old house. Me and Charlie Cooper saw the bugger last night; I'd swear on my mother's grave it was heading to that house of horrors. The kids should be told to stay away."

Jim just rolled his eyes in mock despair; "Not the bloody monster again. If we warned the kids around here to stay away because of the monster; there would be queues forming outside the place. Besides, how do you know the bloody monster lives in Lord Harley-Coats old house?"

Harry sighed; the 'monster' of the east end was apparently a strange and elusive figure that had seen around the place for years. Described as something crossed between Mister Hyde and Jack the Ripper, it was only seen late at night, complete with top hat, dark cape and walking stick. Those who confessed to seeing the creature all commented on his horrific evil features. Most also admitted they had been frequenting the pub just before they caught sight of it. No constable on their night beats had ever reported seeing it. It was becoming bit of an east end legend. Also, no one seemed to know if the 'monster' had actually done anything evil, but that didn't stop the horrific and frightening rumours and stories that circulated about the supposed creature. Between it and 'the Beast', the east end was getting quite a reputation for strange happenings and Harry's case of a 'drowned' women in a derelict house certainly didn't help.

The little man clutched his hat; "We saw the bloody thing heading up Victoria Street – we'd been drinking in the old Queens Head – and it disappeared over the wall of the house. Straight over that bloody big wall like it was on a string. We ran after seeing that." He pushed his hat back on and rubbed his face; "I've got a bloody missus and kids. You should warn people, you coppers should do something about it before women and kids start disappearing." Satisfied he had done his civic duty he headed for the door.

They watched him disappear and Sergeant Rollings chuckled and tore up the sheet of paper he had scribbled something on. "Shall I make out a full report, get his mate Charlie in? Call for bleeding bloodhounds? What do you say Inspector?" The sarcasm in his voice wasn't hidden.

Harry just shrugged his shoulders; "Tell night shift to pay attention to the old house; remember it's a murder scene." Sergeant Rolling wiped his fat face and grinned; "I'll tell them to apprehend any monsters on your say so. That'll make for a lively night shift, I should imagine." Harry and Jim said nothing more and headed down the steps and waited for a cab to appear.

"Right barrel of laughs this case. A woman who drowns found dead in a derelict house and now the bloody monster apparently lives there. What next I wonder?" Jim muttered and held up his hand as an empty cab came into view. Harry shook his head; "Unless we can break Dashwood's water tight alibi, this case is going nowhere. Maybe the monster could be a nice distraction from failure."

The two men jumped in the cab and headed for the theatre.

"You look top notch boss." Skoles commented, adjusting 'Professor Dustin Potts' fez. Uncle William stared in the mirror and grunted. "I understand we're sold out again tonight. That's going to show us if the two new acts are any good; Quite a baptism of fire." Skoles chuckled, "Or rotten fruit." Then added, "One ain't too bad, but I watched the other lot in rehearsal and I hope they like bloody tomatoes!" That made the 'professor' chuckle. The act Skole's was talking about was 'The Alphabet Gang' – a team of five acrobats who formed letters of the alphabet! - Uncle William believed they would be as popular as the pox in a monastery.

Uncle William headed for Dorothy's dressing room and found young Detective Constable Dave Farmer sitting on a rough chair outside. He rose and nodded at Uncle William; "The Inspector has put me on guarding duties whilst Miss Dorothy is at the theatre."

Uncle William thoroughly approved of that idea and knocked, announcing himself. Rose pulled open the door – bat in hand – and grinned; "Already Boss, the bloody place is packed and the new owners are in the Queen's box. Apparently he [the new owner] loves magic shows."

Dorothy, wearing a light summer coat over her flimsy costume, appeared and pushed her arm through her uncles and the pair walked to the rear of the main stage. Constable Farmer and Rosie walked behind. He pointed out to Rosie that carrying the bat for protection could be construed as an offence. She just gave it a few swings and nodded; "Bleeding right son. Anyone comes near my lady will get it straight in the goolies [testicles]." Dave Farmer just had to smile and he said nothing more about the law's view of Rosie's faithful bat.

The little group stood in the wings and was joined by Titus and big Tom. They all watched 'The Nightingales' – three old ladies singing harmonies – they received some applause, mostly out of sympathy. Big Tom shrugged his shoulders and admitted that went better than he expected. "I couldn't turn away three old grannies who were down on their luck, now could I?"

Dorothy patted the little man and he smiled broadly. The next act wasn't so fortunate; 'The Alphabet Gang' performed to an almost silent audience, they only reached 'E' when the crowd reacted. They were booed from the stage under a hail of rotten fruit and a couple of shoes. They did manage to form a large 'V' sign before being dragged off stage. Tom calmed the crowd down and announced the magic act; "Professor Dustin Potts; the magic Master of the Pyramids!' As usual he mentioned that Dorothy's costume was the talk of London. The crowd greeted that with some enthusiasm.

Dorothy handed her coat to Rosie and Constable Farmer smiled; little wonder the young woman had such desperate admirers; she was truly a beauty. Titus and Dorothy made their way to their first stage marks and waited for the 'Professor' who appeared and released half a dozen pigeons into the air....from his little fez! They were about to perform the vanishing trick - where Dorothy was placed in a sarcophagus and replaced by 'Isis' the cat - when the young man jumped on stage from one of the boxes that overlooked it. He ran towards Dorothy clutching a bunch of flowers; he didn't get far. Uncle William shouted; "What's in the bloody flowers!" Rosie was onstage in an instant and delivered a huge swinging blow to young man's crotch with her bat.

 Constable Farmer dragged the screaming man down and the audience cheered and applauded; many thought it was some comedy introduced into the act, following the incident with young Dorothy. Big Tom joined the melee on stage and shouted; "For

Christ sake! It's that dopey infatuated young twat who doesn't know what 'piss off, she ain't interested' means. Get the silly bugger off stage!"

Dave and Titus dragged the sobbing young man into the wings where Miss Player [who doubled as the theatre's First Aider] simply refused to attend his injury. But she did pour a fire bucket over his crotch to help out. Titus returned to the stage and the performance continued uninterrupted and ended with three encores and huge applause. Uncle William walked to the wings with Dorothy and Titus and wondered how he could incorporate something similar into the act; the crowd had loved the little piece of 'comedy'. "Do you know, I think we've discovered a whole new genre of entertainment; Magical Comedy."

Titus was a little concerned that this could mean him getting whacked in the nuts most nights, but the professor shook his head; "No, we would have to employ a stunt man for that." Dorothy chuckled; "Wouldn't it be better if we used a stunt woman?" with some sarcasm that didn't go unnoticed.

Rosie handed Dorothy her coat and slung her bat over her shoulder; "Love lost little twerp, maybe he'll take no for an answer now." Titus actually giggled; "I hope he does or he'll never enjoy the honeymoon when he marries." Everyone laughed and headed for the professors big dressing room for a well earned cup of tea, slightly disappointed that they hadn't caught the other new act: 'The Cable brothers and Rocky the Kangaroo' apparently two Australians and an intelligent Kangaroo who liked to beat them up! They received applause – mostly out of sheer astonishment at Rocky's antics – and some actually cheered when he knocked them down. Meanwhile Dave and big Tom threw the hapless youth out the stage door; followed by his now headless bunch of flowers.

He lay in the gutter and between sobs shouted; "Tell her I love her and will rescue her from her evil Uncle and brother's grasp!" He lay back clutching his testicles and groaned. A couple of old women passing by thumped him with their parasols and called him a dirty little bastard. Young Lord Robert De Salle Barclay's attempts to win the love of his young life definitely hadn't gone too well. He certainly wouldn't mention this little incident to his father; the Duke. He staggered away in the growing gloom of the night; sadly none the wiser for the incident.

The man standing in the tobacconist's doorway, hidden in dark shadows, watched him go with some interest. He stepped from the door and watched with even more interest as the dashing young doctor Paul Shaw disappeared into the theatre. The tall and well built man smiled with some real satisfaction; the dumb Inspector and his hair brained sister had fallen for everything. Now to finish his well conceived plan of revenge and murder: he waved down a cab and headed for the docks.

Doctor Shaw sipped his tea and stared at Dorothy over the cup's rim. They were having what's called 'polite conversation' as Harry read the report that Doctor Shaw had rushed to him. Harry looked up and rubbed his chin; "Industrial cleaning salt? That's in the fluid from the victim and not sea water?" Harry asked and Doctor Shaw placed down his cup; "Most unusual to put that substance in a bath. If one was taking a salt bath for health reasons you would use sea salt or something similar, more pure salt. You certainly wouldn't use Industrial salt, far too coarse and only really used in industrial applications."

Dorothy cradled her cup with both hands and with a small smile asked the doctor how you would actually use industrial salt. He smiled and clasped his hands together; "Well, anywhere food was processed; such as canning factories. The huge cooking vessels would be cleaned regularly with it. It's used in some hospitals along with modern disinfectants and would also be utilized in cleaning the huge fridges and freezers that now store some foodstuffs."

Dorothy leaned forward and placed her cup down; "Would it be used on board those new freezer ships that ply between the continents, carrying frozen meat and such?" The doctor nodded; "Oh yes, it certainly would. Easy to store on board and lasts for a very long time since salt is a preservative in its own right."

Dorothy and Harry exchanged a glance; they had thought the same thing – Dashwood's ship was equipped with huge freezers to carry the beef and lamb to different continents – currently ice cream and vegetables to Argentina and returning with meat. Harry slowly rose from his chair and stood arms folded. He questioned the good doctor further; "Can a human body be frozen months ago and then left to defrost? If so, would anyone notice that the body had been previously frozen and would the decomposition of that body, after freezing, be slower or faster than normal?" The doctor shrugged his shoulders; "Yes a body could be frozen and then defrosted without too many problems. I would need detailed research to answer the part about how fast or slow it decomposed afterwards. But traces of the freezing process should be evident in…." he hesitated and then smiled; "Would be evident in the body such as small amounts of water and salt used to the clean the freezer; just like in those body fluids you provided."

Harry actually smiled broadly; "Dorothy you were spot on about Hanna's winter clothes. She was probably murdered months ago during winter and then placed in the old house to defrost. He [Dashwood] has constructed an alibi that should have fooled everyone. There is a huge warehouse on the docks that the shipping line uses to store the frozen meat when it arrives. I would bet that's where he stored the body. He disposed of it in the old house and sailed away, believing that the police would assume she had only just been murdered. Baby sister; I think we've cracked the bugger's alibi!"

Uncle William sucked noisily on his pipe and smiled; "Bloody incredible piece of detective work you two [indicating Harry and Dorothy] Now that's a stroke of genius. He murdered his poor wife, froze her body and disappeared to sea thinking he had a perfect alibi. Brilliant!" Dorothy just nodded; "But why try to murder me? How could I have threatened such a clever and intriguing alibi?"

Harry had no answer for that. "Somehow, he believes you could have overturned his elaborately constructed alibi. We'll have to work on the why."

"If he went after a woman closely connected with Hanna; then surely, using logic and rational thinking, it should have been Mrs. Lucille Bellman. She and Hanna were childhood friends and she could testify about his violent character and the spankings he gave Hanna. If he wanted to dispose of a real threat, then it should have been Lucille, but that thug attacked me. She was with me that very day, here at the theatre….." Dorothy stopped in mid sentence and sighed loudly; "The thug didn't know Lucille, but obviously had been told to attack a well dressed young woman leaving the damn theatre that day!"

Uncle William coughed and nodded his agreement with that

deduction; Dorothy was almost brutally murdered because the dumb killer had mistaken her for his intended victim. Harry grabbed his coat and hat; "I'm getting a team together and hitting that warehouse and then captain Dashwood's house. This time I won't be so bloody sympathetic with my questions to him."

Harry asked the young doctor to accompany him and the pair left the theatre in a hurry. Dorothy stood by the small window and watched the pair catch a cab. Uncle William patted her shoulder; "I'll get a message to Mr. Bellman that his young wife could be in mortal danger despite the thug being locked up." Dorothy nodded and folded her arms; deep in thought. Surely Dashwood in his elaborate murder plans should have thought that the detectives assigned to his case, would work these clues out? Why leave Hanna in her winter clothes, when it would have taken just minutes to strip the body and place summer clothes on it? Or even easier, leave her nude, there would be few clues then. Dorothy sighed and sat back down and refused Rosie's offer of more tea.

Uncle William gave her a little kiss on the cheek and headed out the theatre to catch a cab to the Bellman house with his warning. Dorothy sat thinking. Had she missed some vital clues? She rose and went to the small desk and pulled several sheets of paper out and slowly sharpened her pencil. 'I'll note down anything relevant from the conversations I had with people that knew Dashwood and his wife….' She stopped and tapped the pencil on the desk.

One conversation came back to her about Dashwood and his first wife who had died in similar circumstances. She scribbled her thoughts down and re-read them. It didn't help. She turned to Rosie who was stitching up a small tear in her stage dress. "Rosie, did you know that Captain Dashwood was married before and his first wife died in the bath?" She asked her, who looked up and smiled. "Oh yes, but the best person to ask about that poor woman would be old Inspector Roy Games; he dealt with the matter all those years ago. Never bleeding solved anything of course."

Dorothy allowed herself a little chuckle at that. "Do you know where he retired too?" Rosie nodded and waved her needle about; "He didn't go far. He still lives down Sebastopol Street, strangely enough around the corner from Captain Dashwood."

Dorothy sat back in her chair and rolled the pencil about in her hand. She read her notes again; the conversation with Captain Roberts about Dashwood's first wife reappeared in her head; her brother clearly and strongly disagreed with the 'accidental death' verdict. Did he suspect that Dashwood had got away with murder? What happened to him? Where is he now? Does he know anything useful or relevant to the current investigation?

She jumped up and said quietly; "Get your hat and coat Rosie; we're going to pay a little visit to old Inspector Games." Rosie packed her sewing kit away and fetched the hat's and coats. She stopped by the umbrella stand and retrieved her cricket bat. Now that did make Dorothy chuckle; "Come on blooming Bobby Abel, let's see what old Games has to say about the first Dashwood case." The ladies grabbed a cab and headed for Sebastopol Street. Dorothy sat and smiled at her maid – no – her friend and lover, Rosie. "How's your sister Gladys's these days? Did she ever marry that boy from Knight's soap factory?" Rosie just sighed and gripped her bat. "No she bleeding didn't. She's staying with us now. Her and the baby; we had to take her in. Put the bleeding cart before the horse didn't she. Still, my little nephew is a real bundle of joy. Lovely little fellow with big dark eyes; his bleeding aunty spoils him!"

"Robert Abel, nicknamed "The Guv'nor", was a Surrey and England opening batsman who was one of the most prolific run-getters in the early years of the County Championship." SJW.

She wondered why Rosie hadn't invited her to more sexual antics at her house: it was bloody full all the time now! Dorothy smiled and stared out the window and wondered how Rosie and her family coped with two extra mouths to feed and where did they all sleep? Rosie had a two bed roomed terrace house in Victoria Dock Road and had two sons herself. Still, there were worse families than that; one of the chorus girls admitted that her mum and dad had five children in the same sized house. But what made it even more remarkable was they had a bloody lodger as well! She sighed; overcrowding was common amongst the poor in London and all the big industrial cities.

They arrived at old Inspector Games modest little house and

Dorothy paid the cabby. Rosie banged on the door with her bat which made Dorothy sigh. A frail looking old man in scruffy trousers and waistcoat opened the door and stared at the women; "What do you want? I don't give to bloody charities for work-shy buggers who should work." He started to close the door when Dorothy stepped forward and smiled; "Mr. Games, I'm Dorothy Hadden; Harry's sister from the theatre and this is Rosie my……" She didn't finish, Roy games jerked the door fully open and just stared at her; he didn't smile.

"I never did like that jumped up little prick, so piss off and leave me alone, I don't know fuck all about that Welsh woman and her bloody stubborn brother." He shook his head and scratched his arms; "Wouldn't accept the bloody verdict. Despite the evidence offered. Oh no, not him, he was bloody obsessed with the notion that Dashwood had killed her. Said he would get revenge for her death. Stupid bastard. Now why don't you people leave me alone." He grunted and slammed the door.

Undaunted, Dorothy shouted through letterbox; "Who else has asked you about Captain Dashwood's first wife's death Mr. Games?" She could just make out the figure shuffling up the uncarpeted hallway. He turned and stuck up two fingers; "Just leave me alone you bastards; I know nothing about any murders." Dorothy dropped the letterbox flap and turned to Rosie; "Murders? Does that mean he knew both Dashwood's wives were murdered?"

Rosie shrugged her shoulders and tapped her bat a couple of times; "If I weren't a real ladies maid, I would have smacked him in the nuts for the way he spoke to you." Dorothy just walked towards the broken gate and stared back at the house; it was in poor condition. It was apparent that retried Inspector Games' pension was inadequate. Dorothy resolved to bring the matter to the attention of the Metropolitan Police Welfare fund; maybe they could help the old man. That revelation made Rosie smile; "Your too bloody soft hearted darling, especially after the way that the old bugger spoke to you." Dorothy just smiled and thought about the old man living in an almost derelict house; practically hidden away. Harry had said that few people saw the old Inspector about the area now. He had become quite reclusive.

The woman reached the street and Rosie held up the bat to wave down a cab. Dorothy stood thinking about what the old Inspector had said. She stared back at his modest house and some strange thoughts about Summerton House came to mind. A cab pulled up and Dorothy told the cabby to head for Summerton House. "Well, if we're going to that house of horror, then it's a good job I have my bleeding bat with me." Was all Rosie muttered as the cab pulled away; watched by old Games from his dirty windows and threadbare curtains. He turned to the silent man standing by the front room door and spat the words out; "Told you that jumped up little prick would be onto you. But this keeps my mouth shut." With a trembling hand he lifted the gold sovereign from his waistcoat pocket and kissed it. Mr. David Jones just nodded and walked to the curtains and made sure that Dorothy and her maid had departed. He left the house without another word and caught a cab to the docks.

As they headed down the road, Dottie had bit of a 'Vision' and gripped the seat, just for a second she was passionately kissing a handsome young Blackman on a park bench on a beautiful sun drenched day. It's wasn't Reggie or Cadbury. Then she saw her hand holding the side of his head as their mouths copulated. There was a gold wedding ring on her finger. At the side of the bench was strange small pram with a sleeping infant. Outside the park were huge buildings reaching up into the hazy blue sky and the noise of motor traffic drifted across the large green space. Beneath his smart jacket the young man carried a shoulder holster with revolver. They broke the kissing and stared at each other with Dottie running her fingers through his thick dark hair. He was saying something and smiling but then it was gone.

Dottie took a breath and eased back in the seat, her mind full of thoughts about the young man. "Who the hell is he?" she whispered to herself, "And why does he keep appearing in my thoughts like this?" She shook the 'day-dream' from her mind, but knew they would return to haunt her again.

Dorothy leaned back in the cab and stared at the people and traffic passing by. She smiled at Rosie and then her memory stirred. "Rosie, what made you say that you thought that Mrs. Bellman's accent was strange for someone from South Africa. Didn't you say that you thought she was Welsh?" Rosie nodded and repeated her story about the South African's now living down Greek Street not sounding like Mrs. Bellman; not sounding like her one little bit.

Dorothy folded her arms and wondered about that remark. The late Hanna Dashwood certainly had a soft accent that Dorothy couldn't identify – at the time – and really wished she had asked Hanna about it. But it was too late now. A tall young man on the opposite pavement watched Dorothy go by and shook his head, "No bloody sign of Davies, yet." He waved down a cab and jumped in saying, "Oddfellows Hall please."

CHAPTER 8. 'REGRET IS A FORM OF PUNISHMENT ITSELF.' Nouman Ali Khan.

Dorothy and Rosie stood outside the old house and Dorothy consulted her little fob watch that she wore on her blouse. That's when she saw the little group of ragged children playing on the corner. "I think we may need assistance and I know where we can get it." She spoke to Rosie who was staring at the old house. "Gives me the bleeding creeps." Was all Rosie replied. Dottie waved the children over to her and spoke to the oldest child; a girl about ten who was watching over her younger brothers. They chatted for a minute or so and Dorothy gave the happy child a silver sixpence and she was gone; dragging her protesting and unhappy siblings behind her. They wanted to stay and play with the others. Rosie chuckled; "Reminds me of me when I was that age. I was always lumbered to watch after me brothers and sisters while mum worked the early shift at the paint factory. Never get born the first girl, my old gran always said that."

"Come on, we'll wait in the doorway for Harry and his merry men." The women walked slowly up the overgrown path and Dorothy suddenly stopped and stood staring at the house. Rosie couldn't see anything amiss with the old place but she could see the look on Dorothy's face. "What have you come up with darling?" She asked gesturing with her bat to the old house.

Dorothy sighed; "I should have noticed it straight away, but I was still thinking about seeing poor Hanna dead on the floor. Look hard at both wings of the house Rosie and what is wrong with what you're seeing?" Rosie stared back at the house for a minute or two and cradled her bat; "No sorry, can't see bloody anything." She said quietly.

Dorothy smiled and gestured to the East wing; "Six upstairs windows on that side and only five on the other; but no sign that a window has been bricked up. Now that's really strange; why would an Architect design a house with such odd numbers of windows?" Rosie actually counted the windows and nodded; Dorothy was right, the west wing was missing a bloody window!

"That means one room up there is lot larger than the others or there is a room up there without a window, which would be really strange." Dorothy explained and Rosie just nodded; she wouldn't have noticed that in a million years of staring at the damn place. But then Dorothy was used to seeing illusions as a magician's assistant.

The women stood in the door way and both noticed that the front door was ajar. Dorothy slowly pushed it open; she knew that was very odd. "Come on Rosie." She said quietly and the pair walked into the not so grand hallway; Rosie gripping her bat tightly."If the monster jumps out, he's getting it straight in the bleeding cobblers." Rosie whispered and she meant it!

They headed up the stairs and walked the top hallway; Dorothy was quietly counting doors. "Five doors and so five rooms I suppose." Dorothy muttered and they checked each room; they were all the same size with a window. They reached the last door, she pushed it open and stared in. There was a window and Dorothy noticed immediately that it was much smaller than the other rooms. They slowly walked in and Dorothy checked the big crumbling bed and wardrobes. "What we bleeding looking for darling?" Rosie asked lifting up part of the carpet. "A secret door or panel that goes…." Dorothy stopped talking and headed for the big fireplace against the far wall. She had realized that the fireplace was far too big for such a small room. She knelt down and stared beyond the empty grate; there hadn't been a fire lit for years. "Careful sweetie you're get your lovely hat and summer coat covered in bleeding soot." Rosie warned and Dorothy pulled off her hat and coat and placed them down. She wriggled into the fire place and felt around in the semi darkness. "It's here somewhere." She spoke softly to Rosie who knelt behind her; bat at the ready.

Dorothy's sensitive hands soon found the little lever and pushed it up. Both girls had to move real quick as the fireplace started to rotate. It opened leaving a gap that the women could squeeze through. They found themselves in a candle lit room. It had a bed, several pieces of furniture and piles of papers and books everywhere. In the far corner was a writing desk and chair, also covered with books and papers. But it was the figure sitting in the chair that caught their attention at once. It was slumped over the desk, back towards them.

Dorothy cleared her throat; "Good afternoon your lordship; sorry for the unannounced intrusion but I think you can help us solve a murder." The figure stirred and slowly turned. Rosie gasped in horror and gripped Dorothy's arm. "Sweet Jesus! Look at the poor buggers face." She whispered, shocked by the man's horrific appearance. It was like his face had simply melted with one eye lower than the other and glazed over.

"It's fucking Quasimodo's brother!" Rosie whispered not letting go of Dorothy's arm. Dorothy just patted her arm and gestured to the figure staring at them. "Rosie, this is Lord Harley-Coats." The man almost chuckled, but coughed and wheezed as he spoke; "No one has said my name in many years my dear. I'm now known simply as the 'monster'. Which is probably more accurate for one such as I." He tried to rise a little and gripped the chair tightly and stood; hunched over and gestured around him; "Welcome ladies to the tomb of Lord David Harley-Coats. Except that the corpse still breaths, a sort of dead man walking." He slumped back in the chair and now the women could see his disfigured hands clearly.

"What happened to you my lord?" Dorothy asked and the man coughed and gasped a couple of times. "Mycobacterium leprae, Hansen's disease or commonly known as leprosy my dear ladies. Totally incurable and you die slowly; a little at a time." He clasped his hands and sat back in the chair. "It creates monsters that people turn away in horror and so far, the only cure was Jesus Christ and I've prayed to him so much that I could be made pope on that fact alone." He tried to chuckle but it was caught in his throat. He lowered his head and sighed.

"I was struck down in Africa, didn't even know I had contracted it until I had been home several months. I had seen what happens first hand to sufferers there. So I simply disappeared and kept well away from people. Only Mr. Brice sees me and brings me what I need. He helps himself to money from the estate which he thinks I don't know about. But in my position you can't really be choosy about the company you keep." He coughed again and patted some newspapers on the desk.

"I've followed the story in the papers that Brice brings. I always wondered when the talented Inspector Hadden would show up. I never thought his beautiful young sister would appear instead. I take it you want to know about the mad Welshman and the poor murdered woman." He said quietly, wiping his mouth with a red hankie. Dorothy nodded.

"Watched it all through a spy hole. This place has secret panels, tunnels and spy holes. I followed him from the kitchen door to the music room carrying the bundle and he dumped it on the floor; that's when I reaslised it was a dead woman. He crept away singing quietly to himself; 'Men of Harlech'. Wonderful singing voice; typical for a Welshman."

Lord Harley-Coats wiped his face again and they could all hear shouting from the corridor outside. "I appreciate any bloody entertainment these days; all I have is the new Harpsichord to play. A little present from the light fingered Mr. Brice and now I play that badly with these hands." He held up his disfigured hands and fingers, adding quietly; "Soon that little pleasure will be gone."

Dorothy patted Rosie and told her to fetch Harry. She was gone in an instant back through the fireplace. Dorothy looked with real sadness at the once handsome and dashing young man, now basically a dead man, but still alive in a terrible strange way.
"I did write a little note for you brother and I would have pushed it through the police station letterbox, I can only visit at night obviously, but some drunks chased me and I had to return here; my strength almost gone." He folded his arms and lowered his head. Dorothy was relieved to see Harry come through the gap and grabbed his arm. He looked as relieved as she was. He stared at the figure and nodded; "Lord Harley-Coats I presume."

The figure looked up and did chuckle as best he could; "You mean what's left of him young man. Now you being a Police Inspector, you can take down my confession to murder."

Harry and Dorothy both looked at each other and stared back at the pathetic figure slumped in the chair and both thought the same thing; another bloody murder!

Rosie had brewed a huge pot of tea and was in her element serving it along with biscuits and cake. Uncle William's dressing room was packed. Harry and Dorothy sat talking closely and quietly together, whilst Uncle William and Jim Grieves read some papers by the fireplace. Constable's Dave Farmer and Edwin Palmer stood by the door, coats and hats on; ready to go at Harry's command. But they enjoyed their tea and cake whilst waiting.

Dorothy sipped her tea and tapped her brother's hand; "So what will happen to that poor sick man now?" Harry shrugged his shoulders; "Well, it's clear that strings have been pulled, despite his confession to murdering the young footman because he had strangled his aunt, he won't hang for it. The Home secretary has said that. Lord Harley-Coats will be sent to a secure hospital for the criminally insane for the remainder of his apparent short life. The case will be held behind closed doors and the press told nothing. The strange thing was that he [Lord Harley-Coats] was not happy about not being hung!"

Rosie handed Harry some biscuits and almost smiled; "So the bleeding young footman was blackmailing his [Lord Harley-Coats] aunt because he knew all about her affairs and when she wouldn't pay up and threatened to have him imprisoned for life; he flipped and bleeding strangled her! What a bloody turn up for the books." She put a large piece of fruit cake on Dorothy's plate and sighed. "I can see why the monster disguised himself and stabbed the blackmailer to death in a bleeding packed pub, then simply vanished. No wonder old Games never had a clue about that murder." She went back to the small stove and boiled some more water for even more tea.

There was a loud knocking at the door and Dave Farmer pulled it open and laughed, calling over to Harry "Your informant is here Guv." Harry jumped up and Dave let the young man in, well boy actually. Charlie Chapman pulled off his rough flat cap and grinned at Dorothy. "Hello darling, when I'm finished with Mr. Hadden here, I'll treat you to a gin at the Denmark Arms and we can take a stroll down the High Street. " Dorothy folded her arms and just sighed. Harry chuckled and pulled the boy over and shoved half a crown into his hand. "What do you have for me?"

The boy did grin and kissed the coin, pushing it into his scruffy jacket. "Got him Mr. Hadden, you know I always come up with the necessary. The bugger is dossing down in rooms at the Royal Standard pub in North Woolwich; Whitey the barman tipped me the wink. He and his lady friend, but she ain't half as pretty as my Dorothy there. They've only had one visitor since he booked in almost a week ago, according to my snout down there; a big ugly bugger who likes to carry a blade apparently. They're still there; well they were half an hour ago when I left there. They were having some strong words with each other."

Harry slapped the boy on the back and shouted; "Let's go!" The room quickly emptied of policemen and Dorothy stood and paced the room. Uncle William finished his tea and looked for a refill whilst young Charlie managed to get a slice of cake off Rosie. He walked to the door and waved goodbye telling Dorothy he'll pick her up at six. He disappeared out the door and Dorothy could hear Rosie chuckling with Uncle William. "Another bleeding admirer of real class and wealth." Rosie muttered and refilled Uncle William's cup. Uncle William sighed and told Dorothy to sit down and relax; they could only wait to hear how Harry's raid turned out. Rosie sat in the chair by the door and sewed; "I wonder who he's lady friend is? I mean this Welsh twat that murdered Miss Dorothy's friend to frame old Dashwood."

Uncle William lit his pipe; "Well, if Harry can grab the pair of them, then we'll know." Dorothy stood by the window, staring down into the street. "I think we could be in for a shock there Uncle William and it may not do the theatre any good." She folded her arms and smiled as she watched Titus and big Tom coming up the steps into the main entrance. The unlikely pair had actually become good friends by all accounts.

"How do you mean, that it could affect the theatre?" Uncle William puffed on his pipe and looked quite puzzled. Dorothy sighed; "I think Lucille Bellman could be the lady visiting with the Welsh murderer." She said and walked back to her chair. Uncle William lowered his pipe; "For once, I hope your wrong about that." He muttered and didn't really want to think of the awful ramifications of the theatre changing hands yet again.

Uncle William dozed in his chair and Dorothy tried to read the local paper. Rosie finished her stitching and washed up plates and cups. Dorothy kept looking at the little wall clock and the hands seem to be crawling around its face. That's when there was a knock at the door. Rosie walked over and shouted; "Who is it?" her yelling woke up Uncle William from his temporary slumbers. "Its PC Tanner Rosie!" came the reply.

Rosie pulled open the door and PC Tanner strolled in, removing his helmet. "Got a message from Mr. Hadden, he says you may be shocked by it." Rosie offered him tea which he readily accepted. Uncle William sat up in his chair and Dorothy stood, putting her paper down. He accepted a cup from Rosie and stirred in some sugar; "Mr. Hadden says brace yourself for a shock, the woman was Mrs. Lucille Bellman the bleeding theatre owner's wife!"

Uncle William sighed and jerked a thumb towards Dorothy; "That's no shock, she told me that half an hour ago!" PC Tanner chuckled; "Funny enough Mr. Hadden said you'd probably say that." He sipped his tea and added; "It turns out their bleeding brother and sister from Cardiff. Apparently the Welsh nutter was Dashwood's first wife's brother and Mrs. Bellman was their older sister. He intended for old Dashwood to hang for a murder that the Welsh loony committed. All sounds a bleeding bit strange to me."

Dorothy sighed and declined yet another cup of tea; "The real tragedy of all this, is that brute Dashwood walks away with no punishment for all the beatings he gave poor Hanna. Talk about coming up smelling of bloody roses." She eased into her chair and wondered about the fate of the theatre now and how its owner would react to his young wife being arrested for assisting a murderer. PC Tanner could only nod his agreement with that statement about Captain Dashwood.

"If they're working together on this dreadful scheme, then why did the Welshman have you attacked? Now that doesn't make sense." Uncle William shifted in his chair and yawned. Dorothy really didn't smile; "I think it was a warning to his other sister – Lucille Bellman – to keep her nose out of his evil plan. I believe he had not counted on her suddenly turning up from South Africa and talking to Hanna's friends. But we'll see what Harry has to say." Uncle William nodded at that and PC Tanner finished his tea and thanked Rosie; he headed back to Brick Lane Station.

Rosie pulled open the changing room door and gestured for

Dorothy to follow; "Best get you ready for this evening's show; big Tom is putting you on first tonight, did you remember that?" Dorothy did smile; "No that actually slipped my mind, still it means an early finish and home early." Uncle William groaned; he had just remembered that change of program. Rosie chuckled at the look on his face; "It's alright boss, I've already told Mr. Skoles and Reggie [Titus] about the change."

The performance was going really well and the vanishing trick was next. Titus had moved the sarcophagus into position and only needed to remove the lid as Dorothy approached. The crowd was silent in anticipation; Titus pulled off the supposed heavy lid and Young Lord Robert De Salle Barclay jumped from the box and grabbed a very shocked Dorothy by the arm shouting; "Run! Run my darling!" Dorothy was dragged a couple of feet by the desperate youth before Titus took hold of the young man and dragged him off stage.

The audience reacted with huge applause, cheering and laughter. Dorothy composed herself and caught Uncle William's signal to start the next trick. She rolled the big urn to centre stage and was relieved when Titus [now grinning] returned and helped her climb in. Professor Potts waved his wand about and 'big Arthur' the snake slowly arose from the large vase and Titus turned the thing over and he slithered out. There was no sign of Dorothy.

The crowd were clapping and cheering. The magic show received four encore's that night. Uncle William was still chuckling about the love sick, daft young man as he and Dorothy made their way home in the cab.

"Big Tom and Titus threw him – again – out the stage door. Apparently big Tom really did put his boot up the boy's arse!" Uncle William sighed and patted Dorothy's hand. She didn't smile and stared out at the early evening traffic. She wondered what Harry would say about the mad Welshman and more importantly; about Lucille Bellman who she had quite liked.

Ellen took their coats and hats. "Mister Hadden is waiting for you." She informed the pair and they walked quickly to the front reception room to find Harry dosed in an armchair, clutching a large brandy. He smiled and raised a class to Dorothy; "Another one chalked up to you my darling little sister!"

Dorothy grinned and curtsied, and then Harry added, "Oh by the way, Sims says to tell you, that you were right about a certain Mister Capstone and he's safely back where he belongs and that includes his wife. Jericho was well pleased with the information and says 'thanks and a job well done!'

Harry waved his glass about, "Now my girl, what on earth was that all about?"

Dorothy took her brandy and smiled, "Just another little mission: snaring someone who actually wasn't very good at covering his tracks. Not really good at all, totally bloody obvious in fact!" She of course, didn't know just how close she [and Rosie] had gone to be embroiled in a sect of particularly evil devil Worshippers. Mister Jericho Tibbs and his team had grabbed 'Henry Capstone' and his wife – who was his English wife from the 1500's – and return them to their ordained time period. He could do nothing about Mrs. Styles and her compatriots as they were all of this time period and temporal detectives do not interfere in the criminal acts of humans in their own time. But he did manage to put the 'frighteners' on the devil worshippers by ensuring that Mrs. Styles knew that temporal detectives were on the case. They would have to close their 'operations' down and sadly, resurrect them at a later date. As Jericho always says, "Once a Devil worshipper, always a Devil worshipper!"

CHAPTER 9. 'INFORMATION MAY INFORM THE MIND, BUT REVELATION SETS A HEART ON FIRE.' Matt Redman.

Uncle William had managed to stop laughing about the love sick boy and slumped into his favourite chair and Ellen handed him a glass of dark rum. He filled his pipe and lit it with some apparent happiness. "Well Harry, what happened?" he asked between puffing his reluctant pipe quite hard.

Harry sat with his glass of brandy, quite grim faced and finally spoke softly; "It was Dashwood's first wife that was the key to all this. The corner was right to declare accidental death; Irene suffered from fits and did indeed have a serious one as she bathed. She drowns in the bath whilst Dashwood was at sea. But her brother David simply could not accept that verdict; he knew Dashwood had beaten his sister several times before, so he believed – in his own mind – that Dashwood had somehow murdered Irene. That festered in his mind and finally he worked out how Dashwood could have done it. So he now set out to revenge his sister, especially when he heard that Dashwood had married again." Harry placed his glass down; he now had their undivided attention.

Dorothy accepted a small glass of brandy from Ellen and made herself comfortable on the sofa. He continued; "He discovered that Dashwood had beaten Hanna again and that the poor woman was practically living in isolation until her bruises cleared up; she was too embarrassed and ashamed to face her friends at the cycling club. That was perfect for his plan and he struck. Abducting Hanna and dragging her to the old house, as soon as Dashwood sailed. He brutally murdered her in the bath, which he filled with salted water. He was a chemist by trade and knew that using industrial salt was key to his plan. He dressed Hanna in winter clothes and dumped her in the musical room, deliberately leaving the kitchen door open. He knew that the local kids couldn't resist going in, looking for the supposed monster. He also knew that Dorothy and I would suspect the captain, especially after Doctor Shaw stated that industrial salt was used to clean the freezers on the refrigerated ships. He wanted Dashwood convicted of murder and hung for the supposed murder of his sister."

Harry eased from his seat and paced the room; "He had a problem when his older sister Lucille [now Mrs. Bellman] turned up back in England. She had been Hanna's friend and he knew that Hanna had told her about the captain's first wife and her fits. He was now in quite a fix; his older sister would have nothing to do with the plan of revenge. Apparently the three girls did know each other back in Wales. That complicated Mr. Jones plan, but he wouldn't be stopped. He panicked a little and hired Max Styles to rough his sister up, to keep her quiet until he could sort things out. Max Styles is a nasty vicious thug and is not too bright. He had been given Lucille's description and the dumb bastard hung about until an elegant young lady appeared from the theatre, where he knew she was visiting and he struck. Except it was our Dorothy and Jim arrived in the nick of time. That left David a little concerned; but he continued on with his plan to get Dashwood wrongly convicted and hung. He would have succeeded but for the 'monster' who had witnessed everything that happened in the old house, through his spy holes."

Dorothy nodded; "Will there be any charges against Lucille over this?" she asked him with some concern in her voice. Harry shook his head; "With the kind of lawyers that old man Bellman could afford and the fact that Lucille took no real part in the actual killing, the Superintendant has decided no action will be taken against her."

Both Dorothy and Uncle William sighed with relief at that. "Max Styles or whatever his name is, now knows that his boss has been apprehended and is singing like a pissed canary in the hope of a reduced sentence. He'll go away for a long time regardless of what he tells us." Harry did smile at the look of relief on his sister's face. "So that nasty piece of work [Captain Dashwood] walks away smelling of roses even though he beat poor Hanna on a regular basis: the brute." Dorothy muttered, clearly unhappy about that.

Uncle William smiled; "Now Harry, what the hell are we going to do about the mad, love sick youth that won't take no for an answer?" The trio started to chuckle and even Dorothy had to laugh about the love sick boy. Harry held up his hand; "Oh, I thought you two should know that I've invited Doctor Paul Shaw over for dinner Saturday night; he really seemed quite happy about that."

Dorothy just sipped her brandy and smiled a little. Then her thoughts turned to her other ardent admirer: Oskar. She had visited his dismal lodgings in Quaker Row, carrying a shopping basket full of goodies from 'Marshal & Snelgrove' of Oxford Street. He was very pleased to see her and her presents. Dottie had decided to thank the man properly for saving her. [See episode **'The workhouse corpse with golden boots.'**]

They had a cup of tea and Dottie was amazed to find he had an incredible knowledge of Botany and he admitted – as a young man – he had worked for a Duke as a gardener, normally in the 'hot houses' [glass houses today] and so knew all about the exotic plants that the Victorian and Edwardian wealthy loved. She placed a gold sovereign on his rough table and asked if he could find a certain individual called 'the beast'. He nodded and said he would make inquiries around the east end underworld. He picked up the coin and kissed it, placing in his little purse, which made Dorothy smile.

"It was common for some working class men to carry such a 'purse' in these times. Nearly all the money they carried was coins. Their cheap clothes had cheap pockets and they soon wore through. The purse was easier to replace! " SJW

She felt it was only fair to offer him the same reward that Reggie received [she was working on how and when to 'thank' Jim Grieves without her brother or Uncle Henry finding out, but it was proving difficult because of the close relationship between him and Harry!] Even if he was ugly and a little bit too old for her: 'fairs, fair' she told herself. A debt was a debt and she would repay his brave actions in saving her from something far worse. While Oskar replenished the tea pot, Dorothy unbuttoned her blouse, she wasn't wearing a corset. In fact she wasn't wearing anything under her blouse and skirt. She pulled her blouse open and when he sat back down, eyes wide, she took his big rough hand and placed it on her heaving right breast. "Now Oskar, I will thank you properly with something that I damn well know you want!" The smile on his ugly brutish face would stay for some days!

The old bed groaned and creaked under the sexual antics of Oskar and Dorothy. He had her first in the Missionary position, fucking her hard and fast with his large fat cock. Then they swapped to 'Doggy' with Dorothy having to grip the shaking iron headboard with both hands, moaning loudly as she had a leg trembling orgasm. After a nip of whisky, they started again and despite his ugly battered appearance, Dorothy agreed to French kiss and that's when the earth really did move. Back in the Missionary position with Dorothy's legs wrapped around his back and both arms gripping his big neck and shoulders tightly, their mouths and tongues crashed together and sparks flew for both of them. The passion was so great that Dottie had a deep orgasm almost immediately and their mouths didn't part until he finished a second time in her. They both lay back panting, gripping hands, both knowing something strange and beautiful had occurred.

Finally Oskar managed to whisper, "If they had written bloody 'Beauty and Beast' like this; it would have been quickly bleeding banned!" Dorothy chuckled and squeezed the big man's hands. She couldn't care less that his face was like a bleeding bulldog chewing rusty wire; he was now something special to her. He whispered if he could have 'a treat' and she slowly nodded, rolling over and pulling her bum cheeks apart. Now ugly Oskar really did smile and mounted her quickly after rubbing his cock vigorously with Vaseline. Dorothy pushed an arm around his neck and turned her head so they could resume their French kissing.

He poked her 'brown flower' for some minutes before groaning and cussing about his ejaculation, admitting that the 'bloody French kissing' was the cause of his quick finish [to him anyway] and Dorothy just stroked his sweaty ugly face and whispered she hadn't noticed the bloody time! Laughing, they cuddled, still physically locked as one. They lay together for some time until Oskar handed her a soft towel and pulled slowly and gently from her much expanded bum hole. She slipped from the bed, the towel pushed between her buttocks and headed for the toilet to find he had an outside privy. He tossed her his old blue dressing gown and chuckled; "My bleeding neighbours are devout bloody Catholic's and old man O'Brian wouldn't object to seeing you stark naked, but Mary his wife would!" Dorothy pulled on the gown and with a big smile headed down the stairs, walking really awkwardly. She had previously entertained Reggie and Albert with her 'brown flower' [which they loved!] but Oskar wasn't only big length wise but had quite a girth and it had certainly stretched her. But she wasn't complaining!

She found the 'privy' at the bottom of the small yard and was actually surprised by how clean it was. But what really impressed her was the toilet paper: it wasn't just some cut up newspaper or magazine but a lovely soft tissue in small sheets and placed in a box.

"It wasn't until the early 20th century that toilet paper became more affordable and widely available to the general public. The introduction of perforated toilet paper rolls in the 1890s by the Scott Paper Company and the subsequent marketing efforts helped popularize its use. By the mid-20th

century, toilet paper had become a standard item in most households." SJW

After a final cup of tea, the new lovers separated and Dorothy caught a cab home and couldn't help but smile. She eased back in the cab seat and slowly grinned, then giggled and laughed. What a strange world sex was! She gripped her handbag and stared out the window with a big smile on her face, after two solid hours of incredible fucking with the ugly man who had played her body like a concert pianist. She had enjoyed two enormous orgasms under his expert handling and indulged in some very naughty – and currently – illegal sex that she thought she would never, ever enjoy so much. She giggled to herself and really did need a bath. Oskar was now third or fourth on her list of lover's despite his rough appearance; just below Reggie and she was undecided where to place Albert! She couldn't wait to tell Rosie, who was the undoubted top of that list.

THE END

EPISODE 4: "THE HIDDEN WINDOW."

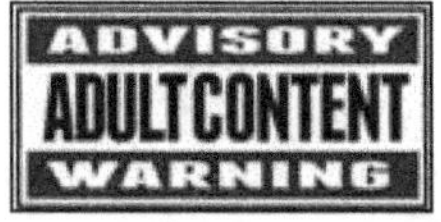

Alcohol – Smoking – Strong language – Strong sexual references [including references to child abuse] – Paranormal & supernatural references – mild horror – Strong violence – Mild Adult Erotica.

Approximately 45 to 60 minutes.

Remember: **Adult Content.**

EPISODE CONTENTS.

1. 'SELF PARODY IS THE FIRST PORTENT OF AGE.'
Start page: 292

2. '...THE LOWEST AND VILEST ALLEYS IN LONDON DO NOT PRESENT A MORE DREADFUL RECORD OF SIN THAN DOES THE SMILING AND BEAUTIFUL COUNTRYSIDE...'
Start page: 298

3. 'SUPERSITION IS TO RELIGION WHAT ASTROLOGY IS TO ASTRONOMY; THE MAD DAUGHTER OF A WISE MOTHER.'
Start page: 304

4. 'AT A DINER PARTY ONE SHOULD EAT WISELY, BUT NOT TOO WELL, AND TALK WELL BUT NOT TOO WISELY.'
Start page: 312

5. NOTHING IN LIFE IS SO EXHILARATING AS TO BE SHOT AT WITHOUT RESULT.'
Start page: 318

6. 'WE ALL HAVE DEMONS...'
Start page: 327

7. 'WE ACCEPT THE LOVE WE THINK WE DESERVE.'
Start page: 332

8. 'GOODBYE SHE SAID, I'M OFF TO JOIN THE GYPSIES.'
Start page: 336

9. 'YOU CAN'T FIND SOMEONE WHO DOESN'T WANT TO BE FOUND.'
Start page: 341

10. 'I WAS PLUNGED INTO WHAT WAS KNOWN AS THE DEBUTANTE SOCIAL WHIRL. THIS WAS ONE OF THE WAYS FATHERS JUSTIFIED THEIR OWN HARD WORK AND SACRIFICES.'
Start page: 348

CHAPTER 1. 'SELF PARODY IS THE FIRST PORTENT OF AGE.' Larry McMurtry.

It was young Frank Wilson – the under Gardener - who found the body of old Mr. Alfred Parks in the small copse of trees by the Tennis Courts. He was cleaning away undergrowth from the gravel path that meandered down from the castle to the seldom used courts. He ran back to the house and crashed through the kitchen entrance shouting and panting. Alice – the young kitchen maid – rushed to find Mr. Paul Gibbs, the Senior Footman and report the dreadful find. Paul was in the Morning Room, slowly spreading out the freshly ironed news papers to accompany the family's breakfast.

 He calmed young Alice down and listened without any real emotion; old Mr. Parks had been the Butler at the castle for nearly twenty five years and now he was laying face down in the small woods; his back torn open by a gun blast. Alice was sobbing and shouting; "Murder! Bloody murder Mr. Gibbs!"

He nodded and told her to fetch Mrs. Calendar – the House-keeper – he would inform the young earl himself. "But we need the blooming police Mr. Gibbs!" She shouted and Paul just patted her shoulder and said quietly; "All in good time Alice, now go fetch Mrs. Calendar." Alice, wiping her tears, left the quiet room and composed herself. She passed one of the upstairs maids – Judith – and didn't say anything to her about what had just happened. She really didn't like either of the upstairs maids.

Alice found Mrs. Calendar in the grand Dining Room, checking the fireplaces and curtains; there was to be a splendid diner given tonight to celebrate the arrival of his Lordship's Fiancé from America; accompanied by her mother and younger brother. Her father had died some years ago; leaving her mother a very wealthy widow and his young son was set to inherit a fortune when he turned twenty one.

Alice whispered to her and grim faced, the women left for his Lordship's study. They met Mr. Gibbs waiting outside. He dismissed Alice and knocked softly on the door. His lordship told them to enter and they did slowly, closing the door firmly behind them. Alice stood some yards away and wiped her face: now what the fuck would happen? She turned, sadly walking away. Mrs. Edna Porterhouse sat at the huge kitchen table and sipped her most needed cup of tea. The normally, cheerful cook wiped a tear away and shook her head, speaking to Alice who gripped her cup of tea with both hands. "Mr. Parks' dead? Oh my Gawd, the place will be crawling with police, bloody reporters and everybody else and we have his lordship's finance and her bleeding family turning up!" Alice nodded; "Do you think his lordship will tell Mr. Gibbs to take over? I mean he'll have to manage several big dinners, all the guests and their servants, then there's the blooming wedding. That's really throwing Mr. Gibbs in at the deep end!"

Mrs. Porterhouse lowered her cup and sighed; "Well, one thing is for sure, his lordship will certainly find out if Mr. Gibbs can do the bleeding job!" She finished her tea and sat back, shaking her head in disbelief; "Who the hell would want to kill old Mr. Parks? I mean, shoot the old boy in the back and leave his body in the woods. I've known him almost five years and there wasn't any harm in him. I would have thought he didn't have an enemy in the world."

Alice finished her tea and placed the cup down; "Well, someone hated him enough to shoot him in the back." Judith and Kate [the two upstairs maids] came rushing through the kitchen door demanding if the incredible story was true. Mrs. Porterhouse calmed them down and told Alice to fetch the girls some tea. She gave a sideways glance at the two girls sitting at the table quietly talking. They both could easily be considered very pretty, quite beautiful in fact; the young Earl would not have a single upstairs maid that wasn't very pretty. Even if they possessed no ability or attitude to be a maid; Mrs. Calendar had already commented on that little problem; several times.

Alice returned with the tea and Judith asked her what would

happen next, what they would do with the body and so on. Alice shrugged her shoulders - she didn't know for sure – but expected the police would be called; almost certainly CID officers from York itself would attend considering the Earl of Barfield was concerned. Both girls sipped their hot tea and talked amongst themselves. Not invited to join the conversation, Alice walked to the back door of the kitchens and stepped out into the rear yard. Open mouthed, she watched the Junior footman running from the back gates; shouting that three carriages had turned into the front gateway of the castle and were headed down the main drive.

She rushed back in and shouted to Judith and Kate; "One of you better find Mr. Gibbs or Mrs. Calendar; I think his lordships finance and her family has turned up!"

Both girls chuckled and just sat drinking their tea. Alice sighed and headed for the back stairs; "Lazy bloody bitches, they think they're so bloody pretty they don't have to do sod all." She muttered to herself and came across young David King [another Footman] carrying a large sealed box. She asked him about the senior Footman and the Housekeeper. He managed to jerk a finger towards the Evening Reception room; "They're all in there, Alice my lovely." He grinned and wandered off down the back stairs, carrying his load carefully.

Alice liked young David – a lot – he had been quite pleasant and hard working; he would always help out when needed. But of course, the two 'sirens' had got their claws into him. Sadly, Mrs. Porterhouse always said that those two [Judith & Kate] would be the ruin of the lad. She knocked on the door and Mr. Gibbs pulled it open and she told him that they had visitors. He just nodded and thanked her, closing the door. Alice had quickly seen that his lordship was sitting in his favourite armchair by the large grand fireplace, with Mrs. Calendar standing in front of him, and old Silas Richards [the Game keeper] next to her.

The conversation between the little group appeared to have been a little 'heated'. Alice made her way back to the busy kitchens; realizing bleeding murder or not; the evening meal would be prepared. She walked back into the kitchens to find that Judith & Kate had gone and PC Richard Holmes sitting at the table with Mrs. Porterhouse. She stood by the sink and poured herself a cup of cold water; she could hear the conversation between the pair.

Apparently Mavis the Postmistress had sent a cable to York Police Headquarters requesting CID assistance. The reply was quick and concise; don't touch anything, no one was allowed to leave and cover the bloody body. A certain detective Inspector Harold Ramsey was on his way.

Alice stood by the huge double fronted stove and sipped her cold water. Apparently old Mr. Parks had been shot in the back at quite close range, almost certainly with a shotgun. He had clearly laid in the woods all night. Mrs. Porterhouse nodded, wiping away a tear and told the officer that the last she had seen him was at about nine o'clock last night; heading up to his lordship's room after being summoned.

Alice nodded her agreement at that; she had watched the old man go, strangely enough his head bowed a little and apparently deep in thought. She had remarked to young David about the Butler's odd appearance. He had just shrugged his shoulders and went back to his magazine about Equine care. Mr. Gibbs quickly appeared in the kitchen doorway and welcomed PC Holmes and asked him to follow to the Earl's study.

The two men left and Mrs. Porterhouse slowly pulled her clean white apron on and gestured for Alice to do the same. "That's an awful omen for his lordships marriage; the murder I mean." She said and started to gather several plates to the table. Alice pulled on her apron and agreed with the cook; "Like old Mister Silas said about those blooming crows gathering on the roof; apparently they haven't done that since 1897 when the old Earl died. My old gran would say they're omens and portents of death or disaster."

Mrs. Porterhouse chuckled, pouring flour into a large porcelain bowel. "Well, I'd keep your omens and portents to yourself Alice; I don't think his lordship will want to hear about them!" Alice managed a smile and started to wash several pounds of potatoes in the deep sink. Both women looked up when Mr. Thomas Blackledge appeared at the kitchen door, cap in hand and looking quite upset. He was the foreman of the men working on the east tower; repairing and strengthening it. Mrs. Porterhouse said quietly; "What is it Thomas, you look like you've seen a blooming ghost." The man walked slowly in and clasped his hands in front of him, gripping his hat. "We've uncovered something at the east tower and it ain't good." He eased himself into a chair and young David slapped down his magazine. "What is it Mr. Blackledge?"

The man pulled a hankie from his trouser pocket and wiped his face. "It, young David, we've found it. I never thought the bloody thing actually existed, but there it is, right there. Sweet Jesus, what a turn up for the books!"

Alice stooped washing spuds and asked what was right there in the east tower. Mr. Blackledge ran his hankie over his face again and sighed;"The blooming devil's window!" he said and shook his head in disbelief. Alice and Mrs. Porterhouse sat back at the table and there was silence for a few seconds, then Alice said softly; "Well, that's one evil omen and portent that his lordship can't ignore." Everyone just stared at her, but they all knew the young maid was right about that. The discovery of the legendary Devil's window after the horrific death of old Mr. Parks couldn't be ignored or dismissed as silly ancient legend and myth now. Mrs. Porterhouse actually crossed herself and slumped in her chair, she slowly shook her head; "Sweet Jesus Christ it cannot be a co-incidence that old Mr. Parks was found dead on the morning that bloody thing was uncovered. For Gawd sake Alice love, make some blooming tea!"

The staff ate their lunch in subdued silence and Mr. Gibbs sat at the head of the table with Mrs. Calendar next to him. Mrs. Porterhouse finally broke the silence; "Mr. Gibbs, are the guests all settled in?" as she pushed the beef sandwich about on her plate. He nodded and sipped his tea; "Yes, Mrs. Porterhouse Miss Charlotte Higgs-Packer, her mother and brother are settled in their rooms, I told her lady's maid to come down for some lunch after she's unpacked. Her name is Miss Harker. She's from New York apparently. The brother is travelling without a valet which is unusual for a young gentleman, so David will have to attend him if necessary."

David nodded and finished his sandwich, starting immediately on his apple. Alice refilled everyone's cups from a huge china tea pot. She really wanted to ask Mr. Gibbs about what troubled Mr. Blackledge had told his lordship, but she knew that the acting butler would put her firmly in place regarding such a question. Mr. Gibbs wiped his mouth and sighed; "I've spoken to his lordship and he's agreed that I will continue to act as butler for the foreseeable future. But because of the wedding, we will definitely need another footman so I've sent a cable to the London house and asked for Mr. Williams to travel up for the next few weeks. He's the senior Footman there and he knows what few weeks. He's the senior Footman there and he knows what he's doing around important and large parties. He should arrive tonight and will share with you David."

David nodded again and ate his apple slowly and quietly. He had heard the gossip about Mr. Williams; apparently a dashing and good looking young man who was already earmarked to rise in the staff ranks; if he could leave women alone! He knew that two other footmen would also be arriving from the family's estate in Norfolk, which had been previously arranged. There was also another cook and her assistant arriving. He wondered how they would get on with Mrs. Porterhouse and Alice of course. Still, they should be grateful for any more hands they could get, considering the amount of work that would be involved with extra guests and the wedding.

Mr. Gibbs tapped the table; he had two more announcements to make. "Some other family guests will arrive tomorrow morning; his lordship's cousin William Hadden with his nephew and niece. The younger man is a London detective and his sister is a stage actress like Miss Higgs-Packer. They will be staying until after the wedding. The young lady will be accompanied by her ladies maid And the two gentlemen will be sharing a valet, so that will make our task easier." Mrs. Calendar nodded her approval at that, especially about the ladies maid, otherwise she would have probably been lumbered with the girl and that would be very unwelcome considering she will have a house full and a wedding to oversee.

Mr. Gibbs finally informed the staff that detectives from York would arrive soon and they would need to speak to everyone and he emphasized 'everyone'. He told the listening staff that they were to go nowhere near the small woods; local uniformed police officers were guarding the body. He asked Mrs. Porterhouse to send them some tea and sandwiches; they were using the old tennis pavilion temporarily.

David whispered to Alice, who refilled his cup; "I do hear his lordship's cousin is a bloody famous magician and his niece is his assistant. Apparently she's a bleeding stunner!" Alice nodded and moved on to refill Judith and Kate's cups. They didn't even bother to say 'thank you', but carried on with their hurried whispered conversation. Alice had picked up on a couple of words; the young earl and the attic's, which were off limits to all staff.

The subject of the 'Devil's window' wasn't allowed or discussed at the table. After lunch, the staff returned to their duties; with the three young Hall Boy's talking about the window, the murder and now a magician and a London detective turning up.

Mrs. Porterhouse shooed the boys from the kitchens and reminded them to keep civil tongues in the heads with so many important guests about the place. They dispersed back to their duties in relative silence.

Alice was slowly peeling potatoes and said quietly to Mrs. Porterhouse; "With the window found, I don't think poor old Mr. Parks will be the only tragedy to hit the family." Mrs. Porterhouse couldn't actually argue with that deduction, by her kitchen maid.

CHAPTER 2. '...THE LOWEST AND VILEST ALLEYS IN LONDON DO NOT PRESENT A MORE DREADFUL RECORD OF SIN THAN DOES THE SMILING AND BEAUTIFUL COUNTRYSIDE...' Sherlock Holmes.

Dorothy walked to the big window and stared out at the rear gardens of Castle Barfield. They were stunning and she could see the woods located near the disused tennis courts. "Apparently that's where they found the dead butler." She gestured out the window as Rosie appeared over her shoulder; "Bleeding fine welcome that. A stiff in the woods and a bloody window discovered that Old Nick himself created which foretells death and bleeding disaster. Lovely time and place for a wedding!" Harry stood in the doorway and chuckled; "That's it Rosie, tell it like it is." He walked in and joined Dorothy by the window.

"Apparently the old butler was last seen at about nine o'clock going to see Cousin David [the Earl of Barfield] over the wedding arrangements. A young Journeyman found the body on a path in the woods by the disused tennis courts. That was the following morning. It appears that the old butler was shot in the back at close range by, probably, a shot gun. He hadn't been robbed; he still had his watch and wallet on him, including keys to the front and rear doors. So what the motive for his killing was remains bit of a mystery." Dorothy nodded and pulled the lace curtains back across.

Rosie pulled the small suitcase open and then looked a little puzzled; "What the bleeding hell is a Journeyman when it's at home Mister Hadden?" Harry chuckled; "It's a fancy name for an apprentice gardener Rosie." She shrugged her shoulders; "Why don't they just bleeding say that instead of dressing it up." They all looked around at the knocking on the door. Rosie wandered over and jerked it open. David the footman smiled and spoke directly to Harry; "Mr. Ramsey, the Inspector from York Police asks if you would join him at the scene sir." Harry nodded and grabbed up his hat. "I'll show you the way sir." David added.

Dorothy told Rosie to fetch her bonnet and joined her brother, much to the astonishment of the young footman. He took the pair through the castle and out into the grounds. They followed the gravel footpath through the woods to the disused tennis courts. They could see several men around the body which was covered with a green tarpaulin. Dorothy stood by the single story pavilion and stared up at the roof. "What's up my girl?" Harry asked and Dorothy gestured towards the roof; "Harry, how long has the pavilion been disused?" Harry shrugged his shoulders; he didn't know.

David coughed and spoke quietly; "Excuse me ma'am, the old pavilion hasn't been used for about twenty years, I think." Dorothy thanked him and turned back to the men standing around the covered body; all staring at her. A quite elderly gentlemen, standing erect with his bowler hat on the back of his grey head, folded his arms and nodded towards Dorothy, but spoke to Harry. "Do you normally have a female accompany you on your investigations mister Hadden?" He didn't look happy.

Harry sighed; "Strangely enough, yes I do. Her mind and eyes are worth a dozen hairy detectives who couldn't detect a bear in their bathroom, until it pulled the bloody chain." He walked over and asked to look at the body. Mr. Ramsey thrust his hands into his trousers pockets and tapped the body with his boot. "Nothing truly mysterious about his death; a shotgun blast to the back is pretty obvious." He informed Harry as he carefully watched Dorothy disappearing into the pavilion. He tapped Harry on the arm; "What the hell is your lady friend up to mister Hadden?"

Harry, kneeling by the body, just smiled; "Don't worry about my sister Mr. Ramsey; she knows her way around a murder scene. Nothing will be disturbed." Harry lifted the body a little and lowered it gently. "Inspector Ramsey is there any reason why the corpse's belt is undone and his flies unbuttoned? Was he found like that?" The Inspector also knelt and told a burly uniform officer to turn the body back over; sure enough, the trousers were gaping open and Harry indicated to the dead man's left hand; "The hand is gripping the trouser's waist band, like he was holding it up." Inspector Ramsey nodded his agreement with that. "Maybe he had been caught short and was taking a dump when he was shot?" ventured the really big man in a tight suit, next to Inspector Ramsey. He was sergeant John Lanes; the York Inspectors assistant. Harry nodded; the big, red faced man could be right; but it was still open for discussion.

Dorothy appeared in the open doorway of the pavilion and gestured for Harry to come over; he rose and was followed by Inspector Ramsey and his burly assistant. Dorothy went back into the pavilion and the three men followed. "Several paraffin lamps – a couple lying on the floor – and take a look at this." Dorothy pulled back a thick dark coloured velvet curtain and everyone stared at the mattress on the dirty floor; there were sheets and pillows laid about the place. There was a distinct smell of perfume or strong soap about the small room, mingled with what Dorothy believed was sulphate or something similar. The single small window had been covered with a dark cloth.

Dorothy pointed to the head of the 'bed'; there were three tin's lying open; all empty. "Someone has a sweet tooth, three empty tins of very expensive sweets." Harry muttered and Dorothy tapped his arm and pointed down at something far more sinister; a couple of soft white towels thrown on the floor; they had little specks of blood upon them. "Touch nothing; I want all this photographed and those bleeding towels looked at." Inspector Ramey wiped his face and stared at Dorothy. At least her brother was right about her; she clearly knew her way around a crime scene. He wondered where that skill came from.

"Well, the poor bugger has lain here long enough." The Inspector gestured to the two big policemen who were holding a wooden and canvas stretcher between them. "Get it shifted boys." He pulled a cigarette case out and offered Harry one, which was politely refused. "Doctor Morrison will do the PM; you just missed him. A busy man is the good doctor; he's off to Drew's farm to deliver an awkward baby. The Midwife has called him."

Dorothy pushed her arm through her brothers and Harry sighed; "I wish your Paul was here to do the PM." Dorothy shook her head and didn't smile; well, not much. "He's not my Paul. We're not engaged or anything." Harry did smile; "Not yet." He chuckled and the pair walked back to the house together.

Dorothy turned back and stared at the 'disused' tennis pavilion; "The chimney is black with soot and the little pot bellied stove looks like it has been recently used. Maybe a vagrant or someone has been rough sleeping there." Harry nodded; he had noticed that too. "Well, we've earned our breakfast. I hope there are some sausages left." He smiled at the face Dorothy pulled.

Mr. Gibbs stood by the large serving table which was laden with breakfast goodies. Uncle William had piled his plate with fat sausages, bacon slices, mushrooms, grilled tomatoes and two fried eggs. He sat quietly at the dining table and sprinkled a little salt on his eggs. Young David the footman poured his tea and Uncle William thanked him. Sitting opposite was Miss Charlotte Higgs-Packer and her young brother. She sipped her tea and stared about the room, trying to avoid eye contact with Uncle William. She wasn't too happy when her brother; George engaged Uncle William in conversation about his magic act. The young man seemed fascinated by it.

Uncle William asked where his mother; Mrs. Higgs-Packer was and the young man chuckled, digging into his huge plate of breakfast. "Apparently widow's still count as married women for breakfast and she had hers in bed." William nodded; they had the same tradition in high born British families; married women almost always took their breakfast in their bedrooms.

The new Earl came through the door and grabbed a newspaper. Mr. Gibbs asked him if he wanted the usual and he nodded yes. He dropped into the seat at the head of the table and smiled at everyone. "We're not going to let the tragedy of poor Mr. parks shocking death overshadow the wedding celebrations and the discovery of that damn window won't affect them either!" he announced and patted his fiancé's hand. That's when Harry and Dorothy entered the room and Harry made straight for the serving table. Mr. Gibbs held the chair next to Uncle William and

Dorothy sat down saying 'good morning' to everyone.

Young George stopped shoveling his breakfast down his throat and slowly smiled at her. "I say, you're a real treat this time of the morning." He now grinned and jabbed a fork at himself, adding; "George Higgs-Packer and this is my sister Lottie. Apparently in three months time I'm going to be stinking rich. Are you spoken for?" his sister just sighed as Uncle William and the young Earl chuckled. "He has a terrible habit of saying whatever enters his head. I do apologize." Miss Charlotte dabbed her mouth and gave her young brother a look that could defrost Alaska. He just grinned and asked Dorothy about the magic act.

Harry joined them, slapping a plate of scrambled eggs and toast in front of Dorothy. His own plate resembled young George's! "Uncle William's and Dorothy's act is well received and very popular. I might be a little biased but I'd say it was one of the best." Harry said and dropped into the seat next to Dorothy and David the footman poured their tea.

Miss Charlotte carefully placed her napkin down and smiled at her fiancé; "My maid tells me the topic of conversation below stairs is about the poor dead butler and some kind of haunted window."

The Earl sat back in his chair and nodded; "Well, the demise of Mr. Parks is clear and not very mysterious; someone shot him in the back. But the window is something else; it was just myth and legend until they found the damn thing!"

Dorothy sprinkled a little salt on her eggs and asked the Earl what the legend actually was. He smiled and waved his knife about; "It's been part of the damn family history for centuries. Apparently during the late medieval Period – the early fourteen hundreds – part of the east tower was a chapel and the third Earl commissioned a French man to create a stained glass for the chapel. Apparently the man was regarded as the best and had worked for the French Royal family. The fellow arrived with his family and workers and set to work. They had almost finished when yet another war broke out between France and England. Sadly, my ancestor thought it was a great opportunity not to pay the poor fellow for his work. So he ordered his arrest and threw the entire family – with their workers – into the dungeons."
  David – the young earl – sipped his tea and continued. "Well, the war lasted a few years and most of the poor man's family and

workers died in the dungeons including his wife and two young children. When the latest war finished, the Earl released the Frenchman and demanded he finish the window. At sword point he did and then threw himself off the east tower; cursing the Earl and his evil deeds for all eternity. When the Earl heard about the tragic death of the Frenchman he just laughed until he saw the window. He immediately ordered it bricked up and over the centuries it was lost. The legends say that the Frenchman came from a gypsy family with dark powers and should the window ever see daylight, then disaster will strike the family."

The Earl chuckled; "A load of old hogwash I believe, but people will – of course- link the discovery with poor old Mr. Parks' death. Except of course, Parks was not a member of the family, so the curse clearly doesn't work!"

"I really would like to see the window, is that possible my lord?" Dorothy asked him and smiled. Lord David nodded; "Yes of course you can and please call me Cousin David." The smile he gave Dorothy didn't go un-noticed by anyone at the table; including his fiancé. "Yes, let's make a morning of it. I would love to see the window." Charlotte slapped her napkin down and rose from the chair so quickly that David the footman didn't even reach her chair. Lord David rose from his chair – his breakfast unfinished – and agreed that everyone should meet up at the stairwell of the east tower in half an hour. He would arrange for the tower to be un-locked and cleaned up for their impromptu visit.

He followed his fiancé out the door opened by Mr. Gibbs. Young George laughed and winked at Dorothy; "I think my future brother-in-law really likes young beautiful women." He wiped his mouth and jumped from the chair; "See you all in the cursed tower my new friends; especially you Dorothy." He was still grinning as he left. Harry leaned back in his chair and said quietly to Uncle William; "Is the seventieth Earl of Barfield trustworthy where women are concerned?" He did smile. Uncle William shook his head; "Young David has quite a reputation for young women; especially beautiful talented young women." Both men looked at Dorothy and smiled broadly. She just sighed and finished her breakfast.

Harry patted her hand; "I would stick to the good doctor if I was you Dotty." He almost giggled and finished his breakfast. Dorothy also finished her breakfast and young David helped her from her chair. "We'll meet up in my room and head for the damn tower." Uncle William said and the breakfast party broke up. Mr. Gibbs opened the door and watched the visitors go. He rubbed his face and sighed, forgetting young David the footman was clearing the table. "I smell trouble there with that young lady; she's what he's really after." Mr. Gibbs followed the group out and headed for the kitchens.

David slowly collected the cups and plates deep in thought. He knew exactly what Mr. Gibbs was talking about. As footman together – sharing a room – they had discussed the very subject numerous times; the young Earl's passion for talented beautiful young women. Well, they didn't have to be that talented; just bloody beautiful and young!

He chuckled to himself and thought about Judith and Kate. The only talent that pair had was their looks. He piled the breakfast plates, cups and glasses behind the ornate screen and then heard the door open; he stuck his head around. It was Miss Harker – the ladies maid – and asked if he could help. The young woman smiled and in an absolutely deep south accent, asked where her lady was. David explained where they going and the young woman gasped and slammed the door; shouting about a change of dresses. David smiled; some ladies maid, surely she knows that women of class and wealth changed their bleeding frocks three or four times a day!

That's when he stared through the big window and saw the gypsy van pulled by two horses, entering the castle's drive. The driver was a big man in his thirties, dressed in a colourful outfit with a vivid red hat and knee length black boots. He looked like he had stepped from a portrait of a classic gypsy traveler. David stopped collecting cutlery and rushed out the room to find Mr. Gibbs.

CHAPTER 3. 'SUPERSITION IS TO RELIGION WHAT ASTROLOGY IS TO ASTRONOMY; THE MAD DAUGHTER OF A WISE MOTHER.' Voltaire.

The little group assembled outside the tower and Mr. Blackledge took them up the well worn stairs to the fourth floor. They gathered around the exposed 'window' – covered with a grey tarpaulin – and waited as two of his men climbed ladder's each side and took hold of the tarpaulin. They loosened a couple of ropes and the sheet fell to the floor. There was silence for a few seconds and finally the Earl said quietly; "No wonder my ancestor had it bricked up despite spending serious money on the damn thing!"

Uncle William had to chuckle a little; "A skeleton strangling the lord of the manor wouldn't have gone down too well in medieval times, that's for sure." Dorothy tapped her Uncle; "What does the writing say; I think it could be old Latin?" Uncle William nodded; "Mortem generat mortem; basically death begets death."

Mr. Blackledge spoke with the earl, saying that Mr. Tuttle had been here earlier taking photographs as instructed. The Earl nodded and turned away telling Mr. Blackledge to 'brick the damn thing back up!'

Strangely enough the man didn't argue that decision and set his men to work. Everyone headed back to their rooms and Harry noticed that Mr. Gibbs had stopped Lord David and was whispering in his ear. The look on the young lord's face betrayed his feelings about what was said. He looked angry and really concerned. That's when Dorothy walked back from the hallway entrance and told Uncle William and Harry there were gypsy vans parked in the driveway. "Strange visitors for a Peer of the realm." Uncle William said and Dorothy shrugged her shoulders; "Maybe they are part of the wedding's entertainment." Her words were overheard by Charlotte who didn't smile; "I really don't think so Miss Hadden. Maybe having dirty thieving gypsies at middle class weddings are the thing, but not for a society wedding." She walked off, not a happy person.

"You know what that is all about don't you?" Uncle William asked Dorothy who shook her head. He smiled; "Jealousy my dear. Plain and simple. She's noticed that her fiancé can't keep his eyes off you." Dorothy just sighed and the trio returned to their rooms. Rosie was waiting with a big pot of tea and Dorothy accepted a cup. "It's all around the kitchens and servants quarters about the young Lord and the way he's been staring at you miss." Rosie chuckled, adding; "The general opinion is that bleeding stuck up Miss Higgs-Packer will be on the next big steamer back to America. Everyone says she's all big hat and no knickers!"

"Rosie's quote was a common saying at the time; it means that the woman pretended to have money and class, but couldn't even afford underwear!" SJW.

Dorothy just sipped her tea and said quietly; "That bleeding may complicate matters somewhat." Rosie eased in the chair opposite and picked up her tea cup. "His mother, the Dowager Countess arrives this afternoon and the word amongst the servants is that she can't stand her future daughter-in-law, so as you say, that will complicate bleedings things, I expect." She slurped her tea and grinned.

Dorothy tapped her cup; "I understand that the old Dowager Countess lives in a big house on the main road to the village. It's called Barfied House and is also medieval. I'm surprised that Lord David didn't borrow her Butler, I mean; I understand he's been in the family for years and was Butler here before even Mr. Parks. Apparently, he wanted to continue working for her ladyship and so became butler in the much smaller household. Now that is odd. Mr. Parks was the Butler at another estate and was given this position when the Dowager's butler moved across to her household."

Rosie nodded; "I heard that he and the new Earl didn't see eye to eye on a lot of things, but the Dowager wouldn't hear of him being dismissed or retired. She's fiercely loyal to staff that have served the family well over the years. So, that makes her a bleeding favourite of mine." Dorothy smiled at that. Then there was a knock at the door. Rosie jumped up and opened it. Titus [Reggie] stood smiling, resplendent in his Valet's suit.

Dorothy waved him in and told him to have a cup of tea with them. The big man sat in a chair opposite the ladies and accepted a cup from Rosie. Dorothy leaned forward smiling and asked how the servants were treating him. He grinned and waved a hand in the air; "Really well, at dinner last night they asked me all about the professor and Mr. Hadden and how I ended up working for them. They really didn't comment on the fact that I'm black as coal!" They all laughed at that. Dorothy was well pleased with that revelation about the staff.

He repeated what Rosie had just told her about the gossip swirling around the castle about the Earl and herself. Dorothy finished her tea and shrugged her shoulders; "I hope you pointed out that it was just nonsense Reggie." He nodded and then turned serious. "Mr. Williams, the senior footman sent up from the London House appears more than happy that old Parks is dead. Didn't even try to hide it. Apparently he couldn't stand the man. He [Williams] was footman here before being moved down south and he doesn't have a good word to say about Parks. He believes that his lordship was going to dismiss him [Mr. Parks] that night he was seen going into his lordship's study all bowed down and unhappy."

Dorothy was now very interested and asked Reggie to continue.

Reggie accepted a refill from Rosie who was hanging on every word. "Apparently there was an incident in the village last month which concerned Mr. Parks and two young girls from the local school. He laughed it off; saying it was a misunderstanding but their fathers came to the castle and demanded to see the Earl. From what I can gather it wasn't the first such incident involving young schoolgirls and the butler."

"Dirty bleeding old sod!" exclaimed Rosie and slurped her tea. Dorothy leaned back in her chair and wondered what – exactly – the butler was doing at old tennis pavilion that night.

"Apparently Mr. Parks had few friends around here, the only person who seemed to like him or rather tolerate him was Mr. Tuttle the Gate-keeper, who lives in the gatehouse cottage. He, Parks and a couple of other men from the village use to play cards at the gatehouse, a couple of times a week. It's rumoured that Park's owed them money from gambling at cards." Reggie finished his tea and placed the cup down.

"Bleeding nice character for a butler to an Earl; likes little girls and won't pay his gambling debts." Rosie muttered and started to clear up the tea cups. Dorothy sighed; "I think there is far more to his murder than we ever suspected. Have you told Harry and Uncle William about this?" Reggie nodded and then tapped his forehead. "That's why I knocked; Mr. Hadden sent me to tell you that he's heading back to the tennis pavilion to have another look around before nightfall."

Rosie draped her arms around a very happy Reggie's neck and kissed his cheek, whilst he pushed a hand up her skirt. "Sneak away tonight when you can darling. You'll be welcomed with more than a bleeding cup of tea!" He nodded and Dorothy leaned over and placed a gentle kiss on his lips, "Make sure you're not seen sneaking about, Miss Higgs-Packer would love to tell that tale to the earl." Reggie squeezed Rosie's bum cheeks and reluctantly withdrew his hand. "I'll be like a shadow, a very black shadow!"

Rosie grinned at Dottie, "I'll make sure the sisters are clean and bleeding serviceable." Dottie nodded; 'the sisters' were the pair's nickname for their 'Dutch caps'. With their evening's sexual entertainment planned and agreed, Dottie stood slowly and asked Rosie to fetch her hat; the weather was so warm she wouldn't need her summer coat. Her and Reggie headed for Harry's rooms, but met him on the stairs. He smiled at them and said quietly; "Do you remember about that strange smell you commented on at the pavilion?" Dorothy nodded and Harry gestured down the stairs. "Well, I smelt the exact same odor this morning when we viewed that strange window."

Dorothy could have slapped herself; she had smelt the distinct odor and hadn't remembered where she had smelt it before and recently. "It's bloody flash powder from a camera flash lamp. Apparently Mr. Tuttle had taken pictures of the window just before we arrived!" Harry said and the trio made their way down the grand stairs and out the castle. They walked in relative silence to the tennis pavilion. They weren't the only people there.

There were several gypsy vans and horses camped around the pavilion. There were barefoot children running about with barking dogs and women were washing and hanging out clothes. The smell of cooking swirled around the camp. Sitting on a bright coloured chair, smoking a cob pipe was a very big man in a red jacket, black knee length boots with a little red hat perched upon his head which was covered with long black hair. He wore a huge gold earring and actually looked more like a pirate than a gypsy chief. He rose slowly from his chair and waved them over as his people gathered behind him.

He offered his chair to Dorothy who politely declined, so he sat back down and puffed on his pipe. "Come to have another look at the place Mr. Hadden?" he gestured to the pavilion and Harry nodded; "So you know who we are, may I ask your name?"

The big man chuckled; "Everyone calls me Gabrielle. I speak for my people when required. How's your little investigation into the old butler's death going mister Hadden?" Harry shrugged his shoulders; "It's Inspector Ramsey's show, I'm just a bystander on this one." Now that did make the big man chuckle. He lowered his pipe and pointed it at Dorothy. "I hear tell that the young lord is having second thoughts about the American woman, now he's seen your lovely young sister. If she plays her cards right, she could easily be the next Countess of Barfield."

"Total nonsense mister Gabrielle, just silly gossip I'm afraid." Dorothy waved a couple of flies away and smiled at the big man. He leaned back in the chair; "That's what I thought until I've seen you for myself. The young Earl is like his father; he knows quality and beauty in a woman and you have it by the bucket full. He'll send that American away and chase your tail my darling." He laughed at his own words and the people standing around him joined in. Dorothy managed to keep her smile.

Harry looked around the makeshift campsite and folded his arms; "I take it Gabrielle that you have his permission to be on his land?" Gabrielle nodded and sucked on his pipe and then – smiling broadly – said quietly; "We were going to provide music and dance for the wedding; part of the entertainment, but now the wedding is cancelled….sorry, delayed, we will move off in a couple of days. The Earl was good about it; he still paid us what was due." He grinned at Dorothy and added; "Some say it's because his heart lies elsewhere now."

Dorothy smiled to herself over the revelation that gypsies would have performed at the wedding; Charlotte would not have been impressed with that. The delay to the wedding didn't surprise her or Harry; they suspected that would happen with the murder of Mr. Parks and finding of the cursed window. What she didn't appreciate was being blamed for the event being cancelled. That gossip was bound to reach Charlotte's ears.

Harry told Gabrielle that they were going to have a look in the pavilion which made the big man laugh again. "You're wasting your time mister Hadden; someone has beaten you to it and stripped everything out. Bare as a baby's bum now." He folded his arms and puffed hard on his pipe. Harry and Dorothy exchanged a glance and Harry told her and Reggie to wait here while he took a look. Gabrielle spoke directly to Reggie; "So you play the valet when not on stage my big friend?" Now that did surprise Dorothy [and Reggie] how on the earth did the gypsies know so much about them?

Reggie explained that he fulfilled both roles as required; but worked mainly on stage with the 'professor' and Miss Dorothy. Gabrielle smiled; "You're a lucky man my big friend to work with such beauty and talent." Reggie agreed with him and thought about Dottie, naked and astride him, groaning and cussing as she rode him. Now that's called working, he thought and couldn't help but smile at his thoughts. Rosie and Dottie's antics with him had not surprised Reggie, he had learnt from quite a young age that white women loved black cock – the bigger the better – and recalled Mrs. Hall, his mother's friend and next door neighbor who had introduced him into the art of fucking. He was thirteen. His happy memories were disturbed by Harry returning, looking a little angry; "Everything has been taken. I think they even took the bloody dust!" They said their farewell's to the colourful gypsy camp and headed back to the castle. "Someone has taken great pains to cover up any evidence left in the pavilion and I wonder why? Harry spoke to Dorothy and Reggie as they climbed the steps into the grand entrance of the castle. They were stopped by Mr. Gibbs, young David the footman and the two upstairs maids coming out. The reason for the staff's appearance turned into the castle driveway. The Dowager Countess's carriage was coming up the drive.

"Now this should be interesting. Uncle William tells me that he knew the Dowager Countess when she was Lady Margret Armstrong back in their youth. Apparently they were quite inseparable until her father married her off – very reluctantly – to the earl of Barfield." Harry whispered to Dorothy as the carriage halted and the footman jumped down and pulled the door open.

Dowager Countess Margret stepped from the carriage and smoothed down her bright summer coat. She slightly lifted the brow of her exquisite broad brimmed hat and stared at Dorothy and Harry. She lifted a gloved hand and gestured the pair over as Mr. Gibbs organized the removal of her trunks and hat boxes.

Harry and Dorothy walked across to her and she offered her hand to Harry, who kissed it whilst Dorothy did a really good curtsey. The Dowager Countess smiled at Dorothy – really smiled – and gestured for them to walk with her. "Your sister is an absolute beauty. I know real class and intelligence when I see it. I drank champagne with my breakfast when I heard the wedding was called off. Maybe finding the Devil's Window didn't bring bad luck after all." She stopped suddenly and patted Dorothy's arm; "You will sit near me at dinner so we can chat. Hopefully, that woman is already packing her bags." She then walked on and Harry and Dorothy exchanged a glance; all that they heard about the formidable Dowager Countess of Barfield was quite true!

Harry glanced behind to see a younger woman in a black dress and white blouse giving instructions to the maids; she wore a neat straw boater and was quite tall for a woman of these times. Harry knew it was Miss Abigail Spencer; the Dowager Countesses ladies maid. He also noticed her and Mr. Gibbs talking quite closely and their hands brush each others. They clearly knew each other well. The Dowager Countess stopped again in the grand doorway and turned back to young David the footman who was carrying a travelling trunk. "Tell Mr. Gibbs that I will require tea in the morning room for some guests and then I will see my son." David nodded and said; "Yes my lady." He staggered off with the case and the trio continued into the castle. She turned to Dorothy and Harry; "You'll take tea with me and please tell William that I would be most pleased to see the old reprobate!" She turned back to Miss Spencer hurrying up the steps with two small bags. "Come on Abby, you need to take my hat and young Dorothy's too. Make yourself useful girl and leave Mr. Gibbs for later!"

The young woman tried to say something but nothing came out; she was blushing. The Dowager Countess turned to Harry and Dorothy; "I may be old, but I can see romance when it appears under my nose. Now how is your Uncle William? I hear he now makes a fine living from his magic tricks. He was always a talent and not just for magic." She chuckled to herself and swept into the morning room, her flustered maid following.

"You keep her company and I'll fetch Uncle William." Harry said quietly and Dorothy could hear him laughing as he walked up the grand staircase.

CHAPTER 4. 'AT A DINER PARTY ONE SHOULD EAT WISELY, BUT NOT TOO WELL, AND TALK WELL BUT NOT TOO WISELY.' W. Somerset Maugham.

Colonel Cornwallis and his young wife [close neighbours] had been invited to dinner and everyone was in the evening reception room before dinner. He certainly had a few amusing stories about his time in India and Dorothy sat with his young wife and chatted politely about the forthcoming wedding and the Colonels family. His son was now in India with his father's old regiment and the Colonel's daughter was now married to a junior Minister in the Colonial Office.

Dorothy quickly realized that his young wife was quite melancholy and seemed a little sad. Dorothy couldn't get anything from the young woman except the odd sigh and very few smiles. Dorothy kept a eye upon her Uncle – with a wry smile – as he sat talking with the Dowager Countess. The way they touched each other's hands and arms as they spoke, sitting quite close together, betrayed their previous intimacy. Dorothy noticed with some surprise that Margret drank dark rum and the pair laughed together frequently. Charlotte sat in almost silence with David who cradled a whisky glass for most of the evening, until Mr. Gibbs announced dinner.

Everyone rose and headed for the dining room. Harry walked with Dorothy on his arm and whispered to her; "Charlotte is not happy. She and everyone else here noticed that cousin David can't take his bleeding eyes off you. Apparently they spent the afternoon arguing about delaying the wedding because of the death of old Parks and the finding of that cursed window which will bring bad luck to the family. I think he will make an announcement soon."

"If the Dowager had her way Charlotte would already be packed and heading back to the USA." Dorothy whispered back to her brother. He chuckled at that; "Yes and If the Dowager had her way you would be fitted out for a wedding dress some weeks later." Dorothy just shook her head; "Not while I still breathe air." Harry had to smile at that.

Young George [Charlotte's brother] announced that he and his mother would be visiting a school friend of his mother's in York and would miss the shoot. They would be return in a couple of days. He smiled at Dorothy and said he would be counting the days until they met again. He reminded her that upon his 21st Birthday; he would be worth over a million pounds and would need a wife!

Dorothy just sighed and didn't smile. But Harry chuckled and asked where his mother was. George just grinned; "Lying down, she has one of her heads."

They were all seated and Uncle William sat next to Margret, whilst Dorothy sat opposite the Dowager Countess – as the Dowager requested – with Harry next to her. On the other side of Harry sat Lady Rosemary; the Colonels wife. The Colonel sat next to Charlotte and – of course – the Earl sat at the head of the table. Young George sat the other side of the Colonel and talked incessantly about money and position. Mr. Gibbs served his lordship and the two footmen [young David and Mr. Williams] – served the guests. The 'Brown Windsor' soup was excellent and everyone commented on it. It had been a favourite of the late Queen [Victoria] and a regular dish on many dinner tables. David suddenly tapped his wine glass with his soup spoon and all conversation died away. He quietly announced that Charlotte and he had decided to postpone the wedding until after Park's funeral and the damn window had been bricked back up. Dorothy briefly glanced across to the Dowager and saw a real broad smile slowly appear on her face. Harry leaned close to her ear; "Careful now girl. I think he's clearing the field for a try at you." Dorothy just shrugged her shoulders and sipped her wine.

David also had another announcement to make; he had cabled to York for the services of a medium! Madame Zodiac would arrive tomorrow with her assistant and it was planned to hold a séance to contact any troubled spirits and persuade them to go away and leave the family in peace. The Earl spoke directly to Uncle William; "I want you and Dorothy there; you're both magicians of some note and you should be able to spot any trickery. I'm paying the woman serious money and I need to know that's it's all above board."

Uncle William nodded his agreement; reluctantly.

Young George thought it was a great idea and went on about a séance he had attended in New York and how the medium changed her voice and sprits tapped the table. "Her Spirit Guide was an Indian called Geronimo and he knew General George Custer!" Harry and Dorothy exchanged an amused glance and couldn't help but chuckle.

The dinner was served and conversations started up again and on a lighter topic, David announced that he had organized a shoot tomorrow for the family and guests. The Colonel thoroughly approved of that idea and asked Harry if he shot. Harry shrugged his shoulders; "I'll give it a try sir." He sipped his wine and smiled at the Colonel's wife who smiled back!

The Dowager lifted her knife and fork; "I'll organize a draw to see which lady accompanies each gentleman as tradition dictates." Lord David thanked his mother for that and Harry whispered to Dorothy; "Somehow, I bet you draw the young Earl." Dorothy just waved that idea away and the meal continued with chatter about the King and who could be the latest mistress.

"Few women would actually pick up a shotgun at these 'shoot's' and their role was largely confined to 'following the guns'. Their names were placed in a Punch Bowl and the gentlemen picked out who would accompany him." SJW.

Dorothy was a little surprised how much lady Rosemary chatted with Harry and the old Colonel didn't seem to mind at all. He actually appeared to encourage the discourse between the two. The Dowager engaged Dorothy in conversation about being a 'working woman' of some obvious independence. She expressed the opinion that was good for all women and that Uncle William and Harry should be proud of Dorothy. She didn't mention that Charlotte was – of course – the same; she was also a 'working woman' as an actress. That didn't go un-noticed by anyone at the table; especially Charlotte herself.

The meal ended with chocolate pudding, followed by cheese and biscuits. Everyone agreed that the dinner was excellent and sent their compliments to the kitchens. Then following tradition, the men and women separated; the men went to the earl's study to smoke cigars, drink brandy and play poker. The woman retired to the library and drank coffee and played Bridge. But that didn't make the Dowager happy.

She convinced the ladies to revolt against tradition and they surprised the men by joining them and indulging in some brandies and to the other women's surprise; the Dowager smoked cigarettes and drank dark rum! Dorothy really had to admire the woman for her show of independence for women, against the social conventions of the day.

What really did interest Dorothy was how Lady Rosemary had opened up with Harry; the pair sat chatting and laughing together for most of the night. The Earl was a little surprised by his mother's revelation that she and Uncle William had known each other in their youth. Especially when she revealed that had she not married David's father – at her own father's insistence – she would probably now be a magician's wife!

On a dour note, the Earl revealed that old Park's had no family and so the Earl had arranged and paid for his funeral with the local undertakers; Joshua Boxhaul & Son's. It would be a small affair and private; just the family and servants. He doubted if anyone from the village would turn up to pay their respects. Mr. Parks wasn't a liked man in the village. Dorothy wondered about that remark, considering how long Park's had worked for the family. The Butler should have been better regarded as the man of influence and position at the castle and estate. Now that was strange.

The forthcoming shoot and séance were the main topics of after dinner conversation; everyone was very discrete and avoided mentioning the 'postponed' marriage. Finally at about eleven the little party broke up and everyone retired to their rooms. Young George was well 'oiled' from the brandy and wine. He drunkenly made some naughty suggestions to Dorothy, who just waved him away. He didn't say anything more after Harry had a quiet word with him.

Dorothy thought it was a little odd that the Colonel and his wife didn't head back to their own estate, but so many rooms had been made up for the wedding guests that their staying overnight wasn't even discussed. A message had been sent to their grand house for Lady Rosemary's maid and the Colonel's valet to attend them. They would – of course – bring all necessary extra clothing as required by the events planned.

Dorothy was a little concerned that the Cornwallis's didn't think twice about dragging their personal servants out in the middle of the night to attend them. But she reasoned; that was probably part and parcel of their jobs. On that note, she told Rosie to make sure the door was locked after Reggie arrived. The girls undressed each other and played on the big bed until they heard the soft knock. A naked Rosie opened it and a very happy Reggie slipped in, just wearing a dressing gown, which he very quickly discarded. Rosie was straight on her knees and attending the big man's urgent erection. Dottie piled up the pillows against the headboard and applied Vaseline to herself. She watched Rosie with some admiration: she certainly could suck cock and quietly chuckled at what Albert had said about Rosie's nickname, when she worked at the shoe factory before they married: 'McHannon's the mouth'.

Rosie rose from the floor and jerked a thumb towards Dottie, "Go to it Reggie, she's been bleeding wet and up for it, all day." Dorothy lay back and opened her leg's as the big man climbed on, she stroked his face and whispered; "Take me like a street whore!" Reggie nodded and did. Rosie watched wide eyed, vigorously rubbing herself as Reggie fucked Dottie like some common street trollop. He handled her roughly and she loved it. She would have small bruises on her arse, tits and back for a few days after this encounter, but her orgasms came quick and hard.

After a break for cigarettes and whisky, it was Dottie's turn to watch as Reggie roughly fucked Rosie, who had to cover her mouth with her hand, to cut off the screams of pain and pleasure. He gave no quarter and Rosie actually cried at one point, but never told him to stop. Well satisfied, Reggie sat back, sipping a well earned whisky and watched the girls cleaning each other up and having quite gentle lesbian sex.

Reggie grunted and grabbed Dottie, roughly pushing her down on the bed into the 'doggy' position and mounted her, with Rosie slipping underneath. Dottie gripped the headboard and within a few minutes had a big, leg shaking orgasm under such rough treatment. He slapped her quivering pink arse and chuckled, "Best fucking dirty little whore I've ever had...and best of all its fucking free!' Dottie just groaned, she was bloody spurting again, much to Rosie's delight as she worked her own magic with tongue and mouth.

It was just over two hours before Reggie left the pair, lying in each other's arms, and sneaked back to his room. But Dorothy wasn't quite a sleep yet and laid thinking about the demise of the old Butler and why he wasn't popular in the village. Someone had hated him enough to shoot the old man in the back. She now wondered what had caused such anger and hatred; how had the old Butler offended someone enough, that they would murder him? On those dark thoughts; Dorothy slipped off to sleep.

It was about two in the morning that Dorothy woke up and sipped some water from her bedside glass. She slipped from the bed and headed for the toilet, returning to quite a surprise.

Sims sat on a chair by the fireplace, knees pulled up and smiling braodly. Dorothy just sighed; "What on earth are doing here and couldn't it wait to a better hour?" she admonished the strange young man who shrugged his shoulders. "Jericho Tibbs sent me with a message and I think you'll agree that visiting you in the night is better that popping up during the day, with so many people around who might see me." He chuckled and stretched out as Dorothy climbed back into bed and pulled the covers up.

Sims was totally unfazed that a naked Rosie lay in Dorothy's bed snoring. "What's the message?" she asked, yawning. Sims folded his arms and didn't smile; "No soul was collected from that old Butler. You know there can be only two reasons for that; he was out of his ordained time period or he had sold his soul to the Dark Prince. I wonder which it was."

Dorothy leaned back on her pillows and knew this was important; such an incident could bring Jericho and his Team on scene to investigate. "What does Jericho want us to do?" she asked and sipped some more water; this was a real turn up for the books.

Sims smiled; "He says to find out if the old bugger was an evil so and so and if he wasn't; then he'll have to investigate the old man as a possible time traveler." Dorothy nodded at that and yawed again. "You had better hang around Sims, we may need you."

Sims nodded and leapt from the chair, rolling himself into a ball

and was gone. Dorothy lay back and drifted off to sleep and slept
really well. As the pair sat in bed sipping tea, Rosie tapped her
cup and looked a little puzzled, "Do you know darling. That I was
half asleep and drifting off, when I would have sworn blind you
were bloody talking to someone and it weren't bleeding me!"

Dottie just leaned over and kissed her, "You were dreaming again
darling. Reggie was long gone." Rosie now giggled a little,
"Yeah, he was long gone but my bleeding honey-pot feels like it's
gone three rounds with Jack Johnson!" Dottie nodded and pulled
the covers back, "Oh my darling, let me kiss it better." Rosie
soon forgot about her tender honey-pot.

*"Rosie is referring to that great heavyweight Boxing
Champion: Jack Johnson, The first 'Black' Champion, he is widely
regarded as one of the most influential boxers in history.
Transcending boxing, he became part of the culture and history
of racism in the United States." SJW.*

**CHAPTER 5. 'NOTHING IN LIFE IS SO
EXHILARATING AS TO BE SHOT AT WITHOUT RESULT.'
Winston Churchill.**

"It appears from my enquiries in the village that the late Mr.
Parks liked to hand sweeties out to the children; like a sort of
early Father Christmas. He may have been popular with the
children but few of the adults liked him. Apparently he only had a
couple of friends, but his best mate – if you want to call him that
– was old man Tuttle, the Gate-Keeper who lives in the lodge by
the gates. Mr. Parks wasn't too forthcoming when it came to pay
his debts." Inspector Ramsey sipped his tea and stared at the
breakfast spread laid out for the shooting party. There was
enough food to feed a poor family for months.

"When we searched his rooms here at the castle we found
nothing. No photographs of any family, no correspondence to

anyone, just bank statements and letters from the Bank Manager about him writing out bent cheques. He appears to have lived way above his means. One actually threatened if he didn't pay up his unauthorized over-draught, the manger would be forced to speak to the young Earl. Not a pretty picture all round." The Inspector placed his cup down and picked up his hat. "All in all; a very strange fellow for a Butler to an Earl. Must have had some Gypsy blood in him by all accounts." He smiled at Harry and Dorothy and then turned to leave.

"Why do you say he must have had gypsy blood Inspector?" Dorothy asked and the Inspector shrugged his shoulders; "He kept making predictions about events and sure enough, they would appear in the papers. Pity he missed the really important one; like being shot in the back." He slapped his hat on and bid them goodbye, with young David the footman showing him to the door.

Harry and Dorothy both watched him go. "Do you think he was a time-traveller? I mean, Sims says no soul was collected and that happens if you die out of your own time. And that was some revelation about his ability to predict events; something a time-traveller from the future would be capable of." Dorothy spoke quietly to Harry who placed his cup down. "Well, we've uncovered nothing that would indicate he sold his soul to the Dark One. Maybe Jericho and his team will have to sort this one out."

Mr. Gibbs appeared in the doorway and announced the 'shooting brake' was ready to be boarded. Everyone started to head for the grand entrance and Dorothy asked Harry, whose name he had drawn from the punch bowl. Harry chuckled; "Lady Rosemary and I understand – surprise, surprise – that Cousin David pulled your name out. Funny that?" Dorothy just sighed and then tapped her brother's arm; "You were getting very friendly with Lady Rosemary last night and her old husband didn't seem to care."

Harry actually grinned and said quietly; "She was very friendly and it appears that her husband likes to sleep alone. I think they have a 'sham' marriage. I know she is just a trophy wife." Dorothy knew all about that; several of her school friends had married much older men for the wealth and security offered. They all have lovers on the side and nothing was said by the 'husbands'. Dorothy walked through the grand doors on her brother's arm and stopped in the courtyard as the Ladies where being helped onto the shooting brake'. She prodded her brother's arm; "Just how friendly my dear brother?" she asked. Harry tapped his lips with a single finger and whispered; "Very friendly, but I don't play kiss and tell." He really did grin!

Dorothy was the last lady on and the gentlemen sat at the open end and smoked. The young earl – satisfied everyone was ready – gave the signal to move off. Now aboard the double horse drawn vehicle, the shooting party set of for Cold Morning Moor. Everyone was chatting and appeared quite happy; except Charlotte who sat with a long face and said little during the journey. They were followed by three other carriages containing beaters and servants. Mr. Williams was in charge of the servants and old Silas –the Gamekeeper – oversaw the beaters. Dorothy gripped Harry's arm as the big vehicle rolled and dipped on the rough road towards the shooting pitches. "I would hope that Cousin David spends some bleeding money on new springs for this old rig." Dorothy muttered; it was tough going on the bum. She was really glad when the rig stopped and she was helped down by Harry who was given his shotgun by his loader; an ancient looking individual from the village called 'Silent night'. Apparently the man's name was Knight and he said very little.

Harry gave Dorothy a peck on the cheek and was joined by Lady Rosemary, who was all smiles and thrust her arm through his and talked quietly to him all the way to their pitch. Dorothy found herself smiling at that; she would certainly interrogate her wayward brother later about what happened between the pair. They kept very few secrets from each other. She watched as Charlotte and the Colonel headed for their position and wasn't surprised that Uncle William had drawn Margret. They walked arm in arm, chatting and laughing to their mark. Cousin David joined her; his shotgun open and lay over one arm. His loader was big rough looking man in a very old fashioned tweed suit called Richard Fallgate. He grinned constantly at Dorothy, revealing a couple of yellow teeth almost hidden by his gray beard. His local accent was so bad that Dorothy believed she would need a translator to have a conversation with the fellow; not that opportunity would actually arise.

"This should be fun." She said quietly to herself as Cousin David started to talk about the responsibilities of the estate. He had been a very happy naval officer until his father had selfishly died and he was 'lumbered' with the multimillion pound estate. He clearly had wanted to remain in the navy. He surprised Dorothy by saying that he knew her brother George: "Always said that his baby sister was something special, a London Hapsburg princess, he always said that and she would probably marry some Duke or Earl. I can see that he didn't exaggerate Cousin Dorothy. And what a prophecy: Duke or Earl!" Dorothy just smiled and knew exactly what he was getting at. She wondered if he would be so enraptured if he knew about her lesbian sex and being fucked like a whore by a big Black man last night!

They reached their pitch and old Silas indicated that all were on their marks. Cousin David gave the start signal and they waited for the birds. Dorothy could hear the noise from the bushes and woods; the beaters were driving the birds towards the guns.

"Let the massacre begin." She muttered and folded her arms. Suddenly, five or six birds appeared above the trees and David fired. He didn't hit anything. His loader had already handed him the secondary gun and was reloading the first; he may not look or sound graceful, but he loaded and handled the shotguns with real smoothness and skill. Dorothy stood with her hands over her ears and could see that one of the dogs had already darted out to snatch a fallen bird. She had to smile; Harry had bagged one! Lady Rosemary was clapping and laughing; Dorothy sighed at that. Harry would have to be very careful with such a liaison. The Metropolitan Police wouldn't approve of such goings on. An unmarried Detective Inspector and a married woman carrying on would certainly incur their wrath.

After just a half hour Dorothy was thoroughly bored and it really showed. She stared towards the little road that ran behind the tree's and saw the Gypsy caravan's on the move. They were heading for the York Road, for an instance she almost envied them the lifestyle they had. Then she had to smile at Uncle William cursing his luck; then a bloody bird practically fell at his feet. The Dowager was laughing and giggling like a lovesick schoolgirl. The scene was completely different with the next pitch down; the Colonel took his shooting seriously and Charlotte stood looking totally bored and unhappy.

Dorothy was truly grateful when she could hear a strident gong being sounded; lunch was served. She was impressed to find that a ramshackle old barn had been turned into a dining room and a hot lunch was on offer. Harry was really happy; chicken curry was available! As everyone chatted and ate; Cousin David called out the scores; The Colonel had bagged four [he received some applause for that], Uncle William had hit one, whilst Harry had downed two and the Earl had hit three. The shooting would continue after lunch and for fairness; everyone would change pitches. Unfortunately – in Dorothy's mind – they didn't change partners and the afternoon basically carried on as the morning left off. Dorothy could have screamed with happiness when the shoot finally closed down and everyone headed back to the castle for the evening meal. They unloaded from the awful old shooting brake and the Colonel was more than happy being branded 'Top-gun' – he had bagged no less than nine birds - The nearest to him was the Earl; who had bought down six.

Harry was next with four and finally Uncle William came plumb last with just one and that apparently gave itself up according to the laughing dowager Countess!

Dorothy was truly proud of her Uncle; he didn't like shooting animals for any reason really; ever mind just for pleasure. Dorothy was rubbing her backside from the journey back from the Moor and really was looking forward to a hot bath and some brandy. That's when she saw Mr. Williams actually running towards the Earl; he was panting and gasping as he stopped Cousin David in the grand archway of the castle entrance. Yes, something was clearly wrong.

The shooting party had arrived back quite late from the Moors and Mr. Williams had brought a paraffin lamp with him. The night was starting to fall early for summertime; but Uncle William had told everyone that a storm was expected tonight or tomorrow night. The sky was burdened with dark clouds. "More bloody bad omens and portents." Mrs. Porterhouse whispered as she headed for the kitchens, head bowed down and walking quickly. The evening meal would probably be delayed now; but for what?

David stood in the doorway and gestured to Harry, who joined him immediately. They spoke briefly and Harry indicated for Dorothy to join them. They walked to the main doors with Mr. Williams – the senior footman from the London House – holding a bright lamp. "Miss Alice the kitchen maid found him; she's in quite a state my lord." He spoke to David and they walked quietly across the gravel path to the foot of the east tower. Mr. Williams held his lamp up high over the body. Lord David loudly groaned and knelt down by the prostrate body that had formed into a grotesque x shape amongst the gravel.

Harry looked up at the dark tower and then joined David by the body. "He must have fallen from the ramparts, the windows are just slits; you couldn't squeeze a rabbit through them." David nodded and wiped his face with a trembling hand; "It's young Albert Dean my senior Hall Boy. He can't be more than bloody seventeen. Sweet Jesus Harry, what the bloody hell is bleeding happening!" Harry patted his shoulder and both men stood. "I'll need to see where he fell from Cousin David, can that be quickly arranged?" Lord David nodded; he was clearly shocked by this latest death. "Gibbs will have a key to the rampart stairs. There are only two in existence. One is held in the Butler's pantry and the other is in the Gate-Keepers lodge with Mr. Tuttle."

Dorothy knelt down and carefully lifted the boy's right hand – the fist was clenched – she tapped Harry and he gently forced the dead fingers open. He held the large gold button which was surrounded by vivid bright red threads, up to the lamp. "Well, that certainly doesn't match what young Albert is wearing. It's possibly torn from the jacket or coat of someone he was with." Harry pushed the object into his pocket.

Dorothy looked down the castle drive and could see the lights burning in the front windows of the small lodge cottage. "Well, Mr. Tuttle is in and awake, the place is well lit up." She told the two men. Harry nodded; "Cousin David, you'll have to get a message to Constable Holmes in the village, to contact York Police again. This could be anything; an accident, suicide or even murder. Dorothy and I will go the gate-keepers lodge and get the key for the tower stairs. Can we borrow Mr. Williams and his lamp?" Lord David just nodded and walked towards the main door shouting for assistance. Harry and Dorothy with Mr. Williams headed for the gate-keepers lodge.

They found the front door wide open and Harry shouted a couple of times and received no answer. They pushed into the small front room and Dorothy held a hand over her mouth. The naked body of a middle aged man lay sprawled before the fireplace. His face had been battered so badly that Mr. Williams took a minute or so to identify the body as Alfred Tuttle; the lodge gate-Keeper.

"I met the man when I was brought up for the old Earl's funeral. He was a very happy man; always smiling and would crack really lame jokes. But he would always stand you a pint in the Barfield Arms." Mr. Williams pulled a shabby hankie from his pocket and wiped his face. "Sweet Jesus sir; three dead bodies around the bloody place in just a few days and all after that damn window was rediscovered."

Harry sighed and looked around the room which had been wrecked; "I don't think cursed windows have anything to do with these deaths Mr. Williams. A human or humans are the best bet for all this." Dorothy walked back into the hallway and called Harry. She slowly pushed open another door which the lock had been torn off. Harry stood behind her and they both stared into the room. The two big wooden cabinets had been broken open and there were ripped up photographs everywhere. A fairly new camera and tripod lay smashed on the floor. Like the front room; the place had been ransacked.

Mr. Williams slowly lowered his lamp; "I heard that Mr. Tuttle was an excellent amateur photographer. He always set up at the village fetes and photographed local weddings and such. I understand that his Lordship had told him that he could join the official wedding photographers and take some pictures too."

Dorothy gripped Harry's arm and whispered; "Do you smell that?" Harry nodded; there was a slight, but pungent smell in the room. Dorothy gestured to the overturned flash lamp, lying on the floor; its powder spilled around it. "Harry; that's the same smell that was apparent in the tennis pavilion, I'm sure of that. Do you think Mr. Tuttle was in the pavilion taking pictures?" Harry nodded; "Yes, but pictures of who or what?" He knelt by the small fireplace and pulled a single sheet of paper from under a small chair and held it up; it was a photograph. He ran a hand over his face and pulled Dorothy to one side and warned her about the picture before she looked. She placed a hand over her mouth and cussed softly. Harry pushed the photograph into his jacket pocket. "It appears that Mr. Tuttle didn't just photograph bloody weddings and fetes, the dirty sick bastard." Harry whispered as they walked to the front door.

Harry stood in the large driveway and stared at Barfield Castle. Someone had brutally battered the pornographer and paedophile to death, then ransacked the place looking for something; but what? A picture? Money?

Dorothy stood in the late evening sunshine and gathering darkness, hands on hips and cussed again – loudly; "That little girl can't be more than nine or ten. No wonder the filthy piece of crap is wearing a fancy dress mask. Sweet Jesus, how could.....I mean, she's just a child for Christ sake!" Harry patted her arm and gripped her hand. "Well, if I'm correct that dirty filth bag won't touch another girl. I recognised those trousers around his ankles and his skinny body and hands. I have seen them before."

Dorothy just stared at him and before she could ask Harry leaned closer and whispered; "The beast in that picture was the now late Mr. Parks. Who the child is, we need to find out urgently." Dorothy leaned against the wall next to the front door and took a breath; "Maybe we now know why someone shot him [Parks] to death. Do you think he had a victim at the tennis pavilion and that dirtbag Tuttle was photographing the whole disgusting sick scene?"

Harry also stood back against the wall and folded his arms; "I think someone is getting revenge on these perverts, maybe relatives of the girl. Her face is quite clear so we may get someone to identify her." Dorothy stared back into the wrecked room and dapped her eyes with a little lace hankie; "Surly that young house boy couldn't be involved in all this?" Harry admitted he didn't know. Maybe the boy's death was an accident. It would have to be closely examined.

They looked back up the castle drive and saw Mr. Williams leading a group of people towards them; headed by a very angry looking Earl. "This won't make our dear Cousin a happy man I'm afraid." Harry said quietly and waited by the door with Dorothy who had dried her eyes and composed herself. Harry was right; the young Earl wasn't happy and sent young David to fetch Constable Holmes – yet again – to the murder scene and the possible accident. "The sooner I brick that fucking window back up the better." He confided to Harry, adding; "I hope that bloody medium can help placate any malevolent forces swimming about the damn place. " Harry said nothing about the medium; he was leaving that one to Uncle William and Dorothy.

The boy's body was covered with blankets from the laundry and young David was posted to see that no-one interfered with it. Mr.

Williams had the same task at the Gate-keeper's lodge. The village would be in uproar over the latest killing and apparent accident.

But Mr. Gibbs had found the key to the tower and Harry, with Dorothy close behind climbed the twisting and turning staircase to the ramparts. Mr. Gibbs unlocked the summit door and shone his lamp through. "Be careful sir and Miss, not too many come up here. Old Tuttle use to raise and take down the flag as the occasion demanded, but that's about all who came up here." They wandered around the small space and Harry could see nothing, even with Mr. Gibbs holding up his quite bright lamp. Harry knelt down and pushed his hand about the stone floor; "Well, there been someone up here, the dust and dirt has been really disturbed. It could easily be a couple of people, but who really knows." Dorothy tapped his shoulder; "Over there, looks like a little pile of very dark dirt." Harry moved over and didn't smile; "Mr. Gibbs, did young Albert smoke a pipe? Someone has tapped out a pipe here."

Mr. Gibbs shook his head; "Young Albert didn't smoke, which was really noticeable because the other Hall boy's all smoke like chimneys!" Harry gathered up the pipe ash and tobacco remains into a little paper bag and stood. "Come on, I think we can say for certain that Albert wasn't alone up here. It could prove totally useless; pipe smoking is extremely popular. Bloody Uncle William enjoys one." Dorothy had to chuckle at that: "I think we can cross him off the list of suspects but there would still be millions on it!" Harry sadly agreed with that deduction and stared about the small space wondering what the hell young Albert was doing up here at nightfall? The answer was suicide or meeting another person: but who? Harry peered over the ramparts and could see the chaos below and little lights everywhere. He saw that PC Holmes had arrived on his cycle; accompanied by another officer, probably PC Kenneth Jones from the next village. With Mr. Gibbs leading with his lamp they made their way back downstairs and re-joined the Earl. Everyone retired to the Evening room and was served fortifying brandies by Mr. Gibbs. That's when he dropped a little 'bombshell' that really interested Dorothy and Harry. The only other relatives that the dead House-boy had were already dead.

Dorothy, being sympathetic, asked how they died and who had been the boys closest relative now. Mr. Gibbs restrained from a smile; "Well Miss, they died in that pneumonia epidemic, you know the one that killed poor Prince Eddy. He [Albert] only had one surviving relative; that was his Uncle, Mr. Parks. I assume that's how he got the job here some months ago. Albert's mother was Mr. Parks' step-sister."

Mr. Gibbs smiled at Dorothy and their hands touched as he handed her a brandy. She returned his smile; Dottie found him quite an attractive man and wondered if Rosie would be happy to sleep in her own bed tonight. The session with Reggie had set fire to her lust and animal passion and she wondered if this young man could quench that fire - for now.

"Prince Eddy was the Heir to the British Throne who died of pneumonia in 1892. He was the eldest son of the future King Edward VII. He would have been King Edward VIII in 1910 when his father died. But with his unfortunate death; his brother became King George V." SJW.

**CHAPTER 6. 'WE ALL HAVE OUR DEMONS....'
Common phrase.**

Everyone assembled in the magnificent library of the castle. The large round table by the big windows would be perfect for the séance. It had been cleared and moved to the centre of the room and eight chairs placed around it. Young David the footman placed the drinks tray on a small serving table by the east window and pulled the curtains. Mr. Williams finished lighting the lamps around the place and the room was bathed in a dull yellow glow.

"Sooner them than me; I wouldn't take part if they paid me in gold bars." He said quietly to David, who vigorously nodded his agreement with that. "Alice said nothing good will comes from it and her granny was medium. She use to read palms and do a crystal ball at the village fete's. Everyone said she was bloody genuine." David whispered and poured several glasses of brandy and placed them on a silver tray. There apparently was very little conversation between the guests as they stood waiting for the arrival of Madame Zodiac [real name Miss Elsie Plumber] who was waiting to be summoned by her assistant; John Gardner. The tall thin man in an ill fitting evening suit was placing a beautiful glass ball sitting on a golden stand, upon the table. He constantly wiped his face and neck with a grubby hankie and looked much older than his thirty five years.

He nodded to Lord David and bowed a little; "Everything is ready my lord. I will fetch Madame Zodiac." David just whispered; "Yes." and the strange man was gone. Uncle William stood next to David and asked – again – if he was sure about this. David nodded and accepted a glass of brandy from his young footman. "Both of you can go now, we'll help ourselves." He told both the footman, who looked quite relieved to be ordered from the room. David turned to Uncle William and said softly – looking about – "I want you here cousin because you're a magician of some good reputation; you'll spot any tricks being played. I want this to be above board. If there is a curse – a real curse – on the bloody place or family, I want to know."

William picked up a glass of brandy and nodded to Harry and Dorothy who were helping themselves to drinks. Dorothy gave one to Lady Margret who was speaking to retired Colonel Frank Cornwallis. Both had attended spiritual readings and séances before. They had both sang the praises of Madame Zodiac to David. Charlotte stood by the door with Lady Rosemary – the Colonel's young wife – chatting very quietly. She was the Colonel's second wife and junior to him by twenty odd years. His first wife had died some five years before the 2nd marriage. She commented on the summer storm a couple of times and wondered if there would be any thunder. Charlotte was half listening to the obviously nervous lady; she was staring at Dorothy with a mixture of jealousy and anger. Especially about the growing friendship between Dorothy and the Dowager Countess; this had become apparent to all present including David, who was more than happy to encourage it.

Mr. Gardner appeared in the doorway and announced in a strange deep voice that Madame Zodiac was here. The little woman swept into the room and bid everyone a 'good evening' and received some very subdued replies. She smiled and sat before her crystal ball. Her assistant pulled up a chair some yards away from her and the guests as they took their positions around the table. He had closed the door and locked it. He made a great show of putting the door key in his pocket, then sat, hands on his knees. Uncle William was staring hard at Madame Zodiac and both Harry and Dorothy noted the brief smile on his face."He's already on the case." Dorothy whimpered to her brother, who sat next to her. Madame Zodiac called the little group to order and asked if any had attended a séance before. The Dowager Countess, Colonel Cornwallis and to Dorothy's surprise; Charlotte all raised their hands. Dorothy smiled a little at her Uncle; she knew full well that he had been present at several séances in his past. He was clearly going to play this one close to his chest.

Madame Zodiac outlined the 'rules' for the evening; very little talking, no one must break the circle of hands after she has started and no one was to leave the table; for their safety. If they needed anything urgently, her assistant would attend them. She made herself comfortable and ran her hands over the ball. She was whispering something and staring hard at the crystal orb. It appeared to fill with a grey mist. She sat back and everyone could see that she appeared a little puzzled "The mirror has shown me bright coloured curtains with horses and dogs; I think it's a tapestry." She leaned forward and nodded; "No, they are stage curtains. I know we have two actors here and the spirits also know this."

She ran her hands over the ball a couple of times and sighed; "My spirit guide Ramses, tells me that we have a connection with the ancient land of his birth; Egypt." She placed both hands on the table and told everyone to hold hands and hold them firmly. She reminded them not to break the circle of hands for any reason. She closed her eyes and sat back; breathing deeply. Everyone sat in silence for some minutes before Madame Zodiac snapped open her eyes. Everyone also heard the rolls and booms of thunder outside; the summer storm was above them.

"Ramses! Ramses! Have you bought any troubled spirits to communicate with us?" She repeated her question twice more and distinct tapping could be heard. She asked her spirit guide who had come to speak. Her eyes rolled up and down and she breathed deep several times, then sat upright and stared around the table. "He is speaking French….old French or it may be Latin.

He is speaking too fast. Wait, he has calmed a little and I can make out that he is full of anger and hate....he is a greatly troubled spirit...He seeks vengeance and justice.....He wants revenge..." Madame Zodiac never finished her sentence because several books feel from a shelf at the rear of the room and crashed to floor causing Lady Rosemary to actually scream. There was silence for a good minute and Madame Zodiac said quietly; "Ramses is trying to sooth the troubled spirit. He's asking how the living can help him?" Madam Zodiac groaned loudly and threw her head back, now almost shouting; "He wants bloody revenge for his family! He says that the Barfield's will pay for their evil deeds." She rolled her head around and gasped several times; like she was struggling for breath. "He says that the living Earl must ask for forgiveness and pay a blood penalty for his ancestor's evil deeds and sins." She lowered her head and sat in silence for some seconds before slowly looking up and all could see the tears falling down her cheeks.

"Ramses tells me he has gone back to the pit of hellfire, where he was cast for the sin of self murder. He says that the curse will remain until Barfield castle falls by God's hand and the Earl pays a blood penalty. He wants death for the deaths of his family." Madame Zodiac sighed loudly and rolled her head several times, shouting; "Blood! Blood! The payment is demanded in blood!"

She lowered her head and was silent for some time. Everyone was staring at her except Dorothy and Uncle William who were staring around the gloomy room. "What the hell is going on?" Harry whispered to Dorothy and gripped her hand tightly. Dorothy almost smiled and whispered; "Here comes the show stopper."

A strange pungent smell seemed to sweep around the room and everyone heard the Colonel say; "Sulfur! Bloody sulfur! The devil's own stink!" Everyone was looking around the room except – again – Uncle William and Dorothy who kept their gaze fixed on Madame Zodiac and her assistant. Dorothy whispered to Harry; "Uncle William has arranged a surprise of his own."

Harry just nodded as Madame Zodiac again called for Ramses, the ancient Egyptian spirit guide to return. He certainly did; but it wasn't actually him! Sims materialized right in the centre of the solid wood table and raised his hands above his head and shouted; "The Frenchman has gone back to Hell and taken his curse with him! The Barfield's are free; the sins have been forgiven!" He then vanished, ducking back through the table top and was gone.

The effect was electric; everyone was cursing and screaming, they ran for the door and David frantically pulled it open and the group spilled out into the corridor. Uncle William, Dorothy, Harry and Madame Zodiac remained in the library. The first three by choice and poor Madame Zodiac because she had fainted!

Dorothy chuckled; "I had arranged with young David the footman to unlock the door as soon as the séance started. Didn't want anyone injured in the stampede!" Harry tapped her arm and really grinned; "Come on, let's get the old con artist up." They helped a babbling Madame Zodiac to her feet; both praising her for the ancient Egyptian spirits appearance. She pulled free from their grip and cursing loudly, ran for the door and disappeared up the stairs, followed by her trembling assistant – who in a deep Welsh accent – was asking her 'what the fuck just happened!'

Uncle William picked up the brandy bottle and filled their glasses and raised a toast; "Here's to Elsie Plumber, the little con artist and big fraud. I recognized her straight away when she arrived. She use to an assistant to Harry Carter and they pulled similar tricks around the Northern theatres years ago. I had heard she had branched out into bent séance's for serious money. She may have to pack it up now because all her clients will demand to see the mummy of her ancient spirit guide and she certainly won't be able to reproduce Sims!"

They all laughed and drank their brandies with Harry jerking a thumb to the windows; "I think the thundery storm tossed background helped!" They laughed again and finished their drinks. "David can breathe now that Sims told everyone that the curse had been lifted. So that's one legend that should fade away now." Uncle William said and finished his drink and headed for the door; saying goodnight to his niece and nephew. They could still hear him laughing as he strode briskly up the stairs. They walked slowly up the stairs arm-in-arm; and Harry dropped Dorothy off at her bedroom. Rosie had the door open and was smiling broadly; she actually loved playing a real 'ladies maid', especially for Dorothy, who she considered a close friend and of course, a lover. She was chuckling as she helped Dorothy from her dress, "Blimey the house is full of talk about the bleeding mummy popping up in the middle of the sodding table! How on earth does Mister Sims do that? Me and Reggie kept our traps shut, don't want to spoil the joke on that bent medium and boy, was it a bleeding cracker!" Dottie turned and kissed her, "And it stays that way darling, so that Cousin David can sleep well of a night now." Rosie smiled, "He certainly will if he gets his hands on you my sweet. Bleeding hell, you could be the next Countess of Barfield." Dorothy just sighed, "Not while I have a say in it."

CHAPTER 7. 'WE ACCEPT THE LOVE WE THINK WE DESERVE.' Stephen Chbosky.

Rosie was pulling the covers back on the big bed and Dorothy was sitting at her vanity mirror, hands on chin, staring at her reflection in the mirror, wearing her short lace nightdress. Everything had been arranged for her 'night caller' to visit. Mr. Gibbs should be here at any moment. Rosie had smiled about this little 'naughty rendezvous', her 'lady' certainly didn't mind fucking the servants: Rosie knew that was a fact, because she was one!

There was soft knock at the door and Rosie sauntered over to open it, whispering, "I think your bleeding stallion is here my lady." and did an extravagant curtsy. Dorothy replied quietly, "I flipping hope so, I need to ride tonight, so he had better be a stallion."

Dorothy was a little surprised to find Lord David standing at her door and Rosie immediately wrapped her in a large fluffy red dressing gown. He held up a lamp and smiled slowly as Dorothy pointed out it wasn't very gentlemanly to visit an unmarried woman in her bedroom at this time of night. A sheepish David mumbled something that is was all right; he wouldn't come in unless invited! Then added that her ladies maid was a married woman and suitable as a chaperone. Dottie calmly asked him what he wanted and David took a deep breath, asking her to consider a very good proposal. She sighed, smiling at a grinning Rosie who stood behind the door listening intently, and asked what his 'proposal' was. He blurted out his undying love for her and that all she had to say was 'yes' and she would be the next Countess of Barfield! Rosie had to slap a hand over her mouth to stop giggles escaping as Dorothy pretended to be interested in such a proposal. Then she let the young man down gently and with some softness which surprised Rosie a little. The young Earl of Barfield walked quietly away, his head bowed down with bitter disappointment. "I bet those two bleeding tarts masquerading as House Maids will soon cheer the dirty bugger up!" Rosie – smiling - announced as she took the dressing gown from a very bemused Dorothy, who agreed with her.

There was a soft knock at the door and Dorothy smiled at Rosie, telling her to retire for the night and the giggling Rosie did as she was asked. Dottie pulled open the door and Mr. Gibbs slipped in and smiled a little; he was carrying a bottle of wine and two glasses. He slowly poured two full glasses and slipped from his dressing gown, Mr. Gibbs was standing by the big double bed - stark naked and fully erect - he certainly didn't disappoint in that respect! - He lifted a full wine glass saying softly; "Come and have a glass of wine my dear." Dottie walked over to him and accepted a full glass of red wine; it was delicious. Mr. Gibbs grinned; "From the Earls private stock. I'm sure he won't mind since it's you my lady."

They both chuckled and Dottie pulled off her night dress and placed the wine glass down. "I best start with some of this." She whispered, quickly kneeling and her eager mouth soon covered his big hard cock. Mr. Gibbs smiled and patted her head, as it moved up and down on his erection. "Good girl, I like plenty of tongue and suck hard; like you're trying to pull a pea up a straw." That made Dottie chuckle and she set to work following the Acting -butler's instructions, who stood sipping his wine and watching quietly.

After some minutes, he too placed his wine down and pulled Dottie to her feet and the pair kissed. Dottie was impressed; he had a tongue like a lizard and it probed her mouth better than a dentist on opium! He pushed her on to the bed and whispered; "Time to reciprocate, my dear." and gently pulled open her legs and he too, set to work on her wet vagina. It took just six or seven minutes before Dottie gripped his head and almost screamed; she had one hell of an organism. He was that good, she almost cried with delight.

He mounted her and the fucking started in earnest, beginning with the good old fashioned 'Missionary position'. She simply couldn't believe the man's incredible stamina and technique. He was trusting deep and hard, yet was gentle about it. He was a highly skilled lover - no doubt about that - they locked in a passionate embrace, tongues in each other's mouths and both were surprised by the intensity of their love making.

They rolled about the bed, groaning, whispering, panting and fucking. At one point, Dottie was face down on the pillows, clutching the blankets with both hands and moaning as he fucked her doggy style. Then she was astride him, riding hard as they clutched hands. She had another huge orgasm which made her collapse on top of him. He simply turned her over and continued to fuck her hard, back in the Missionary position.

"For God sake; cum!" She whispered, sweating and panting with her exertions. Mr. Gibbs just smiled and wiped sweat from his face and continued to thrust deep and hard. Alex found herself crawling about the big bed on all fours with the butler fucking her hard like a dog. She buried herself in pillows and sheets, legs shaking, her entire body quivering under his unbelievable fucking. He still didn't stop and they changed position again; Dottie back on top, almost jumping up and down on that still rock hard cock. She came again and splattered him with her cum. That was it for her; for the first time - in a very long time - she was 'tapped out' and lay on top of him gasping and crying a little. He wiped her face and kissed it. "Roll over sweet one and I'll try to finish." Dottie groaned loudly but did as she was asked. Back in the Missionary Position, she simply lay back and let the happy Butler finish in her. He fucked her for some minutes and she was now crying a little; she hadn't been fucked like this in a long time. He came deep and hard inside and also collapsed. They lay gripped tightly in each other's arms; totally exhausted from the vigor of their love making. They managed some really passionate kissing and Dottie raised her head and looked at the mantel piece clock. "Holy fucking shit! We've been at it for two hours solid!" The butler just chuckled and kissed her face and lips; "Don't worry my dear, with your help and lovely mouth, I'll soon be up and ready again. I always last longer the second or third time." Dottie just stared at him and realized that he meant it!

She pulled him to her and they kissed and caressed, whispering to each other. She and Mr. Gibbs became one on that creaking old bed. They fell asleep, cradled in each other's arms and Dottie slept better than she had done in a very long time. She woke suddenly and sat up a little. The clock was reading almost four o'clock [in the morning] she groaned; Mr. Gibbs shifted and sat up next to her and she pushed into his arms. He kissed the back of her neck and shoulders, cupping her breasts from behind.

Dottie whispered to him that it would soon be morning and he simply smiled and they French kissed. He ran a hand between her legs and chuckled; "Your still quite wet my dear. That's good." He gently pushed her onto the pillows and mounted her again.

Dottie groaned out loud and the love making started again. She made him promise to come quickly and he nodded; "I do sometime come too quick with my early morning riser." She gripped his shoulders and whispered; "Thank fuck for that." and let him fuck her again; she had another two orgasms during this second session. She lay sprawled on the bed, head against a pile of pillows, on her back with her legs open and watched Mr. Gibbs slip on his dressing gown, blow her a kiss and depart. She managed to call for Rosie who appeared and laughed outright, "For Christ sakes! Have you bleeding been at it all night?" All Dorothy could do was nod and ask for a cup of bleeding tea in a whisperer! Rosie leaned over and placed an affectionate kiss upon her lips. "Bleeding good was he?" she asked, stroking Dottie's sweaty face. Dorothy nodded again and whispered; "Bleeding good doesn't cover it Rosie, he was a big bloody gentle animal and I actually don't think I can sodding walk!"

Rosie grinned, "I'll run you a hot bath and while you soak, fetch some tea." She kissed Dottie again and left her to sleep a little. Dottie was a little subdued at breakfast, served by a very fresh looking Mr. Gibbs, who behaved like the pair had exchanged stamp collections and not fucked hard most of the night. Dottie now actually regretted turning Lord David down as her vivid imagination [and sexual fantasies] took hold. The thoughts of her and the butler made her smile broadly: fucking surreptitiously all around the castle whenever they could. Smiling so much, that Harry asked if she was alright!

He reminded her that they would be exploring the village today in search of someone who could identify the poor child in the horrific photograph. That bought her down to earth with a bang when she thought about the little girl and nibbled at her fresh tomatoes and scrambled eggs on toast. "I'll make a list and we'll work through it." She told Harry who nodded his approval.

She walked slowly back to her rooms and simply couldn't shake Mr. Gibbs from her thoughts. She passed 'Madam Zodiac' and her flustered assistant heading down to the front doors and their carriage. They mumbled a 'good morning' and disappeared before they encountered anyone else. She would make sure that Rosie carried a message to Mr. Gibbs inviting him to another 'little rendezvous' tonight and she really couldn't wait for night. Now that did make Rosie's day and she couldn't stop laughing with excitement when she relayed his reply, just before Dottie and Harry left for their mission in the village.

"The bleeding stud agrees and asked if you would let me [Rosie] join in, he says he can manage both of us!" She said smiling broadly and Dorothy joined in her laughter. "Bloody hell Rosie, for once, he's a man whose word you can certainly believe!" Now both women really anticipated the butler's night visit and would warm up for him with some lovemaking: they felt sure he would really like to watch that before servicing the pair. Both also agreed that the service they were receiving at Barfield castle was probably better than Buckingham Palace could provide!

CHAPTER 8. 'GOODBYE SHE SAID, I'M OFF TO JOIN THE GYPSIES.' Unknown.

Dorothy ticked the post office from her list and tapped Harry's arm; "The tobacconists next. Mrs. Gladys Cooper is the proprietor and apparently it has a superb collection of sweets." Harry sighed; "A sweet shop and we're looking for a child. Do you think the sweet shop should have been first on our list and not the last? My bleeding feet are killing me." Dorothy chuckled at that and Harry pulled the shop door open, causing a little bell to tinkle. Dorothy stepped in and bid 'good morning' to the big smiling woman that appeared from the back room and now stood behind her counter.

Harry stuck the photograph – the offending parts discretely covered – under the woman's nose and asked if she knew the child? Mrs. Iris Applegate stared at the picture and adjusted her glasses a couple of time. She didn't smile;"Yes." Was all she said. Dorothy and Harry exchanged a glance and Dorothy took over; "We really need to find her parents, it's a matter of urgency." Mrs. Applegate slowly ran a cloth over her counter; "What's the poor creature done now?" Harry smiled; "Nothing. But we really need to speak to her parents. We think she could be in danger, real danger." He tapped the photograph and asked again if she knew where the child's parents were. Mrs. Applegate sighed; "The poor little thing is pretty as a picture but not right in the head. I think she's a little retarded, but a sweet little girl nevertheless. When her father or her brother's come in for tobacco and matches, she always gets some candy sticks or a little chocolate. They certainly look after the poor unfortunate child, I'll say that for them." Dorothy patted the woman's hand and asked where they could find her father and brothers.

Mrs. Applegate gestured to the door; "I hope you have bloodhounds. Those types of people can be anywhere." Dorothy asked what she meant by that and Iris chuckled; "Gypsies, tramps and thieves. She's the head gypsy's youngest." Harry ran a hand over his face; "You mean Gabrielle, the big gypsy that speaks for them." Mrs. Applegate nodded; "Apparently her mother died having the child and the poor little thing isn't right. But you know gypsies; family comes first."

Dorothy asked if old man Parks had been a regular customer of Iris's and she nodded; "He bought one of those big tins of mixed sweets about a week ago; must have had a sweet tooth." Dorothy said quietly to Harry; "Remember there were empty tins of sweets in the tennis pavilion." They thanked Mrs. Applegate and headed for their next port of call; the police house.

Harry and Dorothy stepped back into the sunshine and Harry slowly pushed the photograph back into his packet. "He [Garberville] must have found out and took bloody revenge. There's not a dad, grandfather, uncle or brother who wouldn't. He killed the pair for what they had been doing to the child."

Dorothy sighed; "So where does that leave Albert Dean and his plunge from the roof of the east tower?" Harry shrugged his shoulders; "Maybe they're unconnected." The pair walked slowly towards PC Holmes's little police house opposite the Butchers shop.

His wife Mavis invited them in and made a pot of tea. She really admired Dorothy's hat and coat. Dorothy neglected her tea to hold the couple's new daughter; just four months old. Little Victoria had been named after her maternal grandmother. It appears that PC Holmes was at the Fisher's Farm; two sheep had disappeared from their pen overnight.

"Richard thinks those gypsies took them when they moved off; either to sell for cash or feed the families." Mavis offered Harry some biscuits whilst Dorothy nursed little Victoria. Dorothy really was reluctant to hand her back to her mum and enjoy her cup of tea. They chattered about the now cancelled wedding and Mavis was surprised that the young Earl had summoned a medium to make contact with the troubled spirits who may inhabit the castle. "Young Alice [the kitchen maid at the castle] could tell his lordship all about spirits and mediums; her granny was a real one and everyone says Alice has inherited her talent. But it was such a shame about young Albert; everyone thought he and Alice would tie the knot in a few years."

Harry placed his cup down and asked about the pair. Mavis smiled; "Everyone knew they were sweet on each other: such a tragedy that the young man fell from the damn tower; what a waste of a young life. Well, at least Alice is young enough to get over it and find someone else." Harry and Dorothy nodded at that and said their goodbyes. Back on the street Dorothy reminded Harry that Alice had found the body.

"Little wonder that Williams said she was so upset." Harry quietly muttered as they started to walk back to the castle. Dorothy asked to see that big ornate button that was found in Albert's hand. She examined it closely as they walked. "Harry where the hell have we seen a vivid red jacket or coat with big gold buttons before?" she asked.

Harry took the button and they pair stopped outside St. Mary's church. He rolled the button around in his hand and sighed loudly. "They are connected Dottie; young Albert's death and the murder of Park's and Tuttle. They're connected by this button; it came from Gabrielle's jacket. Do you remember he was wearing a bright red jacket with big buttons on the day we returned to the tennis pavilion with Reggie?" Dorothy nodded; she did indeed remember their encounter with the big colourful man.

"So what is Albert's connection with Park's and Tuttle? Why would Gabrielle throw the young man from the east tower? What was going on with the pair?" Harry asked and pushed the button back into his pocket. Dorothy gripped his arm; "Harry, I've just remembered that when we met Gabrielle and he spoke to Reggie, he knew that Reggie performed with me and Uncle William! How the hell did he know that? Someone must have already told him who we were and that could only have come from someone at the castle?"

 Harry nodded; "Young Albert of course. It had to be him or…. Alice." Dorothy nodded; "There is your connection right there, except the Gypsy King has disappeared with his clan and young Albert is dead. We need to speak to Alice." She pushed her arm through his and the pair headed back to the castle for a little chat with the kitchen maid Alice. But first they stopped at the post office and sent a cable to Inspector Ramsey at York Police HQ.

Mrs. Joan Cathay – the post mistress – wrote down their urgent message and licked the tip of her pencil. "I can send it normal rates but it wouldn't go until this afternoon or immediately, but it will cost you two shillings." Harry agreed and handed the woman a shilling and two sixpences. She took the money and placed it in a small wooden box at the back of the counter. She gripped the paper and re-read the message that Harry had written. "I'm sorry, but obviously I have read the message and you think that young Alice is somehow involved in all this?" Harry nodded and Dorothy smiled; "We think she is a vital witness and may have some good evidence about the dreadful murders."

The post mistress eased herself down at the small table that held the telegraphic equipment. She wound up the sender with some vigorous turns of the winding handle. She stopped; "I take it you know that young Alice's gran was a traveler. She married Maurice, a local farmer many years ago and settled down here. But her family is still regular visitors to Barfield. They came down to perform at that cancelled wedding of his lordship. Their leader is Alice's cousin." Harry and Dorothy both stared at each other; young Alice was related to the very Gypsy that was suspected of killing the three men!

They were half way up the High Street when they saw PC Holmes jumping down from a hay cart and thanking the tall skinny driver. They walked over and chatted together. He had quite a revelation for the pair; before he went to Fisher's farm, he had searched Albert Dean's room in the castle's attic's – with Mr. Gibbs in attendance of course – and found the incredible sum of ten pounds hidden in his sock drawer. That sort of money would have taken the young house boy several years to accrue and he had only worked in the castle for nine months!

PC Holmes removed his hat and wiped his face and neck in the warm sunshine. He looked carefully about, making sure he couldn't be overheard. "Doctor Kennedy performed the autopsy this morning and as you would expect; death was caused by falling from a great height. But that wasn't the only thing the doctor found." The constable motioned Harry to one side; he certainly wouldn't speak of what the good doctor found with Dorothy standing there. Somewhat annoyed she waited by the church gate and then grabbed Harry as soon as he and Constable Holmes finished their conversation and the PC headed home for his lunch. "Well, what's the big mystery that I wasn't allowed to hear?" She asked.

Harry didn't smile and leaned close to her ear and whispered; "It appears that young Albert was a practicing homosexual. He apparently practiced so much that he anus was immediately noticeable when they stripped the body. It was well expanded and well used for someone so young. Doctor Kennedy was a navel surgeon and had seen the effects of homosexual sex for years and he believes the young man has been having sex for some time; in fact he must have been abused as a child."

Dorothy actually gasped and placed a hand over mouth; "Do you think the money was from clients?" Harry shrugged his shoulders; "Maybe. Or young Albert wasn't adverse to some blackmail. Maybe he tried that on with Gabrielle and picked the most stupid spot in the world to confront someone that had just shot old Parks to death; alone on the top of a bloody big tower at night!"

"Where does Alice stand in all this? She was keen on young Albert and I wonder if she knew he was a homosexual. Did she know that Albert was meeting her cousin, maybe to blackmail him? We really need to speak to her Harry." He nodded; "Well, unless Inspector Ramsey can find Gabrielle amongst the huge numbers of travelling families scattered around Britain, Alice is all we have."

As they walked back to the castle, they saw Mr. Williams with both Kate and Judith heading into the Barfield Arms and Dottie wondered about the girl's employment at the castle. Rosie had told her that the housekeeper had referred to the pair as 'bloody useless'. Maybe Cousin David paid their wages for another kind of service? She smiled to herself over those thoughts, well; it was actually what Rosie thought!

They made their way back to the castle and Uncle William had some news for them.

CHAPTER 9. 'YOU CAN'T FIND SOMEONE WHO DOESN'T WANT TO BE FOUND.' Isabel Allende.

"I've some exciting news for you young lady!" Uncle William could barely restrain himself. Dorothy just folded her arms and said bluntly; "I'm NOT going to marry him. So you can forget that….." She didn't finish as Uncle William roared with laughter; "No! Not that you daft moo! Margret is going to arrange that you're presented this season!" Dorothy stared at him and could hear Harry chuckling. "You'll be presented to their Majesties at this Season's ball. Margret will announce you; she can, being a blooming Dowager Countess. She even insists upon buying your Ball gown for the occasion. I think she'll enjoy all the arranging, dress sessions and practices. This would be a great honour for our struggling family; the last girl we had 'presented' was your Mother's sister Adelaide and she wasn't actually a Hadden."

Dorothy just shook her head; she knew it was pointless to argue against her Uncle on this matter; he had always wanted Dorothy presented at Court since she was a little girl. It did make Harry chuckle and he started to refer to Dorothy as 'your Ladyship' and bowing. The language he received back from her wasn't very lady like, so he dropped that idea quickly.

"We'll have a word with young Alice after Sunday service." Harry concluded the little chat amongst the team and Dorothy headed for a very welcome hot bath after such a long day. Rosie fussed over her with a fresh pot of tea and a bath filled with hot scented water. "Dinner has been put back a bleeding hour and that Inspector from York is apparently on his way again." Rosie passed on the latest gossip to Dorothy who almost dozed off in the bath. She wasn't surprised by the Inspectors return; he had another two murders on his plate now.

Still, the culprit was now known – thanks to Dorothy and Harry – and all that remained was apprehending the fellow; Dorothy knew that was far easier said than done! The Gypsy King had a good day's lead on them and could simply vanish into the travelling community who would certainly close ranks around him. She dressed slowly for the belated dinner and headed for the dining room. The meal was a very subdued affair and it was obvious to all – except the Colonel, who didn't show any concern – that something was going on between Lady Rosemary and Mister Hadden.

Everyone retired quite early and again; Dorothy would sleep really well and wonder what Sunday would bring. She certainly knew what the night would bring: the much anticipated visit of their 'stallion'. He didn't disappoint. He sat naked on a chair watching the girls perform for him, sipping wine and making the odd suggestion to the pair who immediately carried out his wishes. Then with a happy smile, he joined in. He pounded Rosie so hard in the 'doggy' position that she had to wipe her eyes, but she told him to continue regardless. Then had Dorothy stretch over Rosie with her bum facing him and took both giggling girls in turn. He certainly was an imaginative and creative lover and both girls really appreciated that, with Rosie gasping and wondering if he had read the "Bleeding Karma-Sutra cover to bleeding cover!" It turned out that he had.

At one point Dottie found herself sitting backwards on a stiff chair gripping its high back while he stood behind and fucked her hard. Rosie was astride the same chair [keeping it balanced] enjoying Dottie's charms fully. Then the girls swapped over. The happy threesome continued for some two hours with Rosie declaring that the butler had the stamina of a 'bleeding breeding bull.' He was very fair with his seed deposits and finished in each of the girls whilst in the Missionary position with them. Then, calmly announced, as the pair embraced that he could go again: if they wished. Rosie asked him if that was a trick question and the intense fucking started again and carried on for almost another hour. He left the pair sprawled, embracing on the big bed, kissing and whispering together.

"There are police patrols everywhere. I heard Inspector Ramsey has cabled every town and city as far away as Newcastle and Manchester. Do you think they'll get him?" Alice placed the bundle of carrots on the large kitchen table and started to cut the green shoots from each. Mrs. Porterhouse stopped sieving her flour and slowly wiped her hands on her apron; "I can understand why Gabrielle the Gypsy King killed old Parks and Tuttle, but why young Albert? There is no evidence to link him with the other two evil old buggers."

Alice nodded; "Maybe it was an accident; but what on earth was he doing on top of the east tower?" Mrs. Porterhouse sighed; she certainly didn't know what was going through the young man's mind when he plunged to his death from the ramparts of the east tower at sunset. She looked at the clock and smiled; "Well, go on, get your hat and get off to church. Mr. Gibbs will be taking the staff across to the chapel in a few minutes. His lordship and his guests have already left." Alice nodded and pulled off her apron and grabbed up her coat and straw hat. She almost ran through the kitchen door into the yard and could see the other staff gathering by the back gate. She yelled; "Wait for me!" and ran over, joining them as they set off for the Barfield Chapel and Sunday Service with the Reverend John Caulder.

Young David the footman walked next to Alice, smoothing down his hair with both hands. "Do you hear that London copper found something gripped in poor Albert's hand; apparently it will crack the case wide open and expose his murderer!" Alice just stared at him; "What do you mean murder? He bloody fell from the roof!" David chuckled; "Yeah, if that was the case, why was he gripping a button from someone's torn shirt or blouse? It's obvious he was pushed, so it's murder!" Alice just shook her head and stared ahead, at the doors of the Barfield Chapel and two burly police officers who were guarding them.

The staff filed into church and sat behind the family and guests. Alice was admiring Miss Dorothy's wonderful flowery hat and silk coat. "She's a real stunner and a proper lady. Everyone thinks his

lordship will pop the question before she returns to London."
David [the footman] whispered to Alice and pushed his hands
through his unmanageable hair – again. Alice just nodded and
then wondered where Miss Dorothy's handsome brother was.

She found him waiting outside the small chapel and he called her
over; they were quickly joined by Dorothy who managed to
escape the attentions – again – of the young Earl. If anything he
was persistent over getting what he wanted and that was
Dorothy. Alice didn't appear to be nervous or concerned about
answering Mister Hadden's questions about her relationship with
Gabrielle or young Albert. Dorothy was pleased about that; did it
mean that Alice had nothing to hide?

The three walked slowly back to the castle. Alice admitted being
very 'sweet' on Albert and also admitted that Gabrielle was her
cousin and visiting the camp a couple of times with Albert, who
seemed fascinated by the travelling way of life. She said that on
both occasions that old Mr. Park's was indeed at the camp, but
never did find out why he was there.

Harry asked her about the rumours that the night Parks died,
that the Earl was apparently going to dismiss him over the debts
he owed to so many people; including the bank. She looked a
little puzzled by that and stopped walking. "I don't know about
debts Mr. Hadden, but the stories going about the village about
old Park's was that the young Earl was going to sack him over
something far more serious that just owing money." Dorothy
asked what she had heard and Alice didn't smile and looked
about to ensure she wasn't overheard; "That he had allowed Mr.
Tuttle into the castle to take photographs that the Earl didn't
approve of."

Harry nodded and asked if she knew what photographs did Mr.
Tuttle take. Alice sighed; "Naughty ones, dirty pictures. I can't
say for sure but both Judith and Kate were involved for serious
money." She looked quite sad and took a deep breath; "Albert
told me just after they found old Park's body. He admitted that
he had been involved in it for money."

Dorothy asked her outright if she knew that Albert was a
homosexual. Alice nodded and wiped a couple of tears away with
her sleeve; "I thought he could change, you know, get better.
But he never got the chance. He stupidly told me that Gabrielle

was involved in making the dirty pictures and had taken money off both Parks and old man Tuttle. He said that Gabrielle would pay him to keep his mouth shut. But I think Gabrielle had other ideas about that." She was crying openly now and Dorothy gave her a cuddle.

Harry had to ask; "Did Gabrielle kill them because he knew that they had used his young daughter in some of the pictures?" Alice sobbed loudly and clutched Dorothy tightly. She took a couple of deep breaths; "Albert said that old Parks hadn't paid him, refused to pay him for the girl's appearance because she wouldn't behave herself and do as she was told!" Even Dorothy was shocked by that revelation. Revenge hadn't been the driving force for the murders; the gang had simply fallen out over money. Dorothy walked the sobbing girl back to the kitchens and Harry was left to ponder her words.

Harry knew that the manhunt needed to find the little girl above anything else; she was vulnerable, being abused and mistreated by the very people who should protect her. He walked to the post office with great sadness. He needed to send another cable to York Police Headquarters. He knew that the postmistress would open up for him in such an emergency. He almost reached the small silent shop when he saw the carriages sweep by; Charlotte, her mother and brother were heading home; back to America. Apparently the young Earl had called off his engagement.

Harry didn't smile and banged on the door.

Rosie was packing Dorothy's suitcases and was a little sad to give up being a 'proper' Ladies Maid. But she had missed her two boys and she reasoned their bleeding dad also! But she had laughed at her 'lady's' dismissal of the young Earl's offer that the family stay on for a few more weeks. Dorothy had pointed that she was a working woman and needed to return to her 'job'. In desperation the Earl had offered to pay her wages, so that she could stay on. The icy look of disgust from Dorothy ended that idea and he didn't mention it again.

Uncle William took his leave of the unhappy Dowager Countess and with Harry and Dorothy left that afternoon for the train station. Titus was also sad about giving up his 'valet' job, but was looking forward to returning to the stage. He had been really well treated by the staff at the castle and was full of praise for them.

Apparently he confided to Harry that the two upstairs maids had been very kind to him!

They made the London train and were back in King's Cross by evening. They had been informed by Inspector Ramsey that Gabrielle and his family had not been found; which cast a dark shadow over their happy return home; all they could think of was the poor child. But Dorothy allowed herself some thoughts about Mr. Gibbs and then realized that she didn't even know his first name! But her visit to Barfield castle would always remain a happy memory, a very happy memory!

Uncle William sat at the breakfast table and read through his morning correspondence. Dorothy and Harry were having a discussion about the benefits of the Death Penalty! Uncle William looked up and chuckled; "Now, now you two. It won't be abolished any time soon, besides you have something far more important to consider young lady; Queen Charlotte's Ball on the 19th of this month. According to Maggie [Dowager Countess Margret of Barfield] she's will be in London on Friday staying at Barfield House in Piccadilly. She needs to see your dress and coach you in Royal Court protocol."

Dorothy sighed and placed her knife and fork down. "It's just plain daft Uncle William. I see no point or benefit to it." Harry laughed and finished his large breakfast with a satisfied grunt. "It means you're a real lady and can be courted by some very rich men with titles. You know that's been your heartfelt ambition; to marry a wealthy man and lay around a big house, surrounded by servants, doing bugger all!" She just stuck up a single finger and Uncle William – smiling – said "Tut tut my dear, that's not how a debutante behaves."

Dorothy turned to Ellen who was clearing away the breakfast things and asked her; "Ellen, you wouldn't like to marry a very wealthy man and lay around a big house all day with servants doing everything and your only worry would be which dress to wear to make your blooming Lord and master happy, when he comes home?" Ellen stopped loading her tray and stood one hand on hip and stared at Dorothy, she rubbed her chin and replied; "Is that a trick question? Course I would! Do nothing but worry about what bleeding dress I would wear? I'd be happy as a pig in a poke! Just tell me his address and I'd be off and I wouldn't care less if he was old enough to be me father!"

Harry and Uncle William couldn't help but laugh which annoyed Dorothy a little. She waved Ellen away with; "I just picked the wrong person to ask that's all. Most women would steadfastly refuse to be kept in a gilded cage." She folded her arms and then grimaced as Ellen shouted from the doorway: "No they bleeding wouldn't! Not around here anyway!"

Harry lifted up the thick letter he had received this morning and wasn't happy; "It's from Inspector Ramsey and it's not good News I'm afraid. He writes to say there is still no trace of Gabrielle the gypsy King or his daughter. Young Alice has been charged with obstructing justice and he believes she'll get three to five years in prison which will totally ruin her life. "

Dorothy slumped back in her chair; "Charming and certainly not the best news I've heard all week. They must find that poor child for heaven's sake." Harry nodded his agreement with that; "But they can only do what they can do my dear sister." Uncle William tapped another piece of correspondence and said; "On a lighter and much happier note, George's ship will be docking at the Albert Docks near Christmas and he has three weeks leave. So, I think we should have bit of a party for him, what do you say?"

Harry was definitely up for that and Dorothy nodded her approval; she hadn't seen her brother George in nearly two years. He was the third Officer on HMS Colossus and had been in the Royal Navy since he was just twelve years old. Dorothy would admit that she didn't really know her brother George; he was bit of a mystery to her. But ever since he went to sea, he had always sent little china dolls home for his 'baby sister'. She had a wonderful and expensive collection of them. Her oldest brother; Henry was a total mystery to her. She hadn't actually seen him since she was eight or nine years old. Like their father; he was an amateur archeologist and spent all his time in Egypt.

Sir Henry Hadden left all the family business and running of the house to his uncle; William. Both Dorothy and Harry knew that Uncle William had really kept the family together after their parent's untimely deaths. They certainly couldn't have counted on their wayward brother Henry.

Uncle William finished his cup of tea and smiled, pointing to Dorothy; "We have an appointment with Madame Antoinette at ten, so let's get things moving. She has the dress ready for its first full fitting and Maggie will be joining us there." Harry chuckled and made bird noises; "That gilded cage waits with the door open until you're in; you'll love it!" Dorothy just sighed and rose from the table and headed for the door. Uncle William called after her; "In all the excitement of your dress fitting and Maggie turning up, I forget, there's a letter for you from America,"

Dorothy walked back and took the envelope and stared at it; "Who do we know in New York City, New York?" Uncle William shrugged his shoulders; "No one comes to mind." Dorothy quickly opened the letter and it contained just a postcard. She held it out to the others. Harry stared at it; "I've never seen a building so tall, it must a drawing or a painting or something." Uncle William grunted; "I've never heard of the Empire State Building, certainly not in New York."

That's when Harry pointed out that the 'postcard' had the US Mail date stamp of February 14th 1971 and it was from someone called 'Davies Washington'. There was just one line handwritten in the message box; *See you soon my darling Dottie, all my love Davis Washington*. Harry noticed it had a local postmark from a couple of days ago. Strangely enough, they weren't shocked by the date from the future!

Dorothy tapped the strange postcode and said quietly; "Who the bleeding hell is Davies Washington?"

CHAPTER 10. 'I WAS PLUNGED INTO WHAT WAS KNOWN AS THE DEBUTANTE SOCIAL WHIRL. THIS WAS ONE OF THE WAYS FATHERS JUSTIFIED THEIR OWN HARD WORK AND SACRIFICES.' Gene Tierney.

Uncle William relaxed back in his seat and flicked through his notebook – again – checking everything for the big party at the Hadden House after the presentation. He wanted everyone to enjoy Dorothy's big moment and so, had hired caterers with their own waiting staff. [That meant Ellen and Mrs. Harvey could join the party without any worries.] He smiled at Dorothy and said quietly, "Maggie will be there of course and..." he hesitated, "And

Cousin David [the Earl of Barfield] has accepted his invitation too." Dorothy just sighed, but Ellen chuckled, "Well, he's certainly a persistent young man." Dottie grunted – very un-debutante like – "Persistent is not the word I would use. Blind would be a better one."

"You know, Maggie offered Barfield House for the party with everything thrown in. Now that was very generous of her." Uncle William told Dorothy who just nodded and stared out the carriage window at the packed streets, then the carriage rolled to a halt outside a lavish shop which boasted: 'Le masons du Antoinette'. A small sign declared 'dresses and gowns for the New London Season' and 'Continental Travel needs fulfilled'. The doorman was a big man resplendent in an 18th century footman's attire including powdered wig and silk leggings. The cab driver opened the carriage door and removed his hat, while the big footman pushed open the gold gilded door of the fashionable London Salon and bowed a little. He had a really big smile on his quite ugly face. Dorothy now really grinned as uncle William helped her down. She wanted to yell "Hello Oskar!" But restrained herself: how she knew the big man might take some very awkward explanations!

They swept into the salon and were greeted by Maggie and Madame Antoinette [real name Gladys's Shepherd from Tower Hamlets!] the Madame's two assistants [Edith & Clementine] were immediately on hand to get things moving. Madame Antoinette stood hands on hips and deliberately looked Dorothy up and down with a practiced and very experienced eye. She nodded and turned to Maggie, "Your ladyship, this young lady [indicating Dorothy] will be 'belle of the ball' even if I fitted her with a coalman's sack! Utterly exquisite, beautiful, graceful and carries herself like a Hapsburg Princess. It will be an honour for the Le masons du Antoinette to dress her."

Now Maggie did smile, "Hence why I have not scrimped a single guinea on her gown my dear old friend. This little Cinderella will go the ball and illuminate the damn place with just a smile!" Madame Antoinette chuckled and agreed with her. Dottie's gown would cost at least fourteen guineas without any extras!

Ellen whispered to Uncle William, "I think you are right mister William: she [Maggie] has designs on our Dottie as her new daughter-in-law and the next Countess of Barfield!" Uncle William answered with just a very broad smile. He had already confided to Harry if that happened, he would dance around the garden happily naked! Harry had just rolled his eyes because he knew Uncle William would damn well do it.

 *"In today's money that would be about £1,155.00." SJW.*

Uncle William, Harry, Rosie and Mrs. Harvey all waited with real anticipation at the bottom of the stairs and heard Ellen shout, "She's on her way down!" Old Charlie – the Hadden's regular cabby – waited in the doorway, hat off and smiled broadly as Dorothy swept down the stairs, followed by a grinning Ellen. Uncle William grasped both hands together and sighed with pride and happiness. "My little girl looks like a bloody real princess!" He whispered to himself and Harry could only nod his agreement. Dorothy looked stunning in the white silk and lace creation. She stopped and did a respectable curtsey. Everyone noticed that her bodice was low cut, very low cut but all debutantes wore it that way. It was just that Dorothy had more on show than most!

Dorothy kissed her brother, Ellen, and even Mrs. Harvey then kissed Rosie and gripped her hand. Rosie wiped away a tear and whispered, "Go on you daft cow, bleeding knock 'em dead!" Dorothy struggled to stop a few tears appearing and could only smile. Uncle William placed a kiss upon her cheek and said quietly, "Come on Cinderella, let's get you to the damn ball."

Charlie gave a little bow and gestured to the door, "Your carriage awaits your highness." Everyone laughed and with Ellen gripping Dorothy's short train, she made for the door on the arm of her very proud uncle. Waiting in the carriage was Margret, the Dowager Countess of Barfield, who would actually present Dottie to the King and Queen Alexandra. Once settled in the cab, Charlie climbed up to the driver's seat, blew his nose into a clean hankie and flicked his whip. He remembered fondly, running the young Dorothy to school. She was a little beauty then and always polite to him. Once giving him her apple as a tip because she didn't have any money. "One of the best bloody tips I ever had." He thought and guided the carriage through the traffic with quite a smile on his face. A 'fare' like this made his bloody day!

The Mall had been closed and only Debutante carriages were being allowed on it. Two constables were checking everyone attempting to enter, accompanied by a young Palace equerry in a wonderful court uniform who carried a book and a black stick under his arm. Charlie stopped the carriage and shouted down to the constables, "The Dowager Countess of Barfield and Miss Dorothy Hadden!" The equerry removed his hat and peered into the cab, then checked his book and nodded. The carriage was allowed to pass and entered the Mall which was packed on both sides with crowds watching the procession of carriages heading to the palace. Uncle William simply couldn't resist and gave a wonderful graceful wave to the crowd. Several people – to his delight and surprise – waved back.

Maggie carefully checked Dottie's bouquet of flowers and adjusted the three feathers in her hair [Dorothy's] then finally, flicked open the crisp white fan and waved it about. "Keep it closed when actually curtseying to their Majesties." She advised with a smile as Dorothy took a couple of deep breaths, realizing she was nervous about meeting Queen Alexandra and not actually 'Bertie' the king. After all, she could claim she had been a 'royal mistress' after their last encounter! [See episode: **'Miss Pandora and her magic box.'**]

A smart young footman pulled open the carriage door and Dorothy joined the long queue of nervous debutantes awaiting their presentation. That's when an ancient equerry appeared and spoke with Maggie and Uncle William. Dorothy recongnised him immediately: it was the King's servant who had escorted her to the King's private chamber's when Dottie had performed her magic show by 'royal command'.

They were escorted to a nearby antechamber where about a dozen debutantes and their chaperones waited. Both Dorothy and Maggie were overjoyed to see that tea was being served. Uncle William was really impressed, "This is very unusual, you don't normally get tea." He said quietly, but took a cup with a big smile. Maggie chuckled and whispered into a very surprised – and a little shocked – Dorothy's ear. "I strongly suspect that these ladies have already done royal service for the king." and placed a little kiss on Dottie's cheek – now a little red – who could only manage a smile. She sighed; at least the dirty old bugger hadn't forgotten all those women who had served their King and Country...especially the King it would seem!

That's when Dorothy spotted Captain Stubbs in the doorway, dressed in a resplendent court uniform, he gestured for her to attend him, which she did. He removed his fancy hat and spoke softly, "Miss Hadden, I am commanded by his majesty to inform you that your King and Empire requires your talent on a matter of National importance. The very crown jewel of the Empire is threatened and the king and government must act. If we fail, there could be bloodshed on a scale never seen before and could cause the loss of our greatest Imperial asset." He replaced his hat and bowed, adding, "You will be contacted Miss Hadden and the King is confident in your abilities to assist the crown on this matter." He now smiled and departed. Dorothy knew full well that the 'jewel of the British Empire' was India. But what was the threat against it? Her thoughts were disturbed by Maggie who took her arm and the pair headed for the State Chamber and Dorothy's formal presentation to their majesties.

The royal announcer said loudly, "The Dowager Countess of Barfield presenting Miss Dorothy Mary Hadden." Dorothy came forward and curtsied quite low so that 'Bertie' could have a good view of her breasts, which he had declared 'a national asset of his Empire!' the last time they met. The smile on his face proved that he did, indeed, remember and Dorothy was a little shocked, surprised and amused when 'dirty Bertie' [as she called him] actually winked. The dour looking queen just smiled and nodded her head very gracefully. Dorothy and Margret headed for the anti-chamber and were stopped by Captain Stubbs who smiled at Dorothy and complimented both women on their appearance. He slipped Dorothy a note, bowed and stepped away. As they slowly walked to rejoin the very proud Uncle William, Maggie leaned to Dottie's ear and whispered, "Do you know that Miss Elizabeth Kensington-Grove who was also presented today?" Dorothy shook her head, gripping the note. Maggie touched her arm and smiled, "You soon will, she was the other girl that Bertie picked today and received a note from dear Stubby [Captain Stubbs?] I'm sure you'll get on famously. It appears naughty Bertie wants to try that damn chair again!"

Dorothy just stared at her and then both women laughed. It appears that Dottie was summoned to give a second Royal Command Performance!

THE END

EPISODE 5: "A TERRIBLE GLIMPSE OF THINGS TO COME?"

Alcohol – Smoking – Strong language [including racial slurs] – Strong sexual references – Strong violence – Mild Adult Erotica.

 Approximately 45 to 60 minutes.

 Remember: **Adult Content.**

EPISODE CONTENTS.

1. 'WOMEN, UNLIKE MOST MEN, ARE ABLE TO ACCEPT MYSTERY, ACCEPT WHATEVER COMES TO THEM – EVEN IF IT'S NOT LOGICAL.'
Start page: 356

2. 'IT'S THE POSSIBILITY OF A HAVING A DREAM COME TRUE THAT MAKES LIFE INTERESTING.'
Start page: 365

3. 'SOMETIMES WHEN TWO WORLDS COLLIDE, A BETTER ONE IS CREATED.'
Start page: 372

4. 'IF PEOPLE COULD READ MY MIND, I'D GET PUNCHED IN THE FACE A LOT....'
Start page: 379

5. 'ALL THE GIRLS LOVE A SAILOR!'
Start page: 385

6. 'QUAND IL ME PREND DANS LES BRAS, IL ME PARLE TOUT BAS, JE VOIS LA VIE EN ROSE.'
Start page: 394

7. 'IN EVERY CONCEIVABLE MANNER, THE FAMILY IS A LINK TO OUR PAST, A BRIDGE TO OUR FUTURE.'
Start page: 402

8. 'MANDELA EFFECT.'
Start page: 407

IMPORTANT AUTHOR'S NOTE:
"The names and places of some characters have been changed to protect the innocent and ficticious characters created in their stead. Thank you."

CHAPTER 1. 'WOMEN, UNLIKE MOST MEN, ARE ABLE TO ACCEPT MYSTERY, ACCEPT WHATEVER COMES TO THEM – EVEN IF IT'S NOT LOGICAL.' Cher.

"Hey man; what you doing here? Something going down the Prince should know about boy?" the huge man lifted the brow of his enormous hat which boasted a pea-cock feather and grinned. 'The Prince' of 47th street was well known to Detective Davies Washington; he had busted him a couple of times on minor drug and driving stuff. The Prince certainly didn't hold anything against the young cop; he was known to be fair to the 'brothers' and of course; he was a 'brother' himself!

Davies just smiled and they slapped hands; "Ain't nothing going down my man. Waiting for my girl; we're going to see that." He jerked a thumb up at the cinema sign [it was showing 'The French Connection', a big hit from 1971] and the Prince nodded; "I hear its mother fucking bad ass!" Davies nodded; "I hope the girl likes it. On to a Chinese at the Golden Lotus afterwards man. Make a night of it." Davies slapped the big man's shoulder smiling; "She's here." The Prince stared down the crowded pavement and whistled; "Sweet Jesus my man; you've pulled a pretty white princess. Does your mother know?" He chuckled and they slapped hands again. Davies watched him slip into the bright red overloaded; El Dorado Grand and it pulled away and slowly moved off with the traffic. Davies stared down the street and watched her walking towards him; slowly starting to smile.

She was wearing a white t-shirt with no bra and 'hot-pants' that left very little to the imagination. Her hair tied back with a bright red ribbon and Davies had to chuckle as she made a point of touching her throat, a couple of times. She was wearing a small black lace collar. Davies laughed and smoothed his leather jacket down and ran both hands through his short afro hair. He knew that she was wearing the black collar to show that she was a Blackman's little white girl [according to the folk-law of the 1970's.] He wiped his face and grinned. He didn't care about the comments from his black friends and colleagues at the 34th precinct about dating a 'snow bunny'. He really didn't care; he just wanted to be with her.

She threw an arm around his neck and kissed him full on the lips,
He gripped her tightly and breathed deep; she smelt like heaven.
"I thought we could catch a film and then a Chinese sit in, if
that's ok with you?" She nodded and pushed her arm through his
and they walked to the cinema entrance. He looked down at her
backside and groaned; the cheeks of her peach shaped arse were
hanging out the shorts. He reached down and slapped one. "I
really want you baby sister." He whispered.

The girl ran her hand down his shirt; damp with sweat and
brushed against the zipper of his flared trousers. "I think I can
see that or do you keep your service revolver down there!" They
both laughed and found a couple of seats in the back row. The
film was starting and they held hands and kissed a couple of
times. Davies whispered in the darkness; "It doesn't matter
where you go Dorothy, I'll always love you and come and get
you." They kissed quite passionately and his hand disappeared
under her t-shirt. She made no attempt to stop him.

That's when the cinema lights came on and Davies wiped his
eyes and stared at the people passing by him; heading for the
exits. He sat for a few minutes and realized he had been sleeping
in the damn cinema again. He eased himself up and stared down
at the empty seat next to him. He slowly lifted the bright red
ribbon from the back of the chair and lifted it to his nose; it smelt
like heaven. Now totally confused Davies stumbled from the
theatre and headed for his car; parked on a meter with an 'OUT
OF SERVICE' bag on its head. He grabbed the bag and jumped
in; the car was like a sauna and he pulled the window down and
breathed deep a couple of times. New York City, in this summer
of 1971 was steaming in a heat wave.

He switched on his radio and called dispatches to say that he was
back in the green and ready to roll. The woman officer at Control
told him that his partner was ready to be picked up at court.
Davies acknowledged the call and set off. He simply couldn't get
the girl from his thoughts. That was the third dream this week
that she had appeared in. Who the hell was she? He never went
out with white girls – they caused a lot trouble between the
brothers - and his mother wouldn't like it very much!

Dorothy woke and sat up; she was bathed in sweat and lit the
small bedside lamp with shaking fingers. She grabbed the water
glass and drank it down. That was the third bloody dream this

week that the good looking young Black man had appeared in. She leaned back on her pillows and breathed slowly; a black man, in her dreams she's been going with a black man in public, kissing him and holding him close… She actually smiled a little; now that would definitely get her drummed out the Whitechapel Ladies Cycling Club!

She felt cold and wrapped the sheets around herself and stared about her room. At the least the blooming weather in her dreams was a hell of lot warmer than here. The winter snows had come late, but they certainly made up for it now that Christmas was nearly upon them. She leaned over and pulled open the top drawer on her small bedside cabinet and pulled out a notepad and pencil. She started to write down all she could remember about yet another dream concerning a strange looking New York City and the handsome young man who apparently was a CID officer from the 34th Precinct.

Dorothy fell asleep again, but didn't dream and was woken by Ellen with a large cup of tea. She pulled the curtains back and Dorothy saw it was still dark outside. "More snow has come down overnight Miss. Your brother was called out in the night; apparently a couple of Irish fellows were caught down the docks with a crate full of blooming rifles!" She picked up Dorothy's notepad and pencil and sighed; "Another bleeding dream about that young dark man?" Dorothy nodded and sipped her most welcome tea. "Your Uncle William is up already and working in his study. Mrs. Harvey says the breakfast will be ready in about an hour. The milkman was late again because of the snow; apparently his bleeding Horse – called Freddie – doesn't like snow!"

Dorothy smiled and asked if her bath was run; Ellen nodded and replaced the pencil and notepad on the bedside cabinet. She chuckled; "People say that vivid dreams are wishes that go unfulfilled. My Aunt Joyce says that she was chatted up by a couple of black sailors when she was the barmaid at the Royal Standard. But Grandfather would have beaten the crap out of her; just for talking to them, never mind going out with one."

Ellen headed for the bathroom with a couple of towels and Dorothy eased from the bed and stood by the window, watching the snow falling. She slipped off her nightdress and stood naked. She realized that her nightdress was damp from sweat. She dropped it on the bed, to go into the laundry basket. Dorothy stood over the bath and splashed the water; it was wonderfully warm and inviting. Ellen looked a little puzzled; "Have you got a rash or something Miss. That mark on your bum wasn't there yesterday." Dorothy stood in front of the mirror and showed her bum to it. The mark looked like three fingers from a big hand!

"I sat on a bench yesterday. The slats in the seat must have marked me." She muttered and stepped into the bath. Ellen just nodded and laid the towel on the bathroom chair and wandered off. She lay sponging herself and thought about the handsome black detective; Davies Washington. The dreams had appeared far more vivid ever since that mysterious postcard had arrived. Uncle William had given it to Sims to check out if it really was from 1971. The huge building in the photograph didn't exist; well, not currently in 1903.

She also wondered if it would bring Jericho Tibbs and his team to this time to investigate. That would certainly liven up Christmas!

Pushing the sponge over her body, she couldn't drive the naughty thoughts of Davis Washington from her mind, and she realized she didn't want to. She could almost taste his kisses – filled with passion – and feel his big hand on her breast as the moving picture played out. She sighed loudly and smiled, thinking about Rosie, Dottie really wished she was here in the bath, if only to talk to. But their baths together invariably ended up in love making. Dorothy lay back and didn't have a pleasant day dream; she was gently placing a gorgeous little dark skinned baby girl into her push chair and the two shabbily dressed white men – who were rolling dice on the pavement – called out to her and she turned to say something. The oldest man called her a Blackman's mattress and the other one laughed. "So poxed up are you, is a darkie all you could get?" The older man slapped his friends back, "Couldn't find a decent white man after working the streets I expect." They both were laughing and then she heard the shots and the men stopped their game. A young black man ran from the colourful shop, dollars slipping from his fingers with a gun in the other. He turns and fires again, causing the shop window to explode inwards and ran past Dorothy and turned the corner, disappearing. That's when Dorothy saw and heard the little woman standing and screaming in the doorway, shouting for an ambulance and the police. The two men continued playing their game, totally unconcerned by the events surrounding them.

An elderly man appeared from the Ice-cream parlour next door and then ran back inside, shouting he would call the cops. Dorothy picked up the child and walked slowly to the doorway, stepping over broken glass and loose dollar bills, now being scooped up by the two gamblers. The little women was on her knees, cradling a grey haired old man in her arms, she was crying and shaking, looking Dorothy straight in the eyes, "He killed Solomon for thirty one dollars! Thirty one bloody dollars! He had opened the till, he didn't do anything and the ….the black bastard just shot him." She stared at the crying infant and shook her head, waving an arm to the door, "Get out of my shop you fucking bitch and take that little black bastard with you….you fucking whore!....you piece of white crap…." She broke down sobbing and Dorothy could hear the sirens getting closer.

She hurried from the dreadful scene, wiping tears away. Sitting up in the bath, now only tepid, she realized she was shivering and stood up grabbing a towel from the chair next to the bath. And sat on it, slowly drying herself. The daydream had been so vivid and powerful; she had seen the red pool of blood spreading from the old man, feel the heat of the day and smell the sweat and booze on the two gamblers. But all she could think of was the infant cradled in her arms.

Dorothy adjusted her bonnet and looked down the pew and smiled; Reggie had really made the effort and looked every inch the gentleman for his first visit to his new church and new congregation. Harry leaned across and whispered; "You just have to admire him and the reverend; especially the reverend."

Dorothy nodded; "Who would have believed that old Rashwood had such determination and commitment to his principles. It may have taken him two years but he did it."

It had taken that long to get Reggie [Titus] accepted into the congregation at St. Thomas's Church. But the reverend had overcome all objections and Reggie sat proudly with most for the cast and crew from the Paradise Theatre [which was about three streets away]. Harry knew the battle the old clergyman had fought, including denouncing several regular worshippers from the pulpit. "God's children come in all creeds and colours; but they are ALL his children!" he had thundered from the box. It had worked and Reggie was finally accepted into the congregation; the first person of 'colour' to be so welcomed in the small church.

But about a quarter of the good reverend's congregation had moved to St. Margret's in protest. Uncle William patted her hand and gestured with his bible to Reggie; "If pride is a sin; then our Titus is clearly guilty and so am I." Dorothy really smiled at that remark. She knew that her dear Uncle had moved heaven and earth to get Reggie accepted here. Well, so had Harry and her. She glanced back and saw Rosie smiling at her, sitting next to her dozing husband Albert. Her two boys sat either side looking utterly bored. That's when Dorothy caught sight of the young man sitting in the second aisle from the doors.

He was a big man with an expensive suit and hat. He ran a hand through his sandy blond hair and looked about the church. Dottie was well taken by his stunning blue eyes. They almost sparkled with brightness and life. Harry tapped her hand; "Good looking bugger, I bet he's a hit with women; any women!"

Dorothy nodded; "Do you know, I think I've seen him a couple of times at the theatre sitting in one of the private boxes. I've never seen anyone with him." Uncle William casually glanced over his shoulder and rubbed his chin; "I seem to know that face. I think he's been in the local paper." He took a second quick look and nodded. "Yes, that has to be him; he's an American professor staying locally; working on some project in collaboration with some English scientist who lives around here. Apparently he's quite famous in the States." He smiled at Dorothy; "Not married from what I understand and a great fan of magic shows."

Harry chuckled; "Or beautiful women like our Dottie." That made Dorothy sigh and everyone stood as the reverend Rashwood made for the pulpit and told everyone the first hymn was 'Onward Christian Soldiers' and smiled broadly at Reggie with some real satisfaction. He didn't appear upset that a quarter of his congregation had disappeared out the door.

Everyone sat and the good Reverend started his sermon; it was about tolerance and love for fellow men. That made Uncle William chuckle a little. That's when there was an enormous crashing sound and everyone leapt to their feet and stared at the empty seats at the back of the church, by the open doors.

A dark figure lay slumped across a couple of empty pews; he appeared to be smoking hot! There were gasps of surprise, amazement and a little horror as the darkly dressed figure rose slowly to his feet and stood swaying. He appeared to be dressed in a blue 'boiler suit' with small black goggles which he pulled from his face and shouted; "For God sake its total bollocks! Your nothing but ghosts…." He gripped the back of the pew with both hands and shook his head; "Everything you know is bollocks! All this is gone in a ….." he yelled and collapsed on the stone floor with a bang and lay silent.

Harry was already running up the aisle followed by Uncle William, Dorothy and Reggie. The young American professor was already knelling by the still figure. He looked up and said grimly; "I think the poor soul is dead." A little group had formed around the strange figure and Harry turned the man over and nodded his agreement; "He's dead. Someone fetch a constable." Rosie's Albert tipped his hat to Harry and disappeared through the doors.

Rosie gripped Dorothy by the arm and whispered; "What the hell was he talking about; who are bloody ghosts?" She said quietly. Dorothy shook her head; she didn't know.

The impromptu and tragic arrival of the strange young man ended the church service for that Sunday and some of the congregation – who had remained to watch – gathered about the reverend as he stood by the church doors and watched two burly police officers carrying the man from his church on a wooden and canvas stretcher; covered with a white sheet. Harry patted his shoulder and then followed the stretcher to the police horse ambulance.

The young Professor tipped his hat to Dorothy and Uncle William, he smiled a little;"If this was a stage act; that would be a real gold plated show stopper." Dorothy had to chuckle quietly at that. But Uncle William just sighed; "You were nearest the doors; did you see him rush in?" The American shook his head; "No, he just seemed to appear in front of me. He had all that light smoke pouring off him, but he certainly wasn't alight. When I touched him; he was ice cold!"

Uncle William nodded and took Dorothy by the arm; "Let's get back to the theatre. Harry will probably join us there when he's finished dealing with the poor soul." Dorothy agreed and with Reggie following left the chaotic church and hailed a cab. Dorothy glanced back and saw the strange professor standing in the small churchyard; he appeared to be talking to himself!

Uncle William just shrugged his shoulders; "Apparently all brilliant men are a little eccentric." Reggie stared out the window and turned back to his friends; "That young American has been to the theatre at least three times this week. Sits in a private box looking quite bored until our magic act starts, then he sits up and doesn't miss a trick." Uncle William smiled broadly and jerked a thumb at Dorothy. "Maybe your costume is a little too revealing!"

Reggie leaned forward and then sat back. "Old Sean – the stage doorman – tells me that he arrives in a big black carriage with a young woman who always keeps her coat hood up and remains in the carriage until he rejoins her. He always leaves after our spot on stage ends. He doesn't bother to watch the other acts."

Uncle William nodded and tapped Dorothy's hand; "Looks like you have an admirer, but I wonder who the woman is?" Dorothy shrugged her shoulders and then remembered what Rosie had said after last night's performance.

"Rosie tells me that she saw the black carriage with the lone woman waiting and recognized the driver; despite his apparent attempts to keep his face covered. He is a certain Maxwell John Shoemaker – an ex-docker – who's done some time in prison for theft and violence. She believes he was released from Pentonville last year and has kept his nose clean." Dorothy spoke quietly to her colleagues. Uncle William started to fill his pipe; "Our young American keeps some strange company then; a woman of mystery and an ex-felon."

The cab arrived at the theatres stage entrance and Uncle William paid the cab driver. Big Tom was standing by the stage door watching young Arthur pasting up a couple of notices. He smiled at Dorothy and gestured up the stairs; "I had Miss Player put them in your dressing room Miss. They must have cost a fortune!"

The puzzled look on her face made him grin; "Flowers Miss. Bloody loads of them!" Dorothy thanked him and headed up the stairs; the smell of the bouquets was overwhelming and Dorothy pushed open the dressing room door and stood back. The place was filled with flowers; they were everywhere. She also noticed that the floor was strewn with petals. She folded her arms and just had to smile; Isis the cat was having a great time pulling off petals and throwing stems about!

She scooped the mischievous cat up and turned to Uncle William who was behind her; laughing. "Well at least Isis liked them. It's a bit much for my taste." Uncle William strode in and lifted a tag from one bunch of very expensive roses; "From an ardent admirer." He shrugged his shoulders and read some other tags which all had the same inscription.

Dorothy turned to Titus and asked him to fetch young Arthur – reluctantly; as she couldn't stand the nasty little git – and hand out bunches of the damn flowers to the girls in the chorus line and some for Miss Player if she wanted any. Oh, and some for Cedric Barnes, the female impersonator whose act was very naughty and hugely popular with Paradise Theatre patrons. Young Cedric would appreciate the flowers, he regularly received bunches from admirers who simply refused to believe it was a 'drag' act. And he was a man. As Dorothy told him, "Cedric, those are a real compliment to your performance." He had just smiled, "its all pantomime darling, just pantomime without the sarcasm and big breasts!"

"Cedric is probably referring to 'Pantomime Dames' which were and still are, popular on stage. These were male actors playing 'female' roles, normally with well over the top acting!" SJW.

Titus nodded and headed back down the stairs. Uncle William rubbed his nose and sneezed; "Never did like bloody flowers." He muttered and started to shift some of the unwanted blooms outside the door. Dorothy placed the happy cat on a chair and put the kettle on the small stove. "I need some decent tea." She said and stared out the window. There was a big black carriage sitting at the bottom of the small alley that ran behind the theatre. The driver – a big man dressed in black – had his face covered with a scarf; not unusual in the middle of winter; but something disturbed Dorothy and she called her uncle over.

They both watched as a woman – small and slender – wearing a black fur coat with the hood up, stepped into the carriage; the door opening from inside. The carriage rolled away gathering speed. Uncle William tapped the glass; "I think we know who the flowers are from."

Dorothy nodded nonchantilly and stared up at the ever darkening sky; "I think we're going to have some more snow."

![Quill and inkwell icon] **CHAPTER 2. 'IT'S THE POSSIBILITY OF A HAVING A DREAM COME TRUE THAT MAKES LIFE INTERESTING.'
Paulo Coheo.**

Detective Davies Washington lifted the sheet on the late Solomon Rubin and shook his head, turning to the uniform patrolman who was smoking, leaned up against the counter. "So only the old lady witnessed the actual robbery and killing?" The patrolman nodded, his shift was due to end in half an hour and it was bowling night. "Apparently there were a couple of bums [tramps or vagrants] pitching dice a few yards away, near the corner and the perp [perpetrator] ran past them. But the chances of finding them are...well, like zero."

Davies stood and sighed, "Any description of the perp?" The officer shrugged his shoulders, "The old lady said just another black punk kid with a gun." Davies grunted, "Work on her and get a better description than fucking that. That's half the kids in the city." The officer nodded and finished his cigarette. "Oh, the ice cream man said there was a very good looking young white chick near the kerb with a kid in its pushchair. Apparently the bum's were giving her a hard time because the kid was black."

Davies rubbed his chin, "She could be the best witness we have and may give a useful description of the young punk, so we need to find her." The officer chuckled, "Yeah, she's bound to come forward after seeing that punk plug the old man. That's a real incentive to the point the finger and get wasted yourself."
Another young patrolman appeared in the doorway and jerked a thumb behind him, "The photographer is here Davies, and the Coroner's truck is stuck in traffic apparently. A group of bloody faggots are marching today demanding something. Who the fuck knows what those queer bastards are complaining about."

Davies just nodded and pulled out his notebook, scribbling a few sentences, and then thought about him and Dottie. She would

---

have been shopping around here today and certainly would have their daughter – Lilly – with her. "What a fucking shit world." He muttered and the Patrolman leaned against the counter laughed, "You can say that a fucking again!"

Detective Santos Gomez sauntered in and stuck a cigarette in his mouth, "Dispatch is on the horn, shouting, they want us over at Seventieth and Main, apparently some fucking local councilor's daughter has been knocked about by the fucking Hondo's [a Hispanic street gang] and he's screaming down the phone at the Commissioner. What the fuck was the dumb broad doing hanging around their turf is beyond me, unless she likes it rough and Mexican….or trying to score some good Columbian shit."

Davies joined his partner and pushed his notebook away. "Let's go, there's fuck all we can achieve here. But I need to call Dottie." Santos grinned, "Holy mother Davies, soon as you hooked up with that pretty white chick, you've turned into an old married man. Boy, does she have you on a leash." Davies just smiled, "Yeah, but I'm one happy mother fucker of a dog on that leash." They both laughed, giving a wave to Floyd – the police photographer – as he walked up to the door. Santos gestured into the shop, "Nothing great Floyd my man, straight forward plug and run." The old man just nodded and disappeared into the shop.

They walked to Davies's new black and green Plymouth Satellite and slipped in, with Santos grabbing the mic, calling Dispatch that they were rolling on the Seventieth and Main call. Big Delilah [the dispatcher] informed them that Inspector O'Malley was also on that call and wanted their backsides there, like yesterday. They both looked at each other, "Fuck! If 'the mallet' is putting in an appearance, it must be big….and probably political." Santos said, not a happy man. Inspector Michael 'the mallet' O'Malley was their reporting superior officer and made it known he didn't like 'darkies'. So Santos and Davis were not his most favourite detectives. It was also known; he was bucking to be district Chief of detectives and looking to score points whenever he could. He had earned the nickname 'the mallet' from an incident from his patrolman days, apparently three local thugs caught robbing a hardware store, armed with knives, had set about the lone patrolman upon his arrival at the scene. Legend has it, he grabbed a mallet and all three needed hospital treatment and received seven to nine years in Rochester prison. He wasn't a man to upset. He was built like a bear and had the same attitude as one who suffered with constant toothache. But he got the job done and looked after his 'boys'. Both Santos and Davis had to respect the man for that alone.

They joined the slow moving traffic as the city sweltered in the hot weather, passing the Coroner's truck heading to the late Solomon Rubin's Liquor store.

"You really do know how to show a girl a good time." Dorothy muttered to Harry and grinned. He helped her from the carriage and she was really pleased that she had decided to wear her big boots; the snow was at least four inches deep in places and more was forecast for this afternoon. She looked up at the old and imposing building and sighed; fantastic, just where a girl wants to be on her afternoon off; the bloody morgue!

Two uniform constables were coming down the steps towards them; one – the elder one – was smiling, whilst the much younger man looked quite pale; no, he looked a little green. They both saluted Harry who just had to chuckle. He said quietly; "The young probationer's first visit to the morgue; all part of the training." Dorothy just shook her head and pulled her coat tighter.

They walked through the quiet building and Harry knocked on a big black door marked 'PRIVATE' and a young man in a long white coat pulled it open. He nodded; "Hello Mr. Hadden, Doctor Goldstein and Doctor Parish are expecting you." Harry and Dorothy stepped through and Harry turned to her; "That's a bad sign if Doc Goldstein has called on old man Parish for a second opinion."

Dorothy brushed some snow from her coat and said quietly; "Yes, but a second opinion on which corpse?" The young man offered to take their coats, but both declined; the morgue was like a block of ice on warm days and they both would sooner keep their damn coats on. They pushed through another door with a frosted glass panel and were met by Doc Goldstein wiping his hands with a towel. He wasn't smiling. Standing by the two marble slabs was Doctor Gabrielle Parish; the Divisional Surgeon from Forest Gate. He really smiled at Dorothy.

"Which mystery do you wish first Harry?" Doc Goldstein asked with a sigh, Harry rubbed his face and pushed back his hat; "Let's try the 'John Doe' who died in church. Which I'm reliably informed had nothing to do with old Rashwood's bloody sermon!" Now that cheered old Goldstein up and he gestured to the first tray. "Well, to sum it up, both Gabrielle and I cannot find any reason why the young man is dead. Except that he is of course."

That's not a good start mused Dorothy; then wondered who the other corpse was and why were they are a mystery too. "Healthy young man about twenty five years old, he must have been an athlete or something. Can't find a damn reason why he should be dead. All his major organs are in perfect condition. No signs of any previous serious diseases or injuries. He's almost in perfect condition for a man of his age; almost too perfect." Doc Goldstein said and threw in the towel into a small linen basket.

"We've sent some blood to Whitechapel Hospital Laboratory to check for poison or anything else. They may turn up something, but I wouldn't hold my breath." He added and started to roll down his sleeves. Doctor Parish tapped the corpse nearest to him; "I have to agree; he shouldn't be dead. No damage to his brain or vital organs; nothing." He looked down at the body covered with a white sheet and sighed; "To us doctors that's quite something of a mystery."

Harry nodded; "There was nothing on the body to identify him except this." Harry held up a small gold chain with a blood red stone attached. Both doctors stared at it, then Harry pushed it back into his pocket; "We've ran it past a couple of jewelers and they can't identify the damn stone either." He added.

Doctor Goldstein gestured to the other table with its corpse also covered with a clean white sheet. "Another damn mystery right there; though not as perplexing as the first. " He pulled back the sheet a little and lifted a slender, very white arm. "What's the mystery about this one?" Dorothy asked quietly and Doctor Parish smiled at her – again – and gestured to the corpse. He spoke softly: "There's no mystery how he died; a bloody great puncture straight through the heart; clear evidence that he was shot at close range." Dorothy nodded and looked a little puzzled; "What's mysterious about that?" The doctor held up both hands; "No exit wound and no sign of the damn bullet!"

"So we have a magic bloody bullet now." Muttered Harry and

took the files from Doc Goldstein. The second corpse – another young man in his twenties – had been found in Dock Road at midnight; obviously shot through the heart at close range. He still hadn't been identified yet. He also carried nothing that could identify him. Harry gripped the files and thanked both doctors, he nodded to Dorothy that it was time to leave. But Doctor Parish called him back. He pulled the sheet back on the first man [the dead church invader!] and held up a limp white arm. Harry and Dorothy both leaned forward and could see the tattoo on the underneath of the limb.

"Crossed swords and some kind of inscription." Harry said and looked closer. "It's Latin, a motto perhaps; tergum in lumine means back to the light." He added. The Doctor smiled; "Unusual for a copper to speak Latin, but then you've always surprised people Harry." He then gestured to the arm being held up by his colleague; it was the same tattoo!

Doc Goldstein pulled on his jacket; "Now that's some bloody co-incidence; I don't think." He smiled and walked to the door; "Good luck with this one Harry. You'll going to need it I think. Strange co-incidences that both men are young and were very fit and athletic, both carry the same tattoo in the exactly the same place. "

Harry nodded; he now knew full well that the corpses were linked to each other; but how and why?

Doctor Parish chuckled; "Old Goldstein has forgotten to tell you one little fact about the second corpse and I think it may be relevant." Doctor Goldstein stood in the doorway and cursed; but smiled a little. Harry looked up from the files and nodded, Doctor Parish smiled; "The second body was dressed as a very fine young lady of quality!"

Dorothy walked across to the second body and stared at the Pale face and sighed; "Heaven's Harry, he must have been quite beautiful as a woman. I would love to see the outfit he was wearing."

Doctor Parish chuckled again. "Believe me young Dorothy, it was a very expensive ensemble; I know because I have two teenage daughters who are not married and I still foot their clothes bill. That young man was dressed like a Hapsburg Princess. He made a stunning young woman apparently." Harry folded his arms; he made a note to go through the young man's females clothes thoroughly. "Maybe he was killed by a disappointed client. As well you know that some young men importune down the docks dressed up as women. Maybe he just met the wrong client."

The two doctors nodded their agreement with that and tided up their equipment. Dorothy lifted the sheet on the first corpse [the man who died in church] and with her gloved hand, slowly lifted a clump of hair that lay by the man's left ear. She ran a couple of fingers through his hair and lifted up another clump of hair! She showed her hand to the others; "I don't think you can die of alopecia, but our friend had it really bad." Both doctors returned to the corpse and picked at the dead man's head; they both came up with small clumps of hair.

"If he was shedding at this rate, he should be bloody bald." Muttered Doc Goldstein and wiped his hands again. "Come on Dorothy, let's get some breakfast." Harry walked to the door and Dorothy followed. "When will the Coroner convene on these two?" she asked. Harry shrugged his shoulders; "Probably Monday. Means I have a bleeding busy day Monday. I'm at Crown Court in the afternoon." He smiled and the pair left the somber building and caught a cab for home.

Dorothy sat opposite her brother at the breakfast table and buttered her toast liberally, "Harry, does the file on the young man who was dressed as a woman show that he had been having sex with other men?" Harry almost dropped his knife and fork in shock, but recovered and wagged his fork at her; "Dorothy, you're a young unmarried woman and shouldn't know anything about homosexual activities, especially that one!" But he did grin and picked up the file and glanced through it.

He rubbed his chin; "Apparently he was no virgin in that respect, so he could well have been importuning and met the wrong customer, who knows. Do you think that has any bearing on the case?" Dorothy shrugged her shoulders and Ellen came through the door with a covered pan and smiled; "Mrs. Harvey has cooked you a couple of lovely poached eggs Miss. I'll put them on your toast." Dorothy was about to wave the offer away when Harry spoke up; "Yes, that great, slap them on her toast."

Dorothy just stared at her brother as Ellen carefully placed the eggs on her spare piece of toast. Harry grinned; "Get 'em down your neck girl and don't argue about it."

Dorothy sat in silence and sprinkled some salt on her eggs and reluctantly ate them, under the watchful eye of her brother. Ellen poured more tea and cleared away some of the breakfast cutlery. "Oh, there was a delivery for your Miss. From Brem & Haver's; I put it the morning room." Dorothy now smiled; "Hopefully, it's the new trick that Uncle William designed and had them make. I'll unpack it after breakfast." Harry nodded and placed the file down. "How can you shoot someone at close range and there is no exit wound. That's impossible."

Dorothy chuckled; "Gandalf the Great does it most nights at the Empire in Devon Street. That's he's signature trick." Harry just grunted and finished his breakfast.

The front door bell tinkled and Ellen headed for the hallway. Harry pushed his plate away and asked Dorothy if they were expecting visitors. She shook her head and dabbed her mouth with a napkin. They could hear voices in the hallway and Harry rose and went to the door.

Dorothy also rose from her chair and reached the door before Harry turned around and gestured to the smart young man standing in the doorway; "Dorothy, may I introduce Professor John Hammond, from Washington DC. You will remember from the incident in the church." Dorothy nodded and said a quiet 'Good Morning' to the smiling young man.

He spoke directly to Harry; "It was the Reverend Rashworth that handed it me. He seemed to think it was something I may possess, but I believe that young man who collapsed and died in the church may have dropped it." Harry nodded and asked to see the 'thing'. Dorothy was now also interested. The young man fiddled in his coat pocket, still speaking to Harry; "I went down the Precinct Station and they told me you would be at home, so I came straight round." His American accent was clear and quite pronounced. Finally, he pulled the object from his pocket and held it out in both hands.

Harry and Dorothy stared at it and Harry lifted it and held the thing on the palm of his hand. "What on earth is it?" He said softly and Dorothy carefully turned it over on her brother's hand.

"I have never seen glass like that and I have no idea what the rest of it is made of." The professor admitted.

The object was a small rectangle box, incredibly thin and lightweight, with an apparently dark glass front and a silver coloured rear. It was about the size of a cigarette case that gentlemen carried. "It's very difficult to open, if it can be opened and seems quite seamless, not a crack or locking mechanism to be found. What its function is, I have no idea." The professor folded his arms and sighed.

"Whatever it contains – if it contains anything – must be really small and thin." Dorothy concluded; she was utterly fascinated by the strange little box. Harry gestured back to the dining room; "Come in and have some tea." The young professor nodded and everyone returned to the breakfast table. The professor followed them in with quite a smile on his face and wondered just what he will catch with his bait. He accepted some tea and quietly smiled at Dorothy: he's other bait.

CHAPTER 3. 'SOMETIMES WHEN TWO WORLDS COLLIDE, A BETTER ONE IS CREATED'. Susan Gale.

"I'm not sure if your friend Paul will appreciate the good Yankee professor turning up at tonight's performance; just to see you." Harry chuckled and Dorothy sighed; "Stop trying to marry me off Harry. It doesn't suit you. When I meet the right man I'll bloody seriously think about it." She sat in the armchair and wondered about the handsome young professor and his love of H.G.Well's and Jules Verne. He had told her to look out for an exciting writer called Morgan Robertson who had written a book about a tragic shipwreck. It didn't sound that good to Dorothy, but Harry said he would search it out.

Harry accepted his hat and coat from Ellen, who cleared away the breakfast crockery and disappeared back to the kitchens. "Where are you off to now?" Dorothy asked him and Harry didn't smile. "May have a lead about our cross dressing corpse. A Salvation Army captain working amongst the down and outs at the docks told one of the uniform lad's about a young man and woman, apparently searching for someone amongst them. The woman certainly fits the description of our second corpse. Apparently when a couple of more friendly vagrants tried to chat her up; the language was very colourful!"

Dorothy chuckled; "Ah, a lady after my own heart. Did your policeman say who they were looking for?" Harry nodded and started to button up his heavy winter coat. "Yes, an African man in his twenties. Good looking and speaking with a strange accent, believed to be American. I've circulated his name and description to the Dock's police in case he's a sailor." He headed for the door and Dorothy called after him; "Well, what name is he using?" Harry stopped by the door and placed his hat on, he really didn't want to say, but Dorothy insisted; "Oh, apparently he calls himself Davies Washington." He stared at the look on Dorothy's face and slowly walked back over to her.

He unbuttoned his coat and knelt next to her chair; "What the hell is up Dorothy? It just happens to be the same name as on that postcard. That's all; just a co-incidence." Dorothy shook her head and grabbed his hand, taking a couple of breaths and told Harry all about her crazy dreams of the dark stranger called Davis Washington and living in the year 1971 in New York.

Harry sat on the floor and wiped his face. "Sweet Jesus Dottie that cannot be a co-incidence!" She nodded; "Harry, It's quite mad. I mean, women have their freedom and they have thrown all their dignity away, they dress like street whores and behave like them. I can't even describe the clothes I was almost wearing. The world was horrible; noise and filth. Crime everywhere and no one could care less about anyone except themselves. There were strange cars everywhere and so many unhappy people. It was a terrible glimpse of the future and it's only sixty-eight years away."

Harry patted her hand; "It was a just a glimpse, part of a dream and you know how dreams are; they're very rarely based in reality. Did you really want to be with this character - the black detective – in your dream?" Dorothy stared at her brother and whispered; "I think I did." Harry sighed and stood. He gave her a kiss; "I'll see you later and don't fret about a bleeding dream. You know they are all normally quite mad and really don't mean anything."

Dorothy nodded and sat back in the chair and stared at the fire burning in the grate. She could see more snow falling through the big window and muttered to herself that it was a damn lot warmer in her dream!

Dorothy wondered if she had been too harsh in her condemnation of the future in her dreams. After all; it appears a white woman could date a black man but it was met by some with fear and hatred. Despite only having risen from her bed a couple of hours ago; Dorothy felt tired, like she had travelled miles and finally got home to relax. She closed her eyes and thought about heading to the theatre, taking their new trick with her. That would please Uncle William; he had left early to pick up Reggie and go through a couple of tricks with him. He was now playing a far more active role in the show. But Dorothy was now apparently sleeping and dreaming again.

The apartment was in semi-darkness and she could hear the traffic outside despite being on the fourth floor. There was some music playing softly; it sounded quite good, though she didn't recognize it. She was sitting up in bed, her back against a pile of vivid coloured pillows. She ran both hands through her long hair and smiled broadly. The man was stark naked by the window, staring down into the street. He turned and shrugged his big shoulders; "Look's like some idiot jay-walked and got slapped by a cab. He must be Ok; he's standing up." He looked back down at the chaotic scene in the street. "No, a couple of guys are holding him up. Hopefully someone has called an ambulance!" he smiled and walked back to the messed up bed.

She smiled; he was big man in all respects! This was the perfect time to be together – intimately – because Lilly was asleep in her cot. Dorothy let the sheet drop and held out her hands; "Get back in bed, you're on bloody shift in an hour!" Davies just smiled and slipped in beside her; "Baby sister, I have all the time in the world for you." They came together kissing passionately, his big hands running over her naked body. She lay back and giggled. "That's the sort of service I expect from New York's finest."

"Are you Ok Miss? You're not feeling unwell are you?" Ellen was standing over the armchair looking a little concerned. Dorothy eased herself from the chair and yawned. "I'm just not getting a damn proper night's sleep. I best head for the theatre before I blooming drop off again." She muttered and Ellen went to fetch her coat and hat.

Dorothy went to the mirror and adjusted her hair a little; the dream had excited her. She sighed and accepted her hat, while Ellen pushed on her thick winter coat. She stepped outside; it was beautiful morning despite the snow that fell in little flurries. She raised her hand to the handsome cab stopped at the top of the street, then realized she had forgotten the package.

She turned back to find Ellen coming down the front door steps, grinning and carrying the package. "I think you may want this." She said and Dorothy thanked her and jumped with some grace into the cab. She watched the people and traffic passing by the slow moving cab and kept thinking about the latest dream. It's like I'm travelling to another time without leaving this one. She reasoned and gripped the package. But why was she having such strange, bewildering dreams and why now?

The cab pulled up outside the theatre and Dorothy stepped down and paid the cabby fourpence for the trip. That's when she saw the black carriage pull away from the alleyway opposite; she just had a glimpse of the young woman, shrouded in her black hat and heavy coat, then the carriage sped away.

Big Tom was at the stage door; telling young Arthur to clear the bleeding snow from the steps and put some salt down; he didn't want any of the act's breaking their bloody necks on ice. They both greeted Dorothy with a good morning and she swept into the theatre and made straight for Uncle William's dressing room. He was brewing himself a cup of tea and immediately offered Dorothy one. "Skoles has the morning off; he's being fitted for his wedding suit. A brave man that." Dorothy pulled off her coat and hat and then accepted her tea. She sat and watched her uncle open the package. "This should go down well. You are going to adore this." Dorothy leaned forward in anticipation and actually gasped; it was Isis the cat! Well, an incredible life like model of the temperamental creature.

"We can now do the switch twice and much quicker now." He explained and turned the creature in his hands; "They're done a damn good job." He said and placed the cat on the floor. Dorothy couldn't even see the operating string and chuckled as the cat moved its head around and appeared to meow.

"Maybe we won't lose so many blooming pigeons now." She said and sipped her tea. There was a knock at the door and Reggie stuck his head in; "Has the pussy arrived?" He asked with a grin. Even Dorothy managed a chuckle at that and gestured the big man in. Then she wasn't really there anymore.

The small apartment had been decorated by the pair. There were bright coloured paper chains and balloons everywhere. The tiny Christmas tree was covered in tinsel and below, had several well wrapped presents placed beneath it. Detective Davies came through the door and held up a bottle of Bourbon; "Honey, I just made the liquor store, it's like a madhouse out there. Loads of people rushing around grabbing last minute stuff!" He placed the bottle down and pulled off his long dark fur coat, shaking the snowflakes from it. That's when the bathroom door flew open and she stood there, hands on hips. She smiled broadly; "Happy Christmas darling, I thought you could open this present early."

Davies ran both hands through his hair and grinned; "I think I'm about to get the best damn holiday present a man could want." She was wearing a bright red and white Santa hat with a little bell and not much more; just red stockings and a pair of tiny red panties that were tied with a big red ribbon. She walked slowly over and ran her hands down his heaving chest; "Well, aren't you going to open your present baby?" He didn't need a second invitation. She helped pull off his clothes and the pair fell laughing onto the bed, they kissed passionately and he ran a hand over her face; "I have your present here." He held up his big clenched hand and she grabbed it and pulled the fingers apart. He held the open palm up to her; the little single diamond ring was quite beautiful. He smiled; "I thought Valentine's Day would be just right baby." She kissed his hand and nodded; "Let's start the Honeymoon early." Was all she whispered.

"You alright Dorothy?" Uncle William offered her a biscuit and Dorothy slowly took it; then realised her hands were shaking and she muttered about missing breakfast and she would get Rosie to bring some cake in. Her mind calmed down and she reasoned that seeing Reggie may have triggered the vision. Her stomach and crotch felt strange; like she had actually had a man inside her; a big man and they had been making serious love. She suddenly really needed to pee and jumped up, placing her cup down and excused herself. She sat on the toilet breathing quite deeply; her panties had been soaking when she pulled them off and she certainly hadn't pissed herself! The 'Vision' had given her an orgasm and now Dorothy was seriously worried about these dreams and visions. Maybe she was mentally ill? She dismissed that as rubbish, she had orgasms when she fucked, but not like this one! She gripped her stomach with both hands and knew that if the love making had been real; she would certainly be pregnant with the Blackman's child. She groaned and sat on the toilet for several minutes before cleaning herself up and headed back to the dressing room.

Dorothy really needed to push all this from her mind and concentrate on her performance, which she actually managed with a great deal of inner strength. That night she had another dream: she realised she was in bed with the young black man and she knew enough about the mechanics of sex to know that she was in the 'Missionary Position' having serious passionate sex. He was deep inside her; causing her a delightful mix of pain and pleasure. She was gripping his thrusting backside; telling him to give her another black baby. He's mouth found hers and their tongues were exploring each other's mouth with some urgency and desire. She was moaning and pushing her bum upwards to meet his thrusts. The little gold ring on her fourth finger on her left hand seemed huge; she was married and knew she was having honeymoon sex!

"How was the honeymoon big man? I mean, you put the cart before the horse alright having little Lilly first but now you are a married man." Santos hesitated, "How's your mum taking it now?" Davies shrugged his shoulders, "We're working on that. Estelle and Maggie like Dottie, so that's a good start. [They were his two younger sisters] Mum adores Lilly and Dottie's her mum after all." The two detectives walked into the hamburger joint, past a bored patrolman who just nodded a greeting. They were met by a dour faced Inspector O'Malley who folded his arms, "About time you two lazy bastards showed up. I put a call in for you twenty minutes ago."

Santos was about to say something but the Inspector waved that away, "This is right up your street. A real interesting one, three brothers picked on a lone white man who looked like he couldn't tear open a Cornflakes carton and he did this to them. And here's the best fucking bit: he knocked them off using his bare hands, the only weapons used were knives the brother's had." He slowly gestured behind him and Davies stared at two bodies: they were all big men, one was sprawled across a table, with his face looking like he had just been smashed full on with a sledge hammer. The second one was on the floor, laid in an 'X' position, his face contorted and missing both eyes!

Santos whistled, "The fucking dude did this with his bare hands!" he sounded shocked because he was. The Inspector chuckled and gestured to the broken window of the diner, "That's the best fucking one. That brother must weigh in at 200 pounds and the witnesses say that skinny white guy lifted him with one arm – one fucking arm – and threw him with such strength and force, that the bastard travelled thirty feet, straight through a plate glass window, smashing open his skull and back: looks like he was hit by a fucking train. Then the little white guy slowly walks out the joint....this is the best bit - after collecting his fucking take-out!"

The three detectives stood staring about the diner and Santos pushed back his bright red beret, lighting up a cigarette. "Well, I know who we should fucking arrest." Both Davies and the Inspector stared at him. Santos shrugged his shoulders and grinned, "Fucking Clark Kent!"

O'Malley groaned and lit up his cigar, "Just fucking get on with it. I doubt if we can charge the fucker with anything, but I would like to know where such a man is and who the fuck he is."
The two detectives nodded and watched the Inspector walk away. "And where the hell do we start? His description could match a million white dudes in the city. This assignment is crap and O'Malley knows it." Davies stared at the dead bodies as Floyd the photographer unpacked his cameras. "Do you two want to know what's really strange about this job?" he chuckled and lifted his camera, taking shot after shot. "What have you got for us Floyd?" Santos asked and Floyd lowered his camera, "Nothing my friends. There's nothing on the news and fuck all will appear in the papers. Little Graham the dog [an investigative journalist of some merit in the city] has whispered in my ear that the lid has been firmly put on this story, you won't read about: ever."

Davies and Santos stared at each other, then Floyd. "Did he say why?" Davies asked and Floyd shrugged his shoulders, "All the dog would say, is that his editor, told him that the lid came from Washington itself. Yeah, that's right boys, the fucking Fed's are looking at this and that's got up 'the mallet's' nose. Hence you two dumb fucks got lumbered with it." The old photographer coughed and lit up a cigarette, coughing again. "Just tread carefully my lucky lads. The Fed's won't take kindly to you pair sticking your noses into this. Apparently it's going to be all hush-hush."

The detectives stood in the sunshine and Santos lit up a cigarette and took a couple of puffs before speaking, "Davies, this fucking stinks. It's no Federal job unless…..well, why the fuck would they be interested in a self-defense killing in this city? Christ, if they find him, the mayor will pin a medal on the fucker!" He grunted and shook his head. Davies tapped his partners arm and they headed for the car as the Coroner's truck arrived. "It's like the mallet said, he wants to know the name and hereabouts of a man who can kill three armed, well built men with his bare hands, then pick up his take-away as if nothing happened. I strongly suspect the Fed's want to know who he is too."

That's when Davies saw the black Lincoln car and he whispered to Santos, "I recongnise one of those dudes in the black Lincoln: he's fucking CIA!" They climbed into Davies's car and Santos rubbed his face, "So now the fucking CIA is in on the job. All we need now is for the NSA to turn up and we have a hat-trick!"

Davies just grunted, "Guess who's sitting in the red Plymouth outside the Deli?" Santos stared across and swore: it was Special Agent Alexander Corbin from the NSA.

CHAPTER 4. 'IF PEOPLE COULD READ MY MIND, I'D GET PUNCHED IN THE FACE A LOT….' Unknown.

Dorothy and Rosie stood in the wings and watched, with some amazement, the 'Great Zardox' perform his mind reading act. His latest 'victim' – a middle aged woman – stood with her mouth open in genuine shock as he informed the audience that she was having second thoughts about her daughter's wedding; she didn't really like her future son-in-law; she didn't trust him one little bit. That went down well with the audience because the 'son-in-law' was sitting in the audience with her red faced daughter!

She fled the stage to a huge round of applause and everyone enjoyed the ensuing argument between the families, until a couple of stage hands threw them out. "They can't all be bleeding stooges? Can they?" Rosie asked Dorothy; who couldn't answer because she didn't know. "He's bloody good if they're not." She whispered. That's when he gestured to her and announced that the lovely young Egyptian slave of the magic act was next. Dottie shrugged her shoulders; why not?

She walked out on stage and was greeted by a huge round of applause and some cheers. She was wearing her slave costume which the theatre patrons loved; well, the men mostly. Zardox thanked her and told her to relax and went into his mind reading routine. He suddenly raised both arms and said loudly; "The mists of your thoughts are swirling and forming pictures. Pictures that tell a story of lost love, heartbreak and yearning. Your love is far away and separated from your arms and heart. A tall dark handsome man of good character and genuine intent; he lives in a city of noise and crime; a strange city of huge towers filled with hate and suspicion. Yet his love cannot be turned from its true course."

The crowd was cheering and clapping as Dorothy nodded yes. They loved a good tale about lost romance. Zardox slowly lowered his arms and Dorothy could see he looked perplexed; "I see violence, noise and despair on those streets that your young man walks. He yearns desperately to be with his love and will do anything to return to you. But there is another man in the mist of your thoughts." The crowd were now leaning forward on their seats and willing him to continue. Zardox held up a single hand and announced; "You know this man and his machine. He will stop at nothing to prevent you and your true love meeting. For I see he plots to keep...." Zardox started to sway; like he was suddenly drunk. He stumbled forward and whispered; "Beware Dorothy! You must never meet your love in this lifetime.....you must never meet him while living now....." he collapsed upon the stage and lay still.

There was silence for a few seconds and the curtain suddenly dropped and the crowd cheered and applauded. Big Tom quickly appeared and announced the next act while Dorothy and Rosie helped Zardox back stage.

Uncle William had appeared with Reggie and they managed to

get Zardox to Uncle William's dressing room and give him a large brandy. He sat in the chair and everyone could see the colour returning to his face as he sipped the brandy. Finally, he looked up and thanked everyone. "What happened Albert?" Uncle William asked.

Albert Passwell [Zardox's real name] almost smiled; "Sometimes the thoughts I read overwhelm me. Dorothy's were so powerful and real, they swamped my brain and everything went black." He gripped the brandy glass as Reggie poured him some more. "Thank you my friend." He said quietly and turned to Dorothy; "It's so strange my dear, you're thoughts were so strong that I believe they are no dream. Have you been seeing the dark man of your thoughts for real? I saw everything that your mind recorded like I was reading a book already in print. That young man will stop at nothing to be with you again. Yet, I think you don't feel the same? But your reason is strange, for you do love him, but you know you can't be with him."

Dorothy accepted a glass from Reggie and only sipped it. She didn't answer because Peter the senior Stage Hand was knocking and shouting; "Last five minutes Mr. Hadden!" Uncle William cursed and headed for the stage with Dorothy and Reggie close behind. They could hear big Tom announcing their act to a cheering audience.

Dorothy was a little slow with a couple of tricks, but the audience didn't notice and they received terrific applause for the finale with the mummy rising from his coffin. They assembled back in Uncle William's dressing room. Albert Passwell had already left for his lodgings and Rosie dished up fresh brewed tea. Uncle William tipped a little brandy into Dorothy's cup and smiled; "Albert, it is rumoured, is actually the real deal. Now's what's all this about the handsome dark young man your besotted with?" Dorothy eased into a chair and didn't smile, she spoke quietly; "I'll tell you back at home Uncle William." He nodded and slapped Reggie on the back; "I told you that you could handle the extra little bits. You were great my friend." Now that did put a smile on Reggie's face; he had been having some real doubts about his abilities to perform more during the act.

Dorothy sipped her brandy laced tea and thought about what Zardox had said on stage. What did he mean about the man and his machine? More importantly; what the hell did he mean about not meeting in this lifetime? What did that bloody mean? It didn't make sense. Rosie tapped her shoulder; "Come on sweetheart, let's get you changed and got off home." Dorothy nodded and thanked everyone and headed for her dressing room.

She was surprised to find Doctor Paul Shaw waiting for her. He really did smile at her costume until Rosie draped a long dressing gown over her. He kissed her hand and asked if they could talk. Dorothy nodded; "Rosie is a married women so that should be alright. The doctor followed her in and Rosie busied herself making some tea, making a terrible job at pretending not to listen to their conversation. Paul shuffled his feet and held his hat with both hands; "I've been speaking to my father……and my mother of course……about you, well us, really." Dorothy sat slowly and just nodded; she didn't smile.

He wiped his face and smiled again; "Father wants to invite you and your family over for dinner; you know; your Uncle William, Harry, any of your brothers, if they're around. Nothing formal, just a quiet family dinner and that. My two sisters and their husbands will be there and my Grandmother Mary. I thought next Sunday would be fine, if that's OK with you."

Dorothy nodded slowly and smiled a little; "That would be lovely Paul. I'll let Uncle William and Harry know." The doctor looked at the couple of big bunches of flowers on the table and didn't smile. "I thought you didn't like flowers except in the garden." He said quietly, turning his hat in his hands. Dorothy chuckled; "Goes with being on the stage; I get them from all sorts. Most don't even have a name attached to them." Paul slowly lifted the tag on the nearest bunch and smiled; "I bet you have quite a few Ardent Admirers." Dorothy just smiled and accepted a cup from Rosie who was grinning ear to ear.

The good doctor declined a cup and kissed Dorothy's hand; he was doing a shift at the London Hospital for a friend, who would be out celebrating his birthday. Rosie and Dorothy said nothing until the young man disappeared down the back stairs with a little wave of his hat. Rosie quietly closed the door and burst in laughter; "Well darling, I think you're going to be Mrs. Doctor Paul Shaw or whatever!"

Dorothy sat back down and sipped her tea. "Let's not get excited Rosie; he hasn't actually proposed. In fact, he hasn't got near to it." Rosie sat in the chair opposite and slurped her tea; "Gawd my darling, the look he gave you in that costume could have lit a lamp. Believe me Rosie knows; you'll be married in the spring. That young man won't want a long bleeding engagement having seen what he can get his hands on!"

But strangely enough; Dorothy was thinking about young Davies Washington. Rosie slapped her cup down and jumped up; "Come on darling, let's get you changed and we can tell your Uncle and Mister Hadden the good bleeding news!"

They hurried down the back stairs and behind the main stage where they could hear the crowd cat calling and booing the new act performing on stage; 'Vernon Small's the Ventriloquist' wasn't going down too well; apparently his dummy – a representation of a large fat gentlemen with monocle and top hat – had a very pronounced stutter; like Vernon himself…..

Albert [Rosie's husband] was waiting for them – he was going on night shift at the docks – and so Rosie reasoned it had to be a 'bleeding quick one' and Dorothy could take it this time. Albert was happy with that and the trio disappeared back inside, and into the changing room where they soon stripped down, and Dorothy found herself bent over the chaise lounge with Albert behind, fucking her hard and fast with some real pleasure and determination. She was gripping the back and cussing a little as the big rough man took her like a common whore, who plied her trade down the docks. But Dottie always appreciated his rough and ready handling of her body.

They changed position and Albert sat on the chaise lounge and Dottie rode him with some passion. His big hands gripping her swinging breasts, squeezing and kneading them like a happy baker preparing dough for bread. But it was when Dottie leaned her head back, and placed an arm around his neck, and their mouths met, that some real unexpected passion exploded between the two. It actually surprised the pair and their lips and tongues couldn't part. They quickly changed to the Missionary position and Dottie found they were no longer having sex: they were making love! Their passion was so intense that Albert couldn't hold it any longer and finished, cussing and groaning, thanking the Lord Almighty for his generosity. Dottie agreed.

She had enjoyed a couple of very powerful orgasms in his hands which left a warm feeling inside: No, she said to herself, it was a strange contented feeling, a feeling of happiness and solid, real satisfaction. She didn't know how to express what just happened – it was that unexpected – so she said nothing but allowed a couple of happy little tears to roll down her face.

They lay on the chaise lounge in silence, just kissing, running their hands over each other's sweaty and quivering bodies. Albert kissed her face and then her nipples gently now and sighed, "Bloody hell girl, that was – for me – like when Rosie and me were first married. Unbelievable, fucking unbelievable, what the hell happened?"

All Dorothy could do was stroke his unshaven happy face and whisper that they best keep this between themselves. Albert nodded slowly and ran his hand gently over her face, "Christ girl, that's going to be difficult because….because I bleeding think I love you now." Dorothy almost smiled and they kissed – really passionately – again. She whispered they must and that was that. He eased from her and sat on the chaise lounge, slowly picking up his clothes from the floor. Dorothy sat next to him, legs open a little, cleaning herself with a soft flannel. She leaned over and kissed his cheek, "No, this stays between us. We both don't want to hurt Rosie do we?"

Albert nodded and kissed her slowly, lingering on her lips and then they French kissed with some unbridled passion – again – and reluctantly separated. They heard Rosie's soft knock and she peered around the door and smiled, "Come on you bleeding oaf, you'll be late for your shift. And she needs to clean up and get dressed. Off you bleeding go." She carried in a basin and pitcher of warm water and smiled again at the pair, "Go on Bertie, shift yourself, you've had your oats, so get off to bleeding work!" He grinned and without saying anything dressed and left, with a parting look at Dorothy that could have illuminated the North Pole on a real dark night. She watched him go and took a deep breath, looking at Rosie pouring the water into the basin, she went to say something – almost apologise in a strange way – but just smiled when Rosie asked if she enjoyed her 'quickie' with Albert.

"I miss our Sunday sessions darling, we really need to make other arrangements." Dottie said quietly and Rosie – with a big smile – agreed.

Titus pulled open the door and grinned; "Your Uncle William has a very special visitor and Mr. Skoles has been sent to fetch Harry." He stepped aside and Dorothy stared at the tall, very handsome young man in navy uniform; who grinned and held out his arms. "Hello baby sister, sweet Jesus you've grown since I last saw you!" Dorothy rushed over and embraced her 'big brother' George and kissed him on the cheek. "Home port leave for three weeks, couldn't believe it myself. The Colossus is in the Albert and then we're joining the South sea squadron. Apparently There are pirates infesting the waters!" He cuddled Dorothy again and she wiped away a little tear. Rosie stood by Reggie [Titus] and jabbed him with her elbow; "Christ he looks like Mr. Hadden; I mean Mister Harry!" Reggie nodded and handed her a glass of brandy; "Seems a fine young man, serving his King and Country, keeping us safe in our beds." Rosie chuckled; "He could keep me safe in my bleeding bed any day!"

"Admiral of the Fleet 'Jackie' Fisher had calmed Britain's nerves when they found out about Germany's mass building of Battleships in the early Edwardian era. He pointed out that the British fleets were so enormous compared to Germany's that; "everyone should sleep peacefully in their beds" It became bit of a catchphrase." SJW.

Uncle William was really happy about George being home and fussed over him. Dorothy sipped her brandy and smiled at her 'big brother'. He and Harry were both strapping good looking young men that when boys; people would often mistake them for twins. He had – apparently – according to rumours been engaged no less than three times, with none ending in marriage!

Dorothy could understand that, her brother was a charming handsome, dashing figure in his uniform. He was making Uncle William laugh loudly about some visit to a native isle. Rosie slipped next to her and said quietly; "He certainly knows how to tell a story; he won't be short of female company whilst on leave I bet." Dorothy could only nod at that.

Harry couldn't make the drinks in the dressing room but crashed through the evening reception room door at home that night and the brothers embraced with real affection. At breakfast the next morning Uncle William announced that they would have a big Christmas party on Christmas Eve. Everyone would be invited including their friends from the theatre. Harry said he would invite Alistair [his sergeant, now back on duty] big Jim Grieves and Constables Farmer and Palmer – all with their wives or girlfriends – of course. Dorothy would invite Rosie and Albert and Alice, her nurse friend from the hospital.

George struggled to think of anyone to invite because all his friends were at sea or scattered around the country, probably having parties with their families and friends. He grinned; "I'll bring someone along." And winked at Dorothy who groaned; she knew her brother's reputation for picking up women easily and sweeping them off their feet. She really was starting to like her wayward and often absent brother a great deal.

Dorothy also announced the diner with Paul's family on Sunday and hoped everyone could make it. Uncle William raised his tea cup; "Here's to having a Doctor in the family. That'll save us a few bob on medical bills!" George gripped her hand and smiled; "He had better treat you right or me and Harry will sort the bugger out." And he meant it. Harry chuckled; "I've known Paul for a couple of years, he seems a good fellow but like George says; if he raises a hand to our Dorothy, he'll need a doctor himself!"

Everyone laughed at that. But Dorothy thought that domestic violence was no laughing matter; some husbands treated their wives badly. For a moment she thought about the late Mrs. Hanna Dashwood whose husband took a belt to her backside if she displeased him. At least she had two brothers who would not stand for their sister being treated that way. She sipped her tea, but still couldn't smile.

Harry talking about his latest strange case drew her attention back to the breakfast conversations. The two bodies in the morgue had still not been identified and he couldn't even find where the pair had been staying. "It's like they dropped from the bleeding sky; no-one appears to have even seen them about. Even some discrete enquiries in the queer community have drawn a blank."

Uncle William mentioned it might be a good idea to invite Professor John Hammond to the Christmas party, being an American and far from home, it would show him the great British hospitality that we're famous for. He chuckled; "It would also tell him that our Dorothy is taken and he can stop sending all those bloody flowers!"

Harry nodded at that and then noticed the look on his brother George's face, who lowered his tea cup and asked Harry; "Is that Professor John Hammond from New York?

Harry nodded and asked if he knew him. George sat back and didn't smile; "Navel Intelligence sent something out about him last year. Apparently he's being watched by Military intelligence in the States because of the equipment he has been buying and the strange company he's been keeping. He's been spending his time trying to invent a machine that can send objects through empty air and they'll arrive anywhere in the world."

George accepted a refill from Ellen and continued; "If I remember it right, there had been an accident and a couple of his assistants were killed….no, they vanished. Just disappeared and their families reported them missing. I don't think they were found; a young man and a young woman. I think that was the story anyway." Uncle William sat back and rubbed his chin; "That may explain why he's ended up here in London. Maybe they won't let him carry on with his experiments in America now."

Harry said that he would invite him nevertheless. Dorothy tapped her cup with a finger and said quietly to Harry; "I would love to get a look at his machine, wouldn't you?" Harry nodded; "His assistants were a young man and a young woman. Funny how our two unknown stiffs could easily match that description; but if they vanished a year ago, it can't be them…." He stopped talking and picked up a biscuit and nibbled it slowly. Dorothy could see he was deep in thought.

George presented her with two little dolls from his latest trips and she was delighted. She made straight for her rooms and quickly unlocked her display cabinet, and carefully placed the two exquisite little dolls into her cabinet; she now had almost two dozen of the figurines. She closed the door with big smile. "From Japan and China according to George." Ellen peered over her shoulder and grunted; "Mister George looks like his brother Harry but that's where the bleeding resemblance stops." Dorothy turned, a little puzzled by that remark. "What do you mean Ellen?"

Ellen grunted and folded her arms; "He bleeding made a pass at Me this morning, wanted to take me down the Royal Oak for a drink and a knee's up! I put him right in no uncertain terms. I'm a bleeding respectable girl." Dorothy smiled; "Well, he's a young man who's been at sea for a long time; maybe he wanted a lady's company and just have a good night out." Dorothy really restrained from grinning, knowing full well that Ellen was more than happy to share Harry's bed! Ellen was a young widow without children who very rarely spoke about her late husband. Her sad and short marriage remained a mystery in the Hadden household.

Ellen didn't smile; "Yeah and I know the sort of lady's he wanted and I ain't one of them. I had to put up with that nonsense when I was first in service. Just fourteen and his bleeding lordship use to chase me about and if that weren't bad enough his dirty old grandfather would sit in his bath chair and lift the blanket; you know, showing all his bits when I served him his coffee or brandy."

Dorothy tried not to smile; "Did you complain to the House-keeper?" Ellen sighed; "That old cow couldn't care less. Anyway they gave me notice." Dorothy locked her cabinet and asked why Ellen was fired. Now Ellen really did grin; "I gave the old sod his coffee all right; all over his bleeding you-know-what. Apparently you could hear the screams in the kitchens!" Now Dorothy did laugh at that and so did Ellen!

That evening Sims rolled into Dorothy's room and was warmly greeted by George who hadn't seen him for a couple of years. "You're still an ugly bugger!" and embraced Sims like he had the other family members.

Sims pulled the postcard from his bandages and handed it to Harry; "Mr. Tibbs says it genuine; it was printed in 1969 and the big building was completed in 1931. This was posted in New York City in 1971. One of his assistants was a cop in New York in the seventies and he actually knew Davies Washington!"

Dorothy had to sit down; she asked if he was a young black man, quite athletic. Sims nodded; "Wilson [Jericho's assistant] says he played football and kept himself fit. They knew each other because both were a bit unusual for the times; they were both black detectives. He [Wilson] says that there was some gossip about him and a young white woman. But here's the best bit." Sims chuckled and accepted a glass of whisky from Uncle William.

"Well, what's the best bit?" Harry asked, throwing a glance at Dorothy who sat with a real concerned look on her face. Sims downed the whisky in one and would have eaten the glass, but Uncle William took it off him. He folded his arms; "Apparently he's what Jericho calls a missing soul, he should have died in 2003 but missed that one. Jericho says he must have gone time travelling or sold his soul to you know who."

"Do you know anything about the woman he was seeing?" Uncle William asked and Sims shook his head; "Nothing except she was young, white and quite a looker apparently." He scratched his head with both hands and didn't smile; "Wilson did say that his sister-in-law knew the detective's oldest sister and the family weren't happy that he [Davis] was seeing a white girl. All they knew about her was her nickname."

Harry grunted and rubbed his chin; "What was it?" he asked and Sims really smiled in a slightly mad way; "It was Lottie or Dottie apparently. Definitely one of those two." Uncle William and Harry both stared at Dorothy who didn't smile at that revelation.

George interrupted the strange conversation by asking Uncle William if he could bring a friend – an officer in the French navy – who he had met several times over the last year. The officer was on 'Liaison' duties here in London and wouldn't be able to return home for Christmas. Uncle William nodded and said it would fine and who was the officer. George smiled; "Captain Jean-Paul Leon, he's quite a character. He's not considered a coluored man, so he's an officer; I think his mother was white and his father who's really wealthy is mixed race. Anyway; he a good man and an excellent officer. "

Harry nodded; "That's unusual isn't it? A coloured officer?" George agreed and added; "Yeah, but that means he must be bloody good at what he does; bloody good! He's from a wealthy Paris family and his father is a minister or something, so that may explain how he got in, but I like to think it was on ability."

He continued and winked at Dottie, "It's currently fashionable in Paris for some married women to have coloured lovers! Leon told me a couple of stories that would make your hair stand on end." He chuckled, "A big man like your Reggie would be in demand!" Uncle William waged a finger at his wayward nephew, "Now, now young George, Dottie is not a married woman yet, and so those tales are best kept stag." But there was no real censure in his voice.

Dorothy just smiled and thought about Reggie visiting her dressing room for a little 'treat'. They had disappeared into the changing room while Rosie – knitting and smiling – kept watch on the dressing room door. He had fucked her on the Chaise lounge, then the carpet and finally – as the mood took them – against the bloody wall! They were only interrupted once by Rosie, tapping softly on the door and saying, "Keep the bloody noise down girl! Otherwise people will think someone is being bleeding murdered!"

Reggie left with a big smile on his face: oh, he really enjoyed the perks of his job! While a very satisfied Dorothy sat and regaled Rosie of the happenings in the small changing room. She told Rosie about what George had said about the married women of Paris and that made her smile, "Bleeding good for them. Bloody Frenchmen know sod all about fidelity and what's good for the goose is good for the bloody gander." Then kissed Dottie and asked quietly if young George is still looking for a little bit of female company! Dorothy could only sigh, "Rosie, if you got your hands on him, his bloody hair would curl!" Both women laughed and Rosie pushed open Dottie's dressing gown – she was still naked – and kissed her breasts. Dottie took hold of her hand and the pair walked quickly to the changing room.

Dorothy had dozed on the chaise lounge after Rosie went to make the tea and the dream came quickly. She was placing a syrup covered pancake on a plate, testing it with her fork and liking the taste. Her daughter Lilly loved it, grabbing it up, getting sticky fingers and mouth whilst her father just chuckled.

He ran a hand over Dorothy's swollen stomach and then kissed it. "I've told mum if it's a boy, we'll call him after dad. You like the name Charlie don't you?" Dottie slapped a couple of pancakes down in front of him, "And if it's another girl?" Davies smiled, "I thought we would keep up your family tradition and call her Dorothy, after you and your grandmother." Dottie shook her head, "No, I'd like her called Elizabeth, if it's good enough for the English Queen, then its good enough for our little girl. Besides my mum was called Lizzy, so she'll be named after her granny too." Davies just nodded and smiled.

Dorothy awoke gasping a little for breath. She had a strange taste in her mouth; it was like sweet whisky or something similar. She eased from the bed and sat on the edge, drinking water from the glass she always kept on the bedside cabinet.

She lay back clutching the empty glass and stared at the dull white ceiling. She leaned forward and snatched up her little fob watch and saw that it was five o'clock in the morning; Christmas Eve Morning. She stared at the small diamond ring that Paul had given her at the Sunday dinner with his family. They would marry next summer.

She eased from the bed and headed for the bathroom; she was going to help Mrs. Harvey and Ellen with the preparations for the Christmas Eve party, so she needed an early start. She ran her own bath and soaked for about ten minutes, she could hear Ellen pulling open the curtain and shouting that her tea was on the cabinet and that it was snowing again. Dorothy shouted that she would be in the kitchens, apron on and ready to work. She could hear Ellen chuckling at that promise and the bedroom door closing. She couldn't stop thinking about Davies and Paul her new fiancé; struggled to enter her thoughts.

That evening the party started about six o'clock with a grand champagnes toast – provided by Harry & George – to the newly engaged couple. Uncle William made a short funny and very affectionate speech about his niece and Harry played the piano. He changed over a couple of times with Big Tom who really knew the music hall songs and soon had everything singing some very questionable songs!

George was a big hit with the three girls from the chorus line and both Harry and Dorothy commented on that. Her and Rosie stood chatting by the fire place sipping brandies and Ellen told Dorothy that the 'mad professor' had turned up; alone. Dorothy was surprised by that; what had happened to the mysterious women in black? She watched carefully as the professor and Uncle William chatted by the big bay window. They appeared to be getting on like a house on fire. Rosie's Albert joined the girls and asked Dorothy to dance; which she did. She was utterly amazed that the rough coarse docker danced superbly.

Dottie gripped him a bit too tightly and he stared into her eyes with real hidden passion. They passed small talk between themselves whilst both thought of the other naked and making love on the carpet, in front of that big fireplace. It was a difficult dance for both of them and Dorothy knew she had to 'wean' herself off him and that would mean having other men. They were interrupted [Dottie was a little relieved by that] by Paul who insisted on dancing with his fiancé. As the pair now danced Dorothy pointed out that, it would have been the decent thing to do; if he danced with Rosie, since she [Dorothy] was dancing with her husband. Paul just grunted and said that if he wished to dance with her; he damn well would.

It was remarkable that Harry heard the front door bell over the noise of the party and he opened; drink in hand and smiling. It was George's Navel friend who held up two bottle of very [and I mean very] expensive bottles of champagne. Harry introduced himself and Captain Jean-Paul embraced him like a brother; his English was perfect. Harry watched him enter and really smiled; what a bloody treat for the ladies!

Rosie gripped Dorothy's arm as she was pouring more drinks and whispered; "For Gawd sake! Take a look at who has just bleeding wandered in. I never thought I would ever say a man was bloody gorgeous but I will now!" Dorothy sighed; "Men are always referred to as handsome Rosie...." Then she turned and saw the visitor. She said nothing for a few long seconds and said softly; "Rosie, on this one occasion I think you are right." Jean-Paul was tall, dark and handsome with a big smile, he walked with real grace and placed the bottles next to Dorothy and smiled at her. "You must be mademoiselle Dorothy, George told me his young sister looked like a Hapsburg princess and now I know George does not exaggerate." He took Dorothy's hand and kissed it; slowly, adding in his delightful English laced with a little French accent; "I am Jean-Paul Leon; a Captain in the French Republic's navy and I am VERY pleased to meet you mademoiselle. May I have this dance?"

Dorothy found herself nodding at once and he swept her from the makeshift bar and the pair danced together, they danced very close and that didn't go un-noticed by anyone. Rosie really smiled; the pair had locked eyes and an orange elephant could have walked past them and they wouldn't have noticed it!

Ellen whispered to Rosie; "Sweet Jesus, you could make toast with the look that's passing between those two!" Rosie nodded her agreement and few in the room would argue with Ellen's statement for it was true!

Paul was not happy and with the party in full swing, Dorothy tried to cheer him up and showed Paul her collection of dolls. Under the strict social conventions of the day Dorothy, an unmarried woman shouldn't be alone in her bedroom with a man; even if he was her fiancé. They did kiss quietly by the window and he made no attempt to go any further. They re-joined their guests. What concerned Dorothy was she felt very little - except the actual physical kissing – and whilst he clearly enjoyed it – and said so – she now had little doubts creeping into her thoughts about the impending marriage.

The mysterious American professor had a long conversation with uncle William and Harry and they found out that he had rented the large basement rooms of the local 'Odd fellows' Hall; he mentioned he had a couple of assistants but didn't go into details. He confessed that he was working on a device that could change the world by providing a device that would sent parcels, objects, anything really around the world without need for ships or carriages. Harry mentioned that a chap called Tesla had much the same idea and Harry thought he [Tesla] was working with the inventor Edison. John Hammond dismissed the pair; "Amateurs Harry, Edison got lucky with his light bulb and that Tesla is just a foreign crank, probably after money from Edison."

Harry casually mentioned that his brother George was back from the USA and had remembered a strange story about some professor who was working on a similar idea and had 'lost' his two assistants. John Hammond sipped his brandy and didn't smile; "The press in the US will exaggerate or just plain lie to sell newspapers. They couldn't get anything right about what really happened. My two so called assistants were trying to steal the device and sell it; probably to Edison. But it went wrong or they mishandled it and they died. The papers tried to make out I was at fault just by inventing the machine. They got large chunks of the story wrong; both my assistants were men. But they 'sexed' it up by saying one was a beautiful young woman. Newspapers are not my cup tea as you Brit's say."

He didn't stay long and managed one dance with Dorothy and was gone. It was Alistair turning up a little late with his wife Kate, that really grabbed Harry's attention.

He accepted a glass of champagne and chatted with Dorothy, then called Harry over – who was talking to Kate – and rummaged in his pockets. "I picked up the reply from the big post office in Eastham, before it closed up for the Christmas holidays. It came from New York City Police Department by transatlantic cable last night." He pulled the two sheets out and handed them to Harry, who read them with some interest. "It appears that all charges have been dropped against the mad professor. The New York DA has basically dropped the case. They have sent details of his two assistants who are still missing. One is a young white male aged 26 called Gerald Fuxton who played football for his college and majored in Physics. The other is another white male aged 24 who majored in Chemistry. Had a part time occupation as a drag Queen in the city music halls……" he stopped talking and lowered the papers.

"Are you thinking what I'm thinking?" Dorothy asked and Harry nodded. "We need to see his machine." He said softly. Dorothy glanced across at the handsome and dashing French Navel Officer and knew what would happen between the two, and saw him smiling back at her, as if he knew already too.

Plans were set in motion as the pair danced together: again.

CHAPTER 6. 'QUAND IL ME PREND DANS LES BRAS, IL ME PARLE TOUT BAS, JE VOIS LA VIE EN ROSE.' Edith Piaf.

Dorothy walked slowly up the hotel steps and closed her umbrella and shook it. The Doorman had pulled open the door and waited. The two bell boys had grabbed the small suitcases from the back of the taxi and stood behind her. "Come on darling, I'm freezing!" she called down to the man who waved a hand and finished paying the cabbie. Despite the snow and ice he jumped up the steps and Dorothy pushed her arm through his and smiled broadly. They entered the plush interior of the hotel and Jean-Paul signed the pair in, telling the receptionist it was just for the night; they were returning to Paris in the morning and that's why they picked this hotel; it was near the rail station for the trains to Dover and the cross channel ferries. The Receptionist read the entry in the guest's ledger and smiled; "The boys will carry your cases to your suite Captain Leon and you will have a table reserved for dinner if you wish. I'm sure you and Madame Leon will be comfortable." He placed a key into the captain's hand and gestured to the boys to follow the happy couple. He didn't even bother to the check the Captains papers; a high ranking French Navel officer and his wife would be welcomed without fuss. "This isn't bleeding Tsarist Russia." He muttered and closed the book.

Jean-Paul tipped the boys sixpence each which was generous and closed the door behind them. He turned and walked over to Dorothy and pulled her to him; they embraced with some passion. She whispered; "I'm sorry darling, but I need you to play my maid….if you want me out of this dress." He grinned and replied softly; "I would play a monkey in a banana tree for you my sweet." And the pair kissed with Dorothy removing her coat and gloves. She watched from the big bed as Jean-Paul was undressing, carefully placing his uniform on a chair. Their eyes never left each other.

He laughed and said quietly; "My darling, much as it's beautiful like you, but I don't think you need to keep your damn hat on!" Dorothy chuckled and realised he was right and gently removed the hat pins and placed her hat on the bedside cabinet. Now naked, Jean-Paul fumbled in his small suitcase and produced a little black case which he carried over to the bed. Dorothy now naked lay against the pillows and ran her hands over his broad back; "What's in the box darling?" she said quietly and kissed the back of his neck and shoulders. He held it between two fingers; "A condom my darling, so there are no unexpected and stupid consequences of our love making. I'll only need to wear it for proper love making. When I enjoy your mouth and sweet little bum I won't need it. I doubt if any woman in history has become pregnant with oral or anal sex." He held up the other item in the little box; "Vaseline my darling. It will greatly assist your efforts in pleasing me."

Jean-Paul turned and kissed her; placing the condom next to her hat; they lay naked kissed and arousing each other. He certainly knew how a woman liked to be touched. Dorothy was now seriously aroused and agreed to have his erection in her mouth before the love making started. Apparently – according to Jean-Paul she was very good at it for a new starter! Dottie almost choked when he said that but kept her composure and carried on. She wouldn't correct his assumptions of her, well, not today. She lay back as he applied the Vaseline and soon they began the passionate love making. He was very gentle at first, then speeded up and drove deeper into her. They made love for about two hours and Jean-Paul showed his stamina and fortitude by ejaculating twice in that time. They rolled around the bed gasping, panting and moaning; trying several sex positions.

Dorothy was very submissive to his wishes and he loved that. They sat drinking brandy; both propped up against the pillows and shared a French cigarette which made Dorothy cough and decline a second. Jean-Paul sighed and placed both arms around Dorothy and kissed her neck, pulling her to him. "I will arrange for your passage to Paris and then onto my father's Chateaux in Normandy. There you can chose to live in any of five great houses on the estate. You will need to pick a ladies maid..." Dorothy interrupted him, grinning; "I already have a ladies maid!" he chuckled and kissed her again. "You will be a great lady and we will attend the season in Paris and London. You and Isabella will become more than close friends; you are quite up her street as you English say. I will enjoy that show very much!"

Dorothy turned her head and looked puzzled; "Who is this Isabella? Is she your sister?" she asked and Jean-Paul kissed her neck again; "My wife, but she is a very open minded lady who shares my bed with Annette; as I say she will enjoy you as much as I." Dorothy was silent for a few seconds, then asked; "Who the hell is Annette?" Jean-Paul grunted and stubbed out his cigarette in the ashtray. "She is my mistress, well, her and her younger sister Lilly. My wife thinks they are sweet and we have much fun together. You will join in and everyone will be happy." He sighed; "My dear father pays for everything I have, so he will expect you to please him now and again as a thank you; all my other girls do. His favourite is a woman's bum – absolutely loves that – so, I'll train yours my darling so that we both can enjoy it." Dorothy turned and stared at the smiling Frenchman, then saw the small lamp on the bedside. She managed a smile and said; "Oh, I see. I'm to join your harem and have your elderly father poke my bum when he wants and your wife to enjoy my crotch when she wants." Jean-Paul almost smiled and nodded; "But of course my darling….." that was when the normally placid Dorothy exploded. And it started by grabbing the lamp. It wasn't a nice scene.

The cab dropped Dorothy off at home just before ten o'clock and Ellen took her bag, saying that Uncle William wanted to see her. Dorothy just nodded; she was now clam and under control of herself. She checked her make-up in the hall mirror and handed her hat and coat to Ellen, who wondered what was in the case.

Uncle William was poking the fire and puffing his pipe; he looked up and smiled; "Have a good day shopping up west my dear?" Dorothy nodded and walked over and kissed her uncle. "Fancy a rum? I'm going to indulge in a brandy." Uncle William nodded and eased in his chair. Dorothy sat opposite him, sipping her brandy. She sighed; "The French are a strange bunch aren't they?" Uncle William nodded and enjoyed his rum.

Dorothy sat back and somewhere at the back of her mind she regretted a little what she did to Jean-Paul; running naked up and down the hall of the hotel's top corridor with Dorothy also stark naked throwing everything from the room at him. Luckily, the hotel accepted his personal cheque for all the damaged items. They wouldn't press charges against the pair; apparently none of the guests who witnessed the affair were really upset; especially the men apparently!

The hotel manager – a world weary individual – simply explained the incredible scenes with one small sentence, "He's French."

As she strode from the hotel with all the guests standing in silence and just staring at her; two house maids gave her some applause and went back to their duties. Despite the incident, Dorothy was still aroused and now a little unsatisfied – sexually – and stood by the kerb and raised a hand to call a cab. One rolled up and the young driver jumped down, taking her bag and opening the door. Dorothy stared at him: she thought she remembered him from somewhere and had to ask as he helped her into his cab. He leaned on the cab window and rubbed his chin, "Dunno miss, I would remember a real beauty like you – begging your pardon for me boldness – but I don't think we've met before and I'm real sad about that!"

Dorothy had to laugh at his cheek and asked his name, saying that might help. He tipped his hat back and smiled, "Its Theodore – Eddy to my friends – McHannon's miss." Dorothy then realized that he was very similar to Albert, Rosie's husband and her occasional sex partner! She asked if he had a brother: Albert. "Aye, I do miss, are you that magic lady that our Rosie works for?" Dorothy nodded with a smile and the young man slapped the side of the cab and grinned, "Blimey miss, Albert said you were a real cracking piece of cake and he's no liar and that's a blooming fact!" Dorothy leaned over, her face close to his, "What else has dear Albert said about me?" the young man rubbed his chin and thought for a second or two, "Just that when in the bleeding mood you're real game."

Dorothy patted his face and whispered into his ear. He really smiled and slapped his cap back on, "Your wish my lady is my command!" and jumped, whistling, into the driver's seat and flicked the reins. The cab pulled away and Dorothy slowly removed her hat: well, Mister bloody Frenchman and your harem, two can play that game. She still had her 'Dutch Cap' fitted and was now a little wet. She tossed the small jar of Vaseline up in the air and caught it. "My only bloody souvenir of a crappy love affair and I'll put it to some bleeding good use."

The carriage was bouncing gently, parked in the quiet small alley-way. Young Eddy knew exactly where to park for such an impromptu and discrete liaison. He also clearly knew how to fuck a woman like Dottie: hard and fast. To Dorothy's great pleasure, she discovered that Eddy resembled his brother in another very important way: he was hung like a horse too. With her skirt and petticoats pulled up, her feet almost touching the cab's ceiling and both hands gripping his shoulders she let the young man fuck her with some unbridled delight. Fucking like this made her orgasm quickly and she whispered encouragement to her young stud. He certainly responded and they fucked on the floor, with Dorothy bent over the seat. He slapped her arse several times and she orgasmed again under his rough handling. With some desperation in his voice, he finally asked where he could cum and was delighted when she said to finish where he was.

They both sat on the seat, legs stretched out and Dorothy cleaned herself up with his hankies, while he lit a cigarette which he shared. With a big grin, he leaned over and kissed her cheek, "Now that my darling was bloody magic!" they both laughed and he ran her home, refusing to take the fare saying that no tip was also required. He would never have another bloody tip like the one he just received. Dorothy explained why the sessions at Rosie's and Albert home had stopped and he nodded – he obviously knew about his sister and her baby now living there - but he lived alone in an attic flat above the Co-Operative in King William Road and they could use that, if she wished. He pointed out that it only had one bedroom, but came with a bathroom, kitchen and toilet. The living room was really big and had a large fireplace, which when lit, turned the place into a bloody hot house which any gardener would be proud of. Now that really did interest Dorothy and the happy pair parted after kissing quite passionately considering they had just met. Him fucking 'her brains out' had helped break the ice, of course!

As he helped her down from the cab, he further delighted Dottie by placing a finger to his lips and whispering, "Eddy's no fool Dottie, so mum's the word until I'm told otherwise." She wanted to place a kiss on his cheek, or better still his lips, but obviously refrained from doing that in the middle of the street with the neighbours watching. But she did watch him drive off and climbed the steps with quite a smile on her face, really wishing she could rush around to Rosie and tell her everything.

She asked Uncle William about the case and he smiled; "I have some good news on that Dottie; Harry is going to pay the mad scientist a little visit."

Harry had already sent Sims to contact mister Jericho Tibbs about breeches of the time line. Waiting outside their house was PC Allan Coates with the Police carriage; there were few cabs available on Christmas Morning. The Hadden's climbed aboard and set off for 'Odd fellows Hall'. "I've arranged to meet old George Bannister – the hall's caretaker – to open up. He didn't mind; he lives next door." Harry told them, watching fresh snow falling on the deserted streets. He had left the 'bombshell' for Dorothy to the last minute. He handed her the second sheet of the message and she read it; her eyes wide open in surprise. "Hammond is an assumed surname! His real family name is Washington and his family is descended from freed black slaves!" She sat back and stared at Harry who nodded; "There was a lot white blood mixed in with the family. 'Hammond's' older Brother George could easily pass as a Negro and can only teach in black schools. It appears John is a 'throwback'. According to genetics it happens every few generations and it came out on John."

There was silence for a few seconds; "He could easily be related to this 'Davies Washington' who must have been born in the 1940's to be an adult and a detective in 1973. Do you think this is all linked to his damn machine?" Uncle William said quietly and stared at 'Odd Fellows Hall' as the police carriage halted outside.

They stepped into the snow and made their way to the basement entrance at the rear of the building whilst PC Coates knocked up the old caretaker. George wished them all a 'merry Christmas' and commented on how lovely Dorothy looked; wrapped up in her winter furs. He unlocked the doors and pointed down the stairs; "First on the left, you can't miss it."He handed Harry the keys and said that he wouldn't wait for them; he had his large Christmas breakfast to enjoy. Harry thanked him and the team headed down to the basement in silence.

They found the heavy dark door and it took a few seconds for Harry to find the equally large key. He carefully unlocked the door and pushed it slowly open. They stood in the doorway and stared in disbelieve. The machine was no bigger than a bedroom wardrobe with cables everywhere. It had a large mirror fixed centrally and boxes either side. What looked like one of the new 'typewriters' keyboards had been placed below the mirror and a seat pulled up near it.

A young woman with dark hair sat at the machine; she was quite pretty and slim built. The 'mirror' was showing a dark street scene with people walking about. The place was lit with bright street lamps and strange multi coloured machines were moving about. They appeared to contain strangely dressed people. "It's those new moving pictures, isn't it?" whispered Uncle William. He also pointed out the two big lamps nearby and the pile of new mattresses and sacks placed beneath them. That's when the big man in a woolen pullover and dark trousers appeared from a cupboard, carrying a bottle of brandy and a blanket. He stared at the little group standing in the doorway and shouted; "Tess! We have fucking visitors!" The woman on the machine spun around in her big 'captains' chair and grabbed up a small knife that lay on the desk top. The big man threw the blanket down and pulled an evil looking cosh from his trousers.

Harry held up a hand and announced himself. The big man grinned and said quietly; "I fucking hate coppers!" He stepped forward, slapping his hand with the cosh. Harry sighed and pulled his service revolver out. "Now let's keep this civil please people." He said and smiled. The big man lowered the cosh and the woman slapped the knife back down. "Now what the hell is going on here?" Harry asked. He didn't get an answer because there was a flash of light between the lamps and a young woman fell from nowhere and bounced onto the mattresses and sacks.

The big man threw down the cosh and grabbed up the blanket; he rushed to the woman and wrapped her in the blanket; she took a long swig from the bottle of brandy. Everyone just stared at her; she appeared to be smoking hot, but was clearly shaking from cold. Dorothy recognized the clothes; she had seen young women wearing similar articles in her dreams about the 1970's.

The young woman sipped her brandy and stared directly at Dorothy who stared back at her. "Sweet bleeding Jesus! You could be sisters!" exclaimed Uncle William. Dorothy managed to nod; she was looking at an almost mirror image of herself! The woman dropped the blanket and handed the bottle to the big man; she stepped across to the amazed little group and slowly smiled at Dorothy.

"Hello grandma, you don't know how happy I am to meet you. I'm your granddaughter Dottie. Yes, I'm named after you." She now grinned and walked up to Dorothy and held out her arms. Dorothy slowly ran a hand down the girls face and the pair embraced. There was absolute silence until a voice behind them said; "Regretfully this little family reunion should never have happened. It may complicate things. Put the bloody silly pistol away Harry; no one is going to shoot family are they?" It was John Hammond or John Washington.

He walked past the stunned group and up to his machine; he patted the woman on the shoulder; "This is Tess or sometimes she's known as Terry or Terrance. By the way Harry, when you return to work after Boxing Day, you'll find that a certain corpse has vanished from the morgue." He smiled; "I managed to send Tess back to before the dreadful moment, that she met that sick bastard down on the docks and she avoided him. Unfortunately I couldn't do the same for Gerald and thus; he remains very much dead."

Tess grunted, "A vagrant who thought my kindness was an invitation to sex. Carried something like a slide-hammer and I didn't see it until too late. I suspect I wasn't the first woman – or man – he used it on." Harry nodded, little wonder they found no exit wound on the body. Harry ran a hand over his face and pushed his pistol back in his underarm holster. "What the hell have you been doing John and more importantly; why?" John folded his arms; "Like any scientist worth his salt I want to change the world for the better. This machine can do that." He patted the desk and gestured to the 'mirror'. "Show them 1940 Tess." The 'woman' nodded and tapped a few keys; the picture changed dramatically. The Hadden's watched with unconcealed horror as they witnessed the 'Blitz' on the East end in 1940. Then Nazi's and concentration camps flashed across the screen. It finished with the huge explosion on a Japanese city. There was silence until the professor spoke quietly.

CHAPTER 7. 'IN EVERY CONCEIVABLE MANNER, THE FAMILY IS A LINK TO OUR PAST, A BRIDGE TO OUR FUTURE.' Alex Haley.

"Just a terrible glimpse of things to come if I don't change things with this machine." He indicated for Tess to switch the horrific images off. She did so and gripped his hand with some apparent affection. John gestured to the two Dorothy's. "That was my mistake I'm afraid. I travelled to 1971 and met with my descendant Davies Washington who was more than happy to join me and we travelled to 1910. That's where he met Dorothy Hadden performing at her travelling magic show. You can guess what happened; they fell in love and serious complications soon appeared because I knew he would meet Dorothy's very own granddaughter in 1971 and should have fallen in love with her.

But then I realized that the machine wasn't operating as it should; it was mixing up time with some truly bizarre results. Davies wouldn't listen to reason and used the machine to pursue the original Dorothy he fell in love with. He's around here somewhere; that's why Tess and Max [Maxwell Shoemaker – the big rough man] were searching the docks. I believe he's hiding there pretending to be an American sailor who's jumped ship."

Tess eased from 'her' seat; "Gerald and I were at college together; he accepted me as I was and we became more than friends. We even had the same tattoos. But I didn't know that he had been recalibrating the damn machine on the secret. That's when really strange things started to happen." She gestured to the two Dorothy's; "Somehow it was mixing up your past and future lives, somehow it had linked you two over time. Dottie [the granddaughter] started to have dreams about living in Edwardian times. She thought it was just dreams, about what her mother told her about her granny. But it was the damn wrongly calibrated machine behind it all."

John Hammond/Washington sighed; "When I find him, I will send him back to 1971 before I meet up with him and rectify my mistake. He'll fall in love with the correct version of his 'Dorothy' and the time line of humanity will correct itself." He told Max to pass the brandy bottle about; "I think everyone may need a shot of the hard stuff to fortify themselves for what's next. Operate the machine for the alternative version of 1971 if I don't change things back." He said to Tess who nodded and tapped at the keyboard. Another image appeared; it appeared to be New York in the year 1971. Everyone watched with real interest as the images flickered across the strange screen.

"In this version Davies has been with you Dorothy." He didn't smile and looked directly at Dorothy [the granny!]. "There's Davies heading home to meet up with Dorothy who now lives in the 1970's in New York City. She lives in an apartment that is mostly segregated between poor white and black families.

I'm sorry to say that she hasn't quite grasped the way the modern world is and just how dangerous it is. When Davies arrives and parks outside; Merrill walker – an old African-American lady who lives below them - tells Davies that a couple of black guys have just gone to call on him. He's not expecting visitors so he runs up the stairs to find the apartment broken into and Dorothy has been viciously beaten, robbed and raped. He calls 911 and goes with her to hospital. He sits with her all night, but she succumbs to her injuries in the early hours of the morning. He's back out on the streets looking for the bastards." John Hammond had Tess fade out the awful assault scene; he continued.

"The entire human time line now changes dramatically; it took me a while to realize what had happened. There was no world changing event in 2001 when terrorists brought down a couple of skyscrapers in New York by crashing planes into them. It never happened because the damn 'Towers' as they were called, where never built!" John Hammond wiped his face; he nodded at the shocked Dorothy.

"You see, on the night he sat with you dying in hospital, in the original time line he was still on shift and responds to a shooting and robbery in Queen's. He finds a young man on the sidewalk and administers first aid. He knows what he's doing with bloody gunshots and saves the young man's life. Obviously in the new time line he doesn't do that. The young man was a promising architect working for Skidmore, Owings & Merrill who create the twin towers from his idea. That now doesn't happen and the buildings now do not exist. There's no terror attack, no invasions, the Middle East remains as it was. Human History completely changes." He swigged from the bottle and passed it around.

"There was certain Dictator in North Africa who gets his hands on a nuclear device and attacks Israel with it. The world is at war in a matter of days. It doesn't end well." He grunted and told Tess to recalibrate the machine; he handed her a couple of sheets of paper.

The Hadden's stood in total silence and the two Dorothy's gripped each other. Finally Dorothy said quietly; "So if I go back with Davies and live in the 1970's all that will happen?" John nodded; "You must never go there. Your grand daughter will meet Davies, as she should in 1971 and so the time line should be protected. I will jump back and find him before I even meet him [Davies]."

Harry wiped his face and cussed under his breath; "Bloody Christ Dorothy; she must be your granddaughter by a daughter you will have with Paul. But that means, at some stage you move to America?" Dorothy slowly nodded and gripped the arm of her granddaughter. They both watched as John Hammond stood on the pile of mattresses and told Tess to operate the machine as soon as she had made the new settings.

There was a bright flash of light and John Hammond/Washington was gone. The two Dorothy's embraced again and were now chatting like old friends. Uncle William needed to sit down and Tess gave him her seat. Harry stood staring at the machine and wondered if Jericho Tibbs would appear soon. The constant breeches of the time line would surely bring him here.

Harry yawned; he really wished he had waited to have breakfast; the lack of food was probably making him tired. Very tired. He snapped his eyes open; resisting the tiredness that swept over him and yawned again. "I feel knackered and I just got up." He muttered and buttered some toast. The letter from Inspector Ramsey had not been good news about poor Alice.

Dorothy just sighed about that and rose from the table and headed for the door. "Come on you two or we'll be late for church and its Reggie's first appearance at his new church." She smiled at the pair who finished off their toast and enjoyed a final cup of tea.

Dorothy adjusted her bonnet and looked down the pew and smiled; Reggie had really made the effort and looked every inch the gentleman for his first visit to his new church and new congregation. Harry leaned across and whispered; "You just have to admire him and the reverend; especially the reverend."

Dorothy nodded; "Who would have believed that old Rashwood had such determination and commitment to his principles. It may have taken him two years but he did it." It had taken that long to get Reggie [Titus] accepted into the congregation at St. Thomas's Church. But the reverend had overcome all objections and Reggie sat proudly with most for the cast and crew from the Paradise Theatre [which was about three streets away]. Harry knew the battle the old clergyman had fought, including denouncing several regular worshippers from the pulpit. "God's children come in all creeds and colours; but they are ALL his children!" he had thundered from the box. It had worked and Reggie was finally accepted into the congregation; the first person of 'colour' to be so welcomed in the small church. But about a quarter of the good reverend's congregation had moved to St. Margret's in protest.

Uncle William patted her hand and gestured with his bible to Reggie; "If pride is a sin; then our Titus is clearly guilty and so am I." Dorothy smiled at that remark. She knew that her dear Uncle had moved heaven and earth to get Reggie accepted here. Well, so had Harry and her. She glanced back and saw Rosie smiling at her, sitting next to her dozing husband Albert. Her two boys sat either side looking utterly bored. She chuckled to herself and didn't notice the young couple sitting at the very back of the church. The young woman had her arm through the young man's and they sat smiling.

Tess adjusted her bonnet and whispered into her 'husband's' ear; "I think it's sad that they won't be part of the family for another seventy odd years. They're good people." John Hammond lifted his young wife's hand and kissed it. "I suspect that our Dorothy would call herself Ms, if she could get away with it in these very constrained times."

Mrs. John Hammond nodded; "Yes I think you're right darling but we all have to keep our little secrets don't we." John chuckled and gripped his wife's hand tightly; "Amen to that my dear." He said quietly and thought about the crates waiting for him in the basement of 'Oddfellows Hall'. He would start to rebuilt his machine this very night.

Outside, on the snow covered gravel path, Jericho Tibbs pulled his coat tighter about him. He sighed and consulted his beautiful watch. The big man next to him chuckled and slapped his gloved hands together; "Which parts of the story are you leaving out Jericho?" He was quite amused and intrigued about what exactly Jericho was about to tell his human agents – the Hadden family – for this time and place, about their latest mission, which they currently had no idea that they had just undertaken!

Jericho just sighed; "Most of it Wilson, we can't divulge too much about the future, but they deserve to know just how good they were on this one. Not that they'll remember anything about it since the time line has reverted – almost – back to its original form. They did a good job."

Wilson nodded at that and smiled as the parishioners started to file out the church after an undisturbed service. There was a couple in the congregation that would not be pleased to see the temporal detectives.

CHAPTER 8. 'MANDELA EFFECT.' Fiona Broome.

"Hey man; what you doing here? Something going down the Prince should know about boy?" the huge man lifted the brow of his enormous hat which boasted a pea-cock feather and grinned. 'The Prince' of 47th street was well known to Detective Davies Washington; he had busted him a couple of times on minor drug and driving stuff. The Prince certainly didn't hold anything against the young cop; he was known to be fair to the 'brothers' and of course; he was a 'brother' himself!

Davies just smiled and they slapped hands; "Ain't nothing going down my man. Waiting for my girl; we're going to see that." He jerked a thumb up at the cinema sign [the film was 'The Dirty Dozen'] and the Prince nodded; "I hear its mother fucking bad ass!" Davies nodded; "I hope the girl likes it. On to a Chinese at the Golden Lotus afterwards man. Make a night of it." Davies slapped the big man's shoulder; "She's here." The Prince stared down the crowded pavement and whistled; "Sweet Jesus my man; you've pulled a pretty white princess. Does your mother know?" He chuckled and they slapped hands again. Davies watched him slip into the overloaded El Dorado Grand and it pulled away and slowly moved off with the traffic. Davies stared down the street and watched her walking towards him; slowly starting to smile.

She was wearing a white t-shirt with no bra and 'hot-pants' that left very little to the imagination. Her hair tied back with a bright red ribbon and Davies had to chuckle as she made a point of touching her throat, a couple of times. She was wearing a small black lace collar. Davies laughed and smoothed his leather jacket down and ran both hands through his short afro hair. He knew that she was wearing the black collar to show that she was a Blackman's little white girl. He wiped his face and grinned. He didn't care about the comments from his black friends and colleagues at the 34th precinct about dating a 'snow bunny'. He really didn't care; he just wanted to be with her.

She threw an arm around his neck and kissed him full on the lips, He gripped her tightly and breathed deep; she smelt like heaven.

"I thought we could catch a film and then a Chinese sit in, if that's ok with you?" She nodded and pushed her arm through his and they walked to the cinema entrance. He looked down at her backside and groaned; the cheeks of her peach shaped arse were hanging out the shorts. He reached down and slapped one. "I really want you baby sister." He whispered. The girl ran her hand down his shirt; damp with sweat and brushed against the zipper of his flared trousers. "I think I can see that or do you keep your service revolver down there!" They both laughed and found a couple of seats in the back row. The film was starting and they held hands and kissed a couple of times. Davies whispered in the darkness; "It doesn't matter where you go Rosie, I'll always love you and come and get you." They kissed quite passionately and his hand disappeared under her t-shirt. She made no attempt to stop him.

Uncle William tapped another piece of correspondence and said; "On a lighter and much happier note, George's ship will be docking at the Albert Docks near Christmas and he has three weeks leave. So, I think we should have bit of a party for him, what do you say?"

The two detectives walked into the hamburger joint, past a bored patrolman who just nodded a greeting. They were met by a dour faced Inspector O'Malley who folded his arms, "About time you two lazy bastards showed up. I put a call in for you twenty minutes ago."

Santos was about to say something but the Inspector waved that away, "This is right up your street. A real interesting one, three brothers picked on a lone white man who looked like he couldn't tear open a Cornflakes carton and he did this to them. They produced knives and the little guy pulled a fucking Magnum 44 and blew the dumb bastards to hell!" He gestured behind him and Davies stared at two bodies: they were all big men, one was sprawled across a table, with his face looking like he had just been smashed full on with a sledge hammer. The second one was on the floor, laid in an 'X' position, his face contorted and missing most of his skull!

Santos whistled, "The fucking dude did this with a 44, where the hell did he hide that fucking monster?" he sounded impressed because he was. The Inspector chuckled and gestured to the broken window of the diner, "That's the best fucking one. That brother ran for the door and the little guy placed one round through his shoulder blades. He must weigh in at 200 pounds and the witnesses say that he flew through the window like a sack of bricks: looks like he was hit by a fucking train. Then the little white guy slowly walks out the joint….this is the best bit - after collecting his fucking take-out!"

The three detectives stood staring about the diner and Santos pushed back his bright red beret, lighting up a cigarette. "Well, I know who we should fucking arrest." Both Davies and the Inspector stared at him. Santos shrugged his shoulders and grinned, "Dirty fucking Harry!"

O'Malley groaned and lit up his cigar, "Just fucking get on with it. I doubt if we can charge the fucker with anything, but I would like to know where such a man is and who the fuck he is."

The two detectives nodded and watched the Inspector walk away. "And where the hell do we start? His description could match a million white dudes in the city. This assignment is crap and O'Malley knows it." Davies stared at the dead bodies as Floyd the photographer unpacked his cameras. "Do you two want to know what's really great about this job?" he chuckled and lifted his camera, taking shot after shot. "What have you got for us Floyd?" Santos asked and Floyd lowered his camera, "The fucking press loves it and so will every decent New Yorker!"

The two detectives walked from the diner and headed back to their car, but all Davies could think about was meeting Rosie tonight. They passed a large black Lincoln and didn't notice that the big Blackman driving turned away, so he couldn't be recongnised. Wilson turned to Jericho Tibbs and nodded, "With the demon pulled out of that little man [which would explain his 'superhuman' strength!] The time line has restored itself. Three souls still collected and all dispatched naturally, well as natural as a Magnum 44 can be!"

Jericho just nodded, "Dorothy's grand-daughter is now scheduled to have her relationship with Davies as the timeline originally played it. The little changes have been readily accepted by Angel Margret [Jericho's boss!] and most humans won't even notice the small changes" He sighed and gestured for Wilson to pull away, "And those that do, will put it all down to the bloody 'Mandela effect'. Not a bad job all round my friend." Wilson chuckled and felt quite happy about how it had all turned out, for his friend and former colleague [Davies.]

THE END

ADVERTISEMENT BY THE AUTHOR:

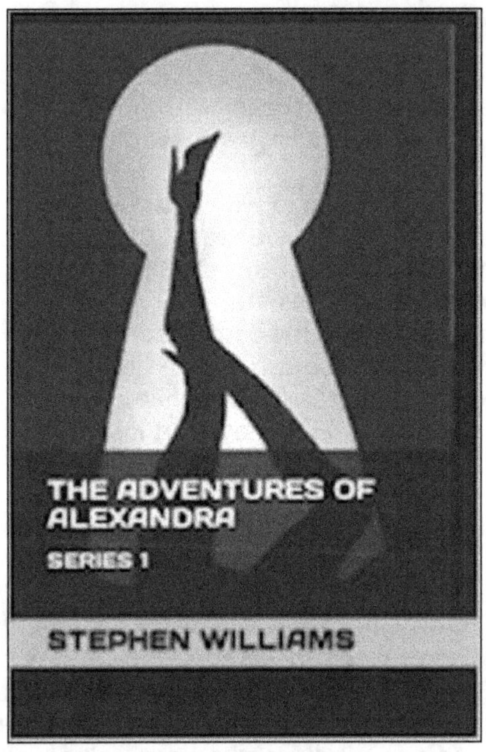

'THE ADVENTURES OF ALEXANDRA: SERIES 1'
the latest book [at the time of going to press!]
of the series by the same author

EPISODE 6: "THE COMPLICATED FUNERAL OF SIR WILLIAM McKENZIE."

Alcohol – Smoking – Strong language – Strong sexual references [including nudity and references to prostitution] – Violence – Mild Adult Erotica.

Approximately 45 to 60 minutes.

Remember: **Adult Content.**

EPISODE CONTENTS.

1. 'ALL I KNOW I READ IN THE PAPERS.'
Start page: 413

**2. 'FORGIVE ME, FOR ALL THE THINGS I DID BUT MOSTLY
FOR THE ONES I DID NOT.'**
Start page: 419

**3. 'LOOK, ALL ADMINISTRATIONS, ALL GOVERNMENTS
LIE, ALL OFFICIALS LIE AND NOTHING THEY SAY IS TO BE
BELIEVED. THAT'S A PRETTY GOOD RULE.'**
Start page: 425

**4. 'ADVERSITY IS THE DIAMOND DUST HEAVEN POLISHES
ITS JEWELS WITH'.**
Start page: 429

5. 'DEATH ENDS A LIFE, NOT A RELATIONSHIP.'
Start page: 433

**6. 'I WAS NOT CONTENT AT HOME....I WANTED TO LIVE
LIKE A COULORFUL BUTTERFLY IN THE SUN.'**
Start page: 440

7. 'FUNERALS...ARE FOR THE LIVING.'
Start page: 446

**8. 'THERE IS NOTHING LIKE A TRAIN JOURNEY FOR
REFLECTION.'**
Start page: 449

**9. 'IN THE GAME OF DECEPTION, THE STAKES ARE
ALWAYS HIGH.'**
Start page: 452

10. 'I AND OTHERS OF MY SEX FIND OURSELVES CONTROLLED BY A FORM OF GOVERNMENT IN THE INAUGURATION OF WHICH WE HAD NO VOICE.'
Start page: 458

IMPORTANT AUTHOR'S NOTE:
"The names and places of some characters have been changed to protect the innocent and ficticious characters created in their stead. Thank you."

CHAPTER 1. 'ALL I KNOW I READ IN THE PAPERS.' Will Rogers.

Dorothy carefully picked at her boiled egg, slowly peeling away little pieces of shell and then sprinkled a little salt on the exposed interior. She picked up her small spoon and dug about inside. That's when Uncle William sighed loudly and slammed the morning paper down with some force.

"I don't believe it! If it wasn't in the bloody 'Times' I would not have believed it." He said and shook his head with some surprise and sadness. Dorothy lowered her spoon and asked what was so unbelievable. Uncle William tapped the paper and sighed again; "My old friend Willy McKenzie is dead. Found dead on a bloody train in Paris; sprawled across the floor of his sleeping apartment carriage - stone cold dead – and his travelling companion, young Robert Laxton, his nephew, is now missing."

Dorothy knew that Sir William McKenzie had been a friend of her Uncle's since their school days. The pair called themselves the 'two Willies' or amongst their school-friends; big Willy and little Willy, for Sir William was a big, strapping Scottish lad from a very wealthy Highland family and Uncle William was a lad of small size in comparison.

"Do they give details of what happened?" She asked and dug her spoon into the egg. Uncle William picked up the paper and adjusted his glasses; "Just that Sir William was returning from St. Petersburg after a business trip – apparently he had clinched a deal to export his family distilled whisky – to Russia. He was accompanied by his nephew, a medical student called Robert Laxton [his late sister's son] who has since simply vanished. No trace was found on the train and the body was found by a conductor who couldn't raise Sir William after the Paris train stopped and all the passengers had departed. There is an international police warrant issued for Robert Laxton on suspicion of murder, which is odd, because there is no cause of death stated. Sir William's widow – Isabella – should arrange for the body to be brought home after the post mortem; if the Paris authorities allow it."

Dorothy nodded and finished her egg; Uncle William sat wrapped in sadness at the passing of his old school friend and Dorothy was really happy when Harry came through the door; shouting for Ellen to bring him some breakfast. He had the paper wrapped up under his arm. He slapped Uncle William on the shoulder; "Sorry about Big Willy; just read about the damn strange thing in the papers. My edition seems to be hinting that the Russian Secret Service could be involved. It appears that the man Sir William was doing business with has been taken into custody by the Okhrana. I take it he [Big Willy?] was no blooming spy!"

Uncle William took the paper and read with great interest. Ellen slapped Harry's breakfast down and handed Uncle William a telegram.

"The 'Okhrana' was formed after the assassination of Tsar Alexander II in 1881. They were known to be totally ruthless and loyal to the Tsar." SJW.

Uncle William tore open the envelope and sighed loudly; but did smile a little. "It's from Edward Collington – Sir William's lawyer – he informs me that according to Willy's last will and testament; I'm to organize the funeral as Willy and I agreed. I'll have to get in touch with Isabella." He rose from the table and headed for his study.

Harry tucked into his bacon and eggs, sipping his tea between mouthfuls. Dorothy sat back and watched her brother enjoying his breakfast; "Won't this Isabella be unhappy by that turn of events?" Harry shook his head; "I shouldn't think so, it was an arranged marriage. Sir William wanted a young trophy wife and she wanted money and position, there's over twenty years between the pair....or rather, there was."

Dorothy picked up the paper and read about the 'Russian' connection. "For heaven's sake he was selling whisky; not bleeding guns!" Harry chuckled at that and finished his breakfast. He wiped his mouth with a napkin and leaned over the table and kissed Dorothy on the cheek; "Must dash, I'm in Crown court in an hour. The case of the headless woman fished from the ruddy Thames. Her old man is guilty as hell and has pleaded not guilty; as usual." He disappeared out the door and Dorothy sat staring at the table; she wondered if she should call on Paul and maybe have lunch together.

Ellen stuck her head around the door and jerked a thumb behind her; "Young Arthur from the theatre just left a message for you miss; says you should get to the theatre as there's someone there who urgently wants to see you." Dorothy jumped up smiling; "I bet its Paul surprising me with a morning visit!" Ellen just smiled and muttered; "I'll fetch your hat and coat then. No one else will."

Dorothy waved a cab down and headed for the paradise Theatre; smiling in anticipation of seeing her fiancé. She had made a momentous decision about her forthcoming marriage. She would try her best to make it work: so she would remain faithful to her new husband – well, with men anyway – she felt he [Paul] wouldn't mind too much about her and Rosie's little playtimes! But Reggie, Eddy and Albert would have to stand back: she was now off limits to other men. Rosie had listened carefully to the new arrangement and slowly nodded; she thought Dottie had made the right decision in the circumstances. Strangely enough, Dottie wasn't surprised by her [Rosie's] reaction.

Dorothy ran up the stage stairs, holding up her skirt and pushed through her dressing room door and found Rosie handing a cup of tea to a strange young man dressed like a street seller. He didn't smile; "Hello Dorothy. I thought it was safest to ask for you rather than your Uncle William; I have police after me. I'm Robert Laxton, Sir William McKenzie's nephew and please believe me I didn't murder him. I need sanctuary and some help. Can you help please?"

Rosie took Dorothy's hat and coat; "Apparently he crossed the bleeding channel hidden in a consignment of smelly French cheese and he's quite ripe." Dorothy didn't have to be told that; her nose had already found that out. She gestured to a chair; "You had better sit down Mr. Laxton before you fall down." He looked like he just taken part in a week long insomnia contest and won. "Please call me Robert." He said quietly and slumped into the chair and downed his tea in one hit, looking for another.

Rosie sighed; "I know this is a silly question; but do you want a bacon sandwich?" The young man grinned and nodded. Dorothy sat in the other chair and stared at the young man; was she sitting face to face with a ruthless murderer who had killed his own Uncle? She actually didn't think so. "What on earth happened in Russia?" she asked and sat back.

"Everything was fine at first; the business was wrapped up in a few days and Mr. Grossvech seemed on the level. He even paid – in advance – for the first shipment - in Russian gold coins. So we all celebrated at a posh St. Petersburg restaurant. Grand Duke Nickolas uses the place. He's the Emperors first cousin once removed, a giant of a man. But I knew were being followed the whole time by Russian secret Service agents. I began to suspect that Mr. Grossvech was far more than he told us; far more, but my uncle wouldn't listen; he trusted the man." He accepted a refill of his cup by Rosie and continued.

"We were staying in his grand house in the city and one night he came rushing into our bedrooms, shouting. He looked afraid, well; terrified would be a better description. He told us to flee the city and get out of Russia as quickly as possible. That's when we could hear gunshots and we didn't hang about. We made the railway station and headed out the city for the German border. For the next three days and nights we were on the run; we didn't know who we could trust anymore. The British consulate and Embassy was always kept under surveillance by them, so we had to avoid them. That's when my uncle pointed out a Russian Newspaper article [he could read Russian] that a certain Mr. Alexander Grossvech had been found dead in the Neva River with several bullet holes in him!" he gulped down more tea and wiped his face. The smell of frying bacon now filled the place.

"We managed to get on the Paris night train from Berlin and we thought we were clear. On the train I met a Russian doctor who "was called – of all names – Doctor Smirnoff. A fat little man who was travelling to Scotland for a big medical conference to be held in Edinburgh; I just didn't trust him and avoided his company. What I did notice was that he had plenty of money and liked the ladies. On the morning we pulled into Paris Central I went to my uncles' carriage and found him dead on the floor; he's face contorted in agony. As I examined him, I noticed a broken needle on the floor and since I knew that my Uncle didn't do drugs; someone must have killed him. That fat little Russian doctor with the evil eyes immediately sprung to mind." He accepted his bacon roll from Rosie and ate it without stopping to breathe!

"The conductor appeared and found me bending over the body and screamed murder. I knew I would be arrested and held; despite my innocence and who would believe such a story? I ran for it and travelled across Paris and onto Calais. I managed to hide amongst some crates of cheese and escape Dover docks. I knew that my Uncle and yours were close and totally trusted each other, so I made my way here. My Uncle William always spoke with some pride about you and your brother Harry. So I thought I would come here."

He sat slumped in the chair and wiped his face; "I think something was going on in Russia with that damn Mr. Grossvech and Uncle and I got caught up in it; that cost the old man his life."

Dorothy quietly asked Rosie if she would grab a cab and leave a message at Brick Lane Police Station for Harry to drop around – urgently – when he finishes at court. Rosie just smiled; "I think you best send young Arthur with that message Miss. You may be engaged, but you can't be alone in your dressing room with a young man. Especially one suspected of murder." Dorothy sighed; she knew that Rosie was right and told her to shout for Arthur. That's when they both noticed that young Robert Laxton had fallen asleep, sitting in the chair.

Rosie threw a blanket around him and folded her arms; "Well, he's either a wronged innocent or he can spin a real yarn and is capable of murdering his old uncle?" Dorothy accepted a cup of tea; "I think it's best for our nerves that we accept he's a wronged innocent, don't you?" Rosie smiled at that and yanked open the door and gestured for one of the maintenance men to come over; she told him to send young Arthur to her. Rosie waited outside the door; leaving it slightly open. Dorothy gave her three pence to give young Arthur for his troubles. He was soon on scene and departed – quite happy to get out the theatre – and was three pence better off.

The two women sat watching the young man; he seemed to be talking in his sleep. He was clearly having a troubled dream. That's when there was soft knock on the door and Rosie quietly opened it. Dorothy waited a minute or two and said softly; "Who is it Rosie?" Rosie opened the door and gestured to the tall man in a neat black suit, who removed his bowler hat; "A bleeding spook. Someone from Military intelligence miss; a captain."

Dorothy went to the door and saw three men standing there. One removed his hat and spoke quietly; "Good morning Miss Hadden. I am Captain Hayward – I believe your brother has spoken about me – so I won't go into the details of what I do for his majesty. I understand that you have a certain Robert Laxton ensconced in your dressing room. We...I am very much interested in speaking with the talented young man; few escape the clutches of the Okhrana and then manage to travel half across Europe with little money and several police forces after him. I just may recruit the young fellow for myself. We always need enterprising, quick thinking people. Like yourself and we are in desperate need of female operatives. You might consider the benefits of serving your King and Country, willingly this time."

Dorothy sighed; she had little choice in this matter, like she had when she last worked for the Special Irish Branch [See episode: **'The workhouse corpse with golden boots'**.] and told the Captain to step in. "He's utterly exhausted and you would expect after such a journey." The Captain nodded and smiled; "You're as clever as you are beautiful Miss Hadden. I do hope you consider my proposition; you will be most welcome."

Dorothy could see two other men outside the door; dressed in similar outfits. The captain gestured for them to remain at the door, but leave it open. She stared hard at the young tall one, who had removed his hat and almost smiled at her. She seemed to recongise him, from somewhere or some place. Dottie groaned to herself: now she would puzzle about that all bleeding day unless she asked him outright. He said, "Hello Miss Hadden." And now smiled, "Don't I know you sir?" she said and slowly smiled. Dottie had recongnised the young man.

Hayward stepped in and smiled; "I see sleeping beauty is here, I guessed he would turn up here sooner or later. He's had quite an adventure; escaping Russia, on the run throughout Europe, dodging the police and smuggling himself back in England. But we need to have words with the young fugitive. You see our agents in St. Petersburg collaborate some of his story. There was indeed a shoot out at Mr. Grossvech's villa between him and the Okhrana. They clearly won; Grossvech turned up dead in the river with several bullet holes in him. It appears that he was considered a bit of a revolutionary. It's his Uncle's connections with the dead Russian that we're interested in and since Sir William can't answer our questions; this young man is the next best thing."

Dorothy stood and folded her arms; she knew who captain Hayward was, Harry had spoken about having dealings with the man and he certainly fitted Harry's description. "He claims or rather believes that a Russian doctor may have murdered his uncle, a...." Captain Hayward smiled; "Yes, the curiously named Doctor, we do know about him Miss Hadden. Now let's wake the young man up."

Captain Hayward shook Robert by the shoulder and he awoke with a start and jumped up, his face filled with fear. Dorothy stepped between them and spoke directly to Robert, telling him who Captain Hayward was and that her brother knew him. Robert wiped his face and stared at the floor.

"Your choices are simple lad. You can co-operate with his royal Majesty's Military Intelligence officers or take your chances with the police forces of two countries and face a murder charge. Not to mention that the Russian secret service may still consider you a threat and take appropriate action. You know that they're not as nice as us." He smiled and gestured to his colleagues to join him.

Dorothy gripped Robert's arm; "I think you can trust him Robert.

I believe that's the advice that Harry would give you." Robert nodded and thanked Dorothy – and Rosie – for help and hospitality. He held out his hands to be handcuffed, but captain Hayward waved that away; "I also believe you're not that dumb Robert. Please go with my associates." Robert followed the two burly men out the door.

Captain Hayward smiled at Dorothy; "I'll speak with Harry, but I think you'll be interested in the proposition I have for you Miss Hadden." Rosie grunted and said quietly; "I can imagine what that bleeding proposition is about." Captain Hayward didn't smile and said to her; "How's Albert Mrs. McHannon's? Still causing trouble down the docks with his union activities? He should be careful about the people he upsets, don't you think?"

He turned back to Dorothy; "This mission may need a lady like you Miss Hadden with your actress talents and beauty. You will hear from me. Give my fond regards to Harry and tell him that I'll be in touch." He slapped his bowler hat on and disappeared through the door.

Rosie slammed it after him; "Bleeding bastards! They know everything about you! How's that possible in a free country?" Dorothy watched from the window as Robert was placed in a big black carriage and driven away. "I think they know everything about everyone because that keeps us a free country. I didn't know your Albert was involved in Union activities?"

Rosie shrugged her shoulders; "All the lad's elected him for a joke and he's taken it really seriously now. I keep telling him to keep his head down, but you know what's he's like. He's always right." Rosie put the kettle back on the small stove and filled it with more water from the big jug. "Do you think there's truth in the story about the Russians and the murdering little doctor?" She asked Dorothy who sat back down. "According to Captain Hayward there is definitely some merit in it or they wouldn't be talking to Robert. They would have just thrown him to the dogs."

Rosie nodded; "So what do you think his proposition is then?" Dorothy shrugged her shoulders; "Well, I know – through Harry – that he's married with two young children and is a former navel captain. Harry says he's very respected by Navel and Military intelligence. He does a lot of work with the Irish branch. Maybe, on certain occasions, they need a woman to play a part in some case that requires it. So I suppose an actress would be the first choice." She sighed and thought back to what she did the last time she worked for them and that didn't make her happy.

"The 'Special Irish Branch' was formed in 1883 to gather intelligence on Irish 'revolutionaries' and later was to become known as 'Special Branch'. It was merged into a counter terrorism unit in 2006." SJW.

Dorothy smiled, "The young man who said 'hello' is the son of George Cabot – he's called George too – who was the head gardener at my old school. All the girls liked young George as he was known and our little connection may prove useful. The last I heard about him, was that he had joined the navy after leaving university. No one knew why, he graduated as a bleeding Archeologist!" Rosie nodded, "Well, he's certainly grown into a big bleeding man and good looking too."

"Like a lot of girls, he's bleeding had his hands in my school knickers and up my blouse on more than one occasion." Dottie said grinning, remembering those warm afternoons behind the sports pavilion and some bleeding cold one's inside during winter. But what she did remember about young George was the kissing: If French Kissing was an Olympic sport; he would be gold medal potential.

The family gathered in Uncle William's dressing room after the evening performance and Uncle William announced they were travelling to France to collect the body and bring it home for burial. He did admit that there was a little difference in Isabella's plans and his. He wanted a full Highland funeral for his friend – as Sir William requested – and Isabella wanted a quiet burial in a Kent churchyard!

Dorothy tugged Harry's arm and smiled; "I don't think there's much common ground between those two ideas." He grinned; "My money is on Uncle William." and quite looked forward to a French day trip.

The ferry had docked at Leith [a port just north of Edinburgh] just an hour or so behind schedule and no really minded; the crossing had enjoyed wonderful weather and Uncle William had a local brewery cart ready and waiting. The four men were quite rough, but handled the coffin with great care. The youngest of them made several desperate attempts to engage Dorothy in conversation and failed miserably. Uncle William did give them a good tip for their efforts. They headed for the railway station; following in a separate carriage with their luggage.

Harry and Dorothy were impressed with the locals; the men removed their hats as the flag draped coffin passed by [it was covered with the old Scottish flag] and they quickly reached the station were the big men carried the coffin unto the platform and took their leave.

Dorothy was really surprised to see that no less than four coffins were waiting to load into the freight carriage of the train. Only one had a grieving widow standing next to it. The poor woman was standing looking around; as if waiting for someone to help her. Dorothy grabbed Harry's arm and propelled him towards the woman; dressed head to toe in morning black; "See if that poor woman needs help for Christ sake Harry." Harry nodded and walked over removing his hat. He spoke to the woman for a minute or so and finally managed to get some porters to load the coffin aboard. He walked back to Dorothy and they watched the women climb into the train.

"It was her brother; died in a fishing accident off the Essex coast a week ago. They came from Aberdeen, so he's being taken there for burial in the churchyard of the village, where he grew up and their parents are buried. He was twenty-three. Her name is Morag and since there is no-one else; it's fallen to her to bury him. Here's the really shitty bit; she's a young widow herself. Her husband died two years ago of blood poisoning from an accident working on their farm. She has two young boys to raise and has to manage the farm herself."

Dorothy felt a wave of sympathy and sadness sweep over her, but she refused to shed a tear. That didn't last long and Harry gave her a cuddle; "Come old thing. Let's get a bleeding cup of tea." They joined Uncle William in their carriage and Harry ordered tea from the attentive steward.

Dorothy wiped her face and checked her make-up in her compact mirror; "There's too much death around these days." She softly muttered and Uncle William patted her hand and smiled a little; "My dear, there IS always too much death around for the living's taste."

Harry stared out the window and said quietly; "Guess who's just climbed aboard the bleeding train?" Uncle William shrugged his shoulders; "King Edward?" Harry chuckled; "No, Robert Laxton and that captain Hayward from Military Intelligence; they just came aboard with another two fellows dressed in similar suits to captain Hayward." Dorothy chuckled; "Must be secret service in disguise. They all wear the same suit apparently. Bit of a joke, if National Security wasn't so bloody important in these dangerous times." Harry had to agree with that. They could hear whistles and felt the train starting to move. The steward appeared with the tea tray and Dorothy filled the cups and wondered about captain Hayward. She couldn't believe that he made a pass at her; despite the fact that he knew that she knew he was married with children!

But one of the agents, who gave Dottie fresh anguished thoughts over where she knew him from, had been solved by Harry; he Pointed out that agent Collins had been a uniform constable at Brick Lane Police Station before joining the department. If Dottie and Rosie hadn't climbed onto a ledge around a hotel, they would have been his 'stag' entertainment!

The train would arrive in Edinburgh central Station in a couple of hours and they [well, Uncle William] would get the coffin transferred to the Highlands Express and onwards to Bray Castle. Joshua Tanner & Sons – the local Undertakers – would meet them at Bray station.

Uncle William sipped his most welcome tea and sighed; "I'm a little surprised that Isabella couldn't even be bothered to attend to husband's funeral. I knew it was bad between the two, but not this bad." Dorothy stirred some sugar into her cup and grunted; "Maybe it would have helped if Sir William had married a woman nearer to his own age; like twenty years nearer." Now that did make Harry laugh. Uncle William just sighed; but knew that his niece was right.

"We will sleep really well tonight after all this travel." Harry was saying as the carriage door opened. Captain Hayward removed his hat and smiled directly at Dorothy. "Thought I'd pop up and keep you up to date with what's going on." He sat down without being asked – next to Dorothy it should be noted – and slowly unbuttoned his black coat. "One of our agents in St. Petersburg confirms that Sir William was indeed carefully watched by the Russian Secret Service. It appears that the man he was doing business with was not considered loyal to Tsar Nicholas."

Dorothy folded her arms and muttered; "From what I hear about Russia; there's not many who are too loyal to him." That made Uncle William chuckle and asked captain Hastings to continue. He gave Dorothy a sideward's look and said; "Our doctors confirm that Sir William was injected with some kind of poison and so it was murder. It appears that he rushed from Russia because he may have stumbled upon something that he shouldn't heard or seen. Aboard the Paris train was a Russian doctor known to us; a certain Doctor Smirnoff who is a Russian Secret Service agent. We strongly believe that he terminated Sir William before he could tell [British secret Service] about what he discovered."

Dorothy had to smile; "Smirnoff? I thought that was Vodka?" Captain Hayward smiled at her; "That's just the name he uses; we believe his real name is Viktor Jerkoff and he is actually a vet." Harry couldn't stop himself having a little laugh at that revelation; "Little wonder he changed his name." he said to himself.

Captain Hayward told them that he was probably travelling to the big medical conference being held in Edinburgh. Now Dorothy was interested in that; her fiancé Paul was also attending that conference and she wondered if they would bump into each other. The captain told Uncle William that Mr. Edward Collington – Sir William's lawyer – would meet them at Bray castle for the funeral. Young Robert Laxton would now attend the funeral. It appears that he was indeed Sir William's heir and stood to gain the Title and estates of his late uncle. Apparently there had been a generous allowance granted in Sir William's will for his young wife. Captain Hayward mentioned that Isabella had wanted her husband buried in Kent; where her family hailed from. Uncle William shook his head and told everyone that Sir William ALWAYS insisted he would have a Highland funeral and be interned in the family crypt. It was specified in the will and He [Uncle William] had been tasked to carry it out.

"Quite so William, we have received information that the doctor may try and contact a man we know to be a double agent; a certain Sir Alistair Growling. He spends far too much money than he earns at the Foreign Office and is known as a 'skirt chaser'. He can't resist beautiful women; especially those of questionable morals. But we need to know where they are meeting up in Edinburgh and catch them together." Captain Hayward stood – ensuring his hand brushed Dorothy's – and pushed his hat back on. He turned to Harry; "I may have need of you Harry and if possible; Dorothy. I have a plan to expose both men and I think that Dorothy could be of real use; if she wishes to serve her King and Country, of course."

Dorothy answered that immediately; "Course I will. I am English and proud of it. If I can play a small part in protecting her, then I will do so." Captain Hayward grinned; "Thank you Dorothy. Spoken like a true woman of the Empire. I'll be back in a few minutes, there's some papers I must look at." and headed back to his carriage. Dorothy just sighed and settled into her seat, watching the beautiful Scottish countryside passing by. She wondered what little part she would be acting. Then she remembered that George Cabot was travelling on this very train and wondered about the young man: he had been friends with Jeb at Dorothy's old school and a little wave of nostalgia swept over her. She decided to seek him out and have a few quiet words, mainly about the past and not the forthcoming mission.

She placed her novel down and adjusted her hat, telling Harry that she 'was popping to the loo'. Harry looked up from his paper and smiled, "Give my regards to young George, I think he's part of the back-up team on this one." Dottie just sighed: it was like her bleeding brother could read her mind at times! She pulled back the door and waited for an elderly couple to pass, the old man tipped his hat and pair disappeared down the corridor.

CHAPTER 3. 'LOOK, ALL ADMINISTRATIONS, ALL GOVERNMENTS LIE, ALL OFFICIALS LIE AND NOTHING THEY SAY IS TO BE BELIEVED. THAT'S A PRETTY GOOD RULE.' Daniel Ellsberg.

She left the carriage and also headed down the corridor saying 'excuse me please' as a big man almost passed her. They both stopped and smiled; it was young George Cabot who lifted his hat and said quietly, "On the job I'm afraid Dottie, keeping an eye on young Laxton." Dorothy had to smile, "If I remember the rumours, you were frequently on the job." He laughed outright at that and gestured down the corridor, "This train has a bar, do you want a drink...for old times' sake?" She nodded and the pair found the dining car and small bar.

They sat chatting about the old days and obviously their little previous intimacies came up in the quiet conversation. He just smiled broadly, a little flattered that Dottie had remembered their almost juvenile groupings behind the sports pavilion. Then a certain Jerome [Jeb] Newgate appeared in the conversation. Dorothy expressed her sincere sadness at the young man's – who she adored – passing in the war. George nodded, and then hesitated before speaking. "Yeah, that was a tragedy; I mean a stupid accident like that." He sipped his whisky and saw the puzzled expression on Dorothy's face as she muttered, "But he was killed in action....it was in the papers."

George sighed and shook his head, "That was the story the War Department put out to keep moral up at home. All the soldiers killed in the train carriage fire were classed as 'Killed in Action'. The papers went along with it of course and the families were told they died fighting for their country. But that's not the real story, not by a long way."

Now utterly intrigued, Dorothy asked what actually happened. George sat back and finished his whisky, ordering another round from the attentive barman: they were his only customers.

"It appears that a company of Manchester boys were being transferred by a small train – perhaps no more than five carriages and a brake car – during the night. They were all settled down for the night journey when – inexplicably - there was a fire in one of the carriages and men jumped for their lives as the flames quickly spread. Sadly half a dozen didn't make it and Jeb was one of them apparently. It appears a faulty hurricane lamp was at fault but the British authorities decided the story might affect moral at home and so the dead men were listed as killed in battle. I do know that the fire was so fierce the individual bodies couldn't be identified and that two men were missing, it was believed they had jumped in the darkness and were lost, never recovered." He accepted fresh glasses from the barman and handed Dorothy one, then continued, "All the dead and missing boys were classified as 'killed in action' and Jeb, sadly, was one of them." He leaned closer and rolled the glass in both hands, "Working for the department [Military Intelligence] I'm privy to something else that wasn't reported in the papers. Military command in South Africa didn't know who ordered the transfer and why. It appears they had been seconded for some kind of secret mission on the orders of Lord Kitchener himself."

"Lord Kitchener was made lieutenant-general in 1900 and posted to South Africa as Lord Roberts's chief of staff. He is – of course – known for his recruitment poster for the First World War. Yeah, that's him with the mad eyes, pointing finger and huge moustache that could hide a family of badgers!" SJW.

Dorothy slowly sipped her drink and asked quietly if George knew anything about the mission the Manchester boys were on. He shook his head, "Still a 'Top Secret' affair apparently. Some of the rumours spread around the department is that Kitchener had some mad scheme to assassinate some senior Boar leader who – apparently – had returned [temporarily and unplanned] to his farm for whatever reasons. It's believed because Kitchener did come up with the 'scorched earth' policy that most of our European allies condemned as barbaric. It appears that his lordship was going to use the Boar's own tactics against them and pursue the war with little or no rules of engagement." He shrugged his shoulders, "With those bloody awful Internment camps, filled with starving and sick women and children, Britain wouldn't have been seen in a favourable light, so I suspect that's the real reason the story of the train fire was hushed up: it was solely to keep Kitchener's reputation intact. He's considered to be a military genus but bit of a loony!"

Dorothy sat back and restrained any fresh tears over her lost love: did it really matter how the poor young man died in that bloody war? He was still dead. She could express no surprise that the British government covered the truth up; no surprise whatsoever, and perhaps it was best that his family thought he died in battle. But the story recounted by George left a bad taste in her mouth. She washed that taste away with whisky and George joined her in that endeavour. The pair was now talking closely and quietly and Dorothy asked George if he knew anything about the 'problems' the British Government was having with India. She had just received notice that she would be required for the 'Indian Mission' by Military intelligence. [See episode: **'The Hidden Window'.**] Dottie didn't mention that she had a role in it.

George leaned real close and whispered, "All I know is that it's big. Concerns some bloody Maharaja who is stinking rich, apparently has his own bloody army and he's suddenly taken exception to British rule in his country. I understand that he's coming to London for secret talks with the Prime Minister and will be entertained at Buckingham Palace by the King." George couldn't refrain from chuckling, adding, "Normally, we would just bump the bugger off and blame the Germans! But, in this case we don't have that option: it would be like putting a match to a powder keg, so heaven's knows how they plan to deal with him."

Dorothy nodded and thanked him, then realized that Harry and Uncle William may be growing concerned over her absence – she was supposed to be using the toilet – and so George escorted her back to her carriage, after Dottie paid a quick visit to the loo. She eased next to Harry and smiled at him. He just shook his head and said nothing. Dottie gripped his arm and placed her head against his shoulder and dozed off. As she drifted into a lovely sleep, all she could hear was Uncle William and Harry laughing quietly.

Captain Hayward folded his arms and looked thoroughly disapproving of Dottie's drinking at this time of day. His wife Maude had tried that caper a few years ago and he quickly put a stop to that by removing her dress allowances and stopping her lady friends calling for a month. He had also spanked her a couple of times when he found she had disobeyed him. She sulked for a good few weeks then things returned to 'normal' in his troubled marriage. He blamed the bloody suffragette movement for all of it. In his mind, women were wives and mothers, well the decent one's anyway. He actually now smiled at Dorothy: and the other type of women was meant to be used and also controlled for the good of the country. And most men of course and she [Dottie] would make a wonderfully slutty, dirty mistress!

The six carriage convoy left Bray Station and headed for the castle. Uncle William, Robert Laxton and captain Hastings sat in the first carriage and watched the castle entrance appear through the spring mist. Uncle William patted Robert's arm, "Well, my boy, you are now in charge of your family's history and there's almost five hundred years of it. You are now the 22nd Laird of Bray-Tulloch and I feel sure that it's in good hands!" Robert just smiled and thanked him for his words. Robert ran a hand over his face as he realized – having now seen the castle - that he had a huge responsibility thrust upon his shoulders and he faced it alone, without his good uncle's guidance. He turned to William, but hesitated, then thought he had nothing to lose. "William, how firm is the arrangement between Dottie and the doctor?"

Uncle William stuck his pipe in his mouth and sucked hard, but didn't light it. "Well, he's given her a ring and they are talking about a spring wedding next year." He shrugged his shoulders and added, "Seems pretty settled to me Robert. What's on your mind?" The young man looked out the carriage window and said quietly, "I'm going to need help William to run all this. A good woman's help: a wife's assistance. That and the pressing and now urgent need to produce an heir, the current one is an American who has no love for the Highlands or its people. He'll sell everything like a damn carpet-bagger and disappear into the night. My dear Uncle William always said it was the first task of the Laird to look after the people who served and worked for him. Can you imagine the damage and despair that would cause?"

"In general, the term "carpetbagger" refers to a traveler who arrives in a new region with only a satchel (or carpetbag) of possessions, and who attempts to profit from or gain control over his new surroundings, often against the will or consent of the original inhabitants." SJW.

Uncle William now lit his pipe, taking measure of the young man he now saw in a different light. His friend 'big Willy' had written well about the boy and always said that he had the right stuff to make a good laird. Now he could see it for himself. "What do you have in mind Robert?" He asked softly sucking hard on his pipe. Robert smiled, "Well, if Dottie should cancel those arrangements – for whatever reason – I would ask your permission to call upon her. I know it would be Dottie that would cancel, the good doctor wouldn't be insane enough to pass up such a woman!"

Captain Hastings nodded; the young man was right about that, but wondered what the new laird would say, if he was allowed to read the file that he [Captain Hastings] held on Miss Dorothy Hadden? That thought made him smile: her growing file and the accompanying photographs and surveillance reports would probably make the young man run for the hills! Miss Hadden was quite the 'liberated' lady of the new century. But she was – it appears - wonderfully discrete and knew how to protect her secrets – so she thought – which made her perfect for the tasks he had planned for her: willingly or otherwise.

Uncle William took a deep breath, a little surprised by young Robert's revelations and he nodded, "Well, Robert, only time will tell I'm afraid. It all seems to be rock solid at the moment."

Robert accepted his words without further comment as a young footman pulled open the door and the new laird was greeted by Mr. Lewis the butler and Mrs. Darcy the housekeeper. There was a line of six maids and two further footmen standing at the bottom of the impressive steps to the castle's huge black doors. Also standing on the gravel were four kitchen maids, the cook: Mrs. Jennings and her assistant, Lucy. Then gathered in a small huddle were four 'hall-boys'. They were busy straightening their jackets and throwing their cigarettes away under the beady eye of Mr. Jerome Fells, now the senior footman.

Standing a little distance away were three grooms and the two game-keepers. All the men had removed their hats and everyone stood in the cold sunshine as a huge, red bearded man played the bagpipes in welcome at the top of the steps. The flag was hanging half way down the pole and Dorothy noted that it was the old Scottish flag and not the Union Jack. The dour butler announced that a hot luncheon was available in the dining room with plenty of tea and coffee, and stronger stuff for those that want it. "Where is Lady McKenzie?" Robert asked the butler as they walked up the steps and Mr. Lewis hesitated then said that her ladyship had already left for London. Robert didn't appear shocked and just nodded, saying nothing more on the subject. But there was plenty of gossip about it amongst the guests, especially the Hadden's. Uncle William was not impressed and said so, saying it was quite shocking and shameful behavior: even if it was a 'sham' marriage.

Those words – for some reason unknown to her – made Dorothy think about her own forthcoming marriage to Doctor Paul! She pushed those thoughts aside and enjoyed a most welcome cup of tea. She and Harry were joined by a handsome young officer from the King's Own Hussars who – unusually – introduced himself to the pair. Apparently his older brother had been at school with Harry and that was good enough to say 'hello'. Harry now smiled, "Good heavens! You're 'Bingo Hope's little brother Brandon?" The young man nodded and Harry introduced Dorothy to the charming and very handsome young man. Harry asked how he was related to the McKenzie family and he sipped his tea and smiled. He really had a wonderful smile and that caught Dorothy's attention, "By granny, our grandmother was the 20th laird's youngest sister, so Robert is our cousin."

Harry asked about his old school pal 'Bingo' [real name Bradley Hope] and Brandon smiled broadly, "The old chap is in Egypt, working for the Colonial office there. I understand he bumped into your brother Henry in Cairo who was making arrangements for an expedition to some obscure place in the desert in search of mummy's and treasure." Harry chuckled, "That sounds like our Henry, he really does have the explorers bug." Dorothy sipped her tea and said quietly, "Or a treasure hunters bug as you call it." That made young Brandon chuckle, "Now I do like a woman of strong opinion. Our sister Catherine is a Suffragette and carry's her political ambitions like a sword. She wants' to be the first woman elected to parliament when women get the vote."

Dorothy agreed with his sister's sentiments and asked if he supports women's rights. The young man lowered his cup, "I most definitely do. Good heavens our mother – Lucille – could make the Privy Council cower and she certainly could run the country while looking after the grandchildren!" Now that did make Dorothy laugh and she really liked this young man. After luncheon she was shown her rooms and found Rosie waiting, busy unpacking the cases, paying particular attention to Dottie's mourning outfit for the funeral.

Rosie was told all about the young mister Brandon and she smiled, kissing Dottie on the cheek, "Is you're bleeding convictions about the good doctor wavering my darling?"

Dorothy shook her head and said 'No.' then added with a smile, "Not yet anyway." She took hold of Rosie's smiling face and pulled it to her and the pair kissed with some passion – as they always did – with Rosie's hand gently slipping under Dottie's dress and between her legs. "Oh my darling, you are a little wet, what bleeding dirty thoughts have you been having?" Dottie grinned and pushed a hand into Rosie's loose blouse. "All about you my love." The pair stepped back and fell gently onto the bed, now French kissing with some passion and their hands frantically undressing each other with some urgency and joy. They were soon both naked and Dorothy lay against the pillows with Rosie's bobbing head between her legs. She groaned loudly a couple of times as Rosie really hit the spot with tongue, mouth and probing fingers. Dottie orgasmed a couple of times under Rosie's delicious assault and then Dottie reciprocated to bring Rosie to a quick climax. Rosie asked – no insisted! – that she have some of her favourite treat and Dorothy, pretending to sigh, rolled onto her stomach and Rosie parted her bum cheeks and set to work on Dottie's 'brown flower'. Dorothy's head lay on her arms, knowing that Rosie would certainly take her time, enjoying her 'treat'. She pushed a hand between her legs and rubbed slowly and firmly, feeling another orgasm was on the way.

Now in the 'doggy position' so that Rosie could get deep between her buttocks it took just another few minutes before Dottie climaxed. Rosie kissed her cheeks with some passion and asked Dottie if she had thought about what she [Rosie] wanted her [Dottie] to do. Dottie shook her head, saying she was still thinking about it. The pair finished their impromptu love-making and lay in each other's arms with Rosie bringing up the subject again and Dorothy stroked her face and finally gave in. She would try it once and if she couldn't bring herself to do it again, that would be that. Rosie kissed her and nodded her agreement.

The girls were in the bath, giggling and splashing water about. Finally Rosie sighed, "Well, that wasn't what it was all bleeding cracked up to be!" Dorothy said 'yes' quietly and giggled some more, kissing Rosie's neck and shoulders. "You smell and taste a lot better now my darling." Rosie chuckled, "Sometimes its better not to get what you bleeding wish for, ain't it?" Dottie nodded her agreement and the pair laughed together – again. Their latest experiment in sex hadn't gone well and both called it a day: 'golden showers' would be someone else's sexual treat as far as they were concerned!

They both fell silent as they heard the loud knock at the bedroom door – the bathroom door was open – and could hear a woman's voice saying that when the gong sounded, it would be time to dress for dinner. When the gong sounded again, it would be dinner being served, or rather time to gather for pre-dinner drinks and conversations. Rosie shouted thanks and she would inform her lady. They sat back and enjoyed their bath.

CHAPTER 5. 'DEATH ENDS A LIFE, NOT A RELATIONSHIP.' Morrie Schwartz.

The convoy left Bray Castle for the family vault at exactly eleven o'clock. Two pipers walked in front of the cortege, playing 'Scotland the Brave' as the hearse slowly trundled towards the imposing stone building. It had an angel standing at each corner; blowing trumpets. The two huge black doors had been pulled to open to receive the latest member of the ancient McKenzie family.

The vicar walked in front of the long string of mourners behind the hearse that was burdened down with flowers and the old Scottish flag. Several professional mourners from the Undertakers flanked it. The Chief Mourner walked in front carrying a dark wooden staff. It was young Mr. Edward Tanner himself of Joshua Tanner & Sons, the local undertakers who had buried McKenzie's for over a century. The service in St. Mary's had been brief – as requested by Sir William – and now the cortege stopped outside the crypt and six pallbearers carefully lifted the coffin from the hearse.

Uncle William stood with Dorothy and Harry nodding with some satisfaction. Young Mr. Laxton made a point of thanking him for his organsiation of the funeral and handed round his silver hip flask filled with whisky. The coffin was carried up the steps of the crypt and then everyone stopped and stared at the black carriage that rolled to halt at the rear of the procession. Someone was shouting and Harry wondered why the little man was waving a paper, whilst flanked by two miserable looking local constables. Panting, the little man stood in front of Uncle William, the Reverend and Robert Laxton. He thrust a piece of paper into Uncle William's hand. "I'm so sorry sir, but there can be no internment today!" A gasp of surprise – and some horror – rippled through the gathered mourners, who now surrounded the little group. Uncle William stared in utter disbelieve at the paper; "A bloody Court injunction to stop the burial!" Everyone groaned in surprise – again. The little man explained; he was a solicitor from Edinburgh and the High Court had granted the injunction to Lady Isabella McKenzie; she had objected to the funeral here in the Highlands and wanted her husband buried in Kent!

Uncle William was clearly angry; but couldn't do a thing about it. The ceremony had to stop until this was sorted out. Mr. Edward Collington – Sir William's lawyer – was shouting that he would go immediately to Edinburgh and lodge an appeal with Judges at the court of sessions; as a matter of urgency. The funeral broke into little groups; all heading back to the castle, all shouting and arguing amongst themselves. Uncle William instructed the dour undertakers to take the body back to the castle. He looked totally devastated and Dorothy gripped his arm. "Come on flipping Uncle William; let's get some bleeding brandy down us." Harry agreed with that and they walked back to the waiting carriage.

After they had received the message from captain Hayward, they arrived in Edinburgh and booked into the newly completed North British Station Hotel in Princes Street. The first thing Dorothy noted and commented on was the clock tower; it was running two minutes late. Harry pointed out that was quite deliberate; "Gives people a few extra minutes to catch their trains."

They settled in their suite and soon captain Hayward appeared with a plan of operation that made Dorothy smile; she was to play the 'honey trap; to get Harry an introduction to the double agent and hopefully, find the elusive Russian doctor.

Dorothy tapped her chin; "Well, This Alistair fellow is bit of a rake, but if he's the only way into this high class brothel then we need to deal with him. He needs an incentive to sign Harry into the club, so I suggest using me as bait." Captain Hayward really did smile at that suggestion, but cautioned Dorothy that she would have to dress as a tart – a high class prostitute – and that would probably mean parading about in her underwear. Dorothy just shrugged her shoulders; "A small price to pay to ensure England and the Empire are safe."

Harry and Uncle William were not happy about it, but in the end, knew that Alistair had to be baited and Dorothy was the perfect honey trap. "I won't let her out of my sight." He placated Uncle William who finally agreed; the security of the nation was in peril and all Englishmen – and women – must do their bit to protect it.

Harry and Dorothy found themselves in Rutherford's Bar and it should be said; thoroughly enjoying themselves, spending the money that Hayward had provided. Harry was playing a rich dissolute rake and Dorothy his questionable 'lady'. The clear photograph of their target had made Dorothy laugh; he looked a complete high class drunken twat!

Dorothy – had already admitted it herself – that she was actually enjoying the bawdy pub. She loved singing the colourful songs that the piano player knocked out and she enjoyed being a little risky in her dress and attitude. She certainly drew some looks from the men in the establishment and all the women. Harry quietly spoke in her ear; "There he is; Sir Alistair Growling, he's suspected of being friendly to any country that can pay him. He's quite a rake about here. If the Russian doctor is looking for female fun around here, then Sir Alistair will be his man."

Dorothy nodded and sipped her gin and stared at the skinny man in an expensive suit with a carnation in his button hole. She had to smile; he looked exactly like the drunken upper class twit that comedians portrayed on the stages of many music halls and theatres.

She stood and brushed down her skirt, making sure that everyone got a very good look at her magnificent breasts, barely restrained by her bodice and sat back down smiling broadly and putting her arm around Harry. It worked; Sir Alistair couldn't take his eyes off her. "Here he comes as the spider said to the fly." Harry whispered. Dorothy adjusted her bosom and grinned as Sir Alistair approached the table.

He introduced himself and slapped Harry on the shoulder as he squeezed next to him; "I only drink champagne and I want you and your lovely lady friend to join me!" and shouted at one of the barmen to bring more bleeding bubbly. It turned out that Sir Alistair worked for the Empire's Foreign office and currently was supposedly supervising the Edinburgh office. He simply couldn't take his eyes off Dorothy – especially those breasts that seemed to hypnotize him – They all chatted and drank champagne which Dorothy quite enjoyed.

Harry played his cover story to perfection; up here for a funeral and away from his miserable wife and troublesome kids. He had brought his 'friend' with him; a music hall actress. Now Alistair was really interested and kept tapping Harry on the back and grinning. The pub was heaving with drunken happy people and the landlord sat cross-legged on his bar with a long white stick; picking out people to do a 'turn'. He pointed to Dorothy and she stood and shouted at the piano man; "Do you know bleeding 'Hold Your Hand Out, Naughty Boy' my friend?" The piano player tipped his bowler hat back and started to play.

Harry sat in some amazement as Dorothy climbed on the table and belted the song out to huge applause and cheering. The landlord joined the applause shouting; "Believe me friends; I'll pick her for another bleeding number!" Now that did receive agreement all around. Sir Alistair grabbed Harry and pushed a piece of paper in his hand; "That's a very special club I know. Tell the receptionist that Mister Black Bunny will sign you in and make sure you bring your bloody friend; suitably undressed!"

The night passed in drunken singing and finally Harry and Dorothy managed to escape when Sir Alistair fell asleep amongst the glasses and bottles. They made their way back to the hotel and Harry read the note; "The Empire & Colonial Coffee House, in Forest Road, which is in the old city. Now a 'Coffee House' is an underworld expression for a brothel. Considering where it's located; it must be a high class establishment." Dorothy just nodded; she needed her bleeding bed if she was going to get up tomorrow.

Both Harry and Dorothy were up late and missed breakfast; but Uncle William did treat them to lunch. He chuckled at their worn appearance and their struggle with hangovers; especially young Dorothy. But they were both young and recovered quickly with plenty of water and tea. They both enjoyed their lunch.

Captain Hayward read his agents report about the Hadden's and their successful link up with Sir Alistair. He particularly liked the part where Dorothy stood on the table singing with her dress pulled up a little and her fine breasts almost hanging out. He really wished he had taken that babysitting job himself but a little something had popped up; that little something being the bloody Russians!

He sipped his dark tea and dipped a biscuit in. The report from Agents in St. Petersburg and Moscow did not make happy reading. Grossvech had indeed been supplying rifles, ammunition and bombs to Russian revolutionaries, intent on bringing down the Tsar. Bolsheviks, socialists and Communists were all the same to British Intelligence. The undeclared aims of the British Government was support for the regime of the Tsar; but not publically. This very year, Britain had signed a very important treaty with France that would make the two countries allies.

But there was a big problem with the treaty; France had already signed a secret Treaty with yet another power; one that the majority of British people didn't really like; Imperial, Autocratic Russia! So now the British Empire was linked to the Russian one; for good or bad via their French allies. The German's knew about it and should war come, would face fighting on two fronts; East and West. They weren't happy about that and made war plans accordingly.

"The 'Entente Cordiale', was a written and partly secret agreement signed in London between the two powers on 8 April 1904. It was mainly against Germany. The French and British agreed to stand together against her in time of war." SJW.

Captain Hayward placed both hands behind his head and sat back in his chair. This was going to be a tricky one; the 'Empire & Colonial Coffee House' was a hot bed of information about the comings and goings of German, Austrian and Russian agents. He wanted to make sure that most people would consider the raid and arrest of the Russian doctor just a police operation to capture a suspected murder; that unfortunately would suffer a massive coronary after arrest and die before any extradition to France. He needed to keep the Russian intelligence services sweet and their flow of secret information about Germany; coming in. He knew full well why they had taken out Sir William McKenzie and he could understand their reasons for doing so. He would certainly keep that little revelation from the Hadden's.

They would be happy that the murderer of their friend had been caught. He didn't need to explain much more than that. This little operation could prove a good training opportunity for Harry and especially Dorothy. The captain knew she could be an effective and invaluable female agent for the crown and he would certainly cultivate that.

Meanwhile, he needed to apprehend the Russian doctor and squeeze out all the information he could, about a very important topic; the proposed assassination of Kaiser William II of Germany and his replacement with his second son. The Crown Prince would perish with his father. The Russians had been working on such a plan to preserve Aristocratic rule in Russia. This, despite the Tsarina [Empress] being German herself. Captain Hayward sighed and slapped the reports shut; he kept thinking about Miss Dorothy Hadden and they were quite disgusting and quite delicious. He stood and pulled on his coat and hat, checking his service revolver. He really couldn't wait to see Miss Hadden in her 'High Class prostitute' outfit!

He leaned down and unlocked his bottom drawer and pulled out a brown file; it was marked; "Assignment 04/132/HADDEN D.M. MISS – Recruitment & Clearance." He placed it on his desk and opened to the first page. He lifted an A4 photograph which showed Dorothy in her stage costume at the Paradise Theatre. He picked the next photograph up of Dorothy in a lovely summer dress and hat feeding ducks in Victoria Park. He picked up another and smiled; this was his favourite: Dorothy quite naked about to step into a bath. He licked his lips and lifted it to his face and kissed it. He had several such photographs of Dorothy undressing or naked. All taken from Barfield Castle where the Hadden's had stayed last year. The Hadden's had never – obviously – caught on that the Earl was an operative of the government and invited all types of people that the Crown was interested in to stay there. Certain bedrooms had concealed camera's which had proved invaluable to Military intelligence and luckily; Miss Hadden had stayed in one. The final photograph was his favourite; Dorothy naked on the big bed with her legs open and Rosie between them. He grinned; she won't need to indulge in that once she was his mistress; willing or not. He wasn't particularly concerned about Dorothy and her lesbian relationship with her 'maid'. Even the report – and photographs – of Miss Hadden entertaining the big black man didn't faze him: if he was honest: it stimulated his sexual appetite for her. A woman who was prepared to fuck like that would make a fine, dirty mistress and of course, a damn fine secret agent!

He then picked up the file marked 'The Jewel' and stared at the contents; the troublesome Maharaja would be arriving soon and everything needed to be in place. He believed that mister Henry Reynolds was a good choice for the camera work and the new girl – formally known as 'shy Mary' – had worked for him [Reynolds] previously. She and Miss Hadden should make a successful team of honey traps and the Indian Prince really did like his white women. It was known he had several in his harem, nearly all purchased from white slavers in Turkey and Egypt. But none were British, so the government ignored their plight, all in the interests of what was best for the British people: of course!

Captain Hayward was concerned about another mission being set up: In Germany itself to discover the contents of the Imperial German War Plan and the big question was, 'Does it involve the invasion of Belgium?' All the British Governments war plans depended on finding the answer to that simple question.

"The Imperial German War Plan for fighting on two fronts was called the Schlieffen Plan' Named after the Chief of the General Staff of the German Army from 1891 to 1906. It appeared to ignore the fact that by invading neutral Belgium it would bring the British Empire into the conflict regardless. And that meant facing the mighty Royal Navy." SJW.

He knew the agent he would deploy but it was getting him into Germany in a suitable disguise. He stared at Dorothy's file and slowly started to smile. [See episode; **The European tour of Princess Isis: Queen of magic.'**]

"I thought I would never say this to my baby sister; but Dottie you make a wonderful Edinburgh whore!" Harry chuckled as the carriage pulled up outside wonderful ornate building, just inside Forest Road. Dorothy had to smile; she only had some very naughty lingerie on beneath her travelling cloak. A dark black corset that had pushed her magnificent bosom up and almost out, with stockings, suspenders and frilly black lace panties with black high heels. That was it.

She had applied her make-up quite thickly for her taste. Especially the bright red lipstick, but that's what top class prostitutes wore; apparently. They had been advised by Mrs. Edna Gunnings; the Matron who supervised women prisoners at Edinburgh Central Police Station. As Harry remarked; she deals with whores and street walkers every day, so she must be bit of an expert on what they wear.

They were followed – discretely – by a couple of carriages containing Captain John Hayward and his men; they were the backup in case things went wrong. Already waiting, a few streets away were two carriages of police from Edinburgh City Police Force who would raid the place; when called. Harry would meet up with Sir Alistair inside the 'Empire & Colonial Coffee House'. Sir Alistair was a member and would sign Harry and his 'friend' in. It was suspected that Doctor Nickolas Smirnoff would be inside and soon as they discovered him; Harry would sound the alarm to raid the place and the pair would get the hell out of there.

They walked into the quiet building and found a nice old lady sitting at a desk. She smiled; "Good evening sir. I know that you're not a member, so may I ask who is signing you in?" Harry smiled; "Sir Alistair....." He stooped and grinned, tapping his head; "Mister Black Bunny will do the honours!" The woman smiled and rang a little bell. A burly footman appeared and she instructed the rough looking man to fetch the member; 'Mister

Black Bunny'. He nodded and disappeared through the heavy black door. The woman gestured to Dorothy; "Madame Anne will expect a little something if you bring your own lady here sir." Harry nodded and dug into his pockets. The woman smiled; "Madame will deal with such matters inside."

The black door opened and Sir Alistair appeared; he had a glass of champagne in his hand. ""Sweet Jesus Harry my boy, She looks even better than the other night! I bet she's a guinea a night!" Harry just smiled and the woman indicated to the door; "You may leave your coats at reception sir."

Dorothy whispered in Harry's ear; "Oh well, I always dreamed of being a stripper as well as a common prostitute!" She pushed her arm through Harry and Alistair's and the threesome waltzed into the 'Empire & Colonial Coffee House'. Alistair slapped her bum and smiled; "You're in for a good night my darling; I'll happy pay a bloody guinea for a little piece of cake like you!"

Dorothy just smiled. Behind the big door was a small cloakroom area; the girl manning the counter was wearing nothing but a small black apron, stockings and high heels. Oh, she also had a small floppy maid's hat on. She smiled broadly and took Harry's coat, indicating to the sign that each coat and hat was a shilling a piece. Harry paid the required amount and Dorothy slowly pulled her coat off and handed it over. The girl smiled at her and whispered; "Love the outfit darling, but you're a bit over dressed for this place!" Dorothy just stared at her. Alistair rubbed his hands together; "At bleeding last, a young tart who knows how to dress properly!"

He guided them through another big door; opened by another burly individual who smiled at Dorothy; really smiled and winked. Dorothy stared about the room which was packed with men – still mostly dressed – and several young women who weren't. Alistair grabbed a young woman by the arm and said; "This is Kate; I've booked a private room my friend with plenty of champagne." The woman smiled; she was stark naked apart from red stockings, a thick red collar, red heels and nothing else. She looked Dorothy up and down and whistled; "Fuck me, I haven't seen a top class tom like that in a while; I bet you earn a fucking guinea a night, you lucky cow!"

Alistair pulled them towards the stairs and shouted; "There's a medical conference going on next to us. Half a dozen bleeding doctors all practicing the kind of medicine even I would enjoy!" they were stopped on the stairs by a very tall, stern looking woman who was actually fully dressed. Alistair smiled at her and introduced his friend. The Madame smiled and held out a skinny hand; "I'm afraid sir that female guests must pay ten shillings. You will understand; to cover the overheads."

Harry dropped four half crowns into her hand and she seemed happy with that. She smiled at Dorothy and whispered in her ear; "Come and have a cup of tea with me love, after you've finished. I may have a serious proposition for you." She disappeared down the stairs, pushing the coins into her little hip purse that hung from her waist.

"That's where we will find our Russian doctor friend." Harry whispered to Dorothy; who nodded. Alistair pushed open a door that had a silver Stork emblem on. "Come on! Last one fucking is queer!" He staggered in, dragging Kate with him. There were four other doors on this landing and Harry gestured to them; "Stick your head in those two over there and I'll check these two."

He pulled the first one open and found half a dozen naked people rolling about the floor; strangely enough singing popular music hall songs. He closed that one and opened the other; four naked young women were having lesbian sex on a big bed while a solitary and quite old man, was sitting naked in a chair; tied up with a gag in his mouth. He appeared to have his aged genitals stuffed into a glass jam jar. "At least there's no bleeding jam in it." Muttered Harry and he quietly closed the door.

Dorothy opened the first door on her side of the hall – very quietly – and found a young couple quite naked having sex on a chair. The girl had her back to Dorothy and didn't even notice. The man was far too busy with the girl's big breasts also to notice Dorothy. She stared and shook her head; he appeared to be in the wrong place and the girl clearly didn't mind such a sex act. Dorothy quietly closed the door and opened the next one.

Four fat men were all naked; being entertained by two young ladies who were naked apart from straw hats. Dorothy quickly recognized the wanted fat Russian doctor immediately from the photograph supplied by captain Hayward. She guessed the others were doctors too; they all had stethoscopes around their necks.

They appeared to be examining the girl's backsides quite closely. She shut the door and gestured to her brother that the Russian was in there. Harry grinned and walked across to the landing window and jerked it open. He waved his red hankie a few times and made a gesture with his hand for five minutes.

Five minutes and it's on." He said quietly to Dorothy who suddenly stopped at the stop of the stairs and walked back to the first door she had opened. Harry was quite puzzled and a little amazed when she pushed the door open and stepped in. Harry shrugged his shoulders and followed.

Alistair appeared in the doorway of his room: quite naked apart from his waistcoat. He shouted at Harry; "My turn with the posh tart!" Harry ignored him and he went back inside muttering something.

Dorothy had recognized the young man who was indulging in illegal sex with the young woman who didn't seem to care. The pair jumped from the chair and the girl rubbed her abused arse, shouting; "Who the bleeding hell are you? This room is booked for the night. Madame Anne will kick your arse's out!"

Paul sat and stared at his fiancé and simply couldn't believe his eyes. Finally he managed to shout; "What the fucking hell are you doing here dressed like that?"

Dorothy folded her arms and stared him full in the face; "You know damn well that I'm part of Harry's undercover disguise! So what the hell are you doing here? I didn't know they held medical conferences in whore houses!" Paul slowly eased himself out of the chair; young Daisy stood arms on hips and demanded to know who this old whore was! Paul was muttering something and trying to cover his nakedness with his hands. Dorothy turned to the girl; "I'm his bloody fiancé!" The naked young girl nodded and wandered over to the bed and sat down; "Well, I want an extra half crown if you and this bloody Harry geezer are joining in!" Paul didn't try to apologies; he just stood gripping his cock with both hands, his mouth opened a couple of times but nothing came came out. Harry walked over to the small table and picked up Paul's discarded trousers and shirt and threw them at his feet. "I suggest you dress and get the fuck out of here Paul; unless you want to be caught up in a raid. Now that won't do your career much good will it?"

Paul just nodded and picked up his clothes. Dorothy saw the open door to the small toilet and strode over to it. She pulled off the engagement ring and held it over the toilet bowl. She turned to Paul and didn't smile; "Strangely enough; the engagement is off!" She dropped the ring into the toilet and walked back to her brother.

Daisy jumped from the bed and dashed into the bathroom shouting; "Jesus girl! You must be nuts, that bloody ring is worth a few bob. If you don't want it I'll bloody have it!" She had one arm down the toilet in an instant. Dorothy smiled; "There we are Paul, she'll make a fiancé more appropriate for a man of your tastes." Dorothy pushed her arm through Harry's and the pair swept from the room.

There were whistles sounding and naked people were running about in panic; well the men anyway, most of the women just sat about talking amongst themselves. The little fat Russian doctor staggered past them, trying to cover his cock with a straw hat. Harry grabbed hold of him and shouted for Dorothy to get help. She strode to the top of the stairs and shouted at two uniform constables who were running up it. "We've got him" Up here lads!" They rushed past her; strangely enough both grinning from ear to ear. They didn't often get the chance to view a beautiful woman in just her naughty underwear!

Harry handed over his prisoner and joined Dorothy downstairs in the now very quiet reception room. Madame Anne was talking quietly to Captain Hayward and the deputy Chief of Police. It was obvious that she knew the police Superintendant very well!

The Captain slapped Harry on the back; full of praise. He stared at Dorothy and a big smile crept across his face. He ordered a uniform constable to give his coat to her; quite reluctantly it should be noted. Dorothy pulled the constables coat about herself and watched as two constables dragged her protesting ex-fiancé – still quite naked – down the stairs. He was followed by Alistair who was asking the uniform constables if they knew who his father was. One smiled; "Ah but, do you know who he was?"

Paul shouted at Dorothy, but she ignored him and chatted with Captain Hayward. The Russian Doctor had a coat thrown over him and rushed into a waiting police carriage. Old sergeant McGafferty chuckled; "Sir, our Russian friend is shouting that he has diplomatic immunity, what will we do with him down the Station?"

Captain Hayward just smiled; "He's not going down the station sergeant, so there's no problem there." The sergeant nodded and walked away. Captain Hayward turned to Harry and Dorothy; "Now we have our little Russian friend, we'll just give all the gentleman caught here a strong warning and the girls can have a free pass too. I think that's fair all round." Dorothy certainly agreed with the girls being released without charges. But she was annoyed about the men being let off.

Harry and Dorothy walked to the door and collected their coats from the half naked girl who was sitting chatting with a big constable who couldn't stop smiling. They retrieved their coats from her and Harry gave her a silver sixpence as a tip. She smiled; "Still, you're on a winner with that one sir [indicating Dorothy] ain't seen a top bit of fanny like that in some time."

Harry smiled and jerked a thumb at Dorothy; "Actually she's my sister who helps me out on occasion." The girl just grinned; "Keeping it in the family are we sir? Makes sense, my dad always did." She sat back down, leaving Harry trying to explain that's not what he meant. Dorothy just sighed and dragged him away; laughing quietly. They slipped into their carriage and it pulled away, leaving a growing crowd on the pavement watching the raid finishing.

He smiled at Dorothy; "You can believe, you know someone and then bang. You bleeding don't!" Dorothy nodded, despite the sheer disappointment in finding out that her ex-fiancé was a liar and a whore monger; she was actually a little relieved that the engagement was off; for good. Harry patted her hand; "Don't worry about it my girl; a little beauty like you won't have to wait for a real good one to come along." She just smiled at her brother's sentiments and wondered what Uncle William would say. She certainly knew what Rosie would say in a most colourful way! But as she sat in the carriage back to the hotel, she groaned inside: her little sexual animal had been aroused by the visit to the brothel and now - she didn't have to hold to her vow about Paul - she wanted a man. She almost blushed openly when her mind added to that dirty thought: any bloody man!

Then young Mister Cabot popped into her head: she smiled.

Mr. Edward Collington had appeared at the hotel and spoke with Uncle William about the aborted funeral and seemed quite relieved that the Judges – sitting at Edinburgh Court of Sessions – had decided unanimously in favour of the petition to overturn Sir McKenzie's wife objections to her husband's Highland funeral and allow the burial to go ahead. Isabella McKenzie was not a happy widow now that her plans had gone astray. She would not even stay for the funeral and arranged to leave Scotland by transatlantic steamer; for good. America beckoned the young widow, now somewhat wealthier by her 'loss'. It appears that she was travelling with quite an entourage: a ladies maid, another maid, a young male servant and a friend called Wilberforce Hoskins who was American by birth. Apparently he was her regular tennis player and coach.

Dorothy was a little ashamed at her ungenerous mind when she said quietly to Harry [who laughed] "Playing tennis my bum, I bet he coaches her ladyship in something quite different!" Even Uncle William had to 'tut-tut' at her remarks, but he did smile.

Uncle William and the lawyer now resurrected the plans for a proper Scottish farewell for Sir William McKenzie. Cables were sent to Mr. Livingston [Sir William McKenzie's Agent] and to Bray Castle for the attention of Sir William's loyal Butler; Mr. Albert Lewis. Dorothy and Harry smiled at their Uncles fervor, as he threw himself in the task of giving his old school friend the send off he had wanted.

They sat in the hotel restaurant and worked their way through a good lunch – well, Harry did anyway – and Dorothy noticed an Advertisement placed in the local paper by the Imperial Russian Embassy in London. She held the paper up to Harry and tapped the advertisement that covered quarter of a page. "Doctor Smirnoff's family has offered a huge reward for information about him; apparently he's missing, last seen in Scotland. The Tsar himself is concerned about the man; well, at least that's what the advertisement says."

Harry couldn't help but chuckle as he helped himself to more smoked salmon; "So claiming Diplomatic immunity didn't help him too much. I suppose a spy is a spy and the Russian's can't shout too loudly about that. They bumped off poor old Sir McKenzie for doing exactly the same thing. Supposedly spying I mean."

Dorothy placed her knife and fork down and Harry could see the look upon her face; "What is it old girl?" he said quietly. Dorothy didn't smile; "Do you realize Harry that we didn't discover a solid piece of evidence that Sir William was actually murdered by the so called Russian spy; the fat doctor? According to captain Hayward he didn't admit the killing. The French Police didn't even have the doctor as a suspect; they went after Robert Laxton, who admitted he was the last person to see McKenzie alive. Then we find out that Robert was the new heir to the McKenzie fortune after the last heir suddenly died whilst fishing in Cornwall. Maybe I'm barking up the wrong tree, but I'm a little unsettled by all this."

Harry sat back and wiped his face with a napkin; he was thinking hard. "So Robert inherits the Title and the McKenzie estates which are worth a small fortune and now intends to give up his medical studies and run the estate." Dorothy leaned forward and really looked quite grim; "Harry, Sir William was killed by a lethal injection of poison that the authorities say was administered by doctor Smirnoff. Robert Laxton was a medical student in his final year; I bet he had access to needles and poison." Harry sat back and folded his arms; it was not a pretty picture. Had they been so caught up in the whole spy thing that they overlooked the basics of gathering real evidence?

Harry sighed; "Well, we are travelling back – again - to Bray castle tomorrow for the new funeral. Maybe we could have a quiet chat with Robert. But I think he won't be too happy about what we have to say."

Dorothy had to agree with that; the new heir wouldn't be too receptive about such deductions. "We catch the train this very afternoon and the funeral will be definitely on tomorrow morning. Apparently Isabella has already left for the docks; the big Cunard steamer SS Lucania sails from Liverpool tomorrow for New York and America." Speaking quietly, Harry checked his fob watch with a little smile.

"SS Lucania was the jewel of the Cunard fleet at this time and regularly made the transatlantic crossing to America packed with the celebrities and wealthy of the Edwardian era. It was sadly destroyed by fire whilst in its home port of Liverpool in 1909." SJW.

Everyone gathered – again – for the funeral re-run. They all hoped this would be the last time. Unlike the original day; the weather had strong winds filled with some rain. That nasty rain that's make you think it's really nothing, but half hour later you realize you're soaking. Everyone stood under their umbrella's and watched the coffin taken into the dark crypt. Uncle William wiped his face – he said from the rain – with his arm through Dorothy's. She gripped his hand and saw that the pallbearers had filed from the crypt and two burly men closed the big doors and resealed it. There was very little talking as the mourners made their way back to the carriages lined up in the small road that lay below the little mound on which the crypt sat. Sir William McKenzie had finally been laid to rest with his ancestors after a very strange and complicated funeral.

There was – of course – drinks and food laid on at the castle, but strangely enough, Uncle William didn't attend. He ordered a cab and with their luggage already packed, the Hadden's left Bray Castle for the railway station. They would be catching the 'Flying Scotsman' back to London that very afternoon. With such a short time schedule Dottie had Rosie fetch Mr. Cabot immediately and they actually didn't bother undressing – well, not very much – and he fucked her on the small sofa of her room with her dress and petticoats pulled up. He wasn't big in the cock department, but certainly knew how to use it and he had to cum when he heard Rosie shouting that the cars were at the front doors to run everyone down the station. Dottie had managed a couple of small orgasms – she was still quite aroused – and admitted her utter enjoyment of the impromptu 'quickie'. George certainly didn't complain! He managed to whisper that he now knew that Dottie was on the 'Indian Mission' and so was he. She replied saying at least they could take their time in future. Now that did make the young man smile in anticipation.

A grinning Rosie tossed Dottie a small soft towel and helped the young man with his coat and hat, then showed him out. "Your brother is on his way up the stairs so you don't have time for a bleeding pee my girl!" Rosie chuckled as Dottie checked her make-up in the mirror and groaned a little: "Don't mention peeing or I'll have to sodding go!" She retorted, then groaned loudly and made for the toilet, leaving Rosie to explain to Harry that he would have wait. He just nodded in total acceptance: after all Dorothy was a woman!

CHAPTER 8. 'THERE IS NOTHING LIKE A TRAIN JOURNEY FOR REFLECTION.' Tahir Shah.

Dorothy sat in the ladies waiting room at Edinburgh Station and watched the several other women also sitting there. All but one had a couple of young children. She thought about her disgraced ex-finance and knew that she had a lucky escape from the marriage; children would have to wait until she could find the right man to be her husband and their father. That was the strict social conventions of her time. And what she desired.

Harry stuck his head through the door and tipped his hat to the ladies; "Come on Dottie; they're loading the flying Scotsman and Uncle William wants to be first into the Dinning carriage." She jumped up and followed Harry onto the very busy platform. She noticed that were several young women kissing men goodbye, including a couple of magnificent soldiers in kilts, their rifles slung over their bags. She wondered which part of the vast British Empire the young men were heading.

Uncle William joined them after supervising the baggage being loaded and they found their carriage – First Class of course – and were surprised to find captain John Hayward sitting there, reading a newspaper. He looked up and smiled, lowering the paper. "Good morning my friends; I'm heading back to London; bit of a flap on with the damn German's I'm afraid." He folded up his paper and raised his hat to Dorothy. "Good Morning Miss Hadden and may I say how lovely you look this morning?"

Dorothy just smiled and asked how his wife and children were!

He didn't smile and immediately turned his attention to Uncle William and Harry, but kept glancing at Dorothy as she placed her coat upon the luggage rack. He couldn't take his eyes off her slim figure and especially her breasts. He had seen the 'goods' that were available to the lucky man she chooses. And he really wanted some!

Not like his wife; Maude. She had taken to reading the evening paper during the once a week sex act!

But back to the business in hand, he had a bit of a proposition for Harry, but knew that Dorothy would probably be involved in it. Women spy's were in short supply and normally turned out to be invaluable for some missions and he had discovered a potential good one in Dorothy. She was quite prepared to strip down to underwear for her country and that did make him smile with anticipation. He and Harry sat talking quietly whilst Dorothy read the new novel by Erskine Childers; 'The riddle of the sands'. She sighed; more bloody German spies and invasion fears. But she was quite enjoying it.

Uncle William lit his pipe and seemed to be in a day dream, staring out the window as the Flying Scotsman headed south. His head was full of his old school days and his enduring friendship with 'Big Willy'. He was a little sad, but had fulfilled the promise he had made when the boys were young. William McKenzie would have a full Highland funeral and be buried in the land he loved so dearly; Scotland. For his part; Sir William McKenzie had agreed that should the task befall him; he would bury 'Little Willy' as he wished. A full Viking funeral with blazing ship and mournful trumpets!

Uncle William chuckled at the prospect of his nephews reading his burial instructions [and Dorothy of course!] and finding they had to arrange a Viking funeral in the bloody 20th century!

The carriage door opened quietly and a big man stepped in. Dorothy looked up from her book and just kept looking. He was well over six feet in height and built like a Greek statue with dark hair and eyes, with a full 'Edwardian' moustache. He must have been in his late twenties. He was also probably one of the most handsome men Dorothy had ever seen. He placed his expensive long dark coat and hat in the luggage rack, but kept the strange parcel with him. Dorothy noticed it at once. Long and thin, whatever it contained had been wrapped with great care. She wondered what on earth it could be. He kept it close and pulled out a book. Dorothy was impressed with the book – but not as impressed as with the man himself – It was Plato's works in the original Greek!

Good looking, well built and intelligent. Dorothy managed a small smile; someone is a very lucky lady if he knows how to be faithful as well. He suddenly looked up from his book and saw Dorothy staring at him; he just smiled a little and returned to his book. Dorothy had gone a little red. Harry and Captain Hayward had finished their quiet discussions and the captain bid them farewell. He stopped by the carriage door and tipped his hat to the handsome stranger. "Good morning my Lord." was all he said and departed.

Harry sat next to Dorothy and whispered; "Good looking fellow and a lord to boot. Some girl is lucky." Dorothy, still a little red at being caught staring at him whispered; "Never mind that, how does Captain Hayward know him?" Harry shrugged his shoulders; "I don't know Dottie, but I can always find out if you really wish me too?" and smiled broadly.

"No don't bother thank you." She turned a page slowly and was caught again by the handsome stranger looking at her, looking at him. She sighed and tried desperately to concentrate on her book. Finally she gave up and sat back. Harry leaned close and whispered in her ear, "Keep this from Uncle William Dottie, I mean it MUST remain just between us, do you understand?" Dottie just nodded and Harry sighed, "Hayward has divulged that bloody Robert Laxton is an agent of the Crown!"

Dorothy had now lost total interest in the book and whispered back, "An agent of the crown? What do you mean by..." Harry held a finger to his lips, "Robert was shadowing his uncle on orders. Intelligence believed that McKenzie was passing information onto his Russian handlers, including the fact that the British Government was playing a double game, saying in private they support the Tsar and in public working against him. That would have been disastrous for us and so they took him out. Then used that to get rid of the only Russian agent that knew: the fat Doctor Smirnoff. Little wonder Robert went with Hastings without any real trouble." Dorothy sat back and shook her head, mainly with disappointment over Robert.

She nodded slowly, remembering the young man in her dressing room. Even Hastings said it was practically a miracle how he escaped and returned to England. Little wonder he succeeded if he had the backing of bloody British Intelligence! Dorothy had to ask, "So our deliberations about Robert's part in his Uncles' death, was that just supposition or did it have factual evidence for it?"

Harry wiped his face, "What do you think? He [McKenzie] had to be stopped from passing on that information and Robert was an agent of the crown, on scene and at the right time and place? I think he carried out his assignment....or duty as he saw it. Again, I think its best kept between us."

 A shocked Dorothy could only nod her agreement: such a revelation would hurt poor Uncle William greatly and achieve nothing now that McKenzie was dead.

She leaned back in her seat and only now fully realized that British intelligence played a dirty brutal game and now both her and Harry was embroiled with it. "Like a bloody basket of two headed vipers." Dottie whispered to herself, then wondered – fearfully – just how much did Hayward and his gang actually know about her private life or as she referred to it: her secret life.

George Cabot had hinted about the existence of an Intelligence file on her and she wondered what it contained. That thought made her shudder a little, then she became her usual resolute self and decided to visit her good friend Oskar, and see how he was progressing in his mission to find out about the strange individual called 'the beast'. Now that damaged man of mystery really did intrigue her.

CHAPTER 9. 'IN THE GAME OF DECEPTION, THE STAKES ARE ALWAYS HIGH.' Unknown.

Dorothy sat at the breakfast table and read the articles on the visit of the Maharaja of Chitral ostensibly here for trade talks. He had been received at Waterloo train station by the Foreign Secretary: Henry Petty-Fitzmaurice, Marques of Lansdowne and taken to 10, Downing Street for a 'chat' with the Prime Minister, Arthur James Balfour. She lowered the paper and didn't smile, wondering what the young prince - Saif Ul-Mulk - would really think of his hosts, if he knew what they were actually planning for his visit.

"When Lord Salisbury retired, Balfour became Prime Minister, but his cabinet split on the free trade issue and his relations with the king were poor. Defeats in the Commons and in by-elections led to his resignation in December 1905. He died in 1930." SJW.

Ellen refilled her tea cup and gestured to the papers, "Who the bleeding hell is prince Saif when he's at home?" Dorothy smiled, "He's a foreign…Indian prince from an Indian state high in the north of the country. It borders Afghanistan and so he's definitely of interest to our government. He is currently our main ally in that part of the world and I have the honour of presenting my magic show to him, whilst he's here: At the Duke of Tyrone's London House no less. He's apparently crazy about magic, the supernatural and all things mysterious, so quite an interesting young man." Ellen nodded and asked how much the government was paying her to entertain him. Dottie smiled, "Twenty-five pounds for the one night show." Ellen whistled and muttered, "Nice work if you can bleeding get it." And cleared away some of the breakfast cutlery.

Dorothy watched Ellen go and sighed. She would like to have thrown those gold sovereigns back in Captain Hayward's face but she needed the money: it was for her independent future. It had caused her a few sleepless nights, since she was expected to have sex with the prince and have it captured on film! If 'shy Mary' was a high class trollop, but a whore nevertheless for charging two sovereigns a time, then what the hell was she, getting paid twenty-five? She had convinced herself that the payment was actually for the magic show and that made her sleep better at nights, but she knew that she was deceiving herself. Then there was meeting bloody Flash Reynolds again and that bought back the fight and killing in her own dressing rooms.

[See episode: **'Miss Pandora and her magic box.'**] She and Reynolds really didn't have much to say to each other. At least 'shy Mary' was a laugh and took it all in her stride. Dorothy found she actually admired the woman and her ambitions to be totally and financially independent of men. The murder and prostitution charges had slightly hampered them, but she was back in the game: this time working with impunity for Military Intelligence. But Mary did make Dottie smile when she said that she would take the prince for the blackmail film and when Dorothy asked why, Mary replied "So that I can say I have performed for fucking royalty!" Now that did make Dottie laugh and she restrained from saying that she had – indeed – performed for royalty already. Much to Dorothy's surprise, she realized that she and Mary could now be called 'friends'.

Dorothy was a little amazed and somewhat pleased with Mary when she finally met Sims [as part of the magic show.] She actually appeared not to be bothered by his appearance and confided to Dottie if the young man needed something for his 'night-starvation', she would take him on and with no fees! Then Mary really dropped a bombshell that had Dottie's undivided attention and interest. She [Mary] had dealings with the character known simply as 'the beast'.

When pressed – repeatedly – by Dorothy to explain, Mary had smiled and recounted her story about the strange man. "After I was acquitted on that ridiculous murder charge and paid my fines, I soon encountered bloody John Vicar who told me in no uncertain terms that I would work for him. Of course, he wanted a fee for his 'protection', nearly half my bloody earnings – the bastard – and you can imagine how I felt about that. But what fucking choice did I have? He could easily have my throat cut and dump me in the Thames like some people would prune their roses. Then I started to hear really strange rumours and gossip about Vicar's old mum; apparently she nearly died in a house fire one Saturday night and had been carried out the blazing building by a passerby who had dashed into the inferno. You can imagine what John Vicar thought of that, he adores his old mum and openly admits it. Well, he wanted to reward the hero, but it was 'the beast' and everyone knew he wouldn't take a penny." Mary stared at the floor and took a deep breath, "Before that, for some months I had been making secret donations to St. Hilda's orphanage and hospital for sick children, you know a sovereign here and again, when I was flush and had a good day. The bloody ragged, disfigured poor little sods had more need of the money than me. I really didn't think much about it as several other high class working girls also donated."

Mary now smiled broadly, "Then I found I had a fucking Guardian Angel, a bloody real flesh and blood one. I was leaving a turn at the Devonshire [an up market hotel] when I find bloody John Vicar himself standing there with a couple of his goons. I nearly wet my knickers but the bastard just smiled at me and removed his hat. I asked what he wanted; I had paid his bloody protection money for the month. He didn't smile and told me that the agreement was off and I didn't owe him a penny and I would still receive his protection, and that I could call upon him for assistance whenever I wanted. At first I thought he was up to something but he was being straight. Apparently 'the beast' had paid him a visit and asked him to leave me alone because my donations at the kid's home were needed. Vicar agreed of course, he owed 'the beast' big time and the whole Eastend knew it. The bloody beast saved my neck, no doubt about it and when I asked Vicar where I could find 'the beast' to thank him, he said simply that I knew 'the beast' and he had given his word never to reveal his identity."

Dorothy had to sit down and slowly whispered to Mary about her encounter with 'the beast' and both women held hands in silence. Dorothy was thinking about the co-incidences in their stories and one important fact leapt straight out: apparently both girls knew or had known the beast! On that revelation they both stared at each other, thinking the same thing: they would have certainly remembered someone like 'the bloody beast!'

But their attention was drawn back to the matter in hand: 'Miss Pandora and her magic box' was about to perform at a private party at the Duke of Tyrone's London House in Piccadilly. The young prince was in attendance of course and so the bait would be placed in the trap. That bait was Dorothy with her additional assistant/distraction for the night: Mary. Both girls were wearing uncensored versions of Dorothy's stage costume and that certainly went down well with the all male audience. Mary confided to Dottie that several high class working girls had been booked for the night as well and would mingle with the men, on hand if anyone suddenly had the urge to fuck. Mary knew this was true because she would have been one of them, if she wasn't appearing in the show.

Dorothy stood back and closed the curtain; she had to admit that the women in the audience were all stunners, especially the dark haired one sitting near the front. Mary nodded, "That's Caroline – nickname 'The Princess' – she's a bloody ten guinea a time girl!" Mary smiled, "I can tell you now Dottie, tricks would easily pay twice that for you. And you've been bleeding giving it away!"

Dorothy made Mary laugh by saying that maybe, honey-pot should be changed to pot of gold. Mary gripped her hand and didn't smile; she was being serious, "I mean it Dottie, just say the word and I could get you twenty or thirty guinea turns, and I mean really easily get you that kind of money." Dorothy just smiled as she heard the act being announced to a cheering and clapping audience. She signaled to Reggie and Sims to take their markers and was pleased to see Mary walk straight to hers. "You actually could be a real magician's assistant, if you wanted." She called softly over to Mary who grinned. The curtains parted and the small five piece band struck up the introduction music: the show was on and so was the undercover mission.

The audience hushed as Titus slowly pulled the lid from the standing sarcophagus to reveal a mummy, fully wrapped with its arms crossed. Then with Mary's assistance laid a carpet over two small tables and stepped back. Dorothy turned to the audience, silent in anticipation, and announced that she would visit the world of the dead with the mummy of the ancient priest. She slowly walked to the sarcophagus and squeezed in. Titus replaced the lid and a little smoke emitted from the bottom, with the band playing sombre, almost funeral music as the coffin shook a little. Then there was silence. Titus slowly removed the lid and pulled it aside to reveal that the sarcophagus was empty.

The crowd cheered and applauded for some time until they realized the carpet thrown over the tables was now moving and lifting. Mary and Titus stepped forward and pulled the carpet away to reveal the mummy standing with Miss Pandora in his arms. She shouted, "Now that's magic!" The audience reacted by standing and cheering with applause thunderous. An incredulous Mary whispered to Reggie, "How the hell does she do that?" Reggie just smiled and said softly, "I haven't a bloody clue. That trick is quite impossible but I believe Mister Sims is the key."

Mary – like most of the audience – could only stare in utter bewilderment and wonder how the hell the young magician could perform such a trick. There was obviously no time to burrow tunnels or build secret trap doors in the Duke of Tyrone's bloody floors!

The young prince sat on the edge of his ornate chair and wiped his face. He had never seen such a trick and his Kingdom abounded in excellent magicians, but they couldn't match this young woman. He was intrigued and totally captivated by her.

Captain Hayward stood by the door to the Duke's study [it was at the rear of the packed reception room] and slowly smiled with satisfaction. George Cabot slipped next to him and whispered that Reynolds and the camera team were in place. Captain Hayward nodded and the pair disappeared into the study un-noticed by the show's audience, with captain Hayward operating the secret switch on the study's large bookcase which allowed them to push the bookcase to one side. They stepped into the dark orifice and it closed behind them. "This was originally the entrance to a 'Priest's Hole', but later Duke's expanded the corridors and built other secret doors for their own nefarious purposes." Hayward explained as they passed down the tunnels with just a small lamp for light. "The Duke may be a Catholic but he is a very loyal supporter of the King and the British Empire." Hayward added, arriving at a small wooden door which he jerked open and the pair squeezed through.

"When Henry VIII broke with the Holy Roman Church in 1534, Catholics almost became criminals and it was worse under Mary I and her half sister, Elizabeth I. Catholic families had these hidden chambers constructed so that Catholic Priests could visit the family for Mass and be relatively safe from arrest and execution." SJW.

'Miss Pandora and her magic Box' was on the final trick and the entire crowd was now focused on the corner of the reception room that had been set aside for the show. Dorothy announced her new trick which would debutante at this very show. It was called 'Isis & Isis' and she went into the act immediately. Titus wheeled the cage from behind the rear curtain and the audience gasped. In the cage was a large totally black leopard with a gold collar. It snarled and slammed it claws against the bars of the cage, showing its fearsome fangs to the apprehensive audience. Dorothy explained that the ancient Goddess Isis liked to appear as cats. Reggie and Mary slowly covered the cage with the red carpet and then wheeled an identical cage – again from behind the curtain – which was empty and threw a matching red carpet over that. She then invited five men from the audience to stand - at a safe distance – between the cages. She wasn't short of volunteers to stand close to her and Mary in those costumes! With five such volunteers now between the cages, Mary helped Dorothy climb into the empty cage and then made a great show of locking the padlock securely. With the carpet now covering the cage, the 'mad mummy' made some magic gestures and quickly disappeared back into his sarcophagus, with Reggie closing the lid. He walked over to the leopard's cage and pulled away the carpet as Mary did the same with Dorothy's cage. There was absolute silence for a few seconds, and then the audience exploded into cheers and applause. Dorothy was now in the leopard's cage and 'the mad mummy' was in hers. There was no trace of the leopard, but then it really didn't exist in the first place! Three and half thousand years ago, Mister Sims had indeed been a very talented magician.....

CHAPTER 10. 'I AND OTHERS OF MY SEX FIND OURSELVES CONTROLLED BY A FORM OF GOVERNMENT IN THE INAUGURATION OF WHICH WE HAD NO VOICE.' Victoria Woodhull.

George stood before the large mirror and gave a little wave, then heard Reynolds's voice saying everything was fine. He made a final check around the bed chamber and then operated the switch at the base of the ornate mirror and it clicked open. He stepped through and nodded at Reynolds, "All ready and make sure you get his face nice and clear." 'Flash' sighed, "I've done this before you know. I'm a professional in this game." That made George chuckle, "So I've heard. Otherwise you would be doing time for a very long period on the charges that Inspector Hadden had on you my friend." Reynolds's just shrugged his shoulders and checked his camera again, giving the handle a couple of cranks. "Just a misunderstanding." He muttered, thinking that bastard

Mosses had stitched him up, good and proper and he [Reynolds] never saw it coming. Then he smiled a little, but he was now fucking dead, so that sorted the problem of revenge out. [See episode: **'Miss Pandora and her magic box.'**]

'Flash' was eagerly waiting to film bloody Miss Dorothy Hadden fucking with the prince and knew that he could get very good money from the stills alone, and fucking serious money for the film itself. Then he sighed again: if bloody British Intelligence allowed him to keep any of his work!

"Heads up, the show's about to start." George said quietly as the door to the bedroom flew open and the prince ran in – hand in hand – with Mary. George grunted and rubbed his chin, "Must be a change in plan. Never mind, she'll do nicely." He then realized he was happy about the switch and smiled, watching Reynolds slowly cranking the camera's handle, a disappointed man over Dorothy's no show. The pair was soon naked and rolling about the bed with the fucking starting almost immediately. "Not one for warming the tart up, is he?" 'Flash' dourly observed and George just nodded in reply, he was thinking about Dorothy: naked on the bed, smiling with her legs open in welcome.

Reynolds's only used three reels because the prince's sexual performance lasted all of fifteen minutes. George stood arms folded and watched the pair share a cigarette, "Well, that wasn't much but it's all we really need." 'Flash' agreed and leaned on his camera after boxing up the reels for development. "They really needed someone to direct the action, that show wouldn't get ten bob on a good day." George had to smile at that.

He opened the small door to the tunnel behind them and 'Flash' quietly and carefully packed up his equipment and the pair left to meet Captain Haywood in the rear yard of Tyrone House. Dorothy watched them go and pulled the curtain back; turning to Reggie asking if everything was packed away. He nodded and asked if they should wait for Miss Mary. Dottie shook her head and the team headed for the rear courtyard with a couple of burly footmen helping them with their props. There was another carriage still waiting in the cobbled and dimly lit yard, with a young footman waiting with the door open. Dorothy supervised the loading of the equipment and quietly instructed Reggie to accompany the wagon back to the theatre. She watched the wagon pull away and disappear through the large stone archway, giving Reggie a little wave, then walked up to the other carriage and stepped in. The footman closed the door and bowed a little, telling the driver to go. The carriage pulled away and Dorothy eased back in the seat and didn't smile at the big figure sitting opposite, smoking a small cigar.

"Thank you Miss Hadden for joining me tonight. There are many organizations that defend our realm and you know most of them. There is the army and navy, the local militias, the various police forces scattered around the kingdom, the Special Irish branch, and military intelligence of course. Then there is the oldest and most secret of them all: 'The King's Men'. In the time of our late Queen, we were known – obviously – as 'The Queen's Men'. We were founded by a very enlightened and brilliant king: Alfred the Great, so we have been around for a very, very long time. We do not answer to the present government or any government that sat in Parliament. The head of the 'King's men' is known simply as the 'The Keeper' and that's the position I currently hold by grace of his majesty, our present King. I held it under his mother too." He blew smoke about, directing it towards the half open window. He leaned forward and smiled; Dorothy was surprised to find that the 'Keeper' was a good looking man in – perhaps – his early forties and clearly looked after himself. Then she realized that his face was familiar – in a vague way – and wondered where she could have seen it before; maybe in the newspapers? Or at the Paradise?

"Alfred the Great [848 - 899] known for his valiant defense of his kingdom against a stronger enemy, for securing peace with the Vikings and for his farsighted reforms in the reconstruction of Wessex and beyond, that Alfred - alone of all the English kings and queens - is known as 'the Great'." SJW.

He continued, "This may surprise you Miss Hadden, but we know about Mister Jericho Tibbs and his merry band, the Holy family that rules everything, even about God and his wayward brother, who's colloquially known as the Devil. Oh, yes, we know all about these things and of course, your dear friend Mister Simhentra-Kara or Sims as you call that most interesting character. He is not alone, there are others like him. But – save one – not so interesting I think! We also know that you, your uncle and brother are agents for Tibbs. Please do not insult our intelligence by denying it."

Dorothy just nodded, totally and genuinely surprised by the man's revelations: especially about Mister Tibbs and Sims. The big man eased back in his seat and opened his fob-watch. He sighed, "There is a meeting I must attend at West...." He stopped and looked up at her, "I have another appointment Miss Hadden, so I will, as our American cousin's say, cut to the chase of this little meeting." He snapped the watch shut and stared hard at Dorothy. "As from this moment in time Miss Dorothy Mary Hadden, you now work for us. You can continue with your engagements for the Intelligence services as you wish or are coerced into. But when we instruct you, you are ours: body and soul. Completely loyal to us in all matters."

She was about to say something, when he held up a hand and didn't smile, "Believe me Miss Hadden, it would be incredibly foolish and downright dangerous to deny us your services. We have never, ever taken 'NO' for an answer. And that record still stands after nearly a thousand years!" Now smiling, he glanced at the window, "Ah, the good old Paradise Theatre, please have a nice night Miss Hadden and I hear that you had quite a thrilling performance thanks to Simhentra-kara....and your own talents of course. Goodnight, we will be in touch."

The door was pulled open and Dorothy stepped from the cab and watched it go, her thoughts were swirling around her brain, mostly dark and forbidding. She ran up the steps and into the theatre. She stood alone in her dressing room lighting a single lamp to illuminate the semi-darkness and called softly for Sims. He appeared – eating an apple! – And asked how he could be of assistance and how well the private show went. She waved that aside and told him about 'The King's men' and meeting 'The Keeper'. He didn't smile and placed the half eaten apple of the small table by the window. With a voice full of concern, he said softly, "Bugger, they are really dangerous people who play by their own rules and apparently don't answer to anyone. Jericho told me himself that they have their own plans for humanity and are far more dangerous than even the 'Priest's of Chronos'. [See Episode: **'The workhouse corpse with golden boots.'**] Jericho has stated that 'The keeper' is probably the most dangerous human alive with regards to the Human Timeline and he's one of a long, long line of them. I'll report all you have said and get back to you with what Jericho wants done."

Dorothy nodded and asked what she should do now and Sims smiled a little, "Whatever they bloody say! Keep yourself safe my girl, that's the main thing right now." She nodded and thanked him, but he just smiled and disappeared. She sat in the darkness and cussed a little: fate wasn't bloody kind to her currently. Then she remembered what 'The Keeper' had said about him [Sims] that there were others like him! Did he [The Keeper] mean other 'mummy's?' Or another creatures with the same or similar powers? Then – with some surprise – she thought about 'The beast'.

THE END

IMPORTANT AUTHOR'S NOTE:

"The adventures of MISS DOROTHY HADDEN continue in book two: SERIES 2; The Early Edwardian adventures – Part 2. Then again in Book Three: SERIES 3; The Late Edwardian adventures – Part 1. It's followed by SERIIES 4: The Late Edwardian adventures – Part 2. It temporally finishes in Book Five: SERIES 5; The Great War years. Then Dorothy appears in SERIES 6: MISS DOROTHY HADDEN' which chronicles Dorothy's post war adventures!

Stephen Williams.

ADVERTISEMENT BY THE AUTHOR:

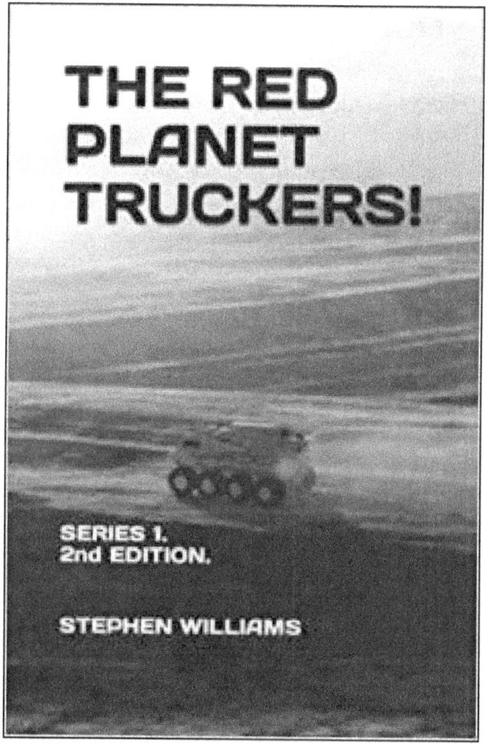

'THE RED PLANET TRUCKERS!' series by the same author.

ILLUSTRATION CREDITS.

"**All Illustrations** are taken from the Public Domain with no copyright details available or they are obscure or have expired. Where available artist and/or photographer details are given: should you claim any copyright as your own please contact the author via:
stephen.williams24@btinternet.com.
Thank you!"

COVER ILLUSTRATION.
The cover illustration of MISS DOROTHY HADDEN: SERIES 1. The Early Edwardian adventures – Part 1 Early 20th century French postcard – part of a small series – by the French photographer Jean Agelou [1878 – 1921] the work itself is in the public domain. The model is currently unknown. Should you have any information about this, please contact the author.

Page 4.
"**Cover illustration of MISS DOROTHY HADDEN: SERIES 1. The Early Edwardian adventures – Part 1 MISS DOROTHY HADDEN.**" Same copyright and history details as the '**Cover illustration**'.

Page 9.
"**THE WORKHOUSE CORPSE WITH GOLDEN BOOTS.**"
A Photograph taken during the late Victorian/early Edwardian period showing police officers apprehending a suspect: it is believed to be staged! No artist details or photographer credited. Copyright is currently obscure or may have expired. Should you have any information about this, please contact the author.

Page 135.
"**MISS PANDORA AND HER MAGIC BOX.**"
Early 20th century French postcard – part of a small series – by the French photographer Jean Agelou [1878 – 1921] the work itself is in the public domain. Also used as the '**Cover illustration**' of **Book 3** of this series. Should you have any information about this, please contact the author.

Page 217.
"THE STRANGE DEATH OF MRS. HANNA DASHWOOD."
A photograph of an Edwardian lady with her bicycle: copyright is currently obscure or may have expired. No artist details or photographer credited. Should you have any information about this, please contact the author.

Page 290.
"THE HIDDEN WINDOW."
A photograph of a stained glass window in the Münster Cathedral Bern, Switzerland; no artist details or photographer credited. Copyright is currently obscure or may have expired. Should you have any information about this, please contact the author.

Page 354.
"A TERRIBLE GLIMPSE OF THINGS TO COME?"
A photograph of 'steampunk' computer, found in the Public Domain with its Copyright currently obscure with no artist details or photographer credited. Should you have any information about this, please contact the author.

Page 411.
"THE COMPLICATED FUNERAL OF SIR WILLIAM McKENZIE."
A photograph of a late Victorian/early Edwardian funeral found in the Public Domain with its Copyright currently obscure with no artist details or photographer credited. Should you have any information about this, please contact the author.

Pages 462 & 466
"STEPHEN WILLIAMS – WORKS BY THE AUTHOR."
This drawing: 'The crazy writer' was found in the Public Domain with its Copyright currently obscure and with no artist details credited. Should you have any information about this, please contact the author.

OTHER WORKS BY THE AUTHOR.

"This contains a listing of some of the major works by the author that are or have appeared in a book format: please scan the QR code below to visit his blog.

Or type: stephenjohnwilliams.blogspot.com in the search bar of your search engine: Bing or Firefox recommended.

Note: Not all Book series have a corresponding 'website' – Sorry about that!

THE TEMPORAL DETECTIVES.

"THE TEMPORAL DETECTIVES. – SERIES 1."

"THE TEMPORAL DETECTIVES. – SERIES 2."

"THE TEMPORAL DETECTIVES. – SERIES 3."

"THE TEMPORAL DETECTIVES. – SERIES 4."

"THE TEMPORAL DETECTIVES. – SERIES 5."

"THE TEMPORAL DETECTIVES. – SERIES 6."

"A GUIDE TO THE SERIES: 2024."

THE RED PLANET TRUCKERS!

"THE RED PLANET TRUCKERS! "

THE GRAVEYARD CHRONICLES.

"THE GRAVEYARD CHRONICLES."

MISS DOROTHY HADDEN.

"MISS DOROTHY HADDEN – SERIES 1: The Early Edwardian adventures – Part 1."

"MISS DOROTHY HADDEN – SERIES 2: The Early Edwardian adventures – Part 2."

"MISS DOROTHY HADDEN – SERIES 3: The Late Edwardian adventures – Part 1."

"MISS DOROTHY HADDEN – SERIES 4: The Late Edwardian adventures – Part 2."

"MISS DOROTHY HADDEN – SERIES 5: The Great War years."

"MISS DOROTHY HADDEN – SERIES 6: The London adventures."

CRABB, POCKETT AND SCARPER!

"GRABB, POCKETT AND SCARPER: THE UNDERTAKERS STORY!"

HARRY BARFIELD.

"HARRY BARFIELD."

SAM DANTE.

"SAM DANTE."

THE ADVENTURES OF ALEXANDRA.

"THE ADVENTURES OF ALEXANDRA: SERIES 1."

"THE ADVENTURES OF ALEXANDRA: SERIES 2."

"THE ADVENTURES OF ALEXANDRA: SERIES 3."

"THE ADVENTURES OF ALEXANDRA: SERIES 4."

"THE ADVENTURES OF ALEXANDRA: SERIES 5."

"A GUIDE TO THE SERIES."

FATHER PARADISE ADAMS.

"FATHER PARADISE ADAMS."

IMPORTANT NOTE:
"NOT ALL BOOKS ARE CURRENTLY AVAILABLE OR STILL IN PRINT – SORRY ABOUT THAT!"
Please enquire about availability at your local bookshop or contact the author:
stephen.williams24@btinternet.com.

www.ingramcontent.com/pod-product-compliance
Lightning Source LLC
Chambersburg PA
CBHW061050210726
48294CB00001B/89